9-12 years

CLASS
ACT

JERRY CRAFT

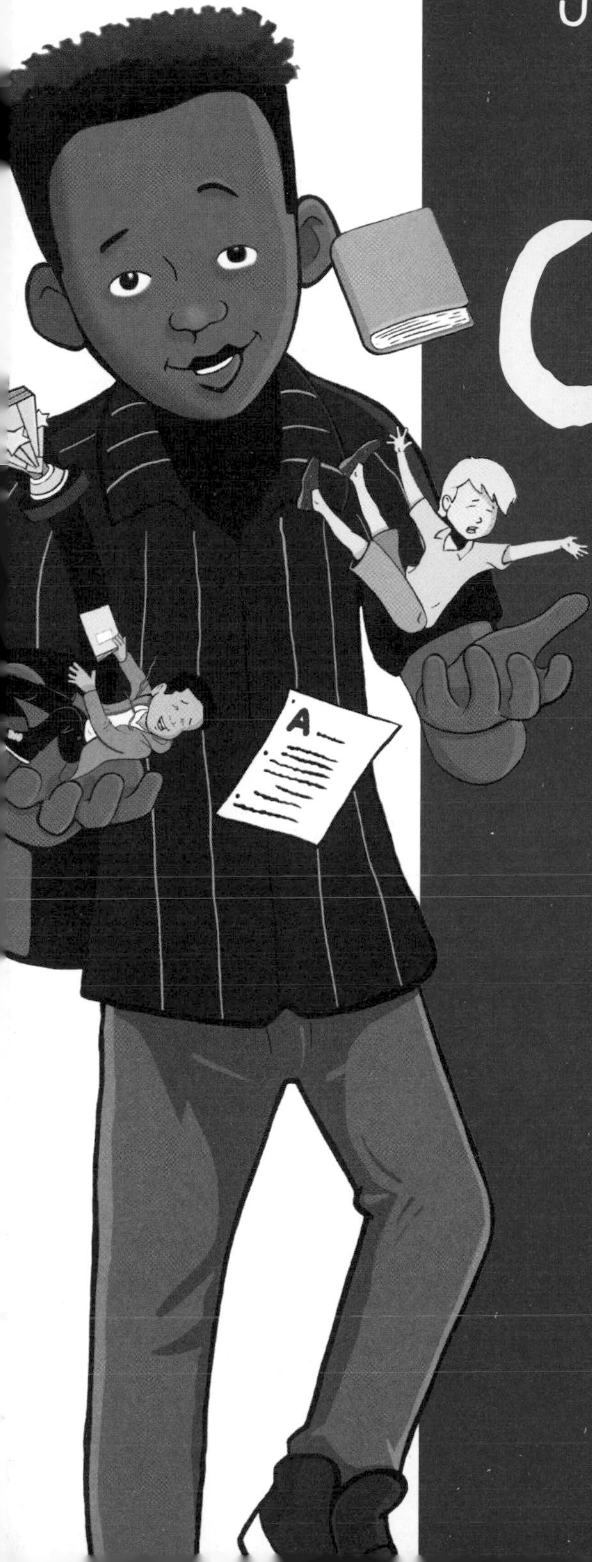

A

CLASS ACT

Quill Tree Books
Imprints of HarperCollinsPublishers
HARPER alley

Quill Tree Books and HarperAlley are imprints
of HarperCollins Publishers.
Class Act
Copyright © 2020 by Jerry Craft
All rights reserved. Printed in Canada.
No part of this book may be used or reproduced in any manner
whatsoever without written permission except in the case of
brief quotations embodied in critical articles and reviews.
For information address HarperCollins Children's Books,
a division of HarperCollins Publishers,
195 Broadway, New York, NY 10007.
www.harperalley.com

Library of Congress Control Number: 2020937195
ISBN 978-0-06-288550-0 (paperback) - ISBN 978-0-06-288551-7
(hardcover)

20 21 22 23 24   TC   10 9 8 7 6 5 4 3 2 1

First Edition

Be kind.
Be fair.
Be you.

SKETCH DIARY

of a

Shrimpy Kid

CHAPTER
1

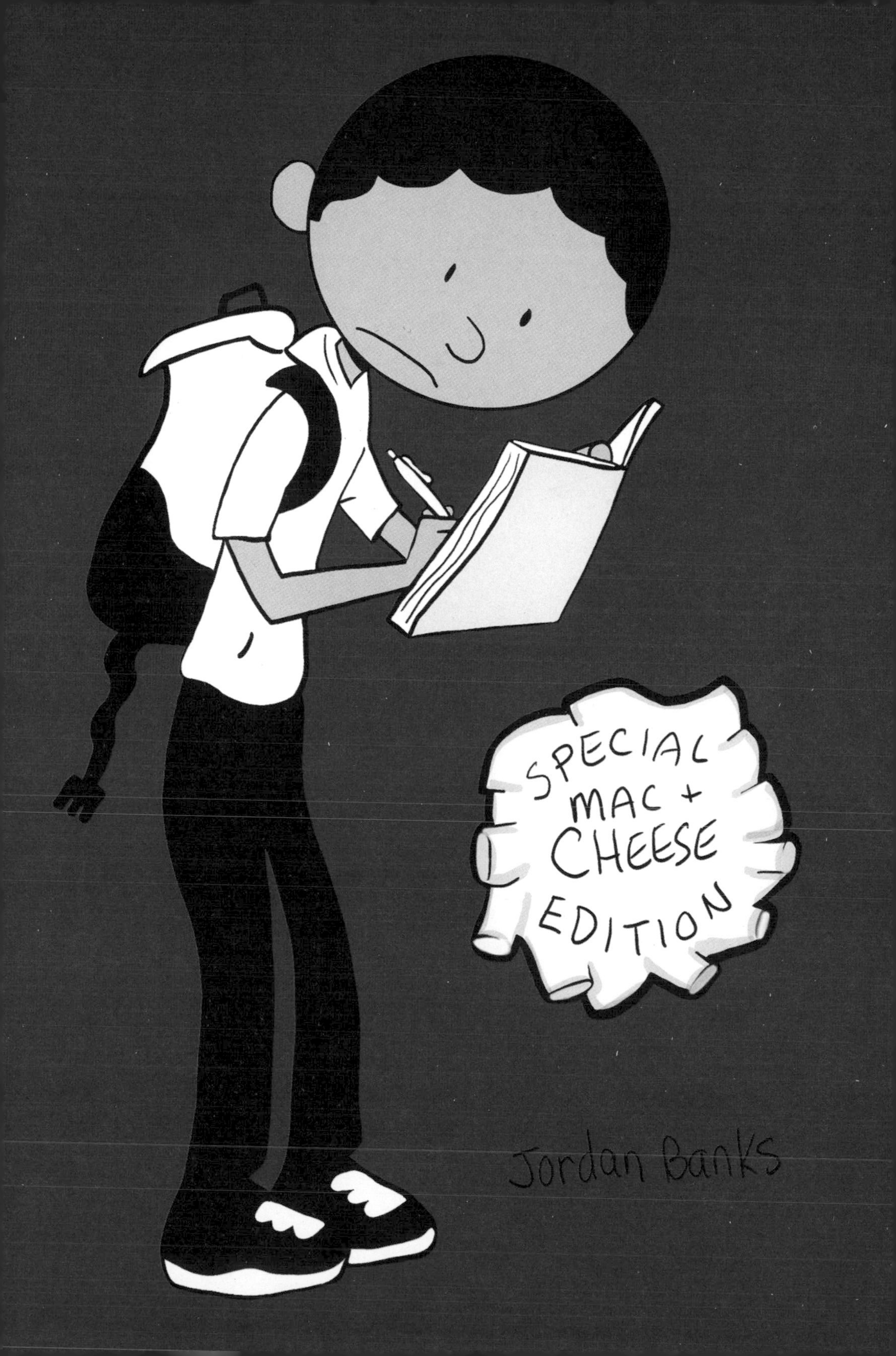
SPECIAL MAC + CHEESE EDITION
Jordan Banks

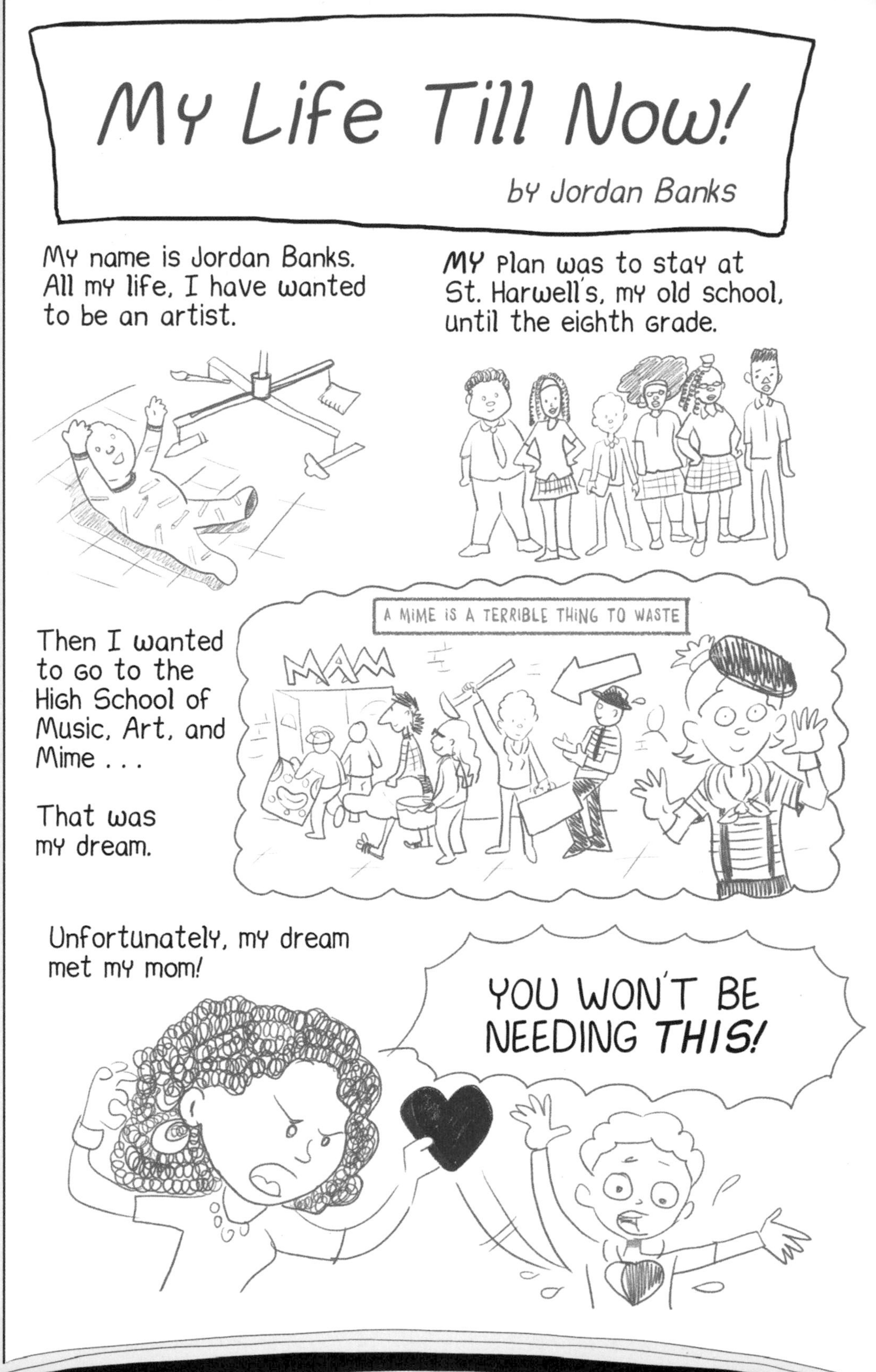
My Life Till Now!
by Jordan Banks
My name is Jordan Banks. All my life, I have wanted to be an artist.
MY plan was to stay at St. Harwell's, my old school, until the eighth grade.
Then I wanted to go to the High School of Music, Art, and Mime . . .
A MIME IS A TERRIBLE THING TO WASTE
MAM
That was my dream.
Unfortunately, my dream met my mom!
YOU WON'T BE NEEDING THIS!

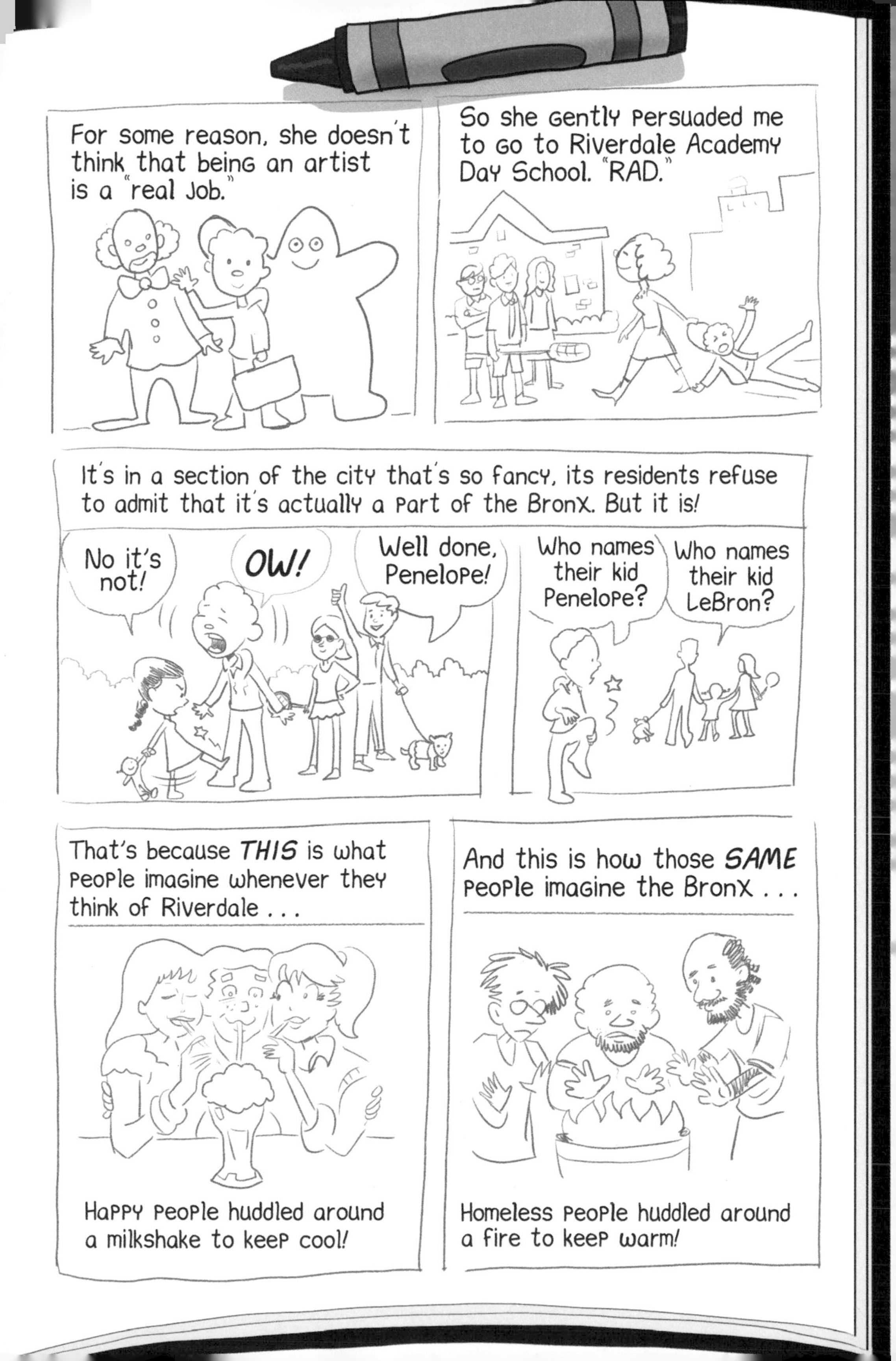
For some reason, she doesn't think that being an artist is a "real job."
So she gently persuaded me to go to Riverdale Academy Day School. "RAD."
It's in a section of the city that's so fancy, its residents refuse to admit that it's actually a part of the Bronx. But it is!
No it's not!
OW!
Well done, Penelope!
Who names their kid Penelope?
Who names their kid LeBron?
That's because THIS is what people imagine whenever they think of Riverdale . . .
Happy people huddled around a milkshake to keep cool!
And this is how those SAME people imagine the Bronx . . .
Homeless people huddled around a fire to keep warm!

WASHINGTON HEIGHTS, MANHATTAN, NEW YORK CITY

HEY, J . . . YOU OKAY?

JUST THINKING ABOUT STARTING SECOND FORM . . .

YOU KNOW, EIGHTH GRADE.

YOU WANNA SHARE?

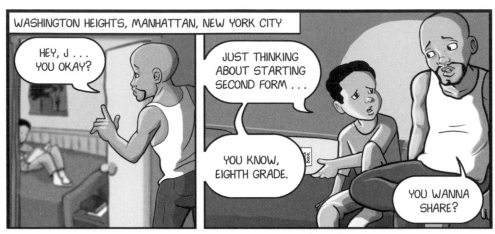

WELL, I HAVE TO MAKE A BIG DECISION AT THE END OF THE YEAR.

IF THE YEAR GOES GREAT, THEN I WON'T WANT TO LEAVE RAD.

BUT IF I DON'T LEAVE RAD, I WON'T GET TO GO TO ART SCHOOL.

AND YOU KNOW IT'S STILL MY DREAM TO BE AN ARTIST.

WE DON'T ALWAYS GET TO LIVE OUR DREAMS, JORDAN.

MY DREAM WAS TO BE A SPORTSWRITER.

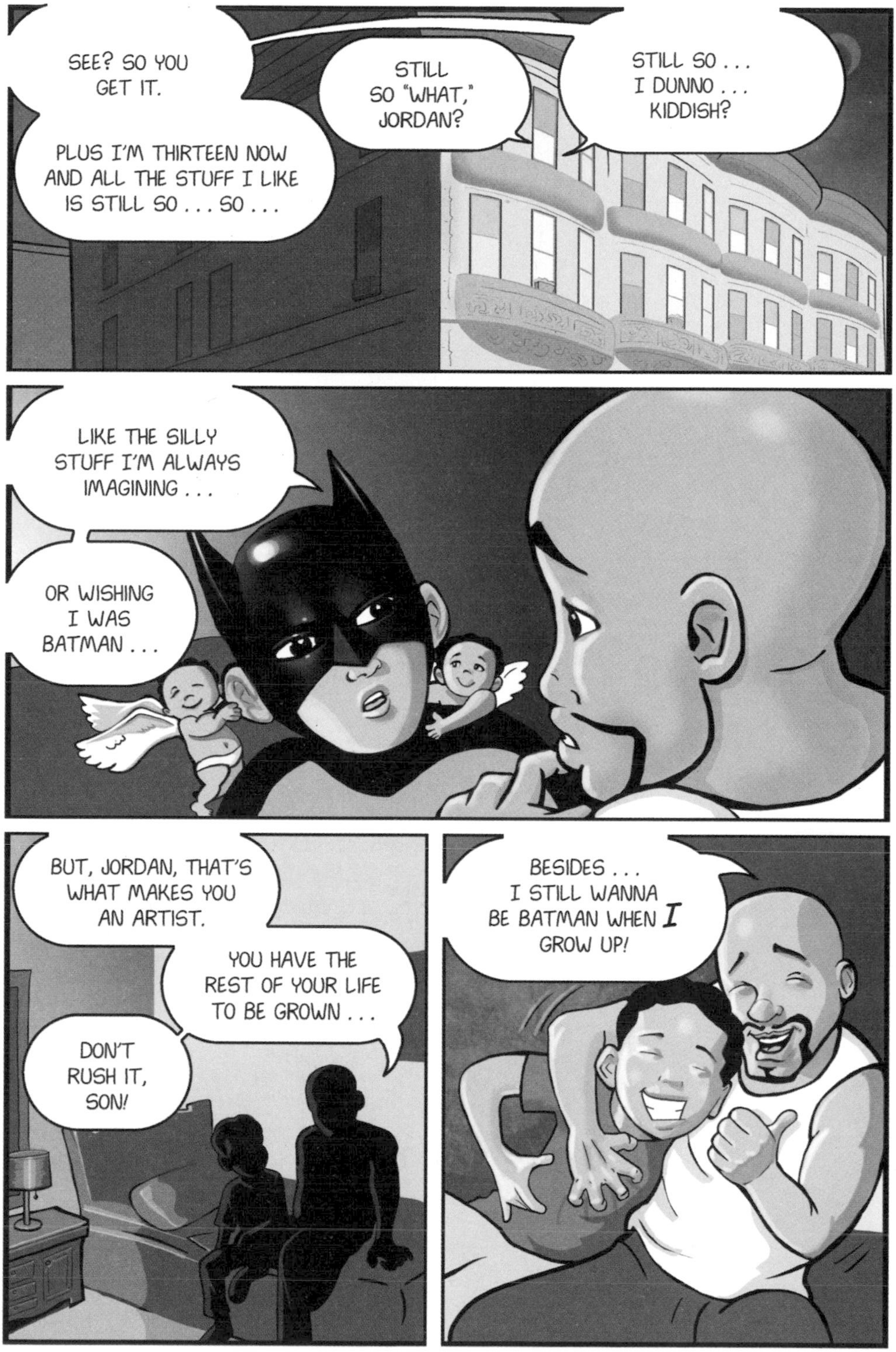
SEE? SO YOU GET IT.
PLUS I'M THIRTEEN NOW AND ALL THE STUFF I LIKE IS STILL SO . . . SO . . .
STILL SO "WHAT," JORDAN?
STILL SO . . . I DUNNO . . . KIDDISH?
LIKE THE SILLY STUFF I'M ALWAYS IMAGINING . . .
OR WISHING I WAS BATMAN . . .
BUT, JORDAN, THAT'S WHAT MAKES YOU AN ARTIST.
YOU HAVE THE REST OF YOUR LIFE TO BE GROWN . . .
DON'T RUSH IT, SON!
BESIDES . . . I STILL WANNA BE BATMAN WHEN I GROW UP!

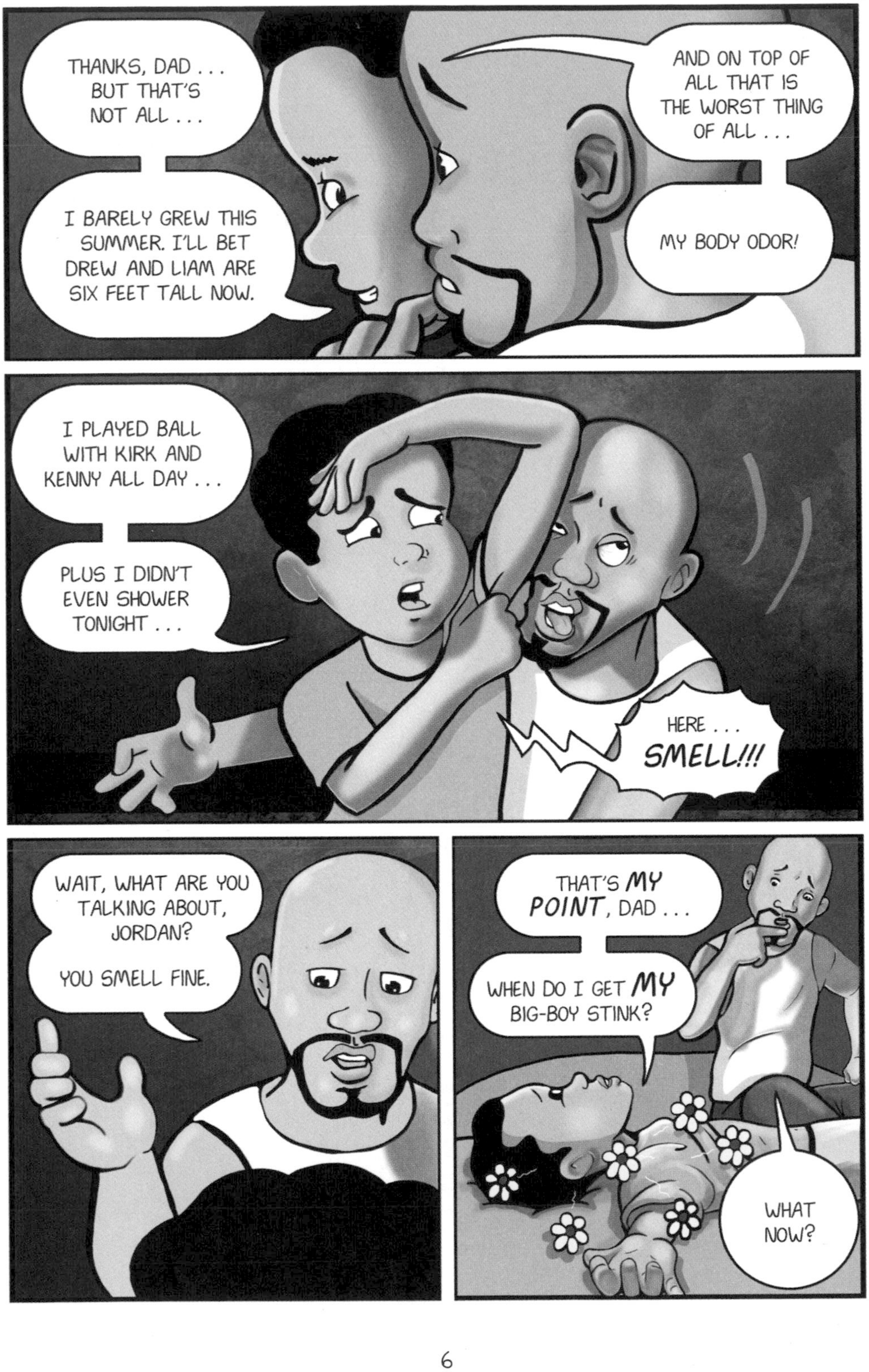
THANKS, DAD . . . BUT THAT'S NOT ALL . . .
I BARELY GREW THIS SUMMER. I'LL BET DREW AND LIAM ARE SIX FEET TALL NOW.
AND ON TOP OF ALL THAT IS THE WORST THING OF ALL . . .
MY BODY ODOR!
I PLAYED BALL WITH KIRK AND KENNY ALL DAY . . .
PLUS I DIDN'T EVEN SHOWER TONIGHT . . .
HERE . . . SMELL!!!
WAIT, WHAT ARE YOU TALKING ABOUT, JORDAN?
YOU SMELL FINE.
THAT'S MY POINT, DAD . . .
WHEN DO I GET MY BIG-BOY STINK?
WHAT NOW?

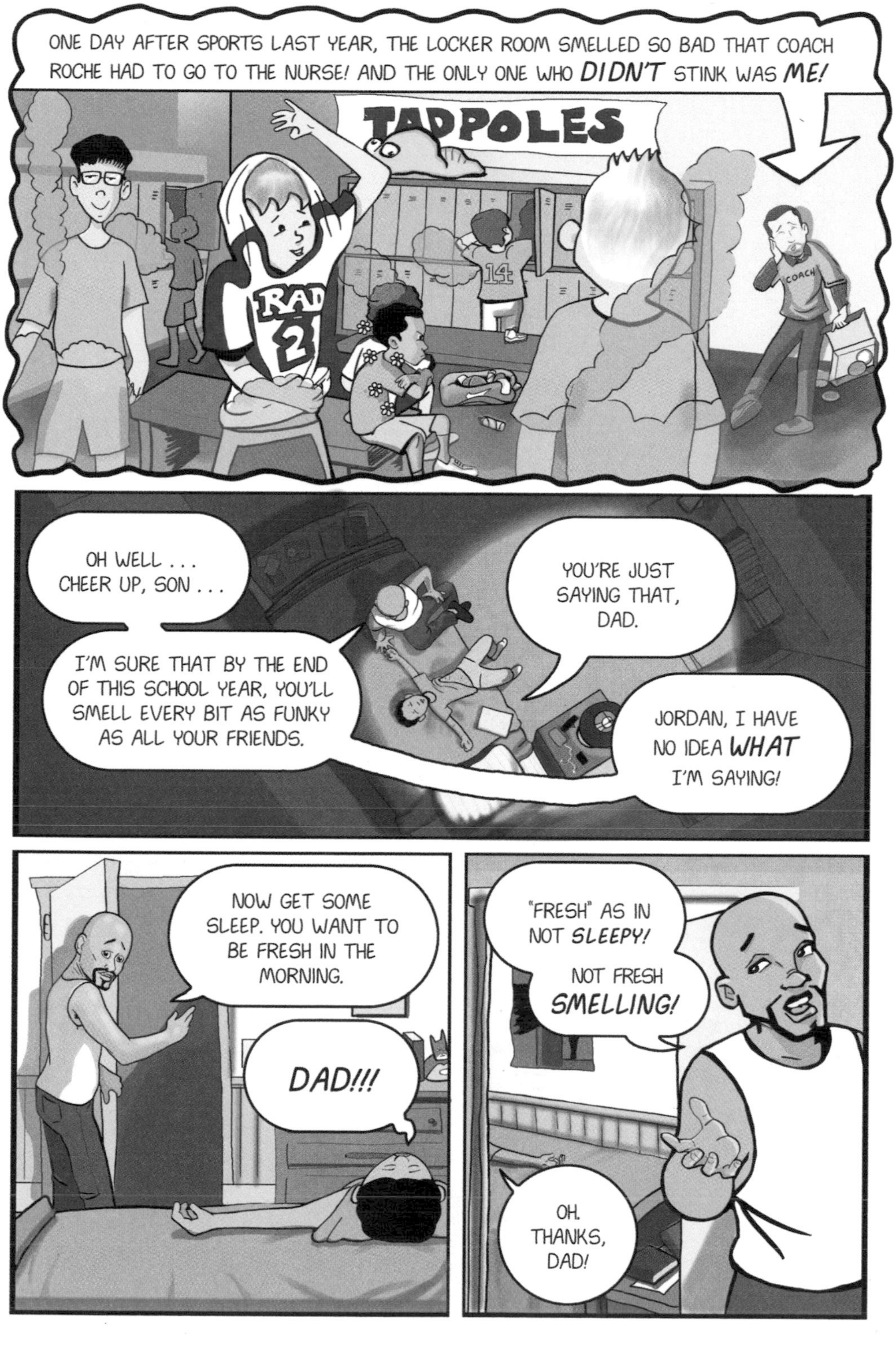
ONE DAY AFTER SPORTS LAST YEAR, THE LOCKER ROOM SMELLED SO BAD THAT COACH ROCHE HAD TO GO TO THE NURSE! AND THE ONLY ONE WHO DIDN'T STINK WAS ME!
TADPOLES
RAD 2
14
COACH
OH WELL . . . CHEER UP, SON . . .
I'M SURE THAT BY THE END OF THIS SCHOOL YEAR, YOU'LL SMELL EVERY BIT AS FUNKY AS ALL YOUR FRIENDS.
YOU'RE JUST SAYING THAT, DAD.
JORDAN, I HAVE NO IDEA WHAT I'M SAYING!
NOW GET SOME SLEEP. YOU WANT TO BE FRESH IN THE MORNING.
DAD!!!
"FRESH" AS IN NOT SLEEPY!
NOT FRESH SMELLING!
OH. THANKS, DAD!

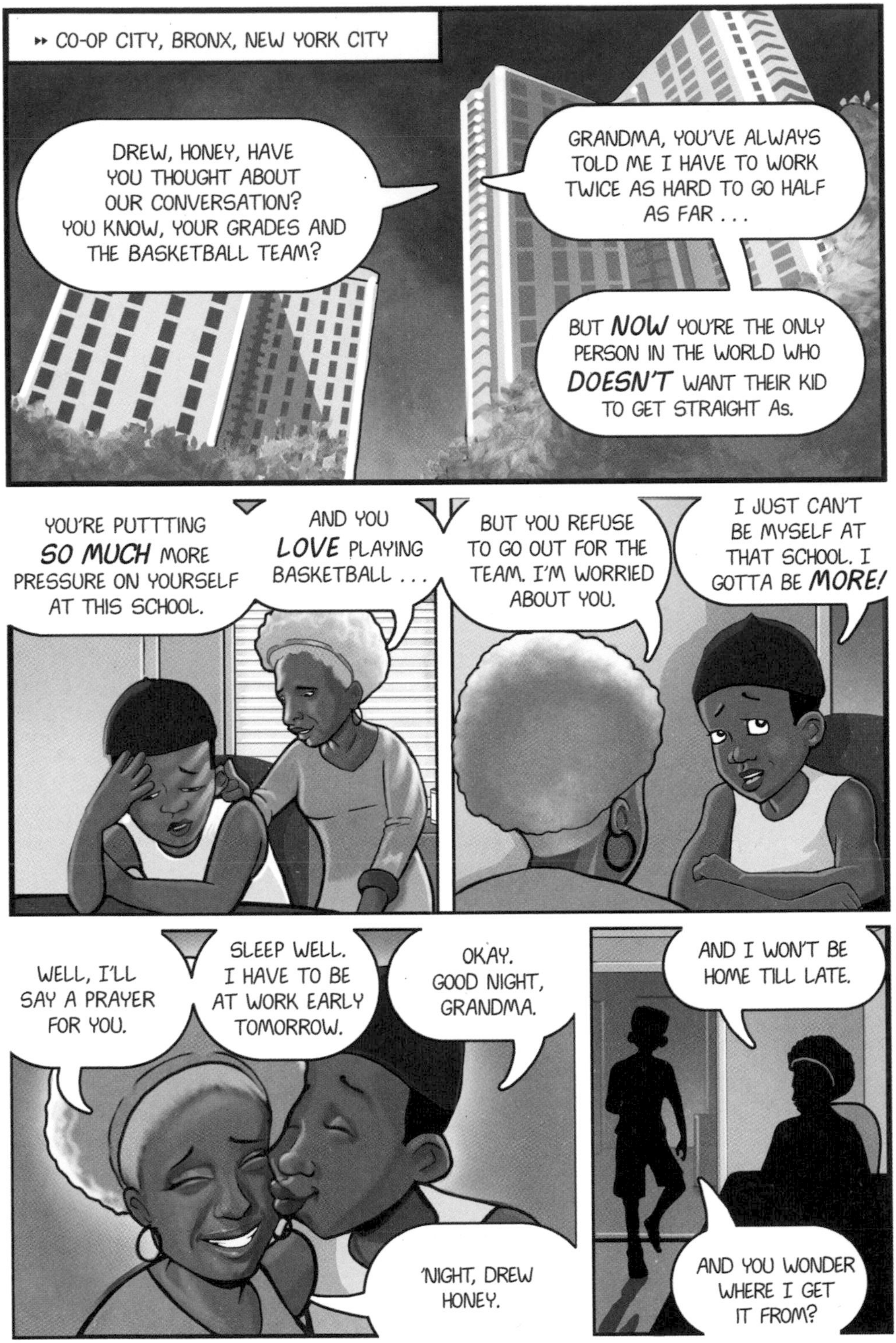
CO-OP CITY, BRONX, NEW YORK CITY
DREW, HONEY, HAVE YOU THOUGHT ABOUT OUR CONVERSATION? YOU KNOW, YOUR GRADES AND THE BASKETBALL TEAM?
GRANDMA, YOU'VE ALWAYS TOLD ME I HAVE TO WORK TWICE AS HARD TO GO HALF AS FAR . . .
BUT NOW YOU'RE THE ONLY PERSON IN THE WORLD WHO DOESN'T WANT THEIR KID TO GET STRAIGHT As.
YOU'RE PUTTTING SO MUCH MORE PRESSURE ON YOURSELF AT THIS SCHOOL.
AND YOU LOVE PLAYING BASKETBALL . . .
BUT YOU REFUSE TO GO OUT FOR THE TEAM. I'M WORRIED ABOUT YOU.
I JUST CAN'T BE MYSELF AT THAT SCHOOL. I GOTTA BE MORE!
WELL, I'LL SAY A PRAYER FOR YOU.
SLEEP WELL. I HAVE TO BE AT WORK EARLY TOMORROW.
OKAY. GOOD NIGHT, GRANDMA.
'NIGHT, DREW HONEY.
AND I WON'T BE HOME TILL LATE.
AND YOU WONDER WHERE I GET IT FROM?

▸▸ RIVERDALE, B~~RONX~~, NEW YORK CITY

I AM NOT HAVING THIS ARGUMENT WITH YOU AGAIN, ZOE! WE DO THIS EVERY SINGLE TIME I HAVE TO

DO YOU THINK YOU'RE THE ONLY ONE WHO IS SICK OF THIS, BILL? YOU'RE GONE ALL THE TIME! WHAT DO

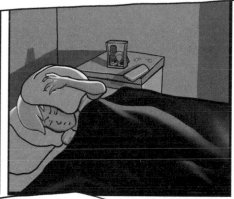

THESE BUSINESS TRIPS OF YOURS ARE REALLY

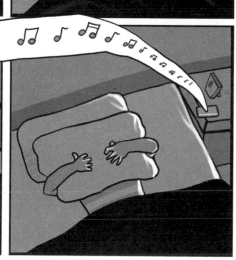

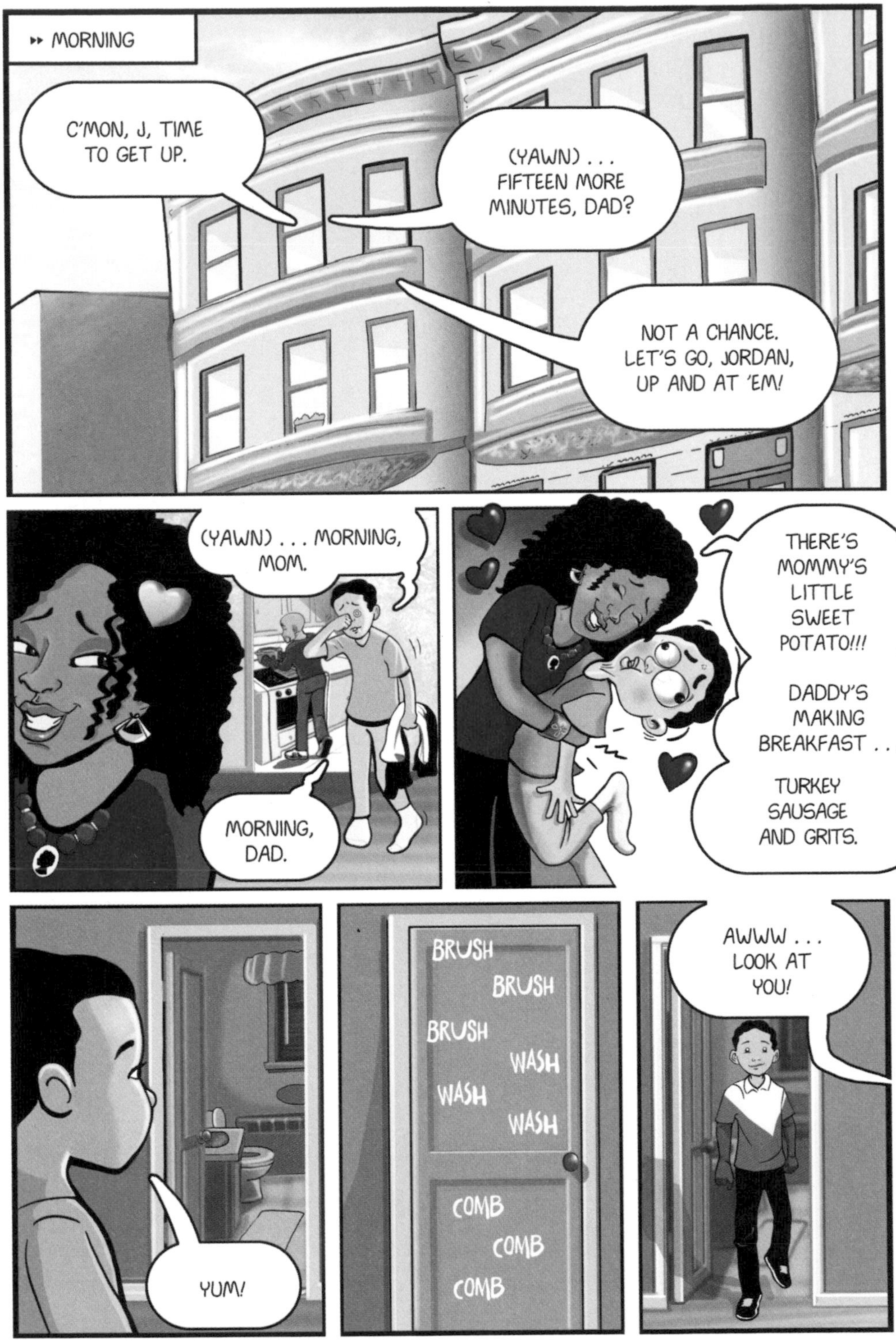
MORNING
C'MON, J, TIME TO GET UP.
(YAWN) . . . FIFTEEN MORE MINUTES, DAD?
NOT A CHANCE. LET'S GO, JORDAN, UP AND AT 'EM!
(YAWN) . . . MORNING, MOM.
MORNING, DAD.
THERE'S MOMMY'S LITTLE SWEET POTATO!!!
DADDY'S MAKING BREAKFAST . . .
TURKEY SAUSAGE AND GRITS.
YUM!
BRUSH
BRUSH
BRUSH
WASH
WASH
WASH
COMB
COMB
COMB
AWWW . . . LOOK AT YOU!

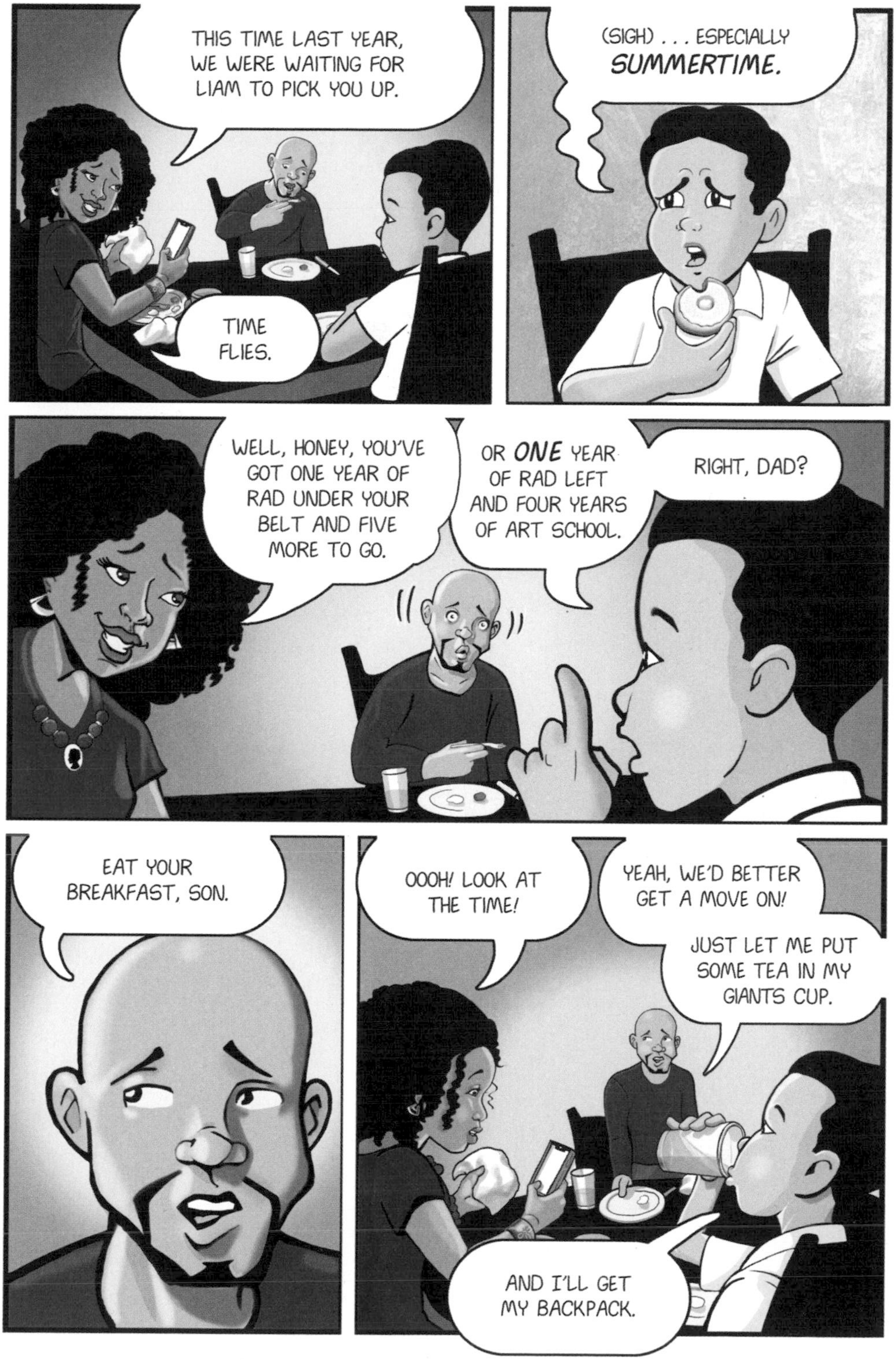
THIS TIME LAST YEAR, WE WERE WAITING FOR LIAM TO PICK YOU UP.
TIME FLIES.
(SIGH) . . . ESPECIALLY SUMMERTIME.
WELL, HONEY, YOU'VE GOT ONE YEAR OF RAD UNDER YOUR BELT AND FIVE MORE TO GO.
OR ONE YEAR OF RAD LEFT AND FOUR YEARS OF ART SCHOOL.
RIGHT, DAD?
EAT YOUR BREAKFAST, SON.
OOOH! LOOK AT THE TIME!
YEAH, WE'D BETTER GET A MOVE ON!
JUST LET ME PUT SOME TEA IN MY GIANTS CUP.
AND I'LL GET MY BACKPACK.

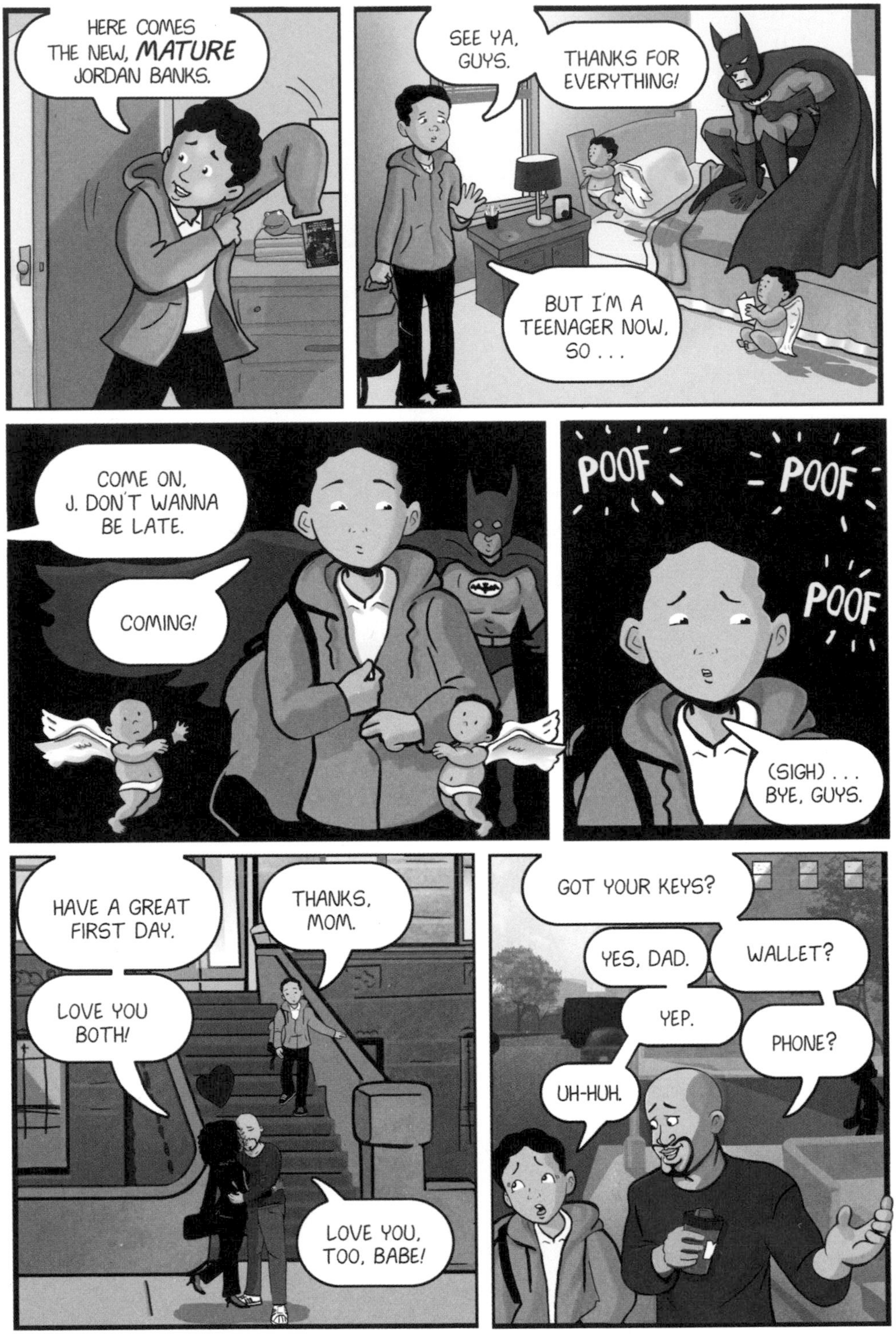

HERE COMES THE NEW, MATURE JORDAN BANKS.
SEE YA, GUYS.
THANKS FOR EVERYTHING!
BUT I'M A TEENAGER NOW, SO . . .
COME ON, J. DON'T WANNA BE LATE.
COMING!
POOF
POOF
POOF
(SIGH) . . . BYE, GUYS.
HAVE A GREAT FIRST DAY.
LOVE YOU BOTH!
THANKS, MOM.
LOVE YOU, TOO, BABE!
GOT YOUR KEYS?
YES, DAD.
WALLET?
YEP.
PHONE?
UH-HUH.

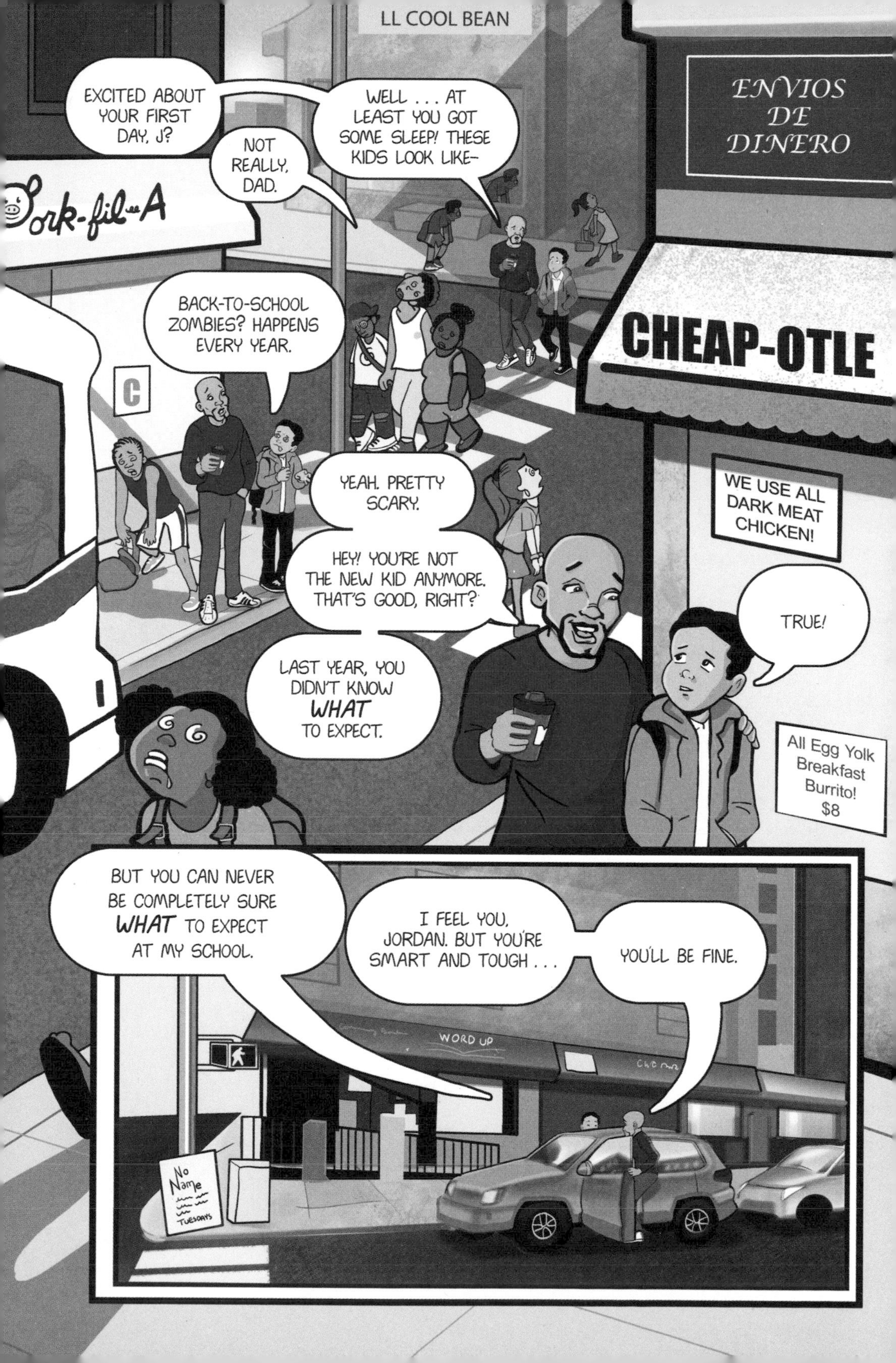
LL COOL BEAN
EXCITED ABOUT YOUR FIRST DAY, J?
NOT REALLY, DAD.
WELL . . . AT LEAST YOU GOT SOME SLEEP! THESE KIDS LOOK LIKE–
ENVIOS DE DINERO
Pork-fil-A
BACK-TO-SCHOOL ZOMBIES? HAPPENS EVERY YEAR.
C
CHEAP-OTLE
YEAH. PRETTY SCARY.
WE USE ALL DARK MEAT CHICKEN!
HEY! YOU'RE NOT THE NEW KID ANYMORE. THAT'S GOOD, RIGHT?
TRUE!
LAST YEAR, YOU DIDN'T KNOW *WHAT* TO EXPECT.
All Egg Yolk Breakfast Burrito! $8
BUT YOU CAN NEVER BE COMPLETELY SURE *WHAT* TO EXPECT AT MY SCHOOL.
I FEEL YOU, JORDAN. BUT YOU'RE SMART AND TOUGH . . .
YOU'LL BE FINE.
WORD UP
No Name
TUESDAYS

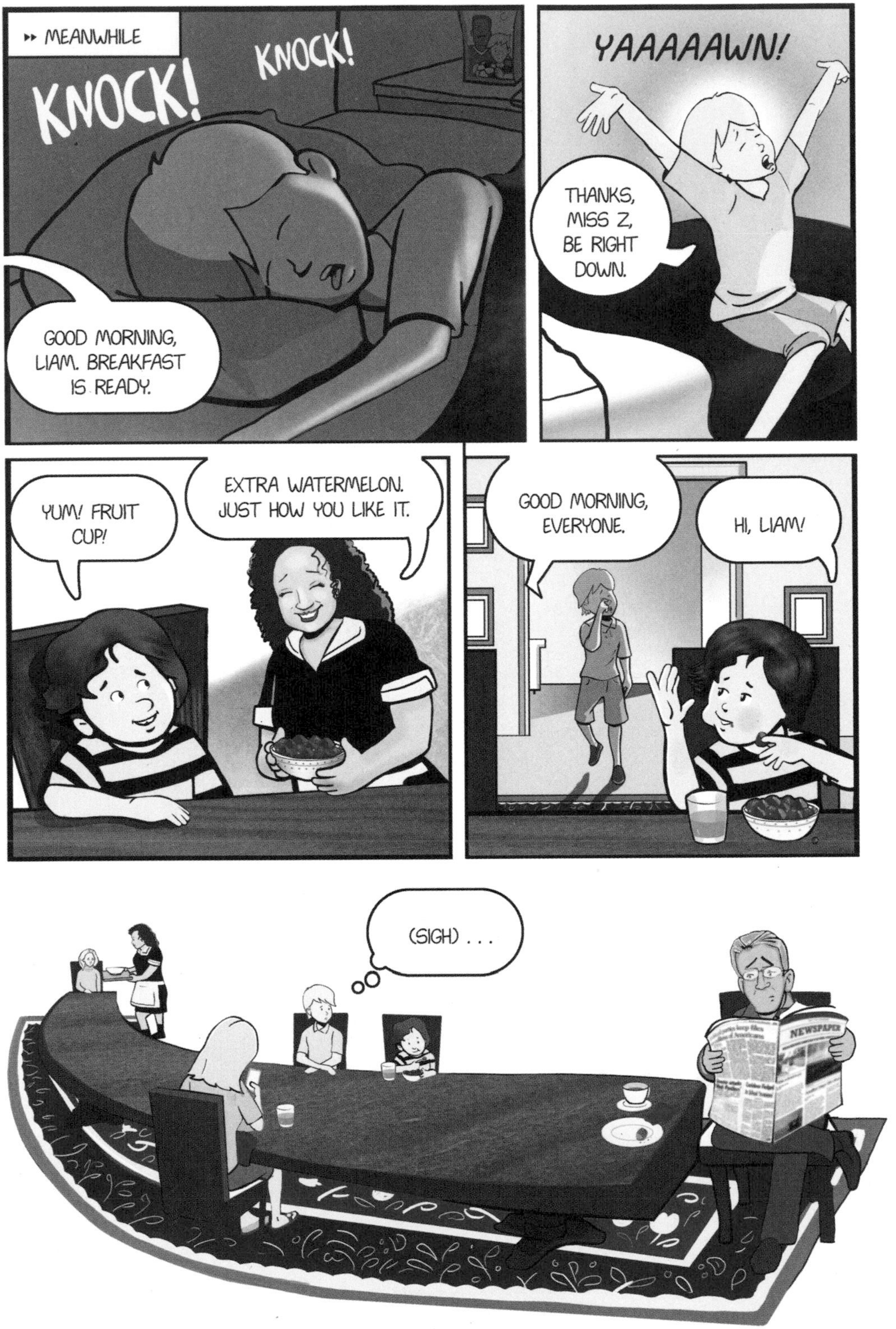

▸▸ MEANWHILE
KNOCK!
KNOCK!
GOOD MORNING, LIAM. BREAKFAST IS READY.
YAAAAAWN!
THANKS, MISS Z, BE RIGHT DOWN.
YUM! FRUIT CUP!
EXTRA WATERMELON. JUST HOW YOU LIKE IT.
GOOD MORNING, EVERYONE.
HI, LIAM!
(SIGH) . . .
NEWSPAPER

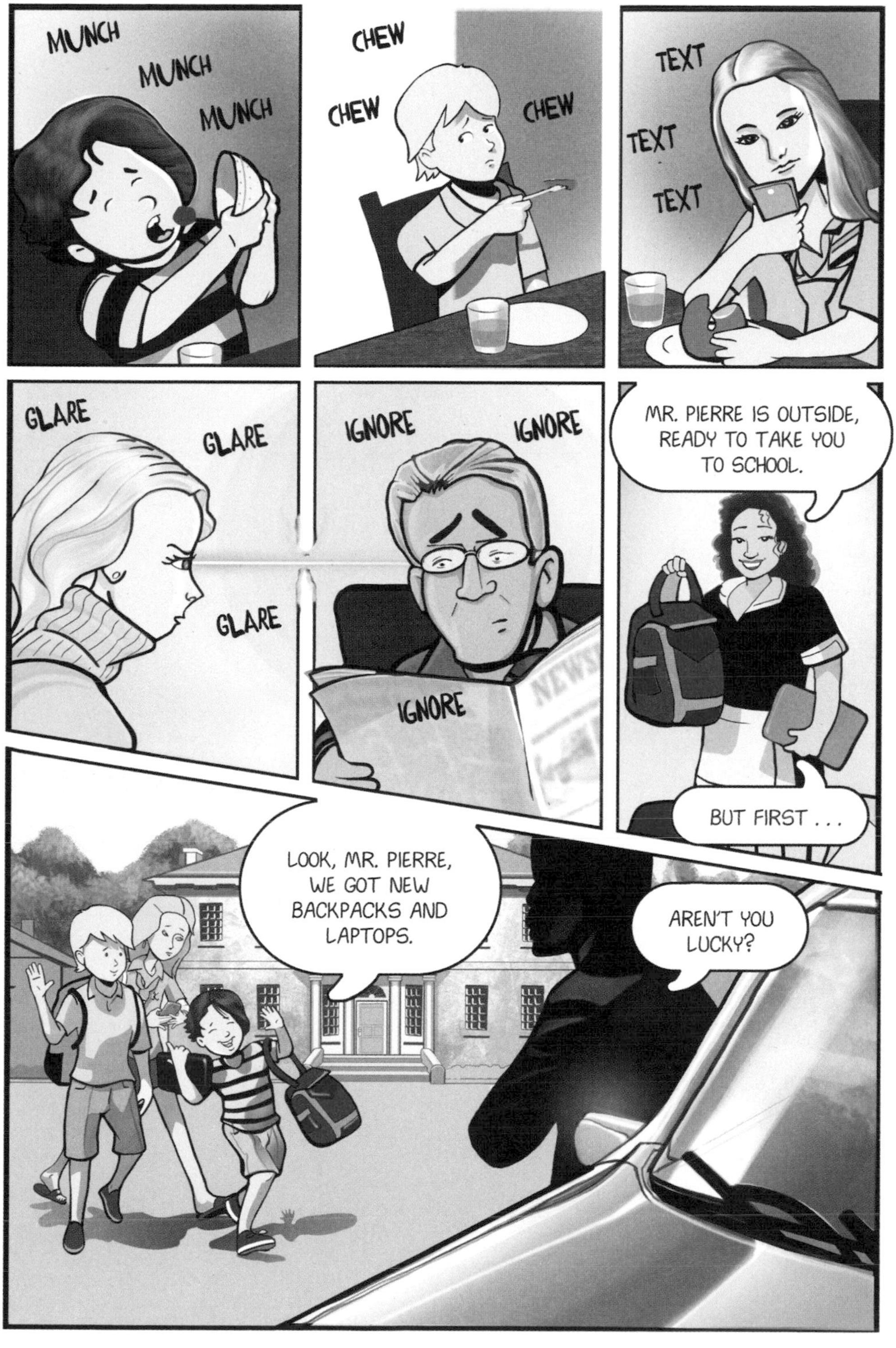
MUNCH
MUNCH
MUNCH
CHEW
CHEW
CHEW
TEXT
TEXT
TEXT
GLARE
GLARE
GLARE
IGNORE
IGNORE
IGNORE
MR. PIERRE IS OUTSIDE, READY TO TAKE YOU TO SCHOOL.
BUT FIRST . . .
LOOK, MR. PIERRE, WE GOT NEW BACKPACKS AND LAPTOPS.
AREN'T YOU LUCKY?

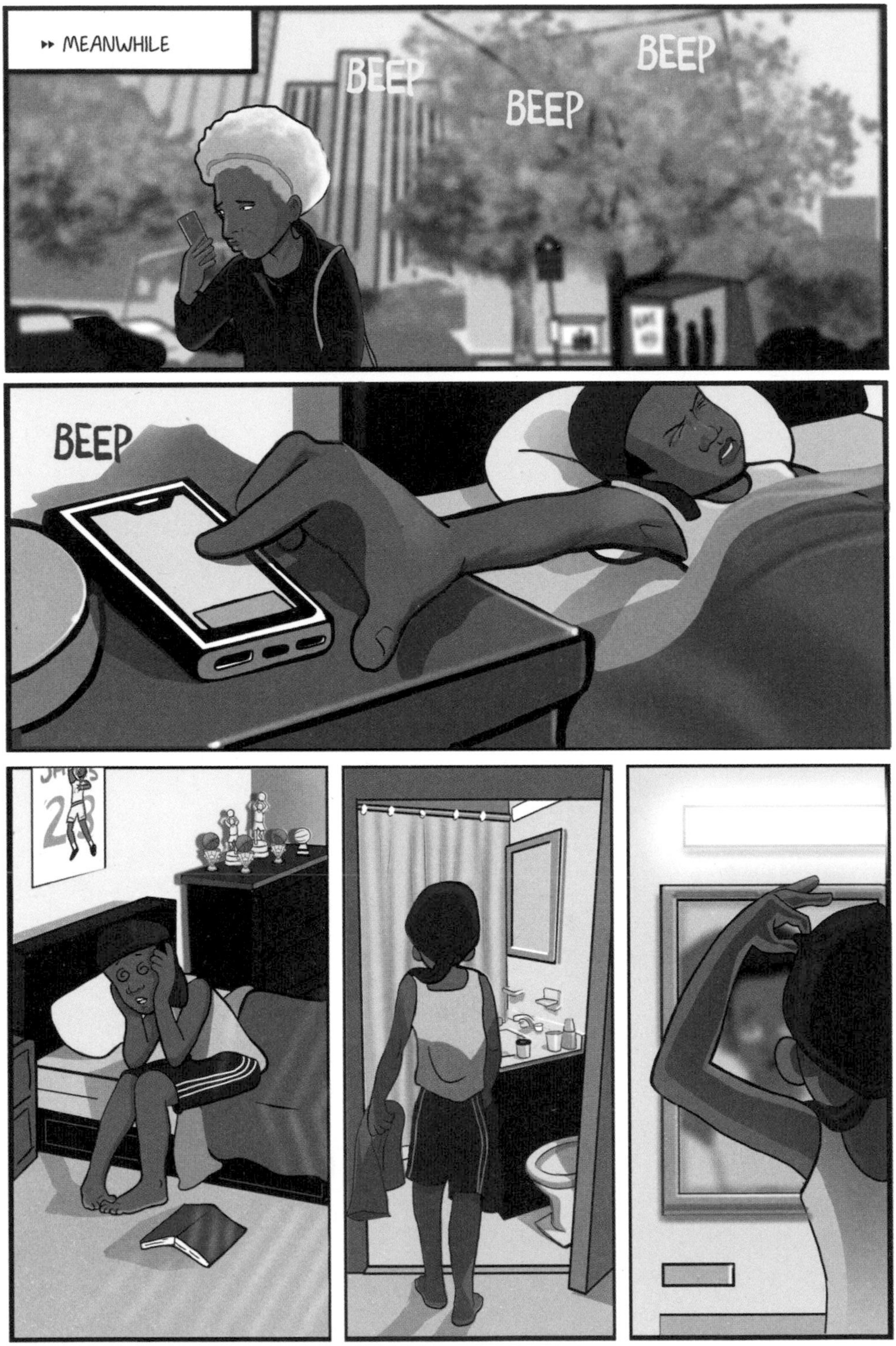
MEANWHILE
BEEP
BEEP
BEEP
BEEP

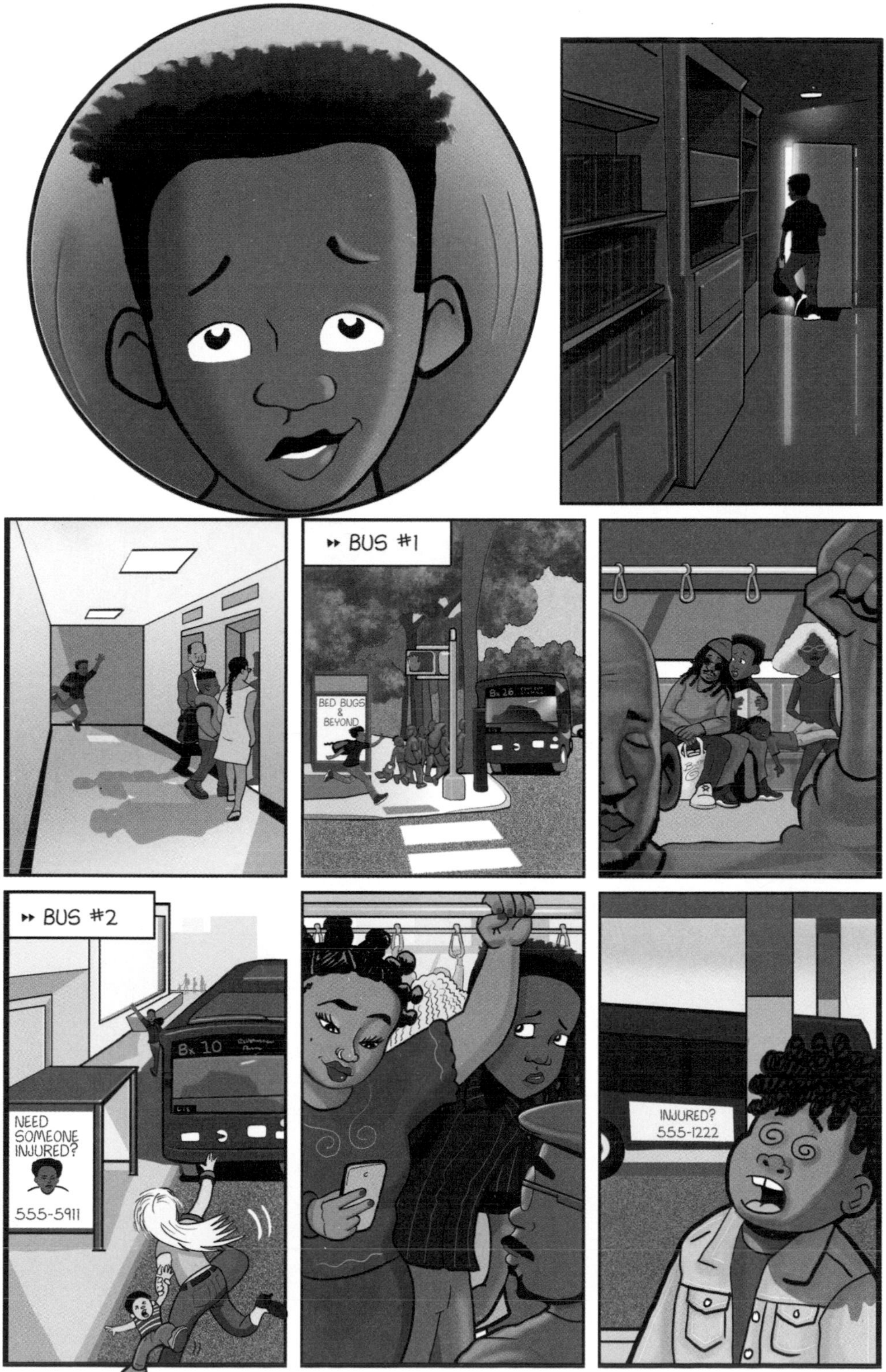
BUS #1
BED BUGS & BEYOND
Bx 26
BUS #2
Bx 10
NEED SOMEONE INJURED?
555-5911
INJURED?
555-1222

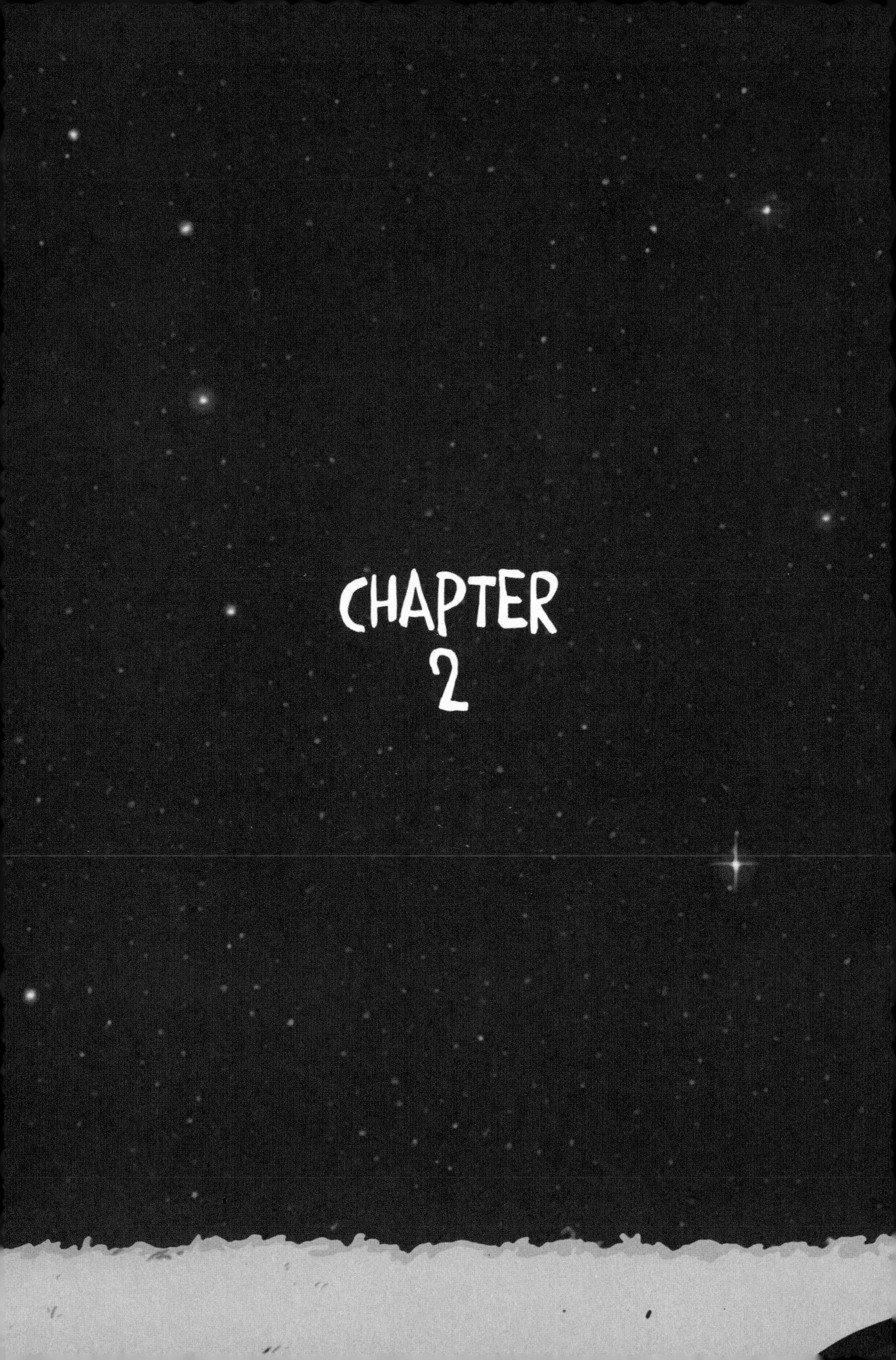
CHAPTER
2

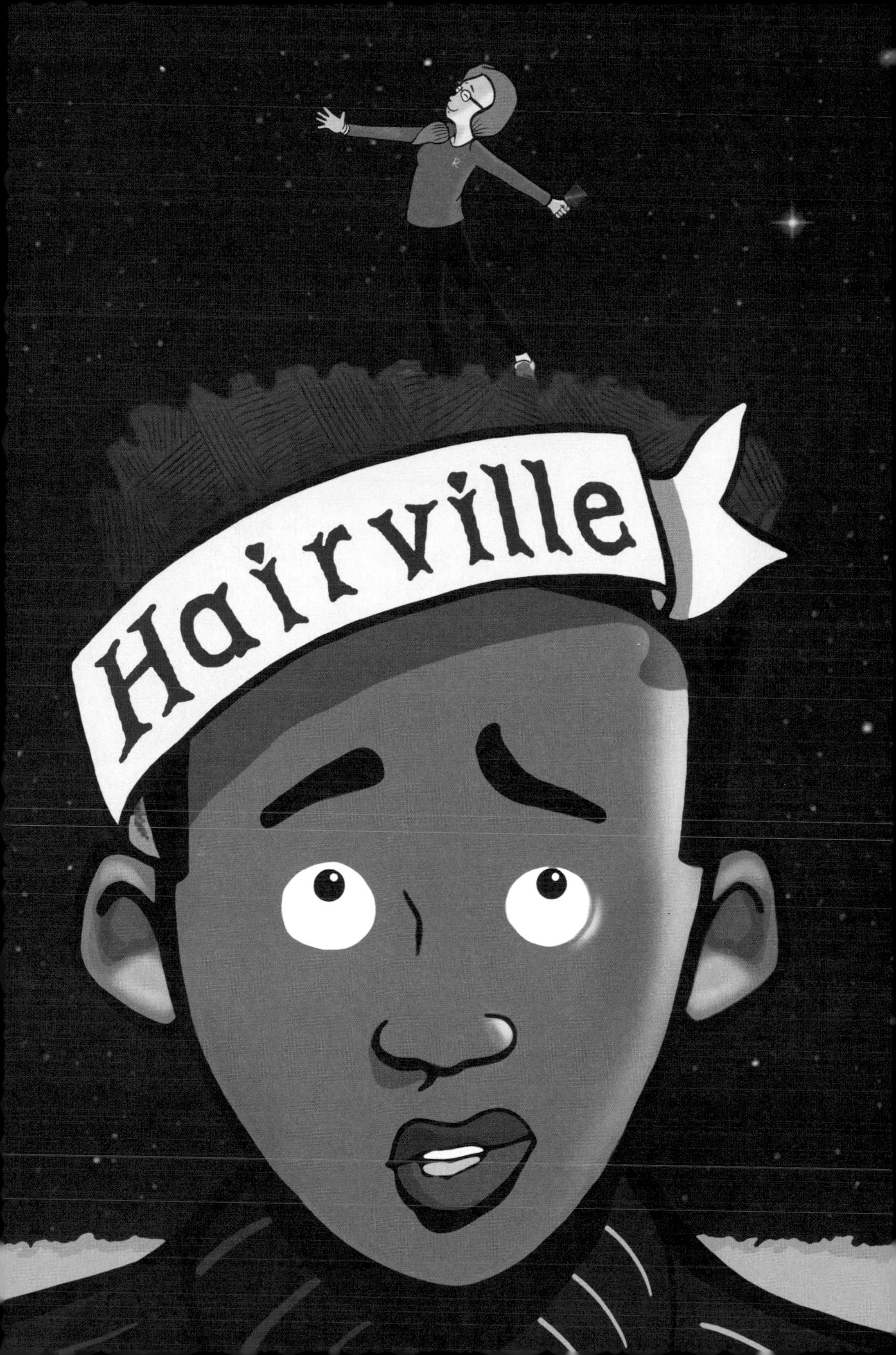
Hairville

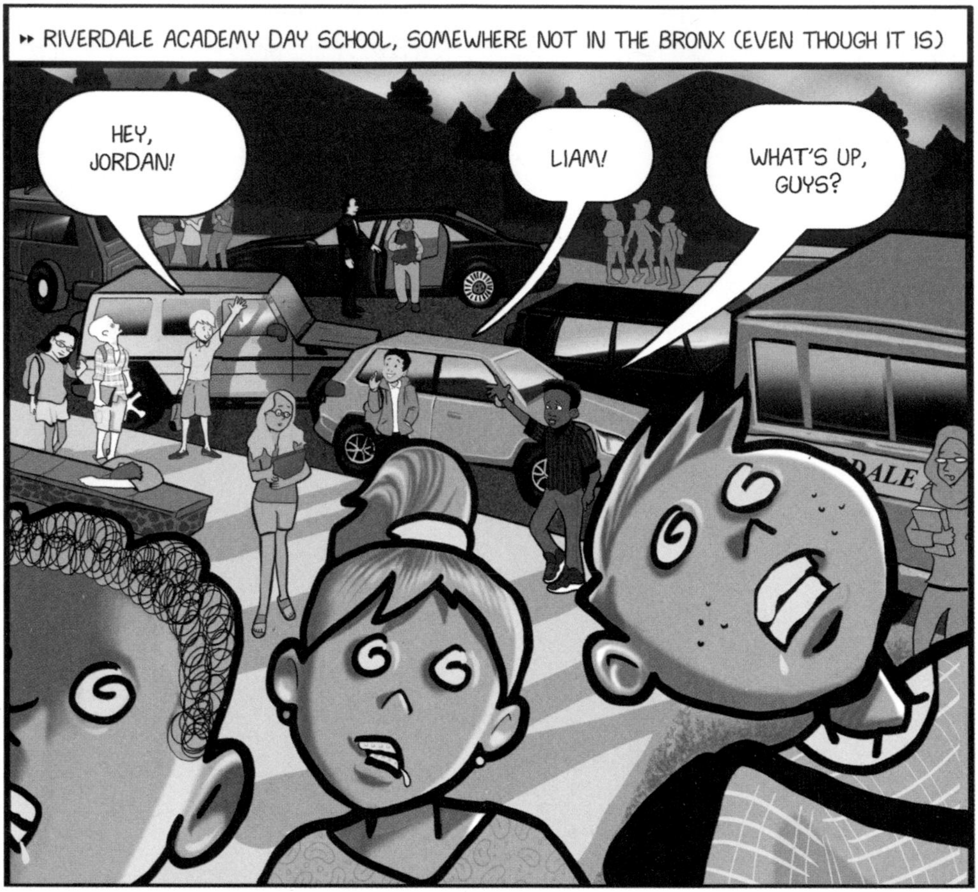
▸▸ RIVERDALE ACADEMY DAY SCHOOL, SOMEWHERE NOT IN THE BRONX (EVEN THOUGH IT IS)
HEY, JORDAN!
LIAM!
WHAT'S UP, GUYS?

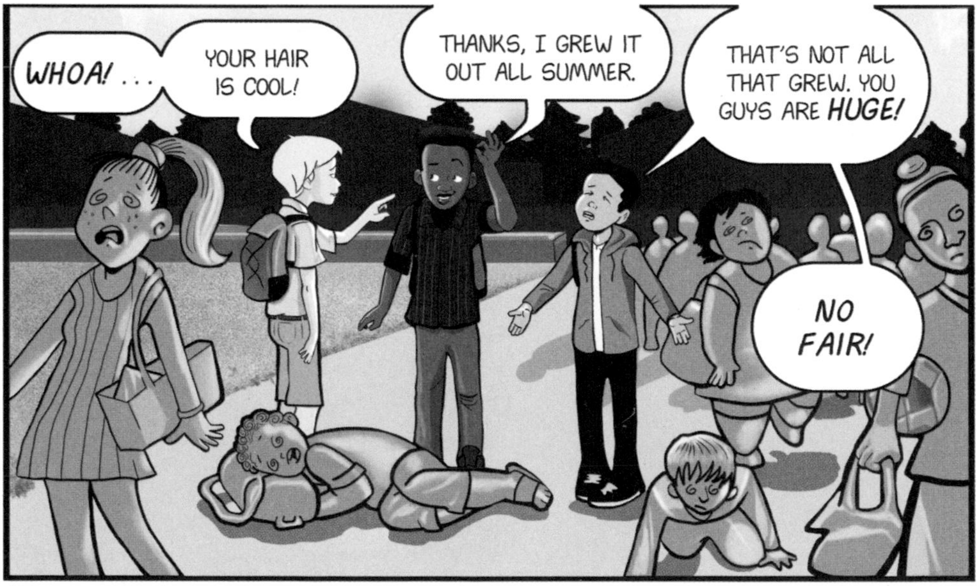
WHOA! . . .
YOUR HAIR IS COOL!
THANKS, I GREW IT OUT ALL SUMMER.
THAT'S NOT ALL THAT GREW. YOU GUYS ARE **HUGE!**
NO FAIR!

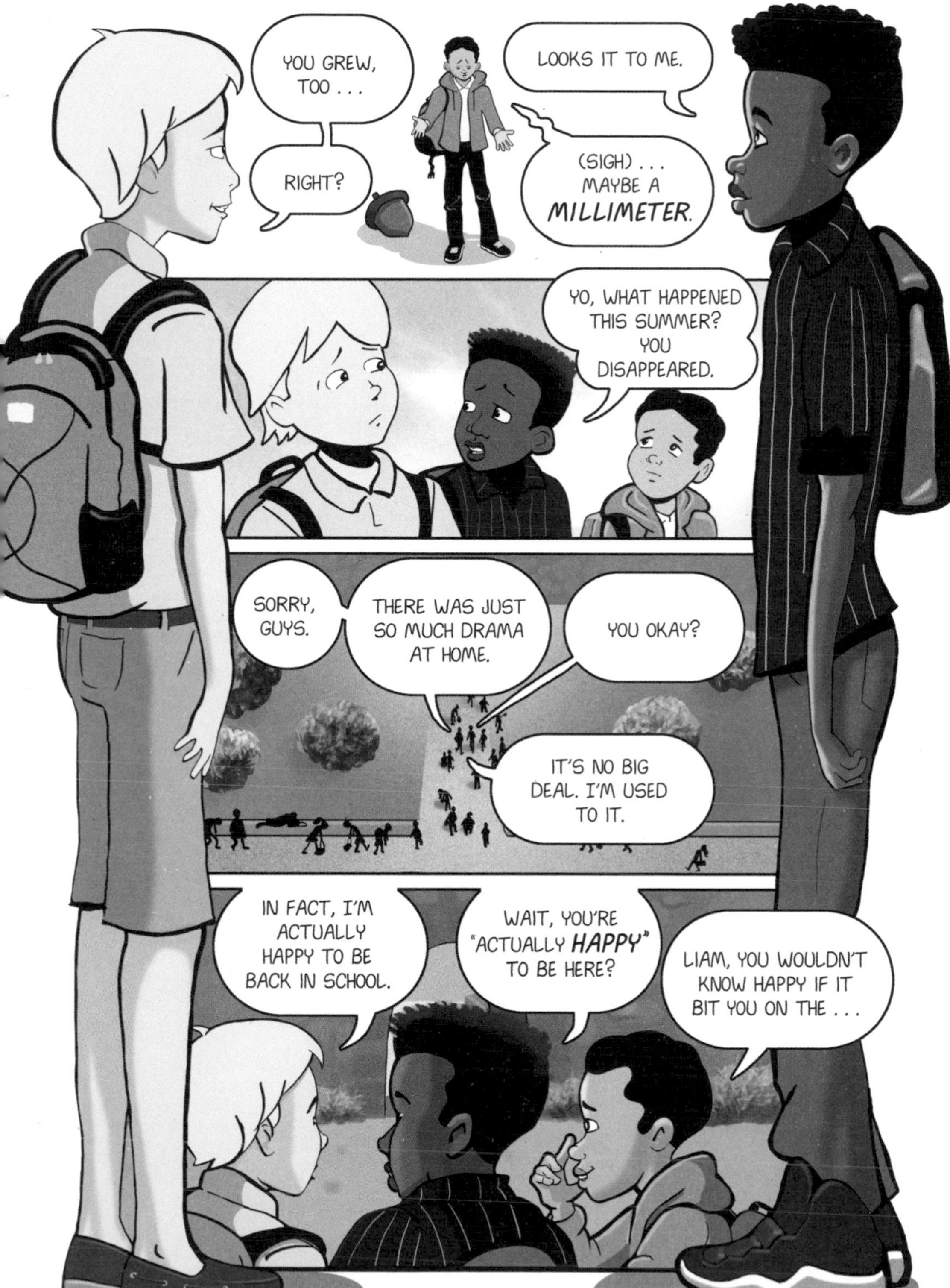
YOU GREW, TOO . . .
RIGHT?
LOOKS IT TO ME.
(SIGH) . . . MAYBE A MILLIMETER.
YO, WHAT HAPPENED THIS SUMMER? YOU DISAPPEARED.
SORRY, GUYS.
THERE WAS JUST SO MUCH DRAMA AT HOME.
YOU OKAY?
IT'S NO BIG DEAL. I'M USED TO IT.
IN FACT, I'M ACTUALLY HAPPY TO BE BACK IN SCHOOL.
WAIT, YOU'RE "ACTUALLY HAPPY" TO BE HERE?
LIAM, YOU WOULDN'T KNOW HAPPY IF IT BIT YOU ON THE . . .

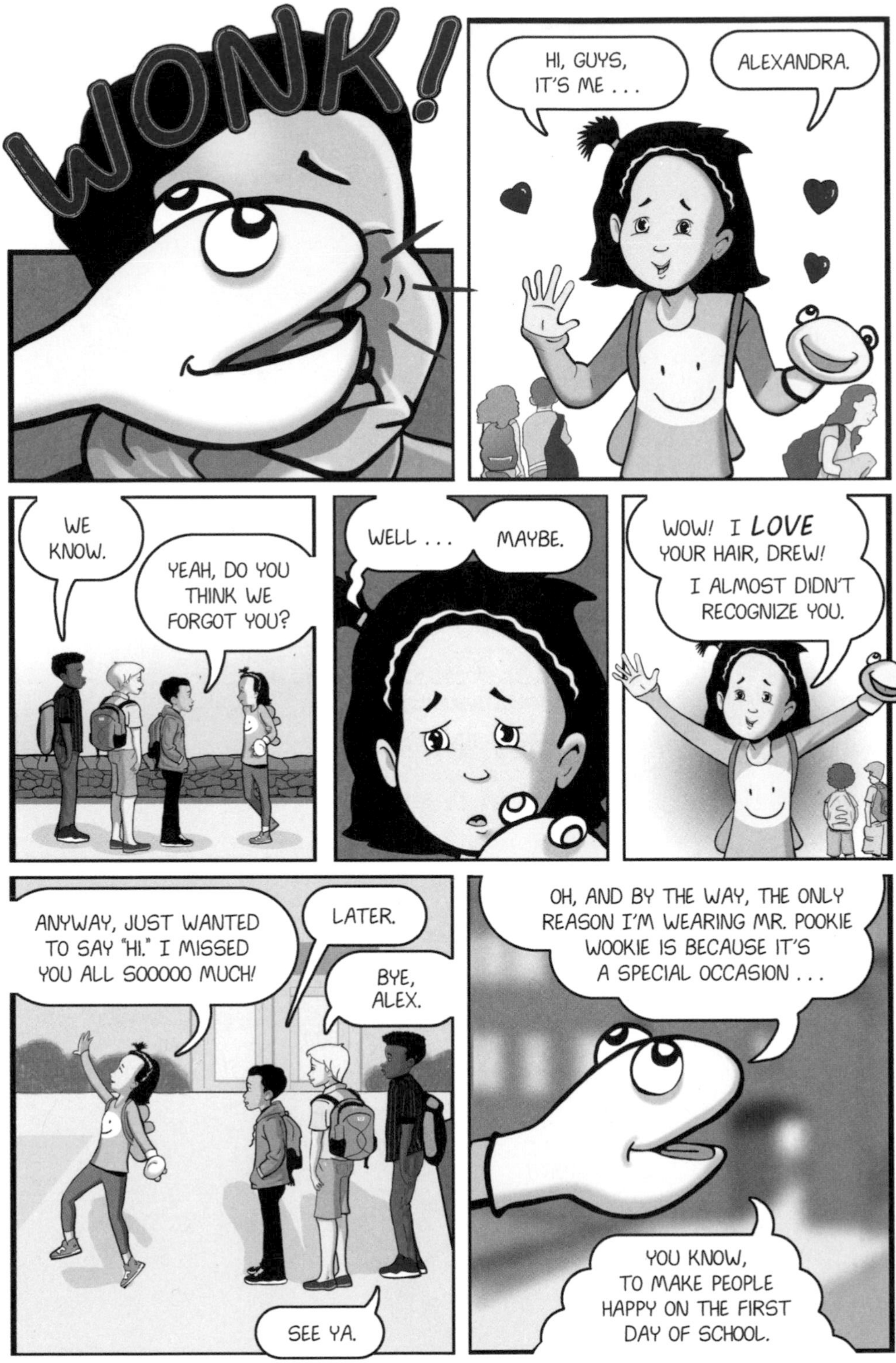
WONK!
HI, GUYS, IT'S ME . . .
ALEXANDRA.
WE KNOW.
YEAH, DO YOU THINK WE FORGOT YOU?
WELL . . .
MAYBE.
WOW! I **LOVE** YOUR HAIR, DREW!
I ALMOST DIDN'T RECOGNIZE YOU.
ANYWAY, JUST WANTED TO SAY "HI." I MISSED YOU ALL SOOOOO MUCH!
LATER.
BYE, ALEX.
SEE YA.
OH, AND BY THE WAY, THE ONLY REASON I'M WEARING MR. POOKIE WOOKIE IS BECAUSE IT'S A SPECIAL OCCASION . . .
YOU KNOW, TO MAKE PEOPLE HAPPY ON THE FIRST DAY OF SCHOOL.

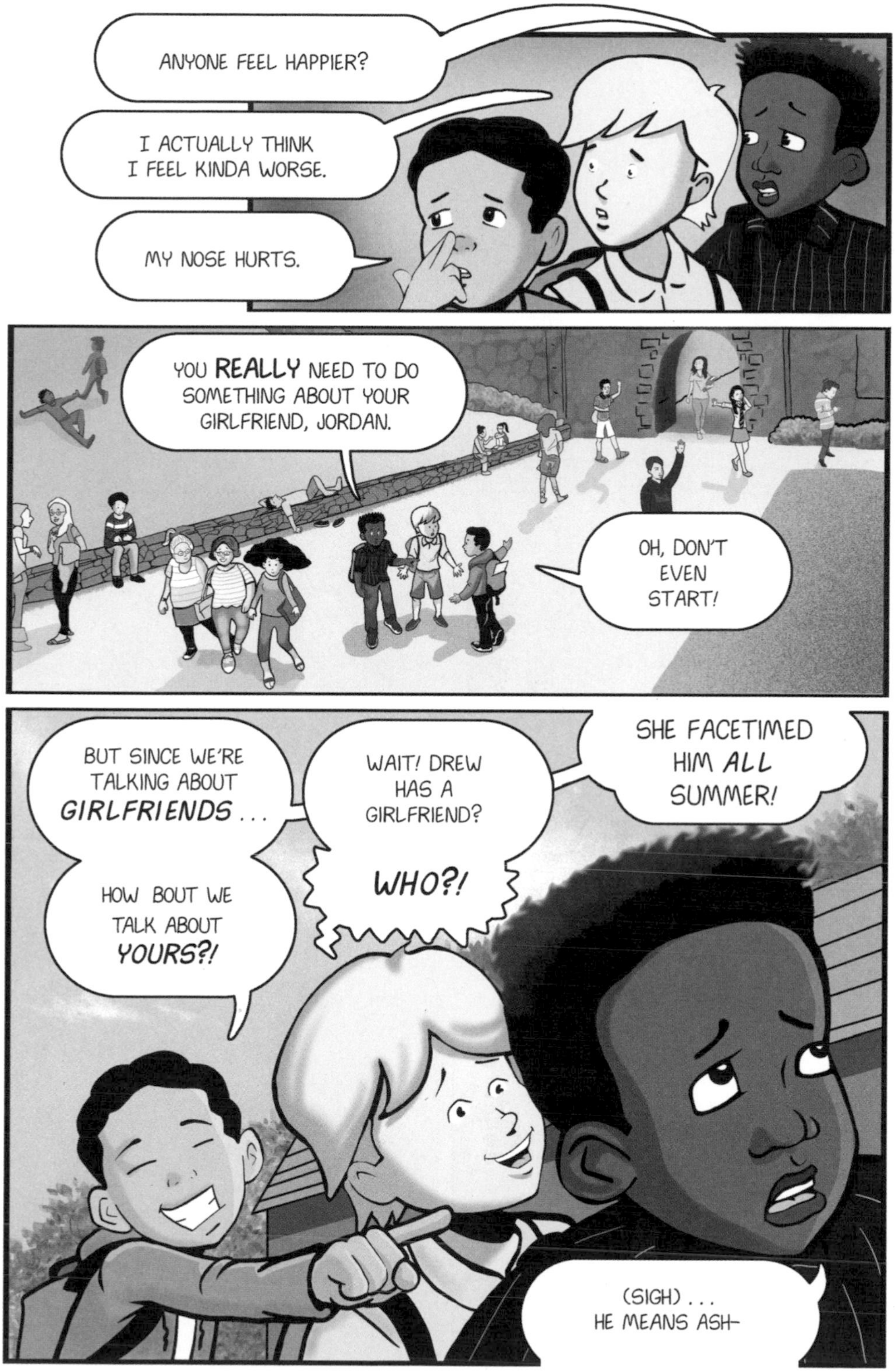
ANYONE FEEL HAPPIER?
I ACTUALLY THINK I FEEL KINDA WORSE.
MY NOSE HURTS.
YOU **REALLY** NEED TO DO SOMETHING ABOUT YOUR GIRLFRIEND, JORDAN.
OH, DON'T EVEN START!
BUT SINCE WE'RE TALKING ABOUT ***GIRLFRIENDS*** . . .
HOW BOUT WE TALK ABOUT ***YOURS?!***
WAIT! DREW HAS A GIRLFRIEND?
WHO?!
SHE FACETIMED HIM ***ALL*** SUMMER!
(SIGH) . . . HE MEANS ASH—

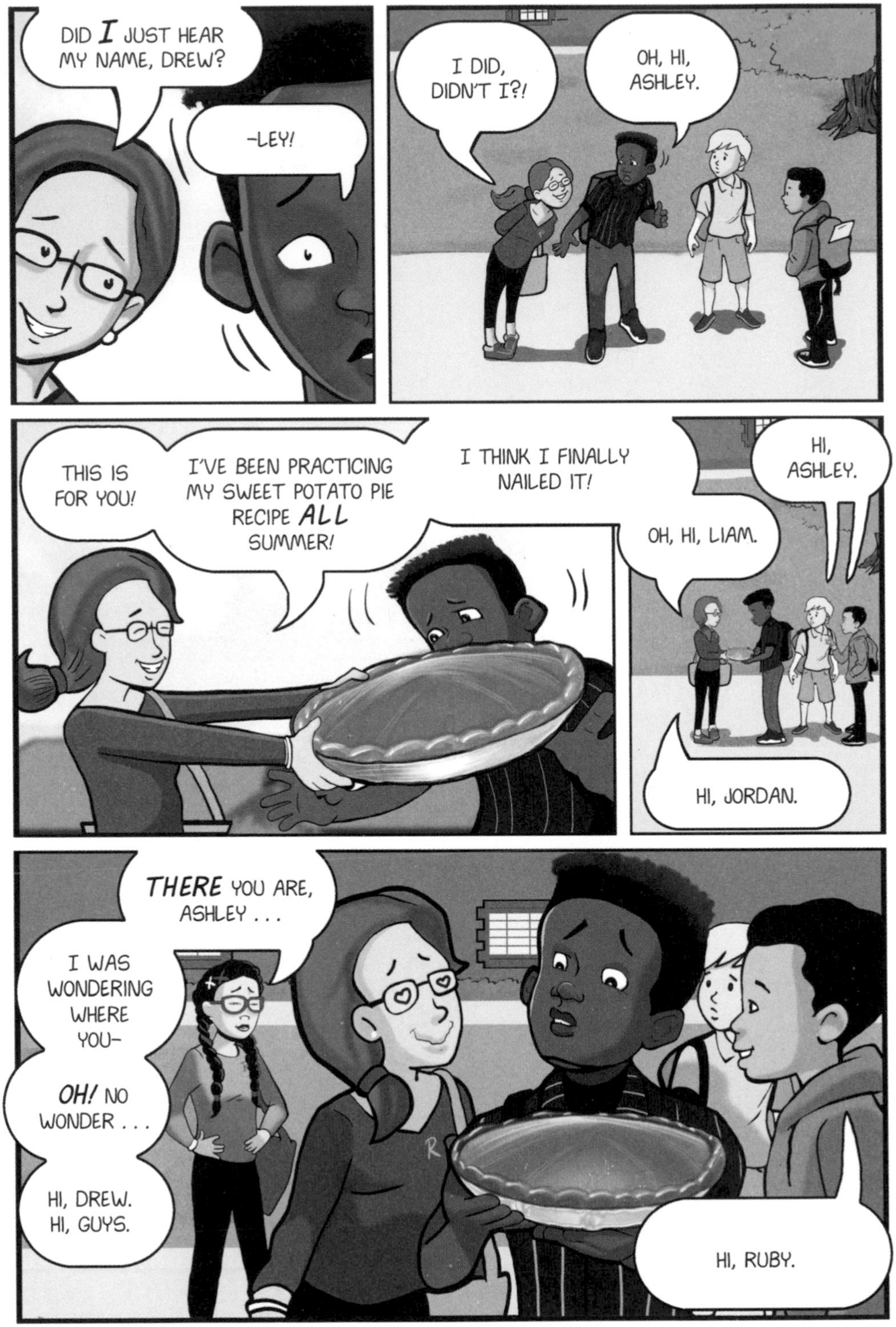
DID I JUST HEAR MY NAME, DREW?
-LEY!
I DID, DIDN'T I?!
OH, HI, ASHLEY.
THIS IS FOR YOU!
I'VE BEEN PRACTICING MY SWEET POTATO PIE RECIPE ALL SUMMER!
I THINK I FINALLY NAILED IT!
HI, ASHLEY.
OH, HI, LIAM.
HI, JORDAN.
THERE YOU ARE, ASHLEY . . .
I WAS WONDERING WHERE YOU-
OH! NO WONDER . . .
HI, DREW. HI, GUYS.
HI, RUBY.

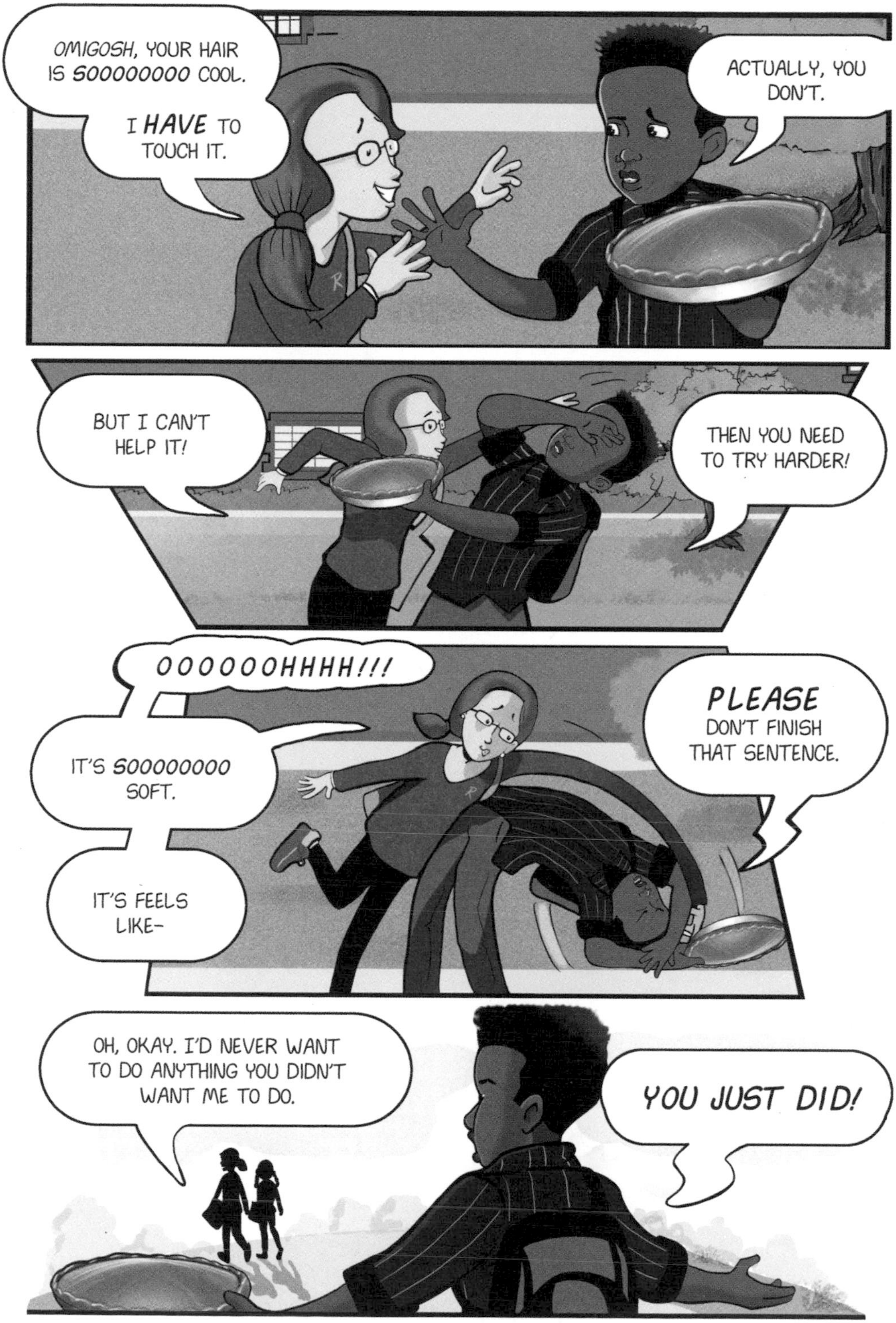
OMIGOSH, YOUR HAIR IS SOOOOOOOO COOL.
I HAVE TO TOUCH IT.
ACTUALLY, YOU DON'T.
BUT I CAN'T HELP IT!
THEN YOU NEED TO TRY HARDER!
OOOOOOHHHH!!!
IT'S SOOOOOOOO SOFT.
IT'S FEELS LIKE-
PLEASE DON'T FINISH THAT SENTENCE.
OH, OKAY. I'D NEVER WANT TO DO ANYTHING YOU DIDN'T WANT ME TO DO.
YOU JUST DID!

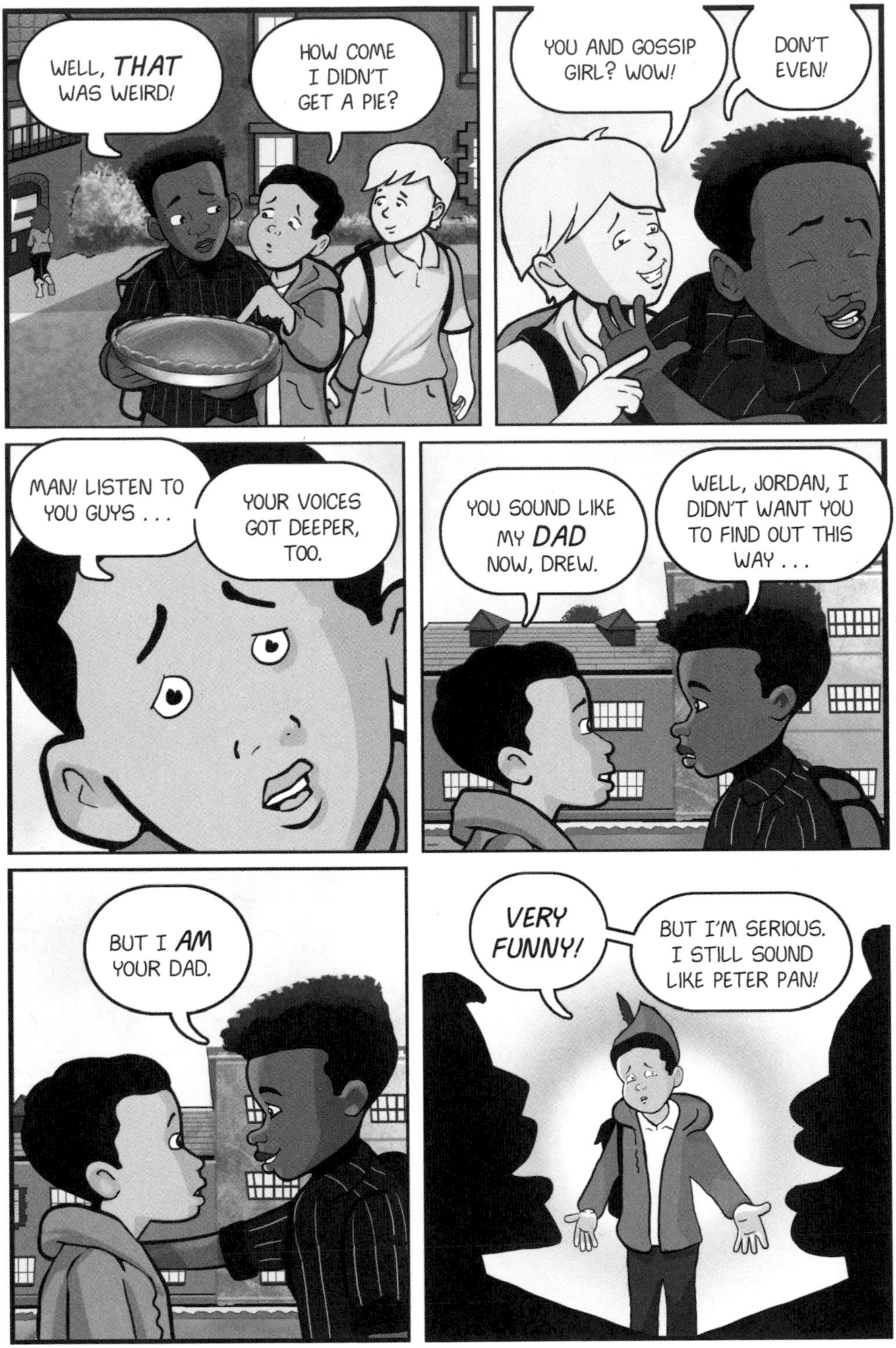
WELL, *THAT* WAS WEIRD!
HOW COME I DIDN'T GET A PIE?
YOU AND GOSSIP GIRL? WOW!
DON'T EVEN!
MAN! LISTEN TO YOU GUYS . . .
YOUR VOICES GOT DEEPER, TOO.
YOU SOUND LIKE MY *DAD* NOW, DREW.
WELL, JORDAN, I DIDN'T WANT YOU TO FIND OUT THIS WAY . . .
BUT I *AM* YOUR DAD.
VERY FUNNY!
BUT I'M SERIOUS. I STILL SOUND LIKE PETER PAN!

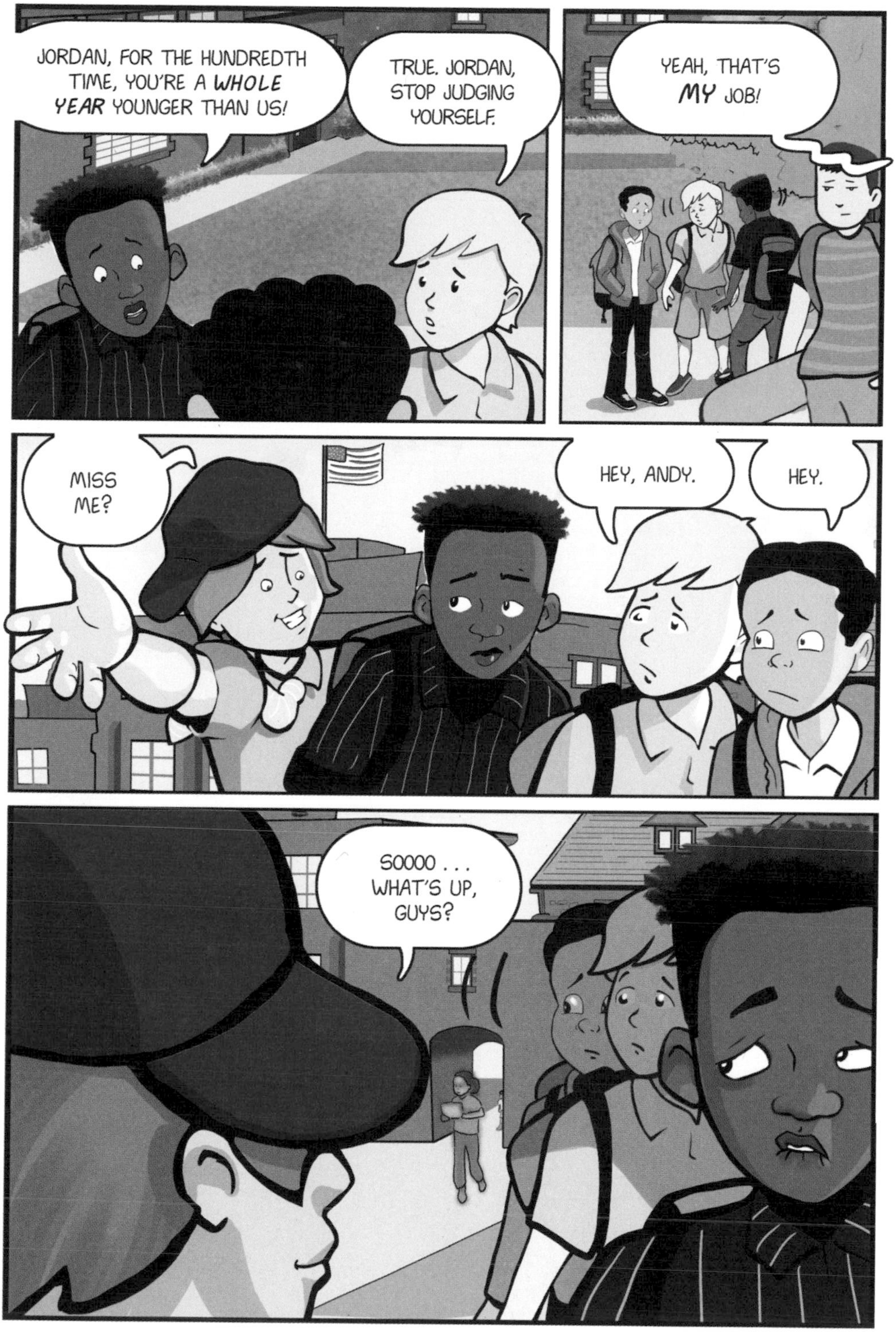
JORDAN, FOR THE HUNDREDTH TIME, YOU'RE A **WHOLE YEAR** YOUNGER THAN US!
TRUE. JORDAN, STOP JUDGING YOURSELF.
YEAH, THAT'S **MY** JOB!
MISS ME?
HEY, ANDY.
HEY.
SOOOO . . . WHAT'S UP, GUYS?

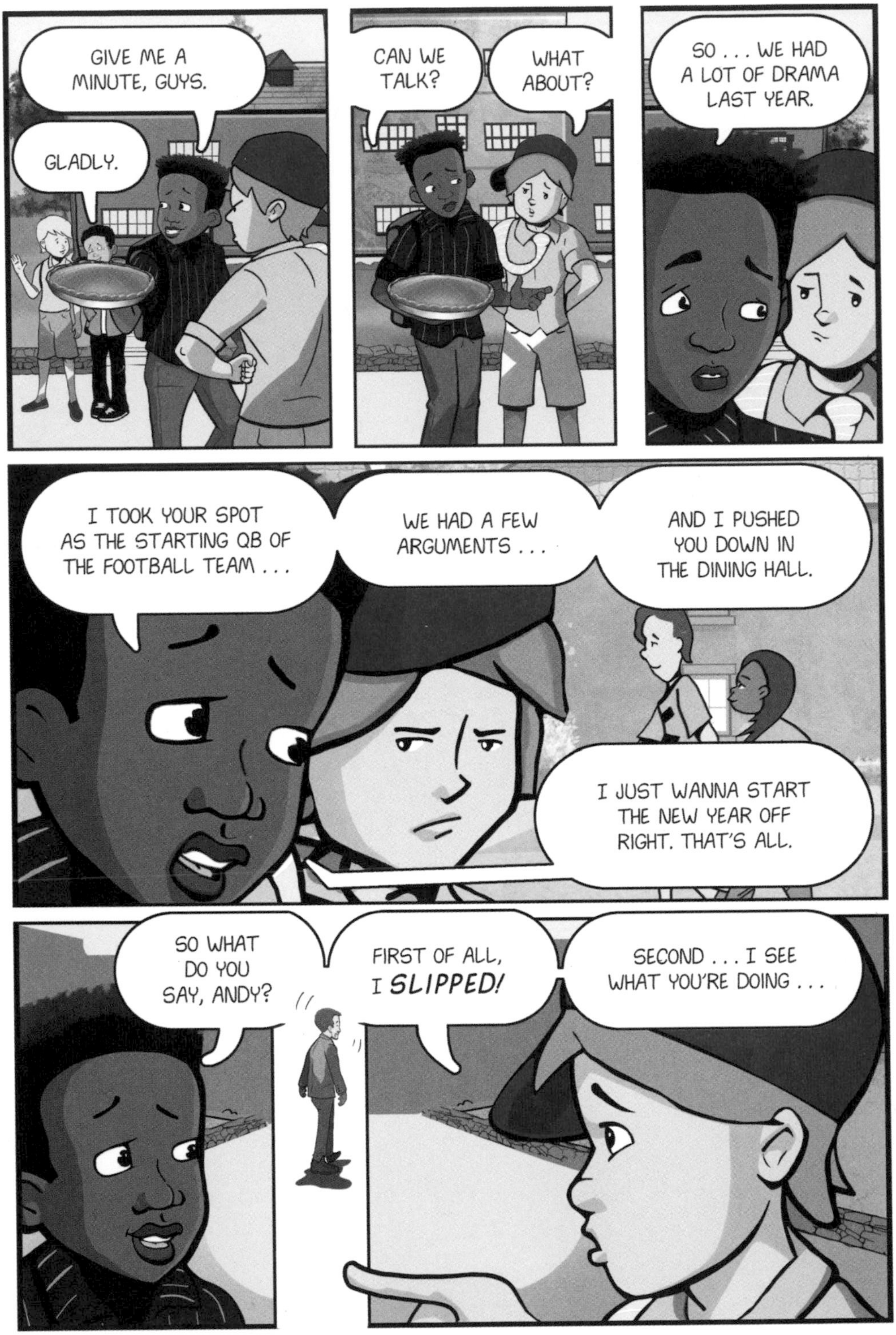
GIVE ME A MINUTE, GUYS.
GLADLY.
CAN WE TALK?
WHAT ABOUT?
SO . . . WE HAD A LOT OF DRAMA LAST YEAR.
I TOOK YOUR SPOT AS THE STARTING QB OF THE FOOTBALL TEAM . . .
WE HAD A FEW ARGUMENTS . . .
AND I PUSHED YOU DOWN IN THE DINING HALL.
I JUST WANNA START THE NEW YEAR OFF RIGHT. THAT'S ALL.
SO WHAT DO YOU SAY, ANDY?
FIRST OF ALL, I *SLIPPED!*
SECOND . . . I SEE WHAT YOU'RE DOING . . .

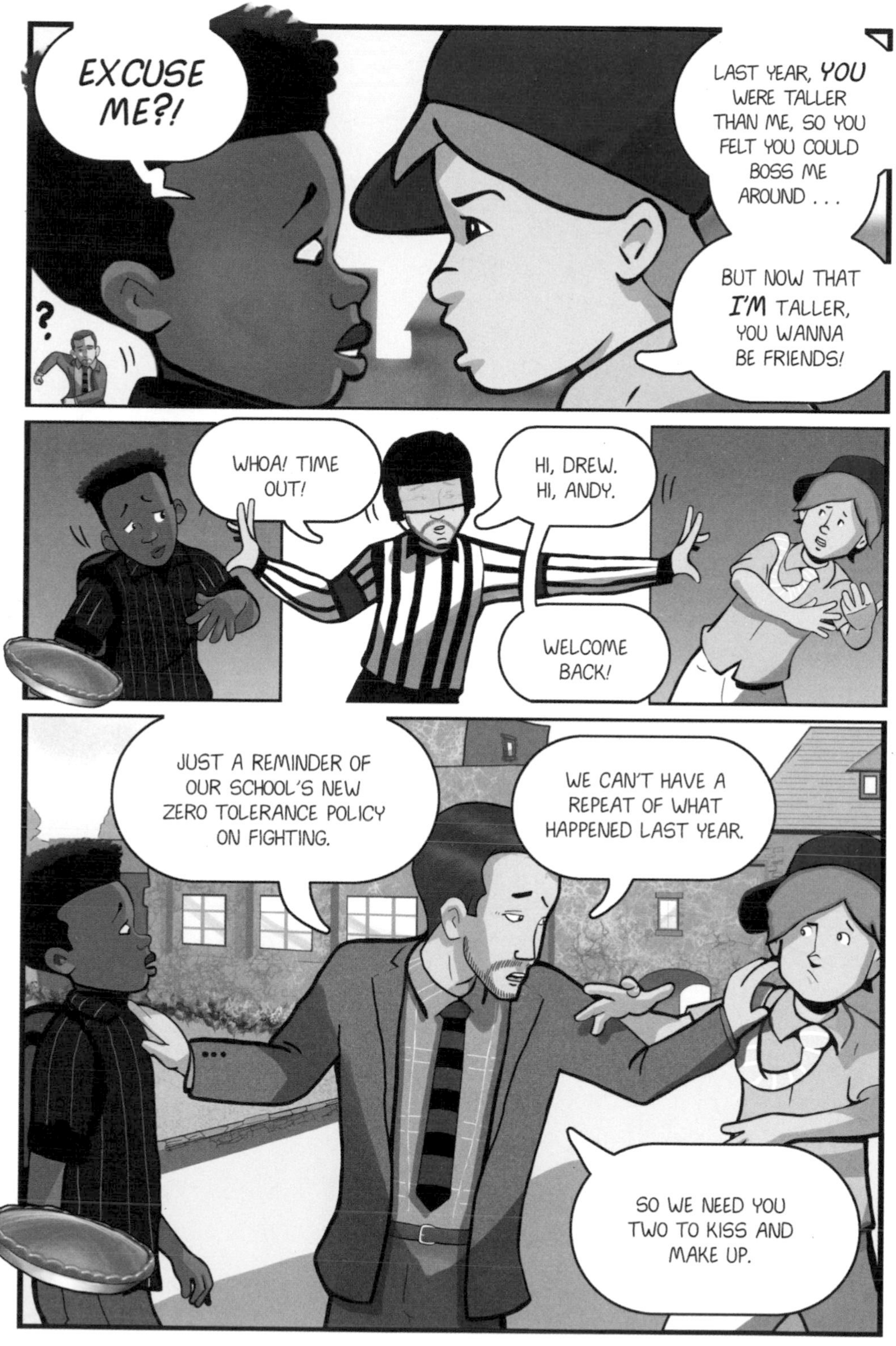
EXCUSE ME?!
LAST YEAR, YOU WERE TALLER THAN ME, SO YOU FELT YOU COULD BOSS ME AROUND . . .
BUT NOW THAT I'M TALLER, YOU WANNA BE FRIENDS!
?
WHOA! TIME OUT!
HI, DREW. HI, ANDY.
WELCOME BACK!
JUST A REMINDER OF OUR SCHOOL'S NEW ZERO TOLERANCE POLICY ON FIGHTING.
WE CAN'T HAVE A REPEAT OF WHAT HAPPENED LAST YEAR.
SO WE NEED YOU TWO TO KISS AND MAKE UP.

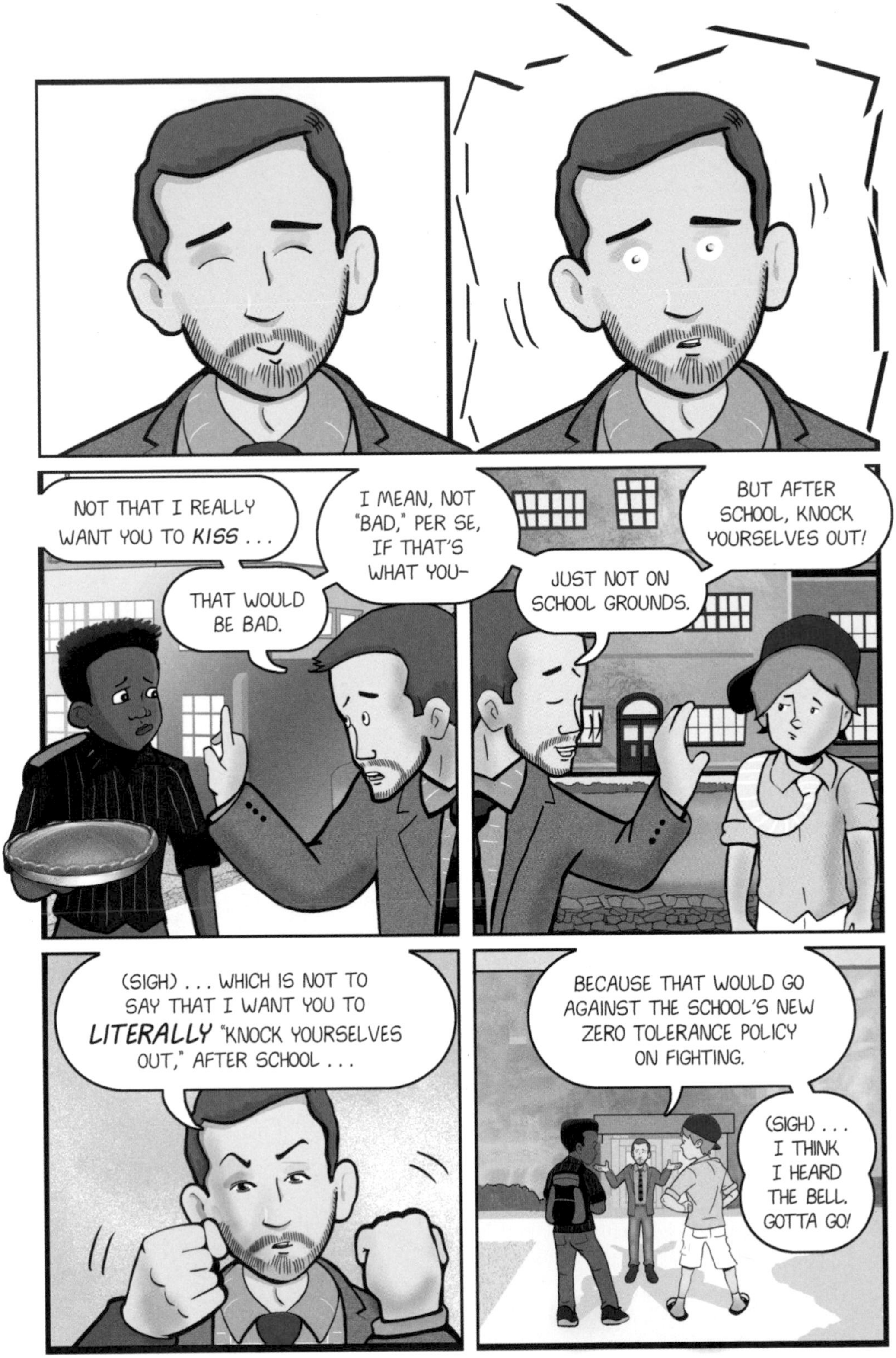
NOT THAT I REALLY WANT YOU TO KISS . . .
THAT WOULD BE BAD.
I MEAN, NOT "BAD," PER SE, IF THAT'S WHAT YOU–
JUST NOT ON SCHOOL GROUNDS.
BUT AFTER SCHOOL, KNOCK YOURSELVES OUT!
(SIGH) . . . WHICH IS NOT TO SAY THAT I WANT YOU TO LITERALLY "KNOCK YOURSELVES OUT," AFTER SCHOOL . . .
BECAUSE THAT WOULD GO AGAINST THE SCHOOL'S NEW ZERO TOLERANCE POLICY ON FIGHTING.
(SIGH) . . . I THINK I HEARD THE BELL. GOTTA GO!

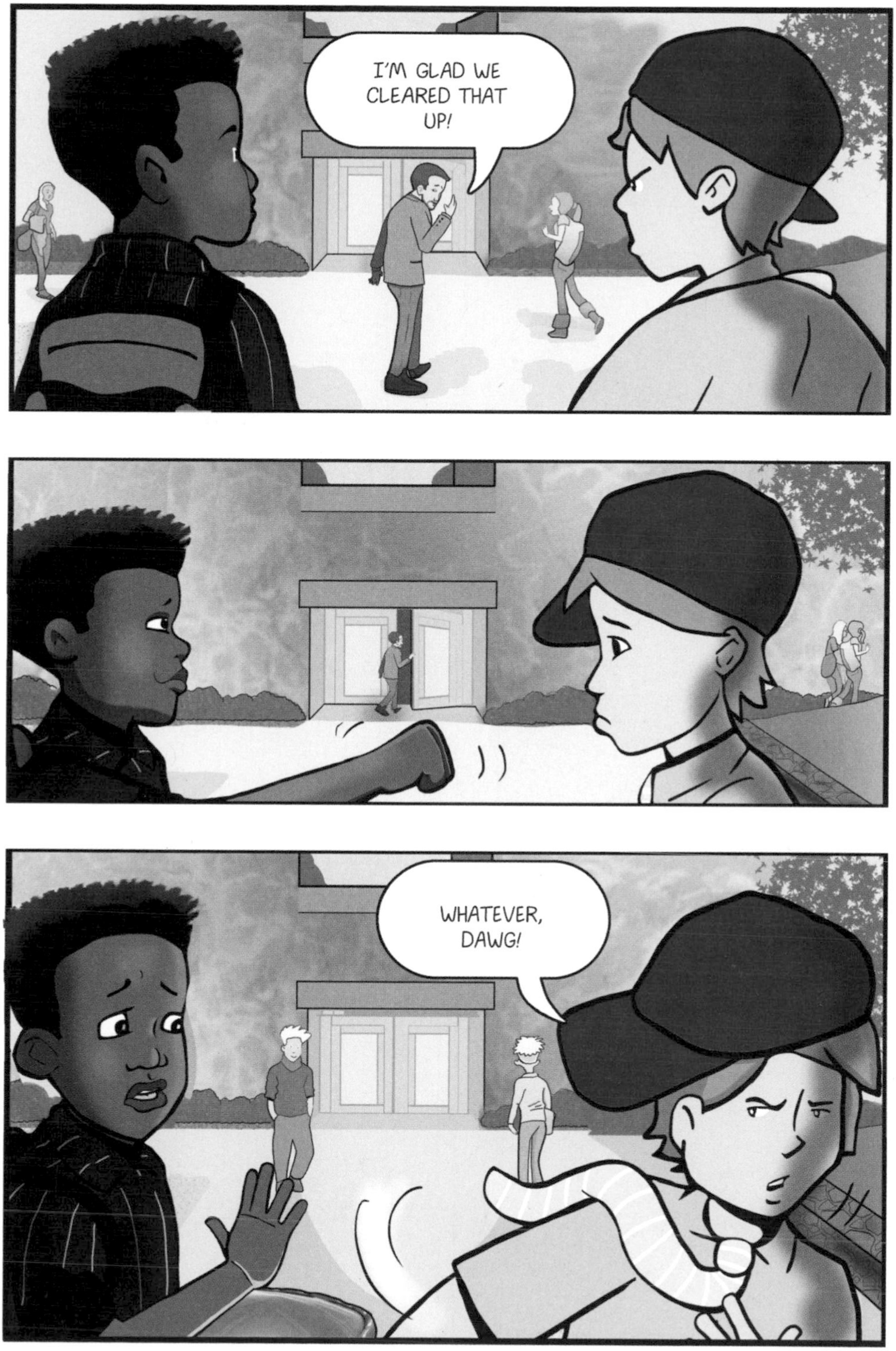
I'M GLAD WE CLEARED THAT UP!
WHATEVER, DAWG!

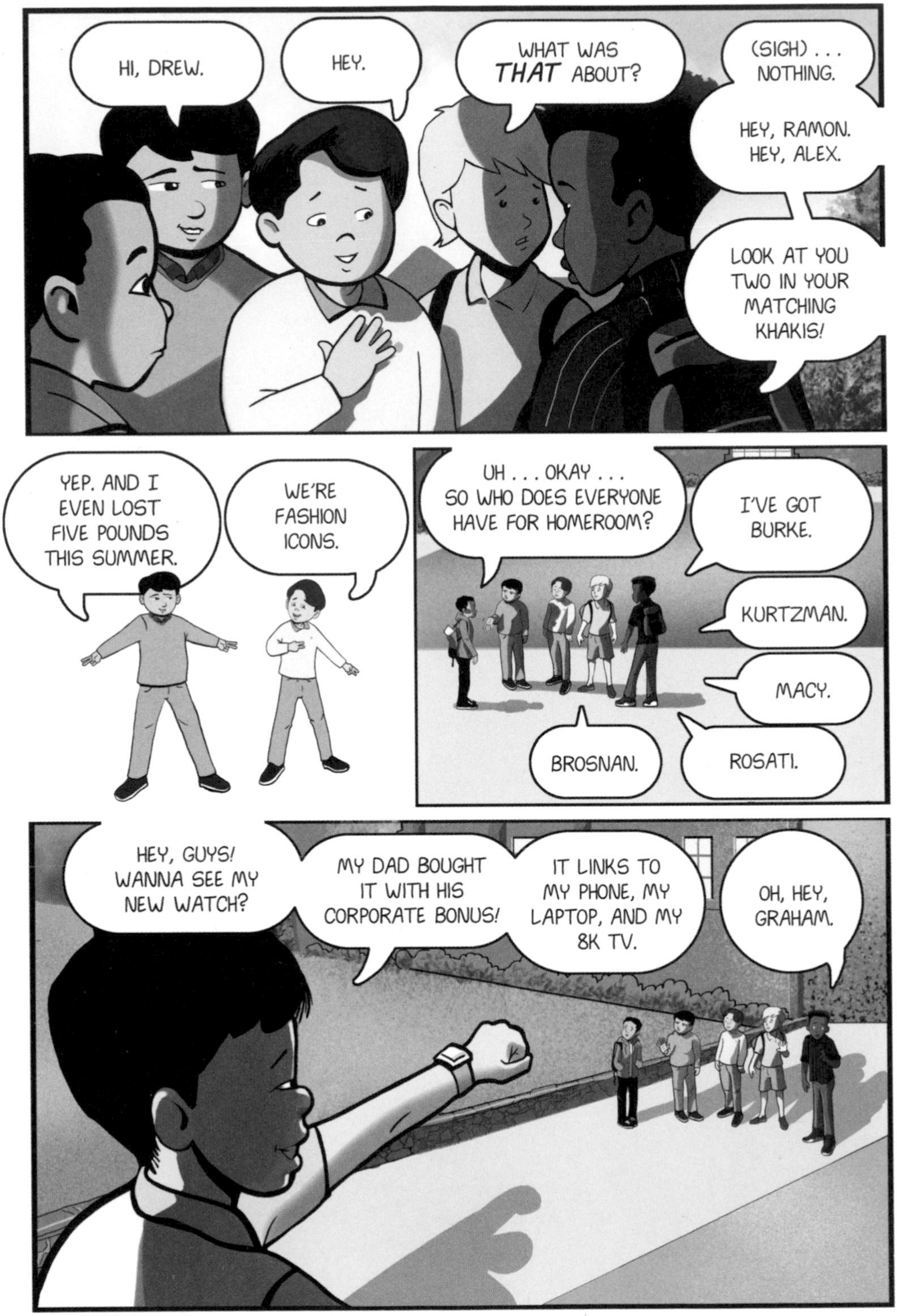
HI, DREW.
HEY.
WHAT WAS *THAT* ABOUT?
(SIGH) . . . NOTHING.
HEY, RAMON. HEY, ALEX.
LOOK AT YOU TWO IN YOUR MATCHING KHAKIS!
YEP. AND I EVEN LOST FIVE POUNDS THIS SUMMER.
WE'RE FASHION ICONS.
UH . . . OKAY . . . SO WHO DOES EVERYONE HAVE FOR HOMEROOM?
I'VE GOT BURKE.
KURTZMAN.
MACY.
ROSATI.
BROSNAN.
HEY, GUYS! WANNA SEE MY NEW WATCH?
MY DAD BOUGHT IT WITH HIS CORPORATE BONUS!
IT LINKS TO MY PHONE, MY LAPTOP, AND MY 8K TV.
OH, HEY, GRAHAM.

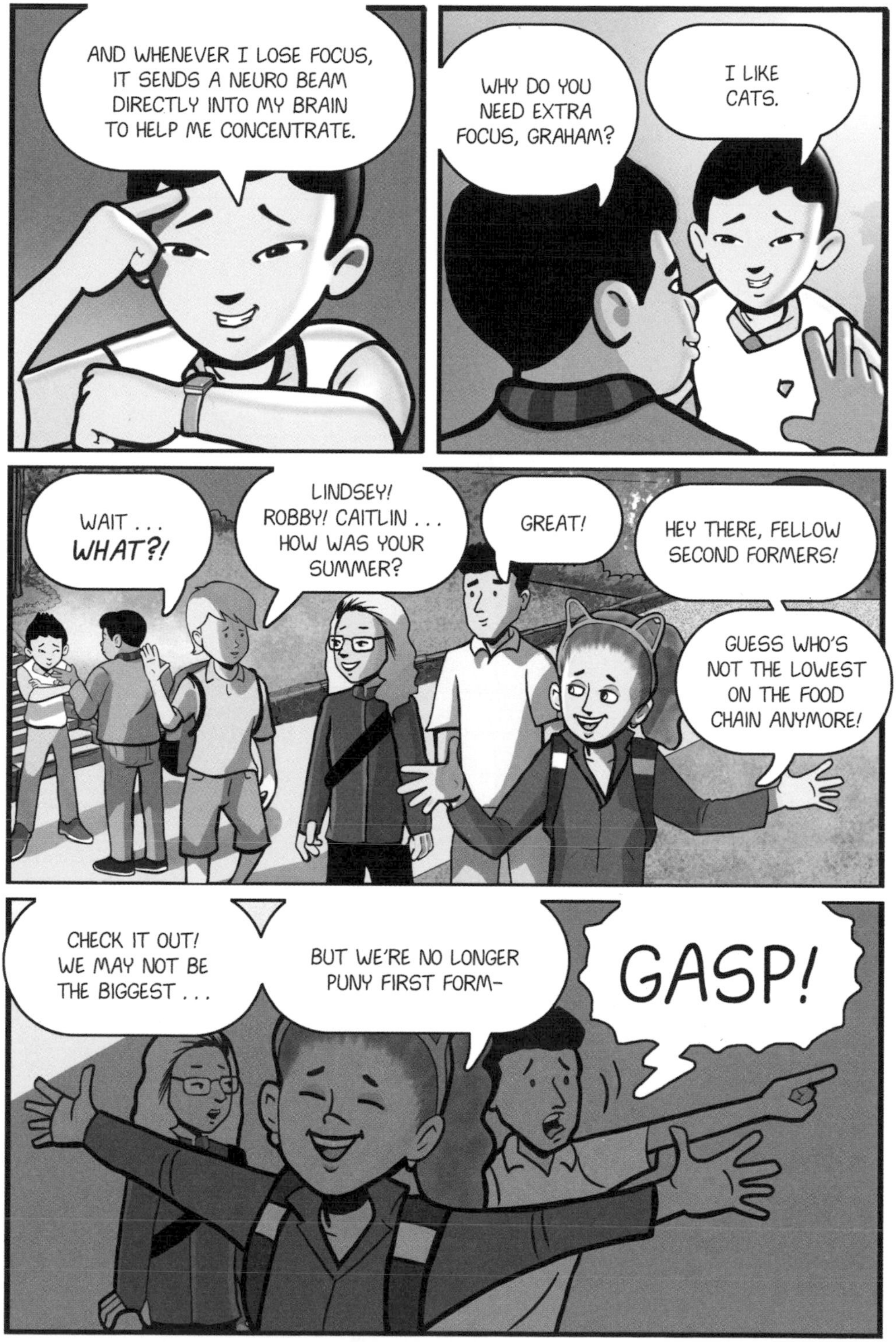
AND WHENEVER I LOSE FOCUS, IT SENDS A NEURO BEAM DIRECTLY INTO MY BRAIN TO HELP ME CONCENTRATE.
WHY DO YOU NEED EXTRA FOCUS, GRAHAM?
I LIKE CATS.
WAIT . . . WHAT?!
LINDSEY! ROBBY! CAITLIN . . . HOW WAS YOUR SUMMER?
GREAT!
HEY THERE, FELLOW SECOND FORMERS!
GUESS WHO'S NOT THE LOWEST ON THE FOOD CHAIN ANYMORE!
CHECK IT OUT! WE MAY NOT BE THE BIGGEST . . .
BUT WE'RE NO LONGER PUNY FIRST FORM-
GASP!

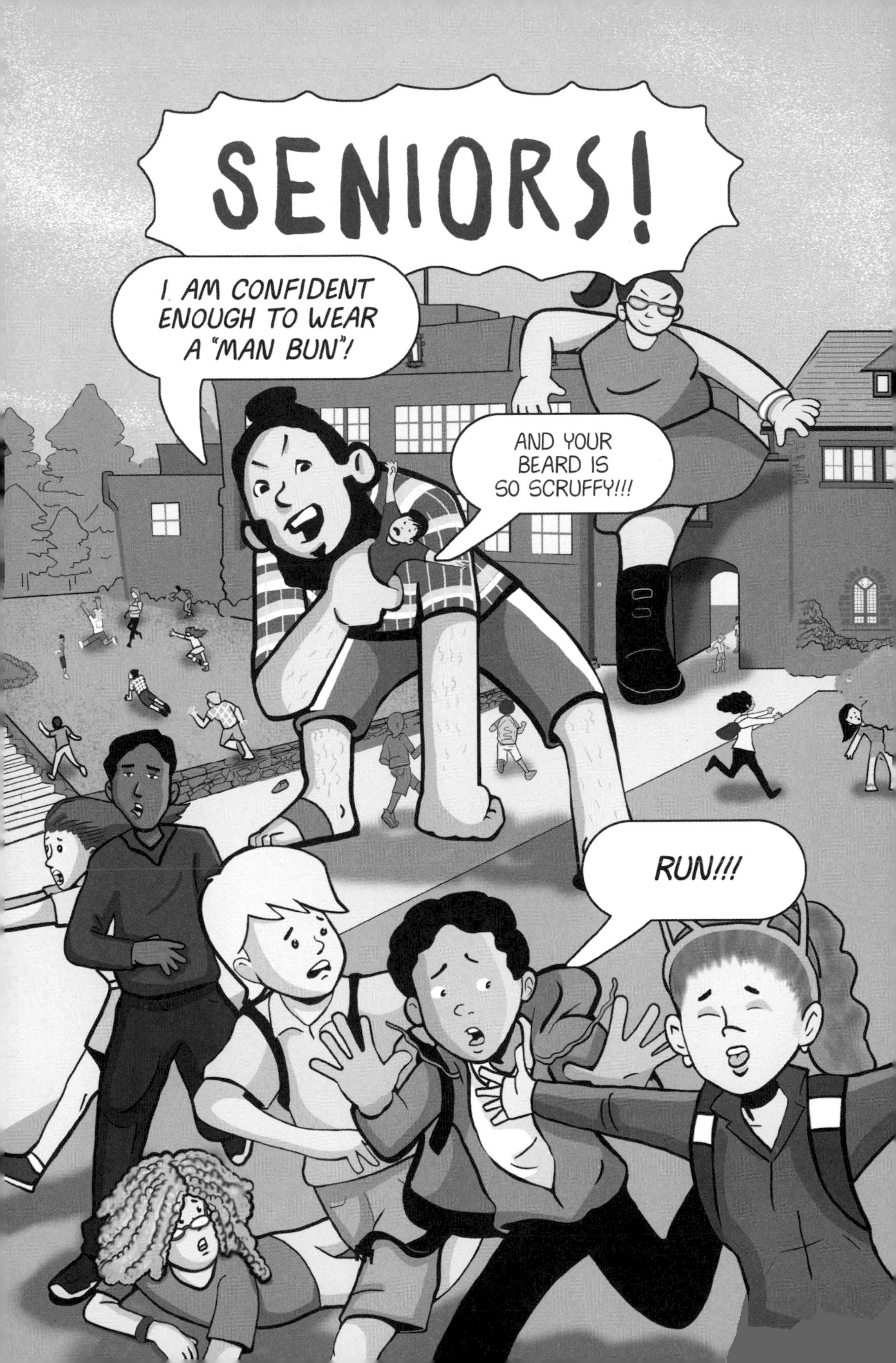
SENIORS!
I AM CONFIDENT ENOUGH TO WEAR A "MAN BUN"!
AND YOUR BEARD IS SO SCRUFFY!!!
RUN!!!

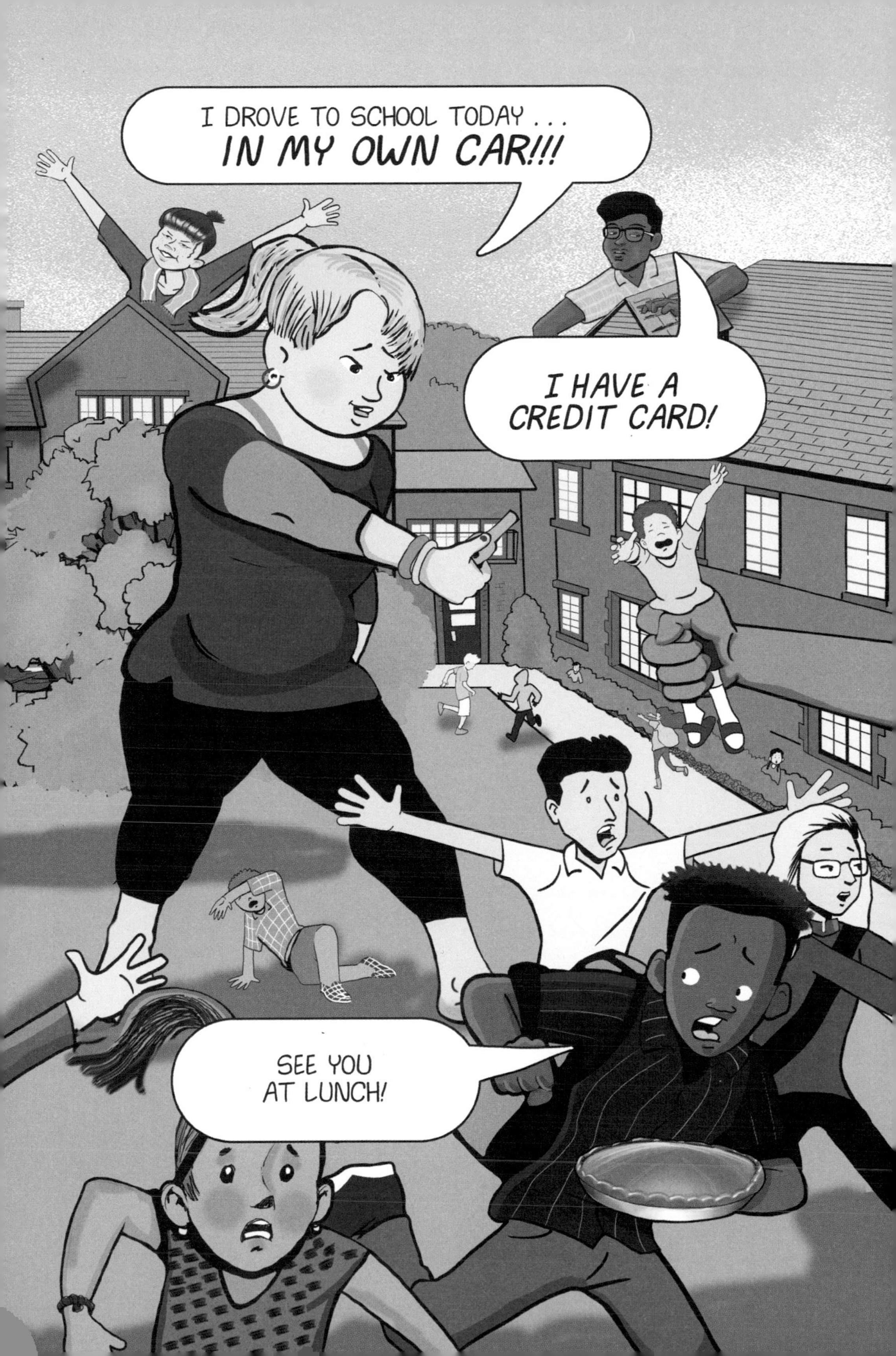
I DROVE TO SCHOOL TODAY . . .
IN MY OWN CAR!!!
I HAVE A CREDIT CARD!
SEE YOU AT LUNCH!

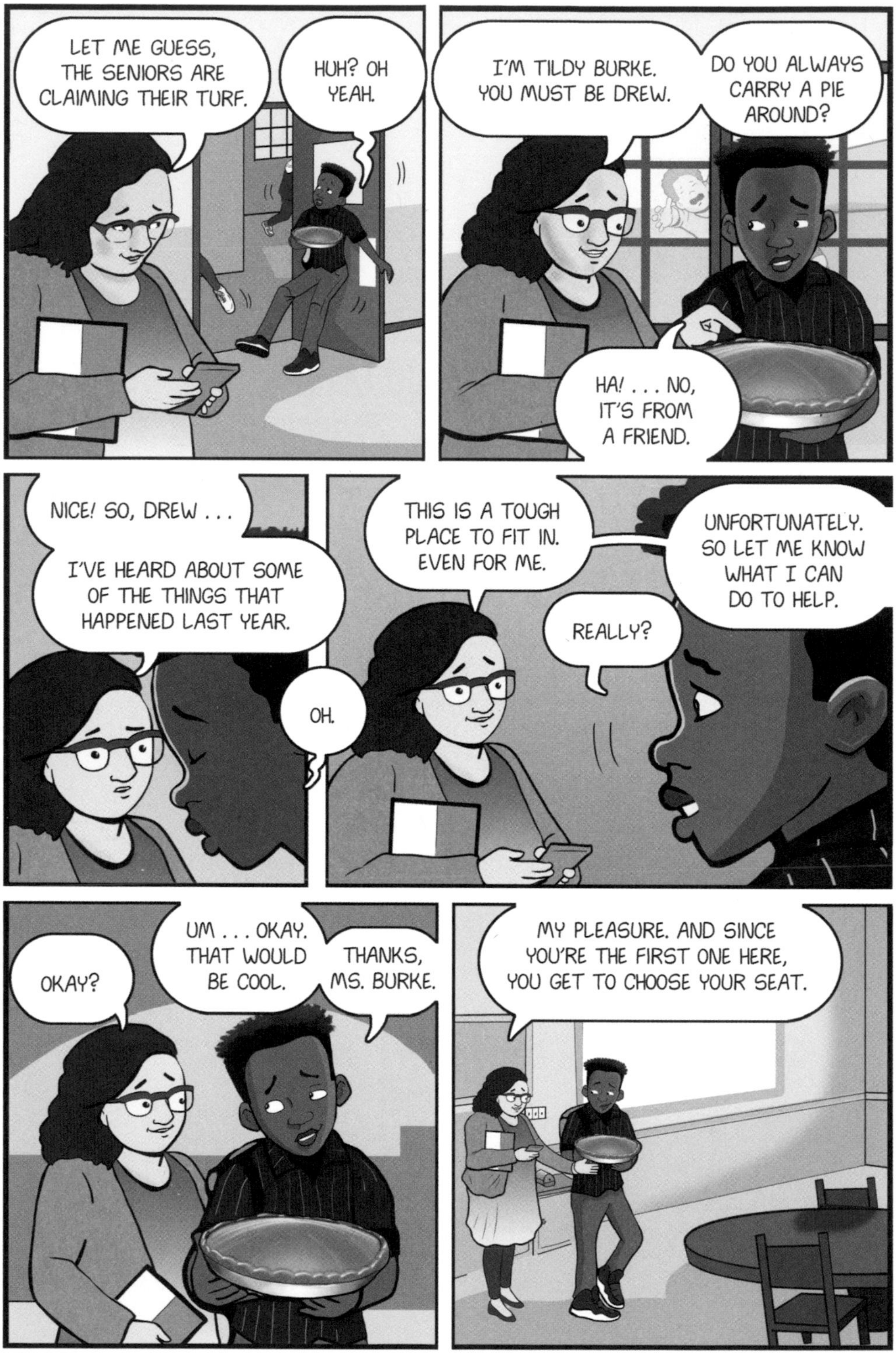
LET ME GUESS, THE SENIORS ARE CLAIMING THEIR TURF.
HUH? OH YEAH.
I'M TILDY BURKE. YOU MUST BE DREW.
DO YOU ALWAYS CARRY A PIE AROUND?
HA! . . . NO, IT'S FROM A FRIEND.
NICE! SO, DREW . . .
I'VE HEARD ABOUT SOME OF THE THINGS THAT HAPPENED LAST YEAR.
OH.
THIS IS A TOUGH PLACE TO FIT IN. EVEN FOR ME.
REALLY?
UNFORTUNATELY. SO LET ME KNOW WHAT I CAN DO TO HELP.
OKAY?
UM . . . OKAY. THAT WOULD BE COOL.
THANKS, MS. BURKE.
MY PLEASURE. AND SINCE YOU'RE THE FIRST ONE HERE, YOU GET TO CHOOSE YOUR SEAT.

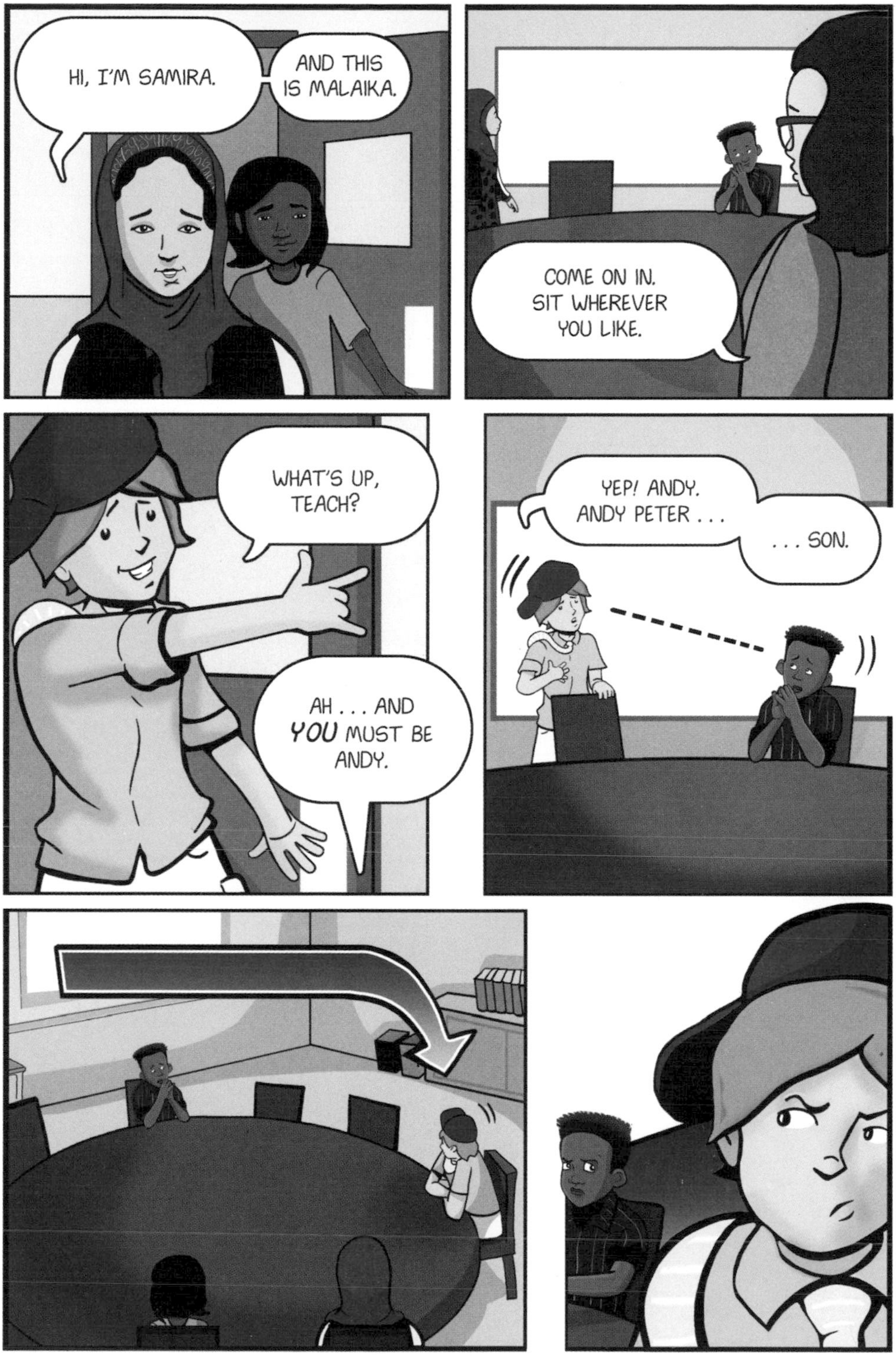
HI, I'M SAMIRA.
AND THIS IS MALAIKA.
COME ON IN. SIT WHEREVER YOU LIKE.
WHAT'S UP, TEACH?
AH . . . AND *YOU* MUST BE ANDY.
YEP! ANDY. ANDY PETER . . .
. . . SON.

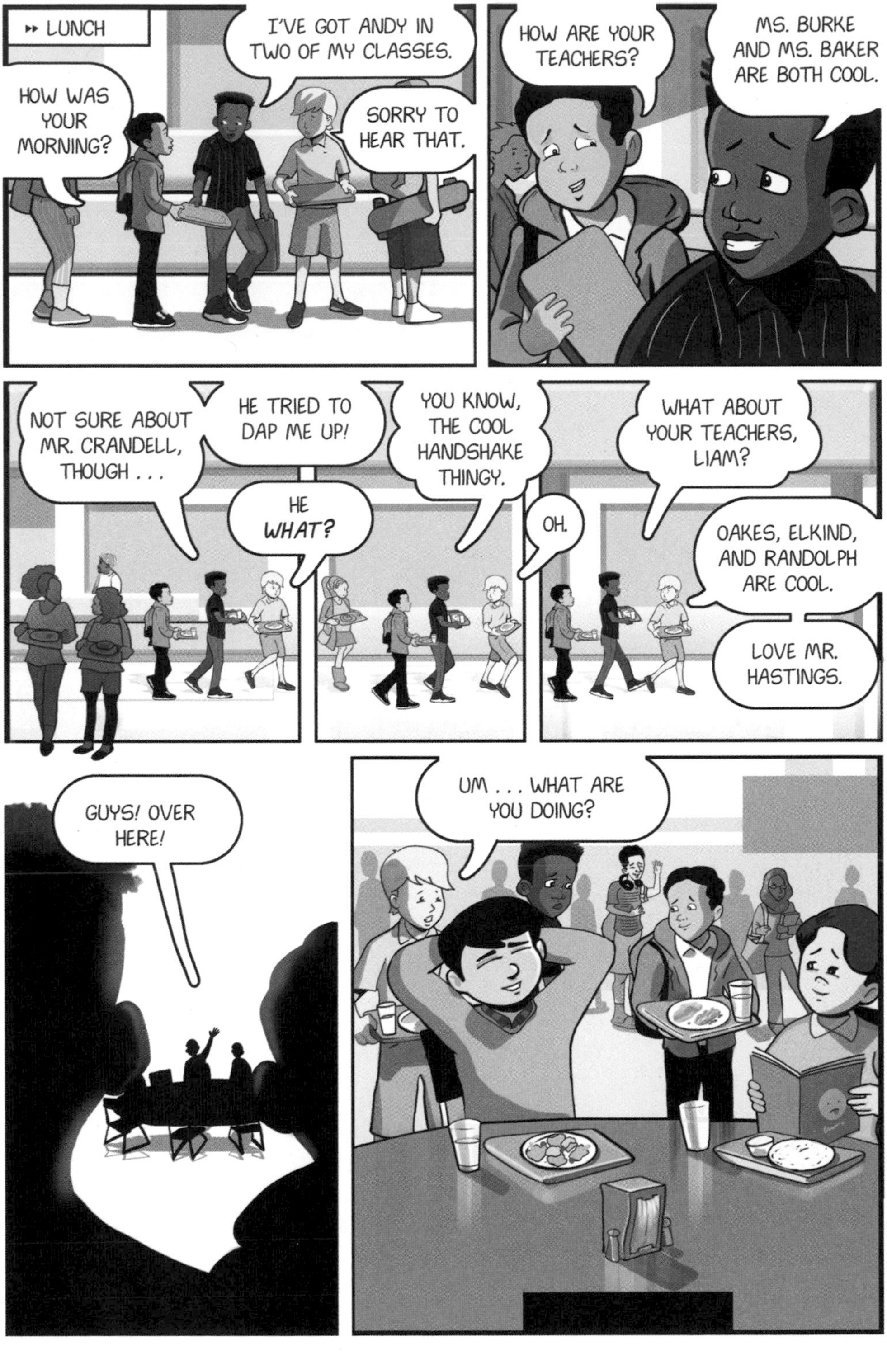
LUNCH
HOW WAS YOUR MORNING?
I'VE GOT ANDY IN TWO OF MY CLASSES.
SORRY TO HEAR THAT.
HOW ARE YOUR TEACHERS?
MS. BURKE AND MS. BAKER ARE BOTH COOL.
NOT SURE ABOUT MR. CRANDELL, THOUGH . . .
HE TRIED TO DAP ME UP!
HE WHAT?
YOU KNOW, THE COOL HANDSHAKE THINGY.
OH.
WHAT ABOUT YOUR TEACHERS, LIAM?
OAKES, ELKIND, AND RANDOLPH ARE COOL.
LOVE MR. HASTINGS.
GUYS! OVER HERE!
UM . . . WHAT ARE YOU DOING?

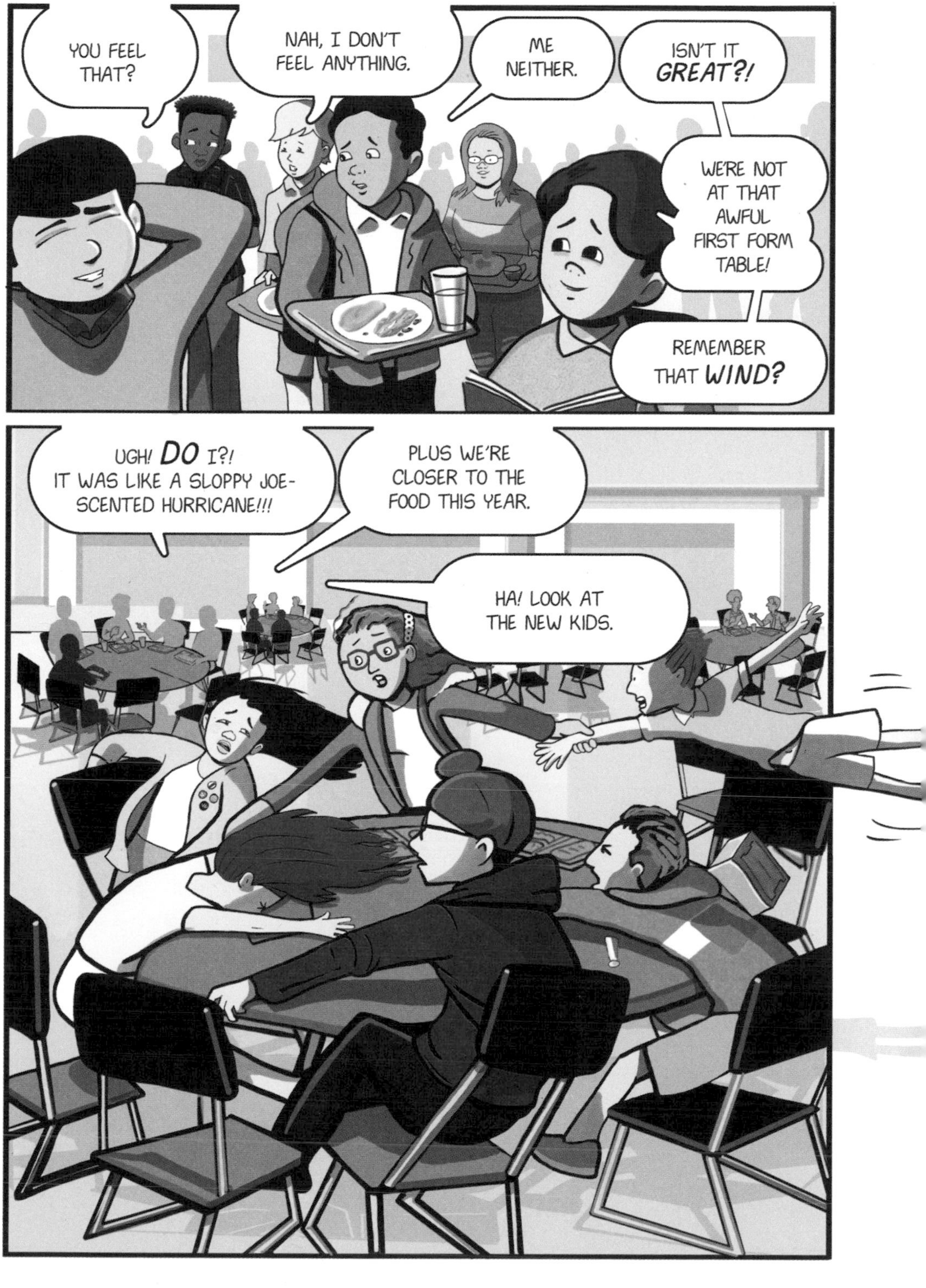
YOU FEEL THAT?
NAH, I DON'T FEEL ANYTHING.
ME NEITHER.
ISN'T IT GREAT?!
WE'RE NOT AT THAT AWFUL FIRST FORM TABLE!
REMEMBER THAT WIND?
UGH! DO I?! IT WAS LIKE A SLOPPY JOE-SCENTED HURRICANE!!!
PLUS WE'RE CLOSER TO THE FOOD THIS YEAR.
HA! LOOK AT THE NEW KIDS.

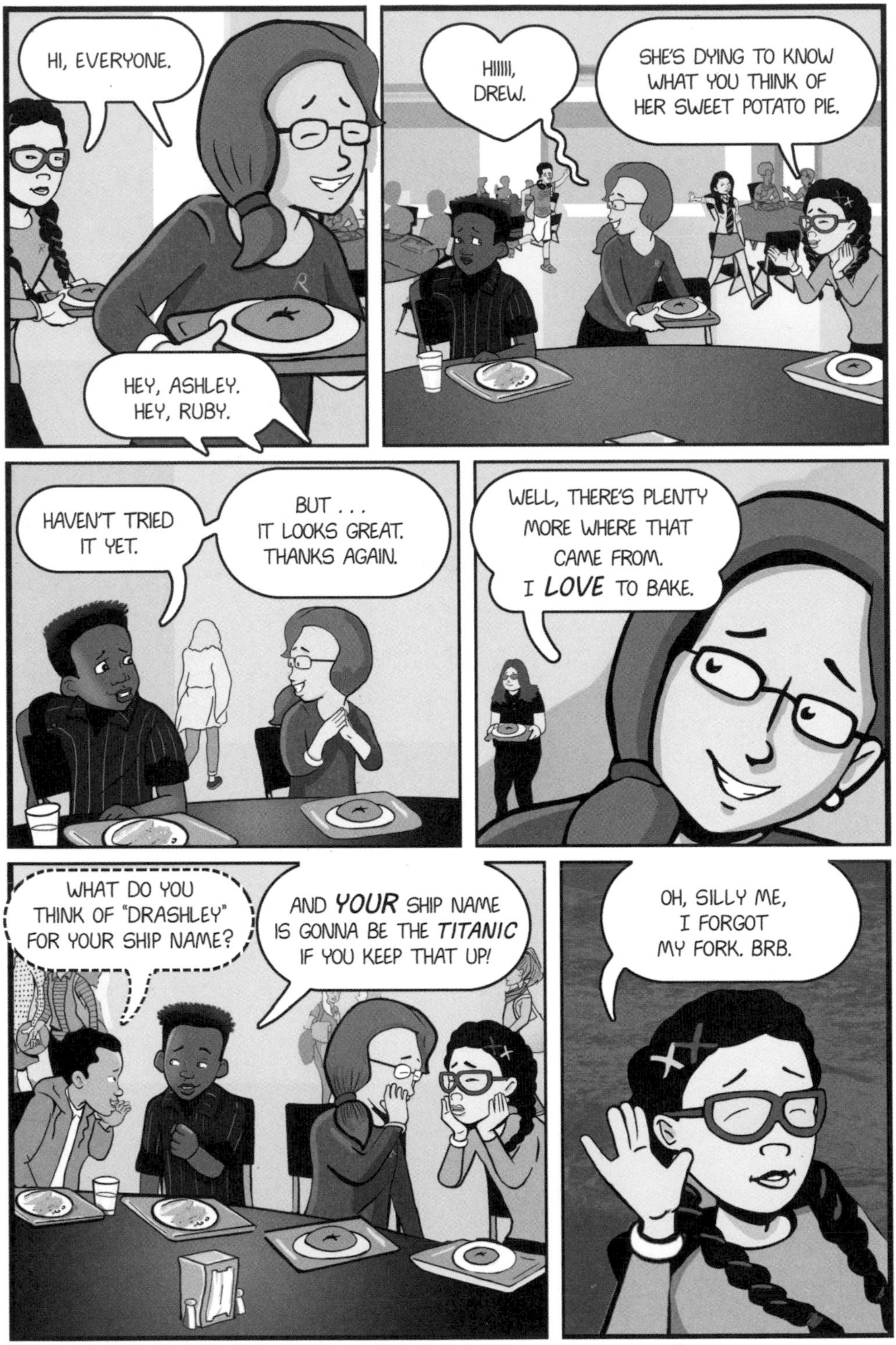
HI, EVERYONE.
HEY, ASHLEY. HEY, RUBY.
HIIIII, DREW.
SHE'S DYING TO KNOW WHAT YOU THINK OF HER SWEET POTATO PIE.
HAVEN'T TRIED IT YET.
BUT . . . IT LOOKS GREAT. THANKS AGAIN.
WELL, THERE'S PLENTY MORE WHERE THAT CAME FROM. I **LOVE** TO BAKE.
WHAT DO YOU THINK OF "DRASHLEY" FOR YOUR SHIP NAME?
AND **YOUR** SHIP NAME IS GONNA BE THE ***TITANIC*** IF YOU KEEP THAT UP!
OH, SILLY ME, I FORGOT MY FORK. BRB.

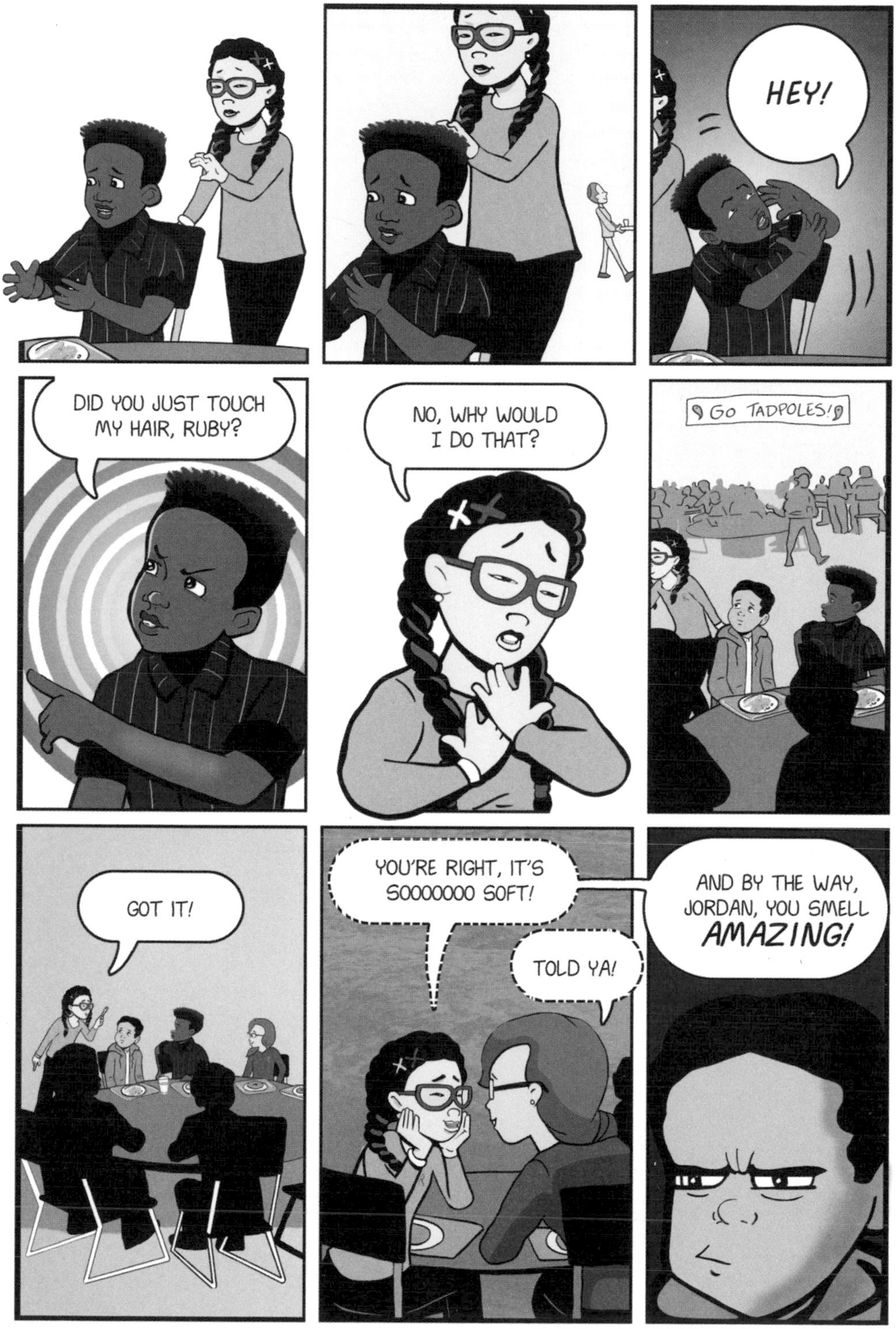
HEY!
DID YOU JUST TOUCH MY HAIR, RUBY?
NO, WHY WOULD I DO THAT?
GO TADPOLES!
GOT IT!
YOU'RE RIGHT, IT'S SOOOOOOO SOFT!
AND BY THE WAY, JORDAN, YOU SMELL AMAZING!
TOLD YA!

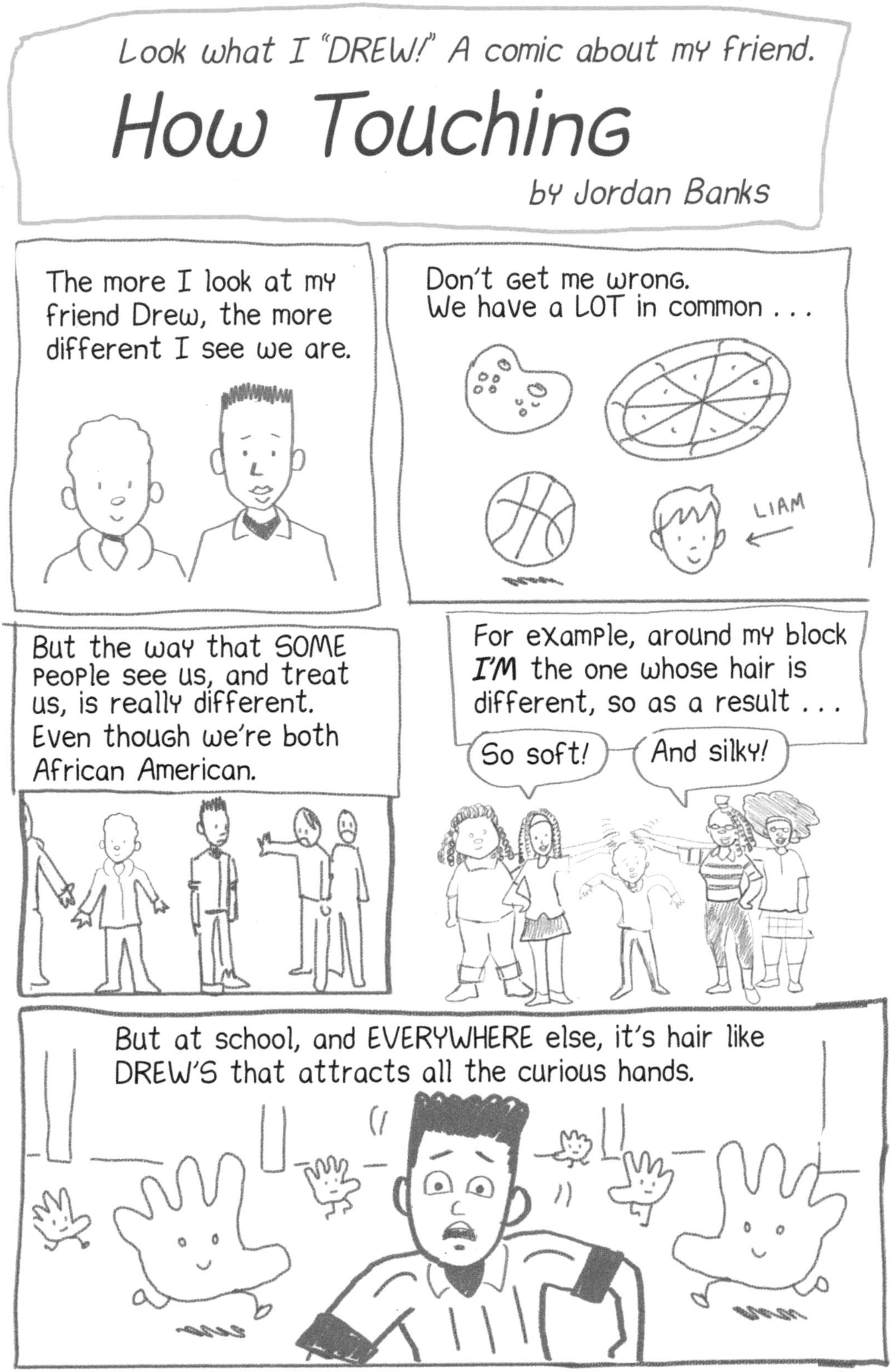

Look what I "DREW!" A comic about my friend.
How Touching
by Jordan Banks
The more I look at my friend Drew, the more different I see we are.
Don't get me wrong. We have a LOT in common . . .
LIAM
But the way that SOME people see us, and treat us, is really different. Even though we're both African American.
For example, around my block I'M the one whose hair is different, so as a result . . .
So soft!
And silky!
But at school, and EVERYWHERE else, it's hair like DREW'S that attracts all the curious hands.

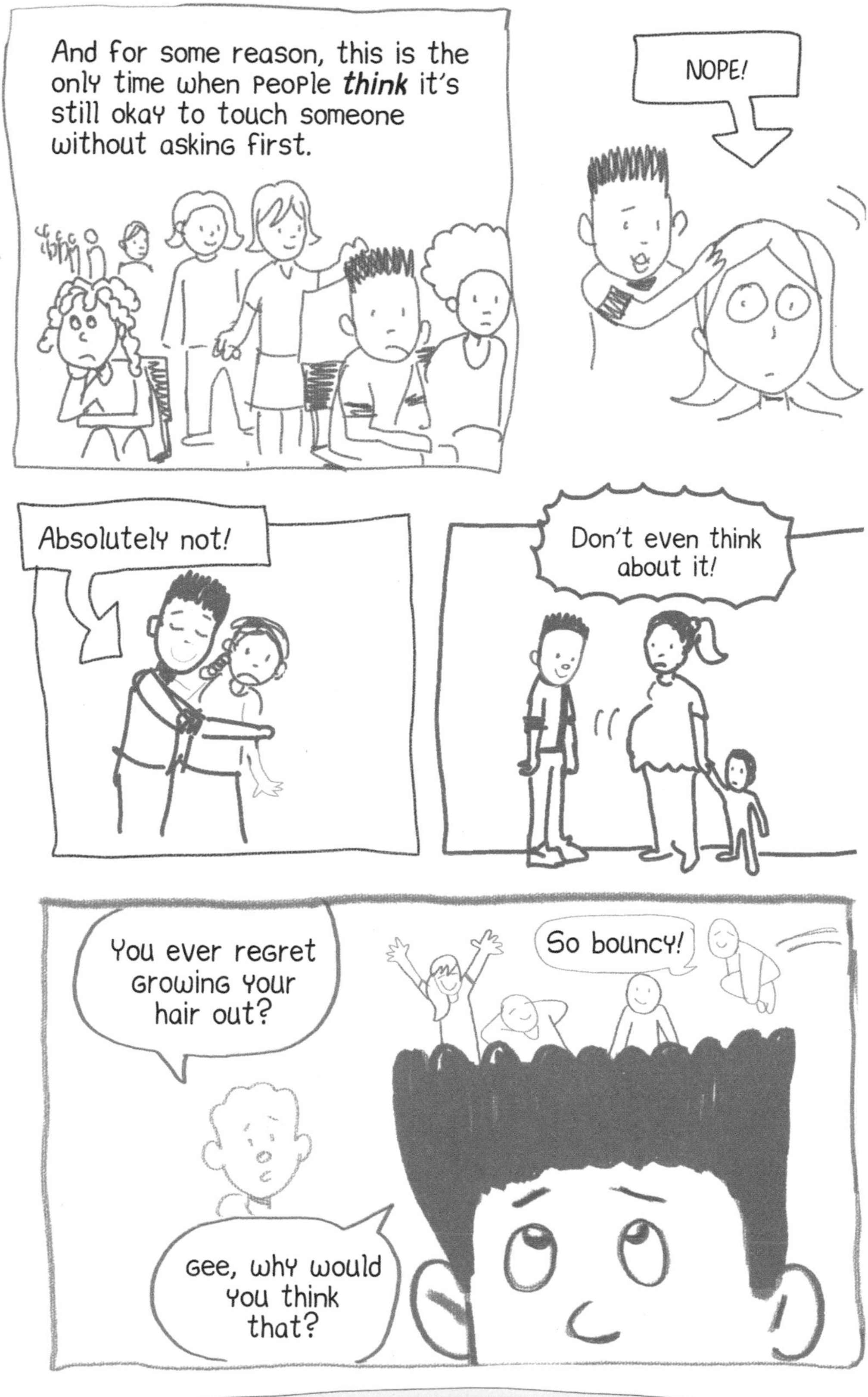

And for some reason, this is the only time when people *think* it's still okay to touch someone without asking first.
NOPE!
Absolutely not!
Don't even think about it!
You ever regret growing your hair out?
So bouncy!
Gee, why would you think that?

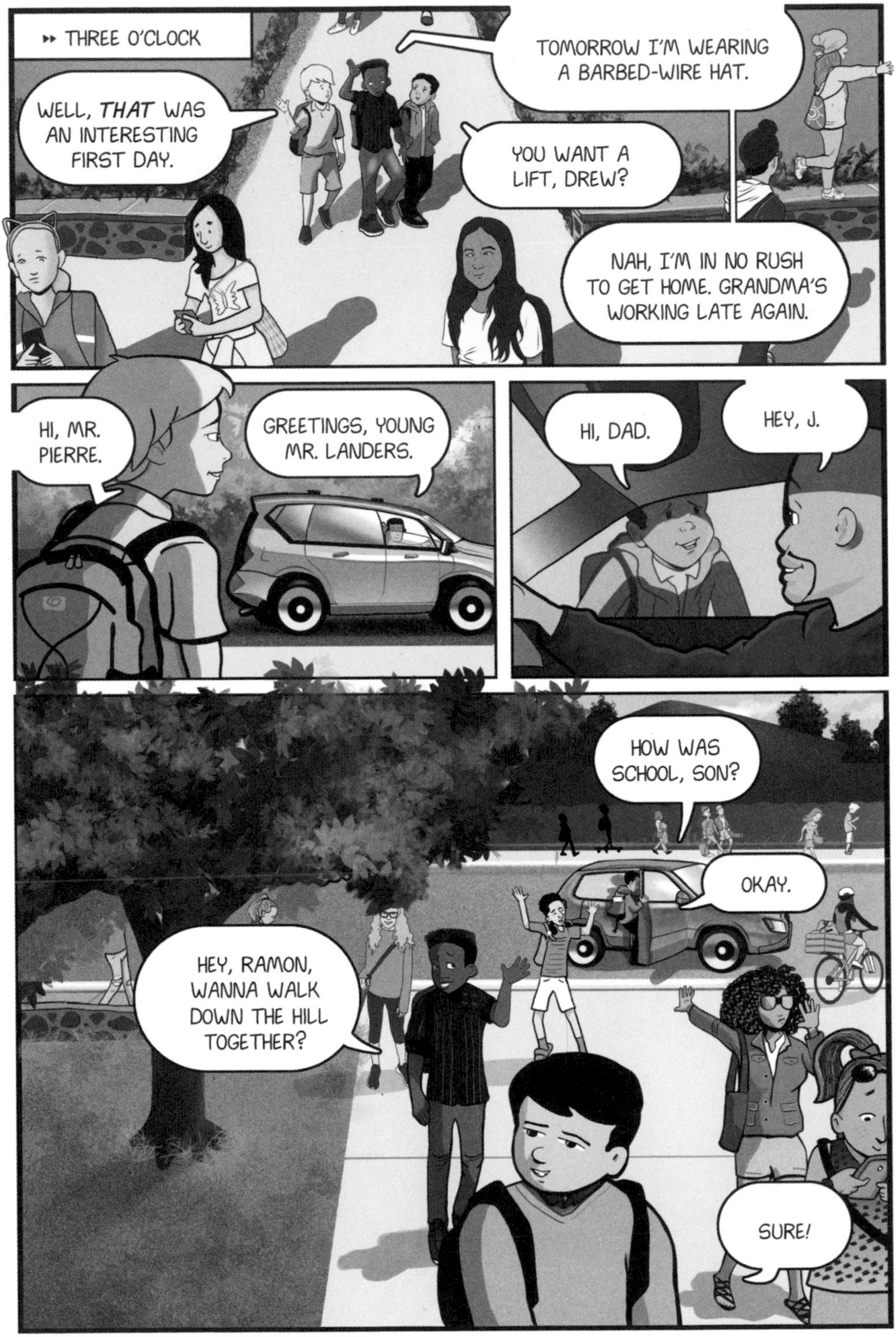
▸▸ THREE O'CLOCK
WELL, *THAT* WAS AN INTERESTING FIRST DAY.
TOMORROW I'M WEARING A BARBED-WIRE HAT.
YOU WANT A LIFT, DREW?
NAH, I'M IN NO RUSH TO GET HOME. GRANDMA'S WORKING LATE AGAIN.
HI, MR. PIERRE.
GREETINGS, YOUNG MR. LANDERS.
HI, DAD.
HEY, J.
HOW WAS SCHOOL, SON?
OKAY.
HEY, RAMON, WANNA WALK DOWN THE HILL TOGETHER?
SURE!

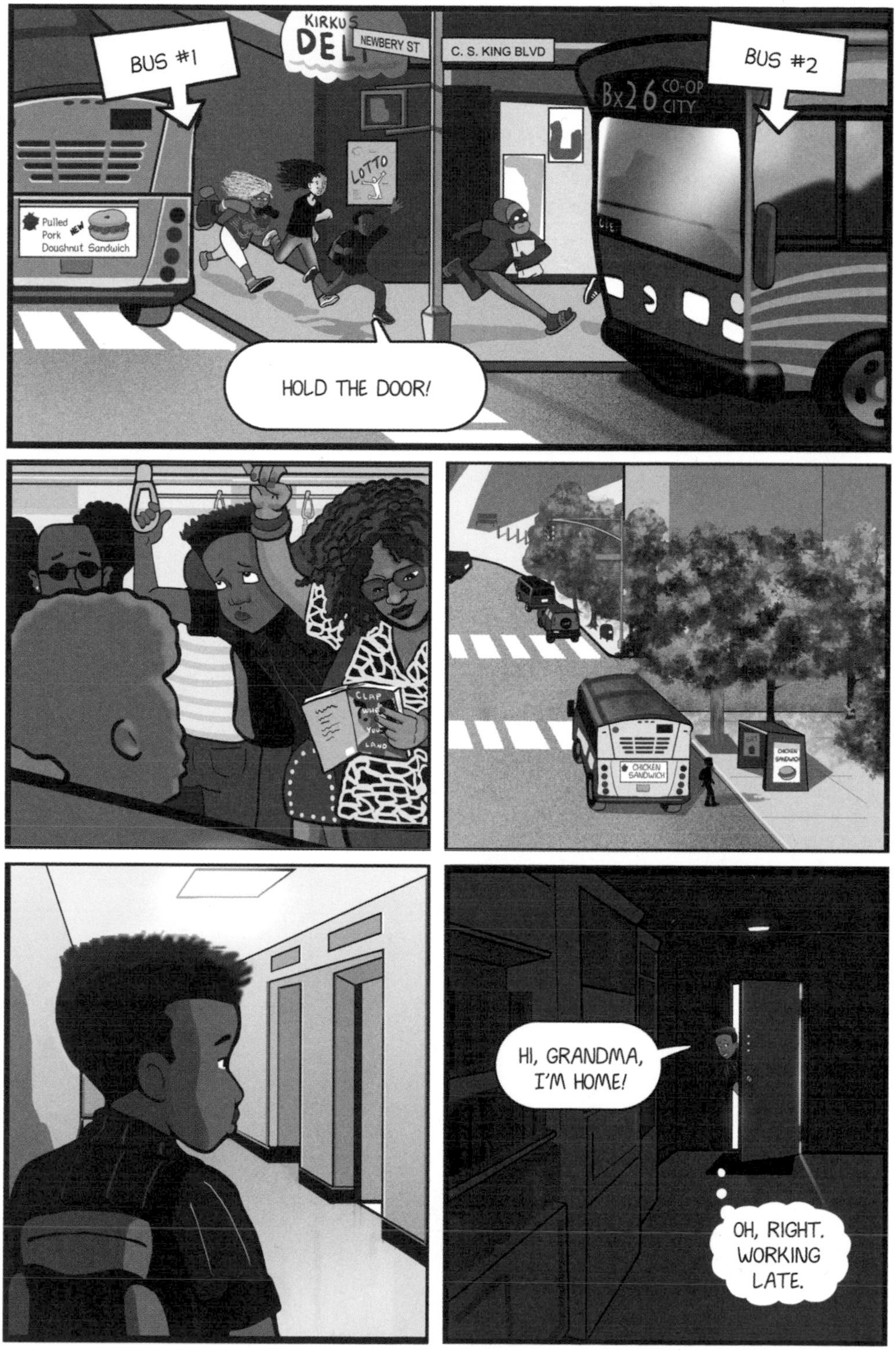
BUS #1
KIRKUS DELI
NEWBERY ST
C. S. KING BLVD
BUS #2
Bx26 CO-OP CITY
LOTTO
Pulled Pork NEW Doughnut Sandwich
HOLD THE DOOR!
CLAP WHEN YOU LAND
CHICKEN SANDWICH
CHICKEN SANDWICH
HI, GRANDMA, I'M HOME!
OH, RIGHT. WORKING LATE.

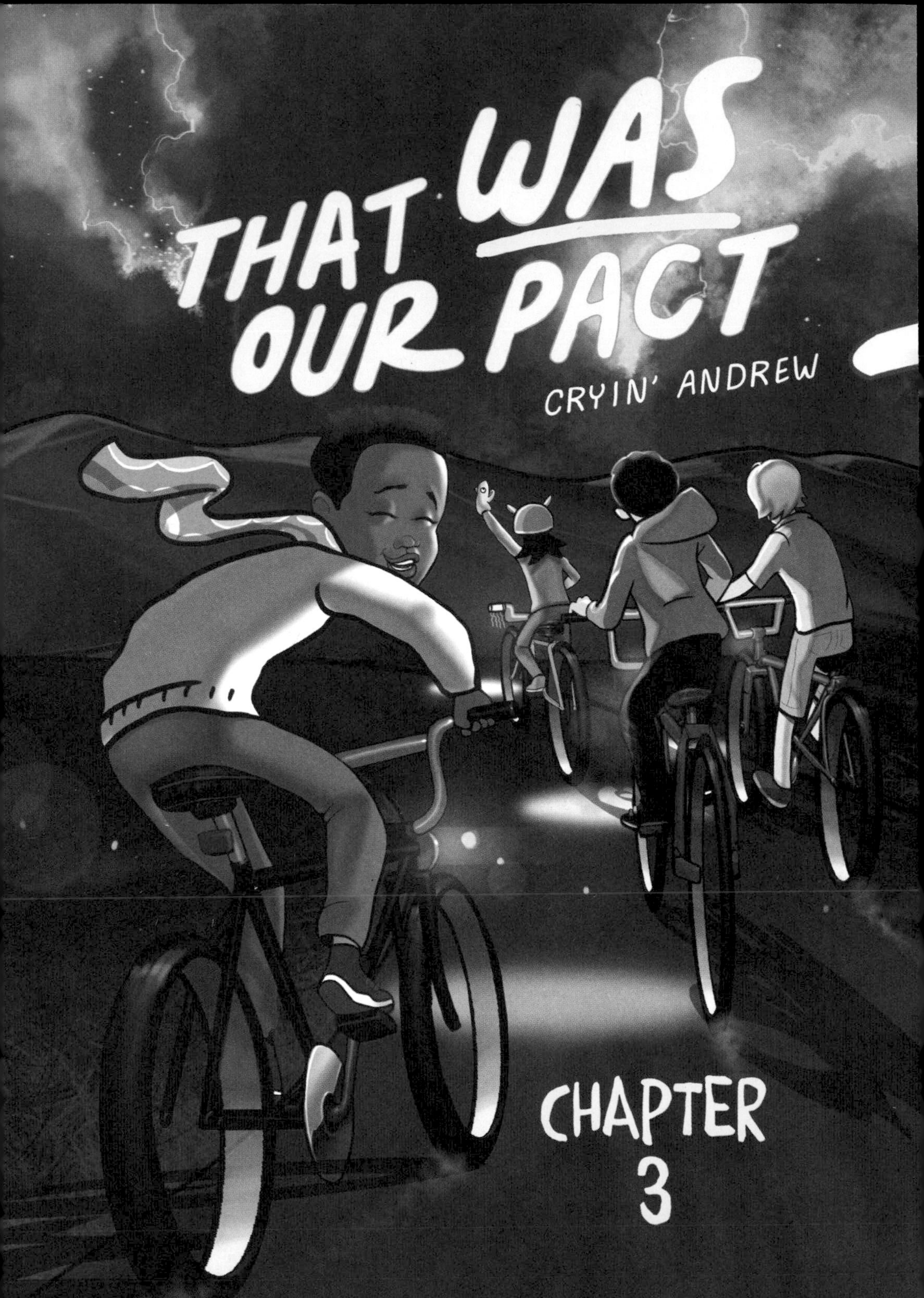
THAT WAS OUR PACT
CRYIN' ANDREW
CHAPTER 3

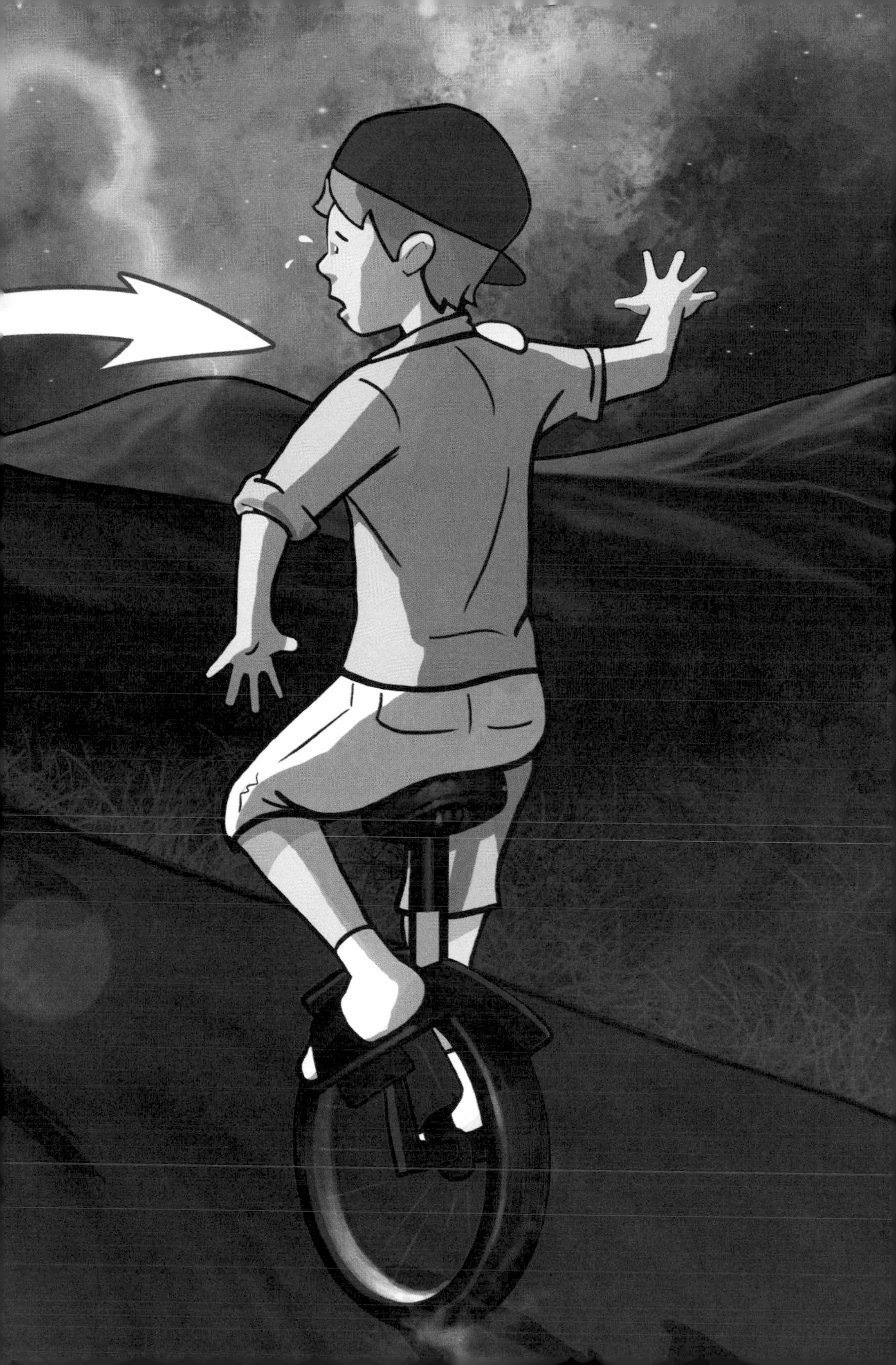

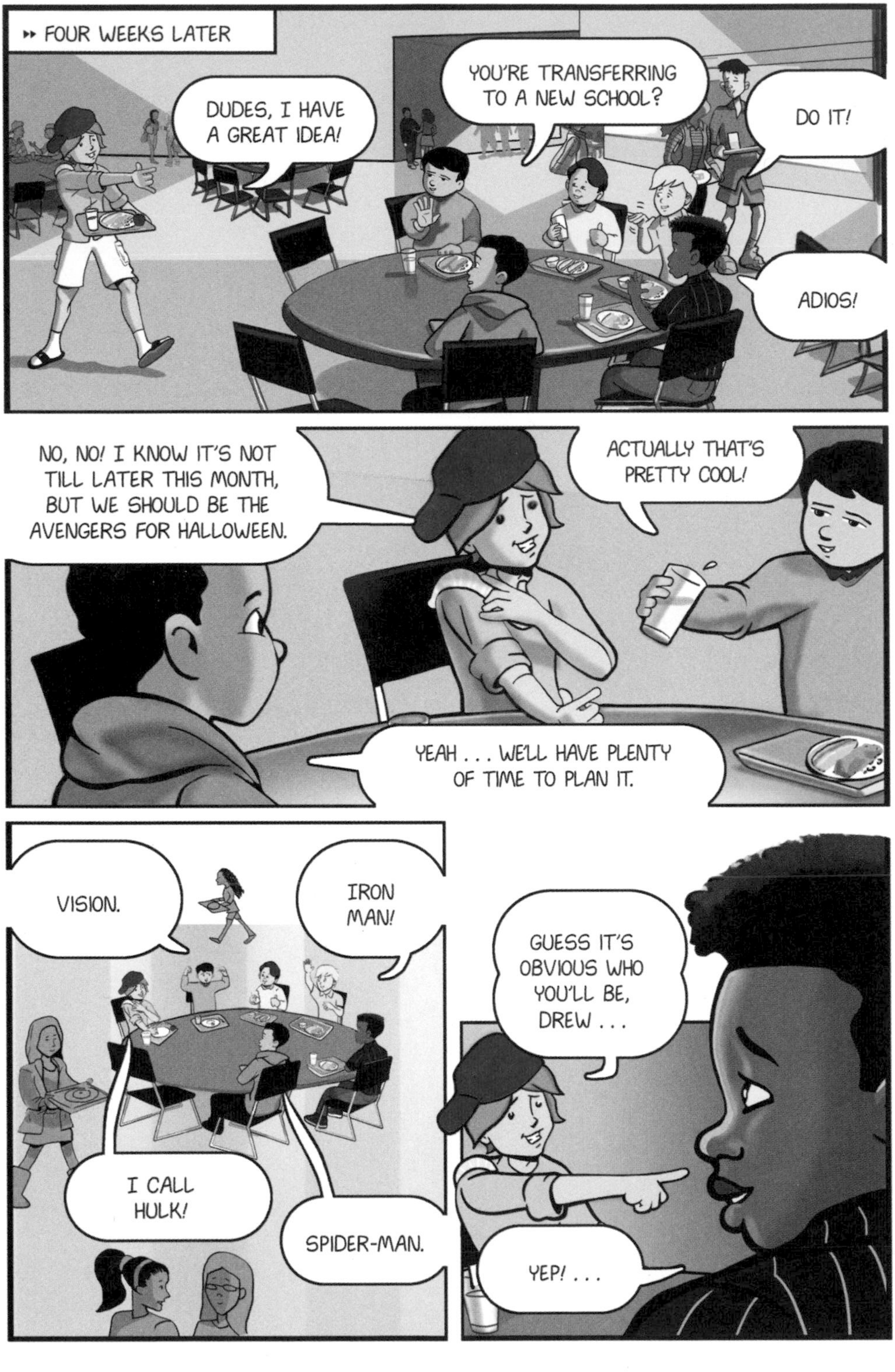
FOUR WEEKS LATER
DUDES, I HAVE A GREAT IDEA!
YOU'RE TRANSFERRING TO A NEW SCHOOL?
DO IT!
ADIOS!
NO, NO! I KNOW IT'S NOT TILL LATER THIS MONTH, BUT WE SHOULD BE THE AVENGERS FOR HALLOWEEN.
ACTUALLY THAT'S PRETTY COOL!
YEAH . . . WE'LL HAVE PLENTY OF TIME TO PLAN IT.
VISION.
IRON MAN!
I CALL HULK!
SPIDER-MAN.
GUESS IT'S OBVIOUS WHO YOU'LL BE, DREW . . .
YEP! . . .

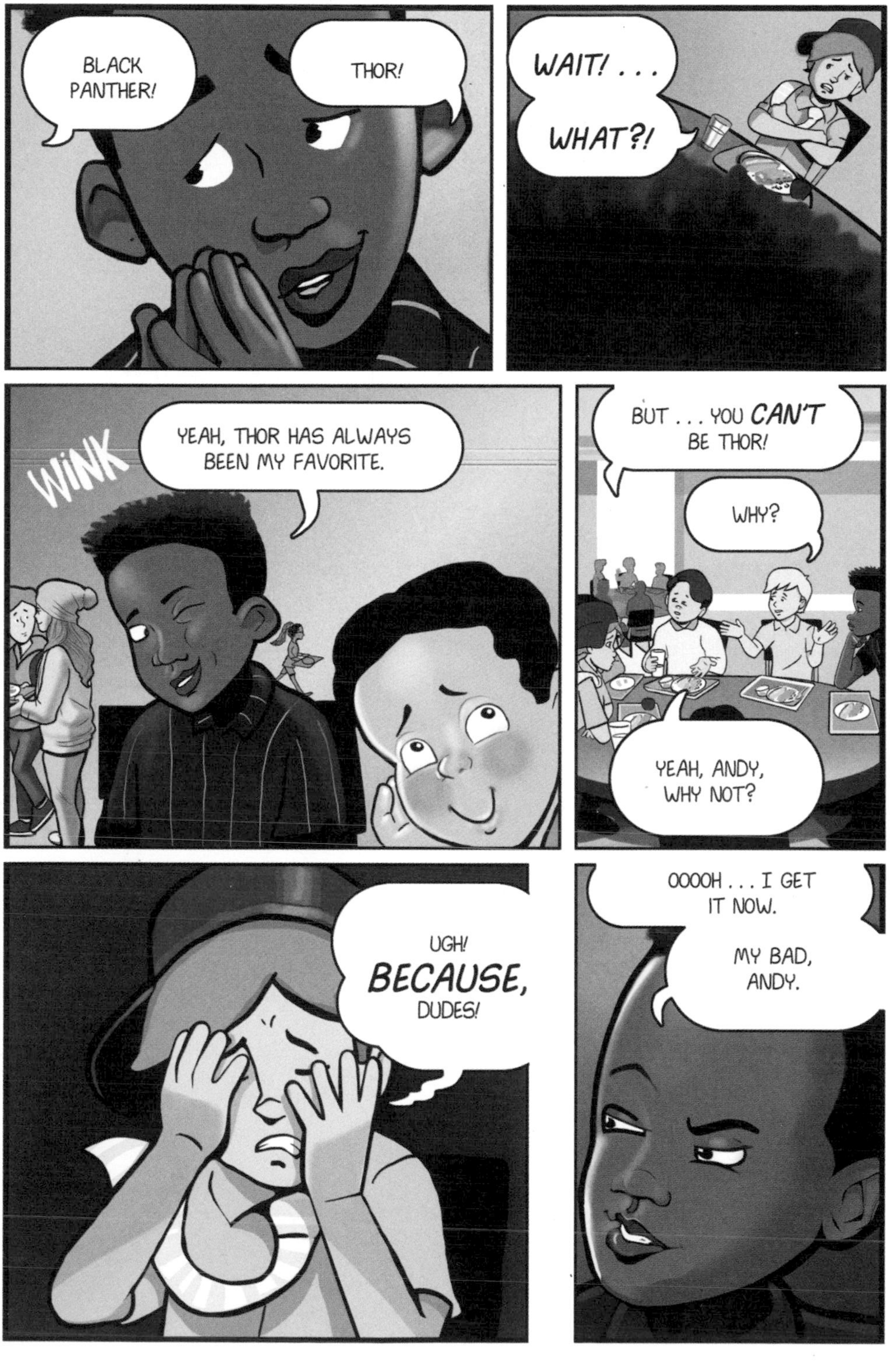
BLACK PANTHER!
THOR!
WAIT! . . .
WHAT?!
WINK
YEAH, THOR HAS ALWAYS BEEN MY FAVORITE.
BUT . . . YOU CAN'T BE THOR!
WHY?
YEAH, ANDY, WHY NOT?
UGH! BECAUSE, DUDES!
OOOOH . . . I GET IT NOW.
MY BAD, ANDY.

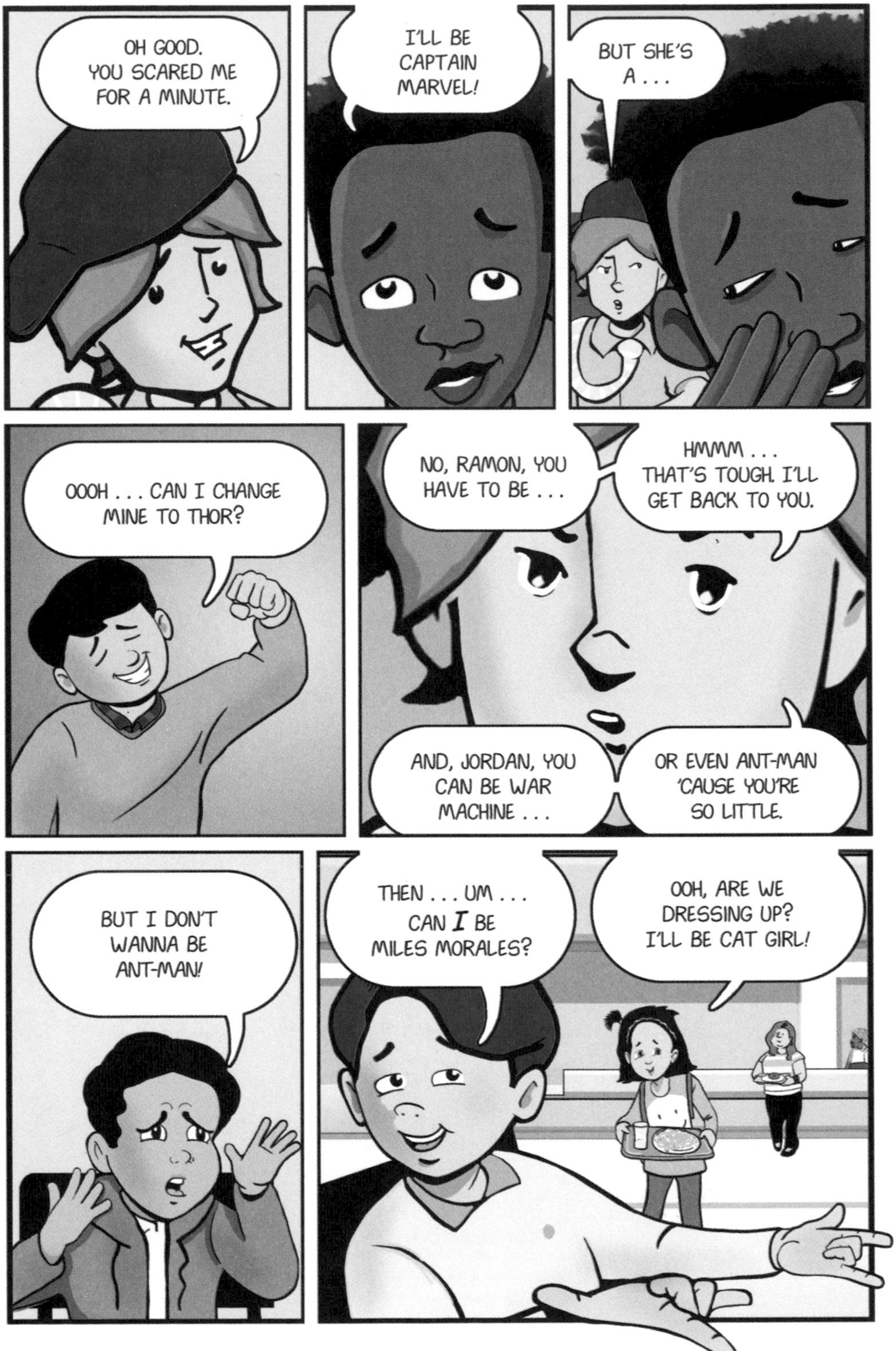
OH GOOD. YOU SCARED ME FOR A MINUTE.
I'LL BE CAPTAIN MARVEL!
BUT SHE'S A . . .
OOOH . . . CAN I CHANGE MINE TO THOR?
NO, RAMON, YOU HAVE TO BE . . .
HMMM . . . THAT'S TOUGH. I'LL GET BACK TO YOU.
AND, JORDAN, YOU CAN BE WAR MACHINE . . .
OR EVEN ANT-MAN 'CAUSE YOU'RE SO LITTLE.
BUT I DON'T WANNA BE ANT-MAN!
THEN . . . UM . . . CAN *I* BE MILES MORALES?
OOH, ARE WE DRESSING UP? I'LL BE CAT GIRL!

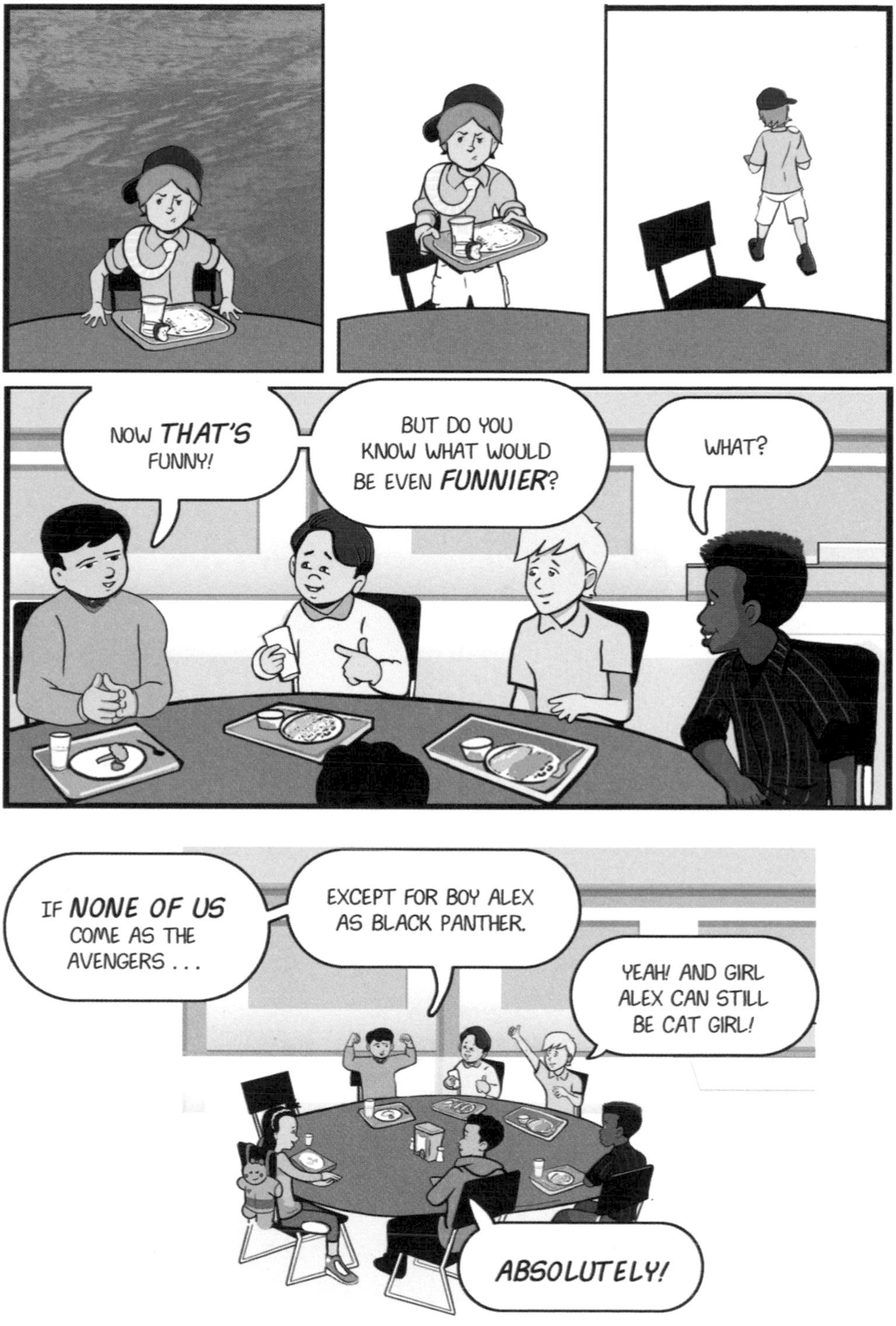
NOW THAT'S FUNNY!
BUT DO YOU KNOW WHAT WOULD BE EVEN FUNNIER?
WHAT?
IF NONE OF US COME AS THE AVENGERS . . .
EXCEPT FOR BOY ALEX AS BLACK PANTHER.
YEAH! AND GIRL ALEX CAN STILL BE CAT GIRL!
ABSOLUTELY!

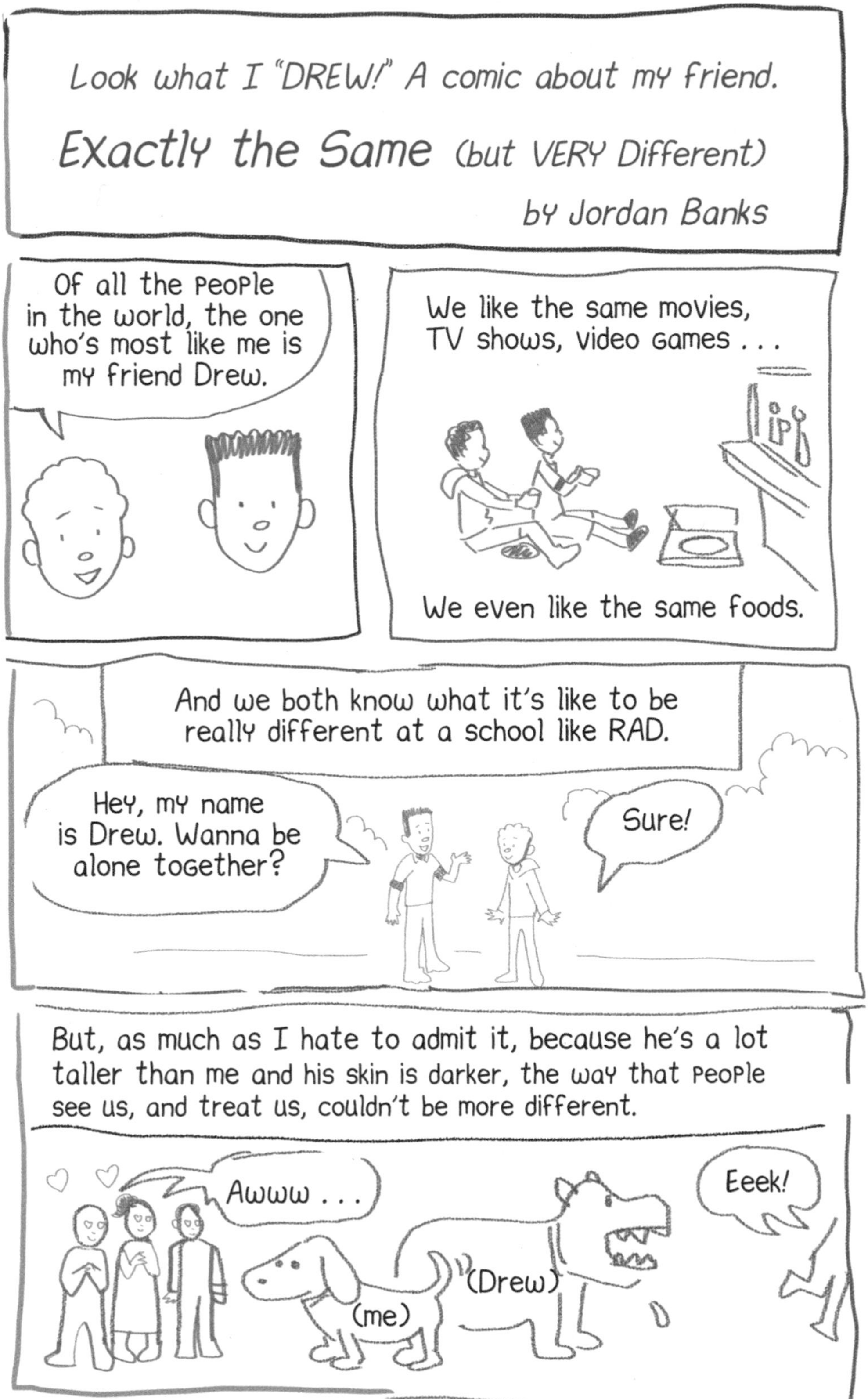
Look what I "DREW!" A comic about my friend.
Exactly the Same (but VERY Different)
by Jordan Banks
Of all the people in the world, the one who's most like me is my friend Drew.
We like the same movies, TV shows, video games . . .
We even like the same foods.
And we both know what it's like to be really different at a school like RAD.
Hey, my name is Drew. Wanna be alone together?
Sure!
But, as much as I hate to admit it, because he's a lot taller than me and his skin is darker, the way that people see us, and treat us, couldn't be more different.
Awww . . .
(me)
(Drew)
Eeek!

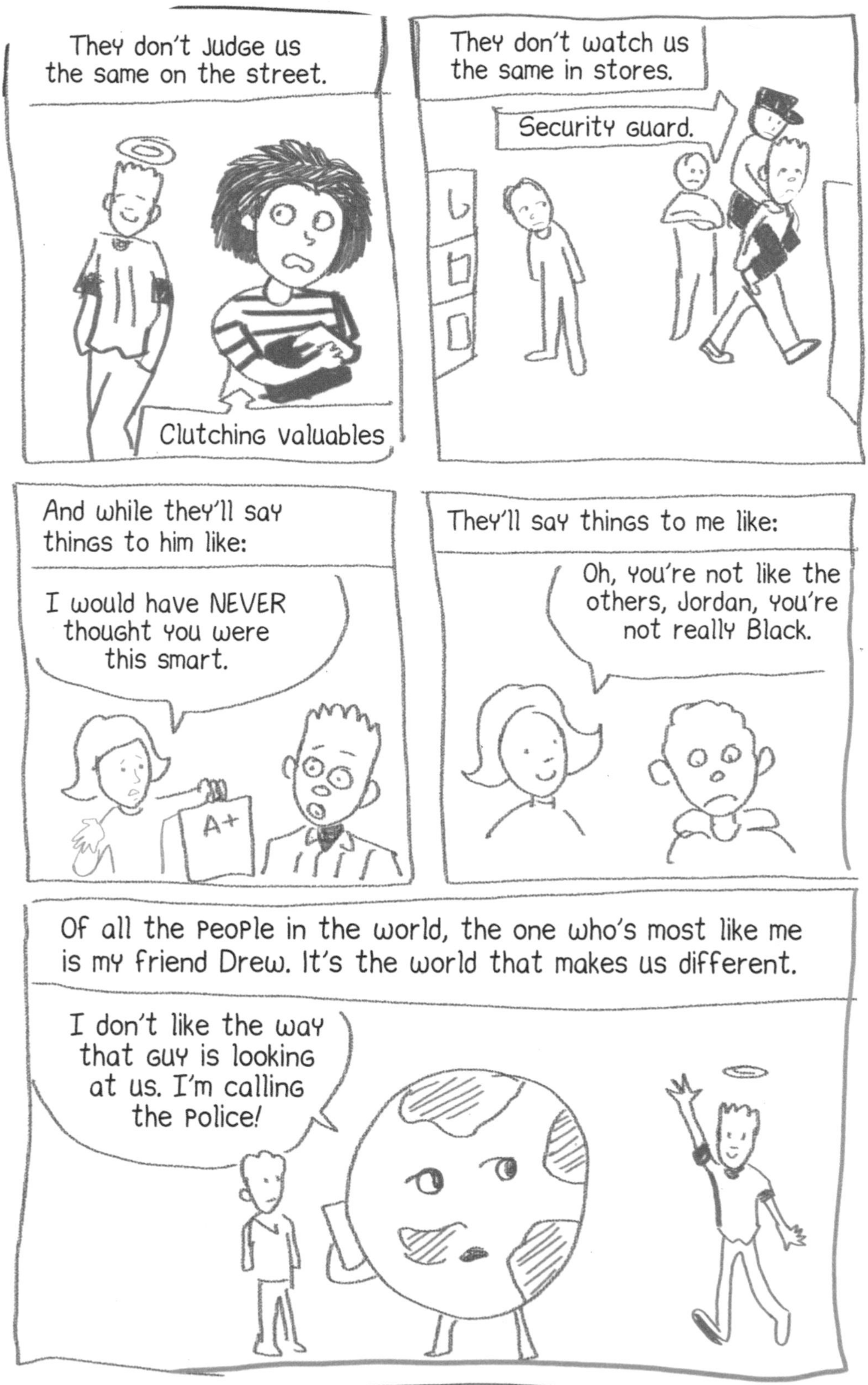

They don't judge us the same on the street.
Clutching valuables
They don't watch us the same in stores.
Security guard.
And while they'll say things to him like:
I would have NEVER thought you were this smart.
A+
They'll say things to me like:
Oh, you're not like the others, Jordan, you're not really Black.
Of all the people in the world, the one who's most like me is my friend Drew. It's the world that makes us different.
I don't like the way that guy is looking at us. I'm calling the police!

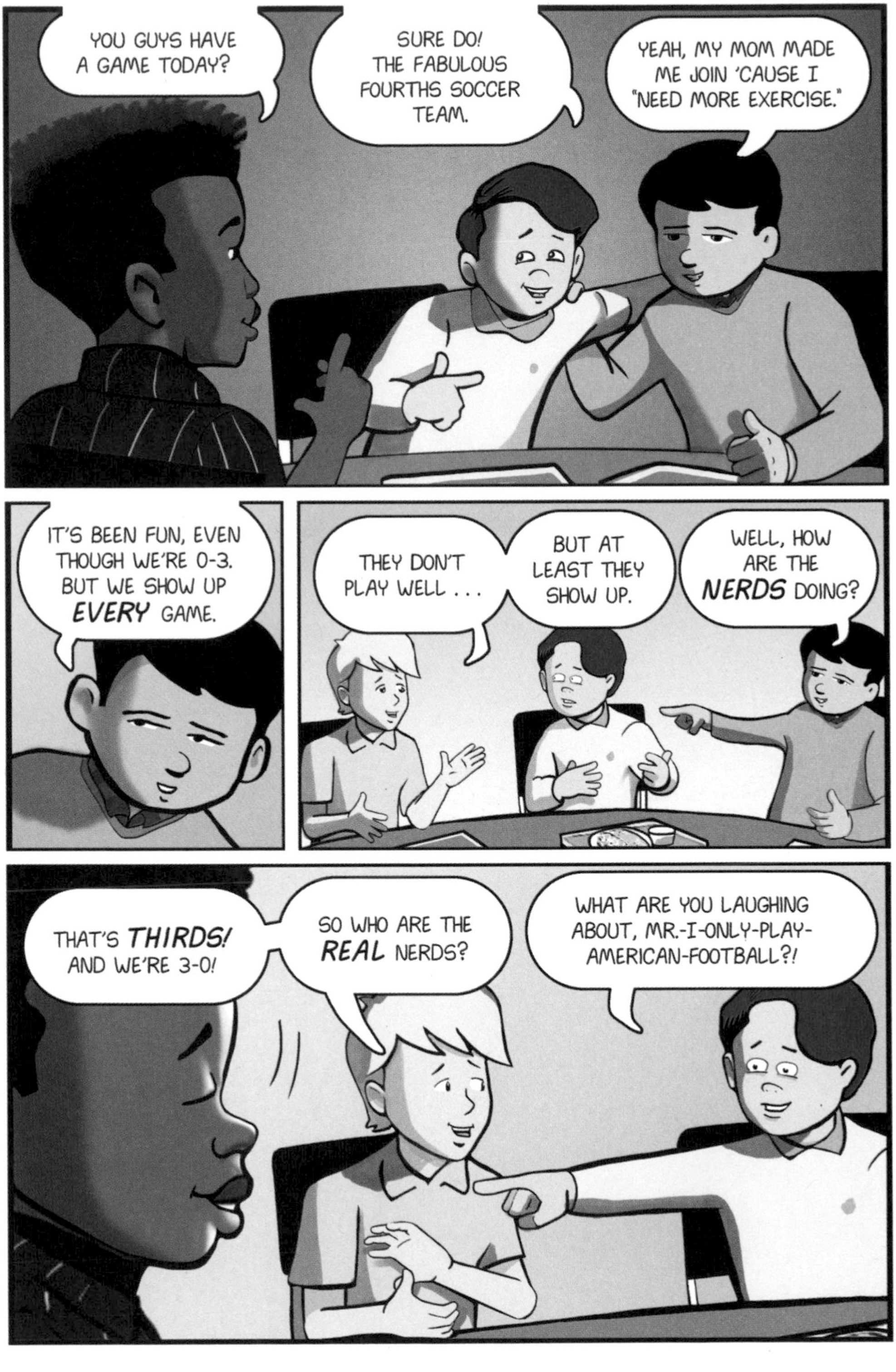
YOU GUYS HAVE A GAME TODAY?
SURE DO! THE FABULOUS FOURTHS SOCCER TEAM.
YEAH, MY MOM MADE ME JOIN 'CAUSE I "NEED MORE EXERCISE."
IT'S BEEN FUN, EVEN THOUGH WE'RE 0-3. BUT WE SHOW UP EVERY GAME.
THEY DON'T PLAY WELL . . .
BUT AT LEAST THEY SHOW UP.
WELL, HOW ARE THE NERDS DOING?
THAT'S THIRDS! AND WE'RE 3-0!
SO WHO ARE THE REAL NERDS?
WHAT ARE YOU LAUGHING ABOUT, MR.-I-ONLY-PLAY-AMERICAN-FOOTBALL?!

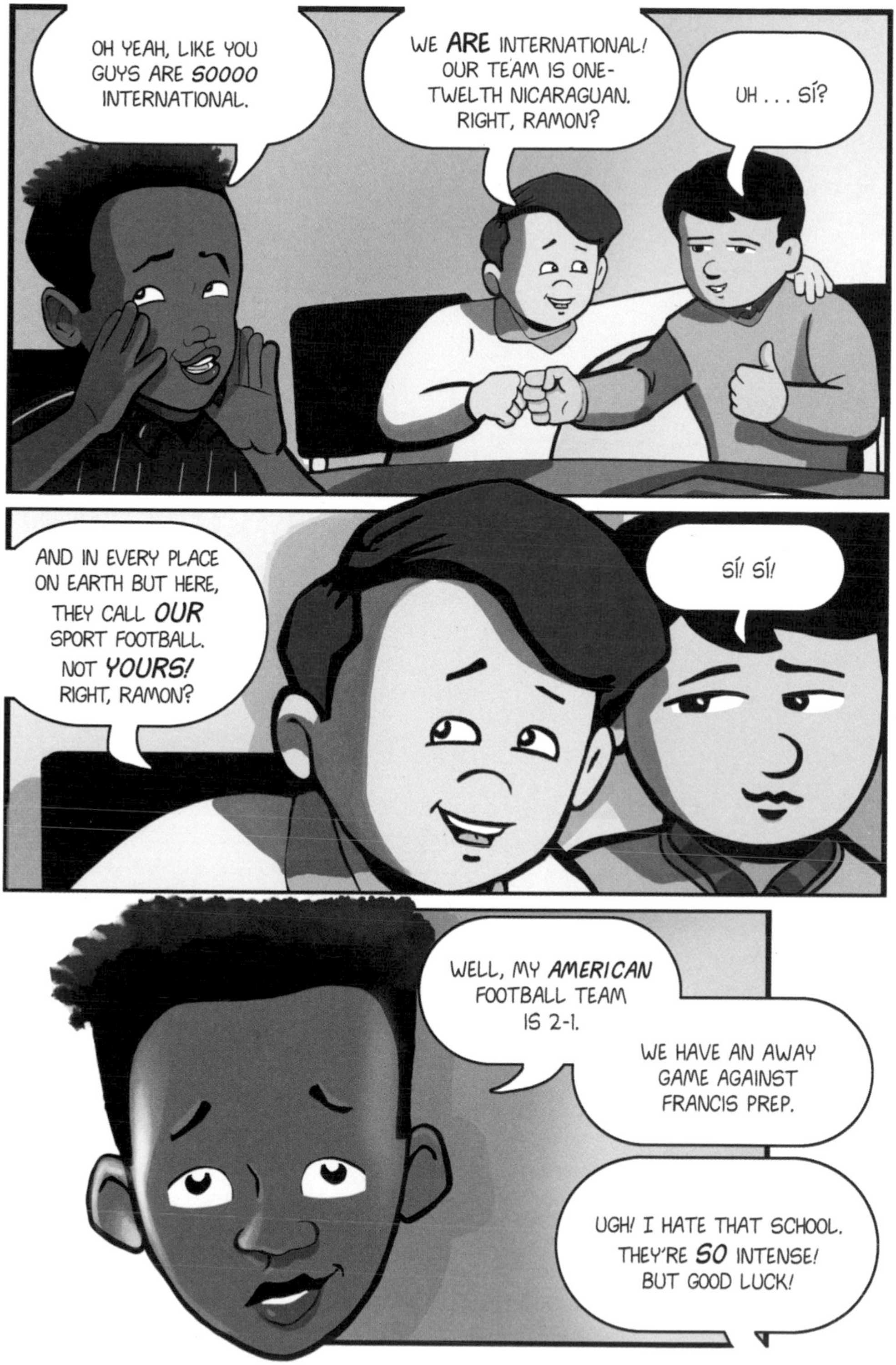
OH YEAH, LIKE YOU GUYS ARE SOOOO INTERNATIONAL.
WE ARE INTERNATIONAL! OUR TEAM IS ONE-TWELTH NICARAGUAN. RIGHT, RAMON?
UH . . . SÍ?
AND IN EVERY PLACE ON EARTH BUT HERE, THEY CALL OUR SPORT FOOTBALL. NOT YOURS! RIGHT, RAMON?
SÍ! SÍ!
WELL, MY AMERICAN FOOTBALL TEAM IS 2-1.
WE HAVE AN AWAY GAME AGAINST FRANCIS PREP.
UGH! I HATE THAT SCHOOL. THEY'RE SO INTENSE! BUT GOOD LUCK!

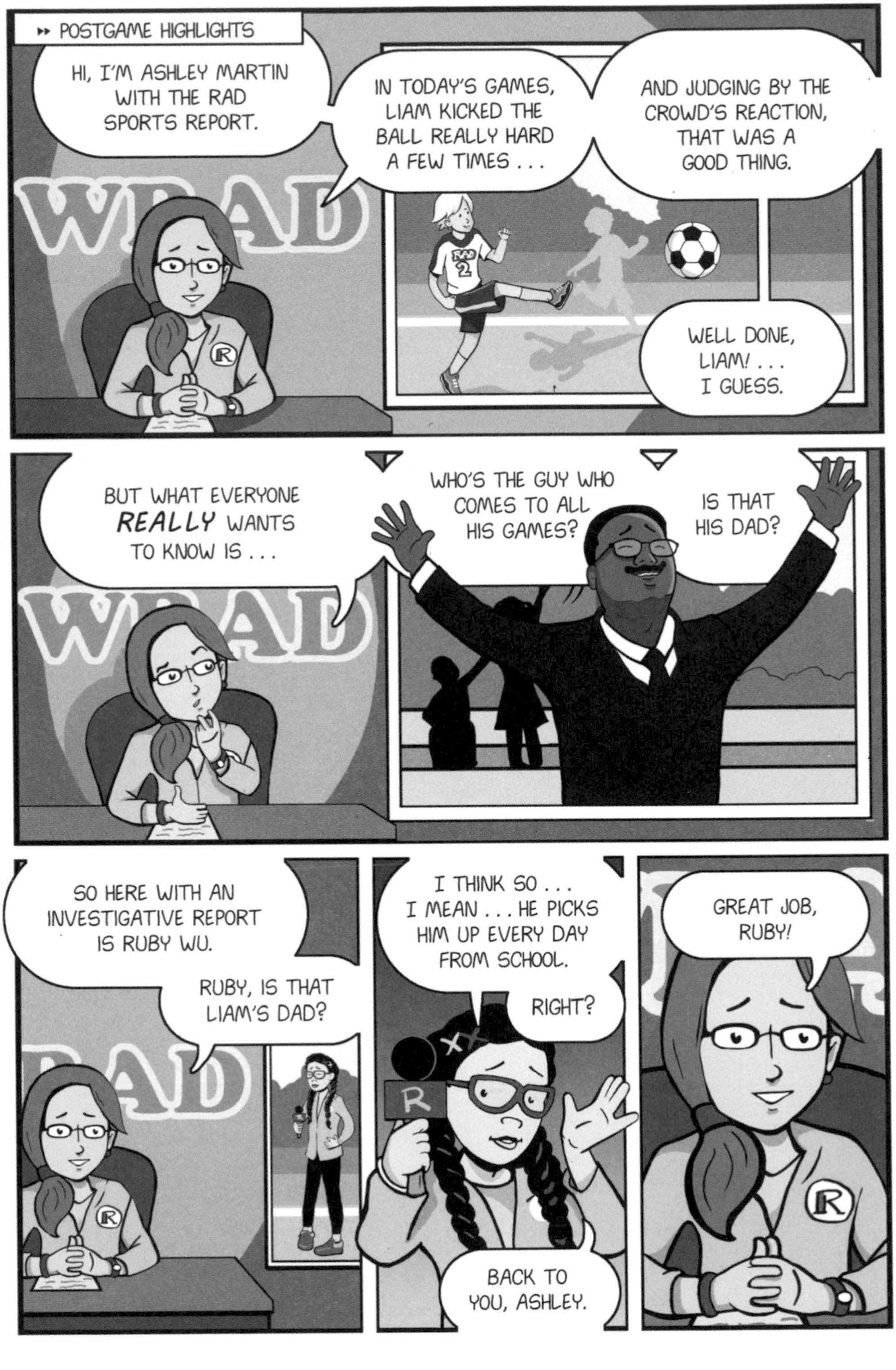

POSTGAME HIGHLIGHTS
HI, I'M ASHLEY MARTIN WITH THE RAD SPORTS REPORT.
IN TODAY'S GAMES, LIAM KICKED THE BALL REALLY HARD A FEW TIMES . . .
AND JUDGING BY THE CROWD'S REACTION, THAT WAS A GOOD THING.
WRAD
RAD 2
WELL DONE, LIAM! . . . I GUESS.
BUT WHAT EVERYONE *REALLY* WANTS TO KNOW IS . . .
WHO'S THE GUY WHO COMES TO ALL HIS GAMES?
IS THAT HIS DAD?
WRAD
SO HERE WITH AN INVESTIGATIVE REPORT IS RUBY WU.
RUBY, IS THAT LIAM'S DAD?
I THINK SO . . . I MEAN . . . HE PICKS HIM UP EVERY DAY FROM SCHOOL.
RIGHT?
BACK TO YOU, ASHLEY.
GREAT JOB, RUBY!

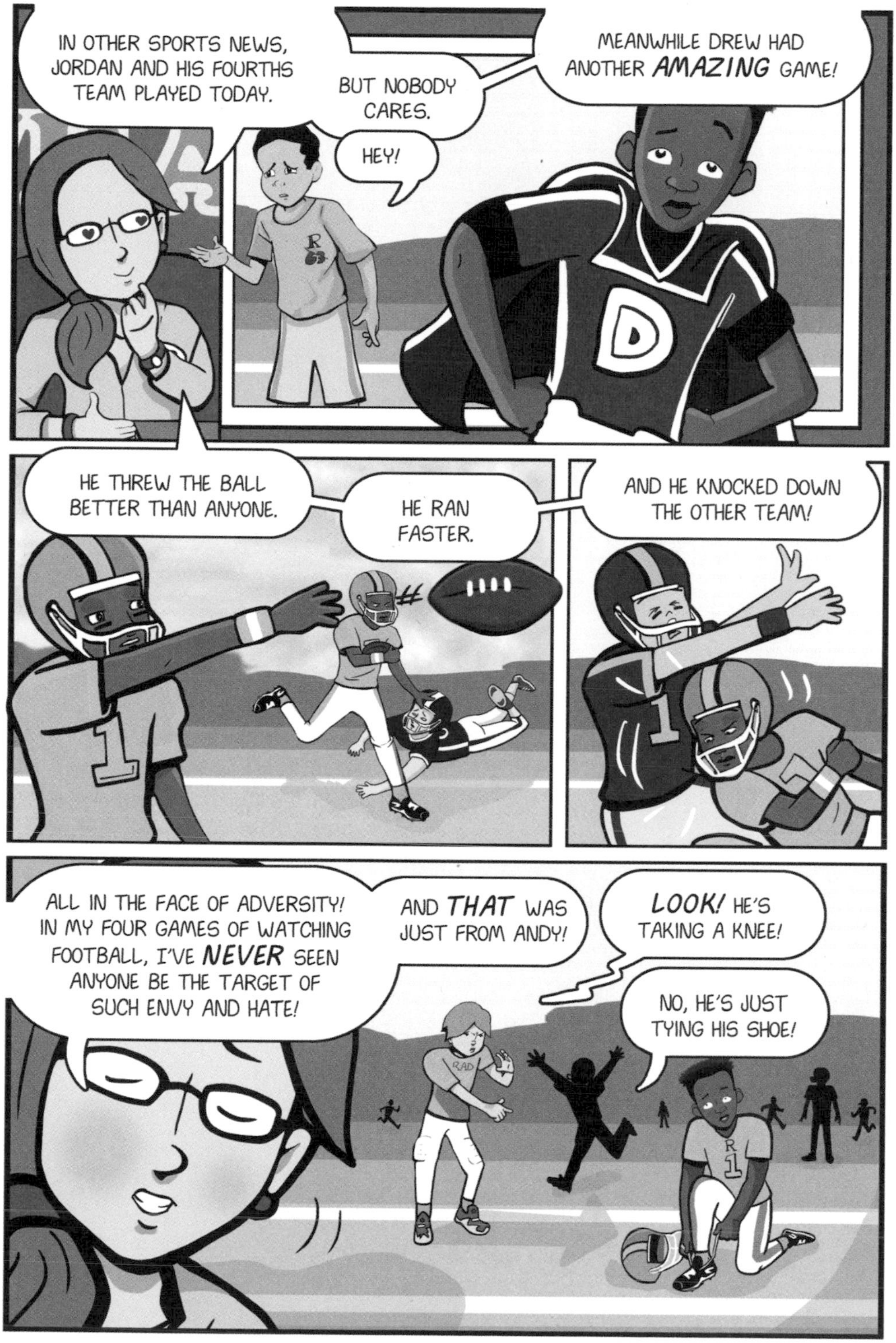
IN OTHER SPORTS NEWS, JORDAN AND HIS FOURTHS TEAM PLAYED TODAY.
BUT NOBODY CARES.
HEY!
MEANWHILE DREW HAD ANOTHER AMAZING GAME!
HE THREW THE BALL BETTER THAN ANYONE.
HE RAN FASTER.
AND HE KNOCKED DOWN THE OTHER TEAM!
ALL IN THE FACE OF ADVERSITY! IN MY FOUR GAMES OF WATCHING FOOTBALL, I'VE NEVER SEEN ANYONE BE THE TARGET OF SUCH ENVY AND HATE!
AND THAT WAS JUST FROM ANDY!
LOOK! HE'S TAKING A KNEE!
NO, HE'S JUST TYING HIS SHOE!

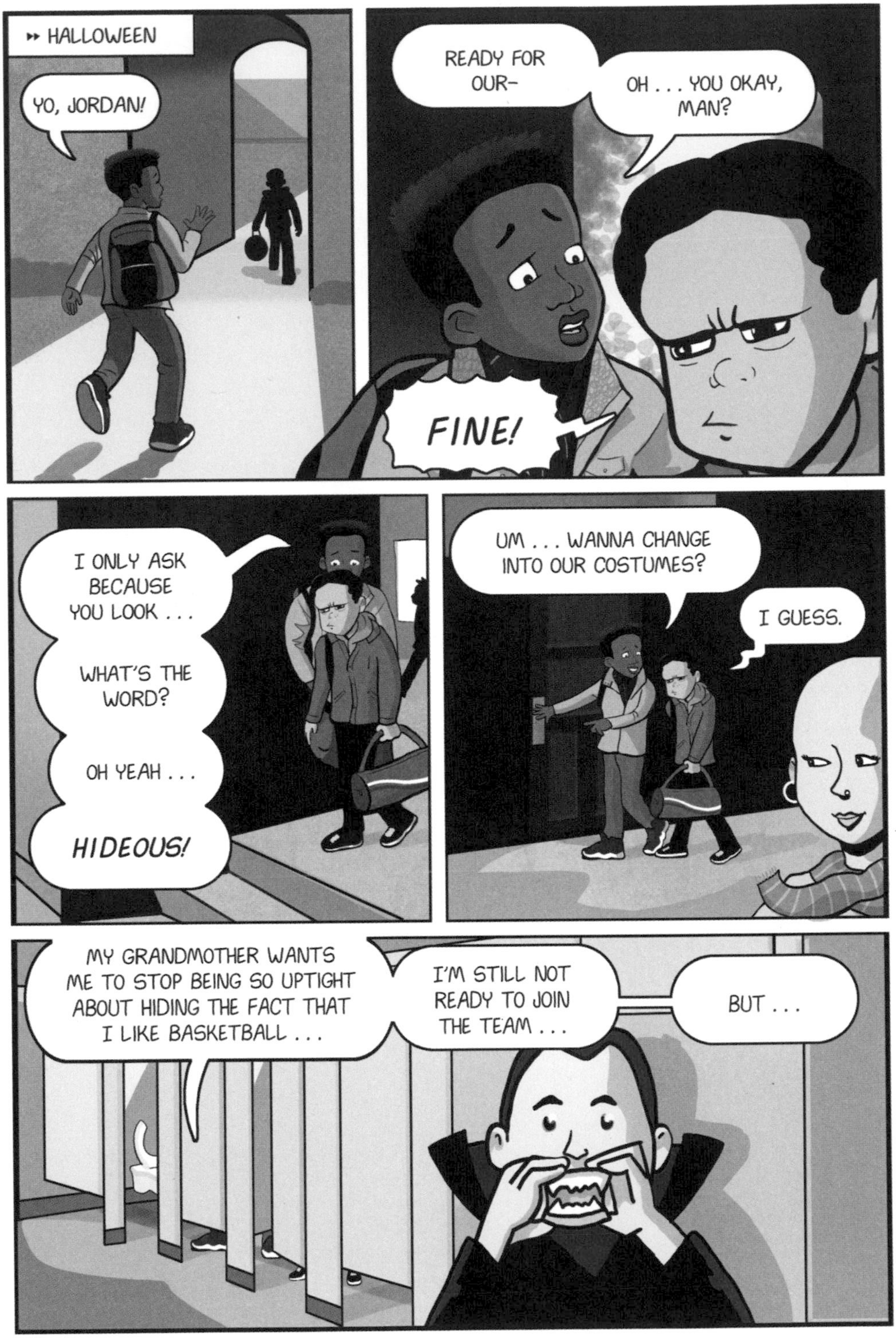
HALLOWEEN
YO, JORDAN!
READY FOR OUR-
OH . . . YOU OKAY, MAN?
FINE!
I ONLY ASK BECAUSE YOU LOOK . . .
WHAT'S THE WORD?
OH YEAH . . .
HIDEOUS!
UM . . . WANNA CHANGE INTO OUR COSTUMES?
I GUESS.
MY GRANDMOTHER WANTS ME TO STOP BEING SO UPTIGHT ABOUT HIDING THE FACT THAT I LIKE BASKETBALL . . .
I'M STILL NOT READY TO JOIN THE TEAM . . .
BUT . . .

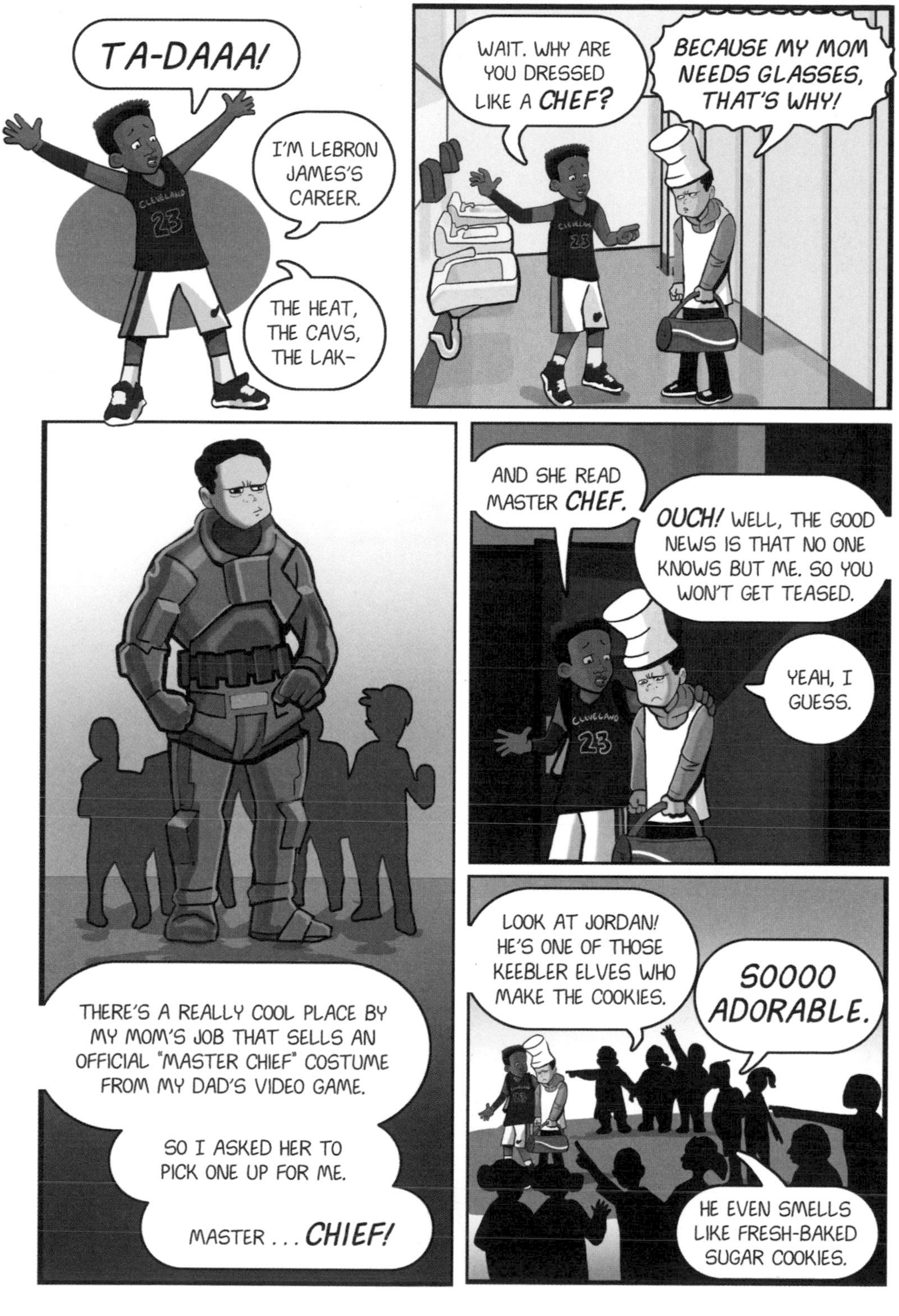
TA-DAAA!
I'M LEBRON JAMES'S CAREER.
THE HEAT, THE CAVS, THE LAK-
WAIT. WHY ARE YOU DRESSED LIKE A CHEF?
BECAUSE MY MOM NEEDS GLASSES, THAT'S WHY!
THERE'S A REALLY COOL PLACE BY MY MOM'S JOB THAT SELLS AN OFFICIAL "MASTER CHIEF" COSTUME FROM MY DAD'S VIDEO GAME.
SO I ASKED HER TO PICK ONE UP FOR ME.
MASTER . . . CHIEF!
AND SHE READ MASTER CHEF.
OUCH! WELL, THE GOOD NEWS IS THAT NO ONE KNOWS BUT ME. SO YOU WON'T GET TEASED.
YEAH, I GUESS.
LOOK AT JORDAN! HE'S ONE OF THOSE KEEBLER ELVES WHO MAKE THE COOKIES.
SOOOO ADORABLE.
HE EVEN SMELLS LIKE FRESH-BAKED SUGAR COOKIES.

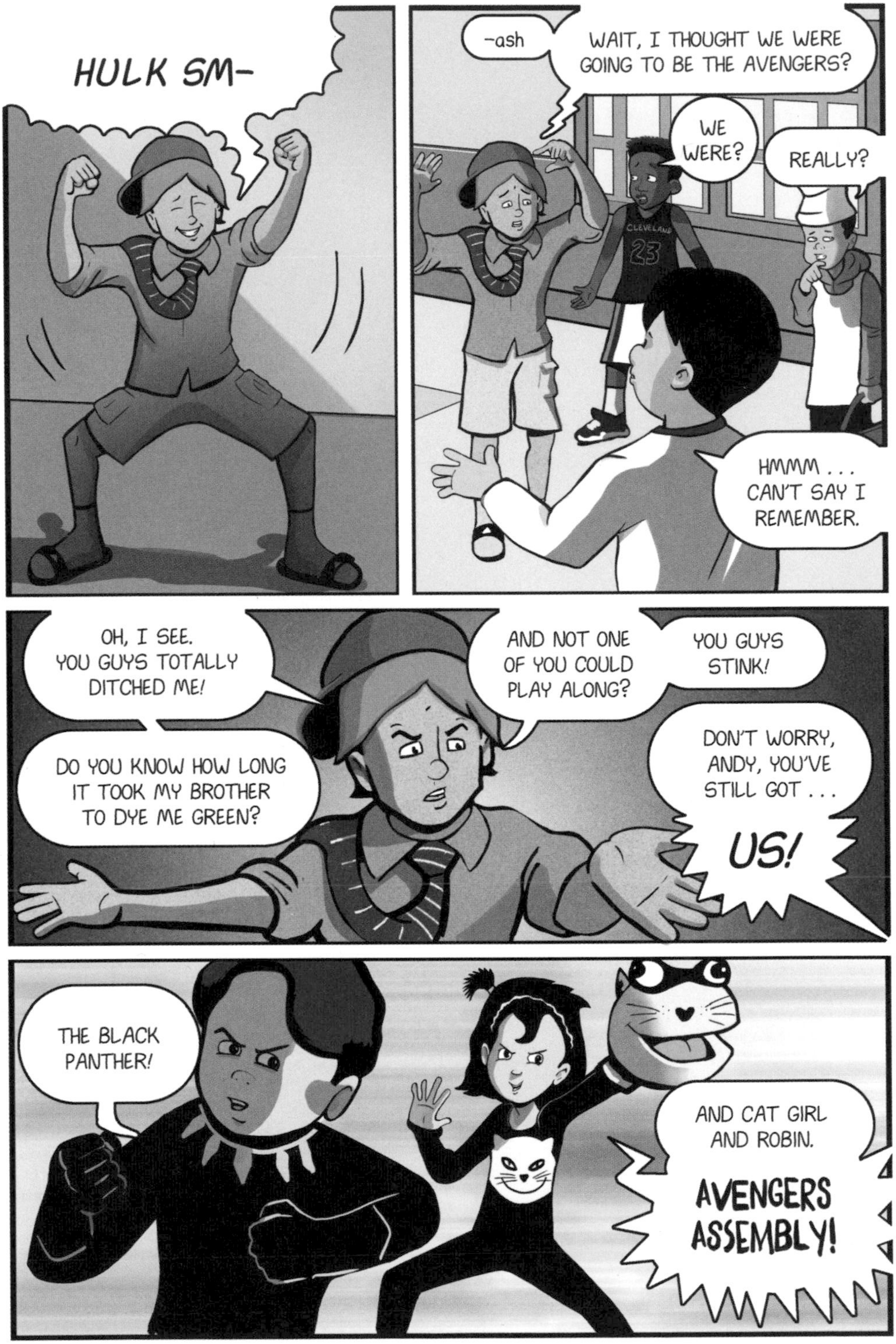
HULK SM-
-ash
WAIT, I THOUGHT WE WERE GOING TO BE THE AVENGERS?
WE WERE?
REALLY?
CLEVELAND 23
HMMM . . . CAN'T SAY I REMEMBER.
OH, I SEE. YOU GUYS TOTALLY DITCHED ME!
DO YOU KNOW HOW LONG IT TOOK MY BROTHER TO DYE ME GREEN?
AND NOT ONE OF YOU COULD PLAY ALONG?
YOU GUYS STINK!
DON'T WORRY, ANDY, YOU'VE STILL GOT . . .
US!
THE BLACK PANTHER!
AND CAT GIRL AND ROBIN.
AVENGERS ASSEMBLY!

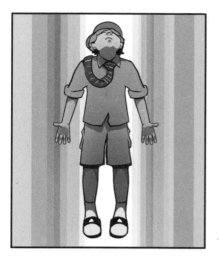

SO WHO IS EVERYONE SUPPOSED TO BE?

ZOMBIE.

ZOMBIE.

ZOMBIES.

I'M A BILLIONAIRE BUSINESS TYCOON.

MAN, WE REALLY SHOULD HAVE COME AS THE AVENGERS.

YEAH.

TEAL FRIENDS

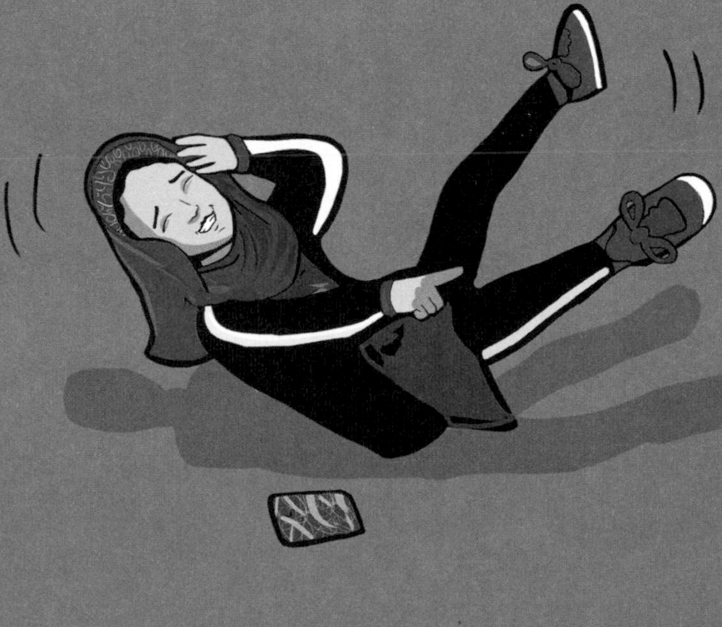

CHAPTER
4

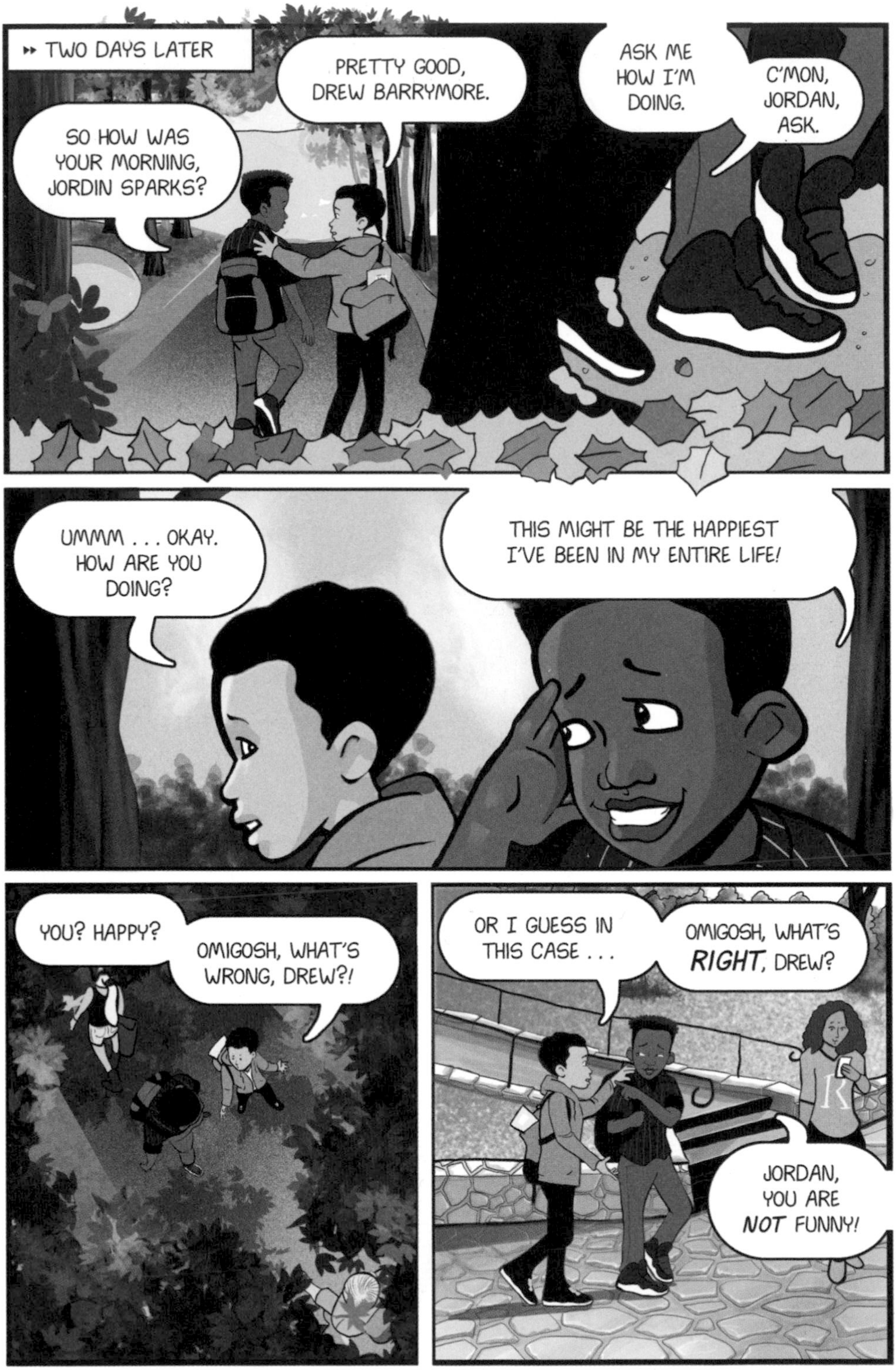

TWO DAYS LATER
SO HOW WAS YOUR MORNING, JORDIN SPARKS?
PRETTY GOOD, DREW BARRYMORE.
ASK ME HOW I'M DOING.
C'MON, JORDAN, ASK.
UMMM . . . OKAY. HOW ARE YOU DOING?
THIS MIGHT BE THE HAPPIEST I'VE BEEN IN MY ENTIRE LIFE!
YOU? HAPPY?
OMIGOSH, WHAT'S WRONG, DREW?!
OR I GUESS IN THIS CASE . . .
OMIGOSH, WHAT'S ***RIGHT***, DREW?
JORDAN, YOU ARE ***NOT*** FUNNY!

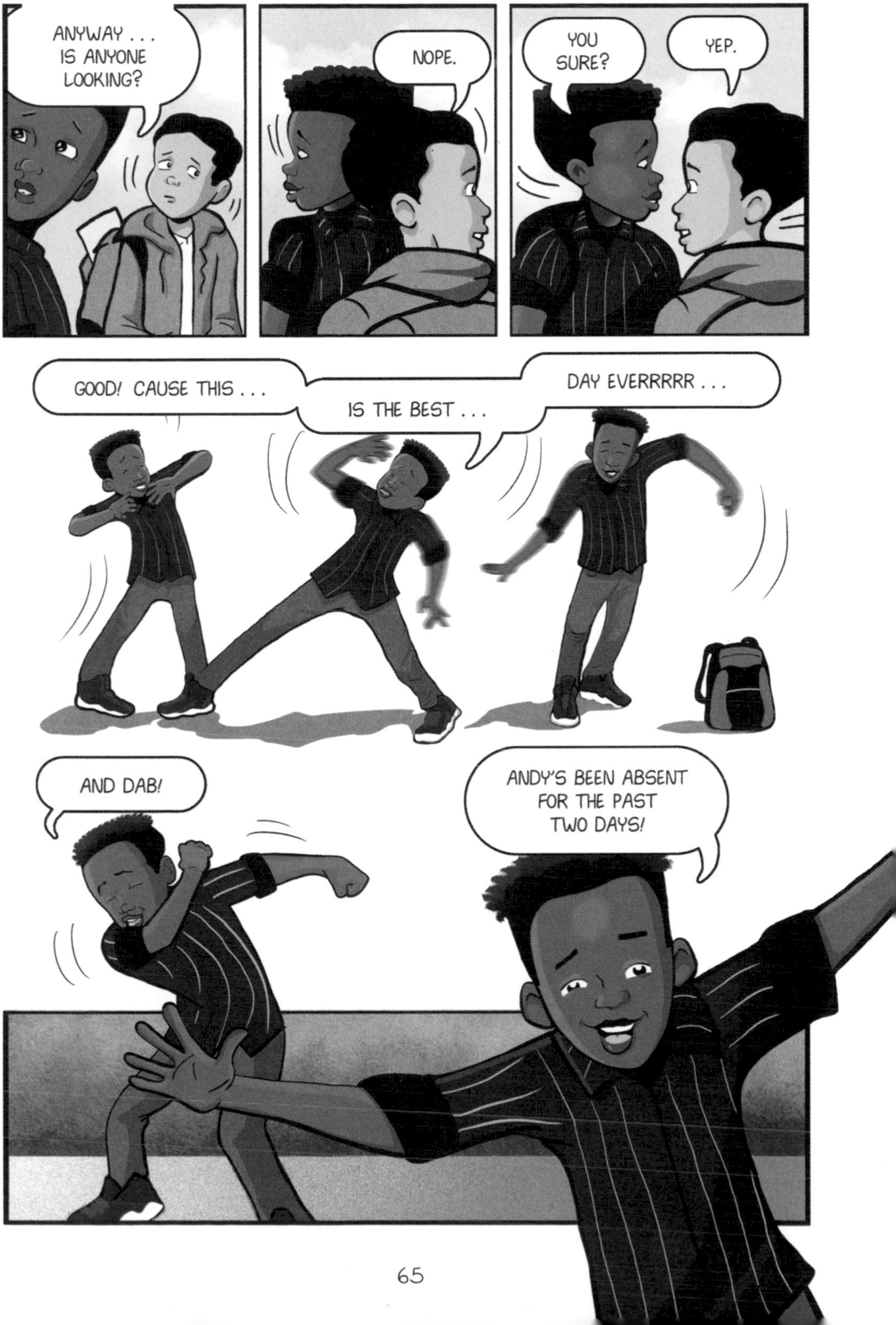
ANYWAY . . . IS ANYONE LOOKING?
NOPE.
YOU SURE?
YEP.
GOOD! CAUSE THIS . . .
IS THE BEST . . .
DAY EVERRRRR . . .
AND DAB!
ANDY'S BEEN ABSENT FOR THE PAST TWO DAYS!

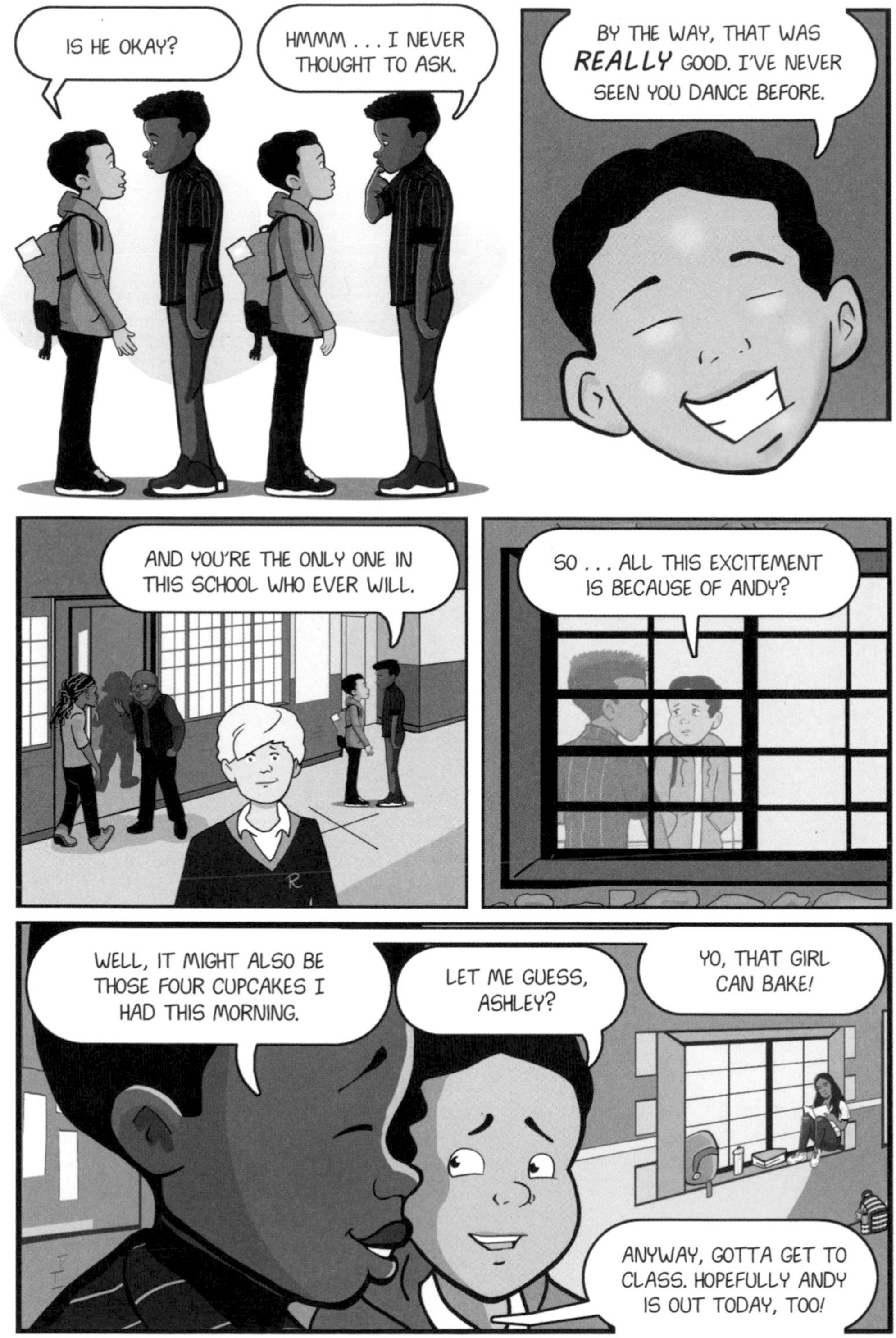
IS HE OKAY?
HMMM . . . I NEVER THOUGHT TO ASK.
BY THE WAY, THAT WAS *REALLY* GOOD. I'VE NEVER SEEN YOU DANCE BEFORE.
AND YOU'RE THE ONLY ONE IN THIS SCHOOL WHO EVER WILL.
SO . . . ALL THIS EXCITEMENT IS BECAUSE OF ANDY?
WELL, IT MIGHT ALSO BE THOSE FOUR CUPCAKES I HAD THIS MORNING.
LET ME GUESS, ASHLEY?
YO, THAT GIRL CAN BAKE!
ANYWAY, GOTTA GET TO CLASS. HOPEFULLY ANDY IS OUT TODAY, TOO!

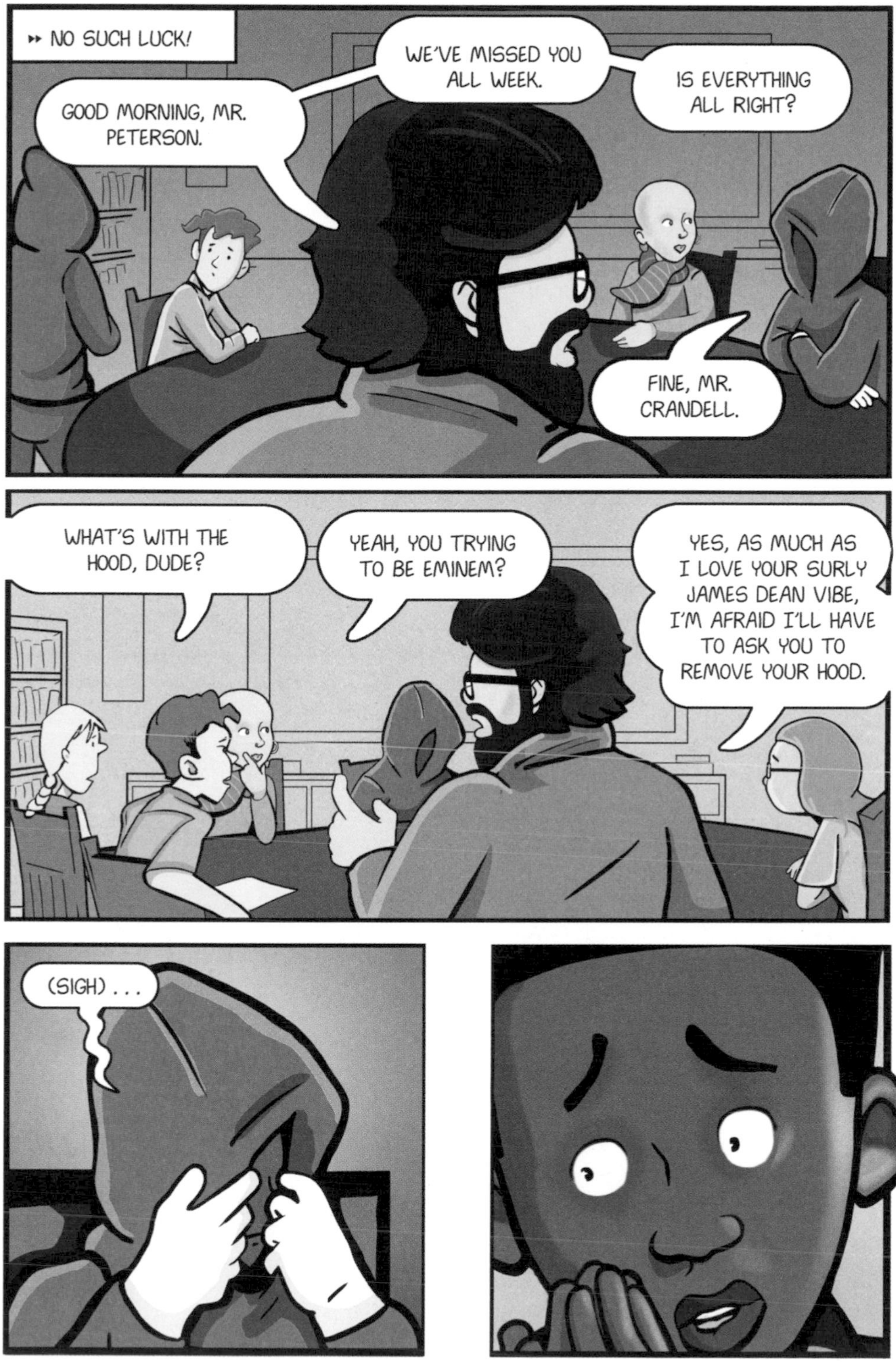
▸▸ NO SUCH LUCK!
GOOD MORNING, MR. PETERSON.
WE'VE MISSED YOU ALL WEEK.
IS EVERYTHING ALL RIGHT?
FINE, MR. CRANDELL.
WHAT'S WITH THE HOOD, DUDE?
YEAH, YOU TRYING TO BE EMINEM?
YES, AS MUCH AS I LOVE YOUR SURLY JAMES DEAN VIBE, I'M AFRAID I'LL HAVE TO ASK YOU TO REMOVE YOUR HOOD.
(SIGH) . . .

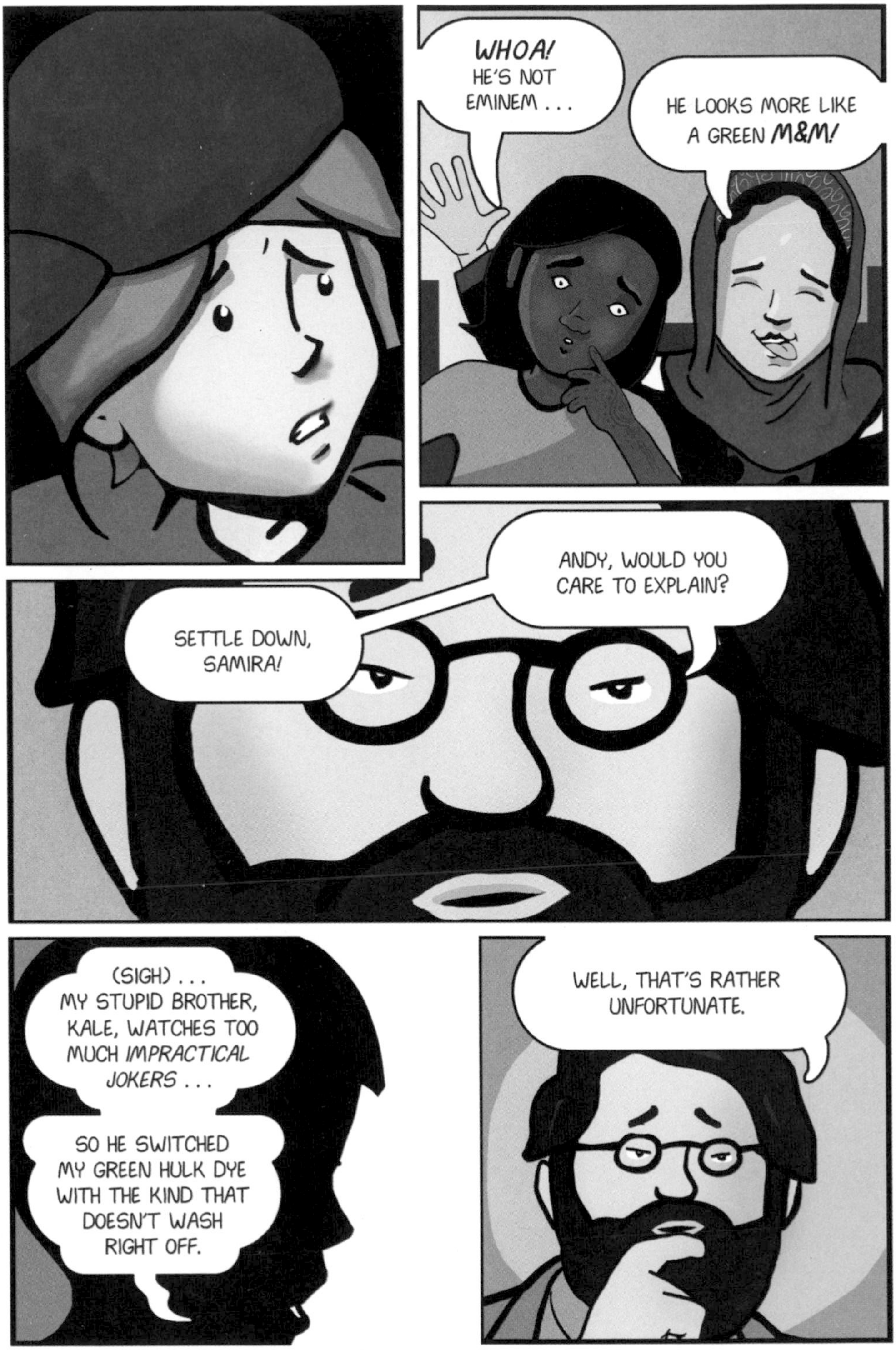
WHOA! HE'S NOT EMINEM . . .
HE LOOKS MORE LIKE A GREEN M&M!
ANDY, WOULD YOU CARE TO EXPLAIN?
SETTLE DOWN, SAMIRA!
(SIGH) . . . MY STUPID BROTHER, KALE, WATCHES TOO MUCH IMPRACTICAL JOKERS . . .
SO HE SWITCHED MY GREEN HULK DYE WITH THE KIND THAT DOESN'T WASH RIGHT OFF.
WELL, THAT'S RATHER UNFORTUNATE.

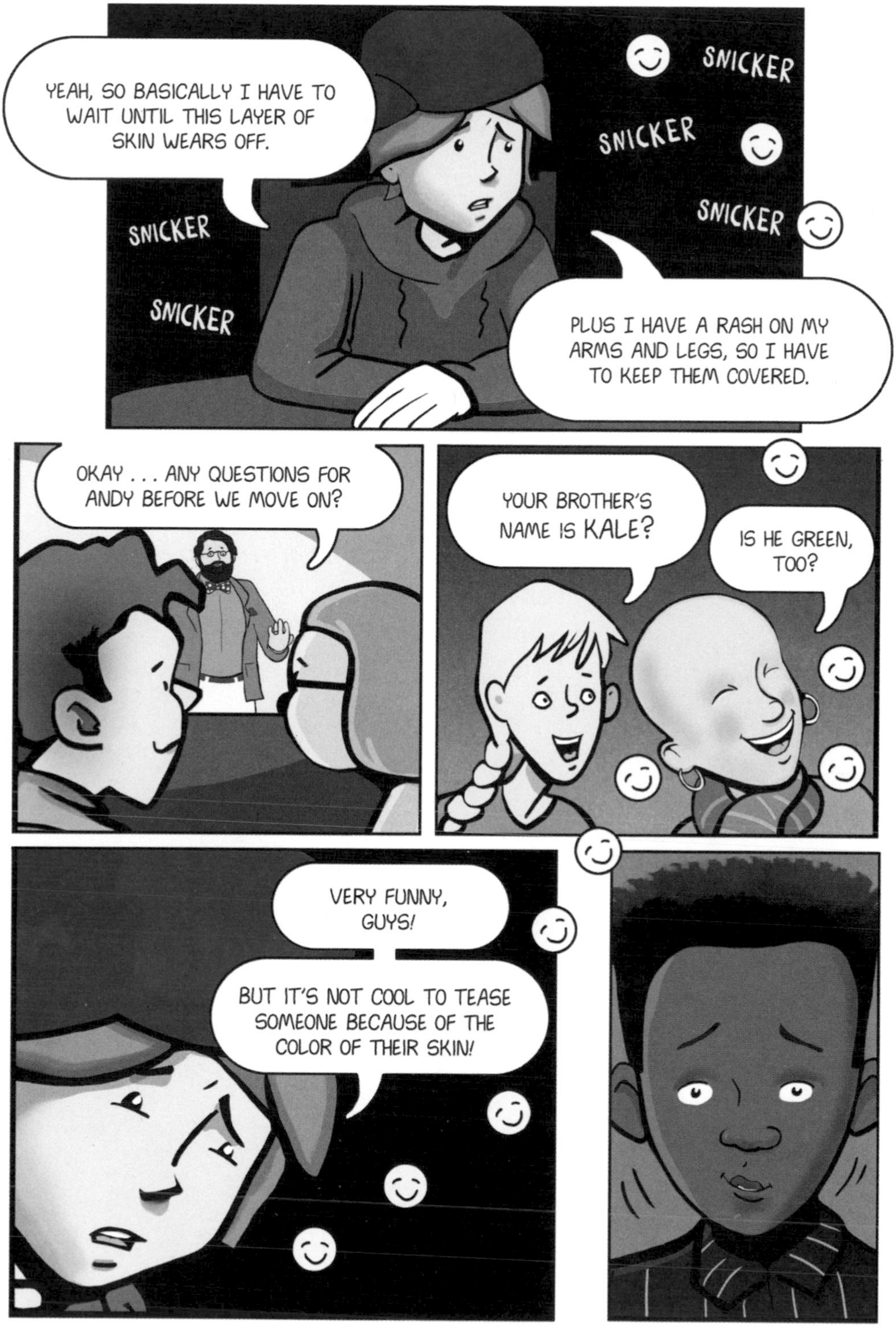
YEAH, SO BASICALLY I HAVE TO WAIT UNTIL THIS LAYER OF SKIN WEARS OFF.
SNICKER
SNICKER
SNICKER
SNICKER
SNICKER
PLUS I HAVE A RASH ON MY ARMS AND LEGS, SO I HAVE TO KEEP THEM COVERED.
OKAY . . . ANY QUESTIONS FOR ANDY BEFORE WE MOVE ON?
YOUR BROTHER'S NAME IS KALE?
IS HE GREEN, TOO?
VERY FUNNY, GUYS!
BUT IT'S NOT COOL TO TEASE SOMEONE BECAUSE OF THE COLOR OF THEIR SKIN!

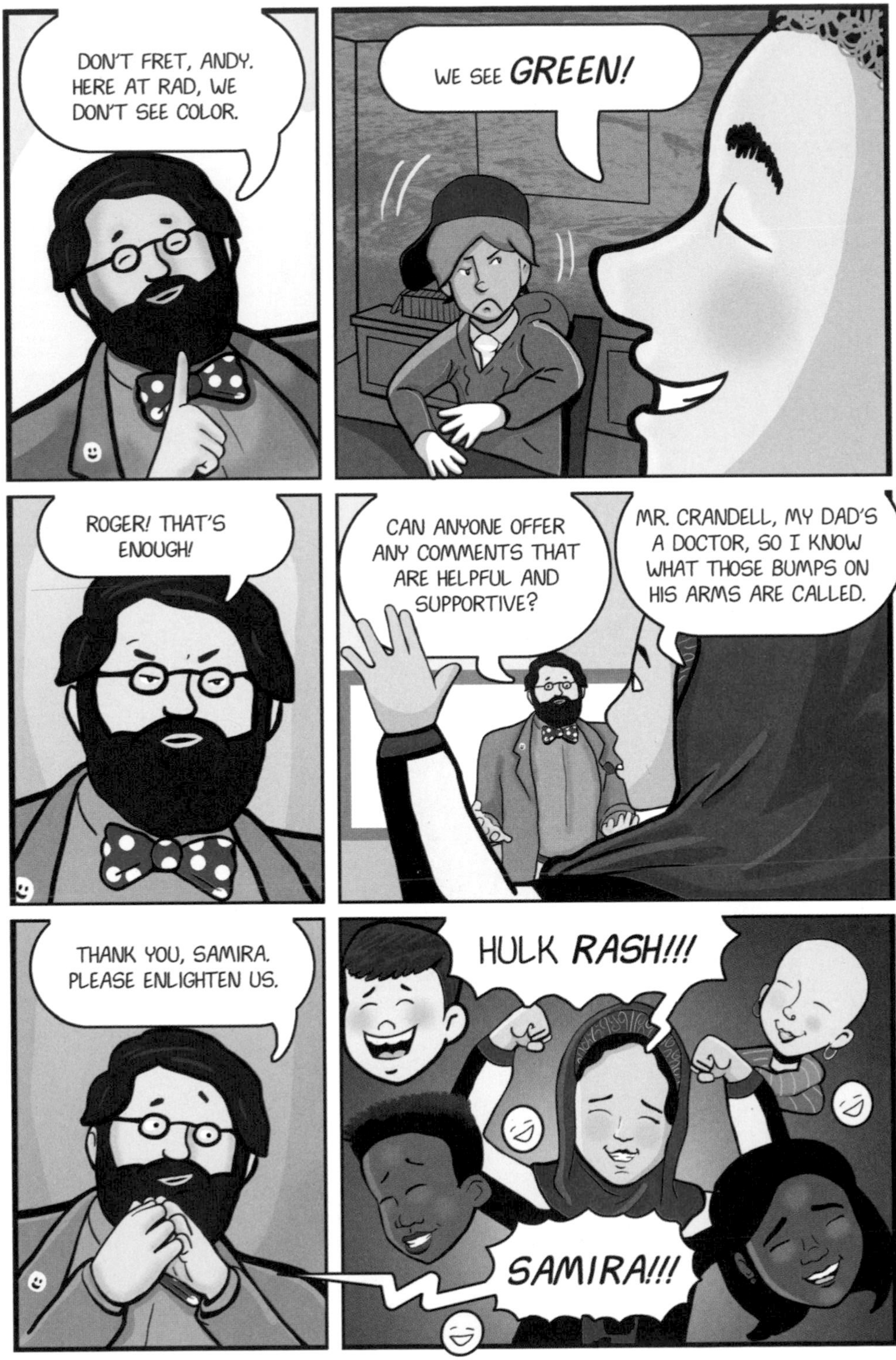

DON'T FRET, ANDY. HERE AT RAD, WE DON'T SEE COLOR.
WE SEE GREEN!
ROGER! THAT'S ENOUGH!
CAN ANYONE OFFER ANY COMMENTS THAT ARE HELPFUL AND SUPPORTIVE?
MR. CRANDELL, MY DAD'S A DOCTOR, SO I KNOW WHAT THOSE BUMPS ON HIS ARMS ARE CALLED.
THANK YOU, SAMIRA. PLEASE ENLIGHTEN US.
HULK RASH!!!
SAMIRA!!!

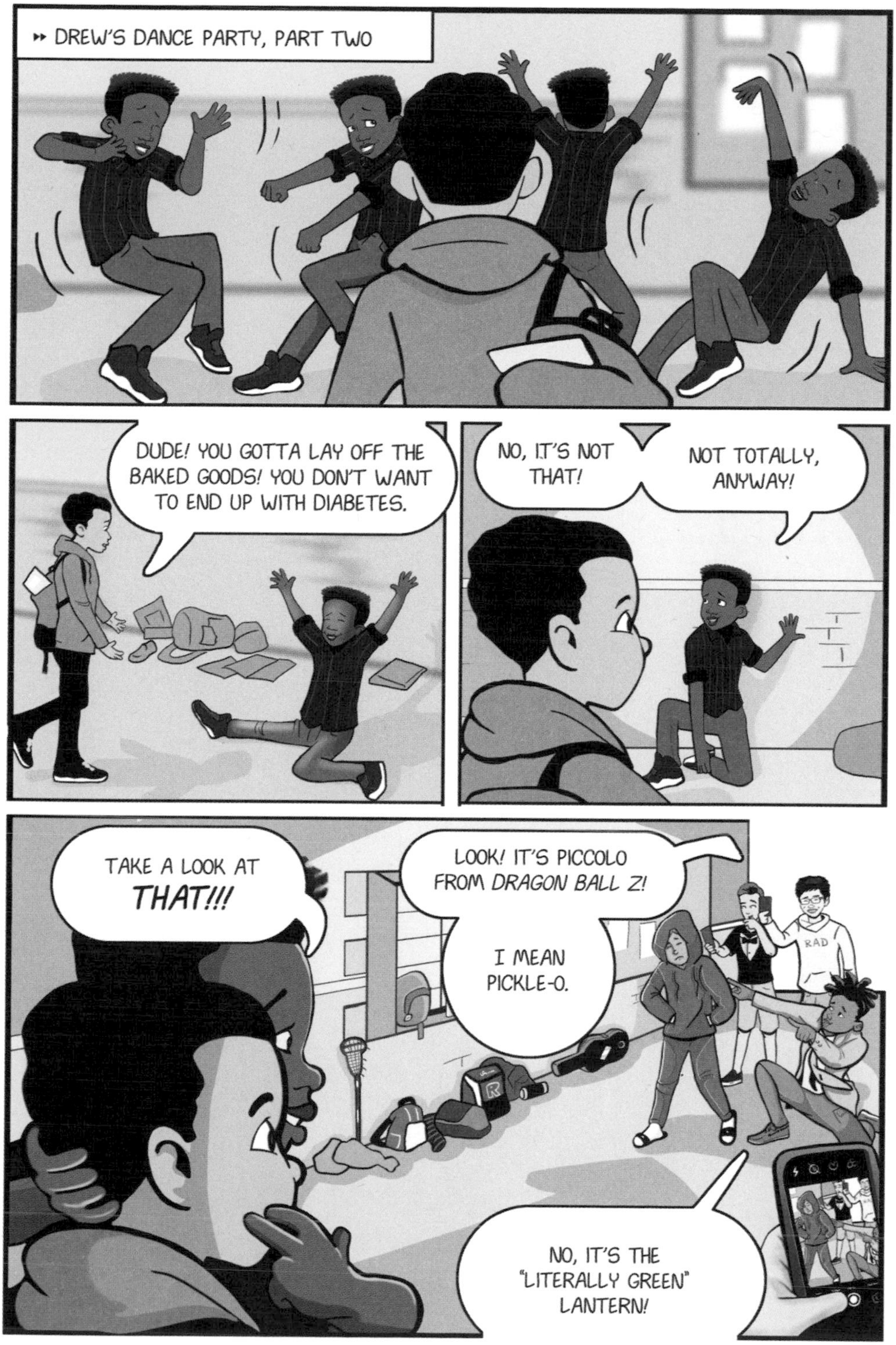
▸▸ DREW'S DANCE PARTY, PART TWO
DUDE! YOU GOTTA LAY OFF THE BAKED GOODS! YOU DON'T WANT TO END UP WITH DIABETES.
NO, IT'S NOT THAT!
NOT TOTALLY, ANYWAY!
TAKE A LOOK AT *THAT!!!*
LOOK! IT'S PICCOLO FROM *DRAGON BALL Z!*
I MEAN PICKLE-O.
RAD
NO, IT'S THE "LITERALLY GREEN" LANTERN!

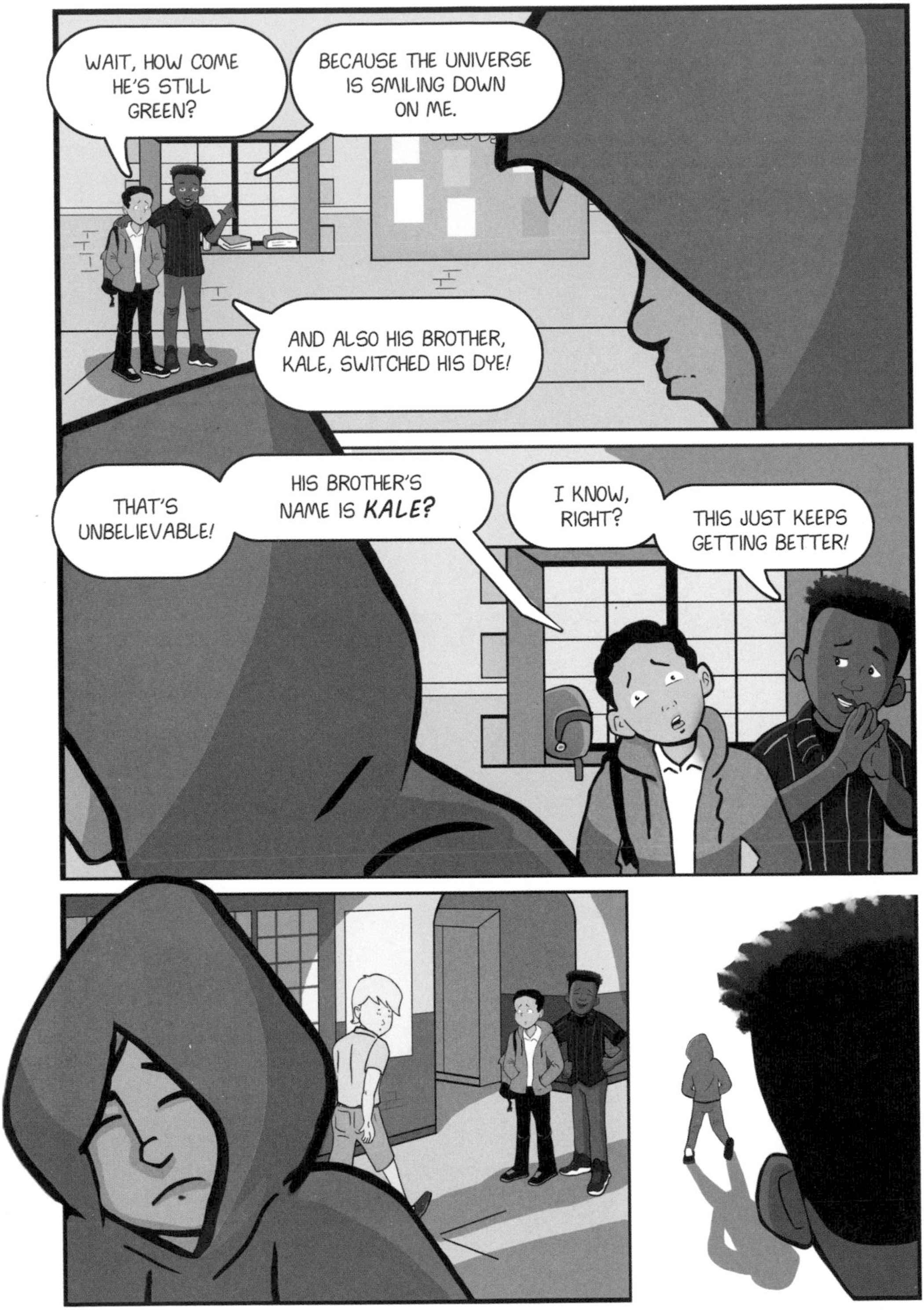
WAIT, HOW COME HE'S STILL GREEN?
BECAUSE THE UNIVERSE IS SMILING DOWN ON ME.
AND ALSO HIS BROTHER, KALE, SWITCHED HIS DYE!
THAT'S UNBELIEVABLE!
HIS BROTHER'S NAME IS *KALE?*
I KNOW, RIGHT?
THIS JUST KEEPS GETTING BETTER!

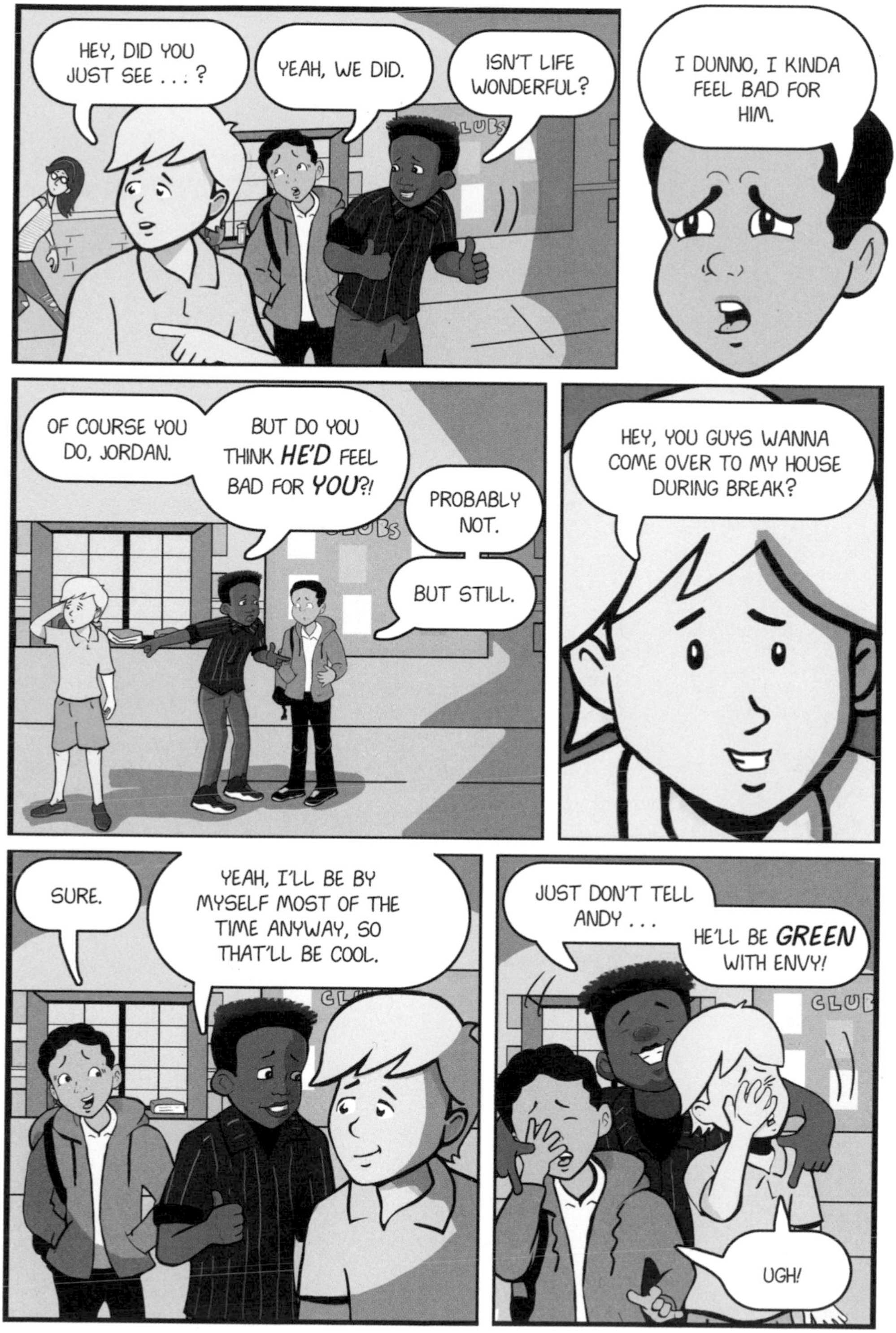
HEY, DID YOU JUST SEE . . . ?
YEAH, WE DID.
ISN'T LIFE WONDERFUL?
I DUNNO, I KINDA FEEL BAD FOR HIM.
OF COURSE YOU DO, JORDAN.
BUT DO YOU THINK **HE'D** FEEL BAD FOR **YOU**?!
PROBABLY NOT.
BUT STILL.
HEY, YOU GUYS WANNA COME OVER TO MY HOUSE DURING BREAK?
SURE.
YEAH, I'LL BE BY MYSELF MOST OF THE TIME ANYWAY, SO THAT'LL BE COOL.
JUST DON'T TELL ANDY . . .
HE'LL BE **GREEN** WITH ENVY!
UGH!

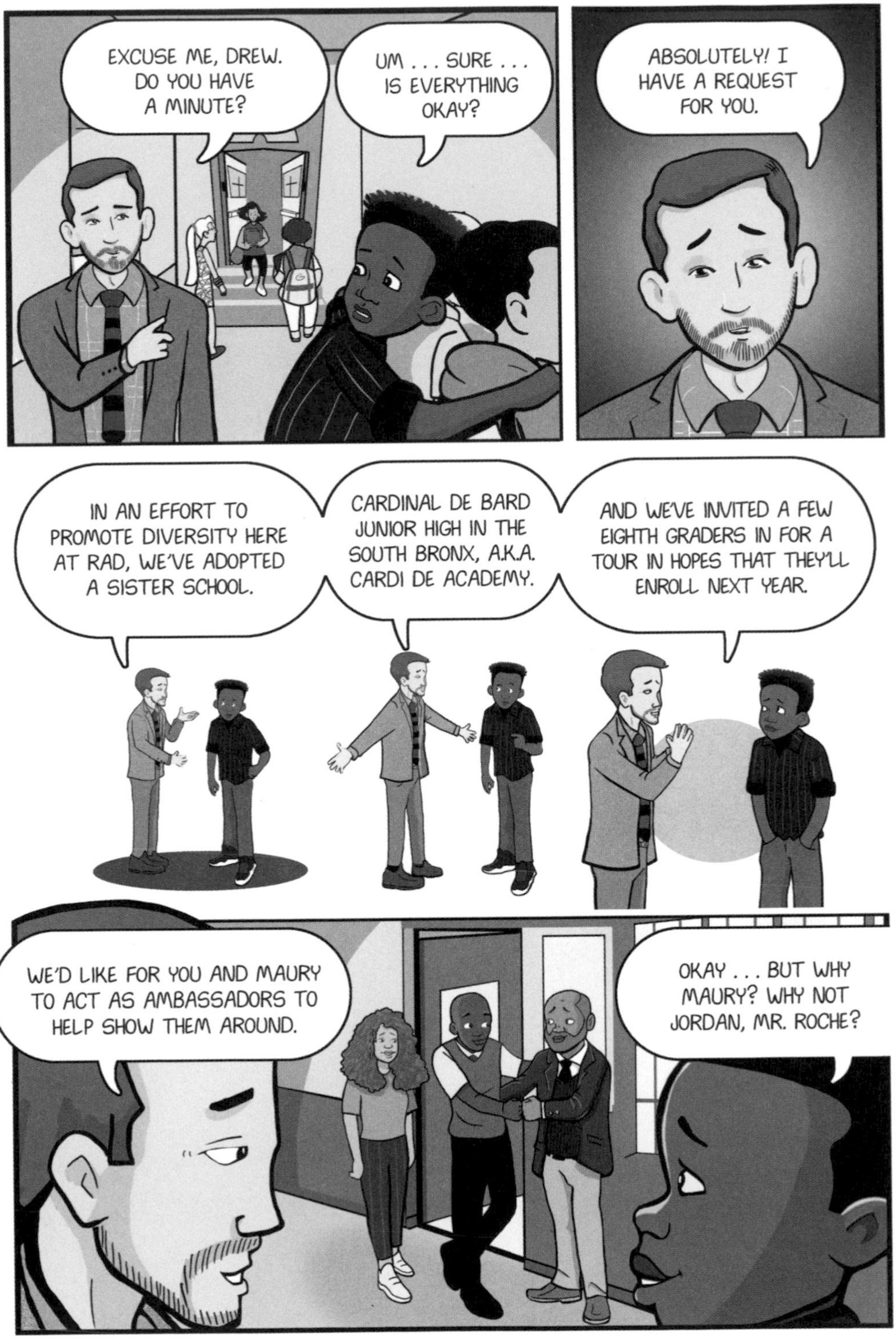
EXCUSE ME, DREW. DO YOU HAVE A MINUTE?
UM . . . SURE . . . IS EVERYTHING OKAY?
ABSOLUTELY! I HAVE A REQUEST FOR YOU.
IN AN EFFORT TO PROMOTE DIVERSITY HERE AT RAD, WE'VE ADOPTED A SISTER SCHOOL.
CARDINAL DE BARD JUNIOR HIGH IN THE SOUTH BRONX, A.K.A. CARDI DE ACADEMY.
AND WE'VE INVITED A FEW EIGHTH GRADERS IN FOR A TOUR IN HOPES THAT THEY'LL ENROLL NEXT YEAR.
WE'D LIKE FOR YOU AND MAURY TO ACT AS AMBASSADORS TO HELP SHOW THEM AROUND.
OKAY . . . BUT WHY MAURY? WHY NOT JORDAN, MR. ROCHE?

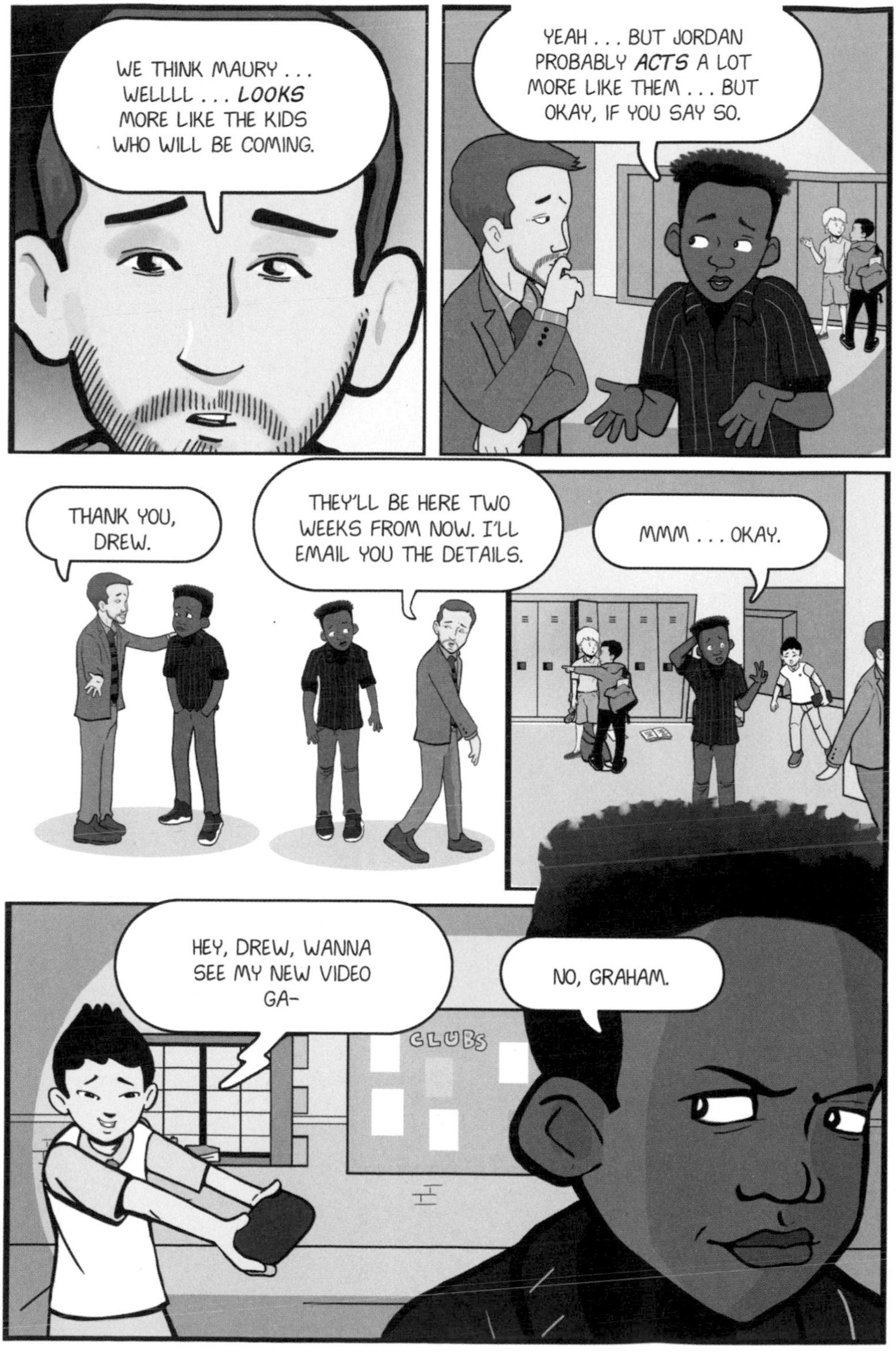
WE THINK MAURY . . . WELLLL . . . ***LOOKS*** MORE LIKE THE KIDS WHO WILL BE COMING.
YEAH . . . BUT JORDAN PROBABLY ***ACTS*** A LOT MORE LIKE THEM . . . BUT OKAY, IF YOU SAY SO.
THANK YOU, DREW.
THEY'LL BE HERE TWO WEEKS FROM NOW. I'LL EMAIL YOU THE DETAILS.
MMM . . . OKAY.
HEY, DREW, WANNA SEE MY NEW VIDEO GA-
NO, GRAHAM.
CLUBS

OMELET

CHAPTER 5

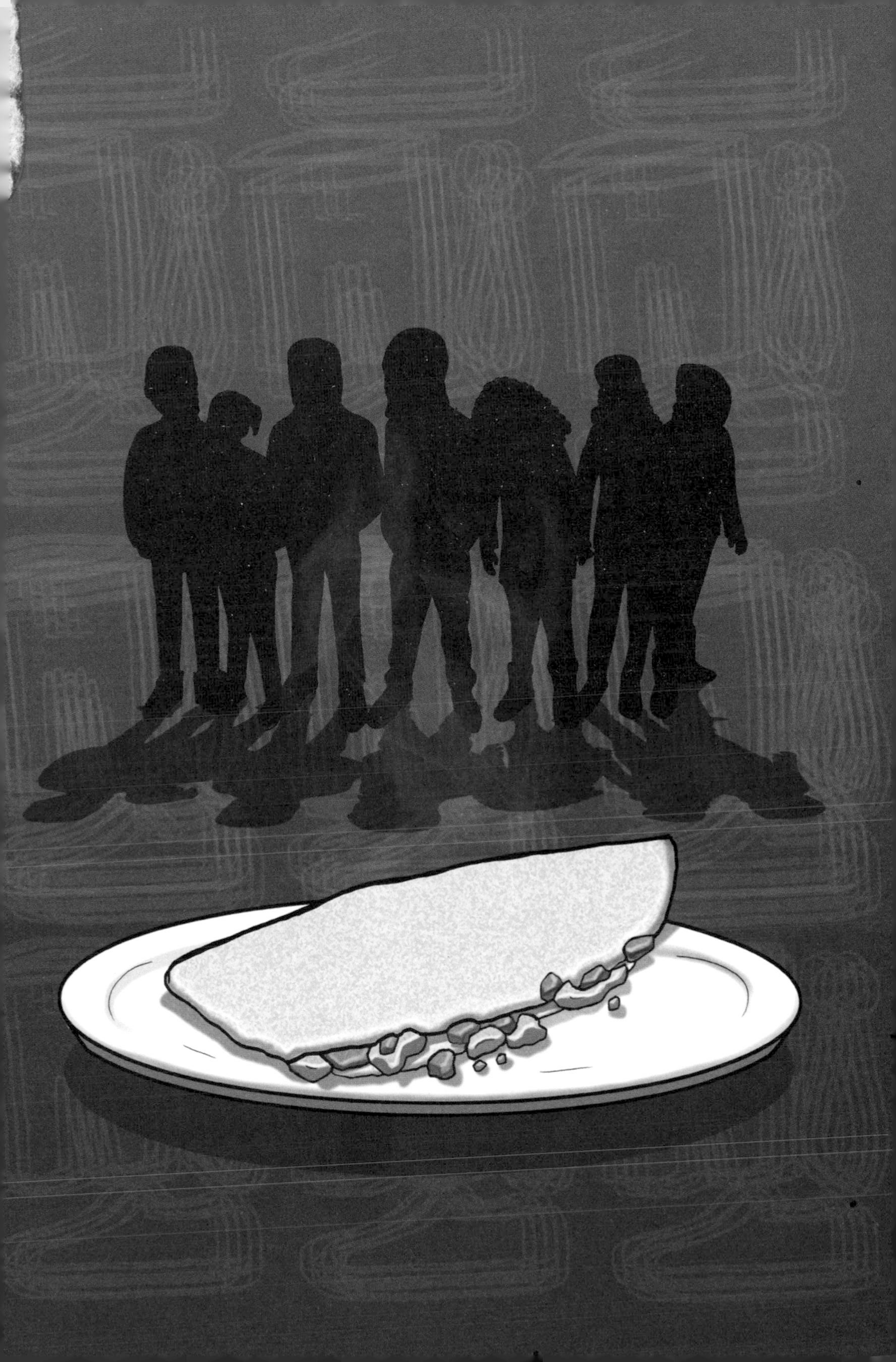

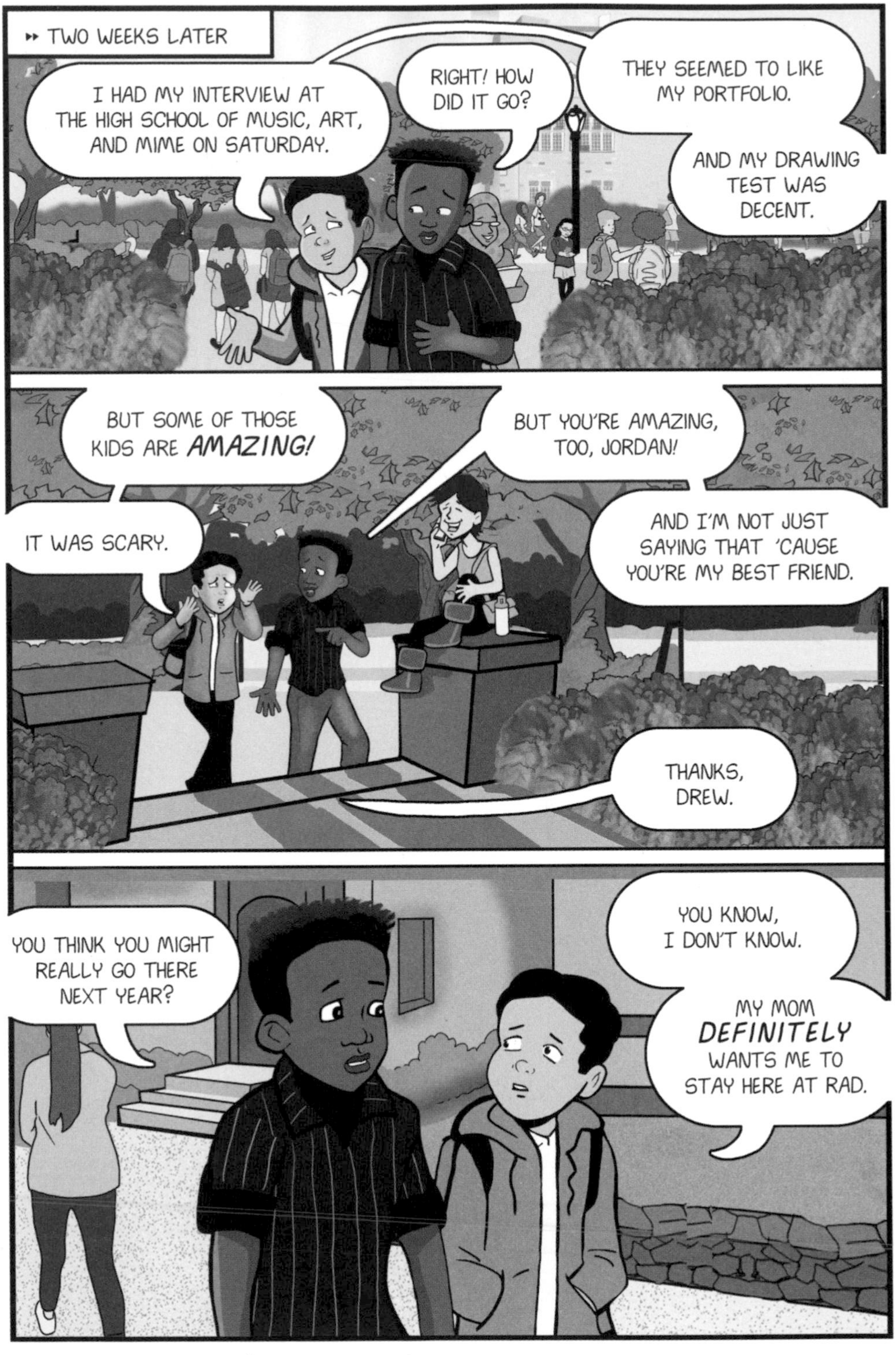
TWO WEEKS LATER
I HAD MY INTERVIEW AT THE HIGH SCHOOL OF MUSIC, ART, AND MIME ON SATURDAY.
RIGHT! HOW DID IT GO?
THEY SEEMED TO LIKE MY PORTFOLIO.
AND MY DRAWING TEST WAS DECENT.
BUT SOME OF THOSE KIDS ARE AMAZING!
IT WAS SCARY.
BUT YOU'RE AMAZING, TOO, JORDAN!
AND I'M NOT JUST SAYING THAT 'CAUSE YOU'RE MY BEST FRIEND.
THANKS, DREW.
YOU THINK YOU MIGHT REALLY GO THERE NEXT YEAR?
YOU KNOW, I DON'T KNOW.
MY MOM DEFINITELY WANTS ME TO STAY HERE AT RAD.

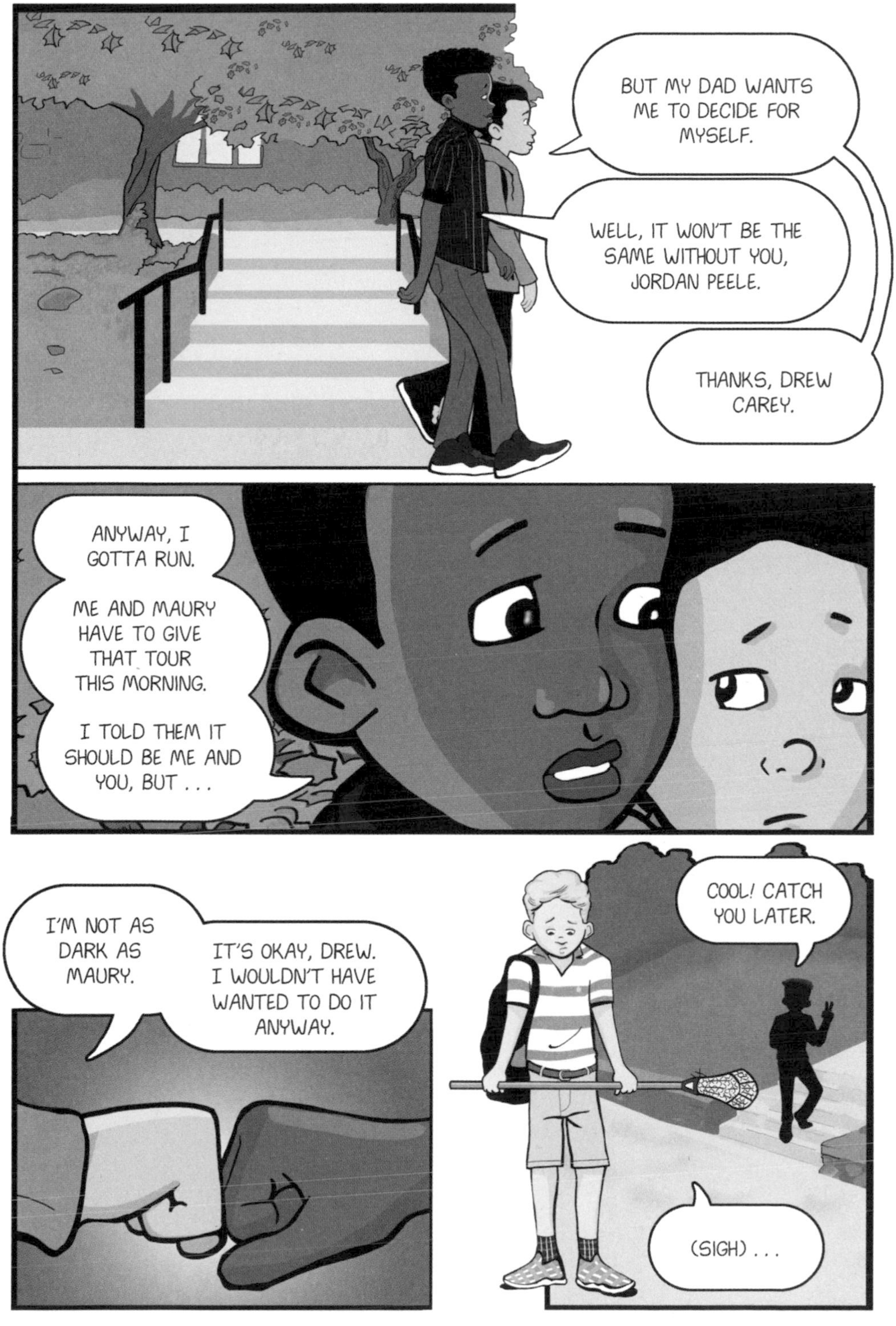
BUT MY DAD WANTS ME TO DECIDE FOR MYSELF.
WELL, IT WON'T BE THE SAME WITHOUT YOU, JORDAN PEELE.
THANKS, DREW CAREY.
ANYWAY, I GOTTA RUN.
ME AND MAURY HAVE TO GIVE THAT TOUR THIS MORNING.
I TOLD THEM IT SHOULD BE ME AND YOU, BUT . . .
I'M NOT AS DARK AS MAURY.
IT'S OKAY, DREW. I WOULDN'T HAVE WANTED TO DO IT ANYWAY.
COOL! CATCH YOU LATER.
(SIGH) . . .

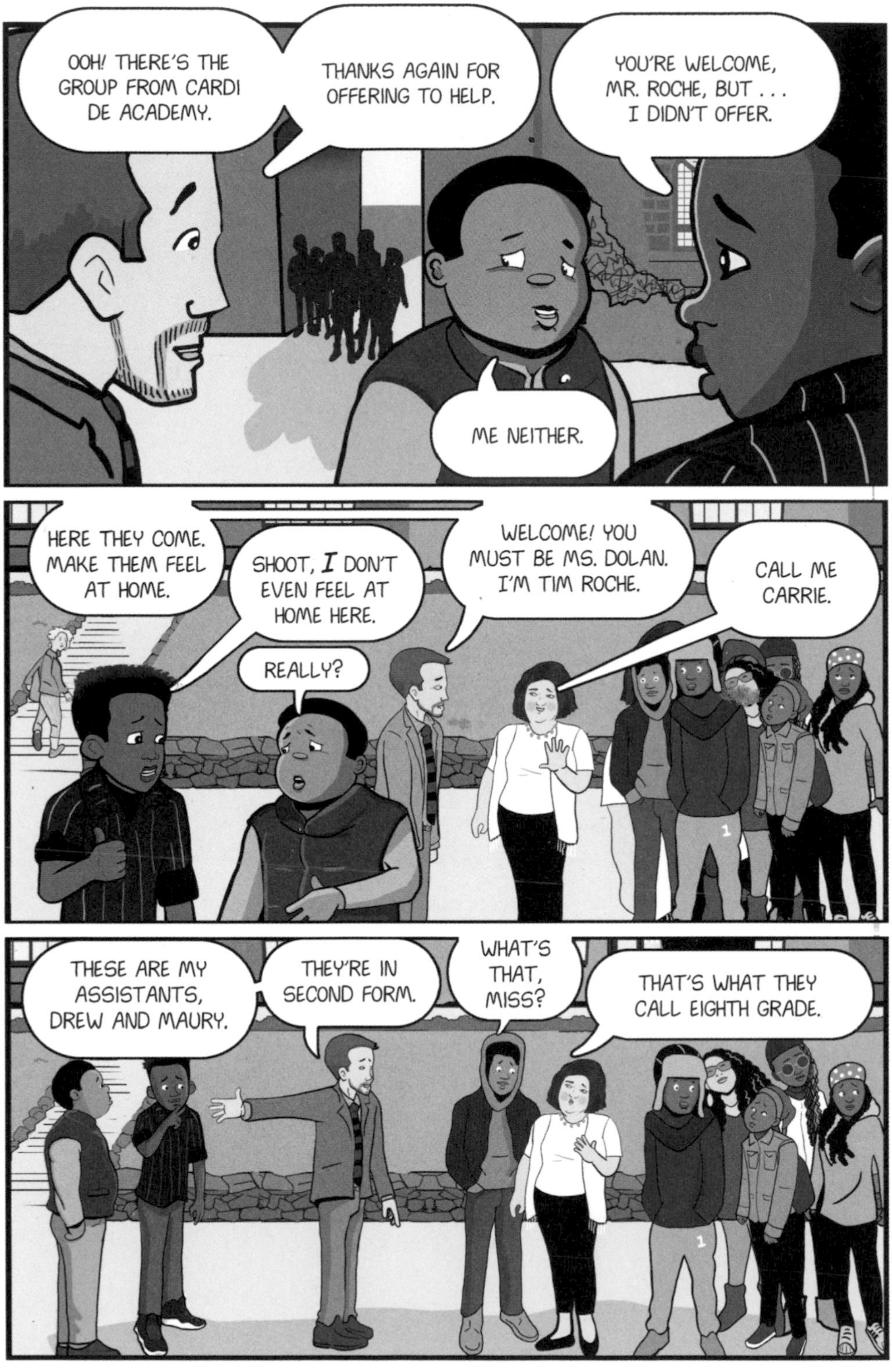
OOH! THERE'S THE GROUP FROM CARDI DE ACADEMY.
THANKS AGAIN FOR OFFERING TO HELP.
YOU'RE WELCOME, MR. ROCHE, BUT . . . I DIDN'T OFFER.
ME NEITHER.
HERE THEY COME. MAKE THEM FEEL AT HOME.
SHOOT, *I* DON'T EVEN FEEL AT HOME HERE.
REALLY?
WELCOME! YOU MUST BE MS. DOLAN. I'M TIM ROCHE.
CALL ME CARRIE.
THESE ARE MY ASSISTANTS, DREW AND MAURY.
THEY'RE IN SECOND FORM.
WHAT'S THAT, MISS?
THAT'S WHAT THEY CALL EIGHTH GRADE.

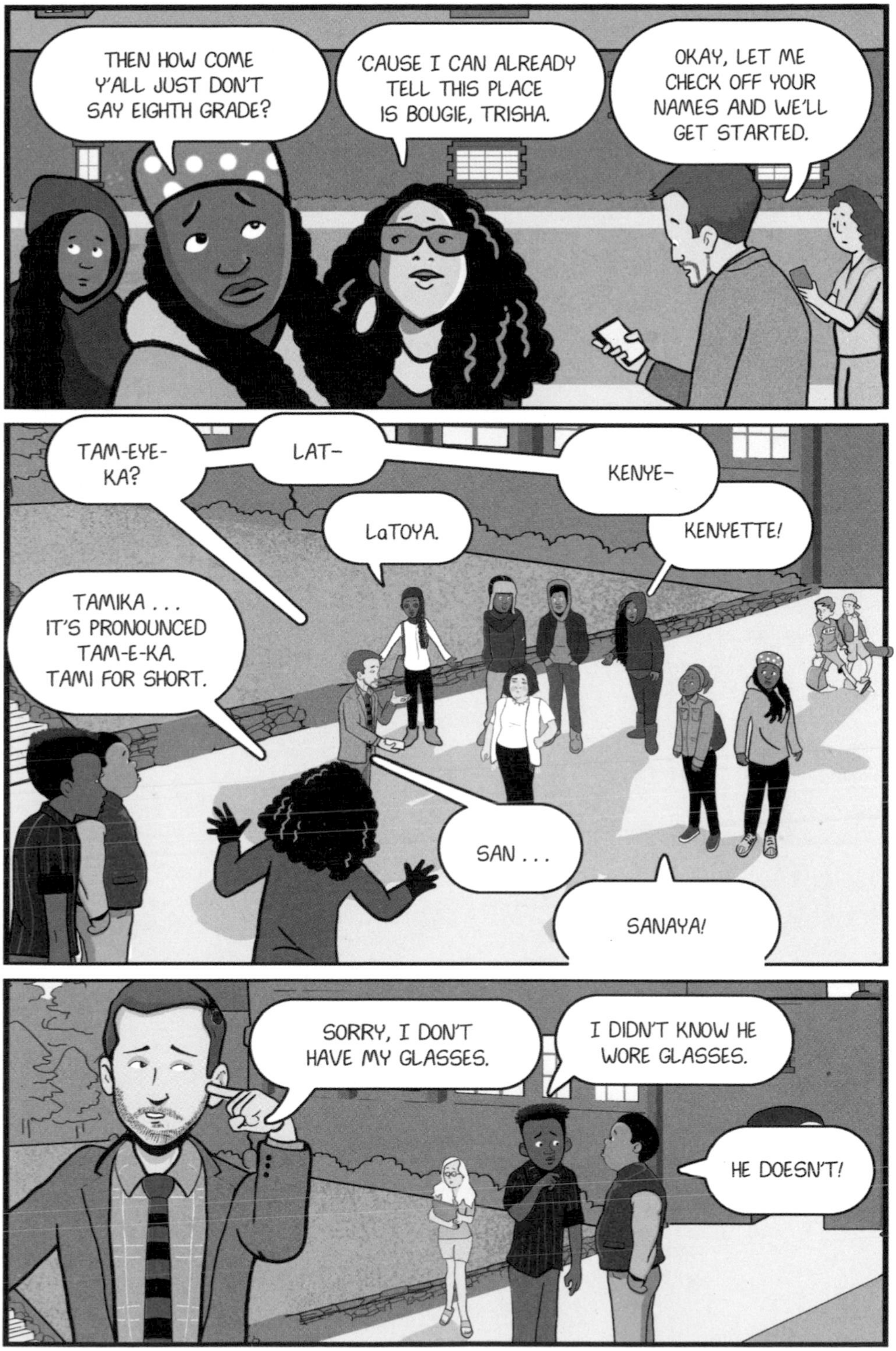
THEN HOW COME Y'ALL JUST DON'T SAY EIGHTH GRADE?
'CAUSE I CAN ALREADY TELL THIS PLACE IS BOUGIE, TRISHA.
OKAY, LET ME CHECK OFF YOUR NAMES AND WE'LL GET STARTED.
TAM-EYE-KA?
LAT-
KENYE-
LaTOYA.
KENYETTE!
TAMIKA . . . IT'S PRONOUNCED TAM-E-KA. TAMI FOR SHORT.
SAN . . .
SANAYA!
SORRY, I DON'T HAVE MY GLASSES.
I DIDN'T KNOW HE WORE GLASSES.
HE DOESN'T!

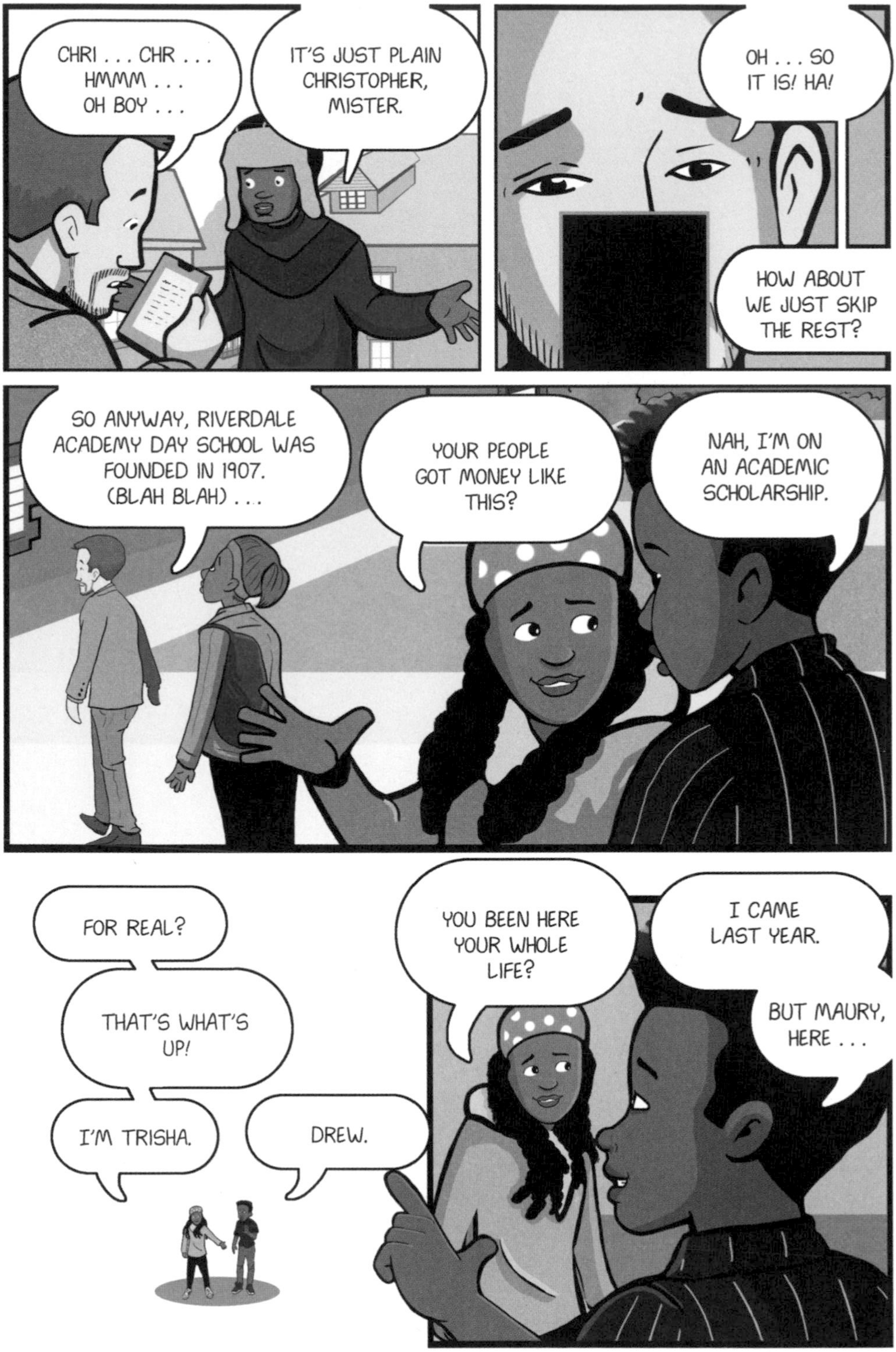
CHRI . . . CHR . . . HMMM . . . OH BOY . . .
IT'S JUST PLAIN CHRISTOPHER, MISTER.
OH . . . SO IT IS! HA!
HOW ABOUT WE JUST SKIP THE REST?
SO ANYWAY, RIVERDALE ACADEMY DAY SCHOOL WAS FOUNDED IN 1907. (BLAH BLAH) . . .
YOUR PEOPLE GOT MONEY LIKE THIS?
NAH, I'M ON AN ACADEMIC SCHOLARSHIP.
FOR REAL?
THAT'S WHAT'S UP!
I'M TRISHA.
DREW.
YOU BEEN HERE YOUR WHOLE LIFE?
I CAME LAST YEAR.
BUT MAURY, HERE . . .

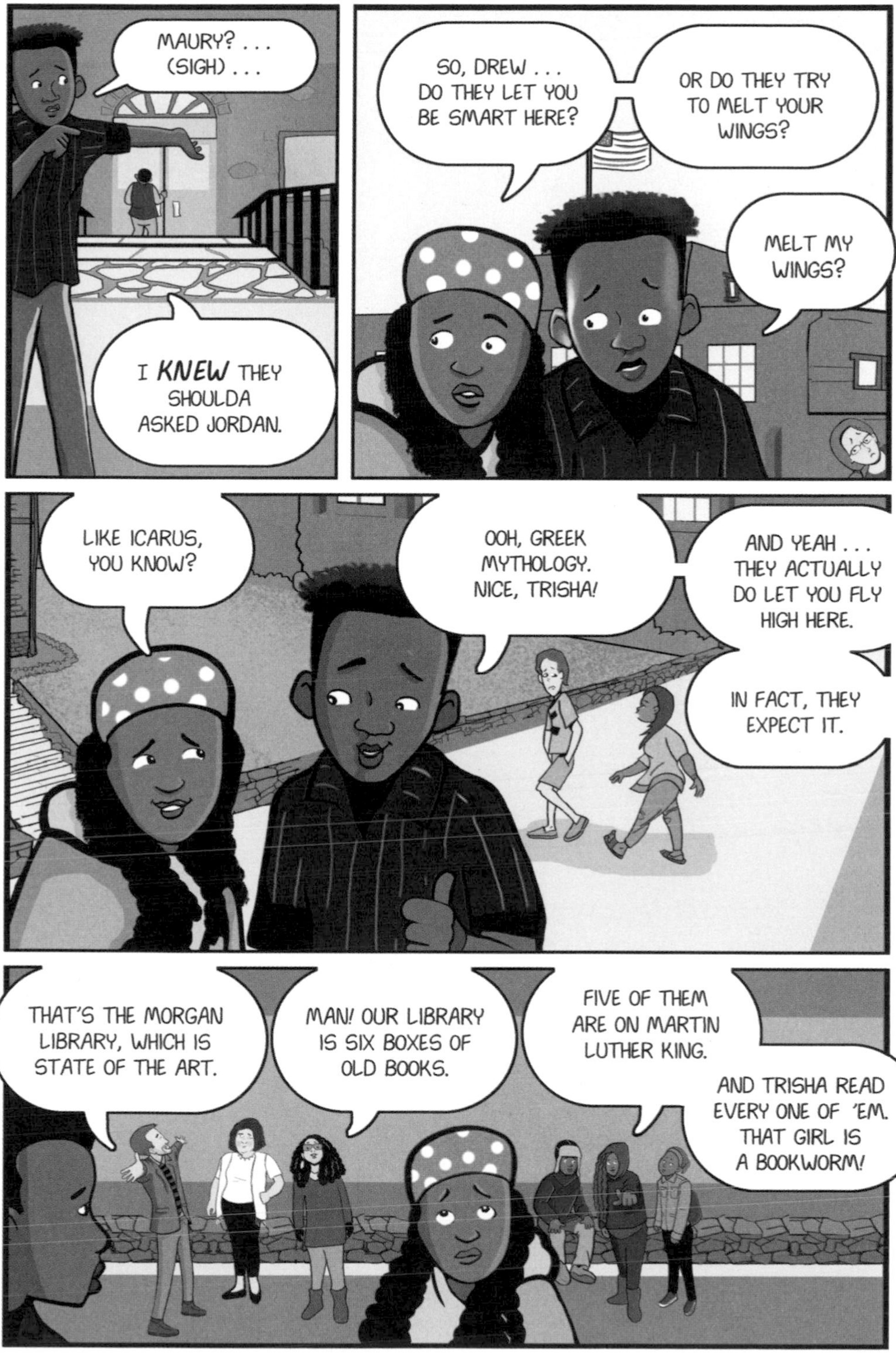
MAURY? . . . (SIGH) . . .
I KNEW THEY SHOULDA ASKED JORDAN.
SO, DREW . . . DO THEY LET YOU BE SMART HERE?
OR DO THEY TRY TO MELT YOUR WINGS?
MELT MY WINGS?
LIKE ICARUS, YOU KNOW?
OOH, GREEK MYTHOLOGY. NICE, TRISHA!
AND YEAH . . . THEY ACTUALLY DO LET YOU FLY HIGH HERE.
IN FACT, THEY EXPECT IT.
THAT'S THE MORGAN LIBRARY, WHICH IS STATE OF THE ART.
MAN! OUR LIBRARY IS SIX BOXES OF OLD BOOKS.
FIVE OF THEM ARE ON MARTIN LUTHER KING.
AND TRISHA READ EVERY ONE OF 'EM. THAT GIRL IS A BOOKWORM!

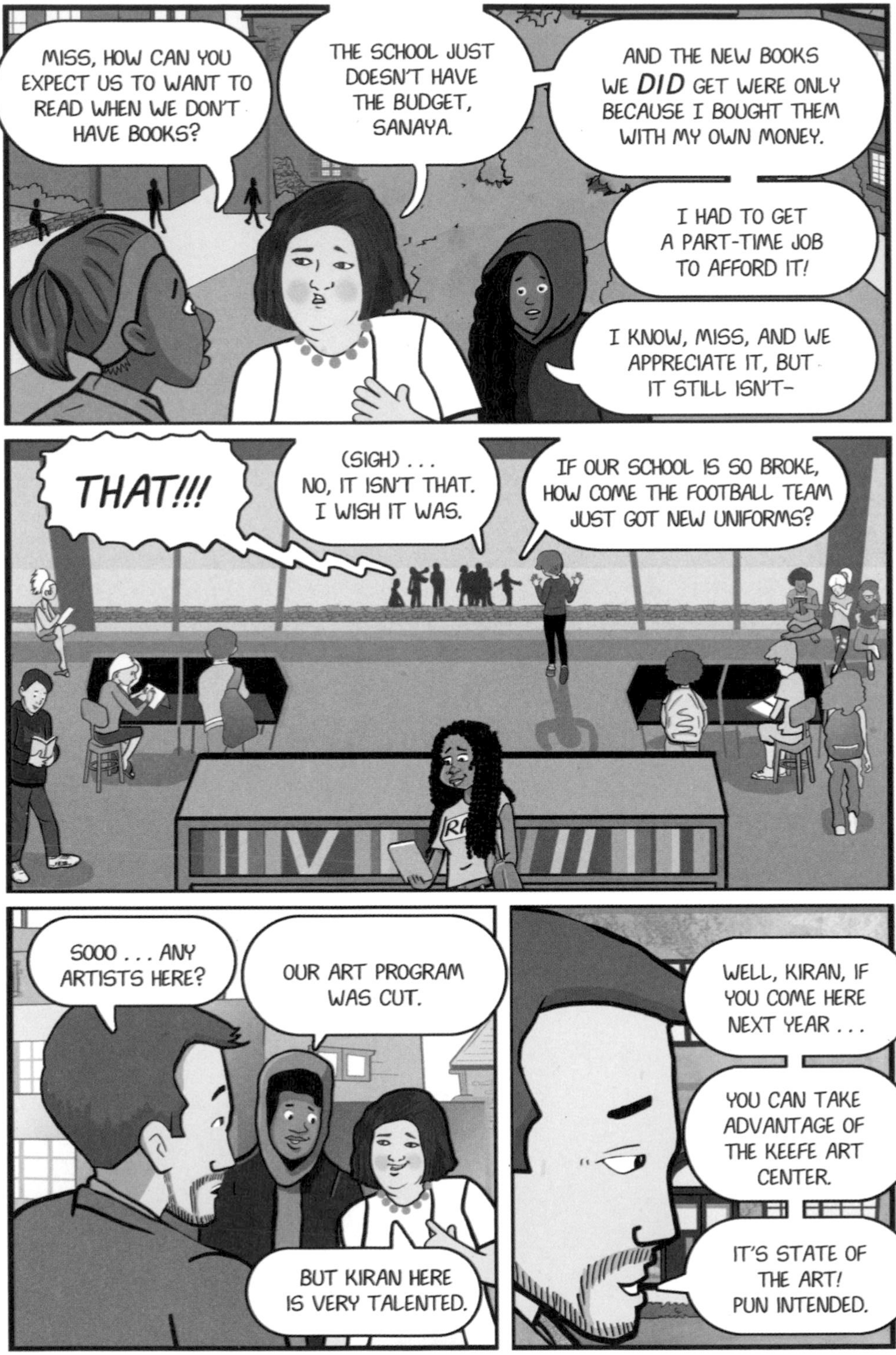
MISS, HOW CAN YOU EXPECT US TO WANT TO READ WHEN WE DON'T HAVE BOOKS?
THE SCHOOL JUST DOESN'T HAVE THE BUDGET, SANAYA.
AND THE NEW BOOKS WE *DID* GET WERE ONLY BECAUSE I BOUGHT THEM WITH MY OWN MONEY.
I HAD TO GET A PART-TIME JOB TO AFFORD IT!
I KNOW, MISS, AND WE APPRECIATE IT, BUT IT STILL ISN'T-
THAT!!!
(SIGH) . . . NO, IT ISN'T THAT. I WISH IT WAS.
IF OUR SCHOOL IS SO BROKE, HOW COME THE FOOTBALL TEAM JUST GOT NEW UNIFORMS?
SOOO . . . ANY ARTISTS HERE?
OUR ART PROGRAM WAS CUT.
BUT KIRAN HERE IS VERY TALENTED.
WELL, KIRAN, IF YOU COME HERE NEXT YEAR . . .
YOU CAN TAKE ADVANTAGE OF THE KEEFE ART CENTER.
IT'S STATE OF THE ART! PUN INTENDED.

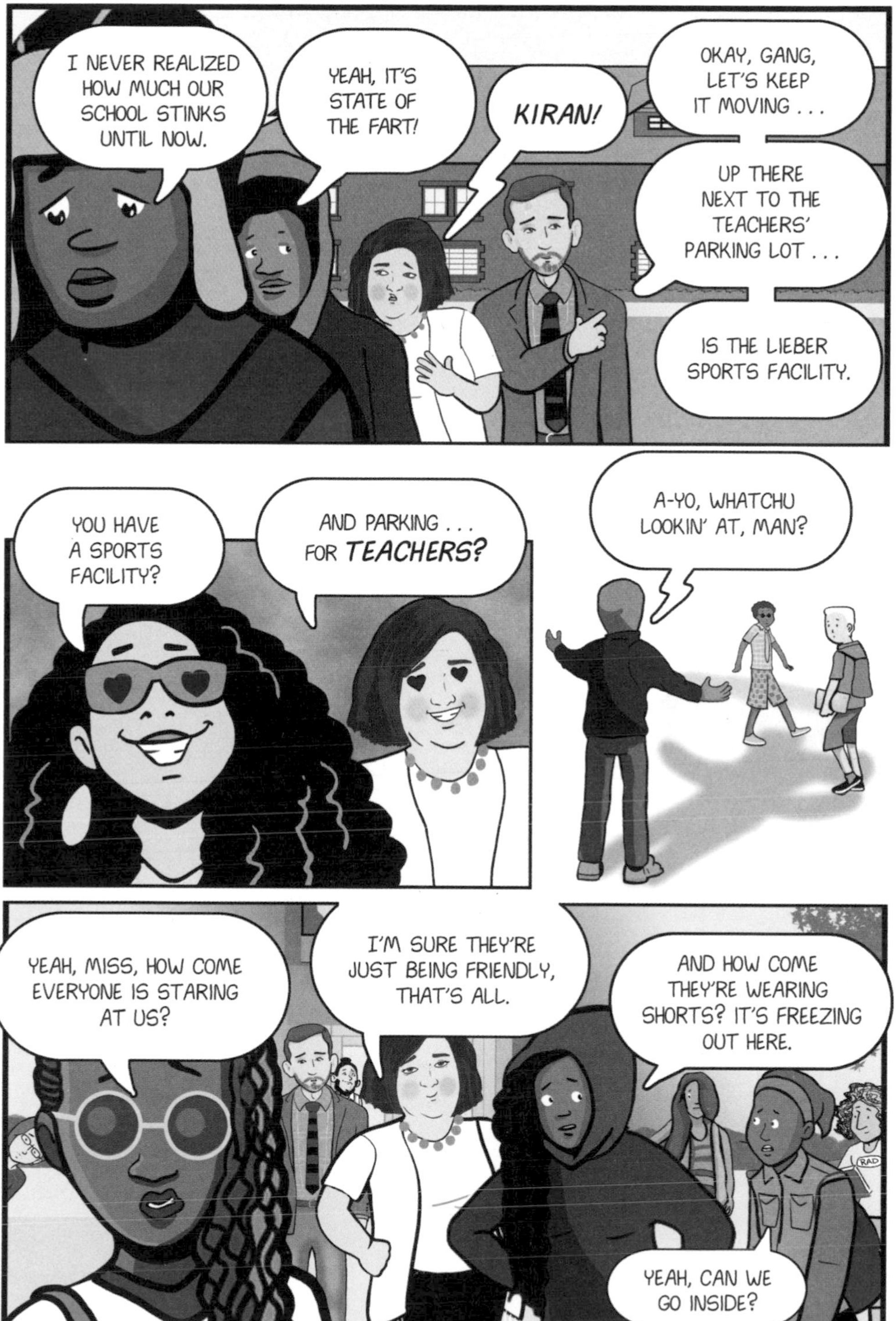
I NEVER REALIZED HOW MUCH OUR SCHOOL STINKS UNTIL NOW.
YEAH, IT'S STATE OF THE FART!
KIRAN!
OKAY, GANG, LET'S KEEP IT MOVING . . .
UP THERE NEXT TO THE TEACHERS' PARKING LOT . . .
IS THE LIEBER SPORTS FACILITY.
YOU HAVE A SPORTS FACILITY?
AND PARKING . . . FOR TEACHERS?
A-YO, WHATCHU LOOKIN' AT, MAN?
YEAH, MISS, HOW COME EVERYONE IS STARING AT US?
I'M SURE THEY'RE JUST BEING FRIENDLY, THAT'S ALL.
AND HOW COME THEY'RE WEARING SHORTS? IT'S FREEZING OUT HERE.
YEAH, CAN WE GO INSIDE?
RAD

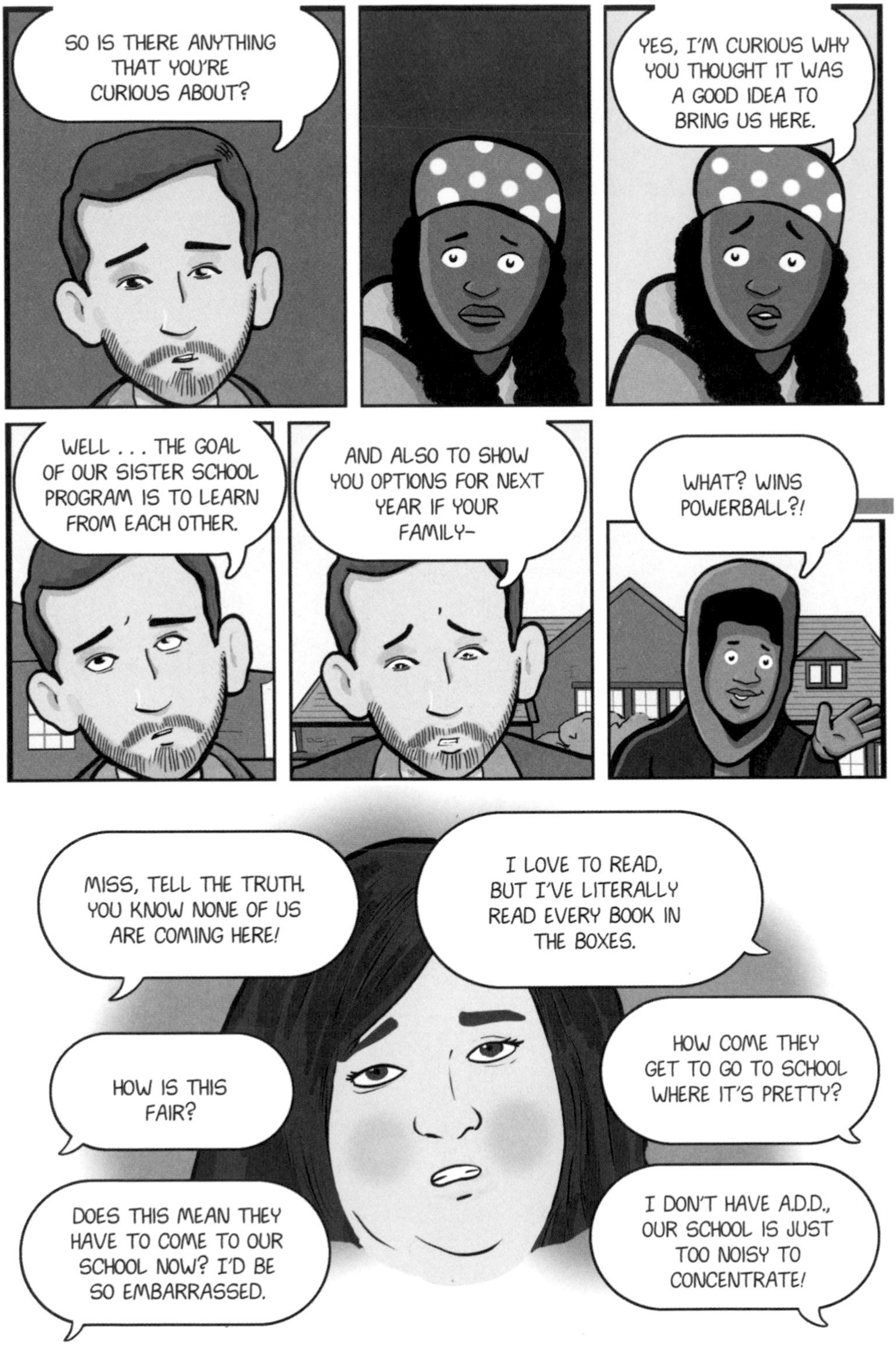
SO IS THERE ANYTHING THAT YOU'RE CURIOUS ABOUT?
YES, I'M CURIOUS WHY YOU THOUGHT IT WAS A GOOD IDEA TO BRING US HERE.
WELL . . . THE GOAL OF OUR SISTER SCHOOL PROGRAM IS TO LEARN FROM EACH OTHER.
AND ALSO TO SHOW YOU OPTIONS FOR NEXT YEAR IF YOUR FAMILY–
WHAT? WINS POWERBALL?!
MISS, TELL THE TRUTH. YOU KNOW NONE OF US ARE COMING HERE!
I LOVE TO READ, BUT I'VE LITERALLY READ EVERY BOOK IN THE BOXES.
HOW IS THIS FAIR?
HOW COME THEY GET TO GO TO SCHOOL WHERE IT'S PRETTY?
DOES THIS MEAN THEY HAVE TO COME TO OUR SCHOOL NOW? I'D BE SO EMBARRASSED.
I DON'T HAVE A.D.D., OUR SCHOOL IS JUST TOO NOISY TO CONCENTRATE!

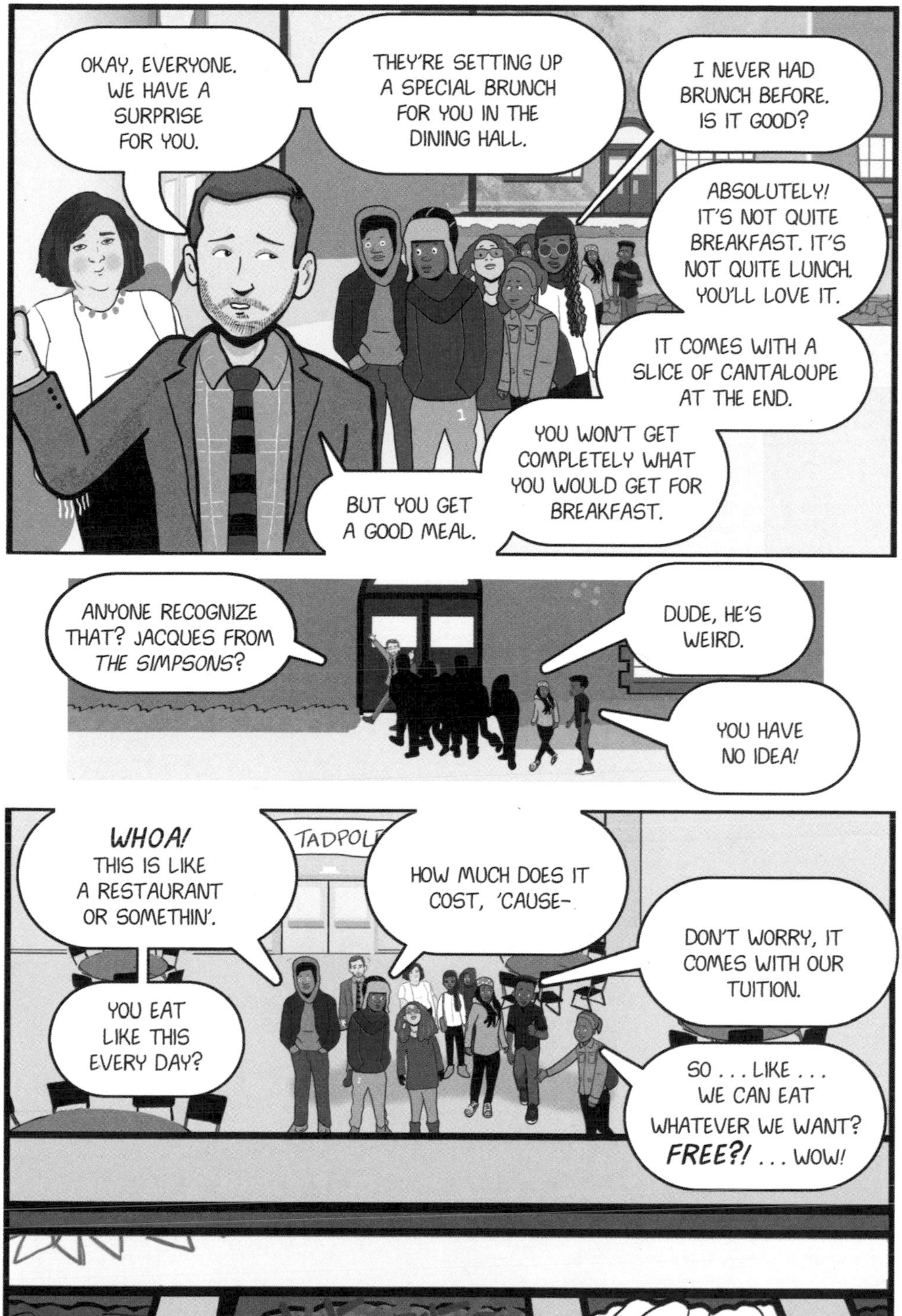
OKAY, EVERYONE. WE HAVE A SURPRISE FOR YOU.
THEY'RE SETTING UP A SPECIAL BRUNCH FOR YOU IN THE DINING HALL.
I NEVER HAD BRUNCH BEFORE. IS IT GOOD?
ABSOLUTELY! IT'S NOT QUITE BREAKFAST. IT'S NOT QUITE LUNCH. YOU'LL LOVE IT.
IT COMES WITH A SLICE OF CANTALOUPE AT THE END.
YOU WON'T GET COMPLETELY WHAT YOU WOULD GET FOR BREAKFAST.
BUT YOU GET A GOOD MEAL.
ANYONE RECOGNIZE THAT? JACQUES FROM *THE SIMPSONS*?
DUDE, HE'S WEIRD.
YOU HAVE NO IDEA!
WHOA! THIS IS LIKE A RESTAURANT OR SOMETHIN'.
HOW MUCH DOES IT COST, 'CAUSE–
TADPOL
YOU EAT LIKE THIS EVERY DAY?
DON'T WORRY, IT COMES WITH OUR TUITION.
SO . . . LIKE . . . WE CAN EAT WHATEVER WE WANT? **FREE?!** . . . WOW!

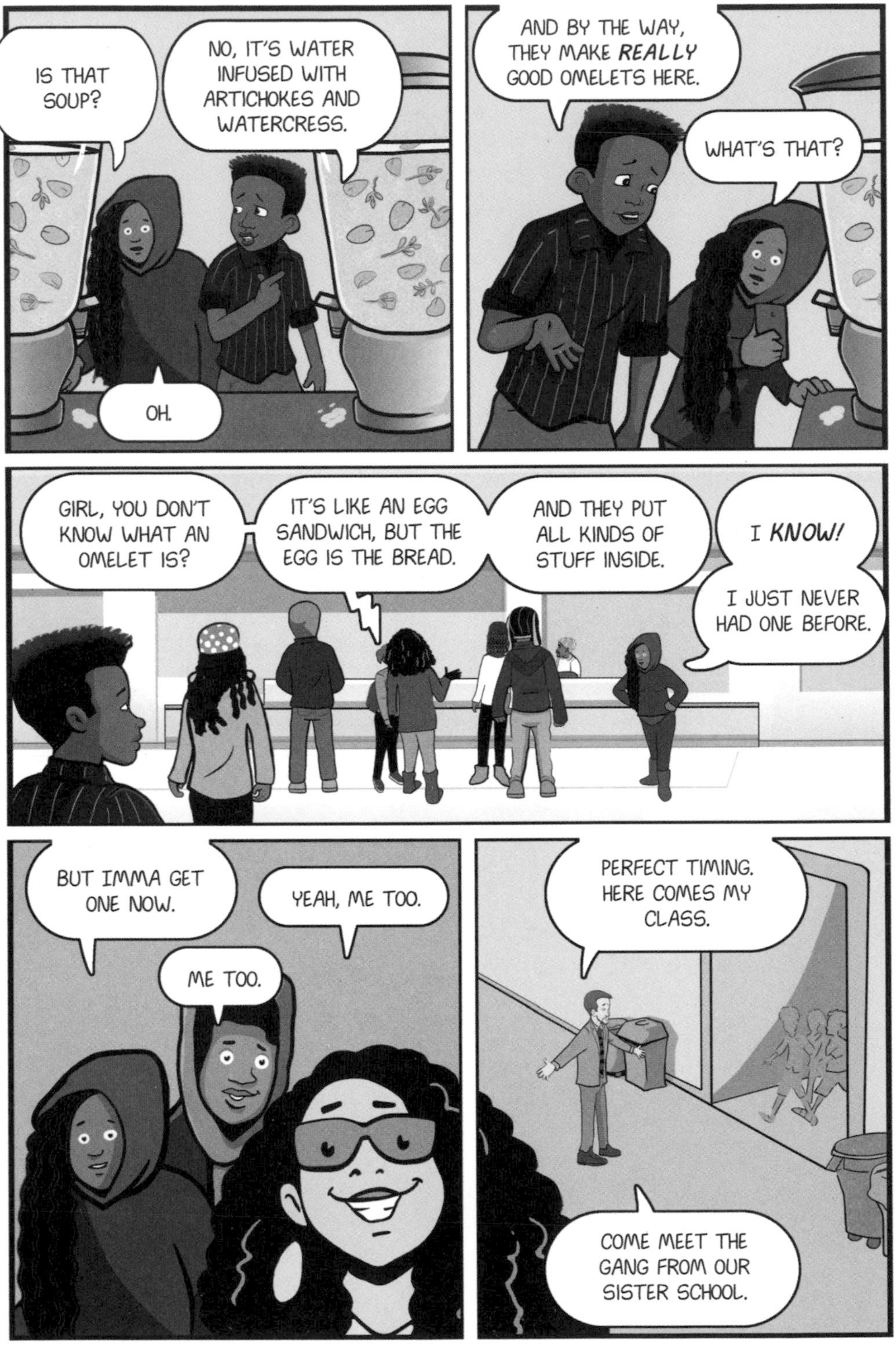

IS THAT SOUP?
NO, IT'S WATER INFUSED WITH ARTICHOKES AND WATERCRESS.
OH.
AND BY THE WAY, THEY MAKE **REALLY** GOOD OMELETS HERE.
WHAT'S THAT?
GIRL, YOU DON'T KNOW WHAT AN OMELET IS?
IT'S LIKE AN EGG SANDWICH, BUT THE EGG IS THE BREAD.
AND THEY PUT ALL KINDS OF STUFF INSIDE.
I ***KNOW!***
I JUST NEVER HAD ONE BEFORE.
BUT IMMA GET ONE NOW.
YEAH, ME TOO.
ME TOO.
PERFECT TIMING. HERE COMES MY CLASS.
COME MEET THE GANG FROM OUR SISTER SCHOOL.

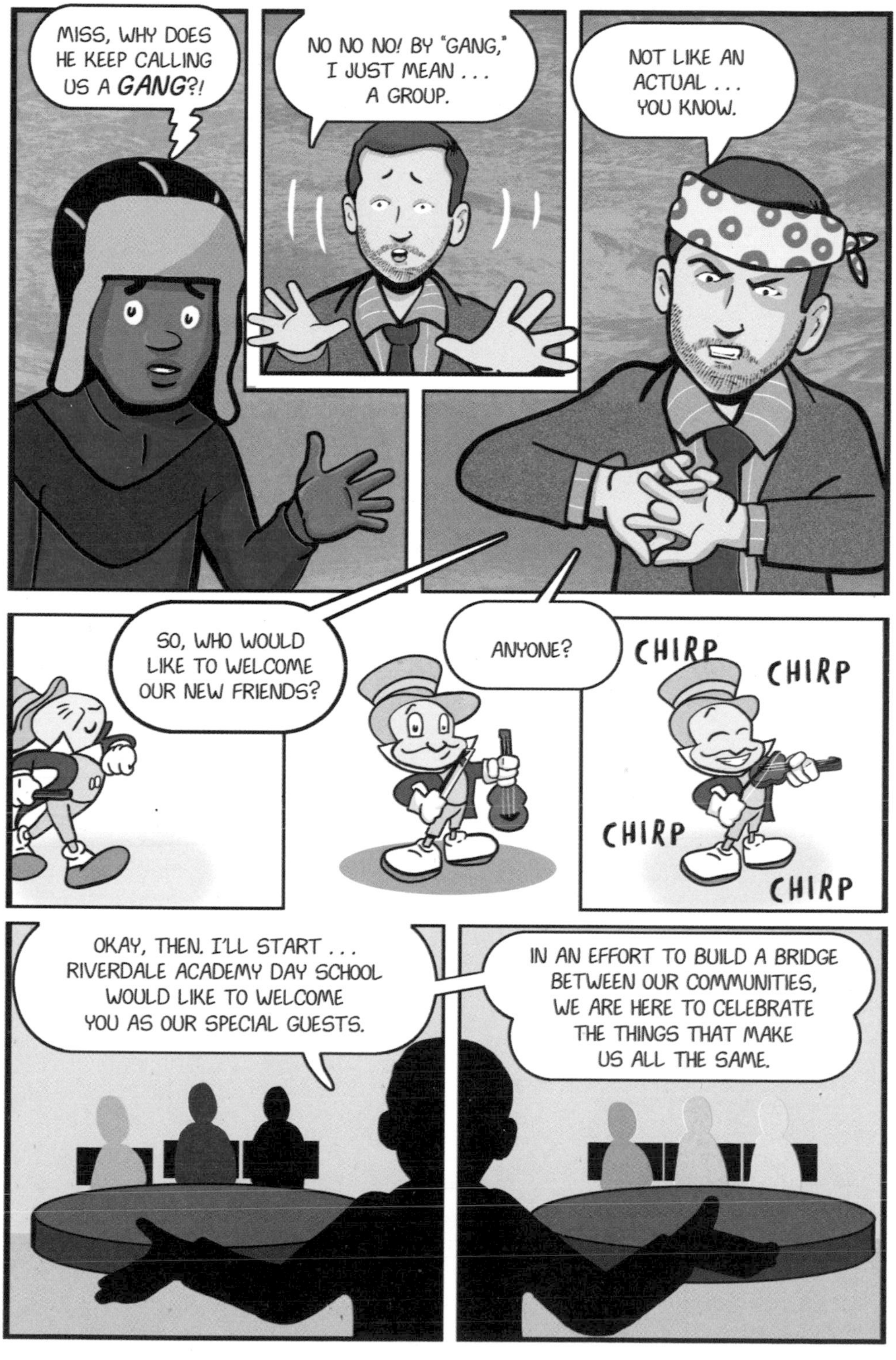
MISS, WHY DOES HE KEEP CALLING US A GANG?!
NO NO NO! BY "GANG," I JUST MEAN . . . A GROUP.
NOT LIKE AN ACTUAL . . . YOU KNOW.
SO, WHO WOULD LIKE TO WELCOME OUR NEW FRIENDS?
ANYONE?
CHIRP
CHIRP
CHIRP
CHIRP
OKAY, THEN. I'LL START . . . RIVERDALE ACADEMY DAY SCHOOL WOULD LIKE TO WELCOME YOU AS OUR SPECIAL GUESTS.
IN AN EFFORT TO BUILD A BRIDGE BETWEEN OUR COMMUNITIES, WE ARE HERE TO CELEBRATE THE THINGS THAT MAKE US ALL THE SAME.

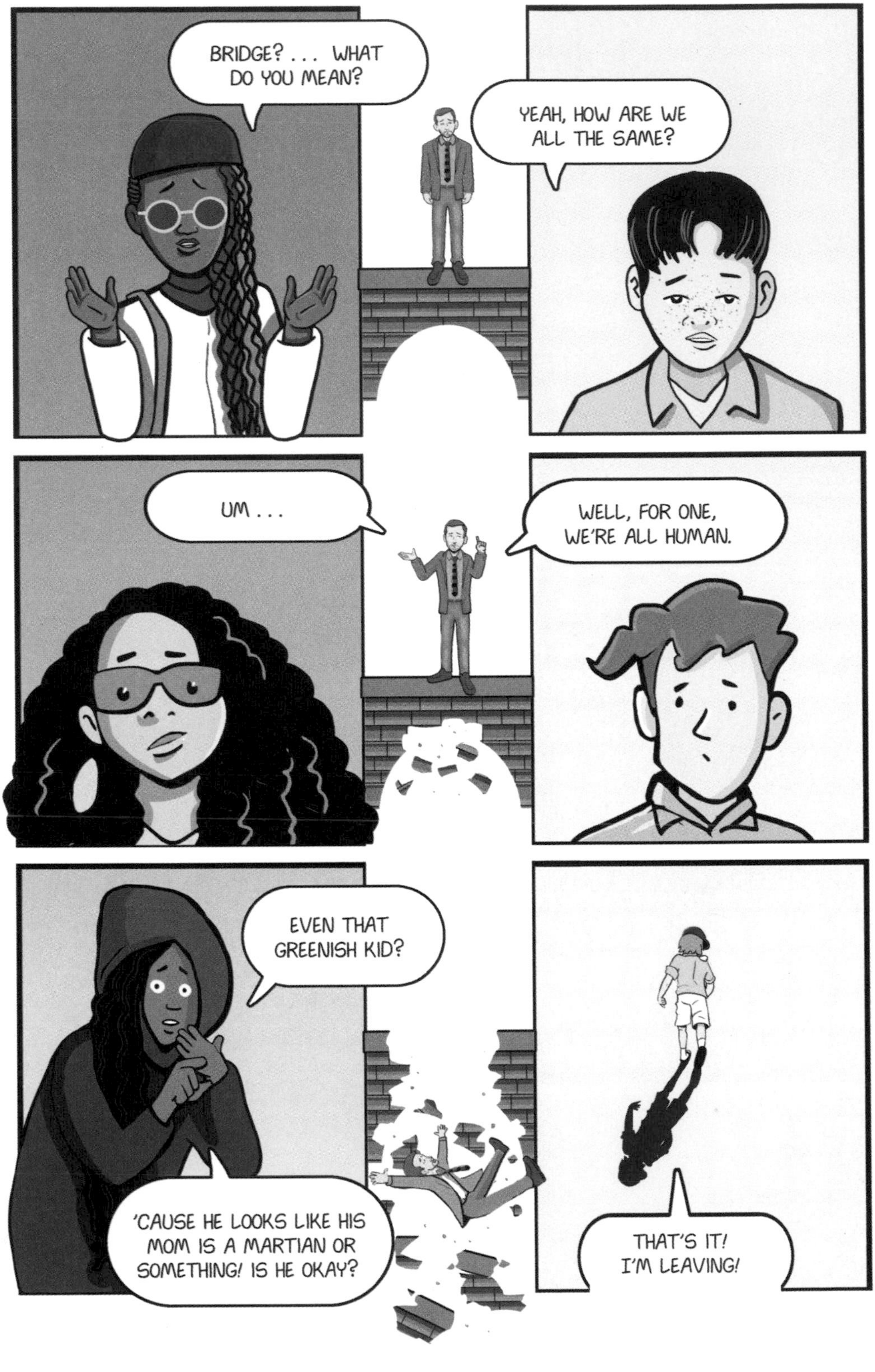
BRIDGE? . . . WHAT DO YOU MEAN?
YEAH, HOW ARE WE ALL THE SAME?
UM . . .
WELL, FOR ONE, WE'RE ALL HUMAN.
EVEN THAT GREENISH KID?
'CAUSE HE LOOKS LIKE HIS MOM IS A MARTIAN OR SOMETHING! IS HE OKAY?
THAT'S IT! I'M LEAVING!

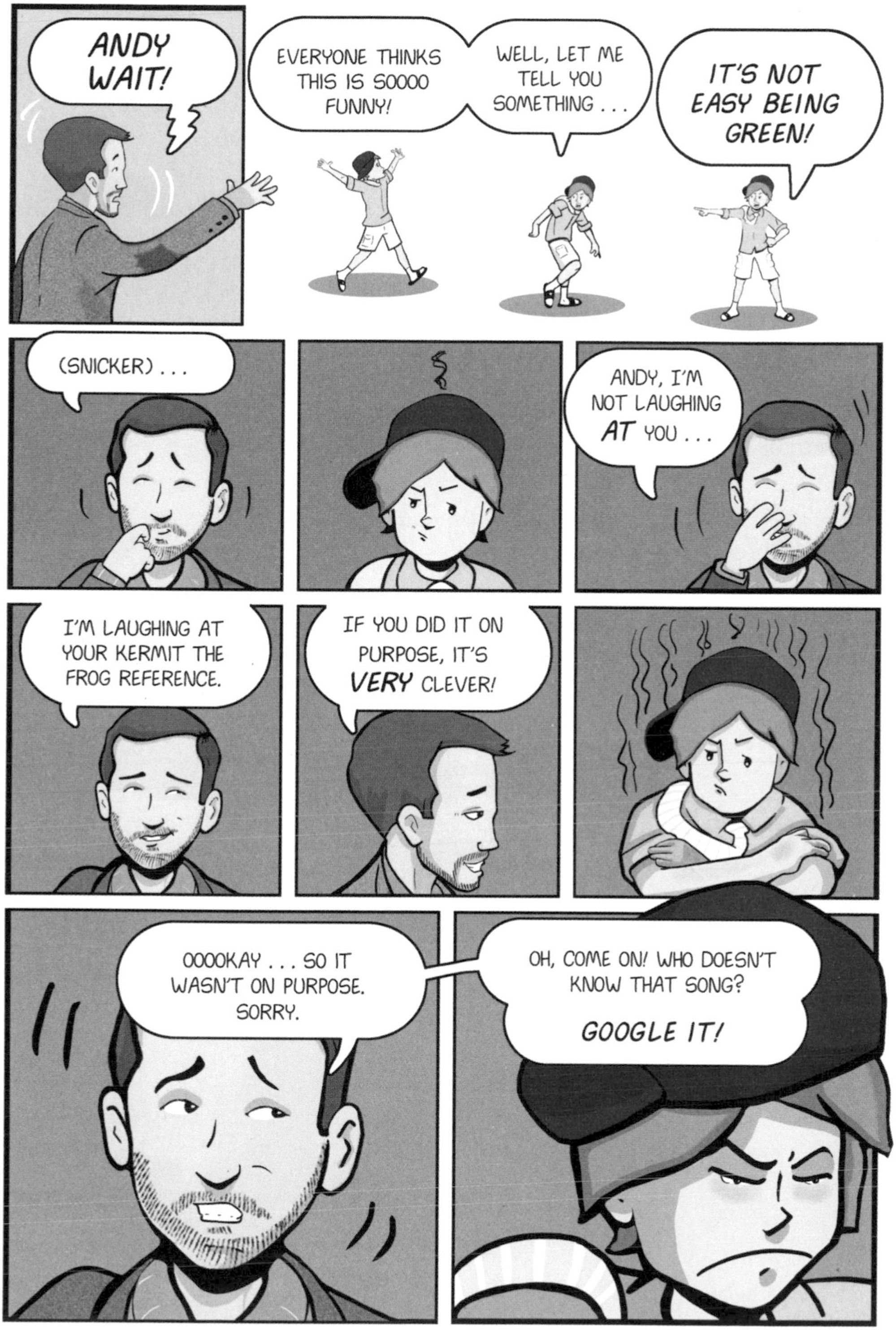
ANDY WAIT!
EVERYONE THINKS THIS IS SOOOO FUNNY!
WELL, LET ME TELL YOU SOMETHING . . .
IT'S NOT EASY BEING GREEN!
(SNICKER) . . .
ANDY, I'M NOT LAUGHING AT YOU . . .
I'M LAUGHING AT YOUR KERMIT THE FROG REFERENCE.
IF YOU DID IT ON PURPOSE, IT'S VERY CLEVER!
OOOOKAY . . . SO IT WASN'T ON PURPOSE. SORRY.
OH, COME ON! WHO DOESN'T KNOW THAT SONG?
GOOGLE IT!

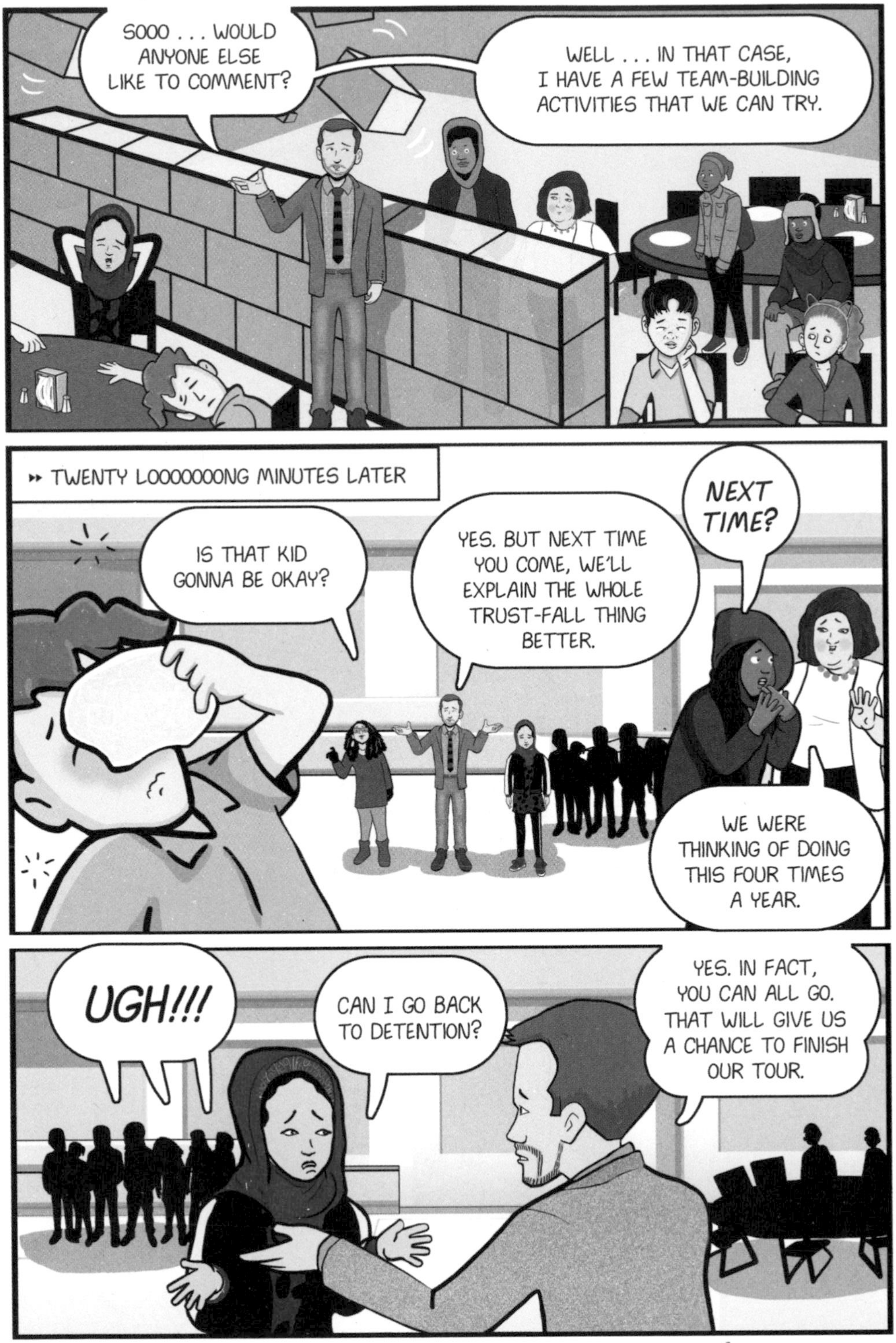
SOOO . . . WOULD ANYONE ELSE LIKE TO COMMENT?
WELL . . . IN THAT CASE, I HAVE A FEW TEAM-BUILDING ACTIVITIES THAT WE CAN TRY.
▸▸ TWENTY LOOOOOOONG MINUTES LATER
IS THAT KID GONNA BE OKAY?
YES. BUT NEXT TIME YOU COME, WE'LL EXPLAIN THE WHOLE TRUST-FALL THING BETTER.
NEXT TIME?
WE WERE THINKING OF DOING THIS FOUR TIMES A YEAR.
UGH!!!
CAN I GO BACK TO DETENTION?
YES. IN FACT, YOU CAN ALL GO. THAT WILL GIVE US A CHANCE TO FINISH OUR TOUR.

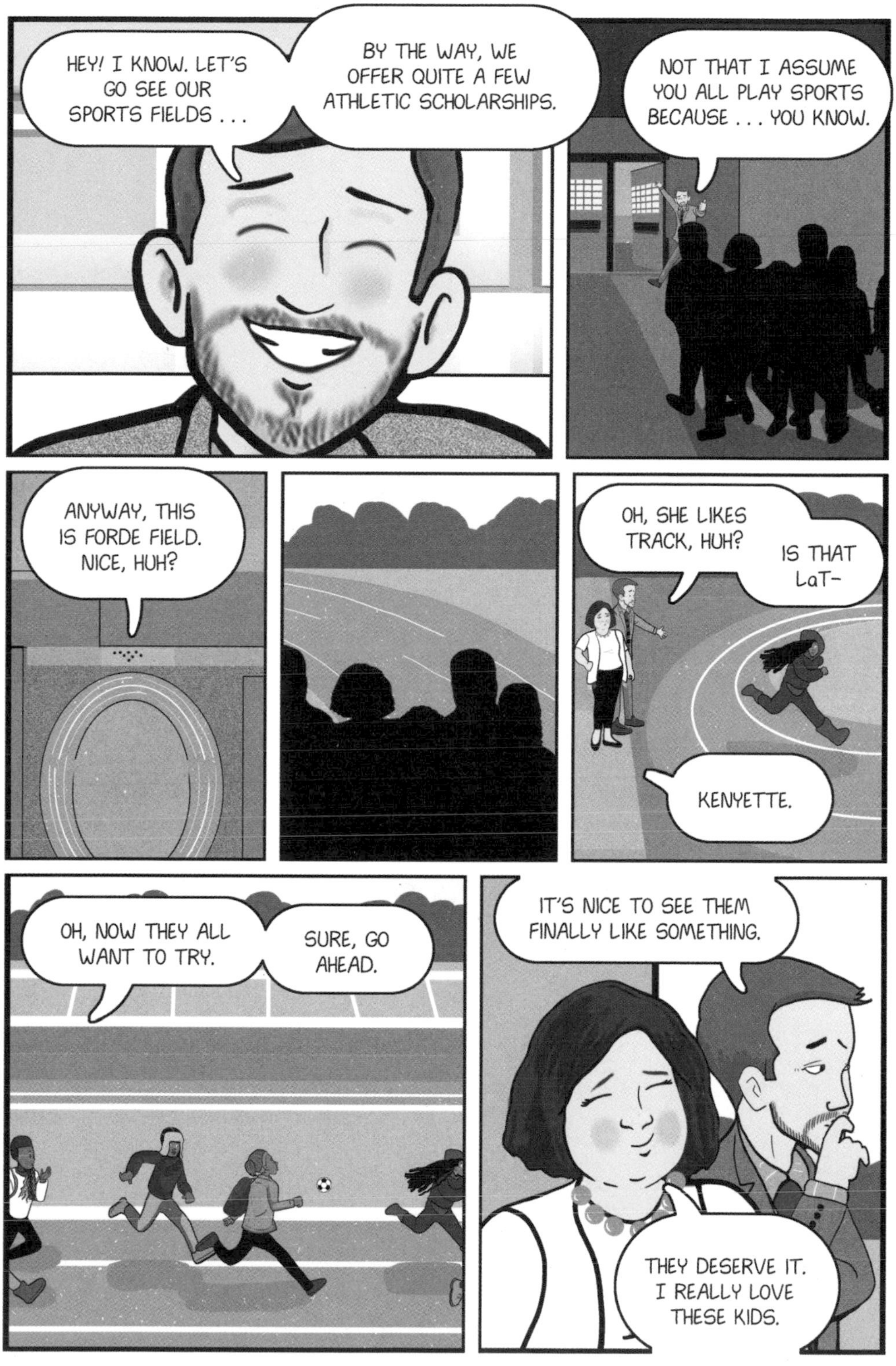
HEY! I KNOW. LET'S GO SEE OUR SPORTS FIELDS . . .
BY THE WAY, WE OFFER QUITE A FEW ATHLETIC SCHOLARSHIPS.
NOT THAT I ASSUME YOU ALL PLAY SPORTS BECAUSE . . . YOU KNOW.
ANYWAY, THIS IS FORDE FIELD. NICE, HUH?
OH, SHE LIKES TRACK, HUH?
IS THAT LaT-
KENYETTE.
OH, NOW THEY ALL WANT TO TRY.
SURE, GO AHEAD.
IT'S NICE TO SEE THEM FINALLY LIKE SOMETHING.
THEY DESERVE IT. I REALLY LOVE THESE KIDS.

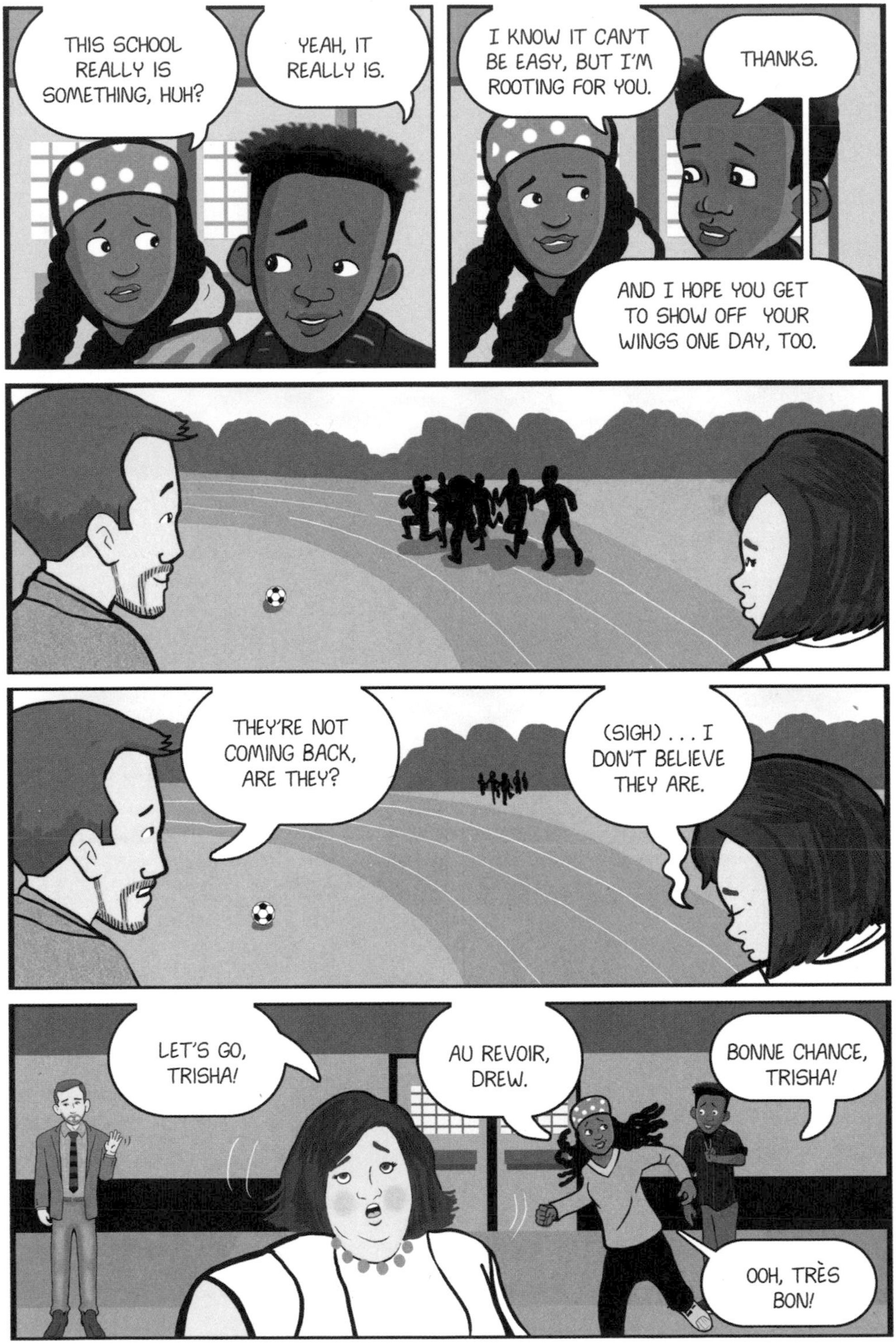
THIS SCHOOL REALLY IS SOMETHING, HUH?
YEAH, IT REALLY IS.
I KNOW IT CAN'T BE EASY, BUT I'M ROOTING FOR YOU.
THANKS.
AND I HOPE YOU GET TO SHOW OFF YOUR WINGS ONE DAY, TOO.
THEY'RE NOT COMING BACK, ARE THEY?
(SIGH) . . . I DON'T BELIEVE THEY ARE.
LET'S GO, TRISHA!
AU REVOIR, DREW.
BONNE CHANCE, TRISHA!
OOH, TRÈS BON!

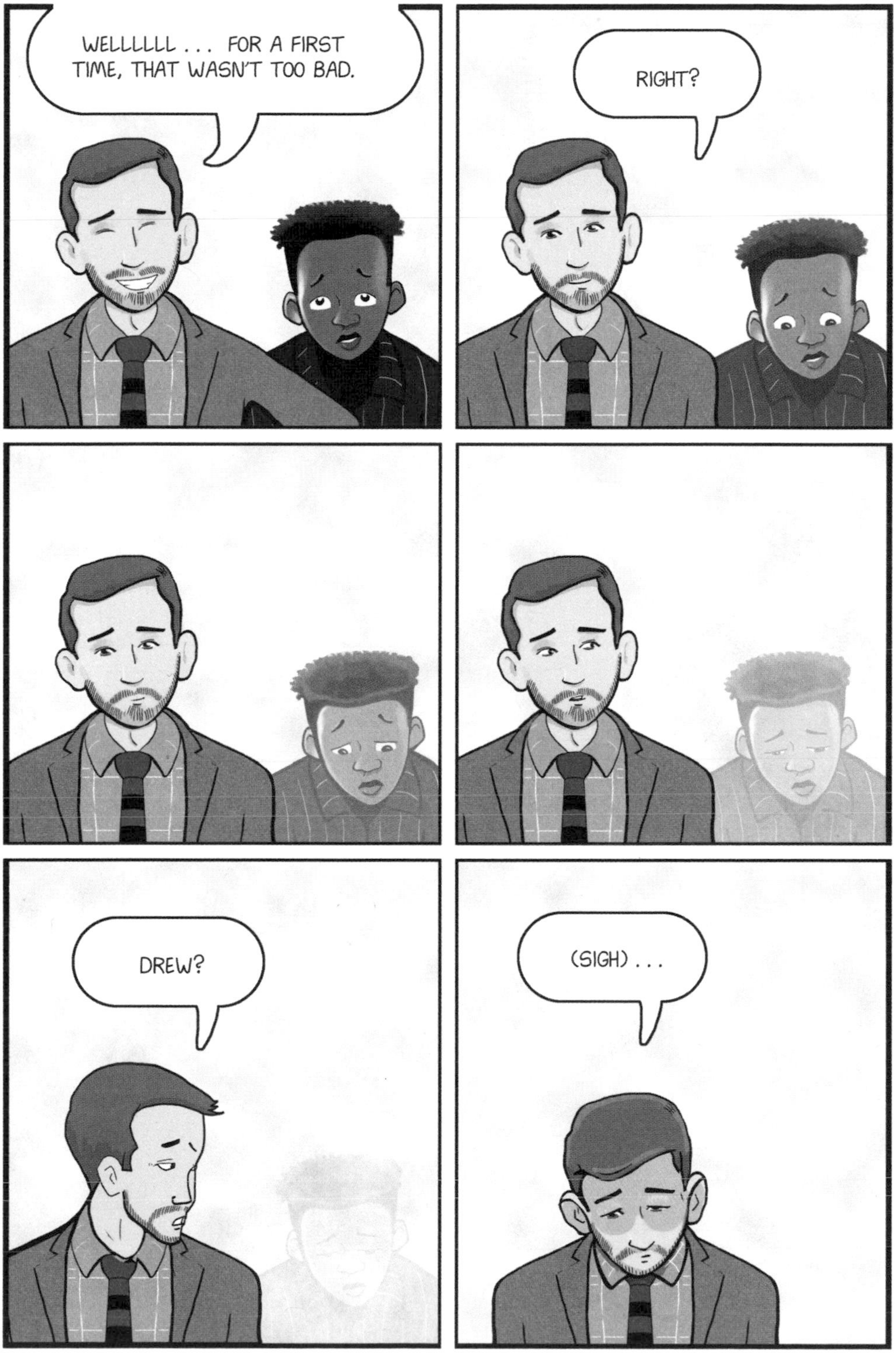
WELLLLLL . . . FOR A FIRST TIME, THAT WASN'T TOO BAD.
RIGHT?
DREW?
(SIGH) . . .

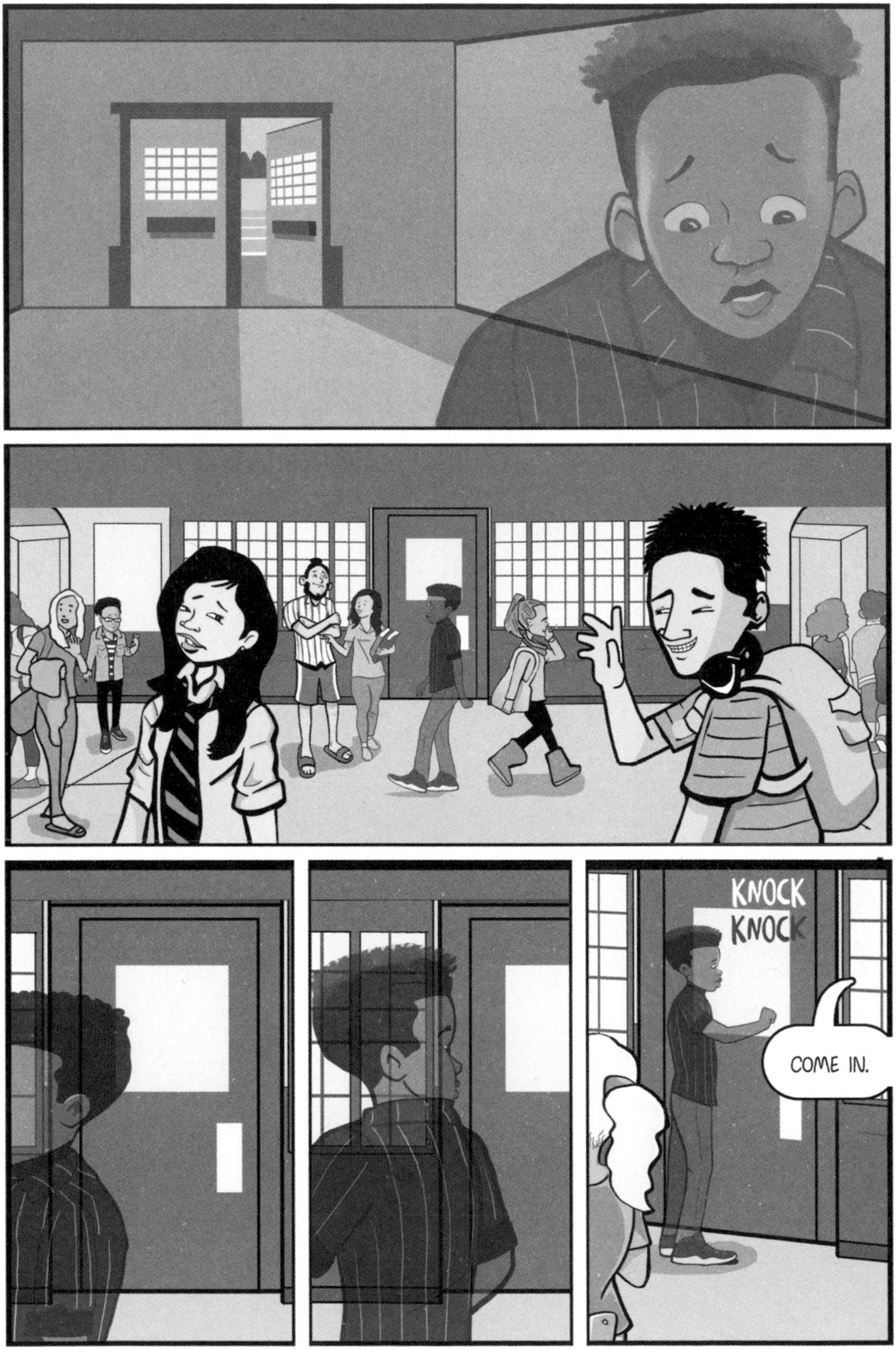
KNOCK
KNOCK
COME IN.

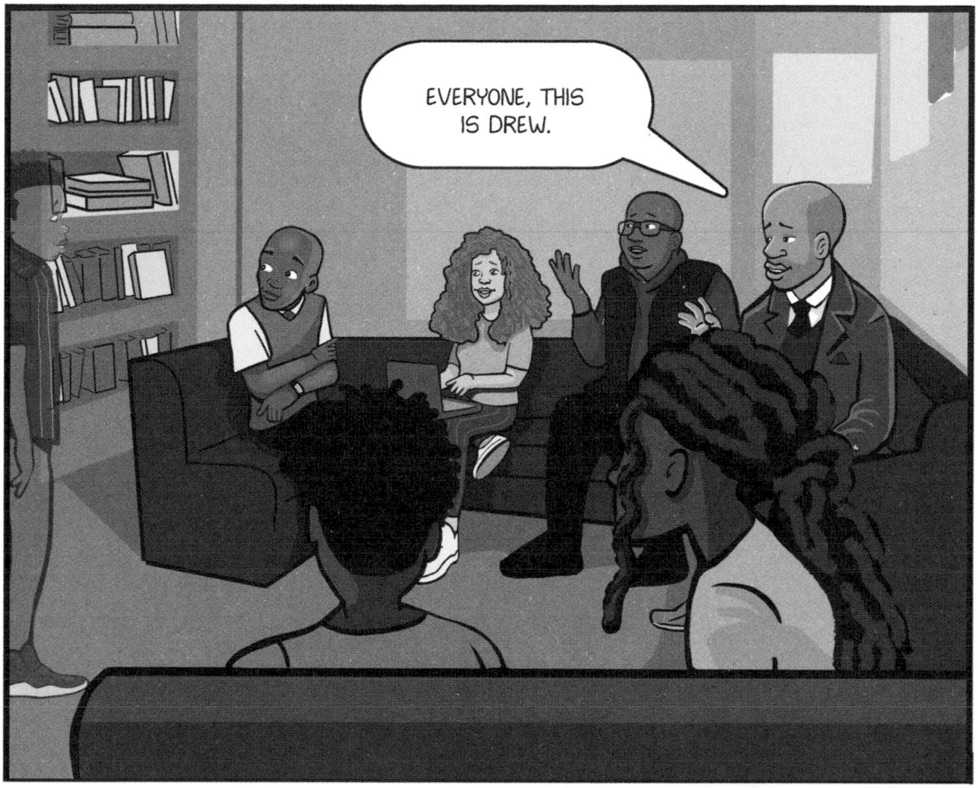
EVERYONE, THIS
IS DREW.

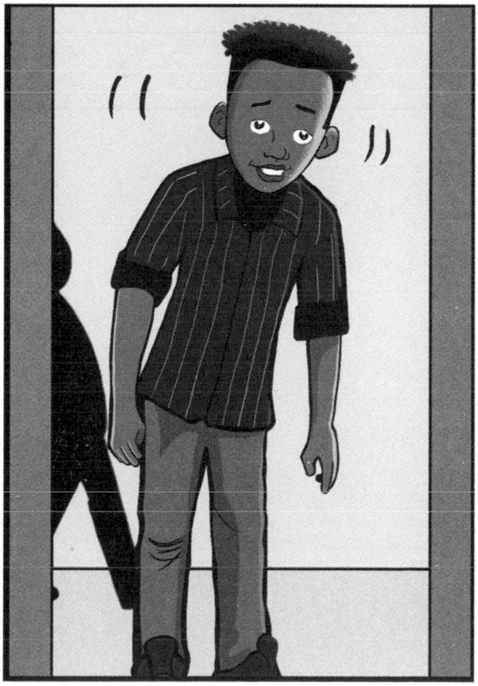

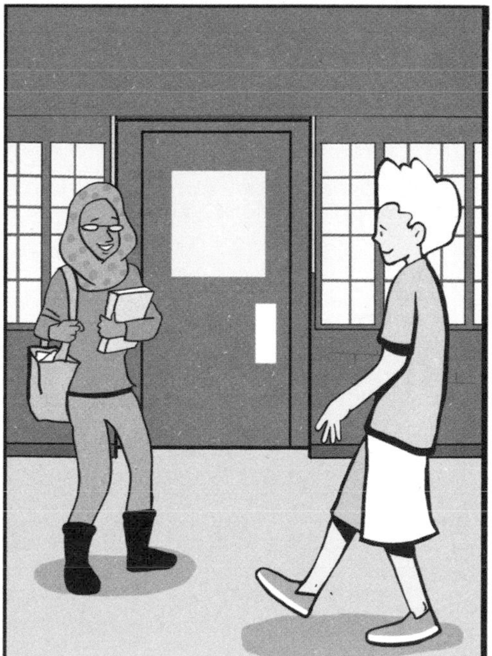

INVISIBLE
m.e.

CHAPTER
6

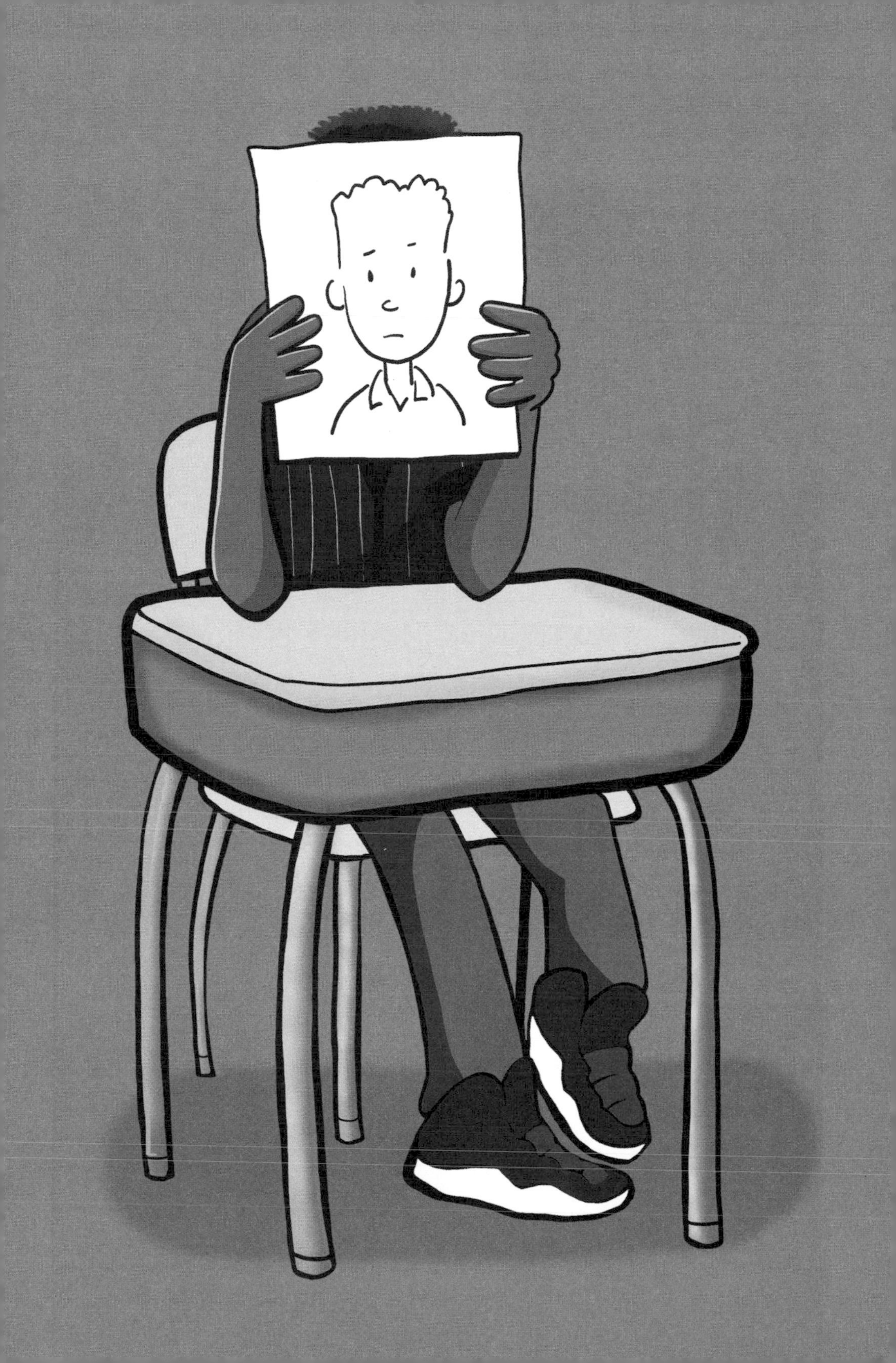

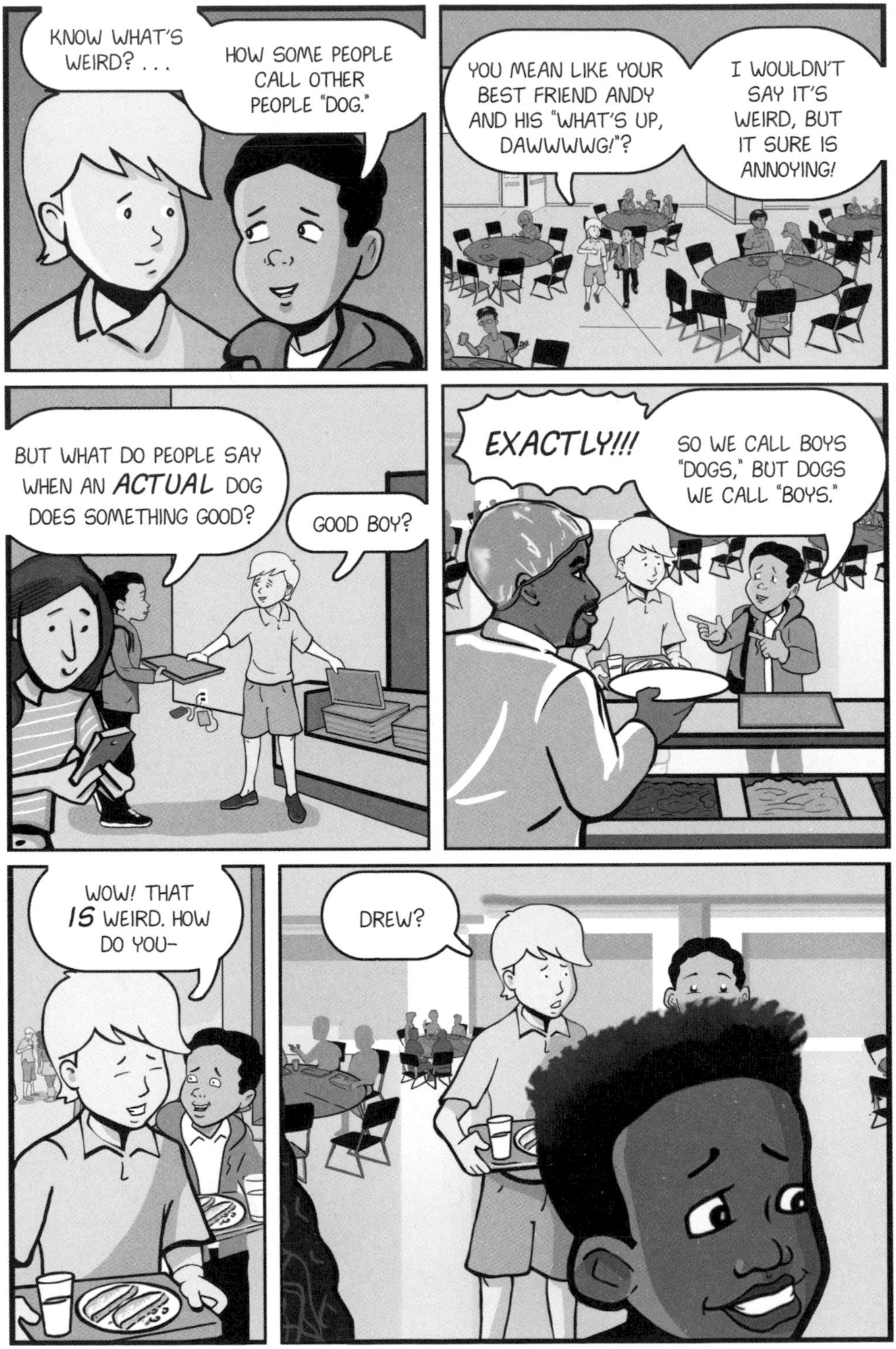
KNOW WHAT'S WEIRD? . . .
HOW SOME PEOPLE CALL OTHER PEOPLE "DOG."
YOU MEAN LIKE YOUR BEST FRIEND ANDY AND HIS "WHAT'S UP, DAWWWWG!"?
I WOULDN'T SAY IT'S WEIRD, BUT IT SURE IS ANNOYING!
BUT WHAT DO PEOPLE SAY WHEN AN ACTUAL DOG DOES SOMETHING GOOD?
GOOD BOY?
EXACTLY!!!
SO WE CALL BOYS "DOGS," BUT DOGS WE CALL "BOYS."
WOW! THAT IS WEIRD. HOW DO YOU-
DREW?

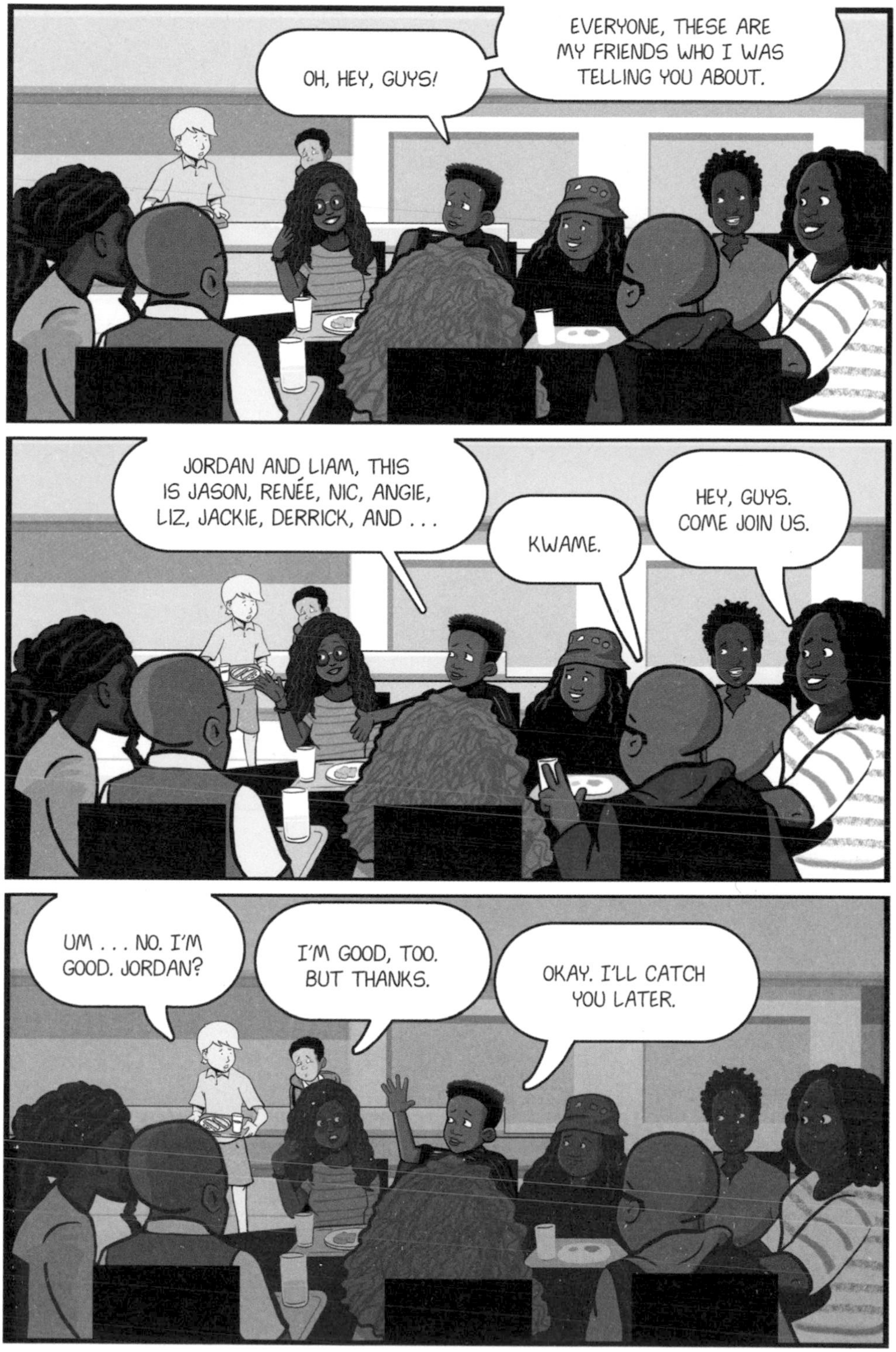
OH, HEY, GUYS!
EVERYONE, THESE ARE MY FRIENDS WHO I WAS TELLING YOU ABOUT.
JORDAN AND LIAM, THIS IS JASON, RENÉE, NIC, ANGIE, LIZ, JACKIE, DERRICK, AND . . .
KWAME.
HEY, GUYS. COME JOIN US.
UM . . . NO. I'M GOOD. JORDAN?
I'M GOOD, TOO. BUT THANKS.
OKAY. I'LL CATCH YOU LATER.

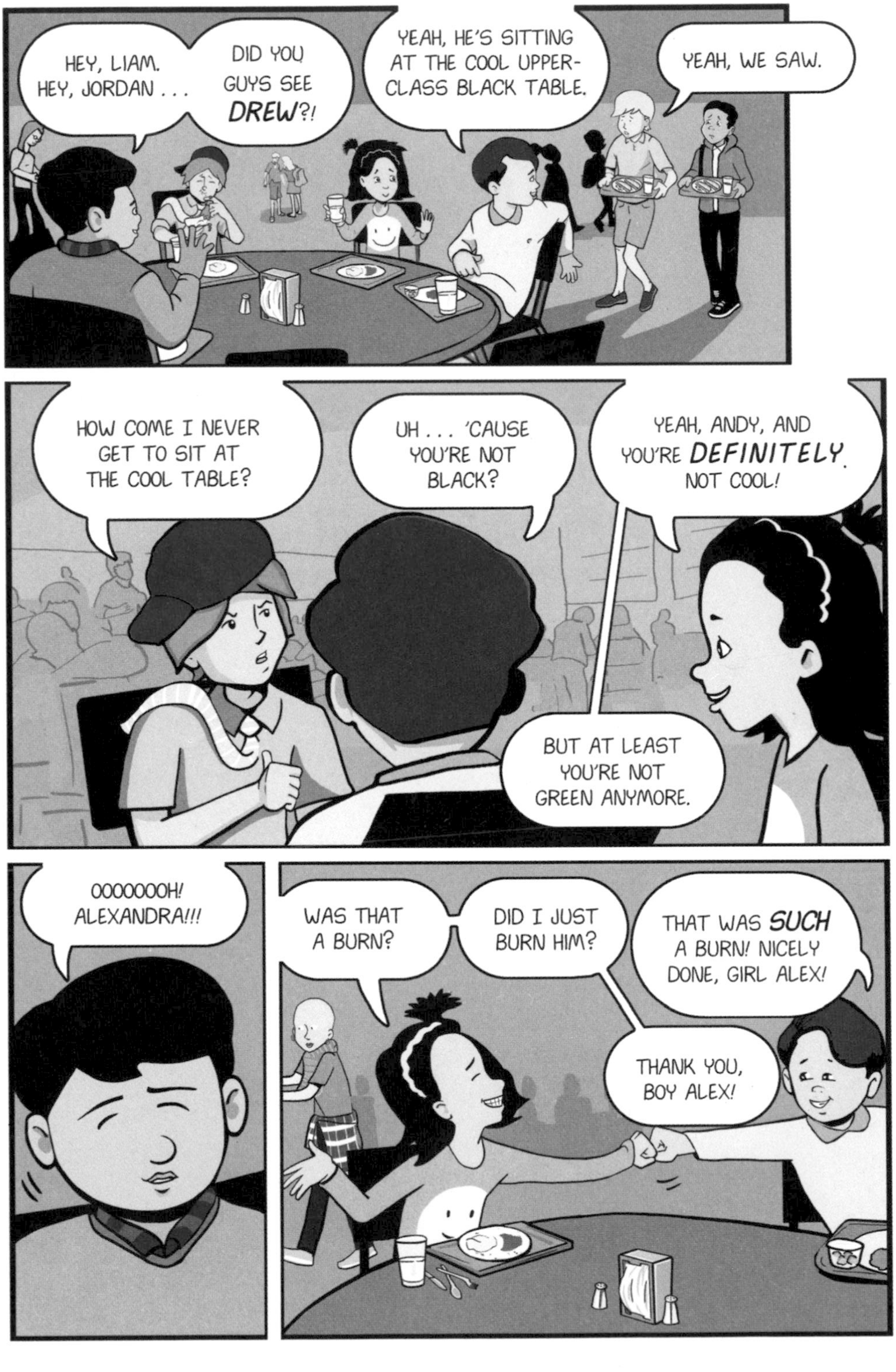
HEY, LIAM. HEY, JORDAN . . .
DID YOU GUYS SEE DREW?!
YEAH, HE'S SITTING AT THE COOL UPPER-CLASS BLACK TABLE.
YEAH, WE SAW.
HOW COME I NEVER GET TO SIT AT THE COOL TABLE?
UH . . . 'CAUSE YOU'RE NOT BLACK?
YEAH, ANDY, AND YOU'RE DEFINITELY NOT COOL!
BUT AT LEAST YOU'RE NOT GREEN ANYMORE.
OOOOOOOH! ALEXANDRA!!!
WAS THAT A BURN?
DID I JUST BURN HIM?
THAT WAS SUCH A BURN! NICELY DONE, GIRL ALEX!
THANK YOU, BOY ALEX!

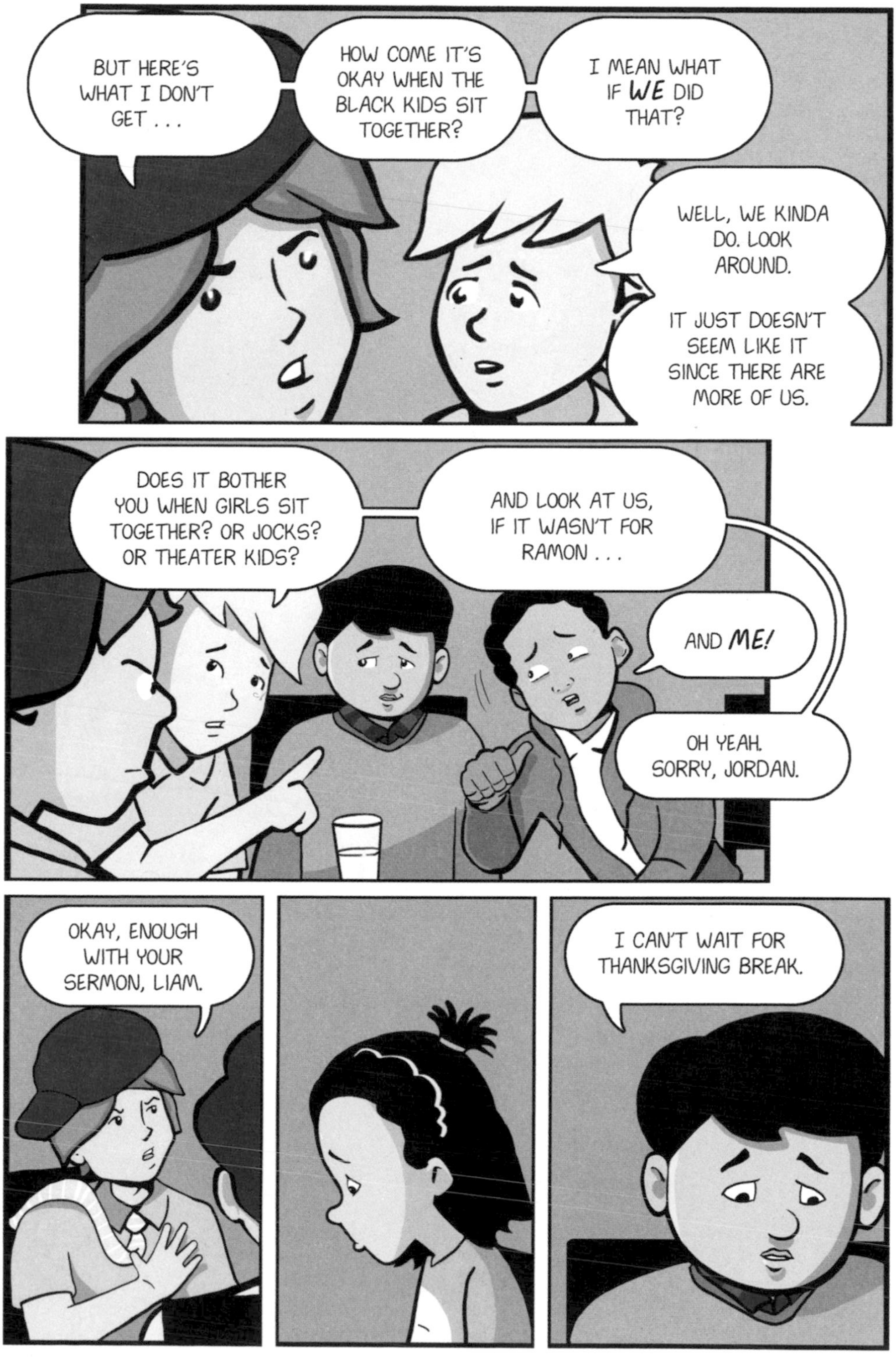
BUT HERE'S WHAT I DON'T GET . . .
HOW COME IT'S OKAY WHEN THE BLACK KIDS SIT TOGETHER?
I MEAN WHAT IF **WE** DID THAT?
WELL, WE KINDA DO. LOOK AROUND.
IT JUST DOESN'T SEEM LIKE IT SINCE THERE ARE MORE OF US.
DOES IT BOTHER YOU WHEN GIRLS SIT TOGETHER? OR JOCKS? OR THEATER KIDS?
AND LOOK AT US, IF IT WASN'T FOR RAMON . . .
AND **ME!**
OH YEAH. SORRY, JORDAN.
OKAY, ENOUGH WITH YOUR SERMON, LIAM.
I CAN'T WAIT FOR THANKSGIVING BREAK.

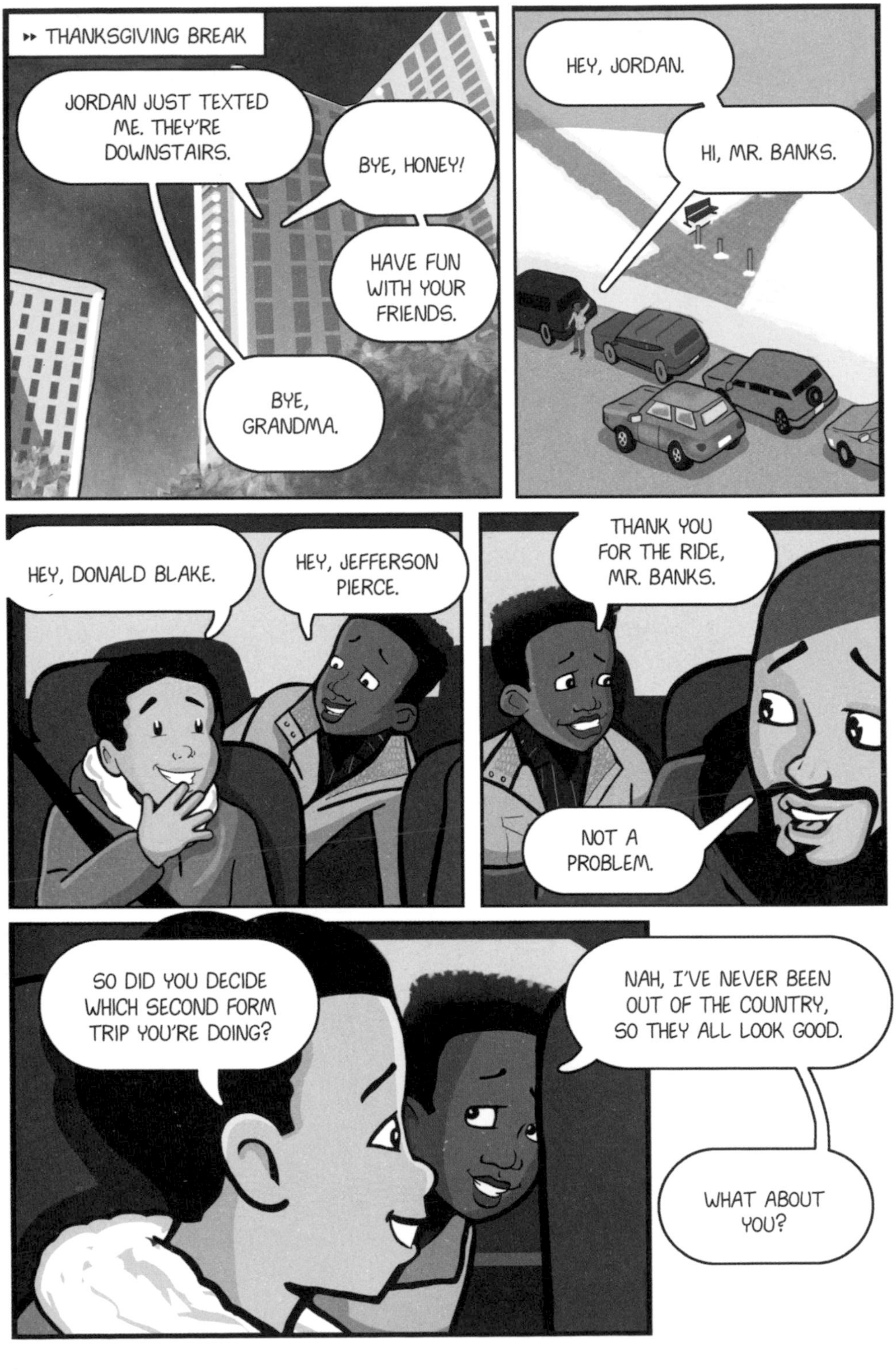
THANKSGIVING BREAK
JORDAN JUST TEXTED ME. THEY'RE DOWNSTAIRS.
BYE, HONEY!
HAVE FUN WITH YOUR FRIENDS.
BYE, GRANDMA.
HEY, JORDAN.
HI, MR. BANKS.
HEY, DONALD BLAKE.
HEY, JEFFERSON PIERCE.
THANK YOU FOR THE RIDE, MR. BANKS.
NOT A PROBLEM.
SO DID YOU DECIDE WHICH SECOND FORM TRIP YOU'RE DOING?
NAH, I'VE NEVER BEEN OUT OF THE COUNTRY, SO THEY ALL LOOK GOOD.
WHAT ABOUT YOU?

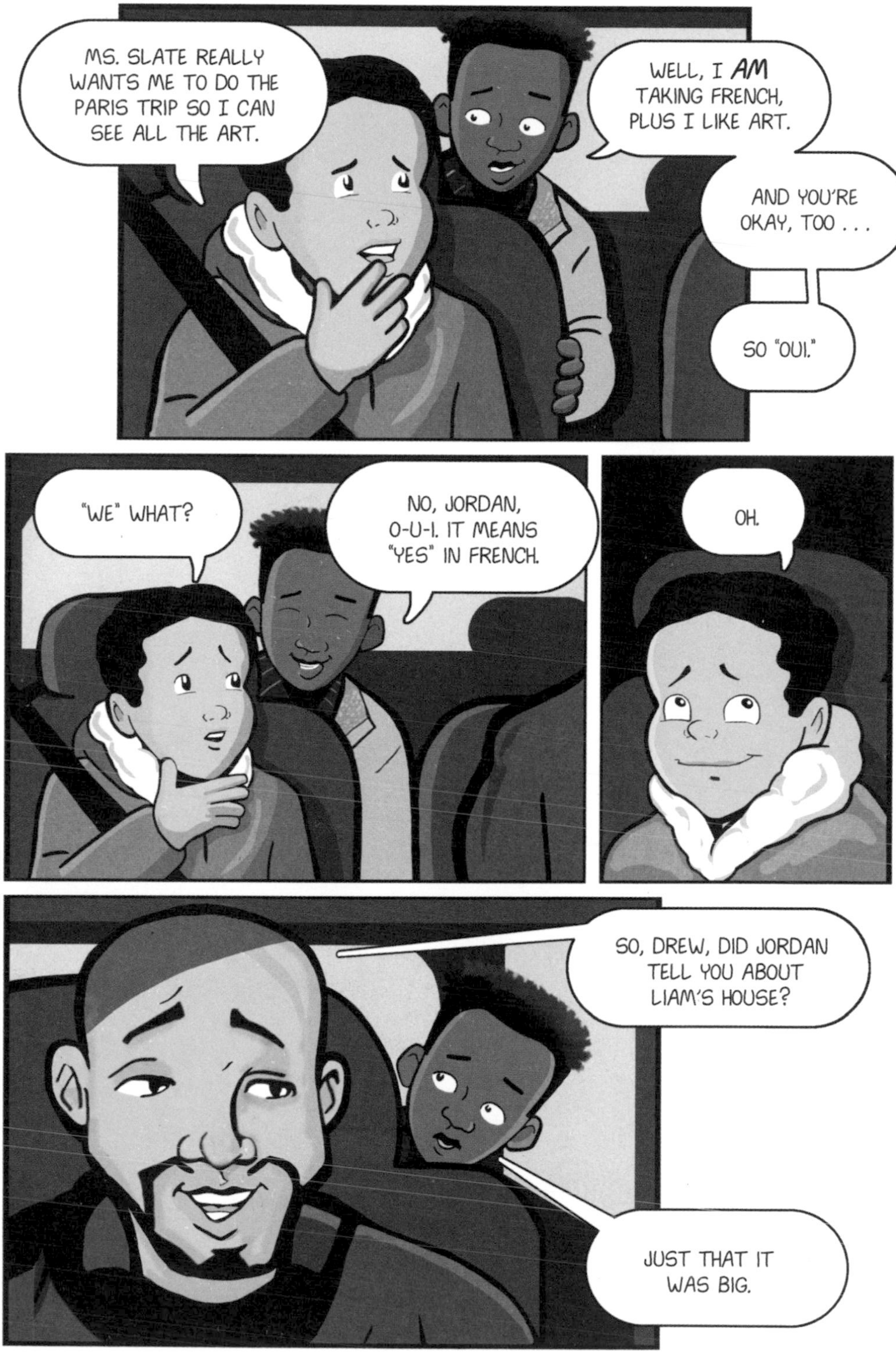
MS. SLATE REALLY WANTS ME TO DO THE PARIS TRIP SO I CAN SEE ALL THE ART.
WELL, I *AM* TAKING FRENCH, PLUS I LIKE ART.
AND YOU'RE OKAY, TOO . . .
SO "OUI."
"WE" WHAT?
NO, JORDAN, O-U-I. IT MEANS "YES" IN FRENCH.
OH.
SO, DREW, DID JORDAN TELL YOU ABOUT LIAM'S HOUSE?
JUST THAT IT WAS BIG.

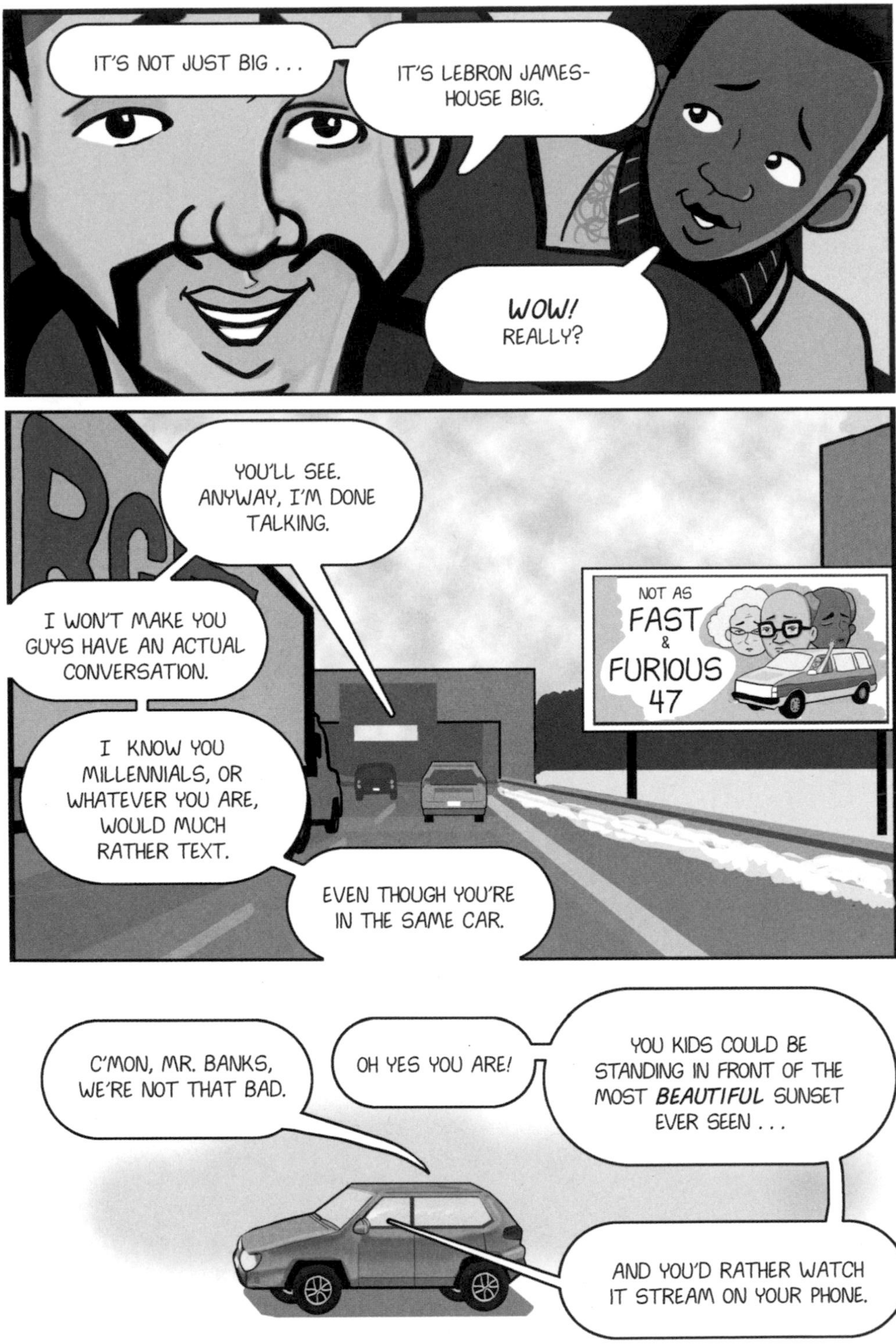
IT'S NOT JUST BIG . . .
IT'S LEBRON JAMES-HOUSE BIG.
WOW! REALLY?
YOU'LL SEE. ANYWAY, I'M DONE TALKING.
I WON'T MAKE YOU GUYS HAVE AN ACTUAL CONVERSATION.
I KNOW YOU MILLENNIALS, OR WHATEVER YOU ARE, WOULD MUCH RATHER TEXT.
EVEN THOUGH YOU'RE IN THE SAME CAR.
NOT AS FAST & FURIOUS 47
C'MON, MR. BANKS, WE'RE NOT THAT BAD.
OH YES YOU ARE!
YOU KIDS COULD BE STANDING IN FRONT OF THE MOST BEAUTIFUL SUNSET EVER SEEN . . .
AND YOU'D RATHER WATCH IT STREAM ON YOUR PHONE.

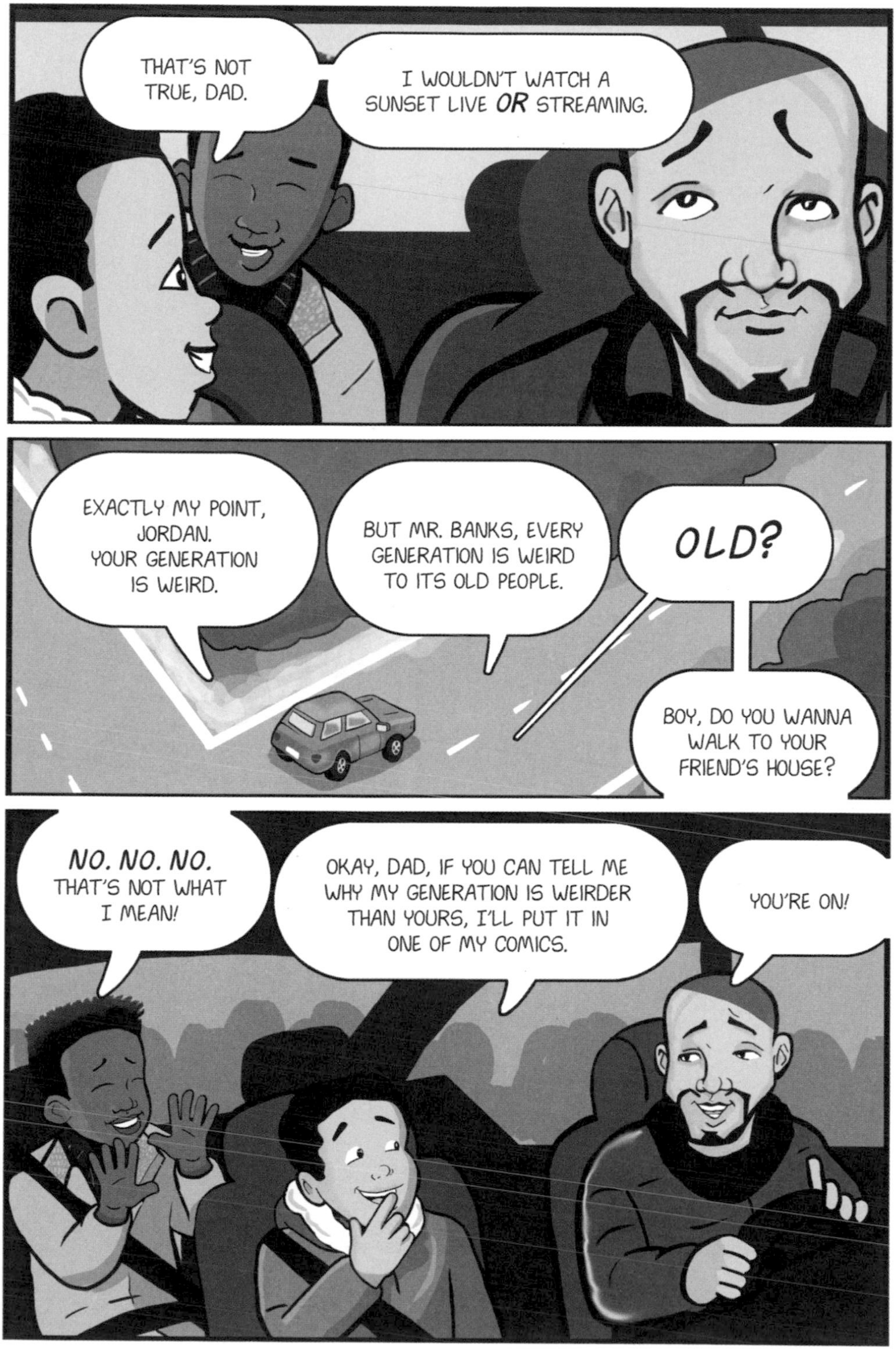
THAT'S NOT TRUE, DAD.
I WOULDN'T WATCH A SUNSET LIVE *OR* STREAMING.
EXACTLY MY POINT, JORDAN. YOUR GENERATION IS WEIRD.
BUT MR. BANKS, EVERY GENERATION IS WEIRD TO ITS OLD PEOPLE.
OLD?
BOY, DO YOU WANNA WALK TO YOUR FRIEND'S HOUSE?
NO. NO. NO. THAT'S NOT WHAT I MEAN!
OKAY, DAD, IF YOU CAN TELL ME WHY MY GENERATION IS WEIRDER THAN YOURS, I'LL PUT IT IN ONE OF MY COMICS.
YOU'RE ON!

I Lost the Bet

written by Chuck Banks *art by Jordan Banks*

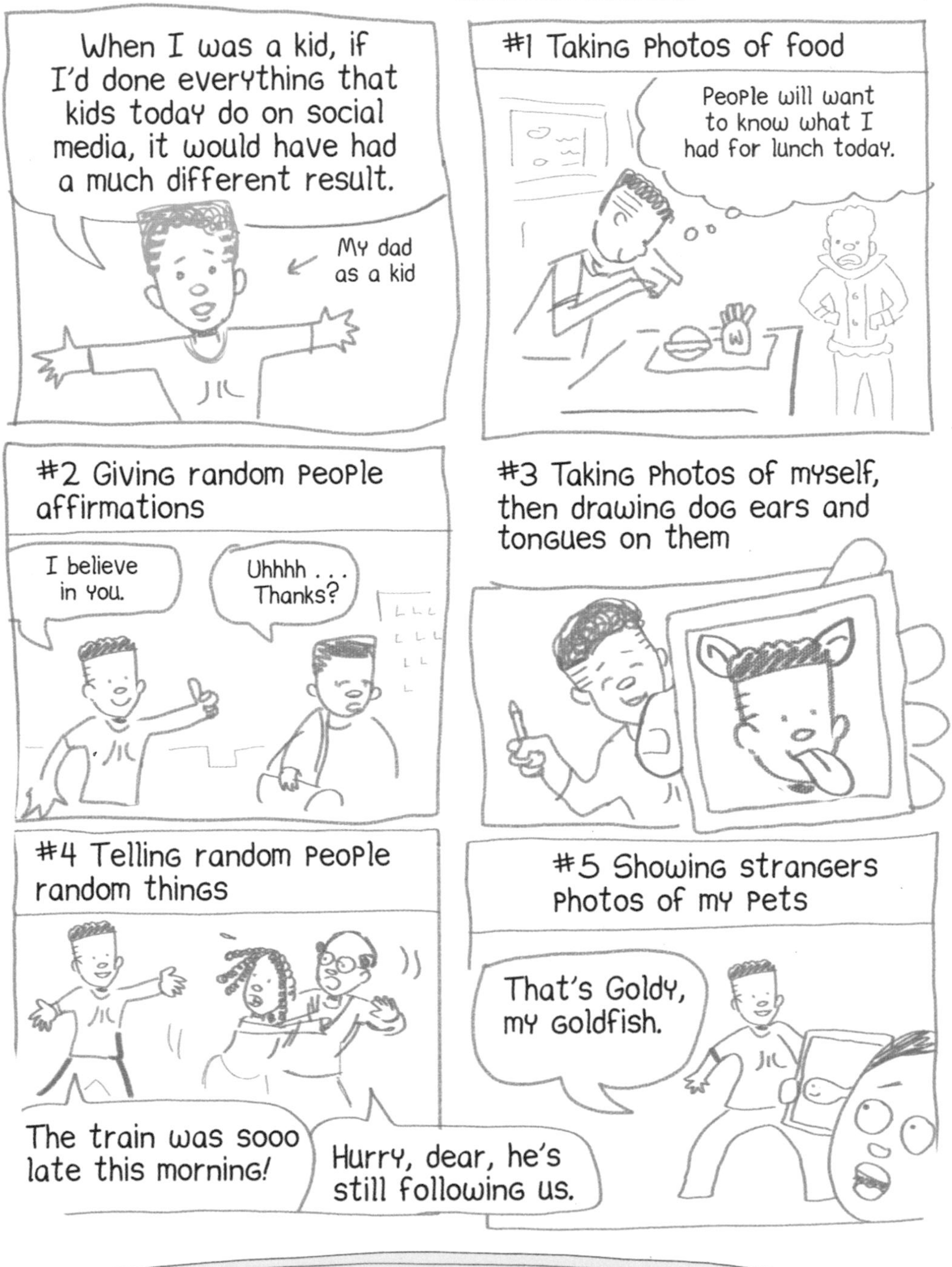
When I was a kid, if I'd done everything that kids today do on social media, it would have had a much different result.
My dad as a kid
#1 Taking photos of food
People will want to know what I had for lunch today.
#2 Giving random people affirmations
I believe in you.
Uhhhh . . . Thanks?
#3 Taking photos of myself, then drawing dog ears and tongues on them
#4 Telling random people random things
The train was sooo late this morning!
Hurry, dear, he's still following us.
#5 Showing strangers photos of my pets
That's Goldy, my goldfish.

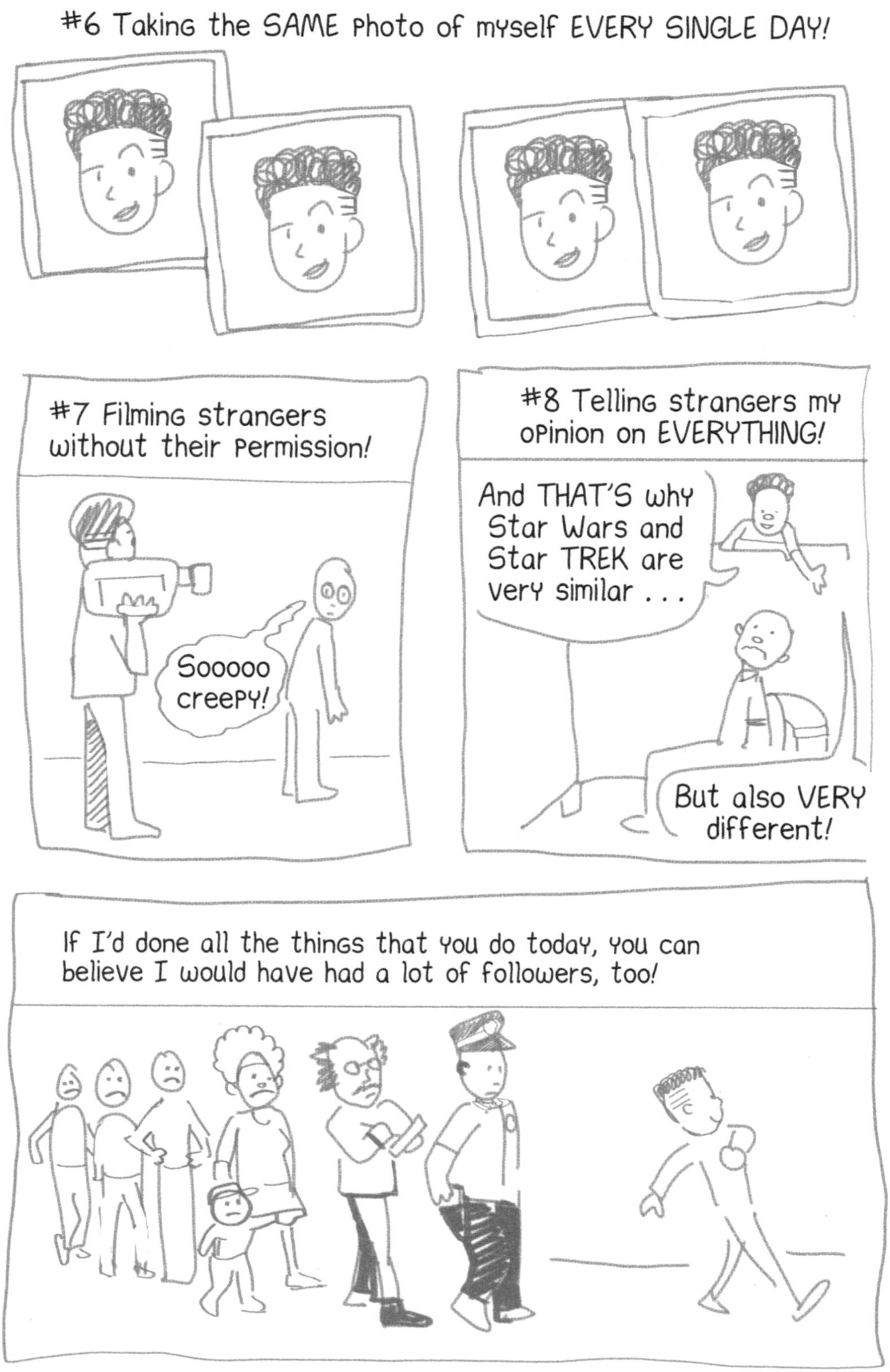
#6 Taking the SAME photo of myself EVERY SINGLE DAY!
#7 Filming strangers without their permission!
Sooooo creepy!
#8 Telling strangers my opinion on EVERYTHING!
And THAT'S why Star Wars and Star TREK are very similar . . .
But also VERY different!
If I'd done all the things that you do today, you can believe I would have had a lot of followers, too!

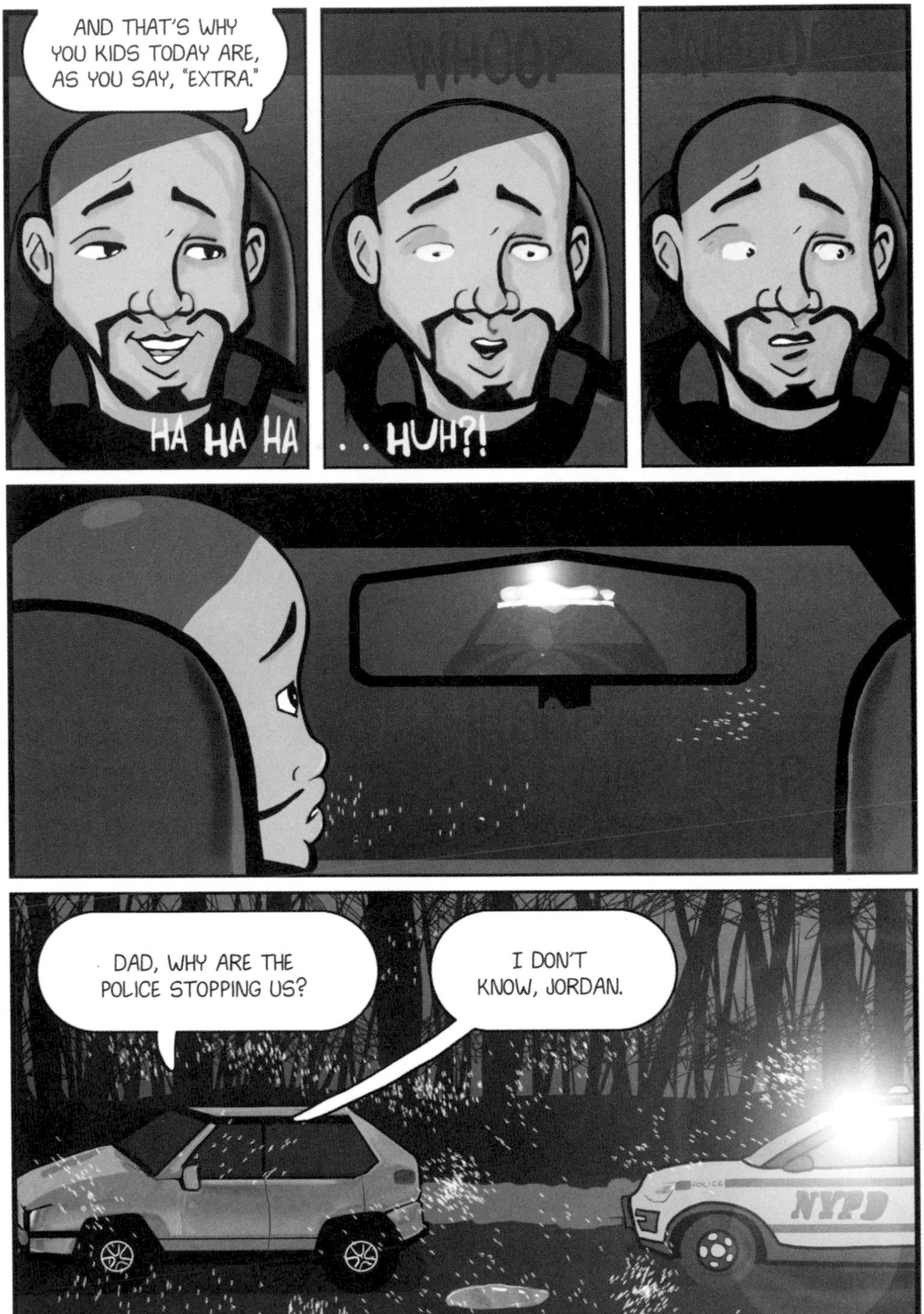
AND THAT'S WHY YOU KIDS TODAY ARE, AS YOU SAY, "EXTRA."
HA HA HA
WHOOP
. . HUH?!
DAD, WHY ARE THE POLICE STOPPING US?
I DON'T KNOW, JORDAN.
POLICE
NYPD

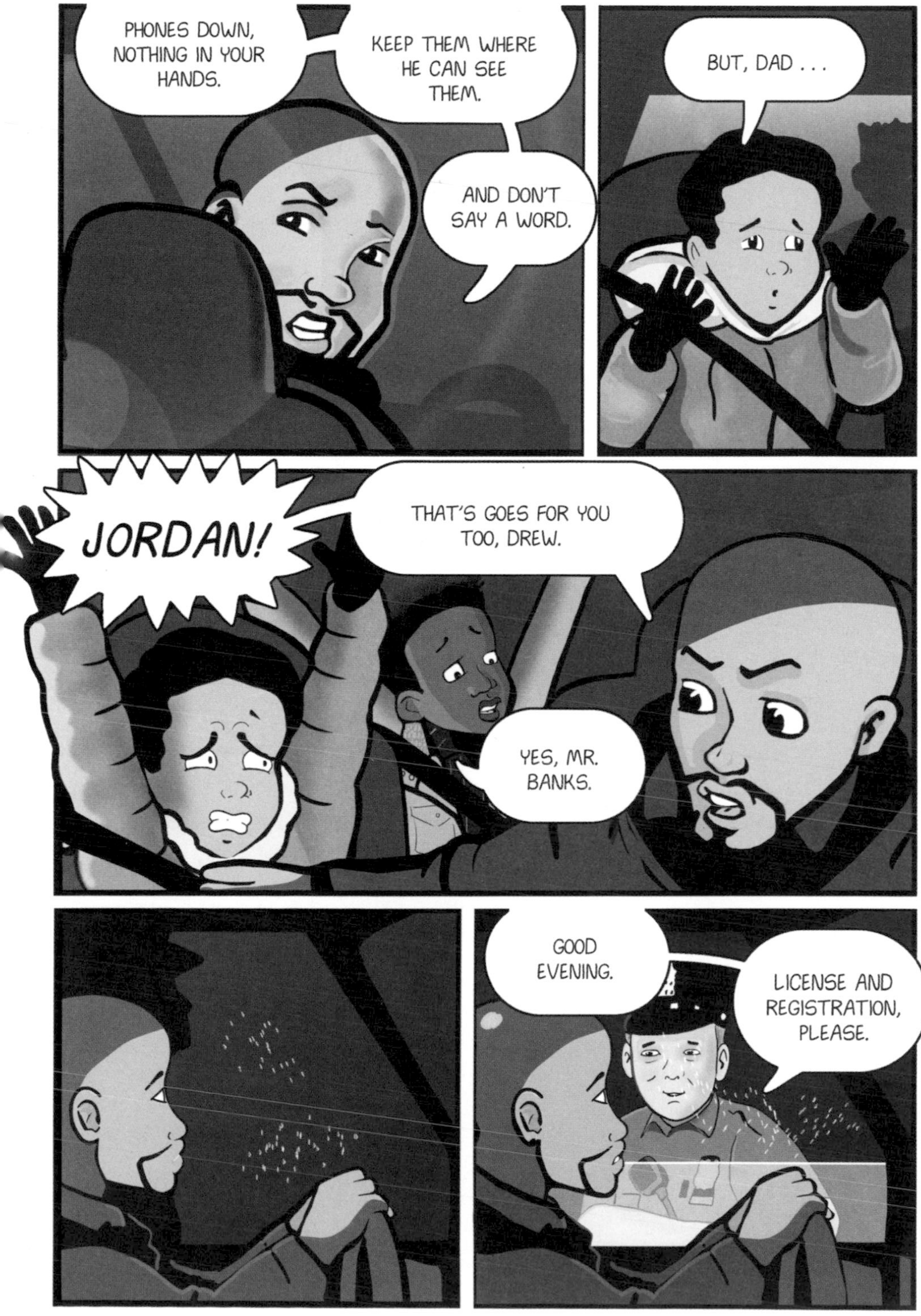
PHONES DOWN, NOTHING IN YOUR HANDS.
KEEP THEM WHERE HE CAN SEE THEM.
AND DON'T SAY A WORD.
BUT, DAD . . .
JORDAN!
THAT'S GOES FOR YOU TOO, DREW.
YES, MR. BANKS.
GOOD EVENING.
LICENSE AND REGISTRATION, PLEASE.

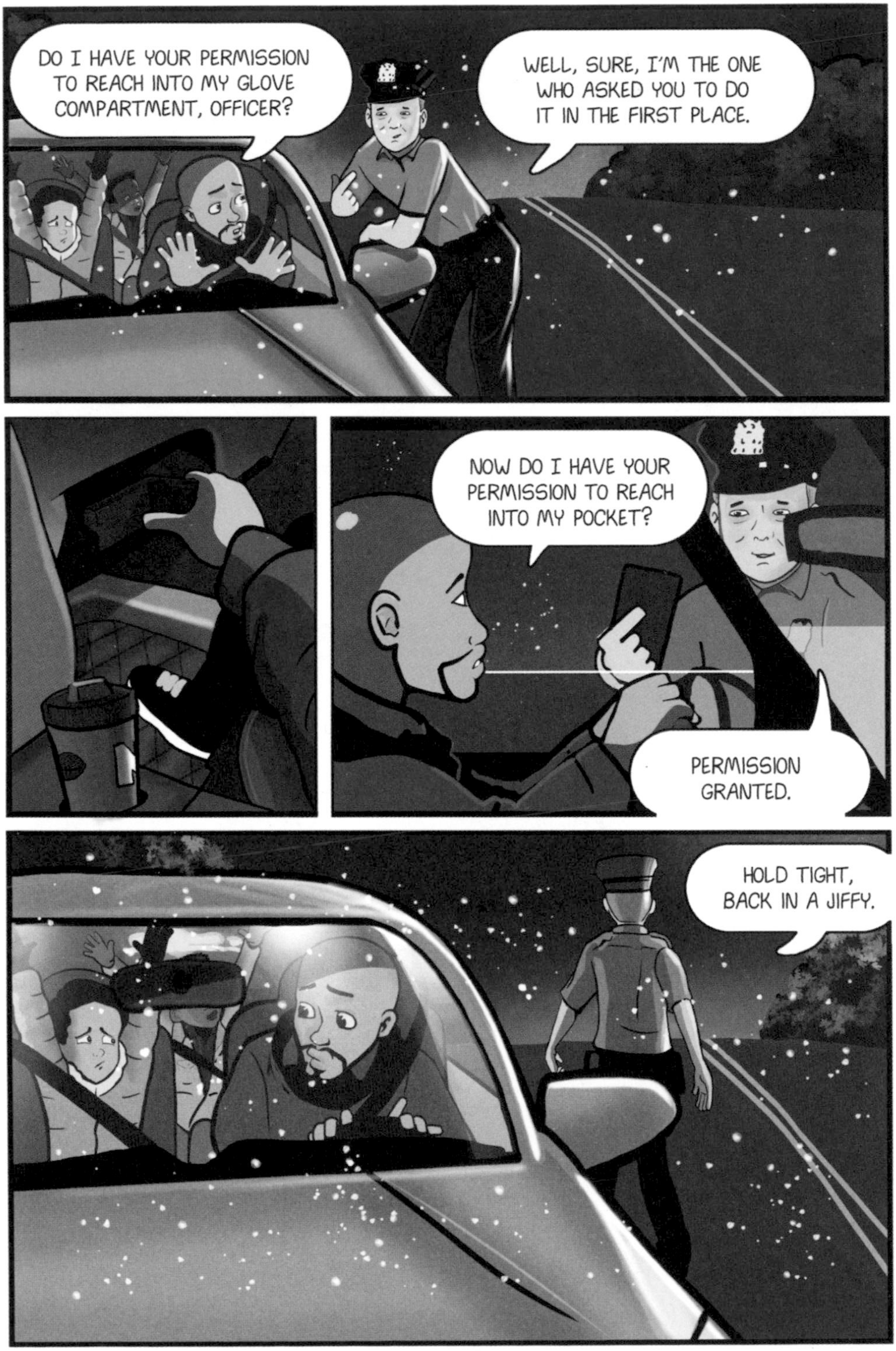
DO I HAVE YOUR PERMISSION TO REACH INTO MY GLOVE COMPARTMENT, OFFICER?
WELL, SURE, I'M THE ONE WHO ASKED YOU TO DO IT IN THE FIRST PLACE.
NOW DO I HAVE YOUR PERMISSION TO REACH INTO MY POCKET?
PERMISSION GRANTED.
HOLD TIGHT, BACK IN A JIFFY.

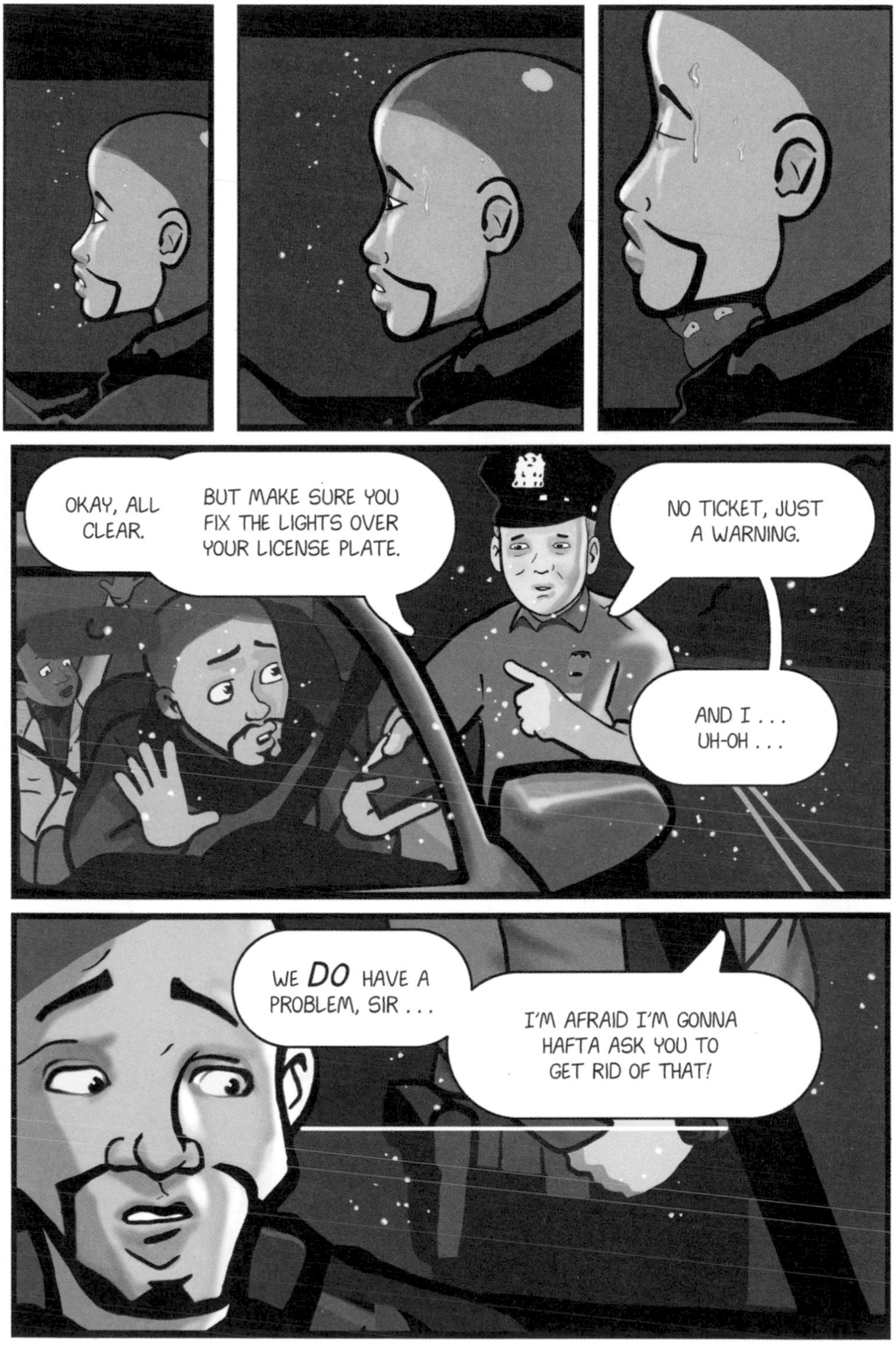
OKAY, ALL CLEAR.
BUT MAKE SURE YOU FIX THE LIGHTS OVER YOUR LICENSE PLATE.
NO TICKET, JUST A WARNING.
AND I . . . UH-OH . . .
WE DO HAVE A PROBLEM, SIR . . .
I'M AFRAID I'M GONNA HAFTA ASK YOU TO GET RID OF THAT!

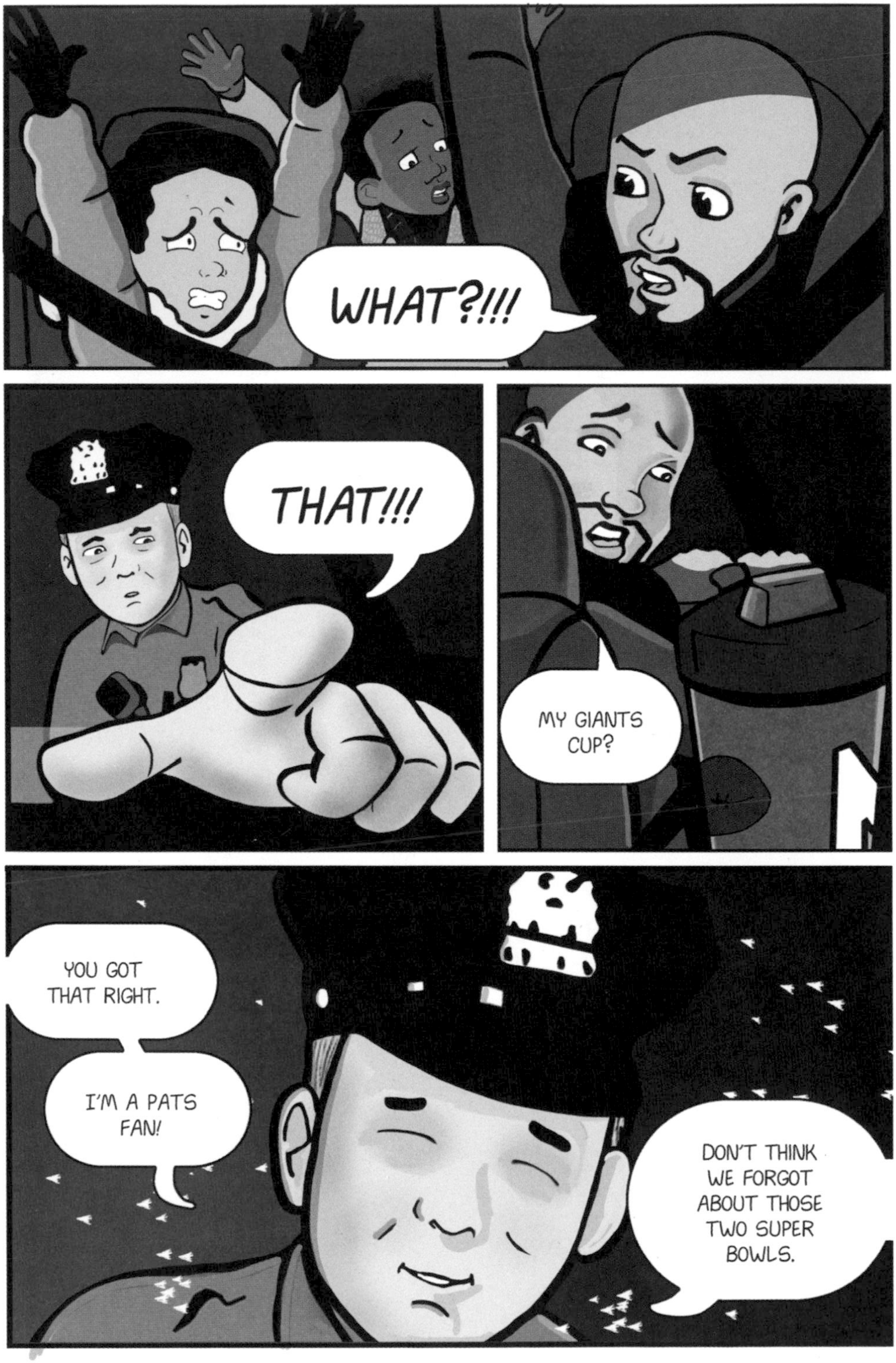
WHAT?!!!
THAT!!!
MY GIANTS CUP?
YOU GOT THAT RIGHT.
I'M A PATS FAN!
DON'T THINK WE FORGOT ABOUT THOSE TWO SUPER BOWLS.

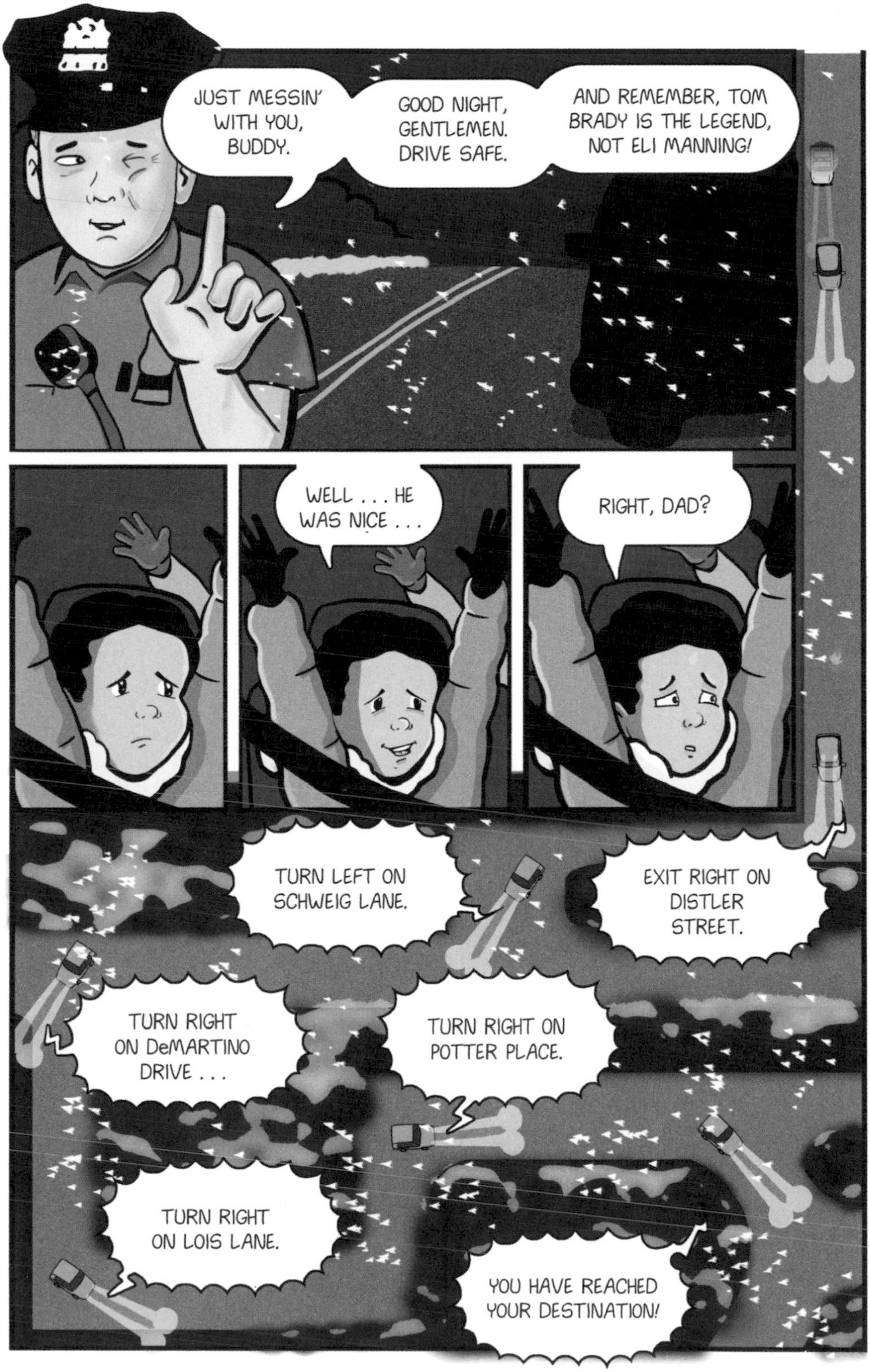
JUST MESSIN' WITH YOU, BUDDY.
GOOD NIGHT, GENTLEMEN. DRIVE SAFE.
AND REMEMBER, TOM BRADY IS THE LEGEND, NOT ELI MANNING!
WELL . . . HE WAS NICE . . .
RIGHT, DAD?
TURN LEFT ON SCHWEIG LANE.
EXIT RIGHT ON DISTLER STREET.
TURN RIGHT ON DeMARTINO DRIVE . . .
TURN RIGHT ON POTTER PLACE.
TURN RIGHT ON LOIS LANE.
YOU HAVE REACHED YOUR DESTINATION!

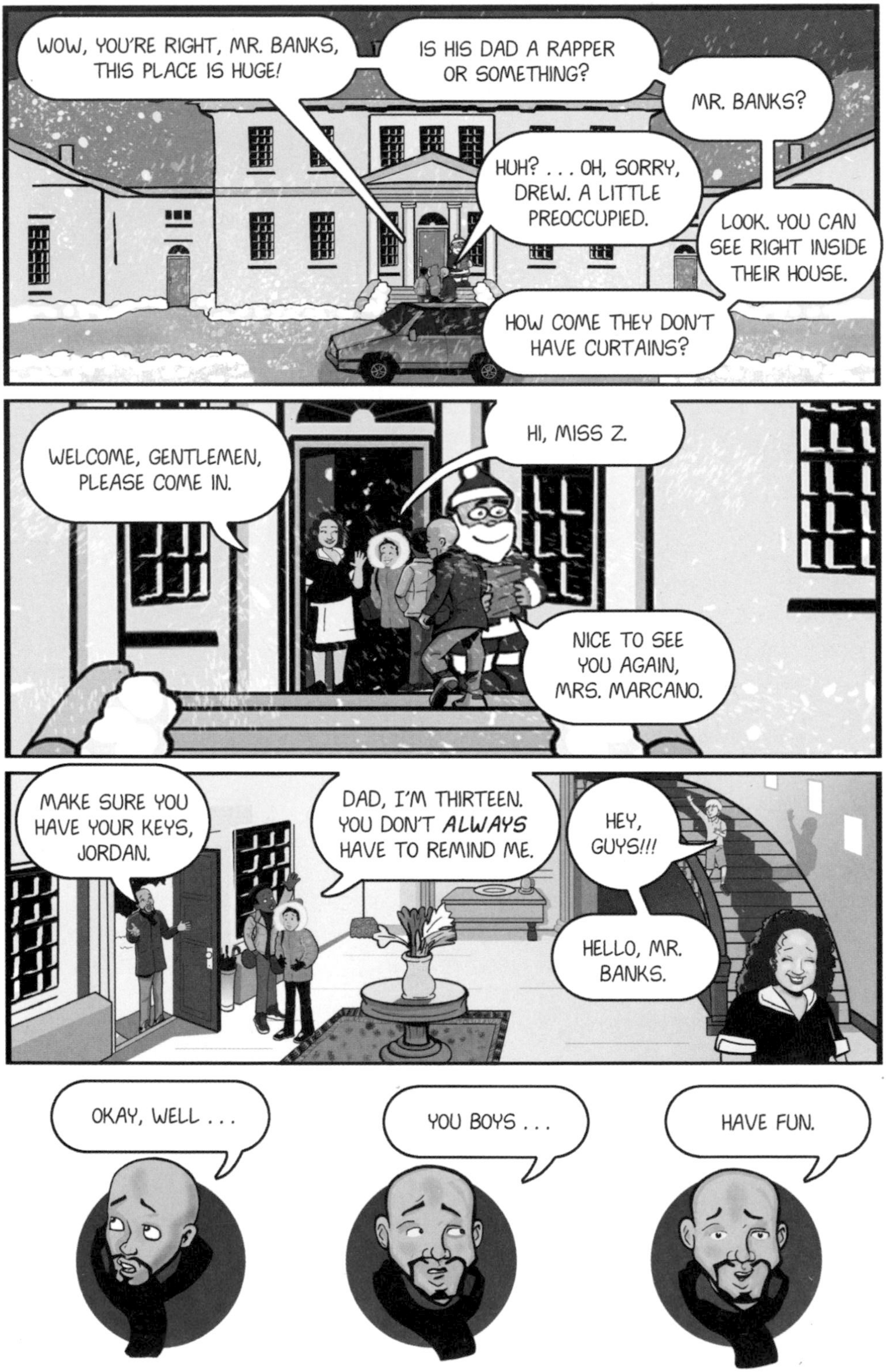
WOW, YOU'RE RIGHT, MR. BANKS, THIS PLACE IS HUGE!
IS HIS DAD A RAPPER OR SOMETHING?
MR. BANKS?
HUH? . . . OH, SORRY, DREW. A LITTLE PREOCCUPIED.
LOOK. YOU CAN SEE RIGHT INSIDE THEIR HOUSE.
HOW COME THEY DON'T HAVE CURTAINS?
WELCOME, GENTLEMEN, PLEASE COME IN.
HI, MISS Z.
NICE TO SEE YOU AGAIN, MRS. MARCANO.
MAKE SURE YOU HAVE YOUR KEYS, JORDAN.
DAD, I'M THIRTEEN. YOU DON'T *ALWAYS* HAVE TO REMIND ME.
HEY, GUYS!!!
HELLO, MR. BANKS.
OKAY, WELL . . .
YOU BOYS . . .
HAVE FUN.

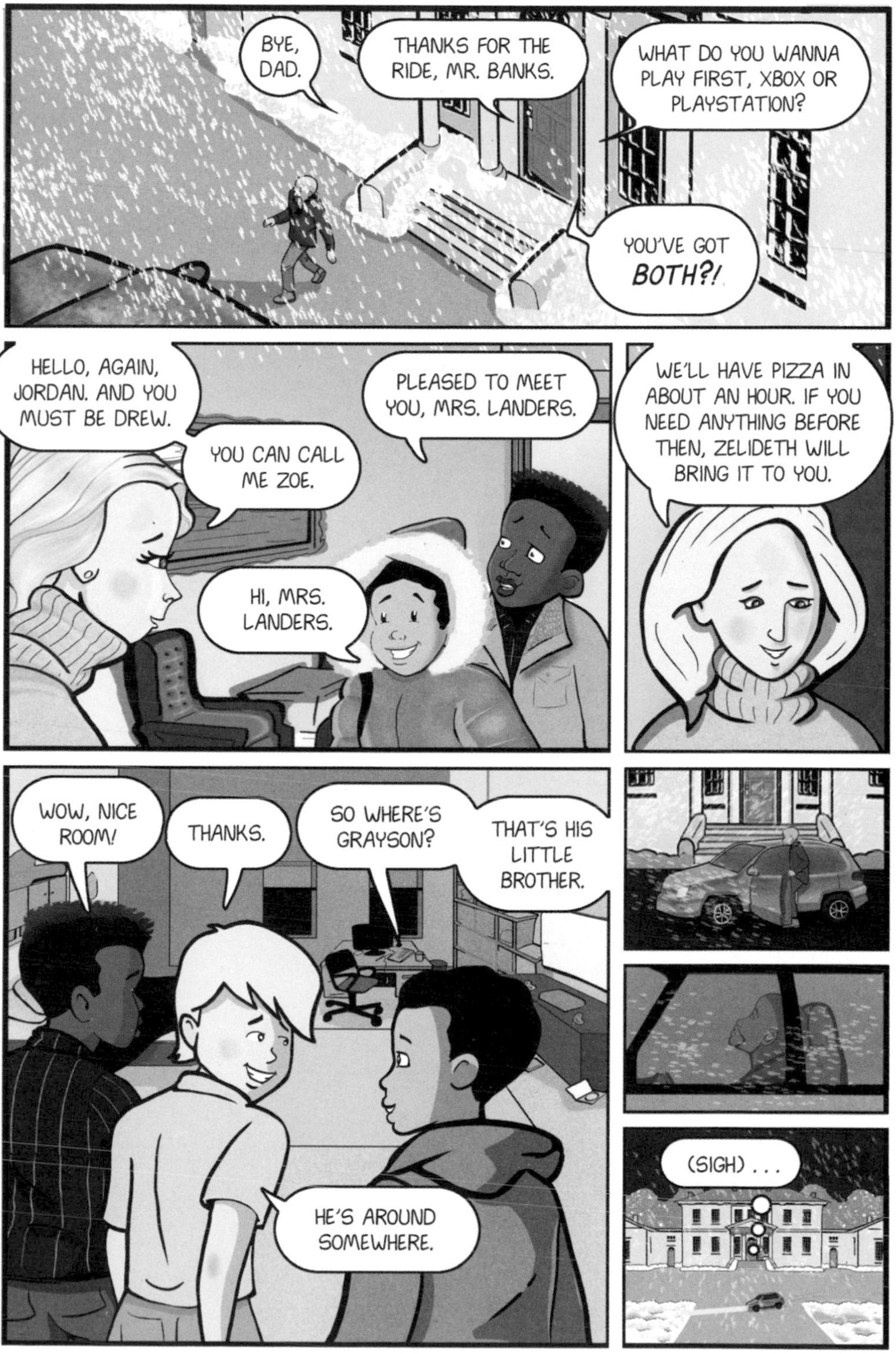
BYE, DAD.
THANKS FOR THE RIDE, MR. BANKS.
WHAT DO YOU WANNA PLAY FIRST, XBOX OR PLAYSTATION?
YOU'VE GOT BOTH?!
HELLO, AGAIN, JORDAN. AND YOU MUST BE DREW.
YOU CAN CALL ME ZOE.
PLEASED TO MEET YOU, MRS. LANDERS.
HI, MRS. LANDERS.
WE'LL HAVE PIZZA IN ABOUT AN HOUR. IF YOU NEED ANYTHING BEFORE THEN, ZELIDETH WILL BRING IT TO YOU.
WOW, NICE ROOM!
THANKS.
SO WHERE'S GRAYSON?
THAT'S HIS LITTLE BROTHER.
HE'S AROUND SOMEWHERE.
(SIGH) . . .

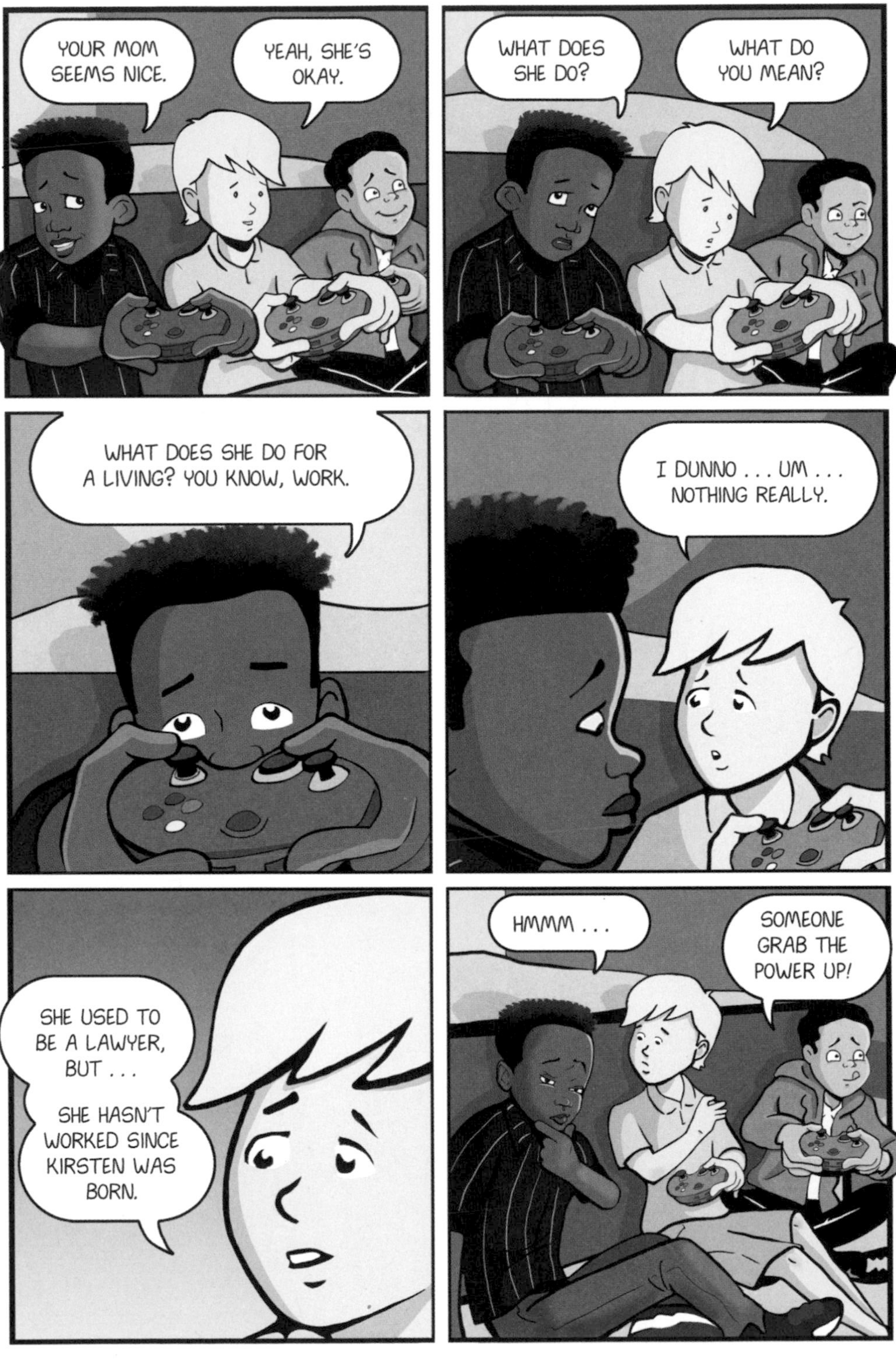
YOUR MOM SEEMS NICE.
YEAH, SHE'S OKAY.
WHAT DOES SHE DO?
WHAT DO YOU MEAN?
WHAT DOES SHE DO FOR A LIVING? YOU KNOW, WORK.
I DUNNO . . . UM . . . NOTHING REALLY.
SHE USED TO BE A LAWYER, BUT . . .
SHE HASN'T WORKED SINCE KIRSTEN WAS BORN.
HMMM . . .
SOMEONE GRAB THE POWER UP!

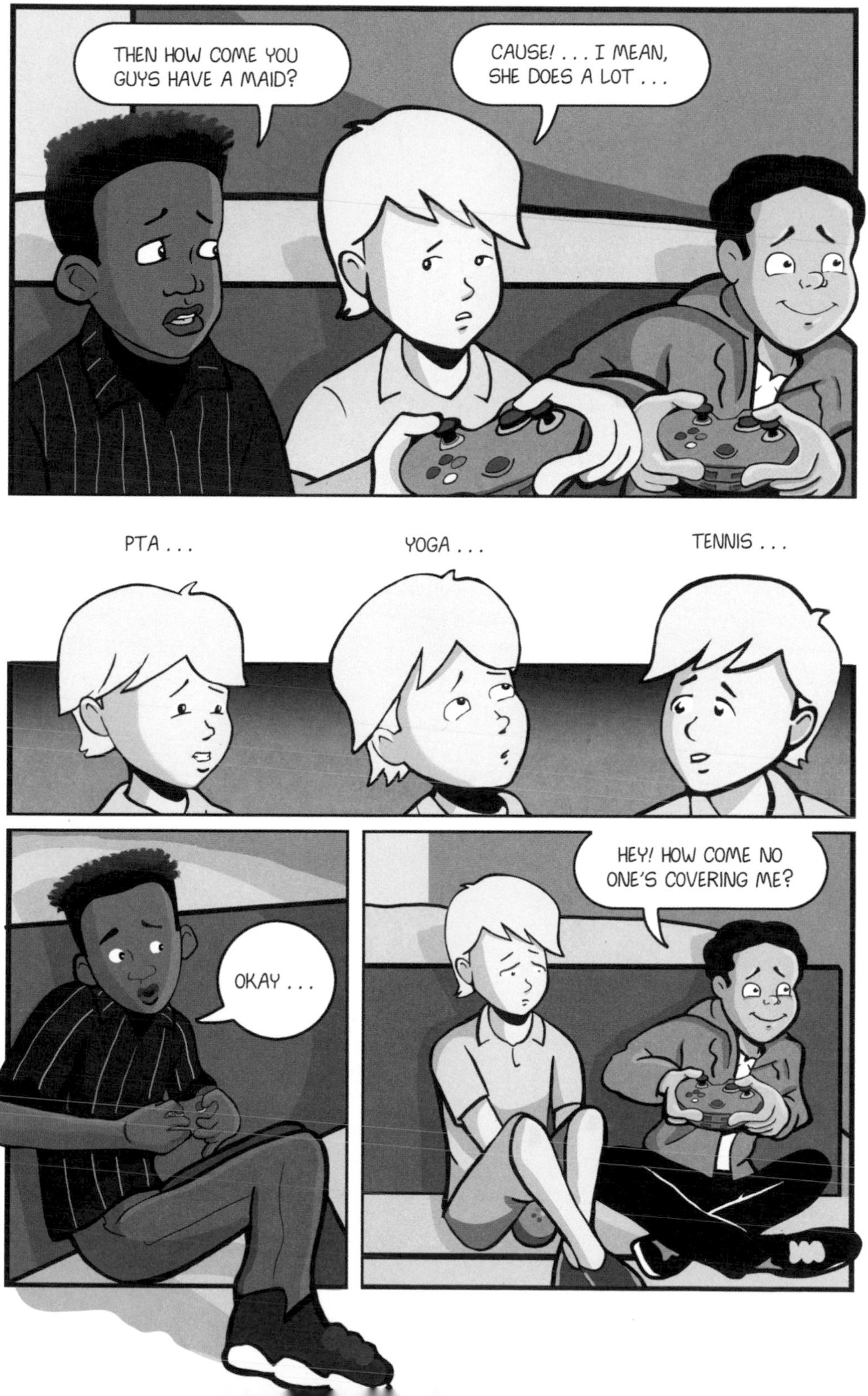
THEN HOW COME YOU GUYS HAVE A MAID?
CAUSE! . . . I MEAN, SHE DOES A LOT . . .
PTA . . .
YOGA . . .
TENNIS . . .
OKAY . . .
HEY! HOW COME NO ONE'S COVERING ME?

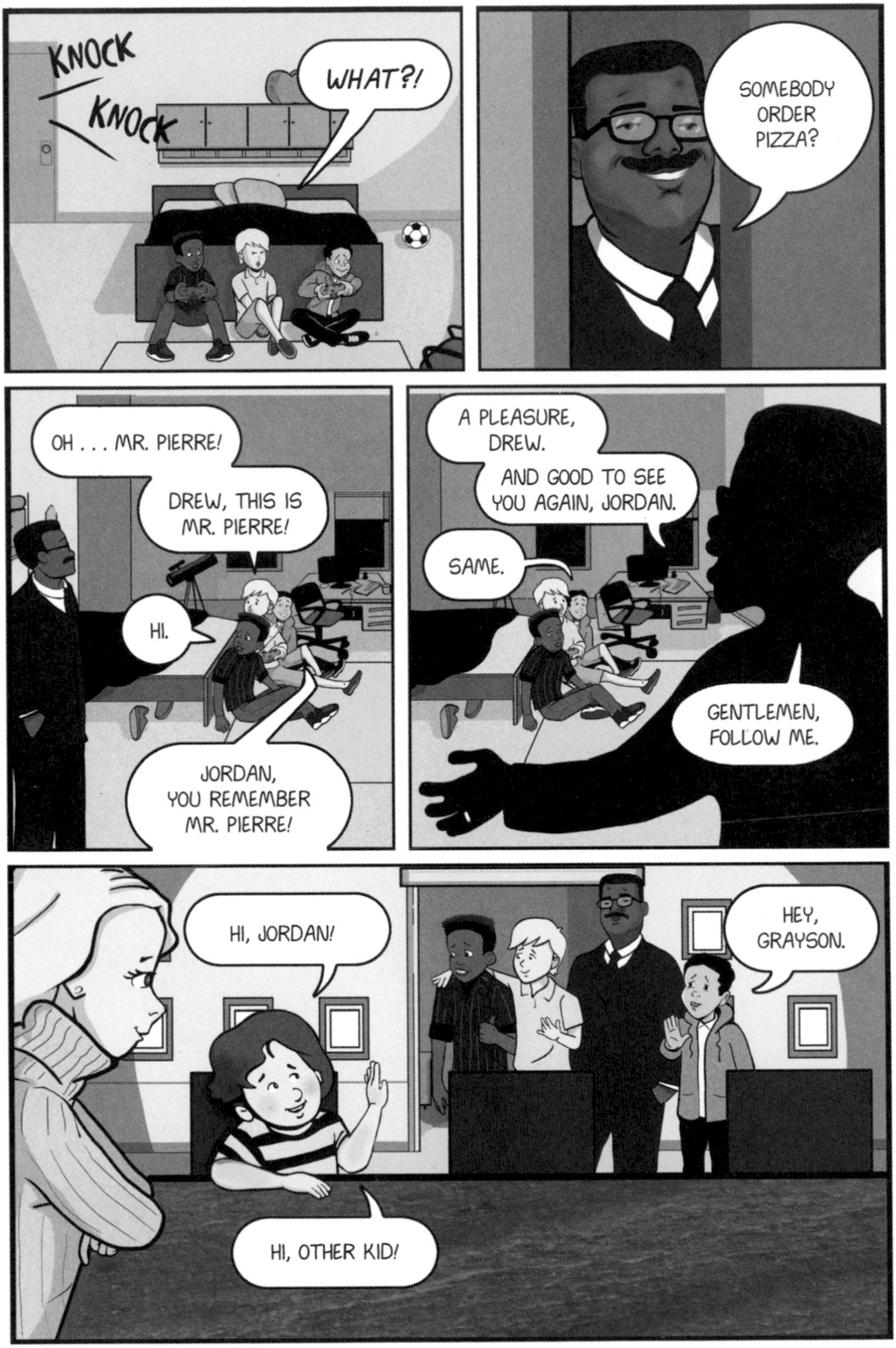
KNOCK
KNOCK
WHAT?!
SOMEBODY ORDER PIZZA?
OH . . . MR. PIERRE!
DREW, THIS IS MR. PIERRE!
HI.
JORDAN, YOU REMEMBER MR. PIERRE!
A PLEASURE, DREW.
AND GOOD TO SEE YOU AGAIN, JORDAN.
SAME.
GENTLEMEN, FOLLOW ME.
HI, JORDAN!
HEY, GRAYSON.
HI, OTHER KID!

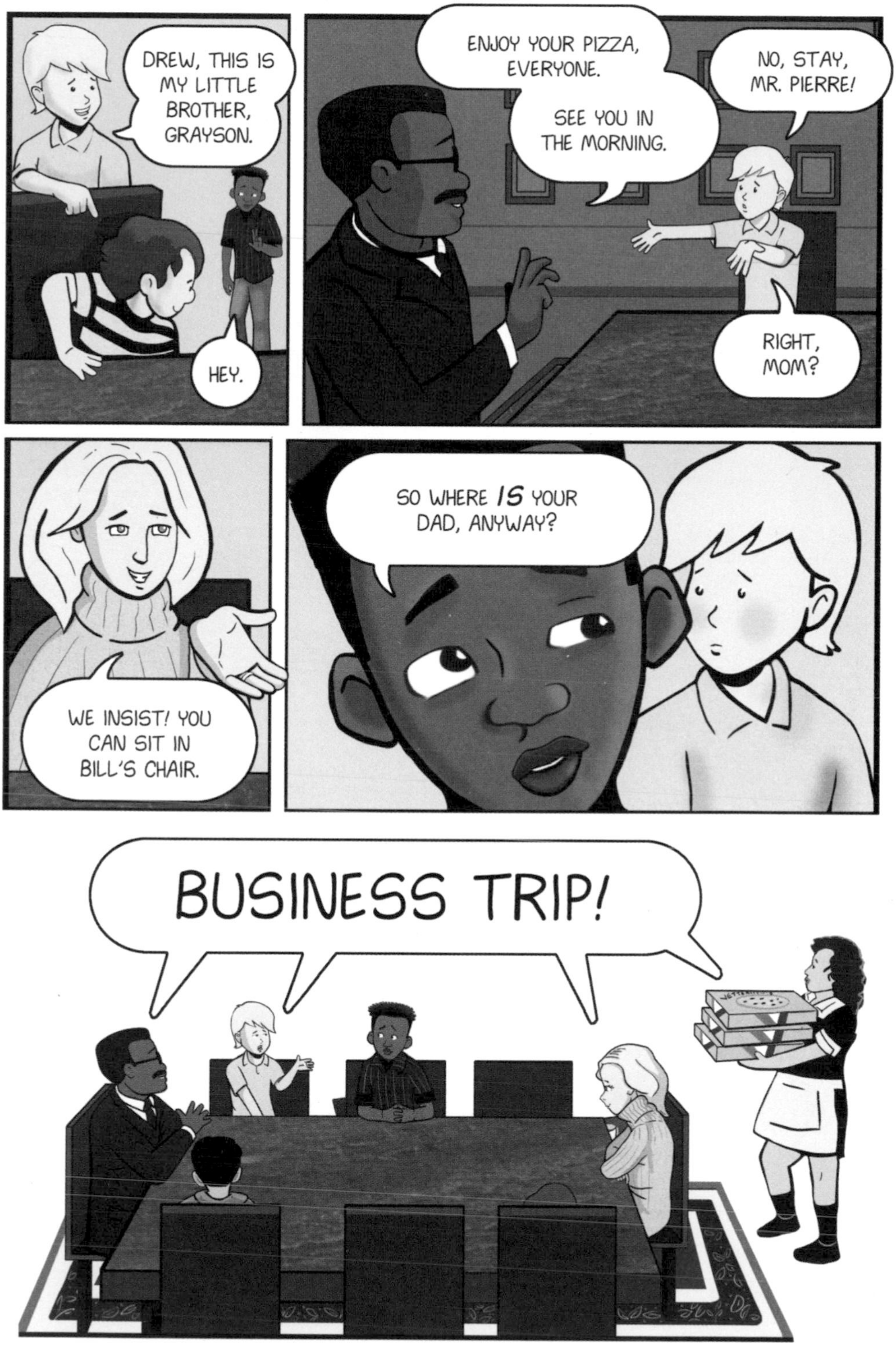
DREW, THIS IS MY LITTLE BROTHER, GRAYSON.
HEY.
ENJOY YOUR PIZZA, EVERYONE.
SEE YOU IN THE MORNING.
NO, STAY, MR. PIERRE!
RIGHT, MOM?
WE INSIST! YOU CAN SIT IN BILL'S CHAIR.
SO WHERE *IS* YOUR DAD, ANYWAY?
BUSINESS TRIP!

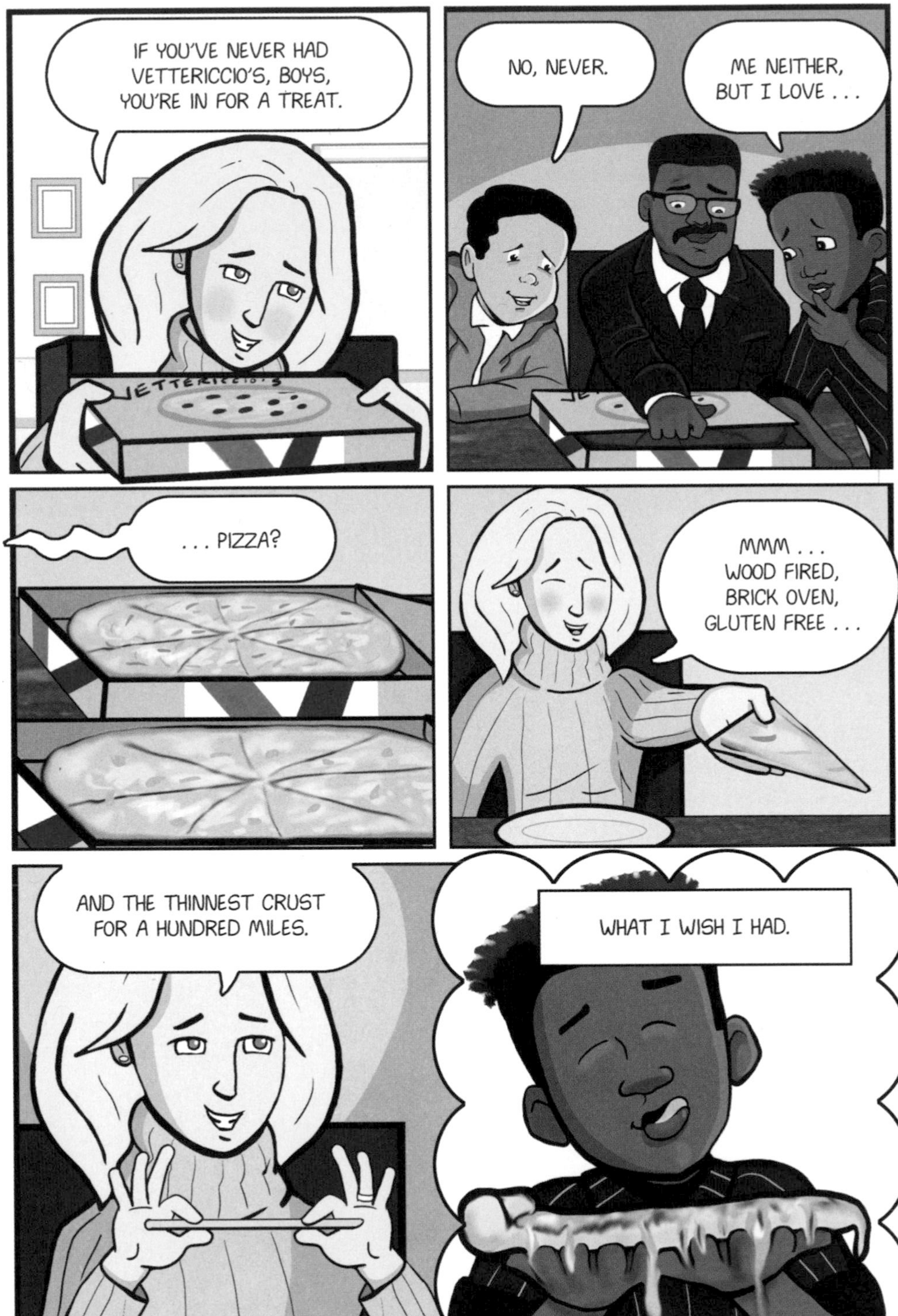

IF YOU'VE NEVER HAD VETTERICCIO'S, BOYS, YOU'RE IN FOR A TREAT.
VETTERICCIO'S
NO, NEVER.
ME NEITHER, BUT I LOVE . . .
. . . PIZZA?
MMM . . . WOOD FIRED, BRICK OVEN, GLUTEN FREE . . .
AND THE THINNEST CRUST FOR A HUNDRED MILES.
WHAT I WISH I HAD.

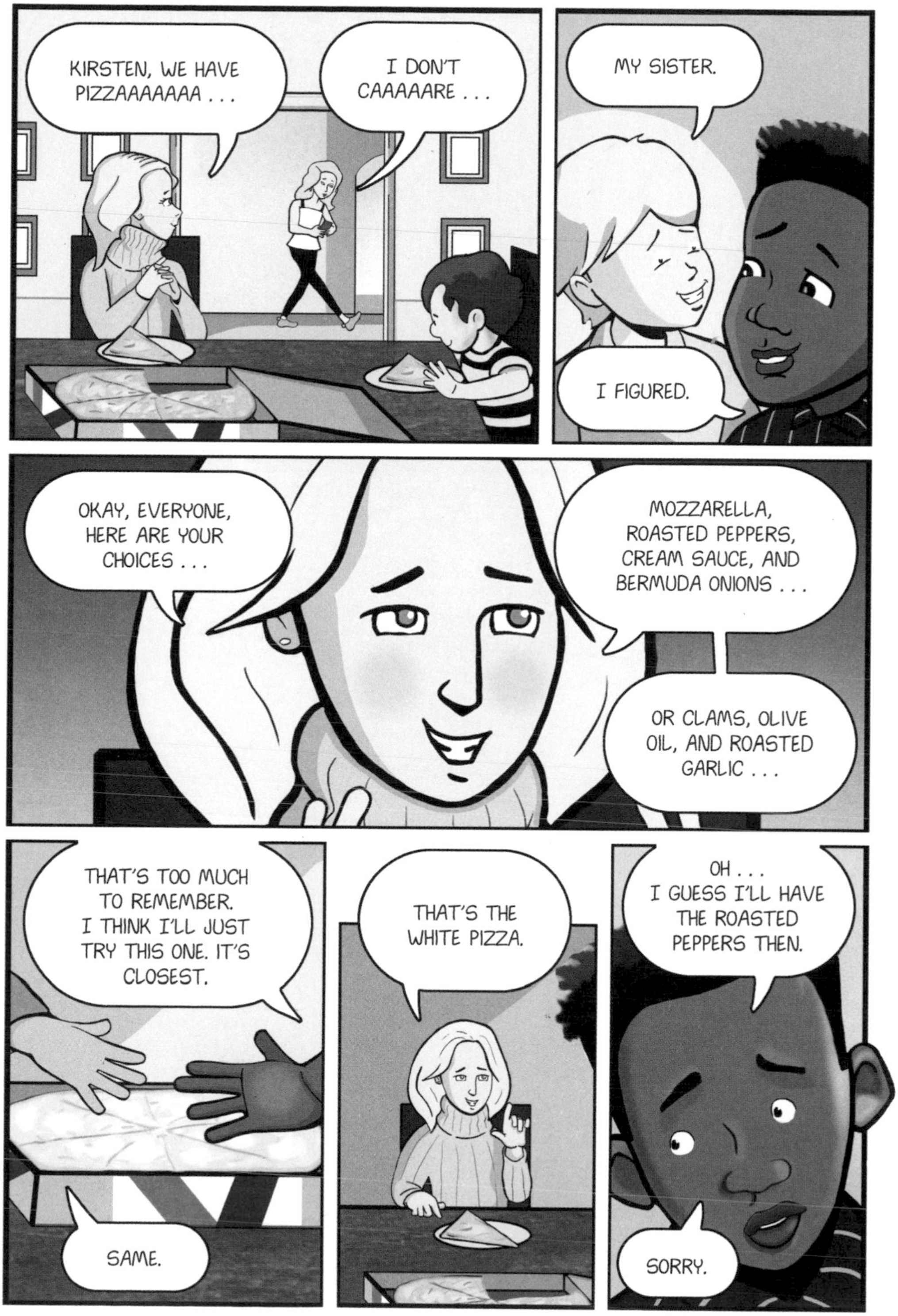
KIRSTEN, WE HAVE PIZZAAAAAAAA . . .
I DON'T CAAAAARE . . .
MY SISTER.
I FIGURED.
OKAY, EVERYONE, HERE ARE YOUR CHOICES . . .
MOZZARELLA, ROASTED PEPPERS, CREAM SAUCE, AND BERMUDA ONIONS . . .
OR CLAMS, OLIVE OIL, AND ROASTED GARLIC . . .
THAT'S TOO MUCH TO REMEMBER. I THINK I'LL JUST TRY THIS ONE. IT'S CLOSEST.
SAME.
THAT'S THE WHITE PIZZA.
OH . . . I GUESS I'LL HAVE THE ROASTED PEPPERS THEN.
SORRY.

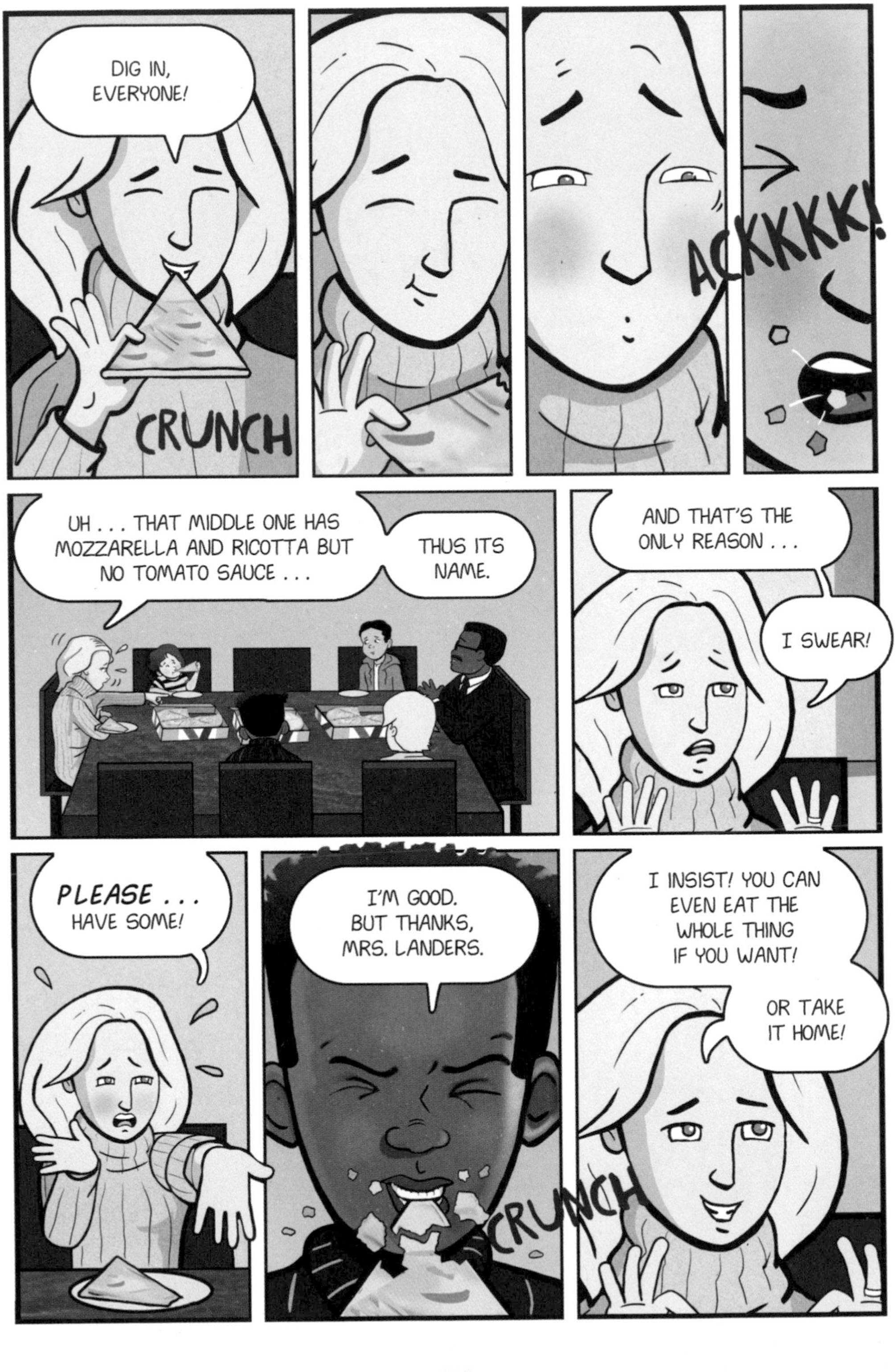
DIG IN, EVERYONE!
CRUNCH
ACKKKK!
UH . . . THAT MIDDLE ONE HAS MOZZARELLA AND RICOTTA BUT NO TOMATO SAUCE . . .
THUS ITS NAME.
AND THAT'S THE ONLY REASON . . .
I SWEAR!
PLEASE . . . HAVE SOME!
I'M GOOD. BUT THANKS, MRS. LANDERS.
CRUNCH
I INSIST! YOU CAN EVEN EAT THE WHOLE THING IF YOU WANT!
OR TAKE IT HOME!

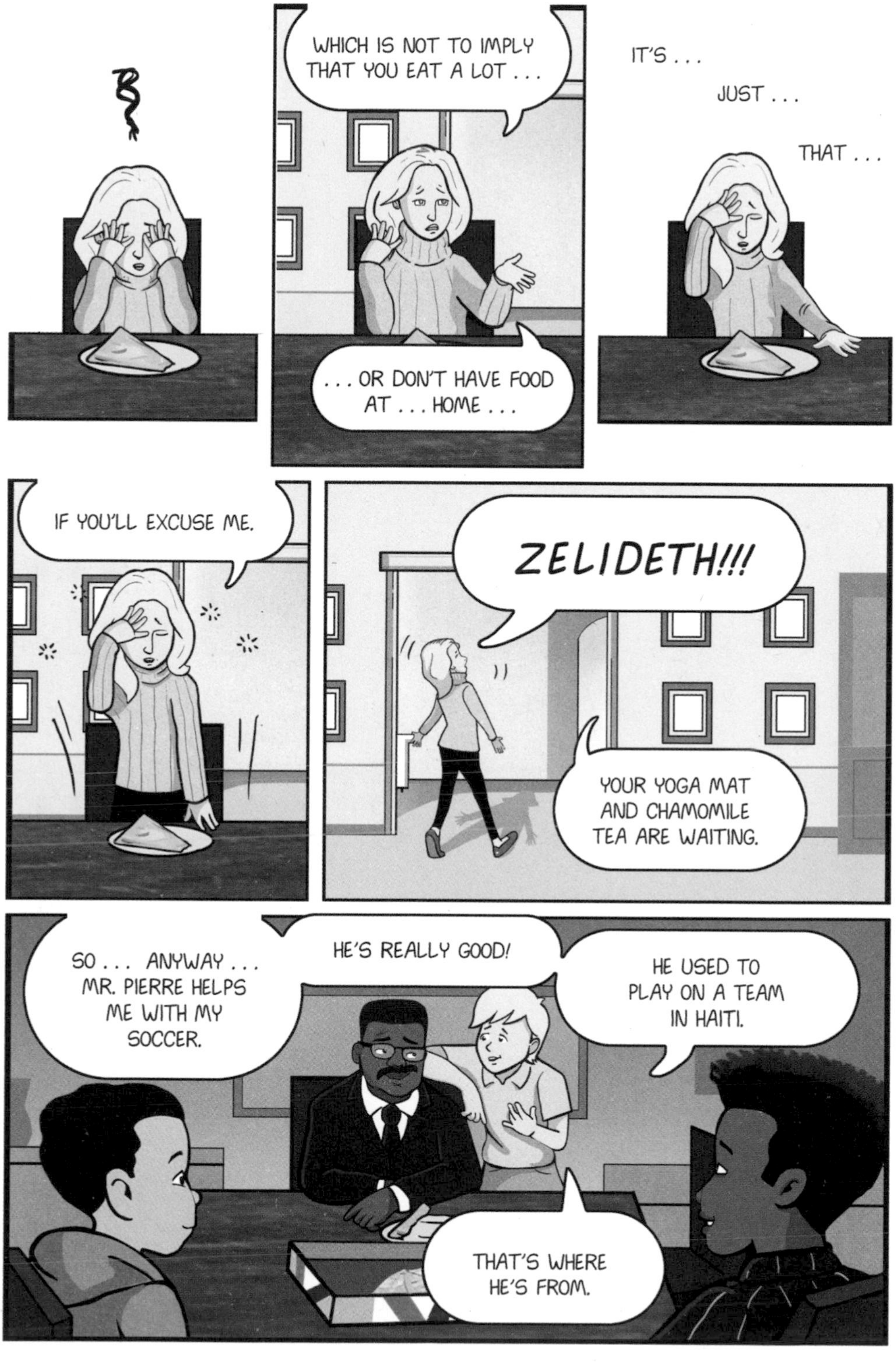
WHICH IS NOT TO IMPLY THAT YOU EAT A LOT . . .
. . . OR DON'T HAVE FOOD AT . . . HOME . . .
IT'S . . .
JUST . . .
THAT . . .
IF YOU'LL EXCUSE ME.
ZELIDETH!!!
YOUR YOGA MAT AND CHAMOMILE TEA ARE WAITING.
SO . . . ANYWAY . . . MR. PIERRE HELPS ME WITH MY SOCCER.
HE'S REALLY GOOD!
HE USED TO PLAY ON A TEAM IN HAITI.
THAT'S WHERE HE'S FROM.

OH, SO *YOU'RE* WHY LIAM IS SO GOOD.

LIAM IS A GREAT STUDENT.

MR. PIERRE HAS A SON MY AGE.

HIS NAME IS JULIAN AND HE STILL LIVES IN HAITI.

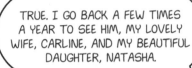

TRUE. I GO BACK A FEW TIMES A YEAR TO SEE HIM, MY LOVELY WIFE, CARLINE, AND MY BEAUTIFUL DAUGHTER, NATASHA.

WOW! YOU MEAN YOU LIVE HERE AND THEY LIVE THERE?

WHY?

THERE IS STILL A LOT OF REBUILDING BECAUSE OF THE EARTHQUAKE . . .

SO I WORK HERE AND SEND MONEY HOME.

BUT ENOUGH ABOUT ME. YOU SHOULD GO AND HAVE FUN.

OH, OKAY. NICE MEETING YOU.

LIKEWISE.

WOW! YOUR "DAD" IS COOL!

UGH! I CAN'T BELIEVE RUBY IS TELLING EVERYONE THAT.

SO *ANYWAY* . . . YOU WANNA PLAY XBOX OR PLAYSTATION?

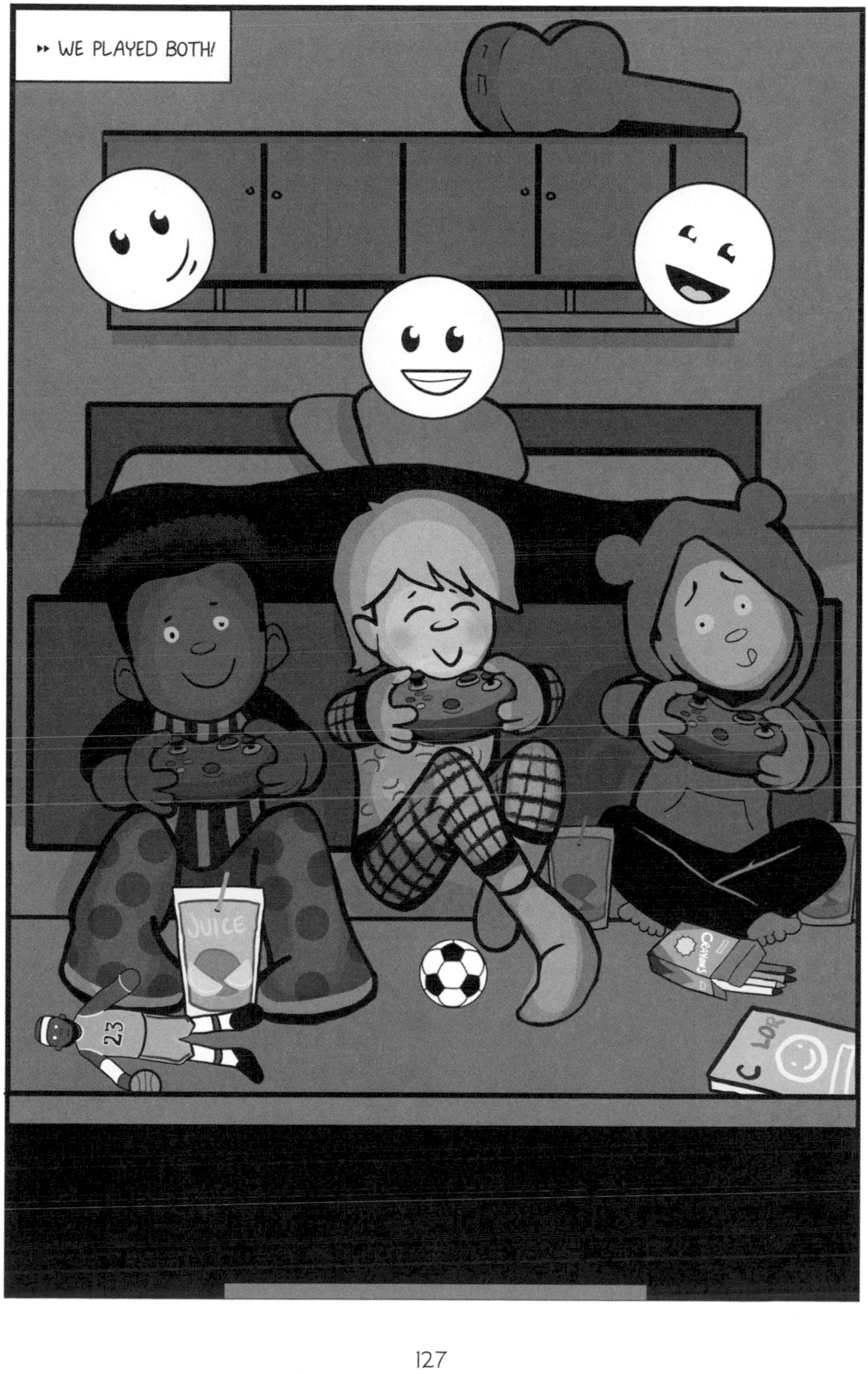
▸▸ WE PLAYED BOTH!
JUICE
23
CRAYONS
C LOR

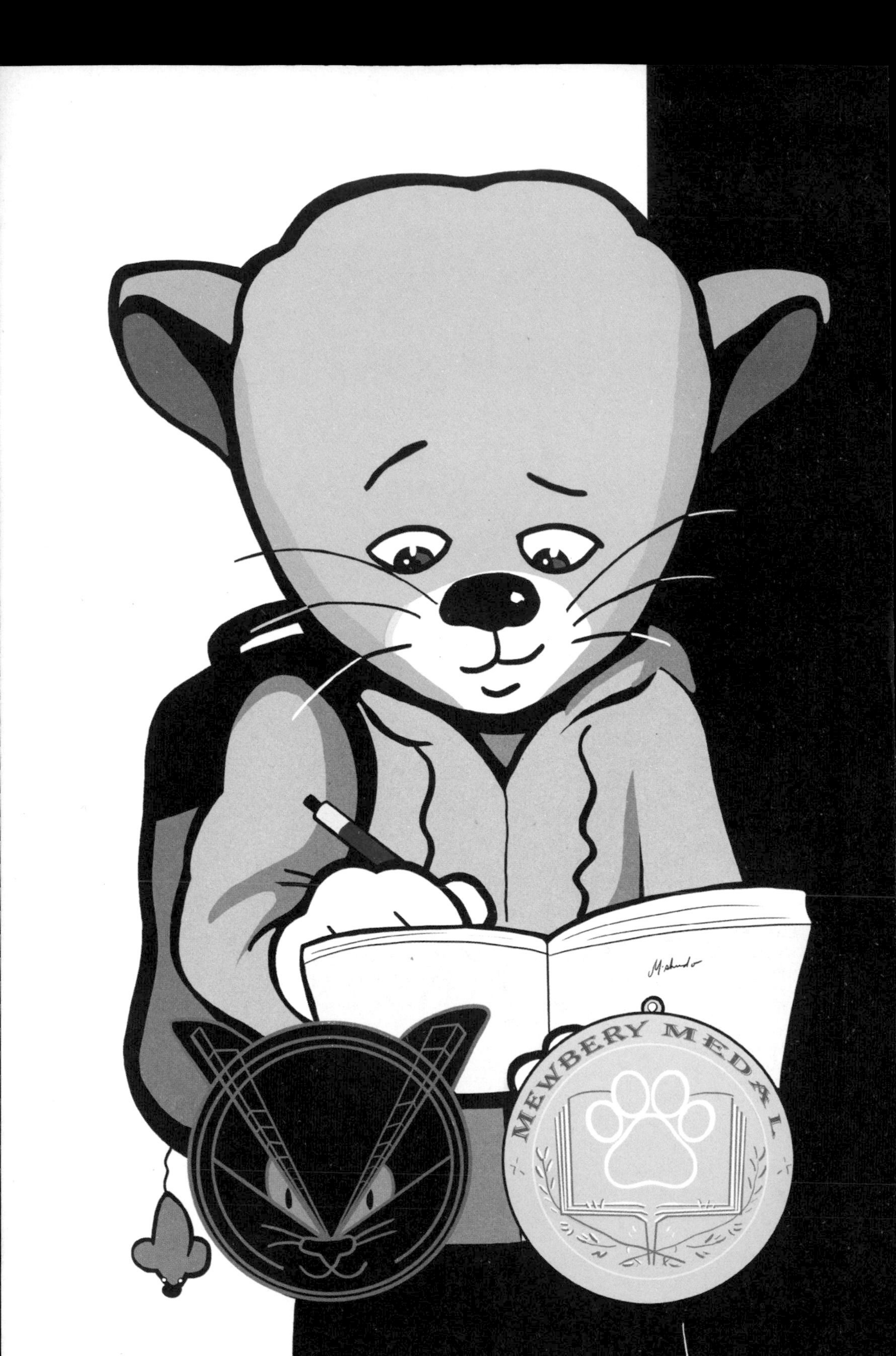
MEWBERY MEDAL

Obedience school
is hard enough
without being the . . .

MEW
KiD CHAPTER 7

Mew York Times bestselling pawthor

FURRY CRAFT

"Furry, sharp claws, and totally real.
Jordan Manx is the cat
everyone will be talking about."
-Jeff Kitty
Author of *Diary of a Wimpy Cat*

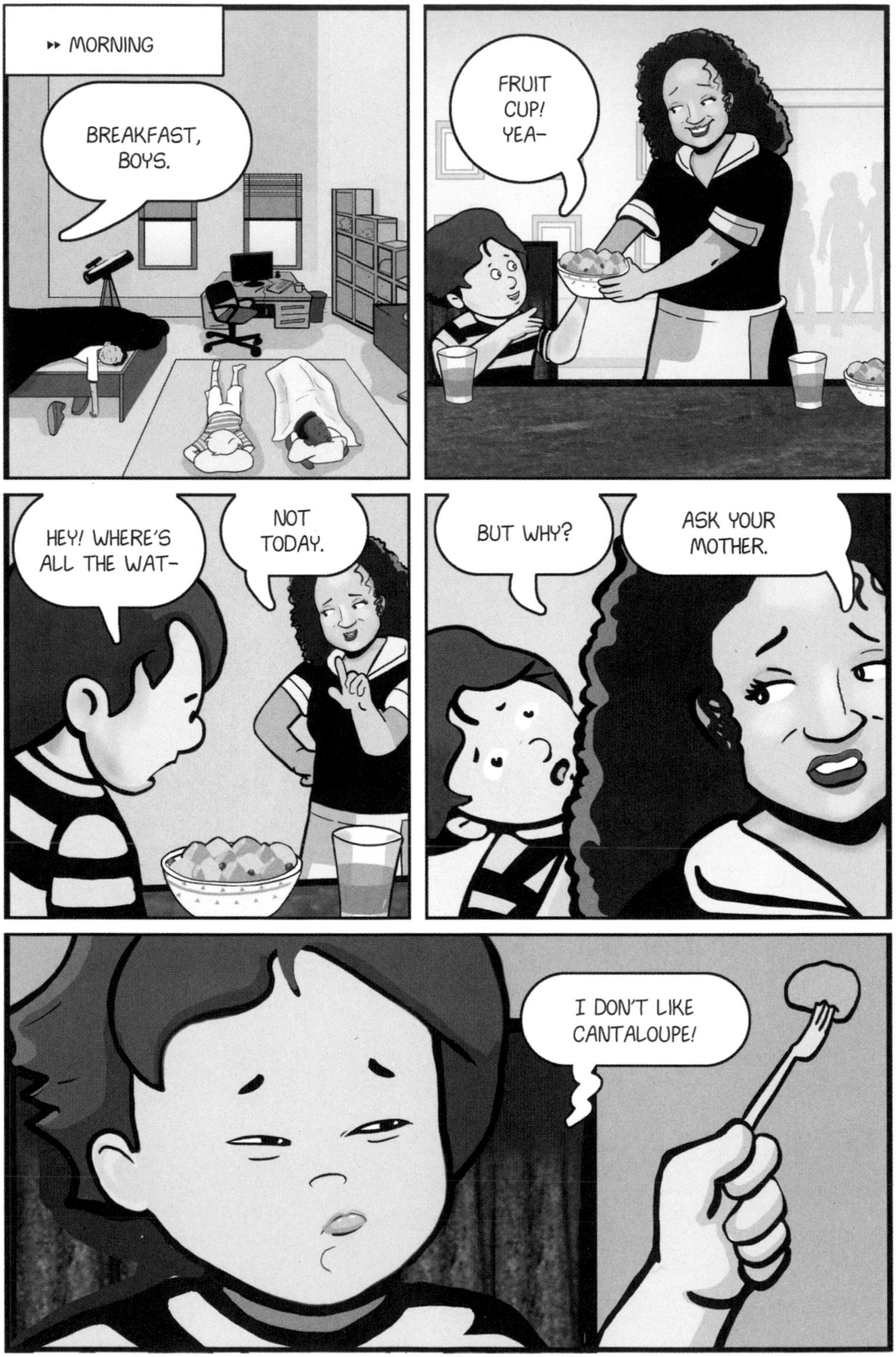
▸▸ MORNING
BREAKFAST, BOYS.
FRUIT CUP! YEA-
HEY! WHERE'S ALL THE WAT-
NOT TODAY.
BUT WHY?
ASK YOUR MOTHER.
I DON'T LIKE CANTALOUPE!

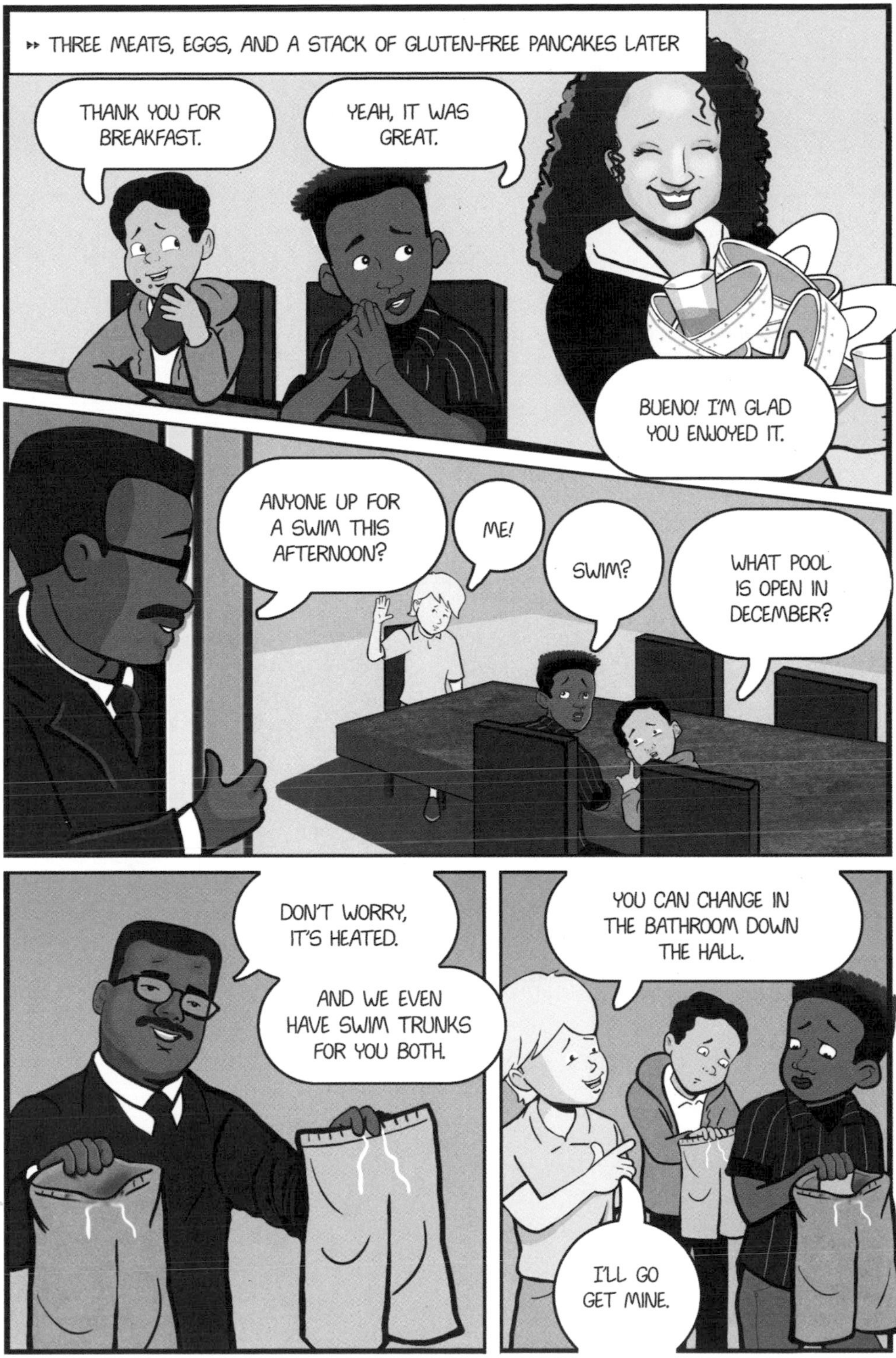
THREE MEATS, EGGS, AND A STACK OF GLUTEN-FREE PANCAKES LATER
THANK YOU FOR BREAKFAST.
YEAH, IT WAS GREAT.
BUENO! I'M GLAD YOU ENJOYED IT.
ANYONE UP FOR A SWIM THIS AFTERNOON?
ME!
SWIM?
WHAT POOL IS OPEN IN DECEMBER?
DON'T WORRY, IT'S HEATED.
AND WE EVEN HAVE SWIM TRUNKS FOR YOU BOTH.
YOU CAN CHANGE IN THE BATHROOM DOWN THE HALL.
I'LL GO GET MINE.

MAN! THEY'VE GOT A POOL, TOO?

APPARENTLY. HE NEVER MENTIONED IT THOUGH.

DID HE SAY THE DOOR ON THE LEFT OR ON THE RIGHT?

I WASN'T LISTENING.

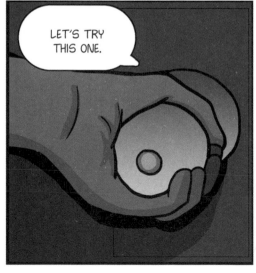

LET'S TRY THIS ONE.

JORDAN!

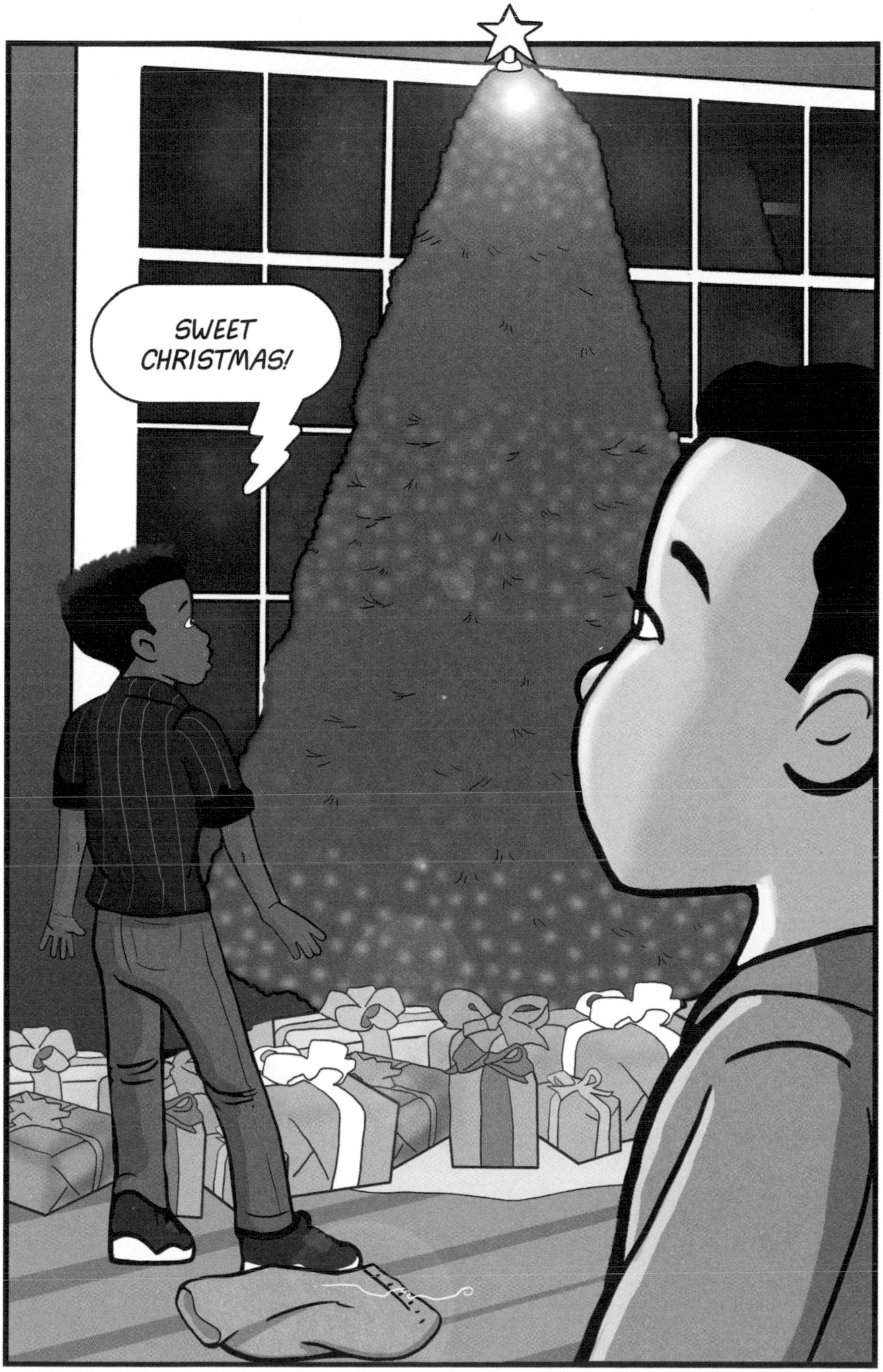
SWEET CHRISTMAS!

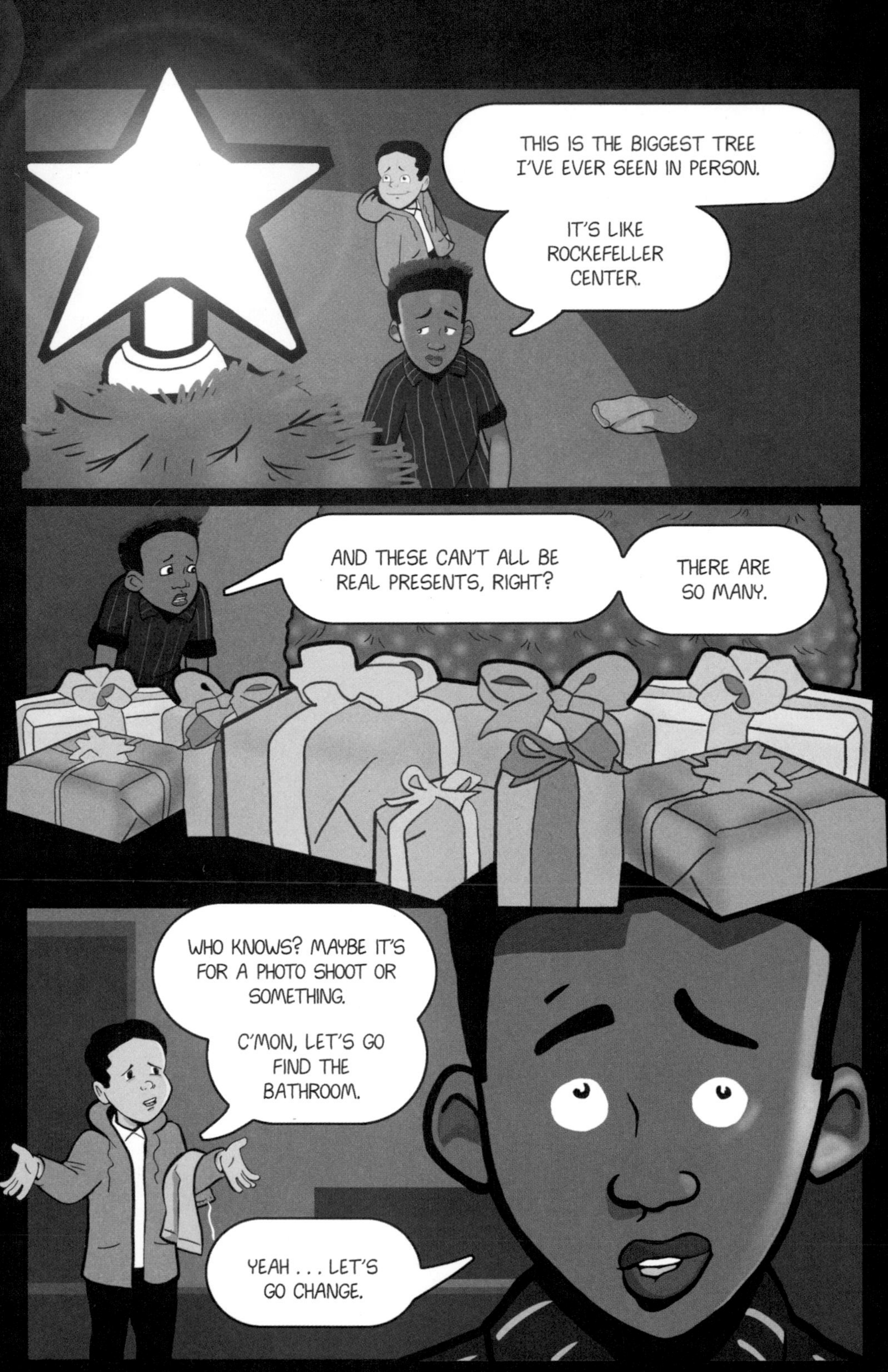
THIS IS THE BIGGEST TREE I'VE EVER SEEN IN PERSON.
IT'S LIKE ROCKEFELLER CENTER.
AND THESE CAN'T ALL BE REAL PRESENTS, RIGHT?
THERE ARE SO MANY.
WHO KNOWS? MAYBE IT'S FOR A PHOTO SHOOT OR SOMETHING.
C'MON, LET'S GO FIND THE BATHROOM.
YEAH . . . LET'S GO CHANGE.

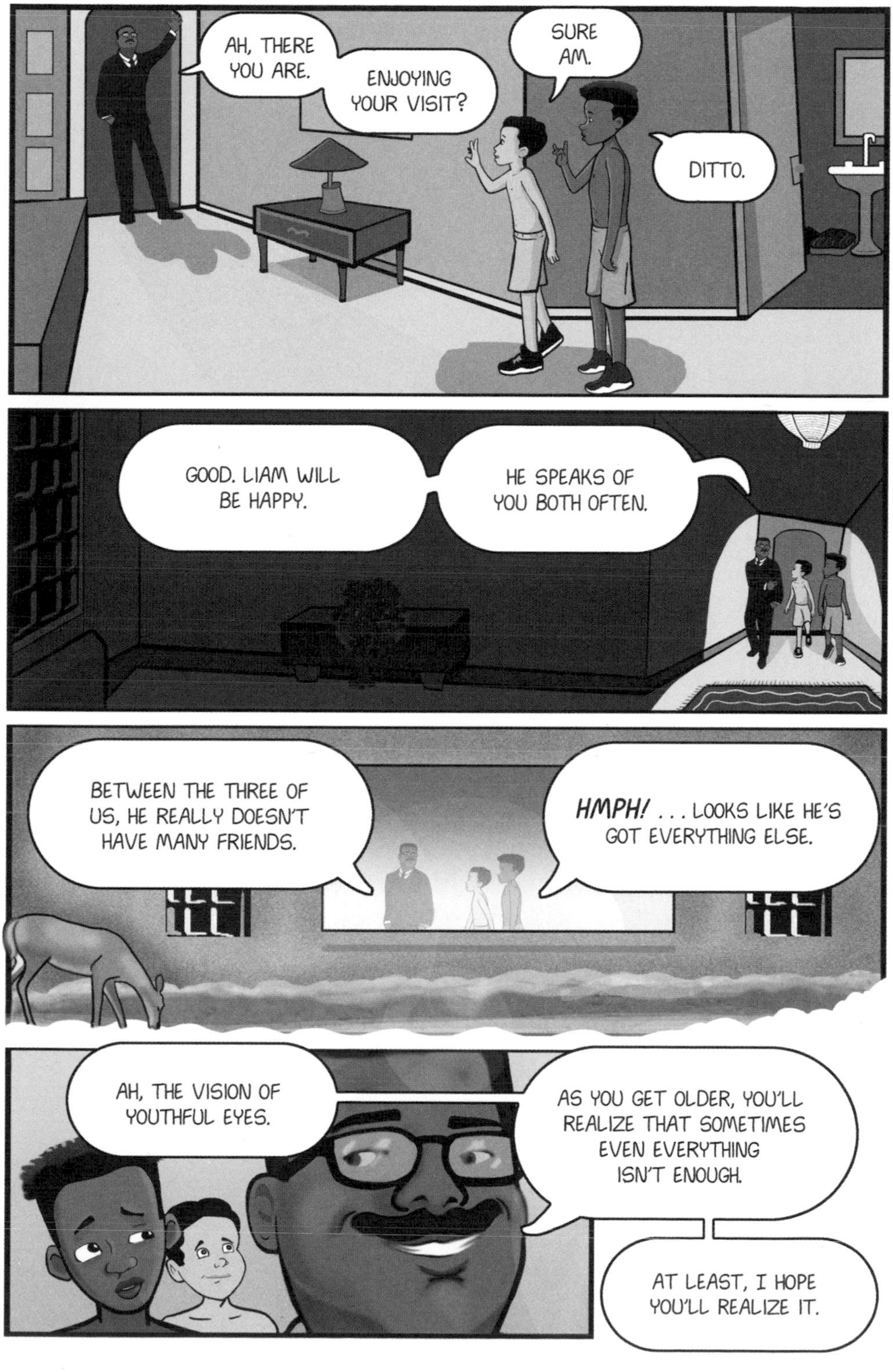
AH, THERE YOU ARE.
ENJOYING YOUR VISIT?
SURE AM.
DITTO.
GOOD. LIAM WILL BE HAPPY.
HE SPEAKS OF YOU BOTH OFTEN.
BETWEEN THE THREE OF US, HE REALLY DOESN'T HAVE MANY FRIENDS.
HMPH! . . . LOOKS LIKE HE'S GOT EVERYTHING ELSE.
AH, THE VISION OF YOUTHFUL EYES.
AS YOU GET OLDER, YOU'LL REALIZE THAT SOMETIMES EVEN EVERYTHING ISN'T ENOUGH.
AT LEAST, I HOPE YOU'LL REALIZE IT.

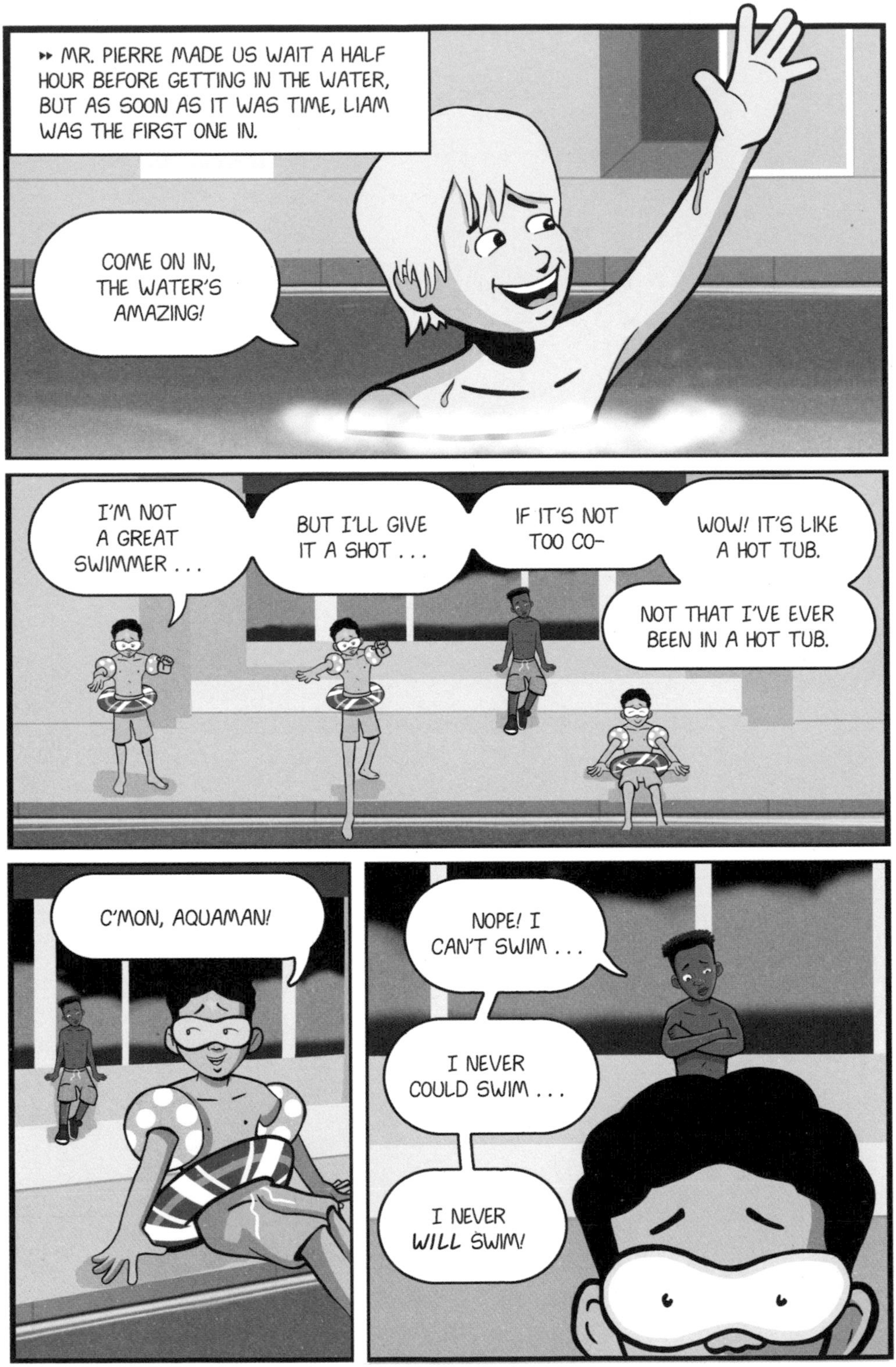
MR. PIERRE MADE US WAIT A HALF HOUR BEFORE GETTING IN THE WATER, BUT AS SOON AS IT WAS TIME, LIAM WAS THE FIRST ONE IN.
COME ON IN, THE WATER'S AMAZING!
I'M NOT A GREAT SWIMMER . . .
BUT I'LL GIVE IT A SHOT . . .
IF IT'S NOT TOO CO-
WOW! IT'S LIKE A HOT TUB.
NOT THAT I'VE EVER BEEN IN A HOT TUB.
C'MON, AQUAMAN!
NOPE! I CAN'T SWIM . . .
I NEVER COULD SWIM . . .
I NEVER ***WILL*** SWIM!

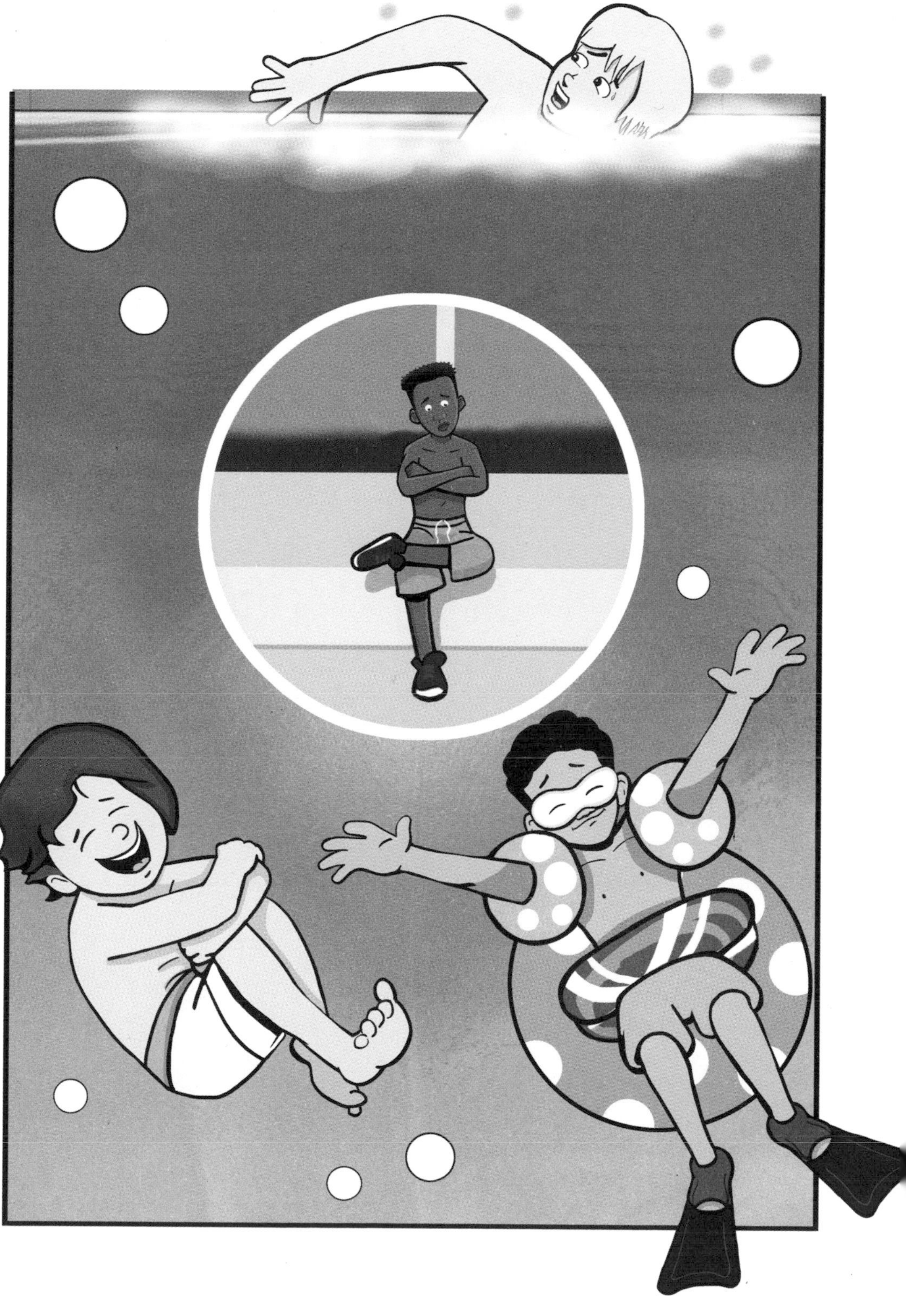

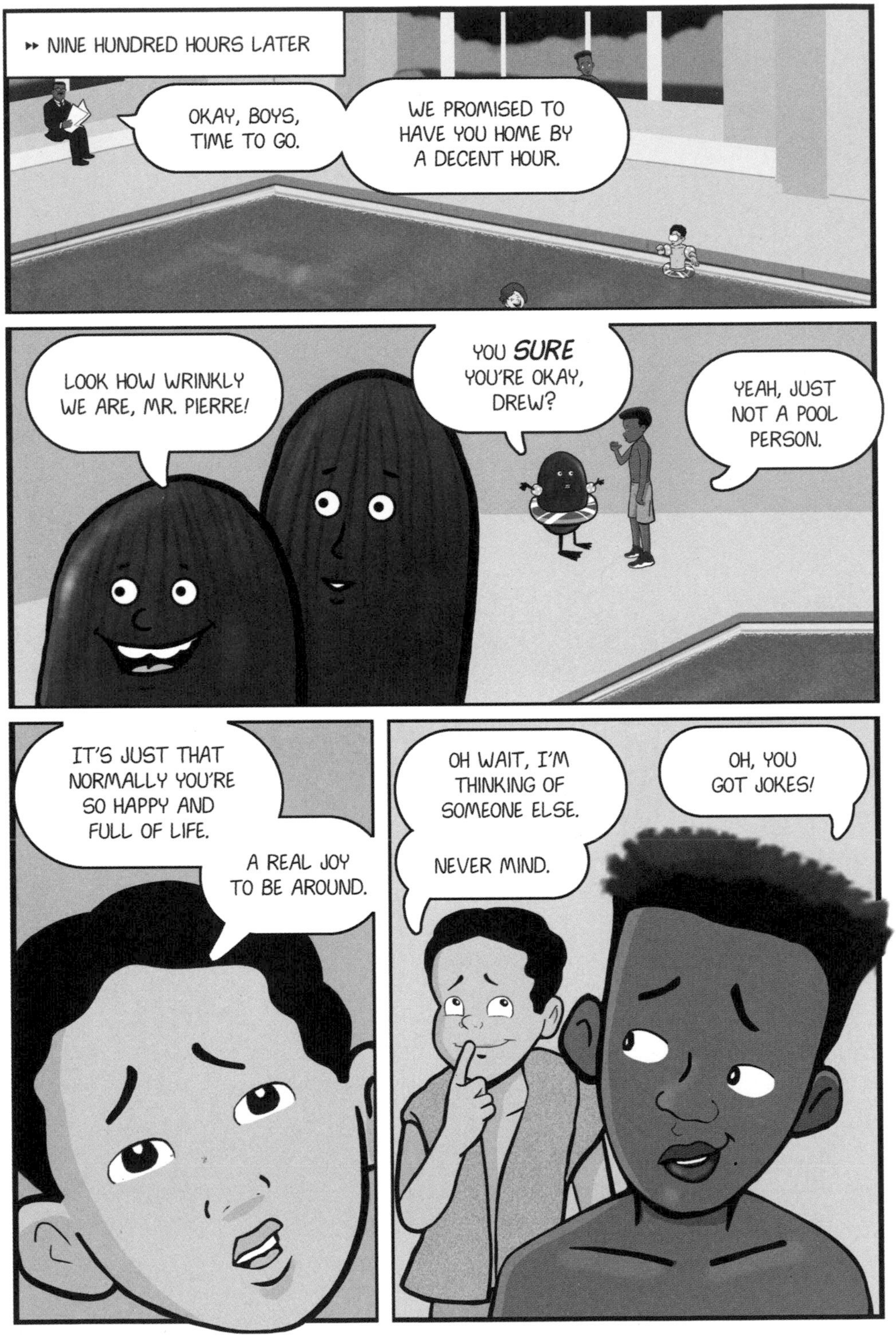

▸▸ NINE HUNDRED HOURS LATER
OKAY, BOYS, TIME TO GO.
WE PROMISED TO HAVE YOU HOME BY A DECENT HOUR.
LOOK HOW WRINKLY WE ARE, MR. PIERRE!
YOU **SURE** YOU'RE OKAY, DREW?
YEAH, JUST NOT A POOL PERSON.
IT'S JUST THAT NORMALLY YOU'RE SO HAPPY AND FULL OF LIFE.
A REAL JOY TO BE AROUND.
OH WAIT, I'M THINKING OF SOMEONE ELSE.
NEVER MIND.
OH, YOU GOT JOKES!

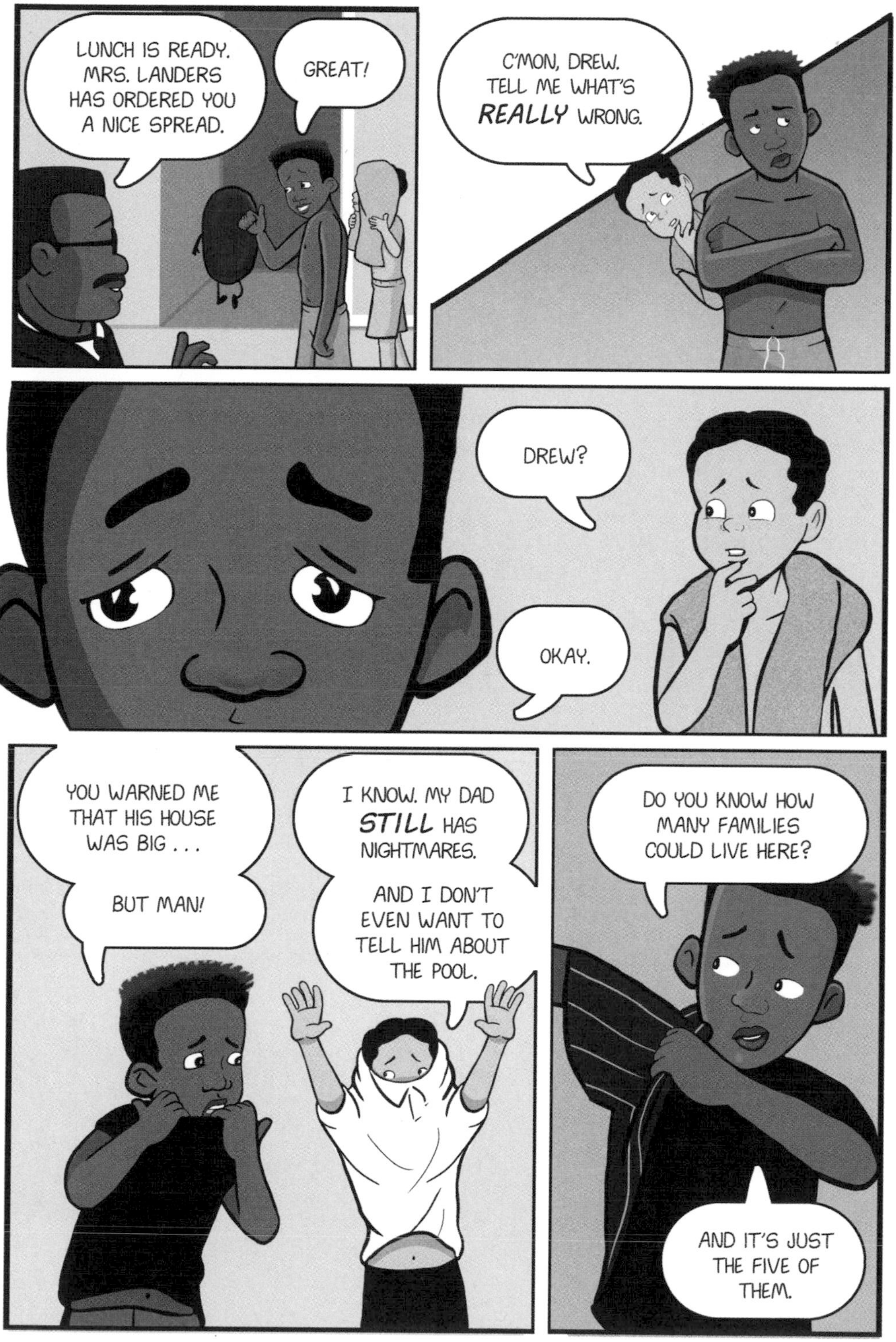
LUNCH IS READY. MRS. LANDERS HAS ORDERED YOU A NICE SPREAD.
GREAT!
C'MON, DREW. TELL ME WHAT'S REALLY WRONG.
DREW?
OKAY.
YOU WARNED ME THAT HIS HOUSE WAS BIG . . .
BUT MAN!
I KNOW. MY DAD STILL HAS NIGHTMARES.
AND I DON'T EVEN WANT TO TELL HIM ABOUT THE POOL.
DO YOU KNOW HOW MANY FAMILIES COULD LIVE HERE?
AND IT'S JUST THE FIVE OF THEM.

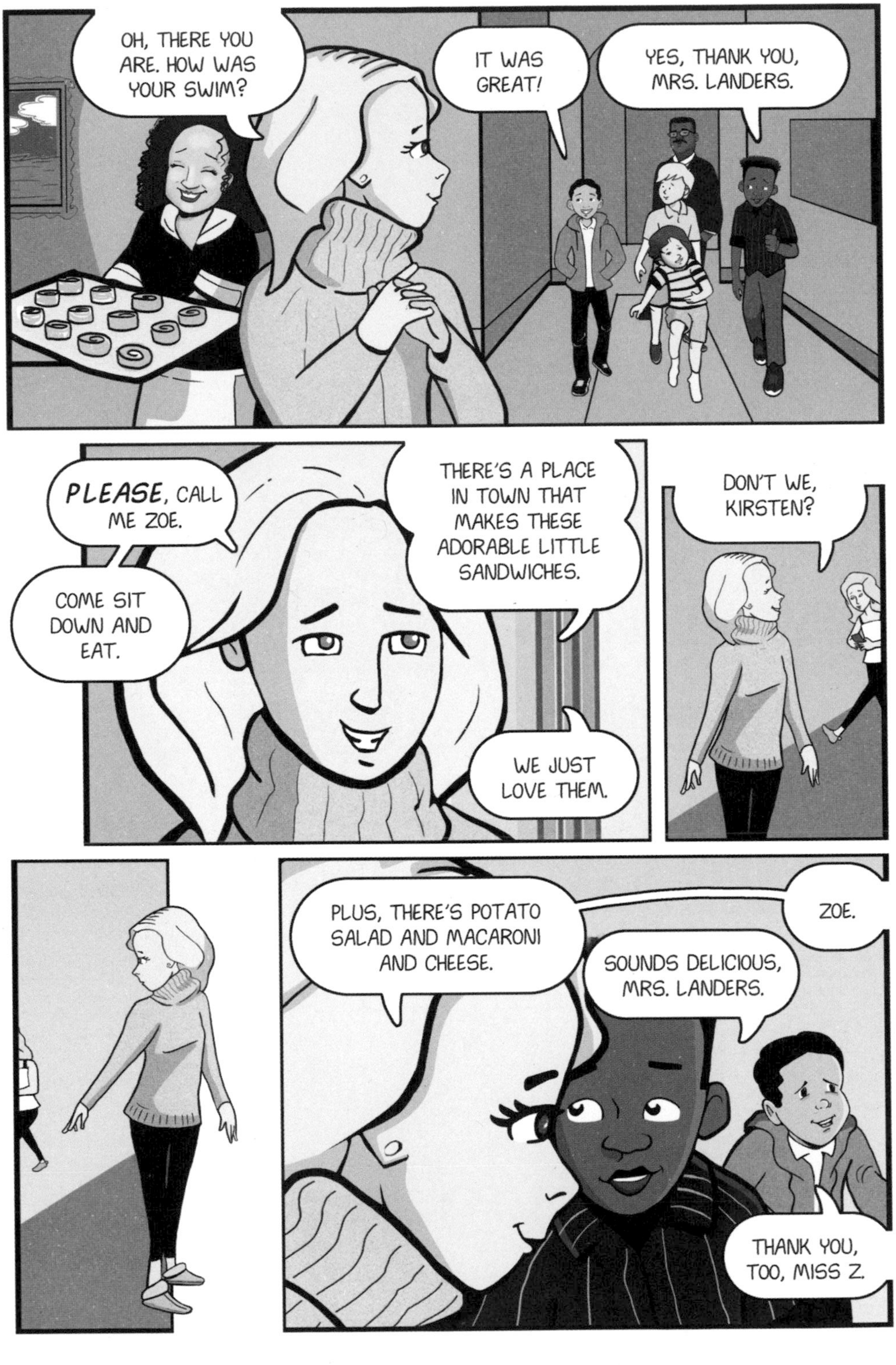
OH, THERE YOU ARE. HOW WAS YOUR SWIM?
IT WAS GREAT!
YES, THANK YOU, MRS. LANDERS.
PLEASE, CALL ME ZOE.
COME SIT DOWN AND EAT.
THERE'S A PLACE IN TOWN THAT MAKES THESE ADORABLE LITTLE SANDWICHES.
WE JUST LOVE THEM.
DON'T WE, KIRSTEN?
PLUS, THERE'S POTATO SALAD AND MACARONI AND CHEESE.
SOUNDS DELICIOUS, MRS. LANDERS.
ZOE.
THANK YOU, TOO, MISS Z.

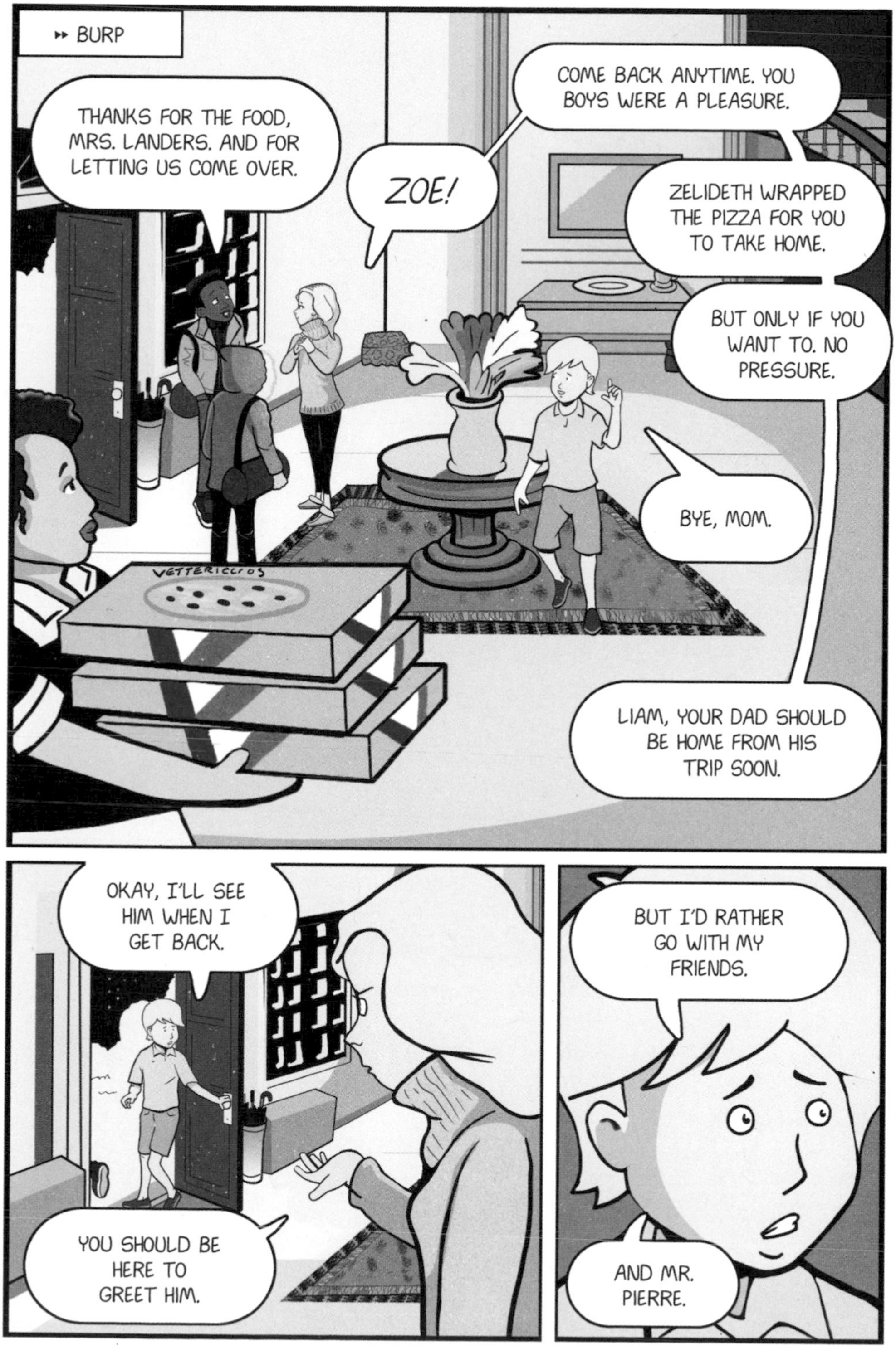
▸▸ BURP
THANKS FOR THE FOOD, MRS. LANDERS. AND FOR LETTING US COME OVER.
ZOE!
COME BACK ANYTIME. YOU BOYS WERE A PLEASURE.
ZELIDETH WRAPPED THE PIZZA FOR YOU TO TAKE HOME.
BUT ONLY IF YOU WANT TO. NO PRESSURE.
BYE, MOM.
LIAM, YOUR DAD SHOULD BE HOME FROM HIS TRIP SOON.
VETTERICCIOS
OKAY, I'LL SEE HIM WHEN I GET BACK.
YOU SHOULD BE HERE TO GREET HIM.
BUT I'D RATHER GO WITH MY FRIENDS.
AND MR. PIERRE.

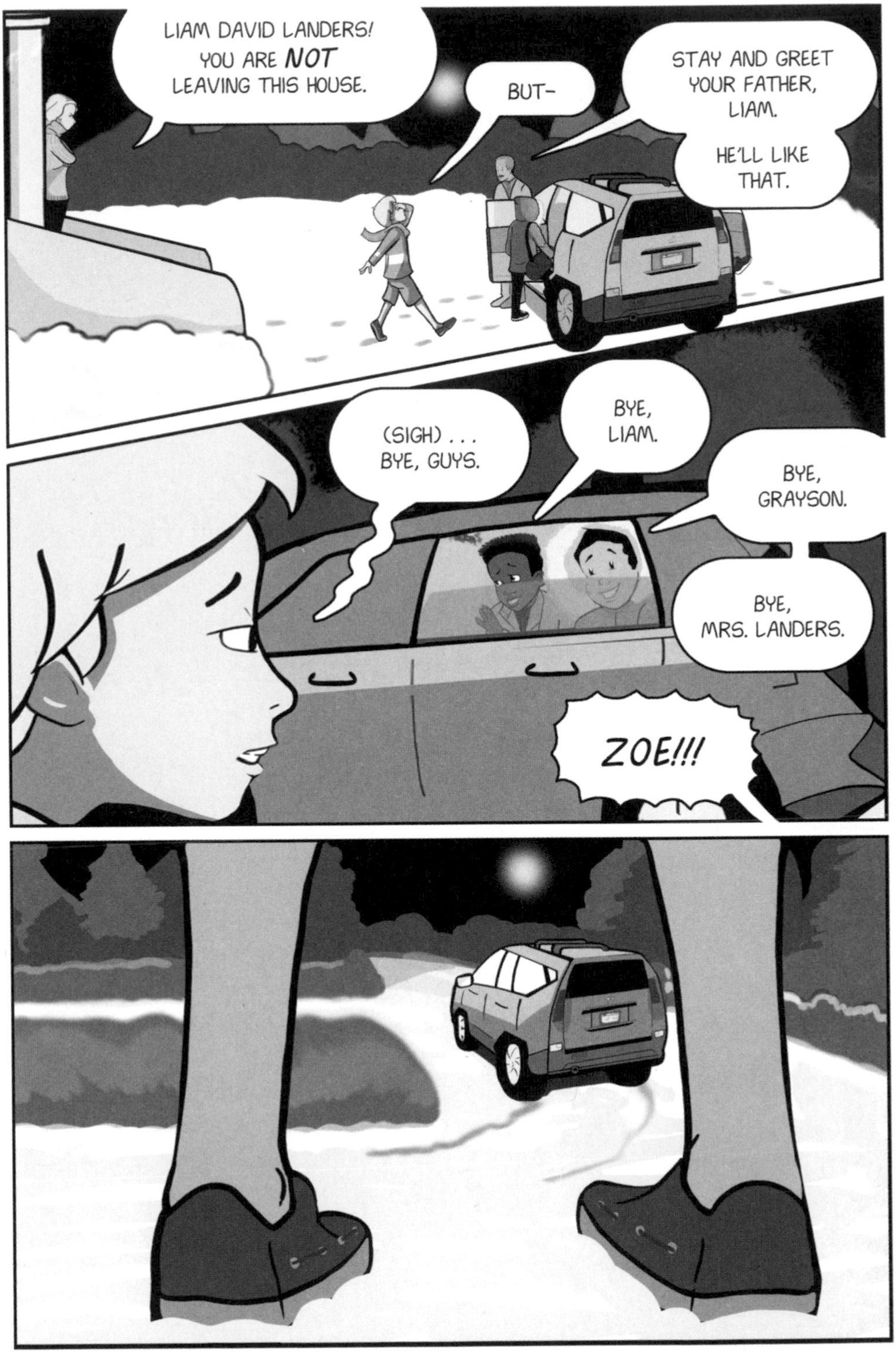
LIAM DAVID LANDERS! YOU ARE NOT LEAVING THIS HOUSE.
BUT-
STAY AND GREET YOUR FATHER, LIAM.
HE'LL LIKE THAT.
(SIGH) . . . BYE, GUYS.
BYE, LIAM.
BYE, GRAYSON.
BYE, MRS. LANDERS.
ZOE!!!

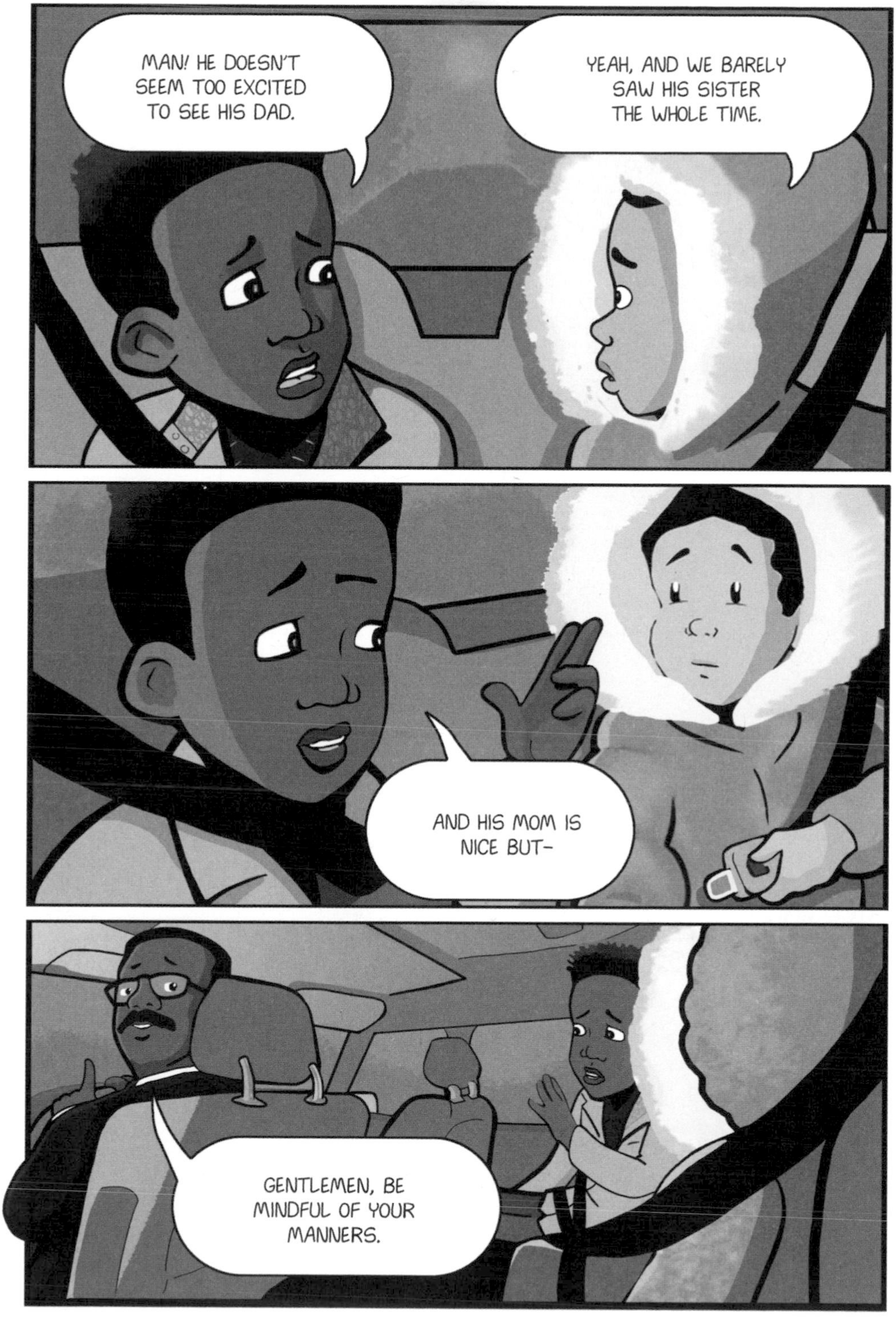
MAN! HE DOESN'T SEEM TOO EXCITED TO SEE HIS DAD.
YEAH, AND WE BARELY SAW HIS SISTER THE WHOLE TIME.
AND HIS MOM IS NICE BUT-
GENTLEMEN, BE MINDFUL OF YOUR MANNERS.

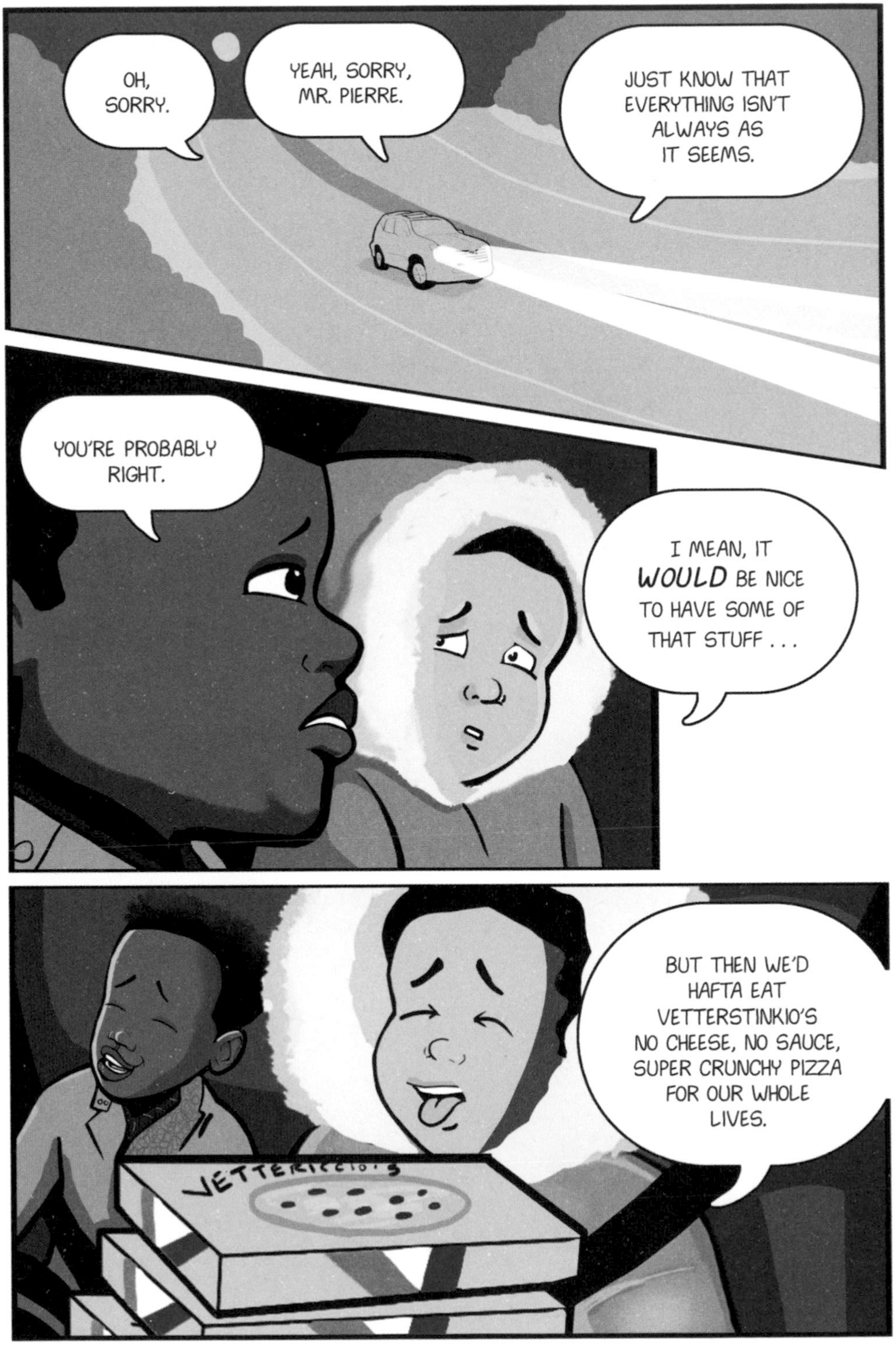
OH, SORRY.
YEAH, SORRY, MR. PIERRE.
JUST KNOW THAT EVERYTHING ISN'T ALWAYS AS IT SEEMS.
YOU'RE PROBABLY RIGHT.
I MEAN, IT **WOULD** BE NICE TO HAVE SOME OF THAT STUFF . . .
BUT THEN WE'D HAFTA EAT VETTERSTINKIO'S NO CHEESE, NO SAUCE, SUPER CRUNCHY PIZZA FOR OUR WHOLE LIVES.
VETTERICCIO'S

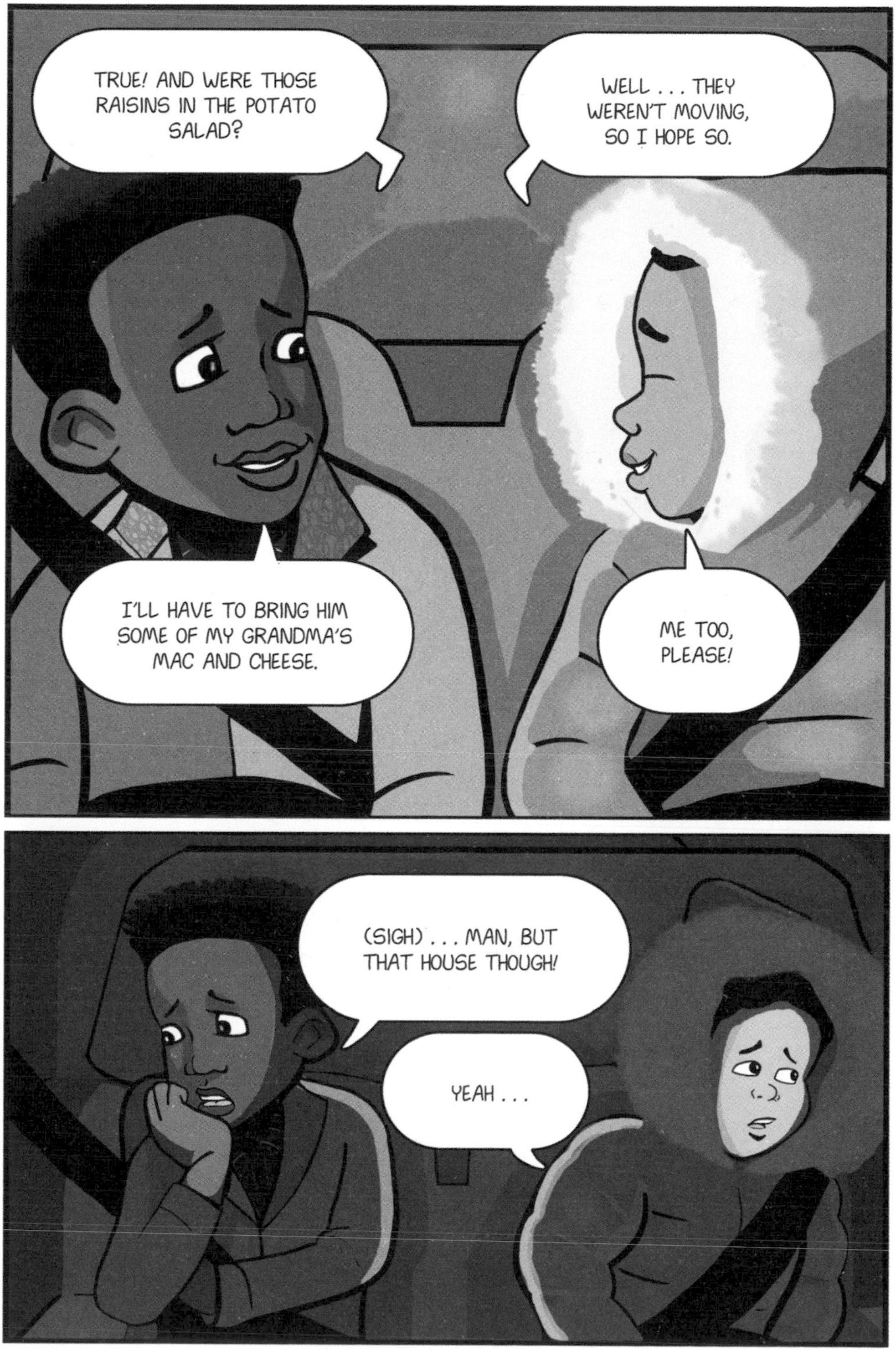
TRUE! AND WERE THOSE RAISINS IN THE POTATO SALAD?
WELL . . . THEY WEREN'T MOVING, SO I HOPE SO.
I'LL HAVE TO BRING HIM SOME OF MY GRANDMA'S MAC AND CHEESE.
ME TOO, PLEASE!
(SIGH) . . . MAN, BUT THAT HOUSE THOUGH!
YEAH . . .

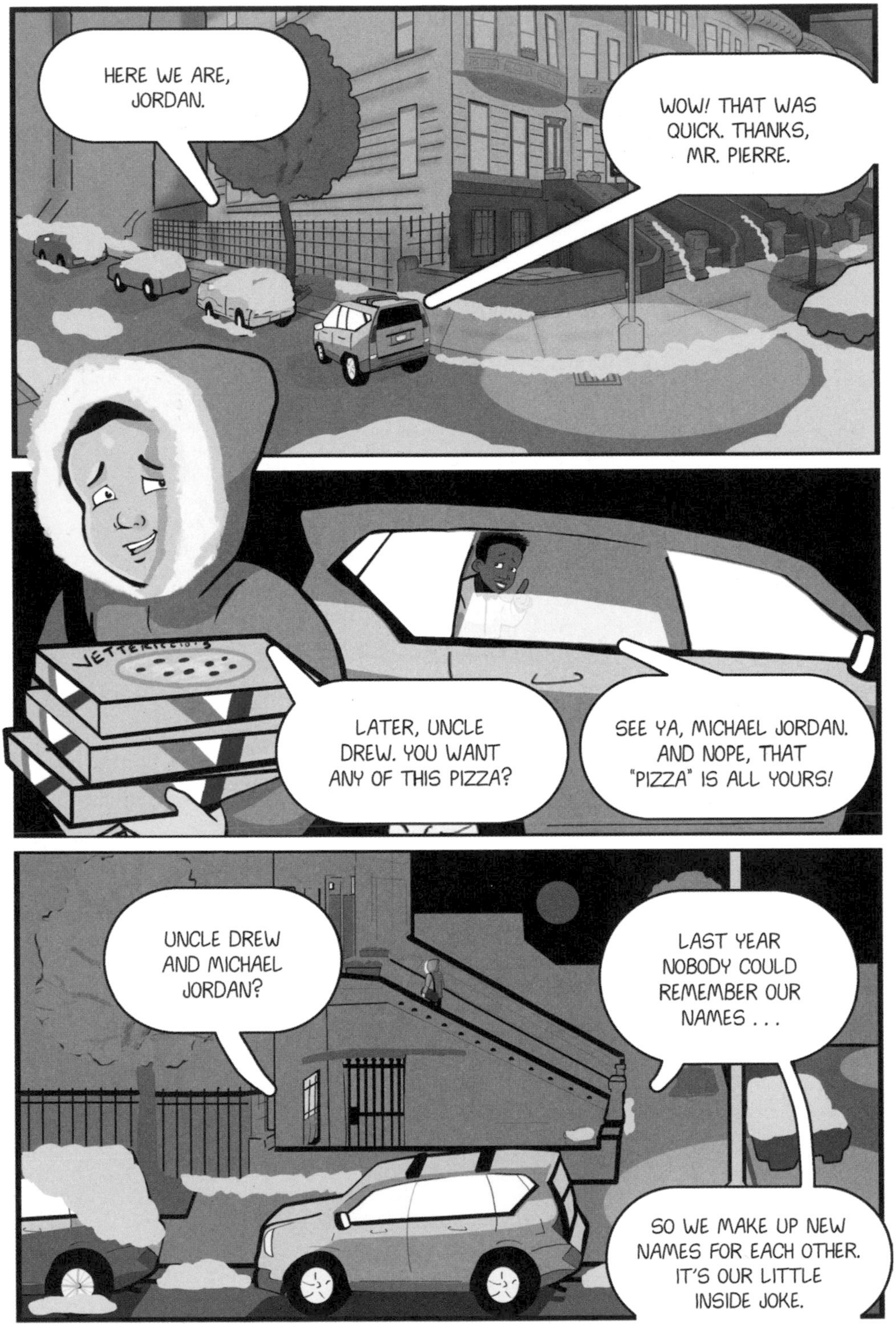
HERE WE ARE, JORDAN.
WOW! THAT WAS QUICK. THANKS, MR. PIERRE.
LATER, UNCLE DREW. YOU WANT ANY OF THIS PIZZA?
SEE YA, MICHAEL JORDAN. AND NOPE, THAT "PIZZA" IS ALL YOURS!
UNCLE DREW AND MICHAEL JORDAN?
LAST YEAR NOBODY COULD REMEMBER OUR NAMES . . .
SO WE MAKE UP NEW NAMES FOR EACH OTHER. IT'S OUR LITTLE INSIDE JOKE.

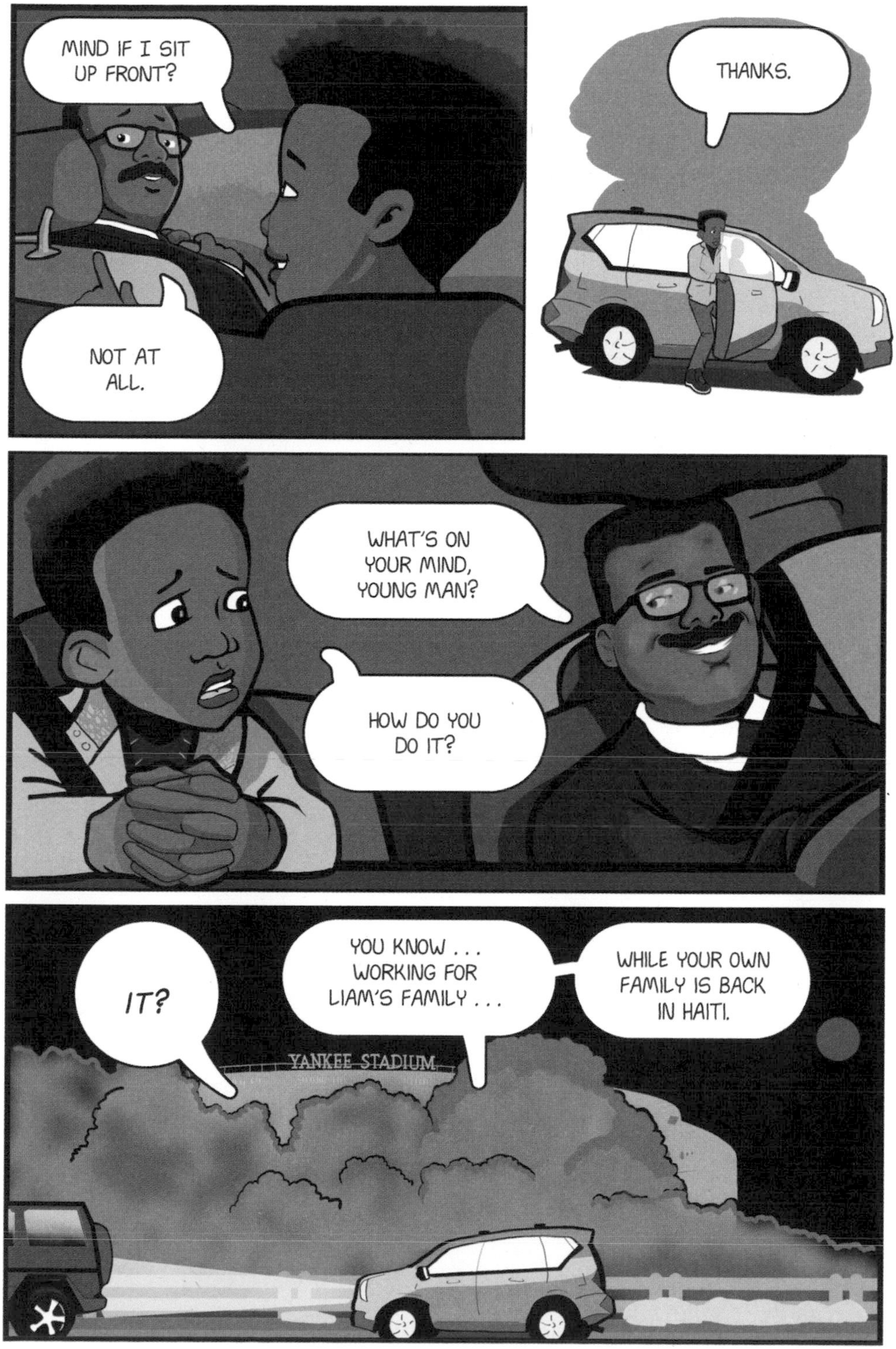
MIND IF I SIT UP FRONT?
NOT AT ALL.
THANKS.
WHAT'S ON YOUR MIND, YOUNG MAN?
HOW DO YOU DO IT?
IT?
YOU KNOW . . . WORKING FOR LIAM'S FAMILY . . .
WHILE YOUR OWN FAMILY IS BACK IN HAITI.
YANKEE STADIUM

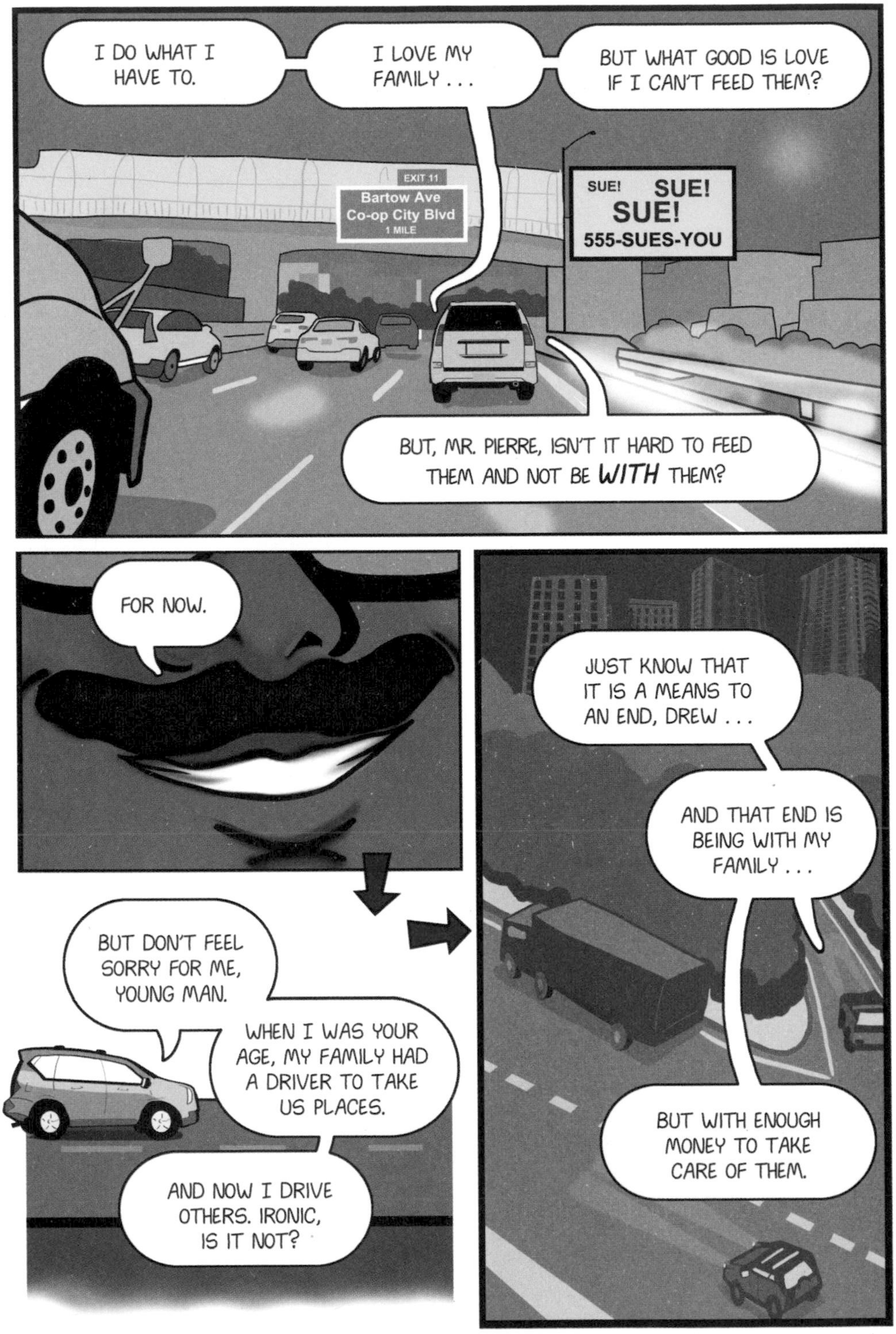
I DO WHAT I HAVE TO.
I LOVE MY FAMILY . . .
BUT WHAT GOOD IS LOVE IF I CAN'T FEED THEM?
EXIT 11
Bartow Ave
Co-op City Blvd
1 MILE
SUE! SUE!
SUE!
555-SUES-YOU
BUT, MR. PIERRE, ISN'T IT HARD TO FEED THEM AND NOT BE *WITH* THEM?
FOR NOW.
BUT DON'T FEEL SORRY FOR ME, YOUNG MAN.
WHEN I WAS YOUR AGE, MY FAMILY HAD A DRIVER TO TAKE US PLACES.
AND NOW I DRIVE OTHERS. IRONIC, IS IT NOT?
JUST KNOW THAT IT IS A MEANS TO AN END, DREW . . .
AND THAT END IS BEING WITH MY FAMILY . . .
BUT WITH ENOUGH MONEY TO TAKE CARE OF THEM.

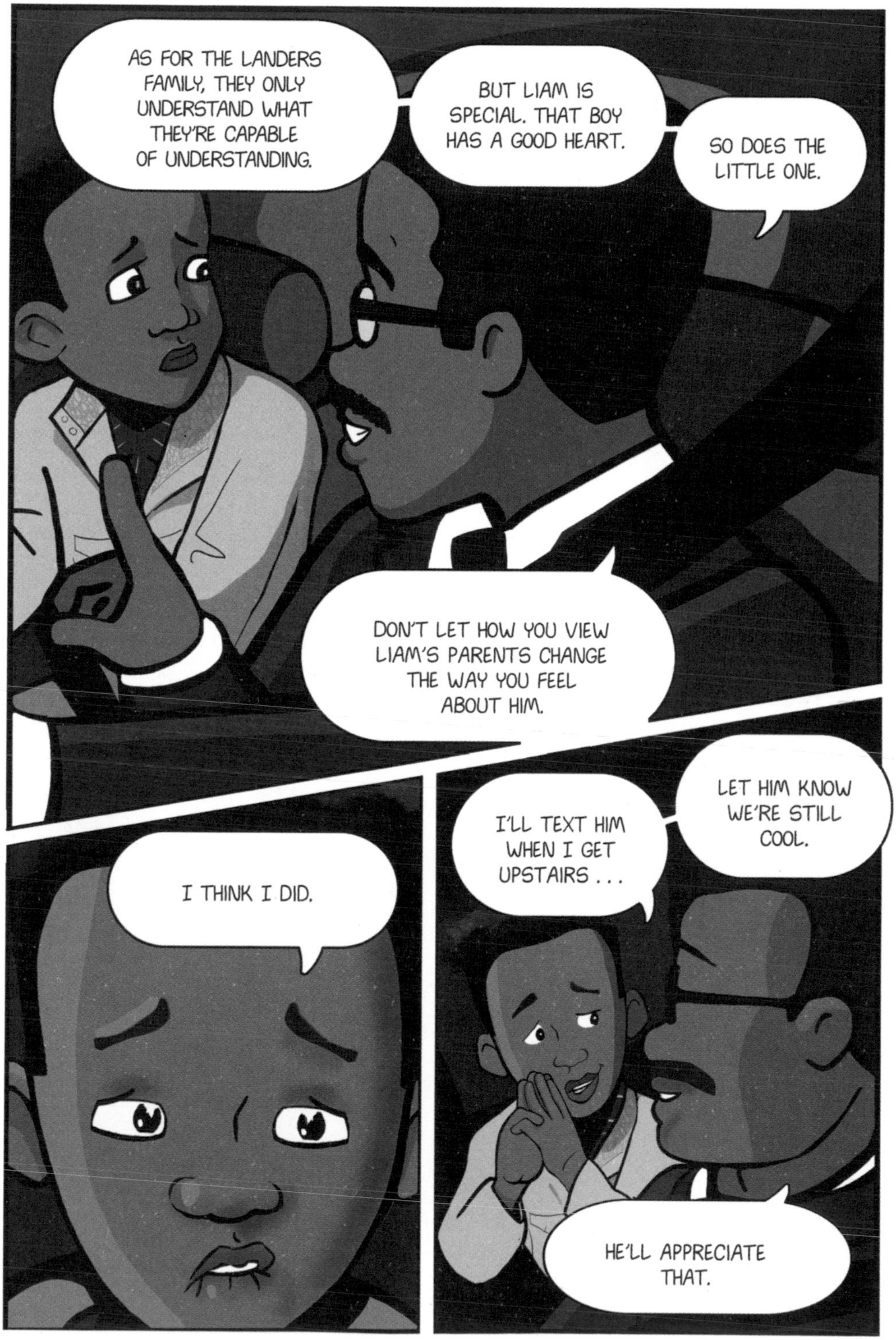
AS FOR THE LANDERS FAMILY, THEY ONLY UNDERSTAND WHAT THEY'RE CAPABLE OF UNDERSTANDING.
BUT LIAM IS SPECIAL. THAT BOY HAS A GOOD HEART.
SO DOES THE LITTLE ONE.
DON'T LET HOW YOU VIEW LIAM'S PARENTS CHANGE THE WAY YOU FEEL ABOUT HIM.
I THINK I DID.
I'LL TEXT HIM WHEN I GET UPSTAIRS . . .
LET HIM KNOW WE'RE STILL COOL.
HE'LL APPRECIATE THAT.

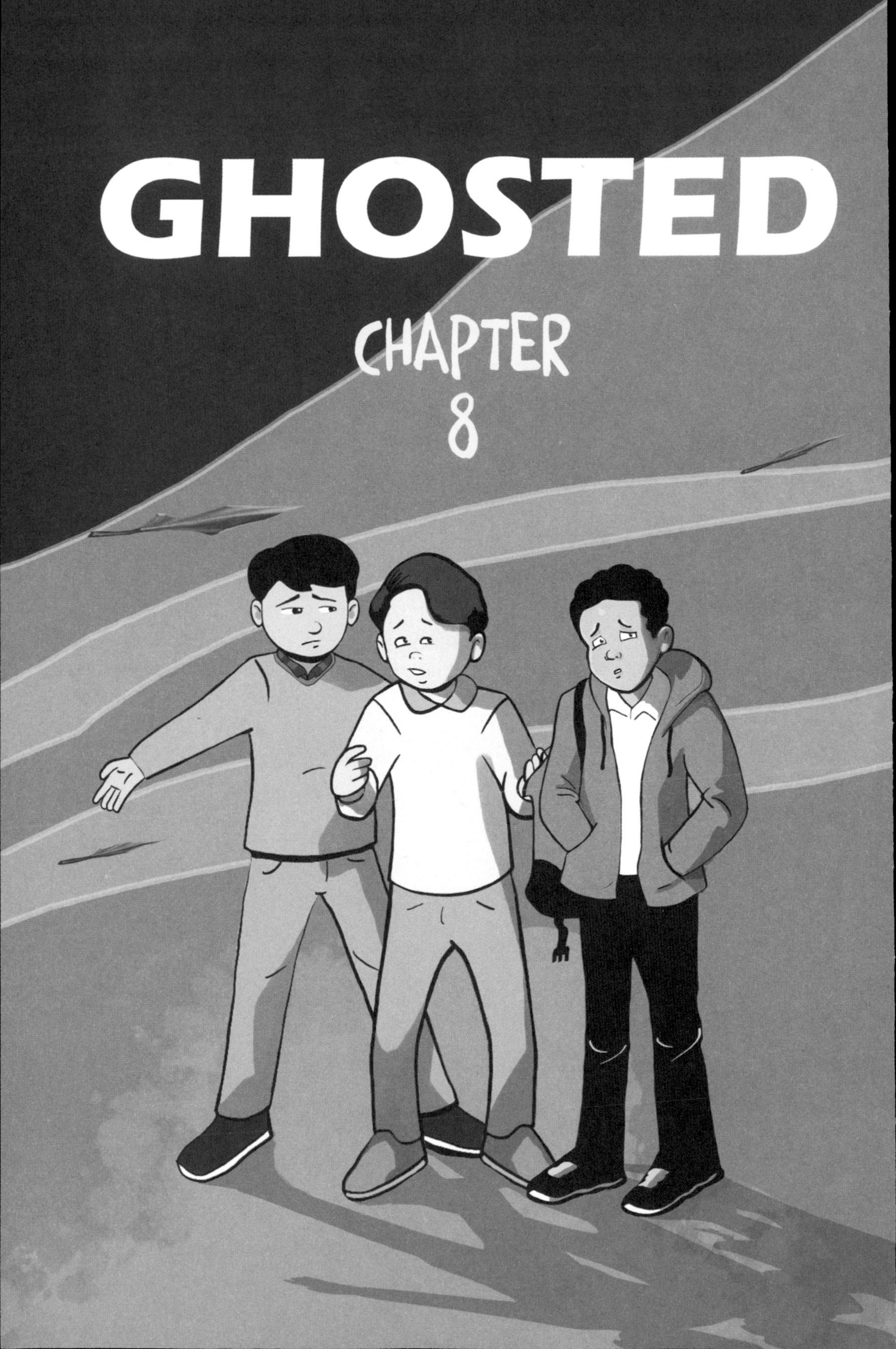
GHOSTED
CHAPTER
8

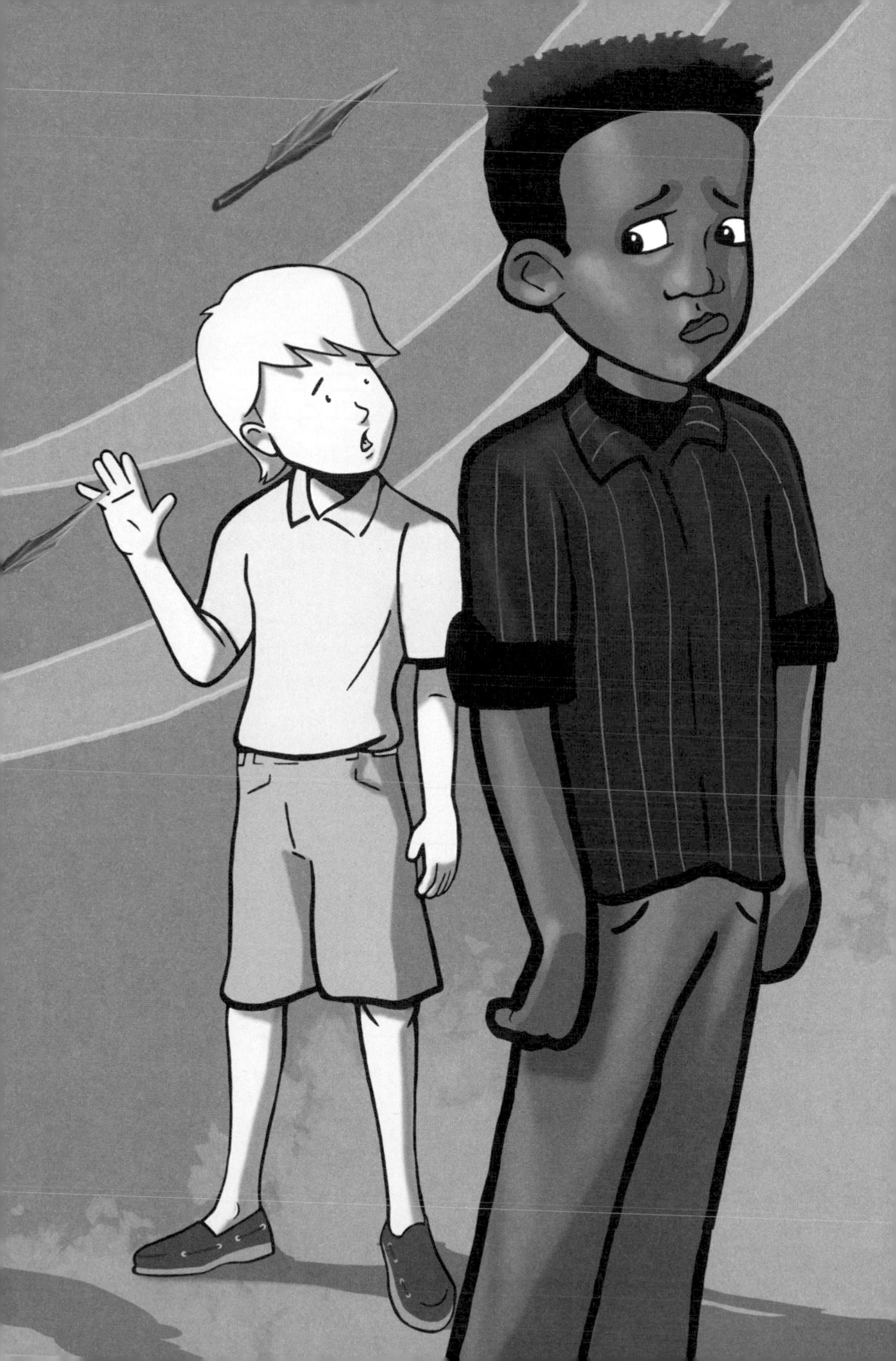

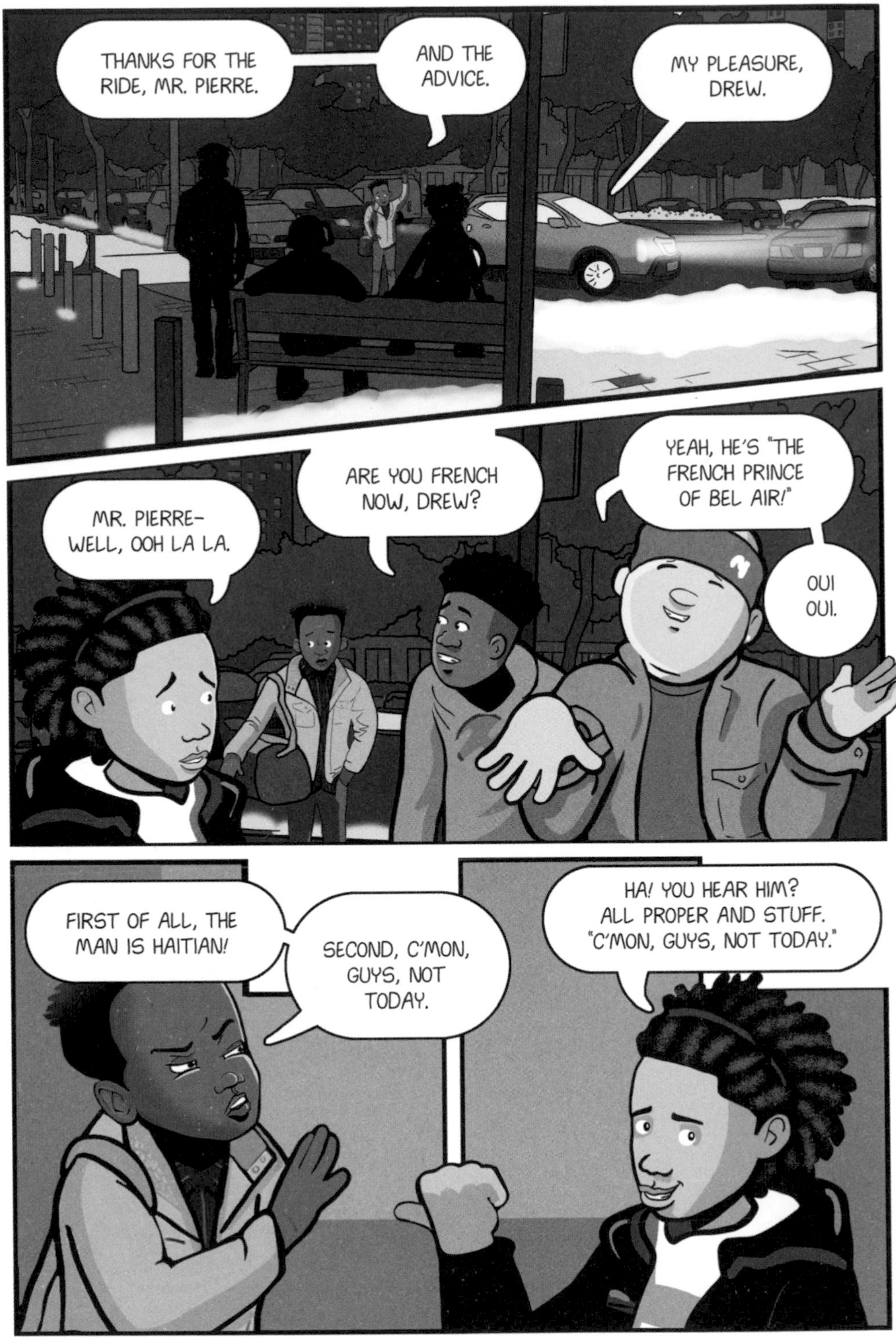
THANKS FOR THE RIDE, MR. PIERRE.
AND THE ADVICE.
MY PLEASURE, DREW.
MR. PIERRE-WELL, OOH LA LA.
ARE YOU FRENCH NOW, DREW?
YEAH, HE'S "THE FRENCH PRINCE OF BEL AIR!"
OUI OUI.
FIRST OF ALL, THE MAN IS HAITIAN!
SECOND, C'MON, GUYS, NOT TODAY.
HA! YOU HEAR HIM? ALL PROPER AND STUFF. "C'MON, GUYS, NOT TODAY."

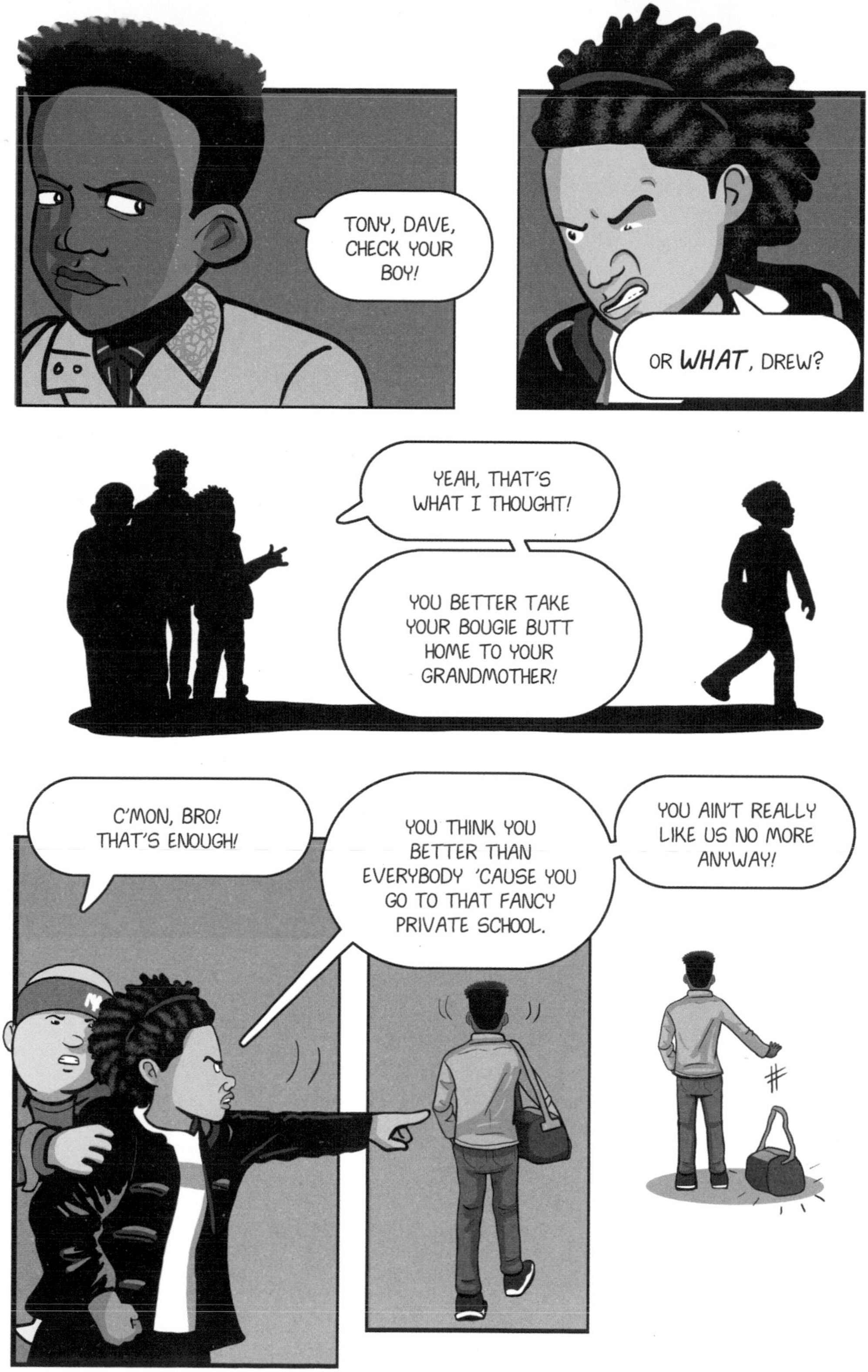
TONY, DAVE, CHECK YOUR BOY!
OR WHAT, DREW?
YEAH, THAT'S WHAT I THOUGHT!
YOU BETTER TAKE YOUR BOUGIE BUTT HOME TO YOUR GRANDMOTHER!
C'MON, BRO! THAT'S ENOUGH!
YOU THINK YOU BETTER THAN EVERYBODY 'CAUSE YOU GO TO THAT FANCY PRIVATE SCHOOL.
YOU AIN'T REALLY LIKE US NO MORE ANYWAY!

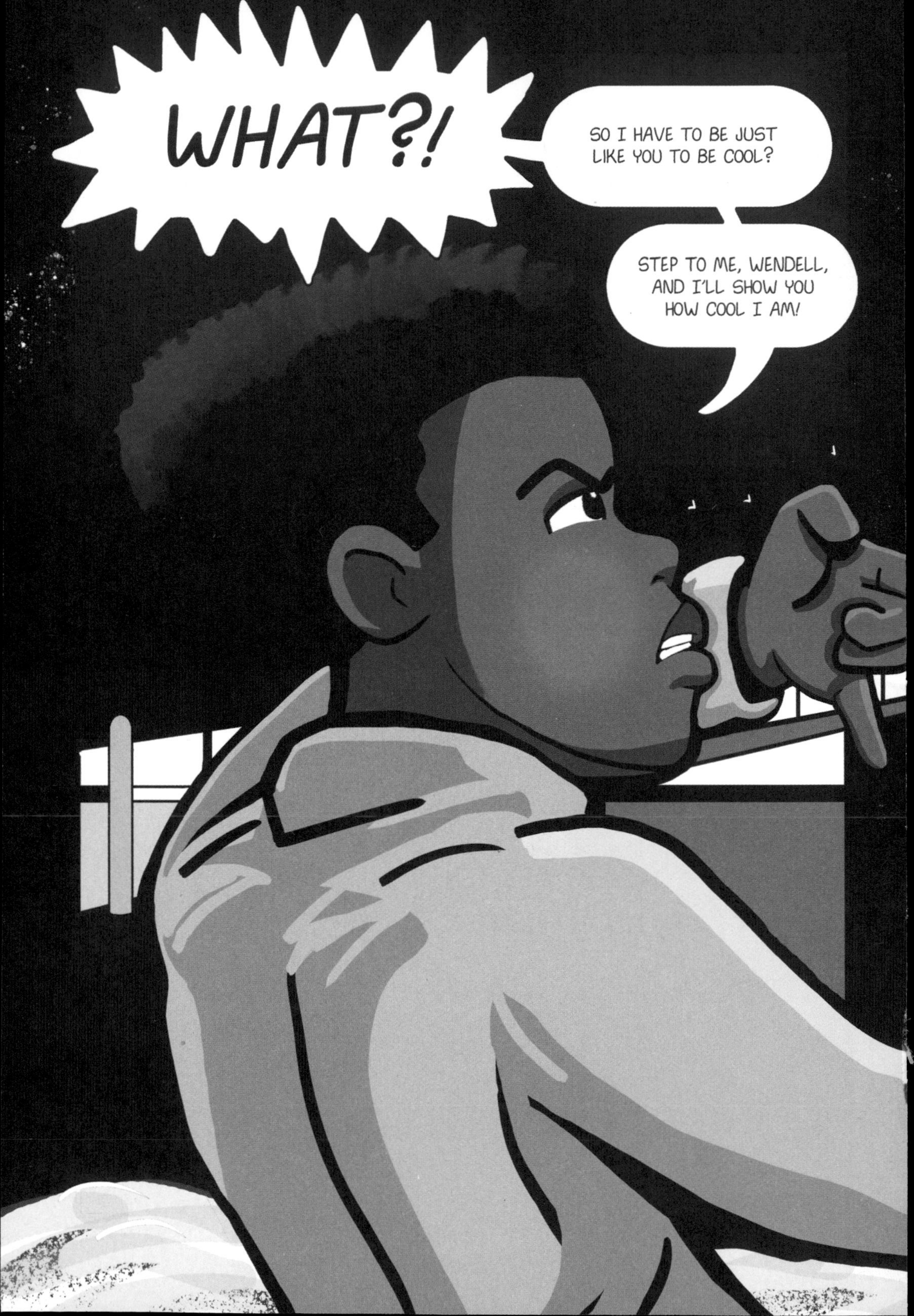
WHAT?!
SO I HAVE TO BE JUST LIKE YOU TO BE COOL?
STEP TO ME, WENDELL, AND I'LL SHOW YOU HOW COOL I AM!

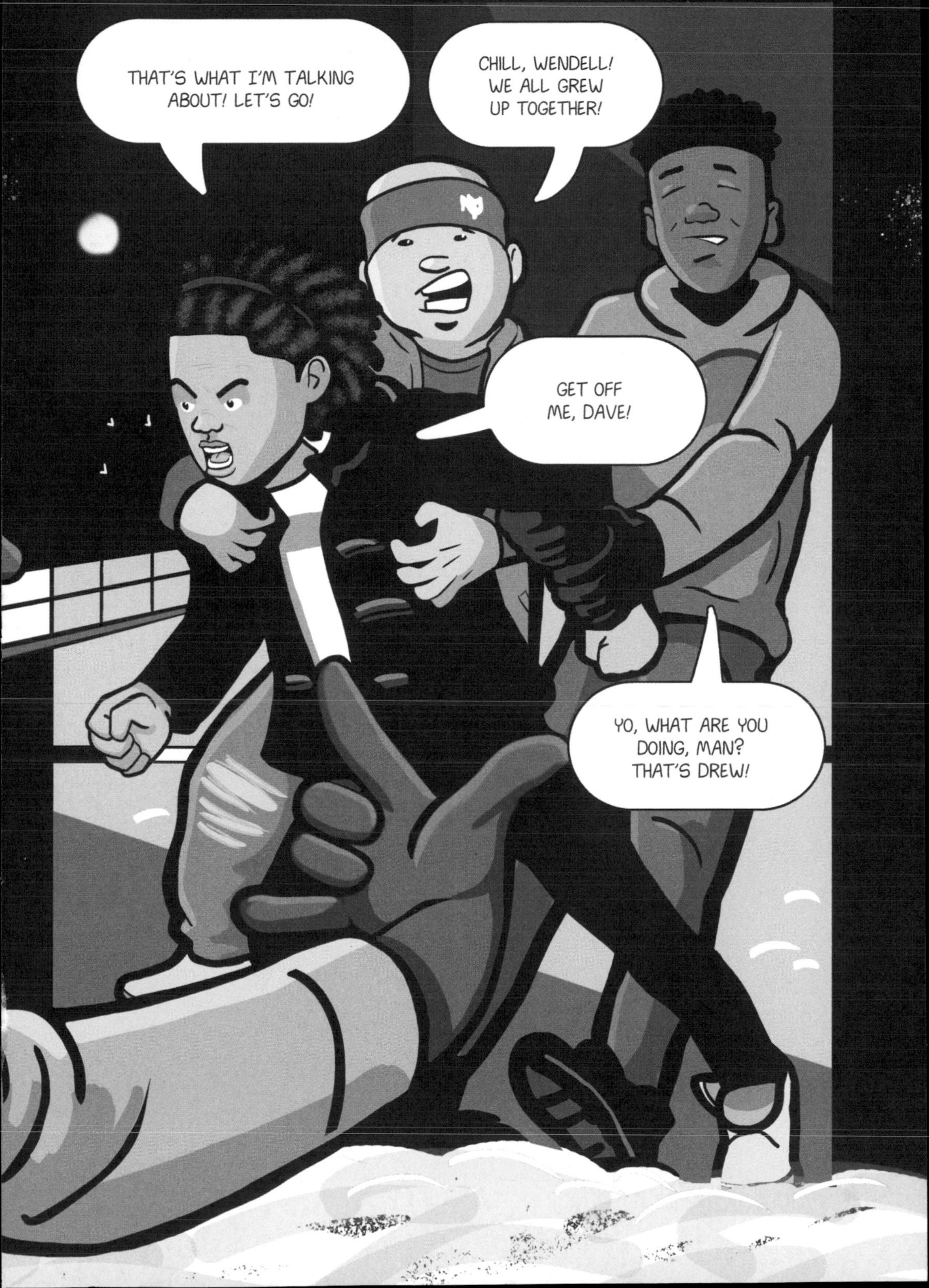
THAT'S WHAT I'M TALKING ABOUT! LET'S GO!
CHILL, WENDELL! WE ALL GREW UP TOGETHER!
GET OFF ME, DAVE!
YO, WHAT ARE YOU DOING, MAN? THAT'S DREW!

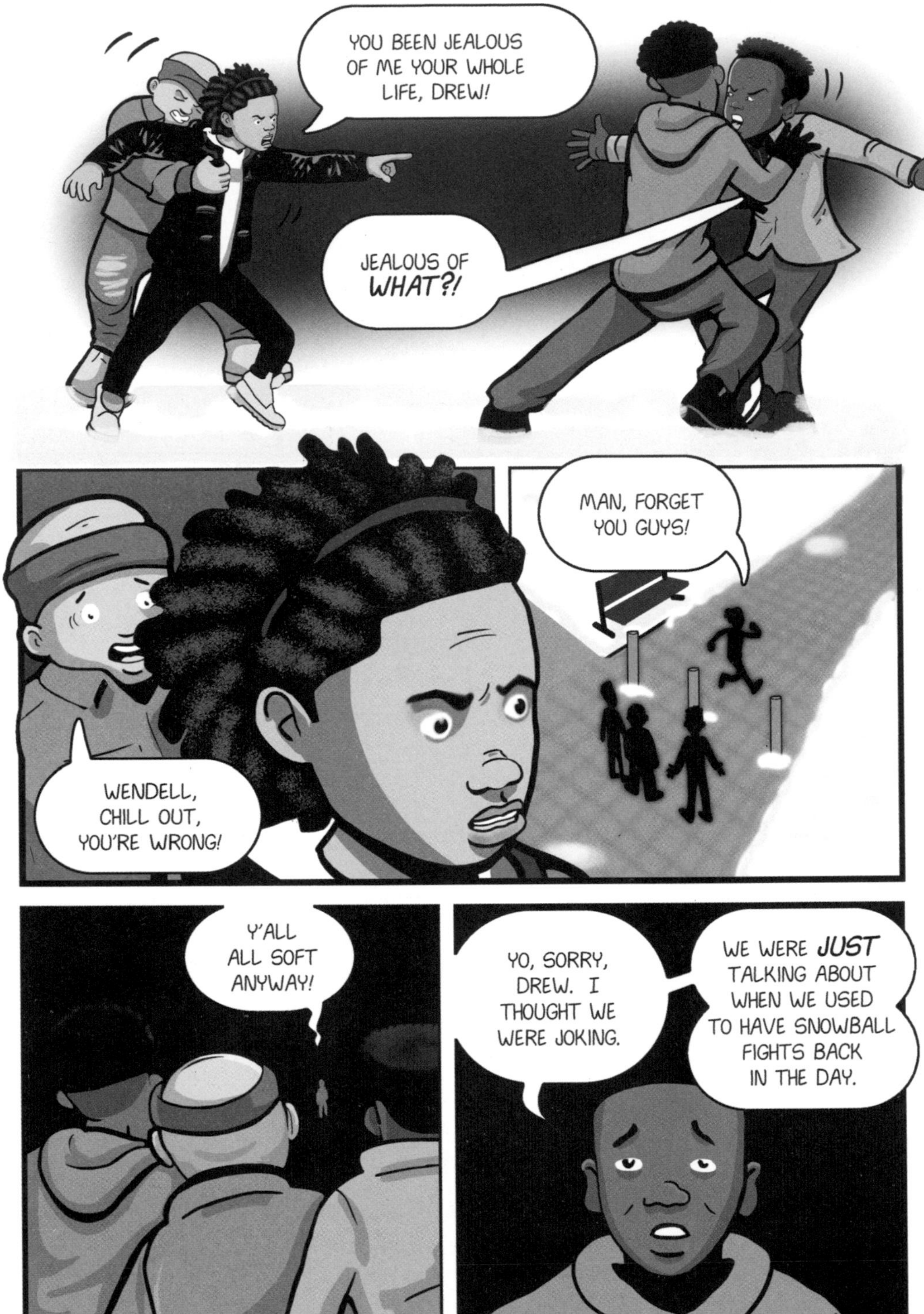
YOU BEEN JEALOUS OF ME YOUR WHOLE LIFE, DREW!
JEALOUS OF WHAT?!
WENDELL, CHILL OUT, YOU'RE WRONG!
MAN, FORGET YOU GUYS!
Y'ALL ALL SOFT ANYWAY!
YO, SORRY, DREW. I THOUGHT WE WERE JOKING.
WE WERE JUST TALKING ABOUT WHEN WE USED TO HAVE SNOWBALL FIGHTS BACK IN THE DAY.

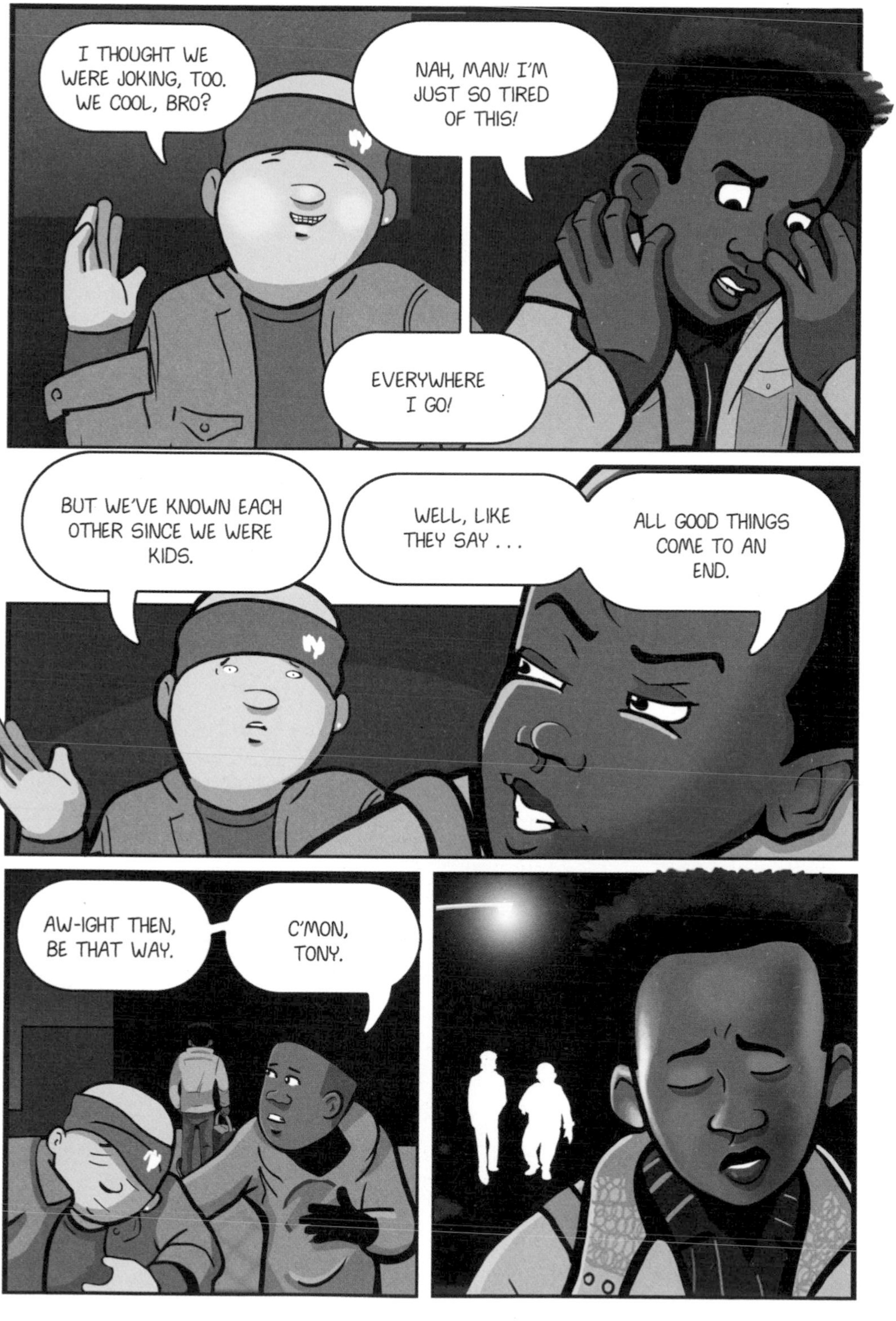
I THOUGHT WE WERE JOKING, TOO. WE COOL, BRO?
NAH, MAN! I'M JUST SO TIRED OF THIS!
EVERYWHERE I GO!
BUT WE'VE KNOWN EACH OTHER SINCE WE WERE KIDS.
WELL, LIKE THEY SAY . . .
ALL GOOD THINGS COME TO AN END.
AW-IGHT THEN, BE THAT WAY.
C'MON, TONY.

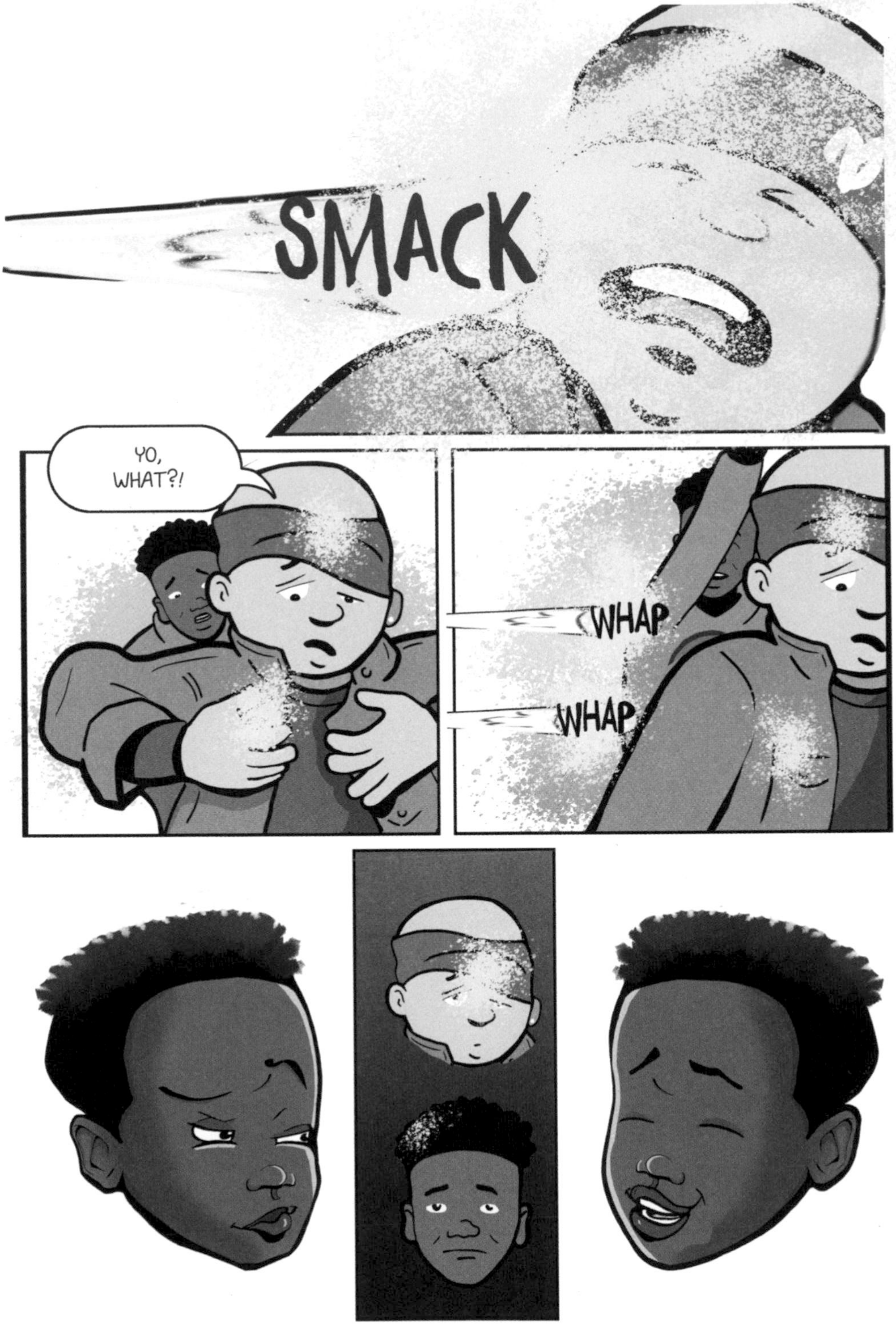
SMACK
YO, WHAT?!
WHAP
WHAP

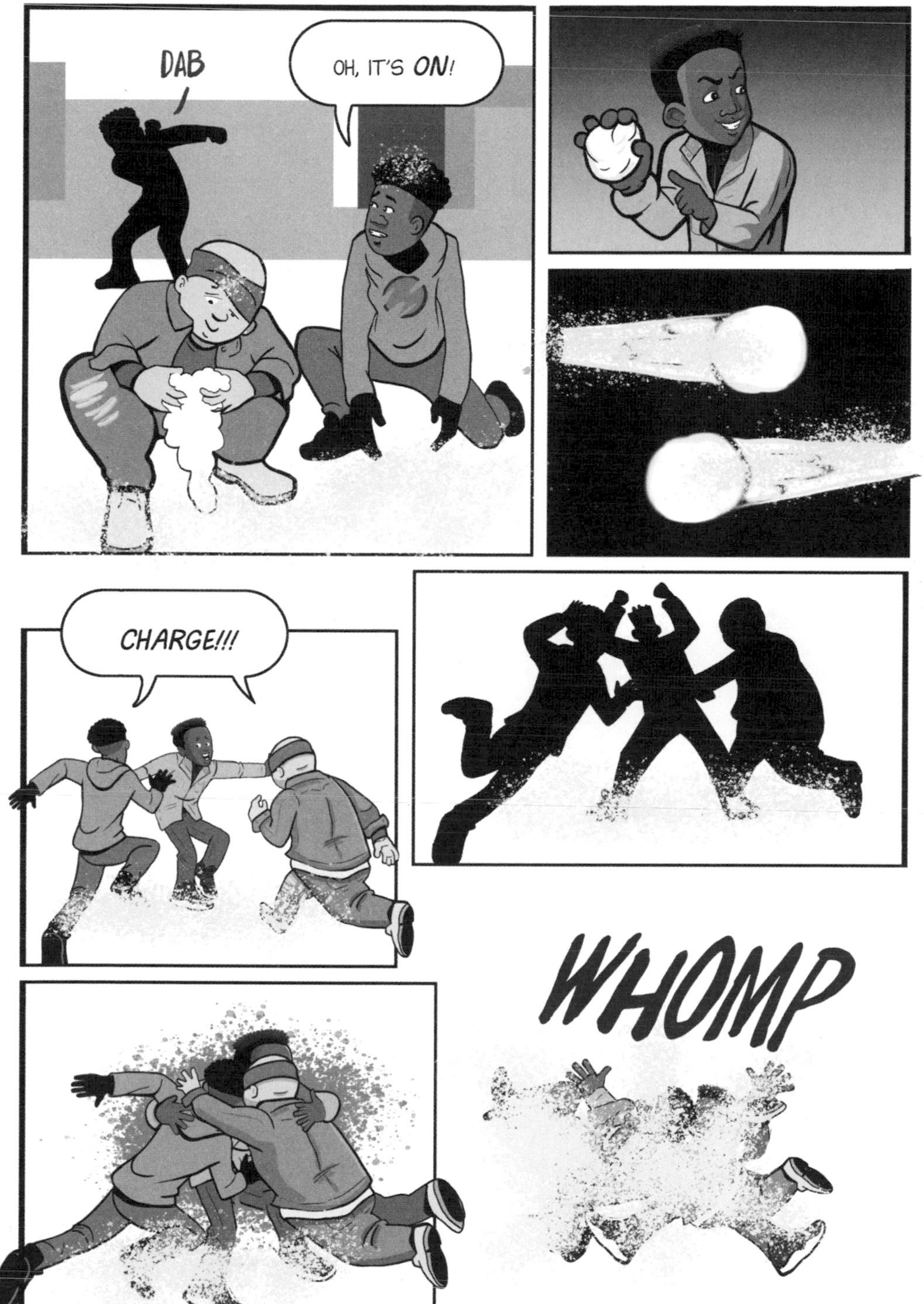

DAB
OH, IT'S ON!
CHARGE!!!
WHOMP

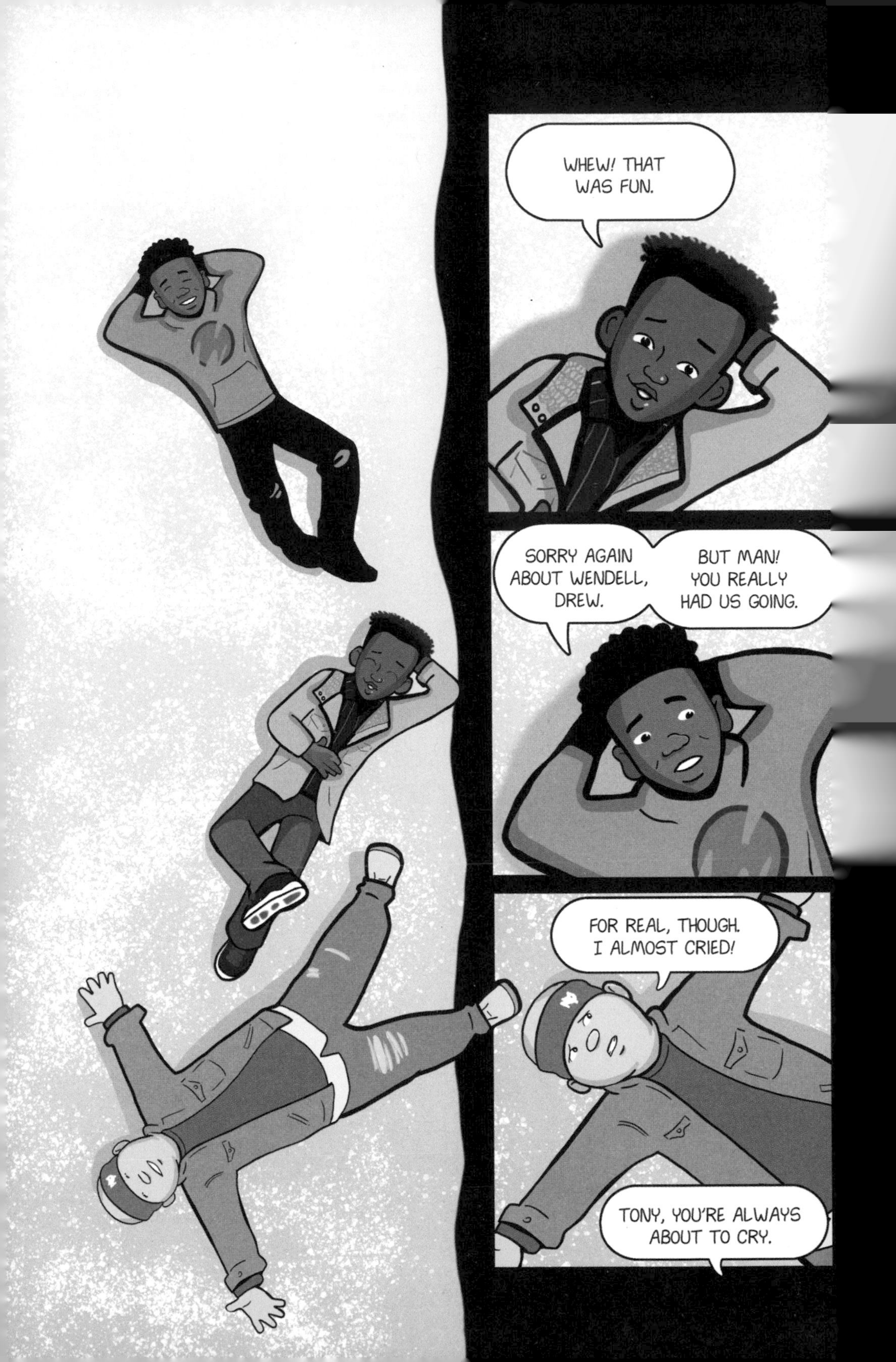
WHEW! THAT WAS FUN.
SORRY AGAIN ABOUT WENDELL, DREW.
BUT MAN! YOU REALLY HAD US GOING.
FOR REAL, THOUGH. I ALMOST CRIED!
TONY, YOU'RE ALWAYS ABOUT TO CRY.

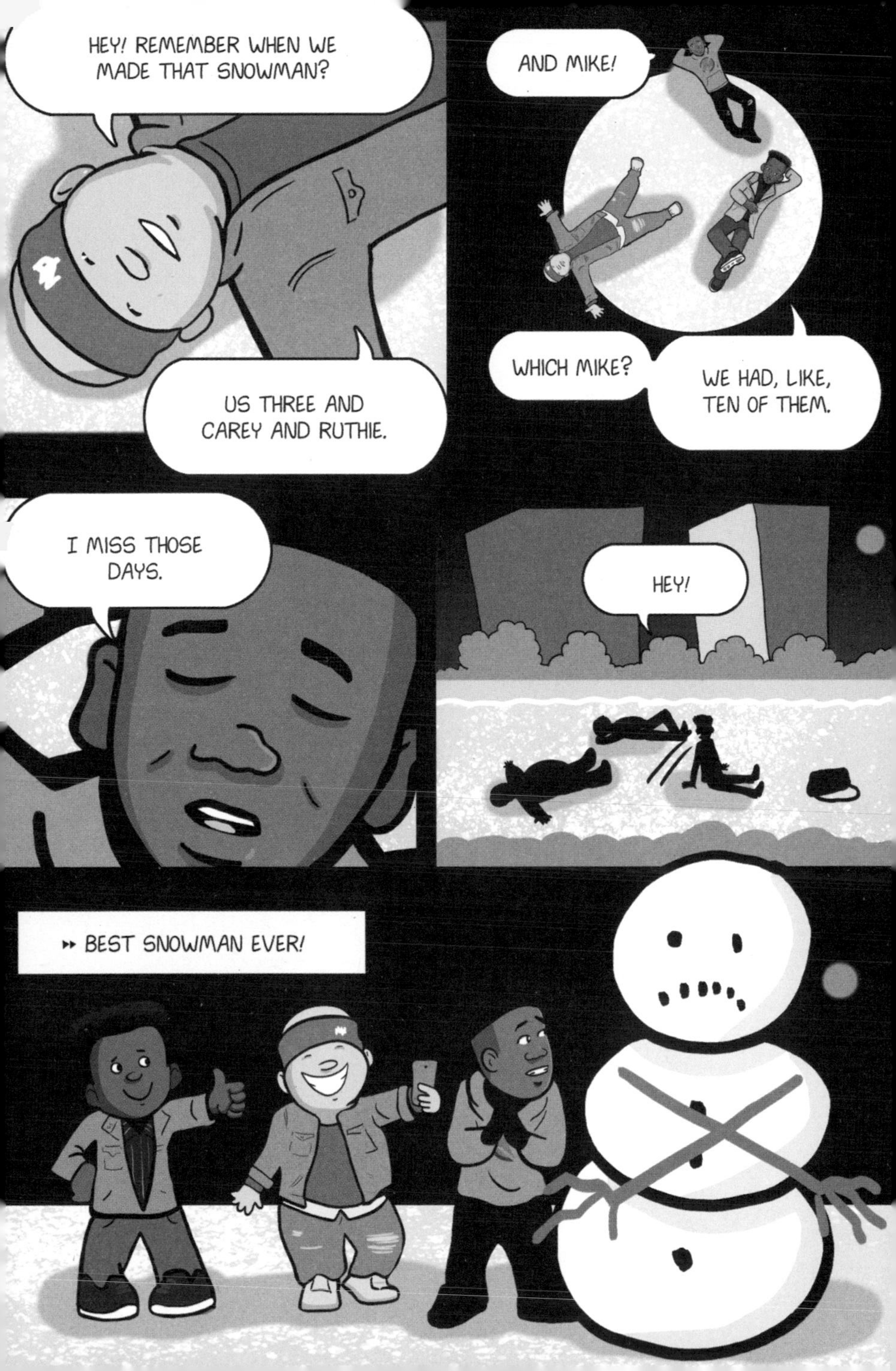
HEY! REMEMBER WHEN WE MADE THAT SNOWMAN?
US THREE AND CAREY AND RUTHIE.
AND MIKE!
WHICH MIKE?
WE HAD, LIKE, TEN OF THEM.
I MISS THOSE DAYS.
HEY!
▸▸ BEST SNOWMAN EVER!

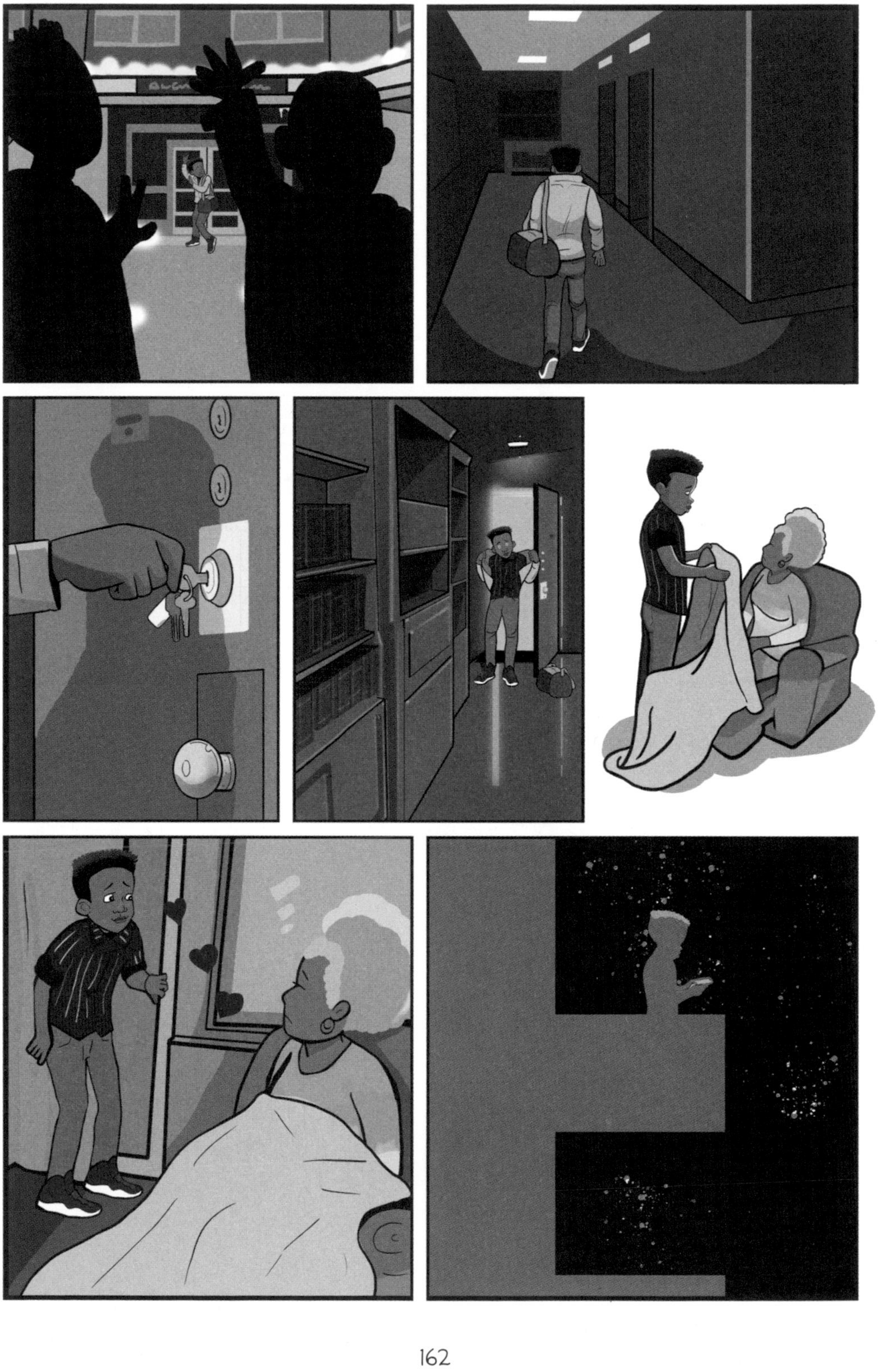

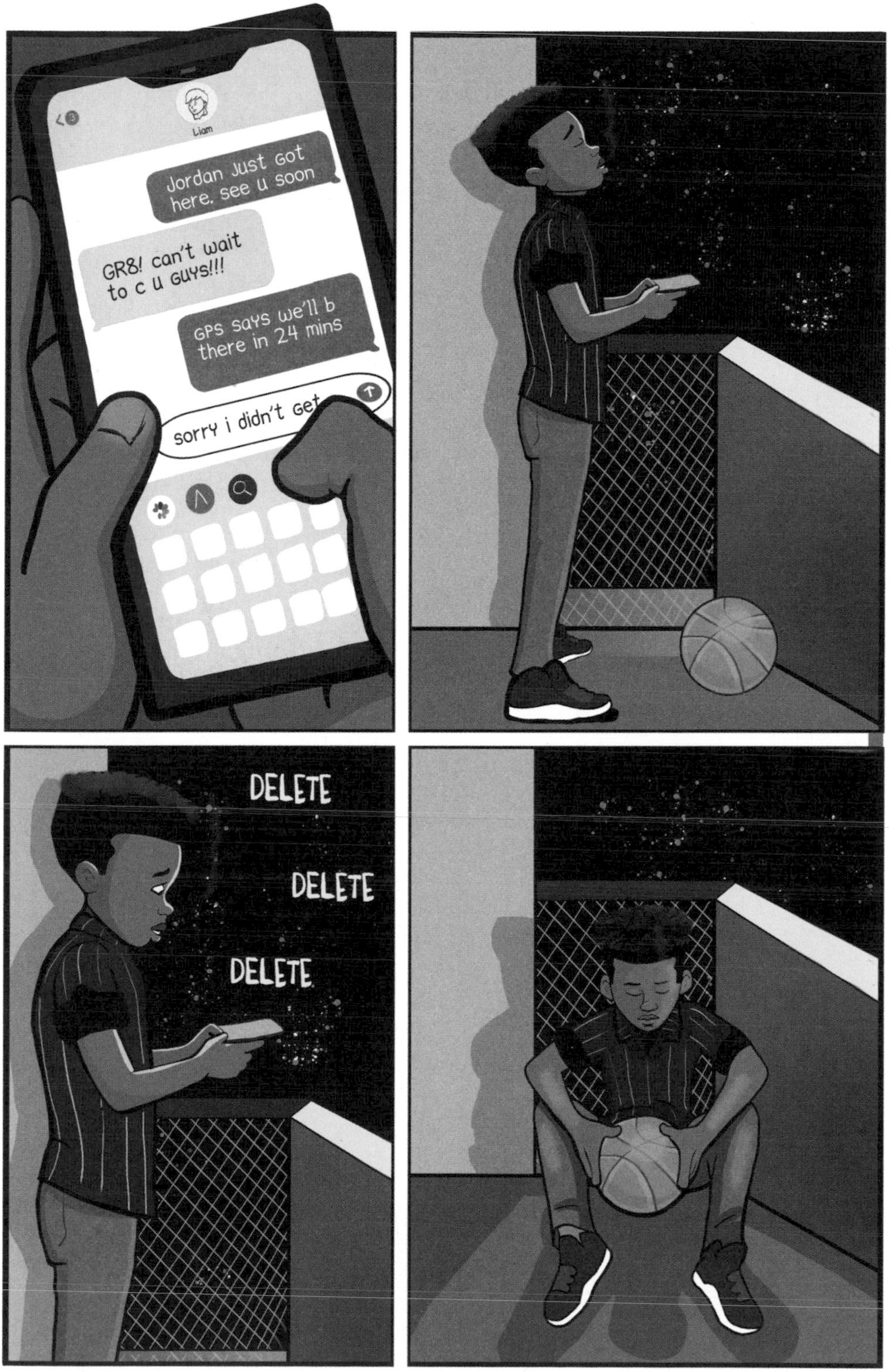
Liam
Jordan Just Got here. see u soon
GR8! can't wait to c u GUYS!!!
GPS says we'll b there in 24 mins
sorry i didn't Get
DELETE
DELETE
DELETE

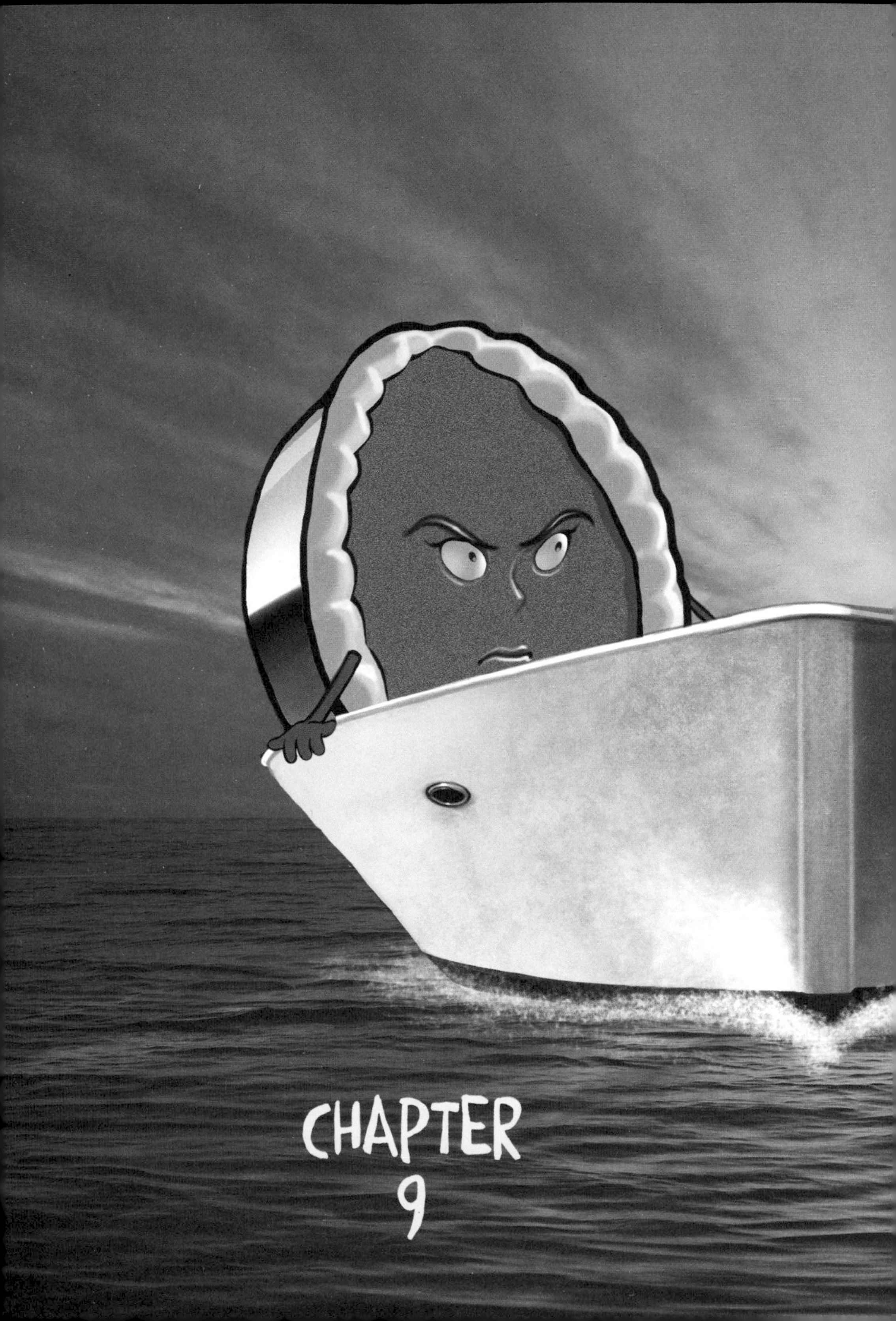

CHAPTER 9

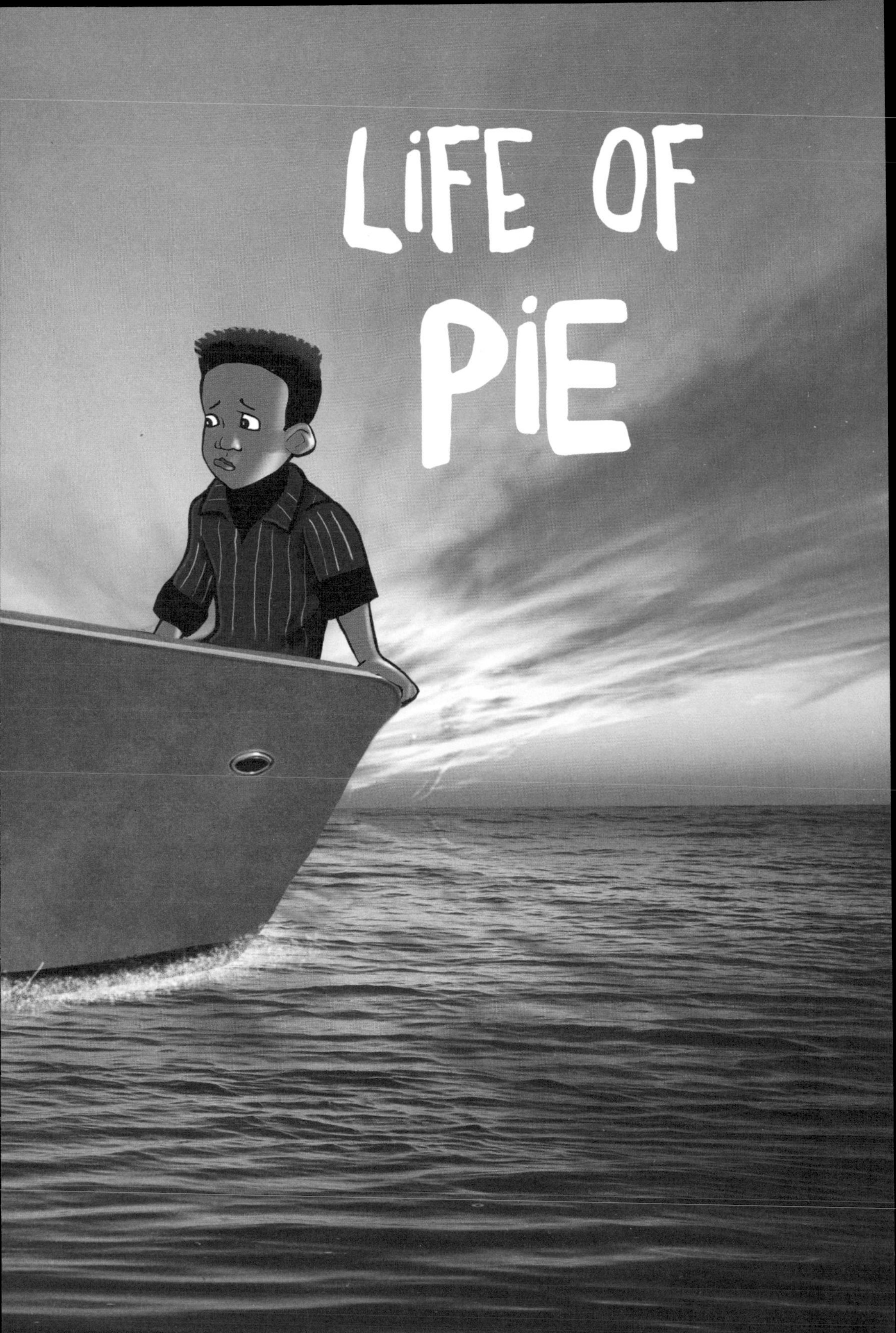
LiFE OF PiE

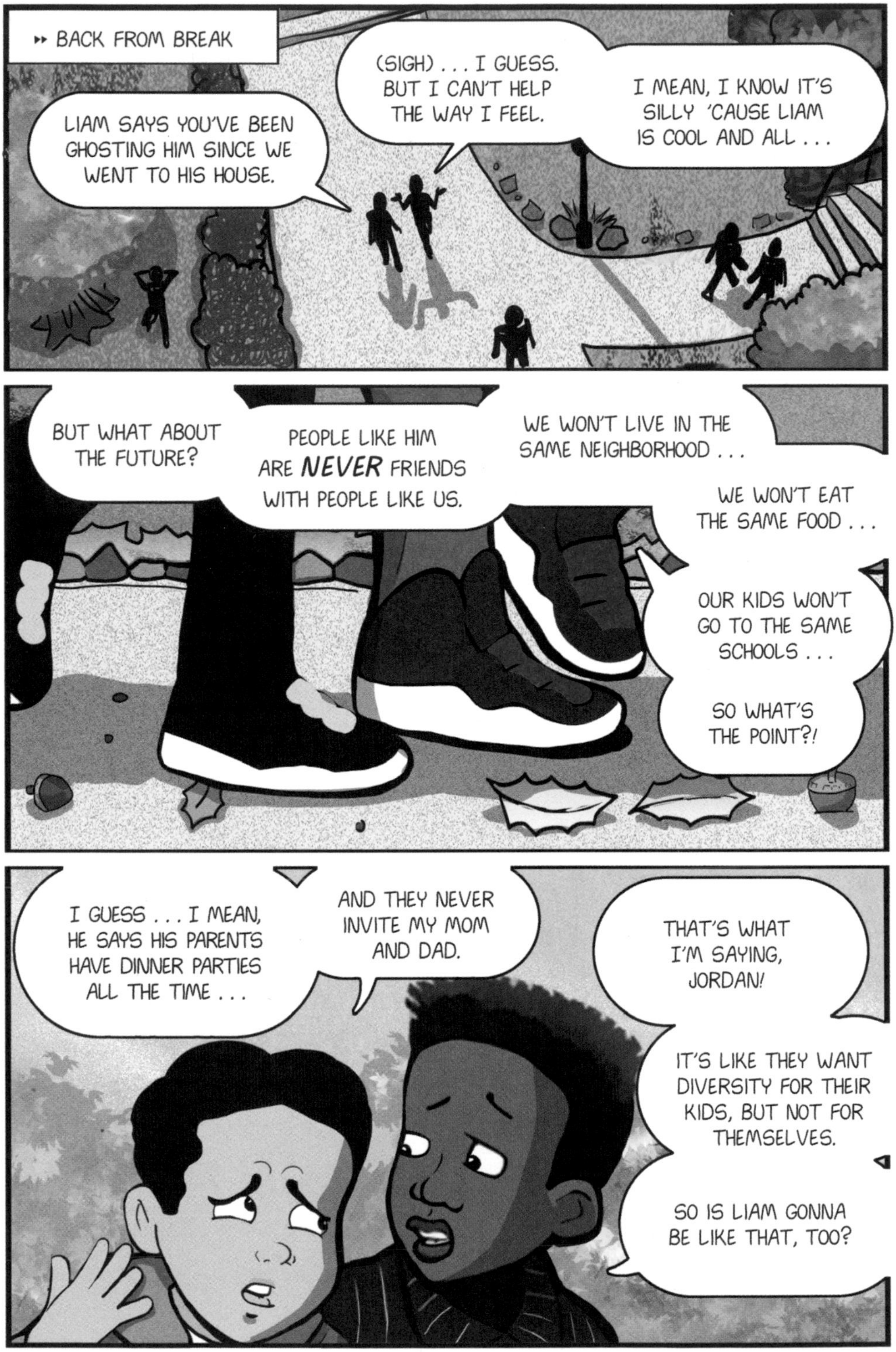
▸▸ BACK FROM BREAK
LIAM SAYS YOU'VE BEEN GHOSTING HIM SINCE WE WENT TO HIS HOUSE.
(SIGH) . . . I GUESS. BUT I CAN'T HELP THE WAY I FEEL.
I MEAN, I KNOW IT'S SILLY 'CAUSE LIAM IS COOL AND ALL . . .
BUT WHAT ABOUT THE FUTURE?
PEOPLE LIKE HIM ARE ***NEVER*** FRIENDS WITH PEOPLE LIKE US.
WE WON'T LIVE IN THE SAME NEIGHBORHOOD . . .
WE WON'T EAT THE SAME FOOD . . .
OUR KIDS WON'T GO TO THE SAME SCHOOLS . . .
SO WHAT'S THE POINT?!
I GUESS . . . I MEAN, HE SAYS HIS PARENTS HAVE DINNER PARTIES ALL THE TIME . . .
AND THEY NEVER INVITE MY MOM AND DAD.
THAT'S WHAT I'M SAYING, JORDAN!
IT'S LIKE THEY WANT DIVERSITY FOR THEIR KIDS, BUT NOT FOR THEMSELVES.
SO IS LIAM GONNA BE LIKE THAT, TOO?

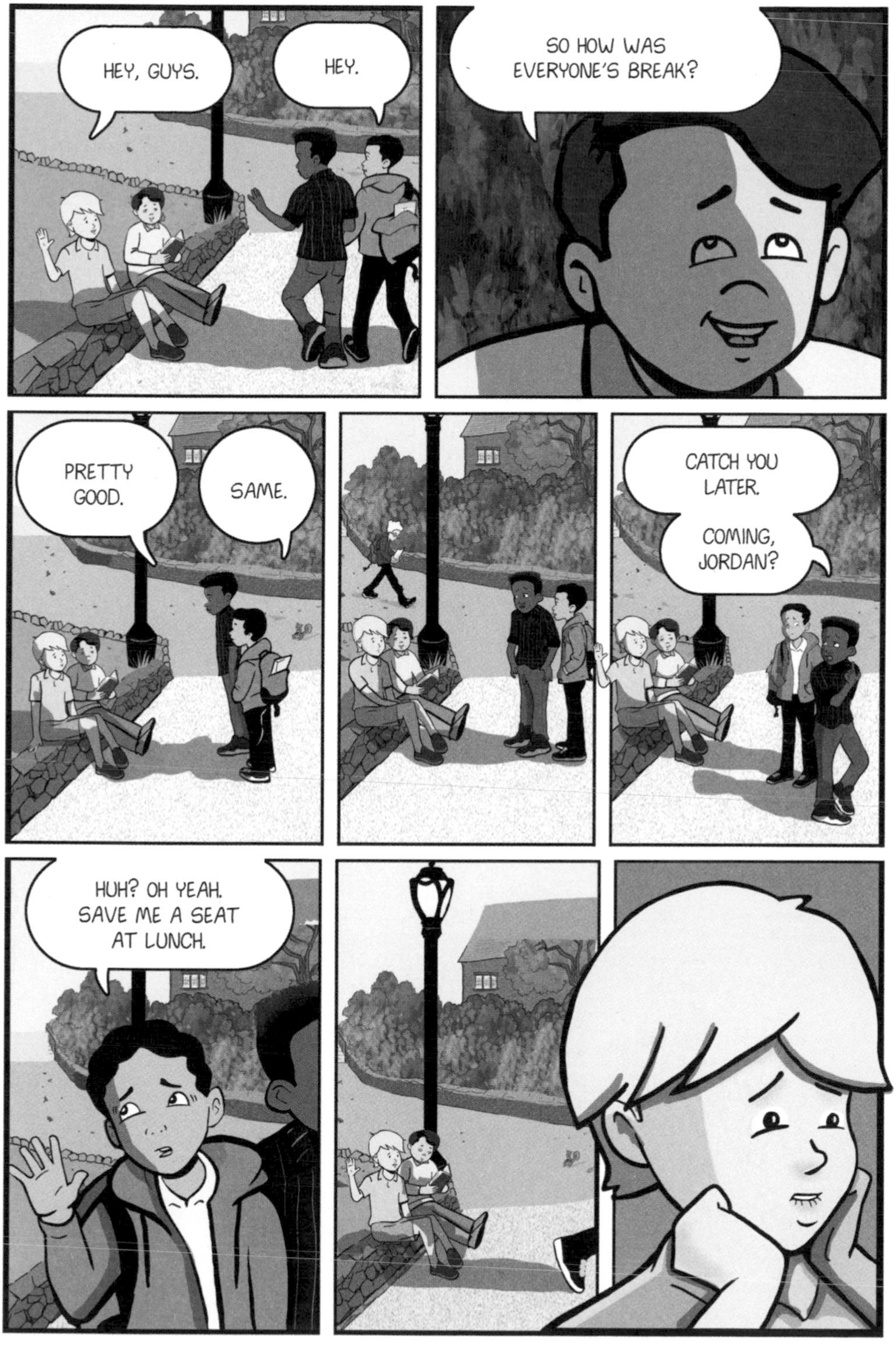
HEY, GUYS.
HEY.
SO HOW WAS EVERYONE'S BREAK?
PRETTY GOOD.
SAME.
CATCH YOU LATER.
COMING, JORDAN?
HUH? OH YEAH. SAVE ME A SEAT AT LUNCH.

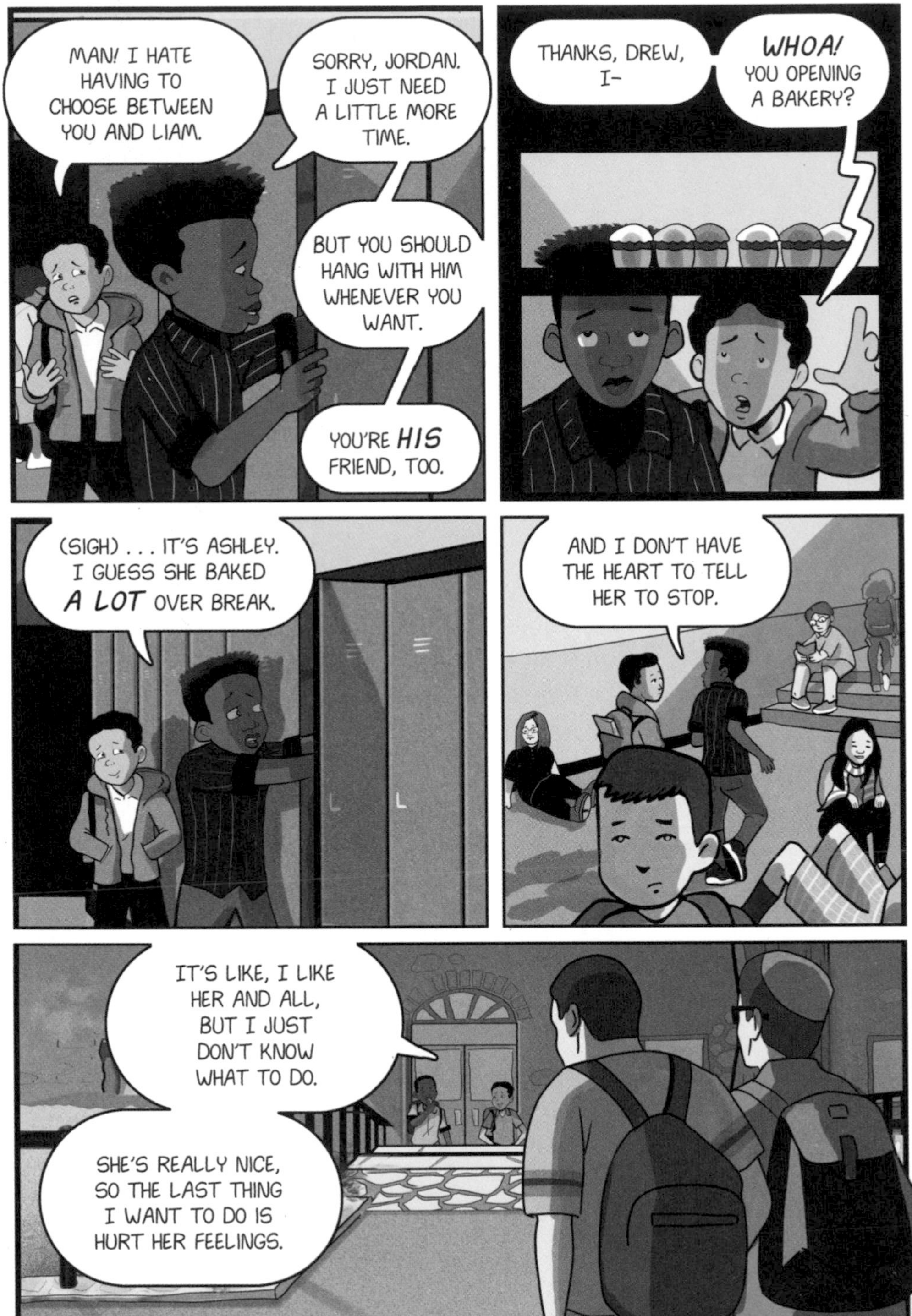
MAN! I HATE HAVING TO CHOOSE BETWEEN YOU AND LIAM.
SORRY, JORDAN. I JUST NEED A LITTLE MORE TIME.
BUT YOU SHOULD HANG WITH HIM WHENEVER YOU WANT.
YOU'RE HIS FRIEND, TOO.
THANKS, DREW, I–
WHOA! YOU OPENING A BAKERY?
(SIGH) . . . IT'S ASHLEY. I GUESS SHE BAKED A LOT OVER BREAK.
AND I DON'T HAVE THE HEART TO TELL HER TO STOP.
IT'S LIKE, I LIKE HER AND ALL, BUT I JUST DON'T KNOW WHAT TO DO.
SHE'S REALLY NICE, SO THE LAST THING I WANT TO DO IS HURT HER FEELINGS.

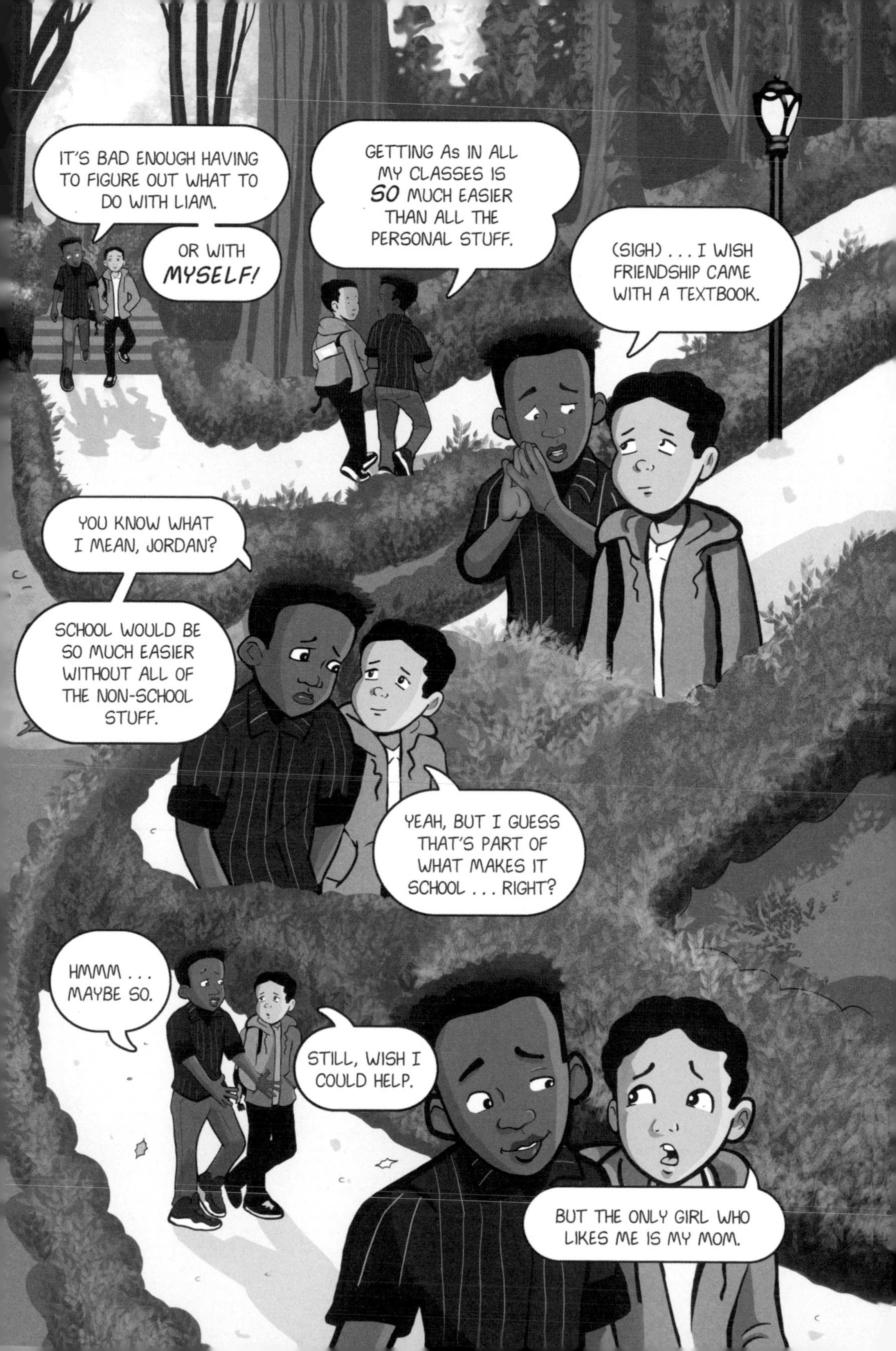
IT'S BAD ENOUGH HAVING TO FIGURE OUT WHAT TO DO WITH LIAM.
OR WITH *MYSELF!*
GETTING As IN ALL MY CLASSES IS *SO* MUCH EASIER THAN ALL THE PERSONAL STUFF.
(SIGH) . . . I WISH FRIENDSHIP CAME WITH A TEXTBOOK.
YOU KNOW WHAT I MEAN, JORDAN?
SCHOOL WOULD BE SO MUCH EASIER WITHOUT ALL OF THE NON-SCHOOL STUFF.
YEAH, BUT I GUESS THAT'S PART OF WHAT MAKES IT SCHOOL . . . RIGHT?
HMMM . . . MAYBE SO.
STILL, WISH I COULD HELP.
BUT THE ONLY GIRL WHO LIKES ME IS MY MOM.

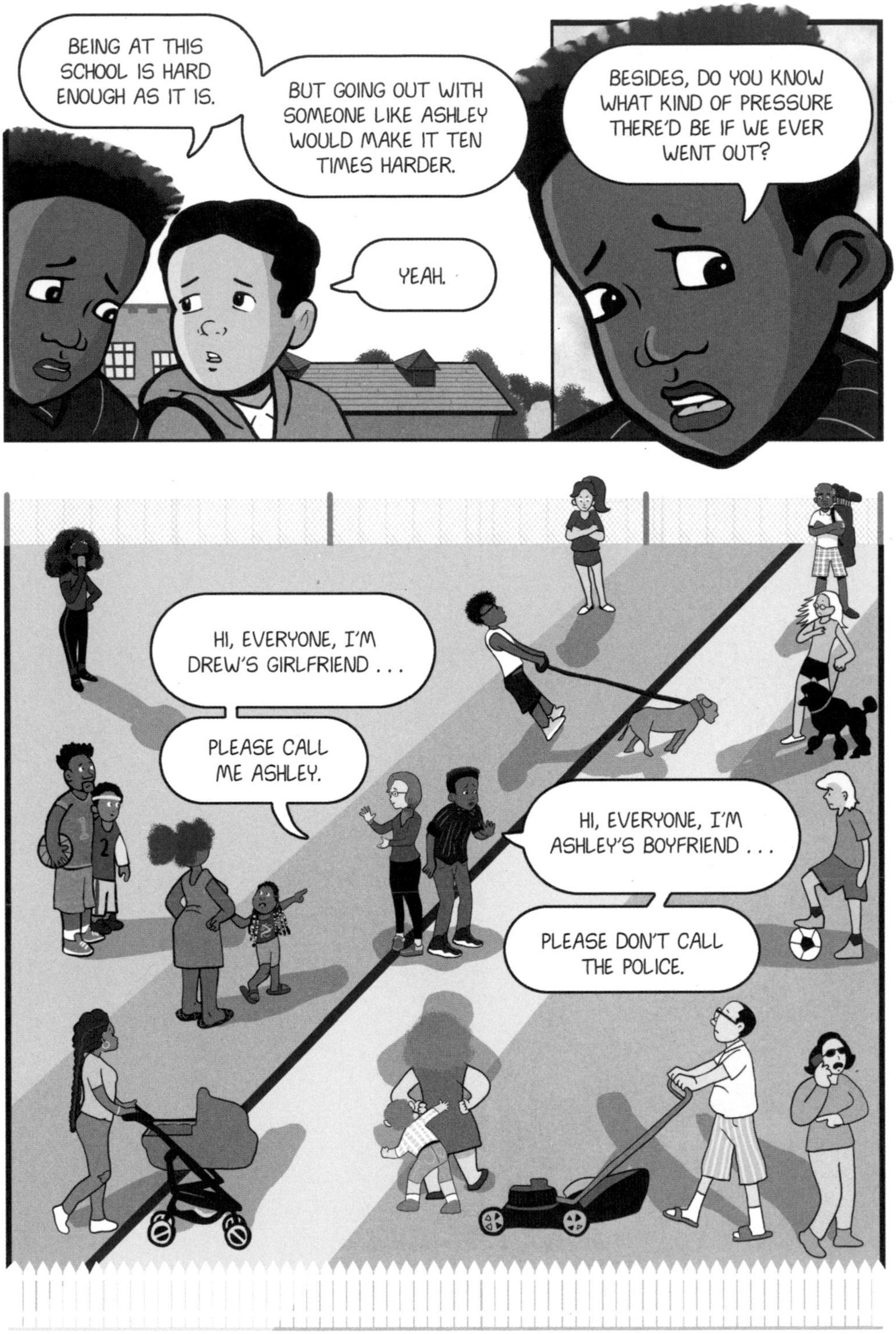
BEING AT THIS SCHOOL IS HARD ENOUGH AS IT IS.
BUT GOING OUT WITH SOMEONE LIKE ASHLEY WOULD MAKE IT TEN TIMES HARDER.
YEAH.
BESIDES, DO YOU KNOW WHAT KIND OF PRESSURE THERE'D BE IF WE EVER WENT OUT?
HI, EVERYONE, I'M DREW'S GIRLFRIEND . . .
PLEASE CALL ME ASHLEY.
HI, EVERYONE, I'M ASHLEY'S BOYFRIEND . . .
PLEASE DON'T CALL THE POLICE.

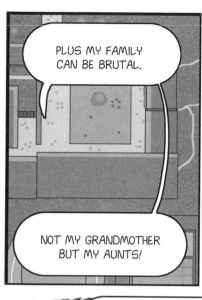

PLUS MY FAMILY CAN BE BRUTAL.

NOT MY GRANDMOTHER BUT MY AUNTS!

I'D *NEVER* HEAR THE END OF IT!

GRANDPA DREW, DID YOU REALLY DATE A GIRL NAMED ASHLEY IN THE EIGHTH GRADE?

OH, WILL YOU GIVE IT A REST, CAMRYN?!

I'D BE SCARED, TOO, IF A GIRL HERE LIKED ME.

ACTUALLY, I'D BE SCARED IF A GIRL *ANYWHERE* LIKED ME.

DO YOU THINK BEING AN ADULT IS EASIER OR HARDER?

PROBABLY THE SAME. BUT YOU HAVE TO PAY BILLS.

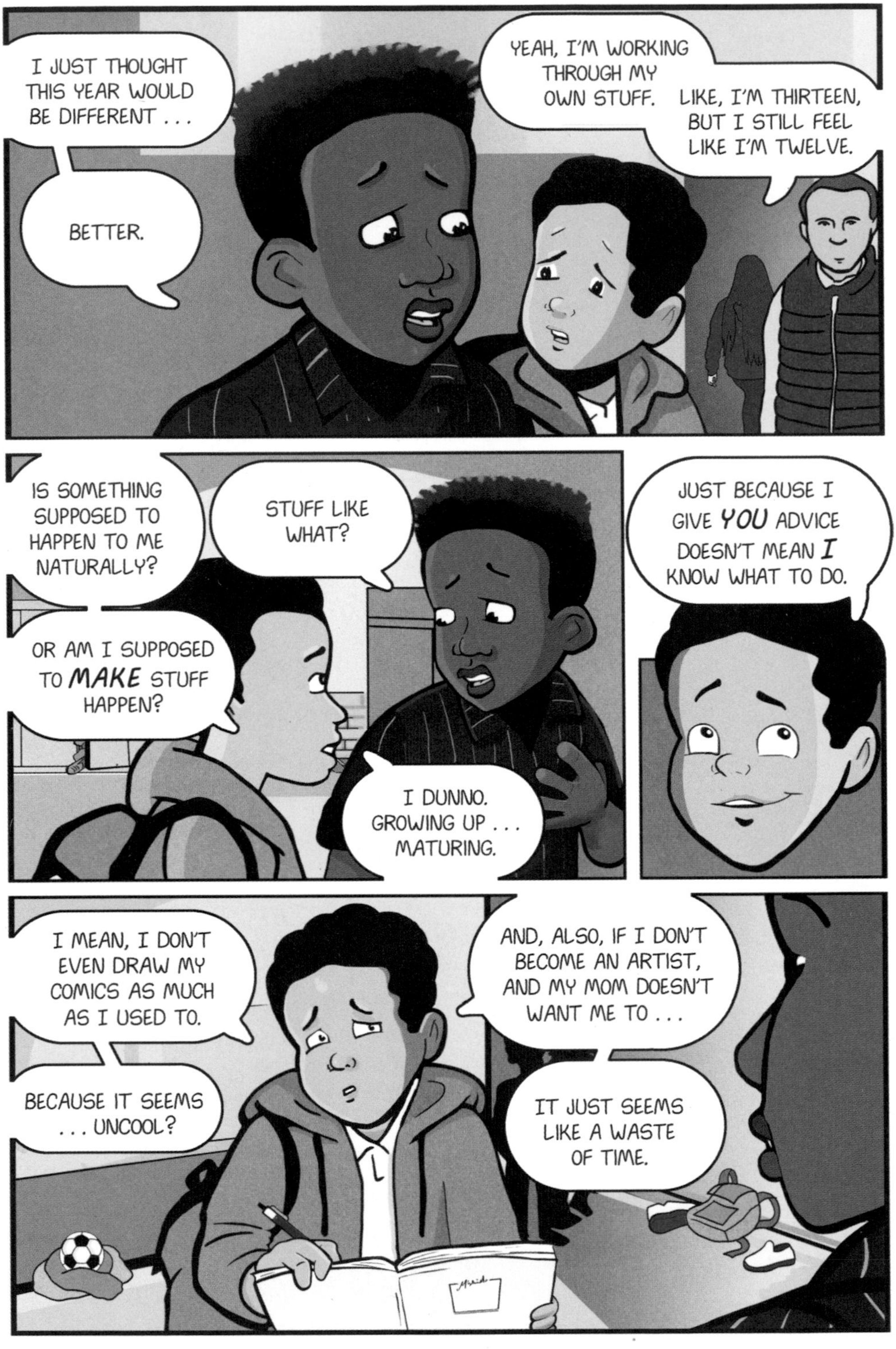
I JUST THOUGHT THIS YEAR WOULD BE DIFFERENT . . .
BETTER.
YEAH, I'M WORKING THROUGH MY OWN STUFF.
LIKE, I'M THIRTEEN, BUT I STILL FEEL LIKE I'M TWELVE.
IS SOMETHING SUPPOSED TO HAPPEN TO ME NATURALLY?
OR AM I SUPPOSED TO MAKE STUFF HAPPEN?
STUFF LIKE WHAT?
I DUNNO. GROWING UP . . . MATURING.
JUST BECAUSE I GIVE YOU ADVICE DOESN'T MEAN I KNOW WHAT TO DO.
I MEAN, I DON'T EVEN DRAW MY COMICS AS MUCH AS I USED TO.
BECAUSE IT SEEMS . . . UNCOOL?
AND, ALSO, IF I DON'T BECOME AN ARTIST, AND MY MOM DOESN'T WANT ME TO . . .
IT JUST SEEMS LIKE A WASTE OF TIME.

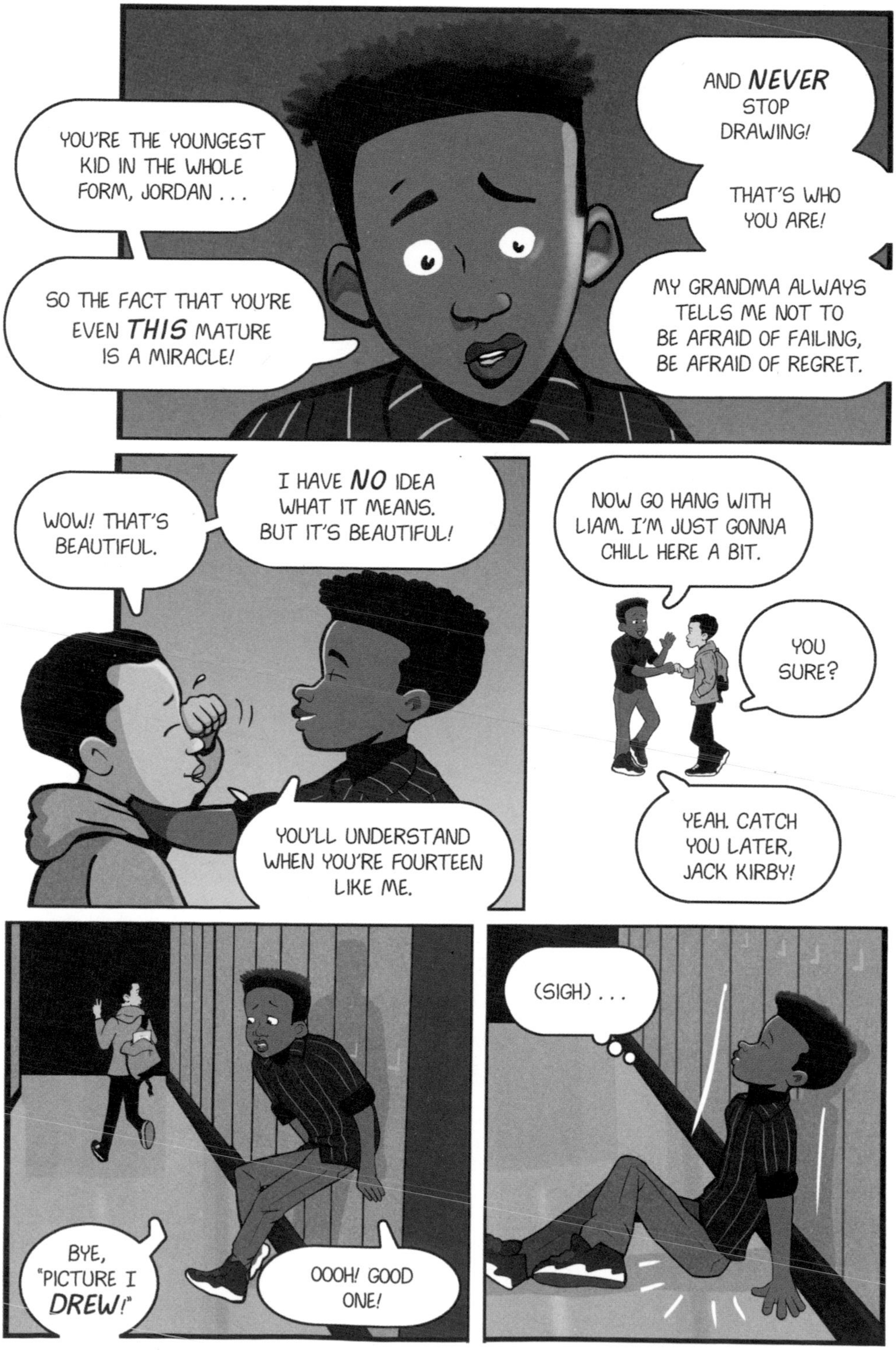
YOU'RE THE YOUNGEST KID IN THE WHOLE FORM, JORDAN . . .
SO THE FACT THAT YOU'RE EVEN THIS MATURE IS A MIRACLE!
AND NEVER STOP DRAWING!
THAT'S WHO YOU ARE!
MY GRANDMA ALWAYS TELLS ME NOT TO BE AFRAID OF FAILING, BE AFRAID OF REGRET.
WOW! THAT'S BEAUTIFUL.
I HAVE NO IDEA WHAT IT MEANS. BUT IT'S BEAUTIFUL!
YOU'LL UNDERSTAND WHEN YOU'RE FOURTEEN LIKE ME.
NOW GO HANG WITH LIAM. I'M JUST GONNA CHILL HERE A BIT.
YOU SURE?
YEAH. CATCH YOU LATER, JACK KIRBY!
BYE, "PICTURE I DREW!"
OOOH! GOOD ONE!
(SIGH) . . .

THE HAND-PUPPET'S TALE

CHAPTER 10

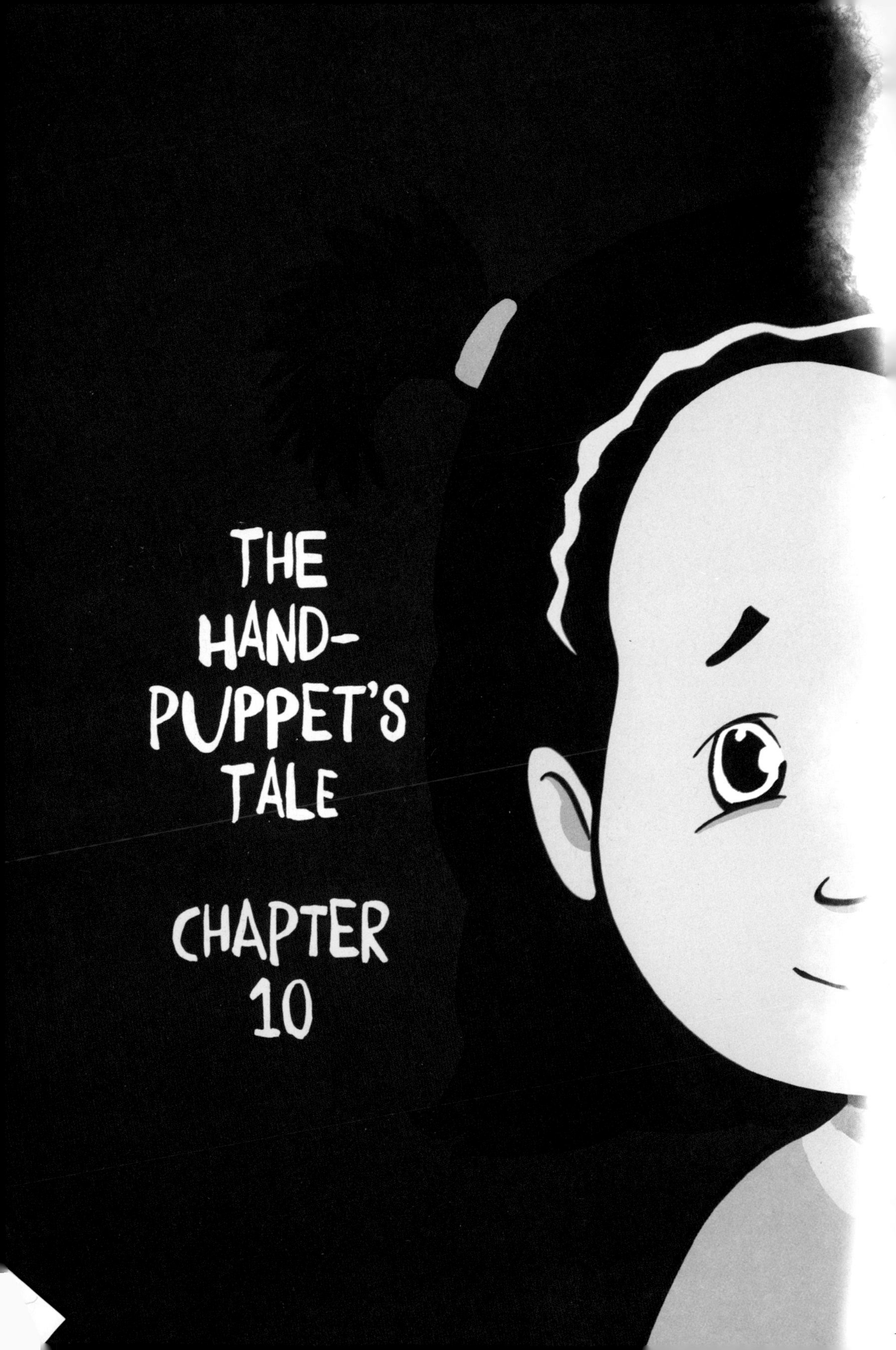

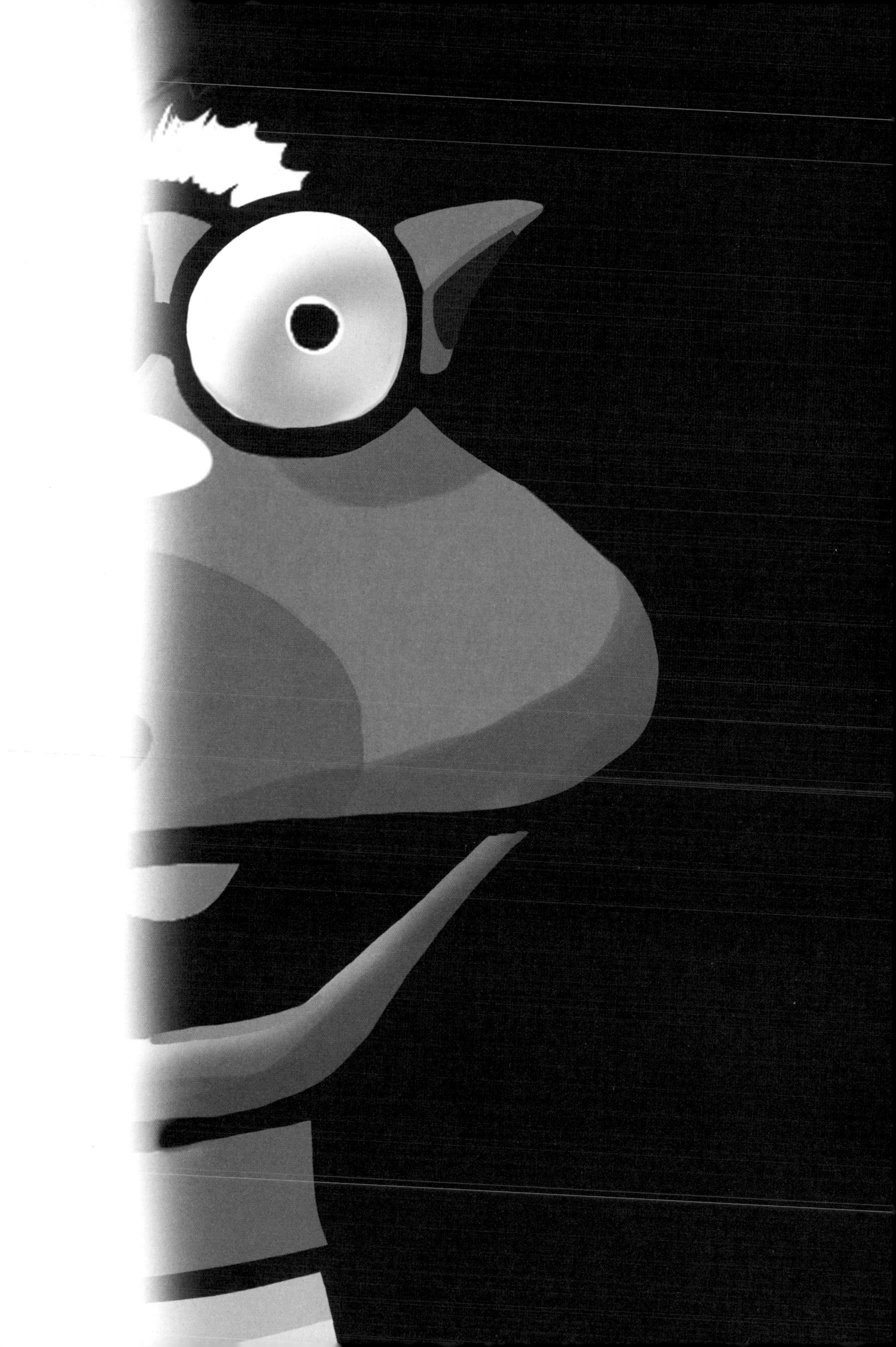

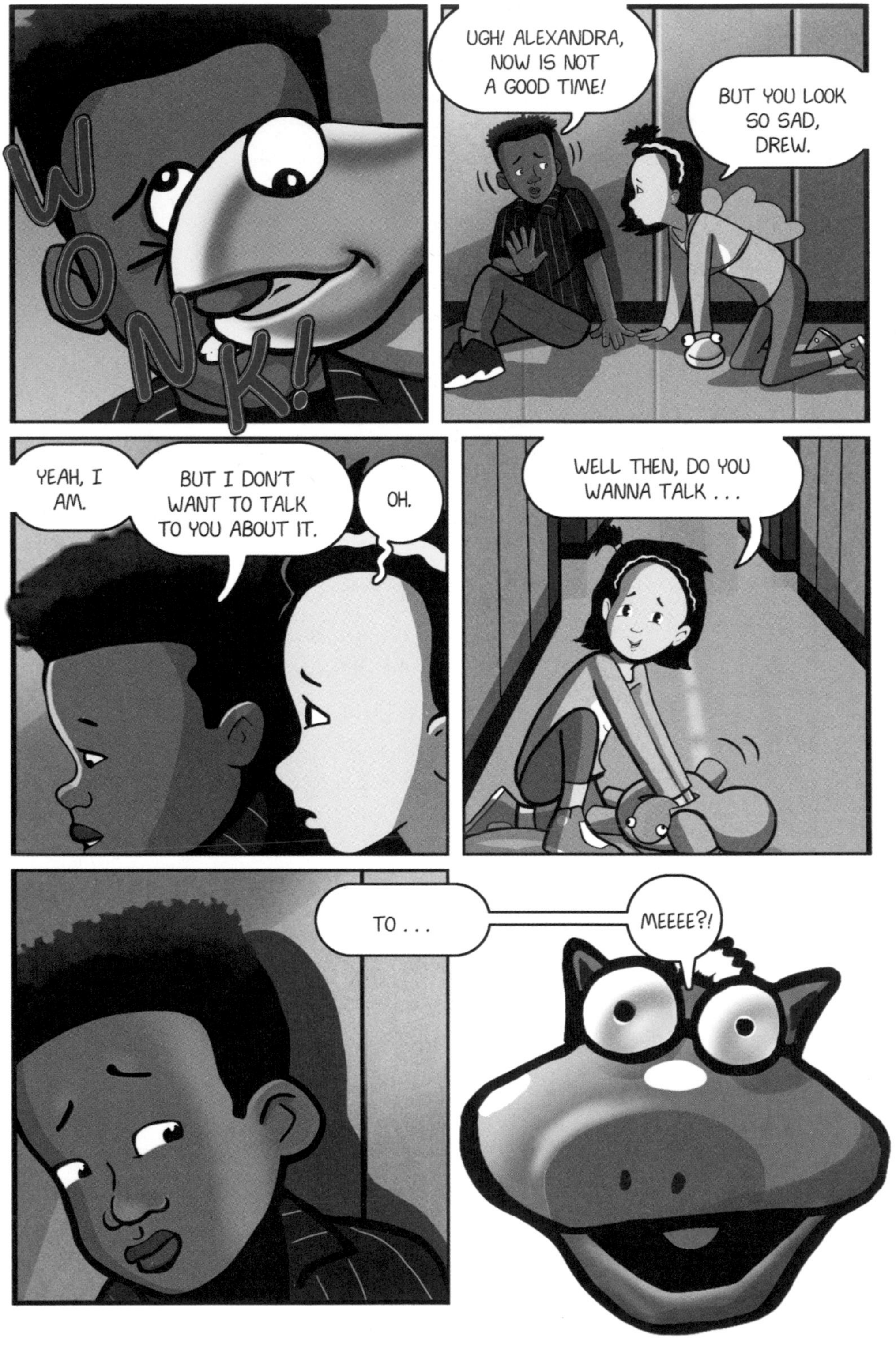
WONK!
UGH! ALEXANDRA, NOW IS NOT A GOOD TIME!
BUT YOU LOOK SO SAD, DREW.
YEAH, I AM.
BUT I DON'T WANT TO TALK TO YOU ABOUT IT.
OH.
WELL THEN, DO YOU WANNA TALK . . .
TO . . .
MEEEE?!

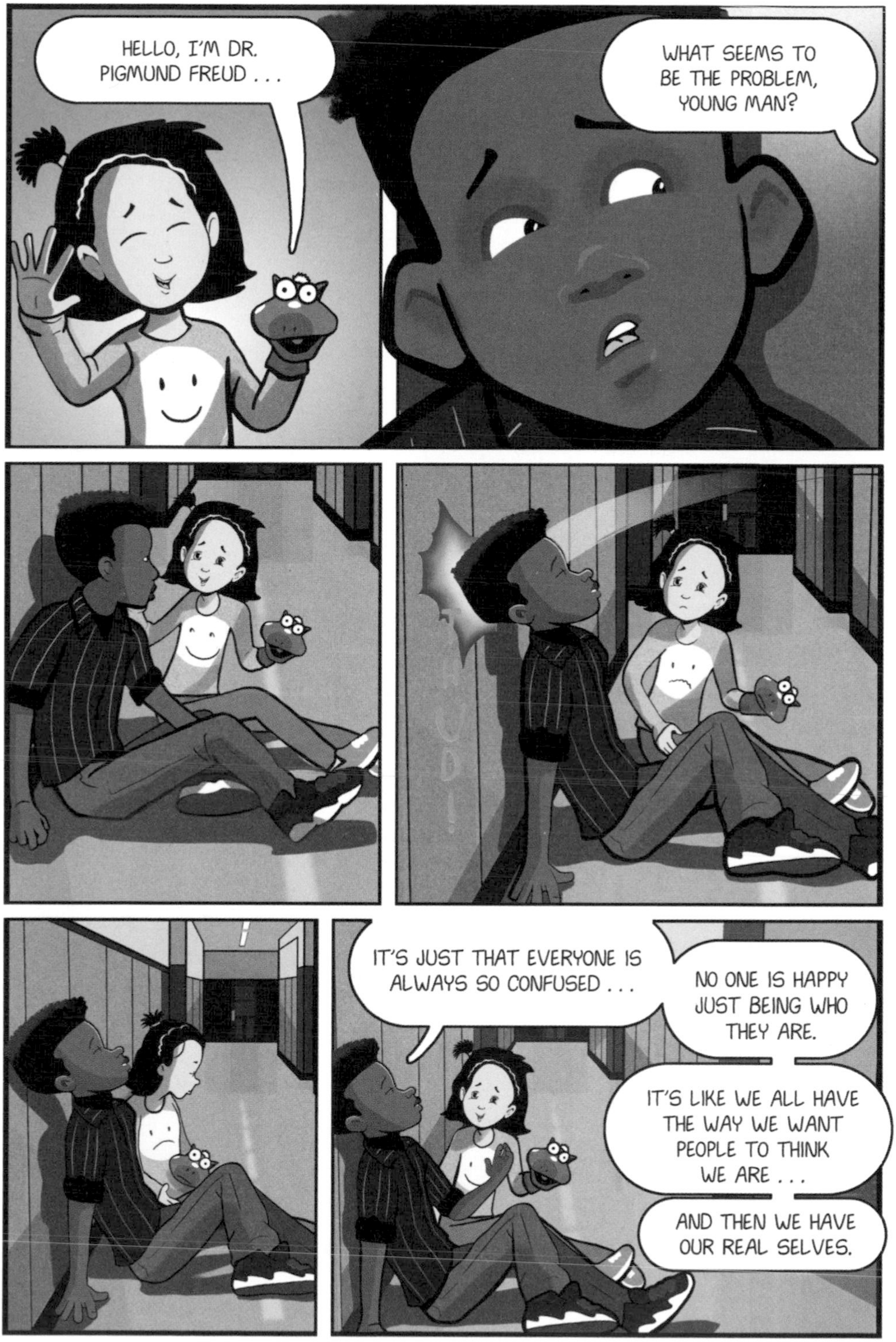
HELLO, I'M DR. PIGMUND FREUD . . .
WHAT SEEMS TO BE THE PROBLEM, YOUNG MAN?
IT'S JUST THAT EVERYONE IS ALWAYS SO CONFUSED . . .
NO ONE IS HAPPY JUST BEING WHO THEY ARE.
IT'S LIKE WE ALL HAVE THE WAY WE WANT PEOPLE TO THINK WE ARE . . .
AND THEN WE HAVE OUR REAL SELVES.

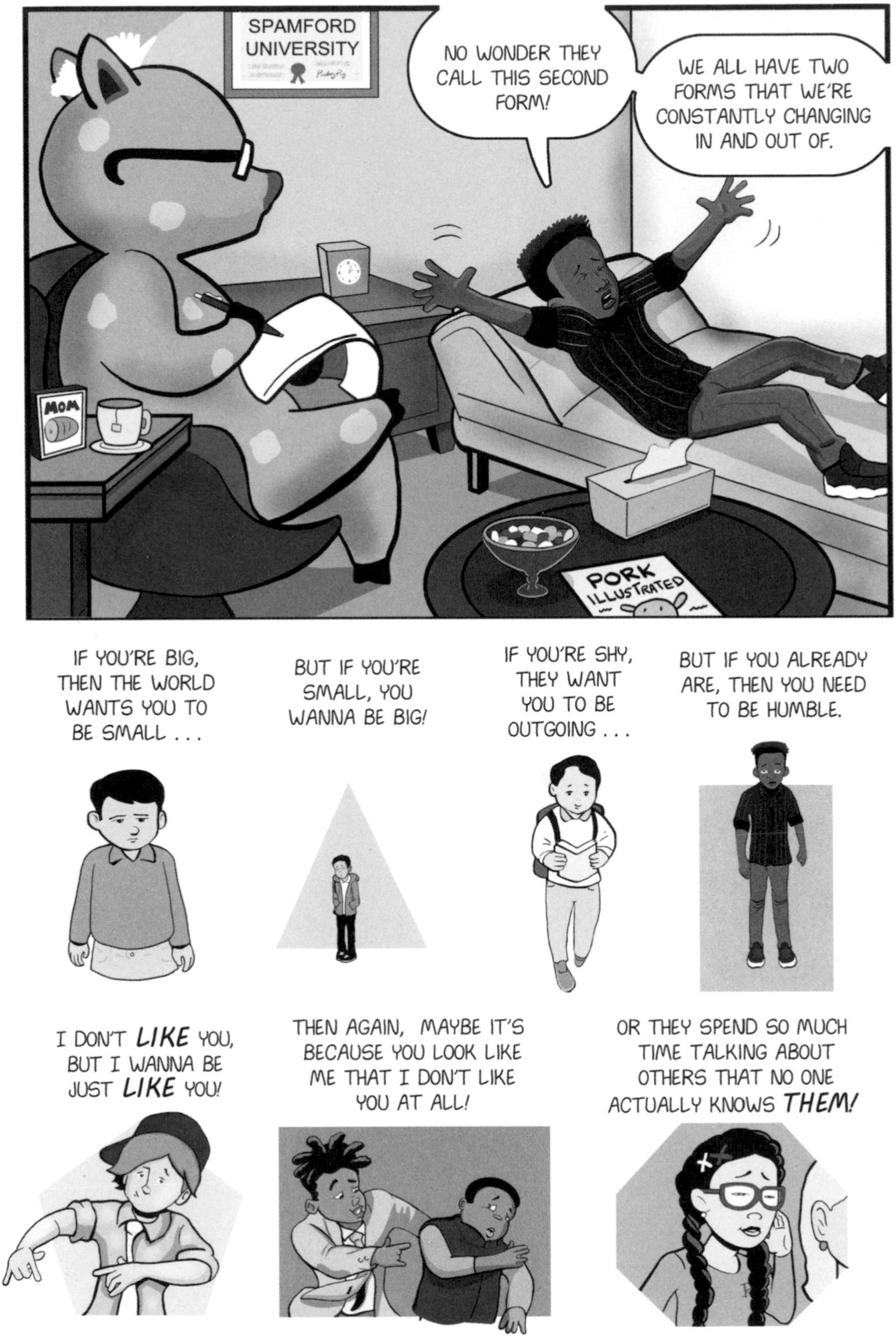
SPAMFORD UNIVERSITY
NO WONDER THEY CALL THIS SECOND FORM!
WE ALL HAVE TWO FORMS THAT WE'RE CONSTANTLY CHANGING IN AND OUT OF.
MOM
PORK ILLUSTRATED
IF YOU'RE BIG, THEN THE WORLD WANTS YOU TO BE SMALL . . .
BUT IF YOU'RE SMALL, YOU WANNA BE BIG!
IF YOU'RE SHY, THEY WANT YOU TO BE OUTGOING . . .
BUT IF YOU ALREADY ARE, THEN YOU NEED TO BE HUMBLE.
I DON'T **LIKE** YOU, BUT I WANNA BE JUST **LIKE** YOU!
THEN AGAIN, MAYBE IT'S BECAUSE YOU LOOK LIKE ME THAT I DON'T LIKE YOU AT ALL!
OR THEY SPEND SO MUCH TIME TALKING ABOUT OTHERS THAT NO ONE ACTUALLY KNOWS **THEM!**

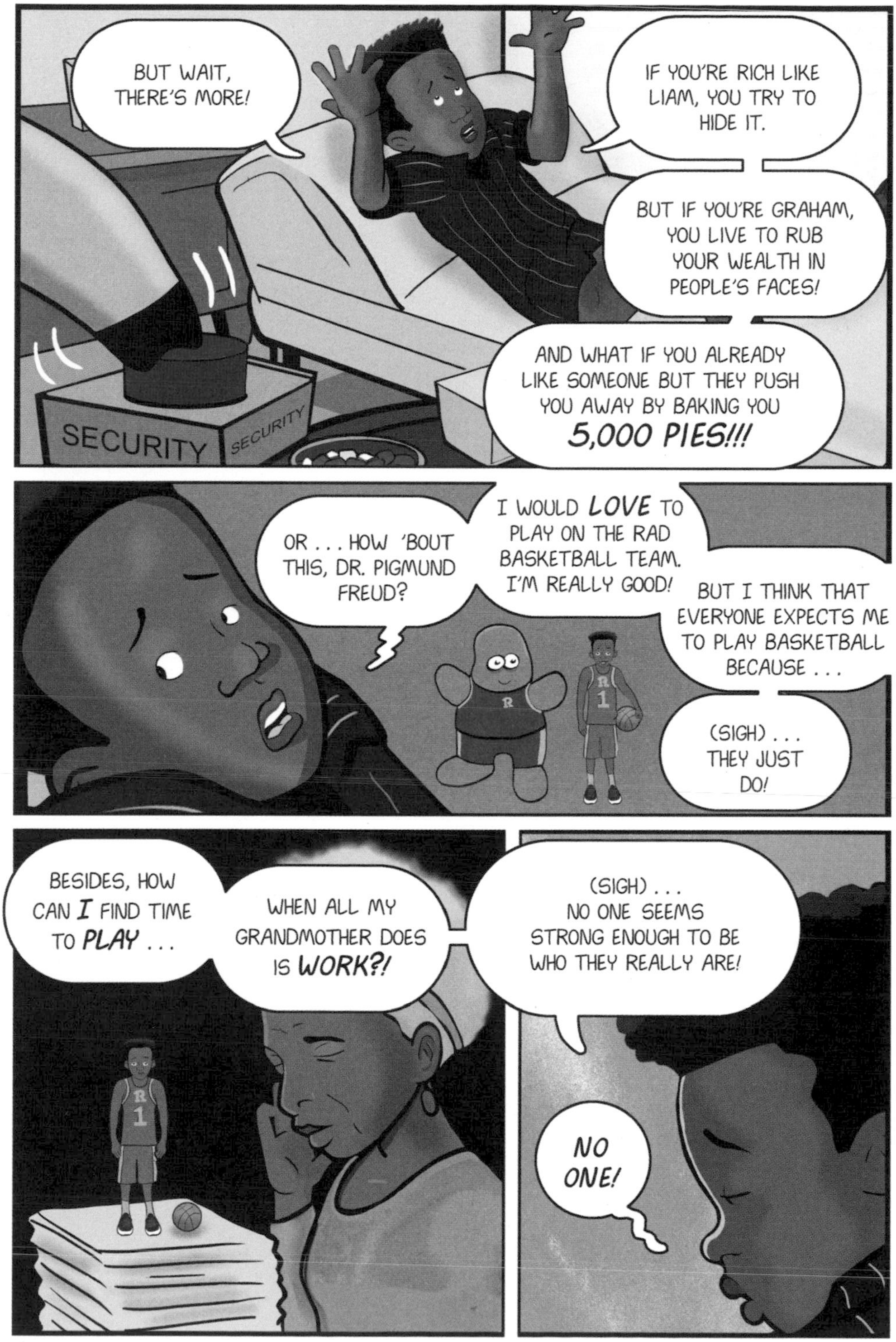
BUT WAIT, THERE'S MORE!
IF YOU'RE RICH LIKE LIAM, YOU TRY TO HIDE IT.
BUT IF YOU'RE GRAHAM, YOU LIVE TO RUB YOUR WEALTH IN PEOPLE'S FACES!
AND WHAT IF YOU ALREADY LIKE SOMEONE BUT THEY PUSH YOU AWAY BY BAKING YOU 5,000 PIES!!!
SECURITY
SECURITY
OR . . . HOW 'BOUT THIS, DR. PIGMUND FREUD?
I WOULD LOVE TO PLAY ON THE RAD BASKETBALL TEAM. I'M REALLY GOOD!
BUT I THINK THAT EVERYONE EXPECTS ME TO PLAY BASKETBALL BECAUSE . . .
(SIGH) . . . THEY JUST DO!
BESIDES, HOW CAN I FIND TIME TO PLAY . . .
WHEN ALL MY GRANDMOTHER DOES IS WORK?!
(SIGH) . . . NO ONE SEEMS STRONG ENOUGH TO BE WHO THEY REALLY ARE!
NO ONE!

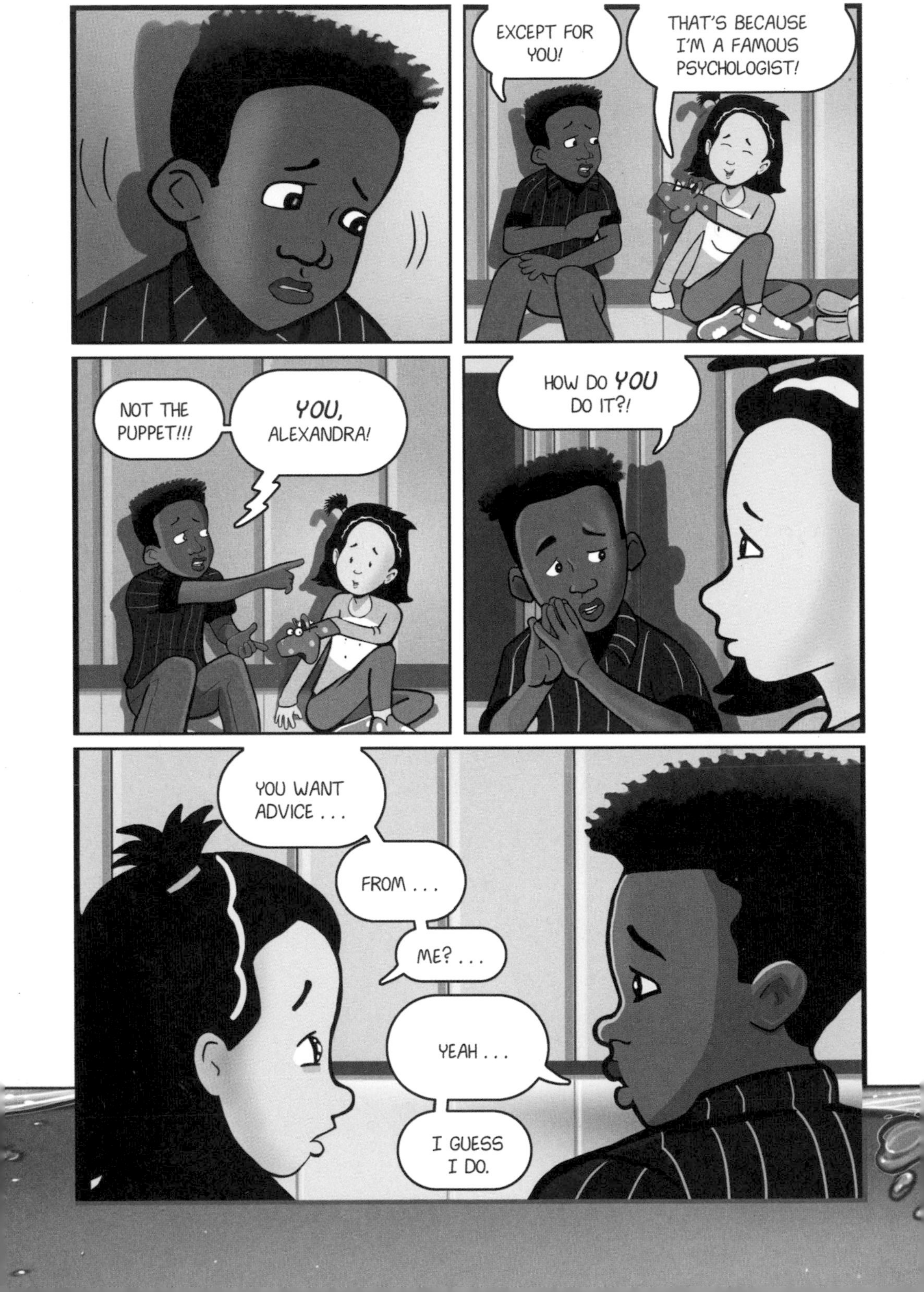
EXCEPT FOR YOU!
THAT'S BECAUSE I'M A FAMOUS PSYCHOLOGIST!
NOT THE PUPPET!!!
YOU, ALEXANDRA!
HOW DO YOU DO IT?!
YOU WANT ADVICE . . .
FROM . . .
ME? . . .
YEAH . . .
I GUESS I DO.

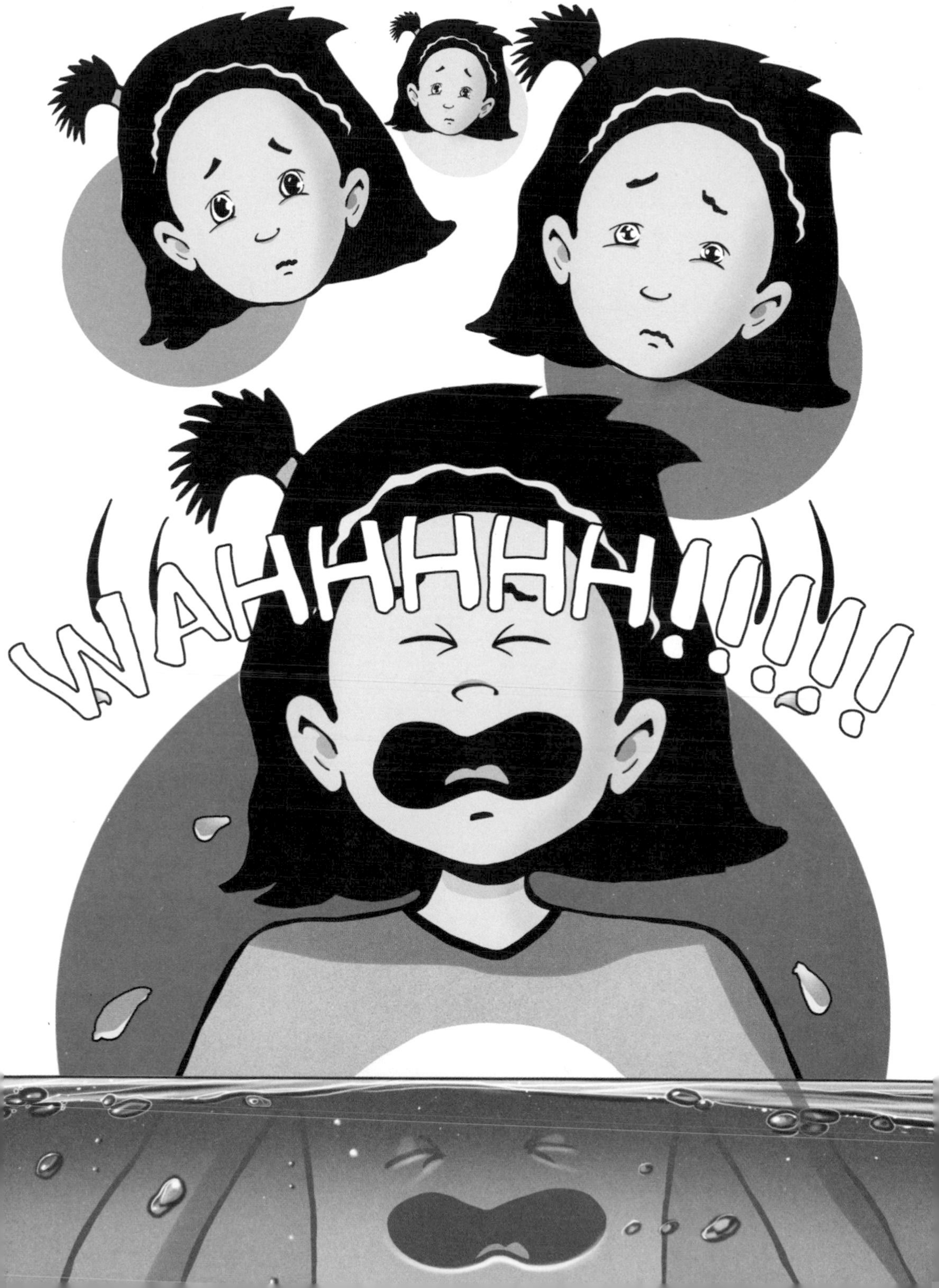
WAHHHHH!!!!!!

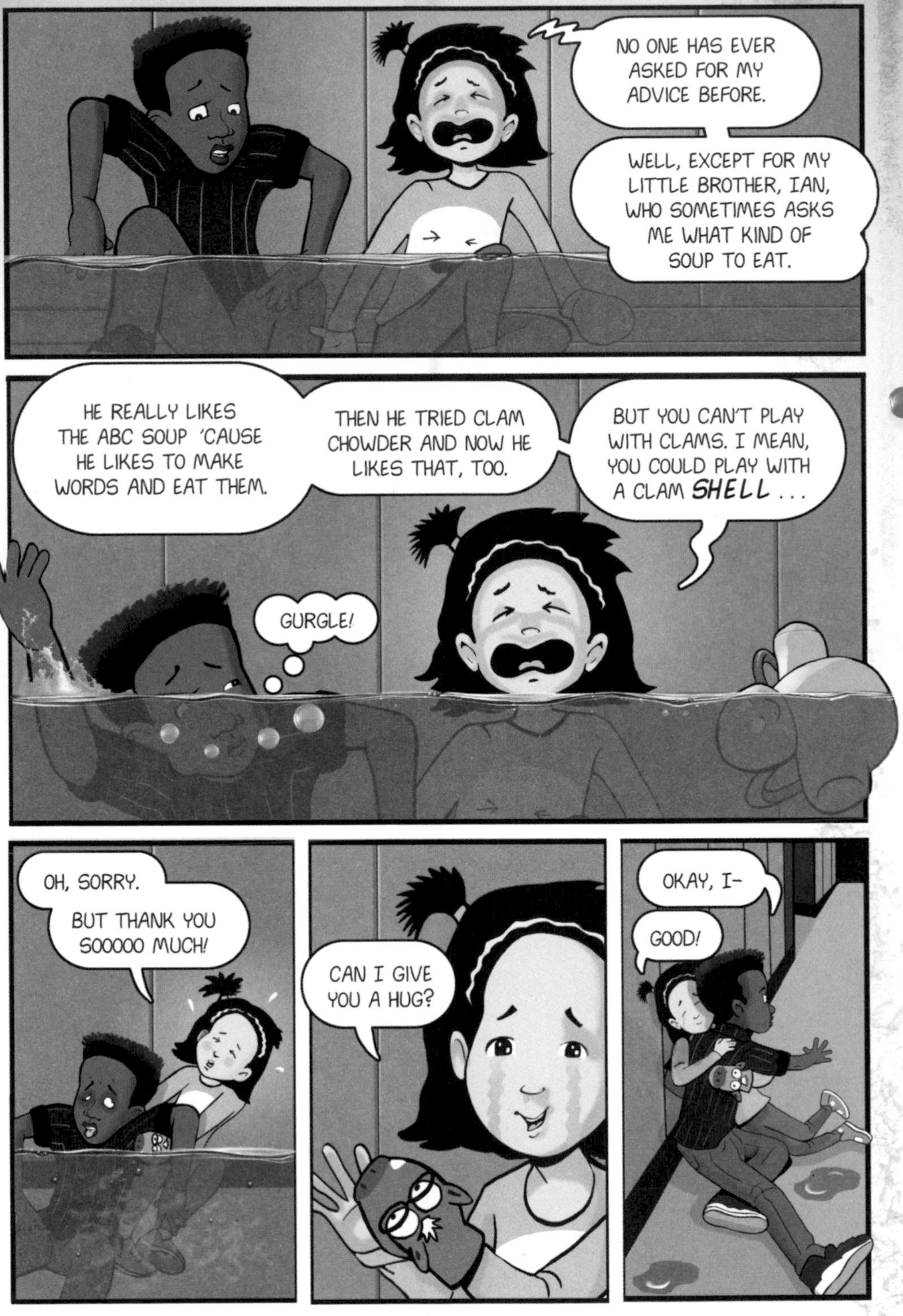
NO ONE HAS EVER ASKED FOR MY ADVICE BEFORE.
WELL, EXCEPT FOR MY LITTLE BROTHER, IAN, WHO SOMETIMES ASKS ME WHAT KIND OF SOUP TO EAT.
HE REALLY LIKES THE ABC SOUP 'CAUSE HE LIKES TO MAKE WORDS AND EAT THEM.
THEN HE TRIED CLAM CHOWDER AND NOW HE LIKES THAT, TOO.
BUT YOU CAN'T PLAY WITH CLAMS. I MEAN, YOU COULD PLAY WITH A CLAM SHELL . . .
GURGLE!
OH, SORRY.
BUT THANK YOU SOOOOO MUCH!
CAN I GIVE YOU A HUG?
OKAY, I-
GOOD!

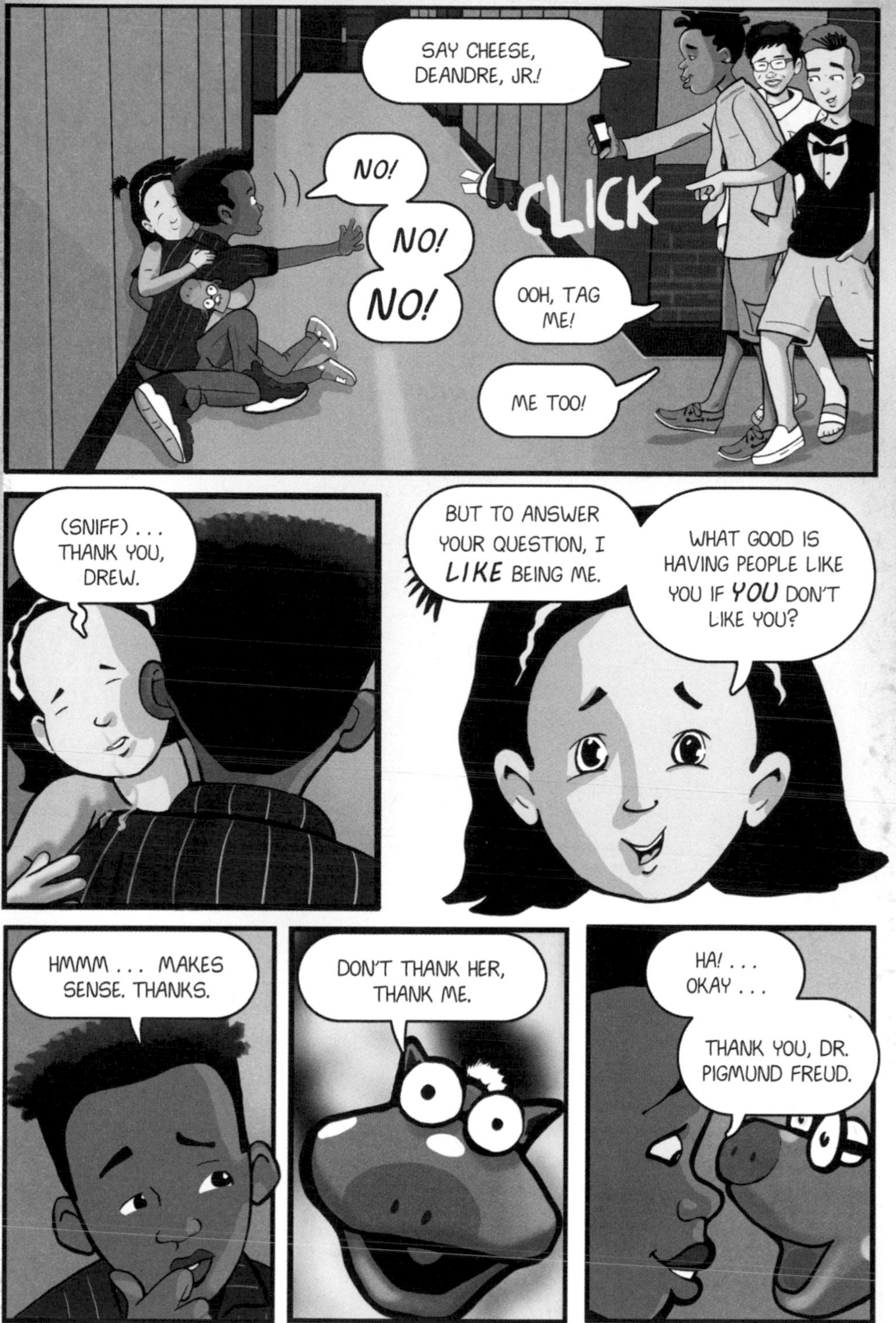
SAY CHEESE, DEANDRE, JR.!
NO!
NO!
NO!
CLICK
OOH, TAG ME!
ME TOO!
(SNIFF) . . . THANK YOU, DREW.
BUT TO ANSWER YOUR QUESTION, I LIKE BEING ME.
WHAT GOOD IS HAVING PEOPLE LIKE YOU IF YOU DON'T LIKE YOU?
HMMM . . . MAKES SENSE. THANKS.
DON'T THANK HER, THANK ME.
HA! . . . OKAY . . .
THANK YOU, DR. PIGMUND FREUD.

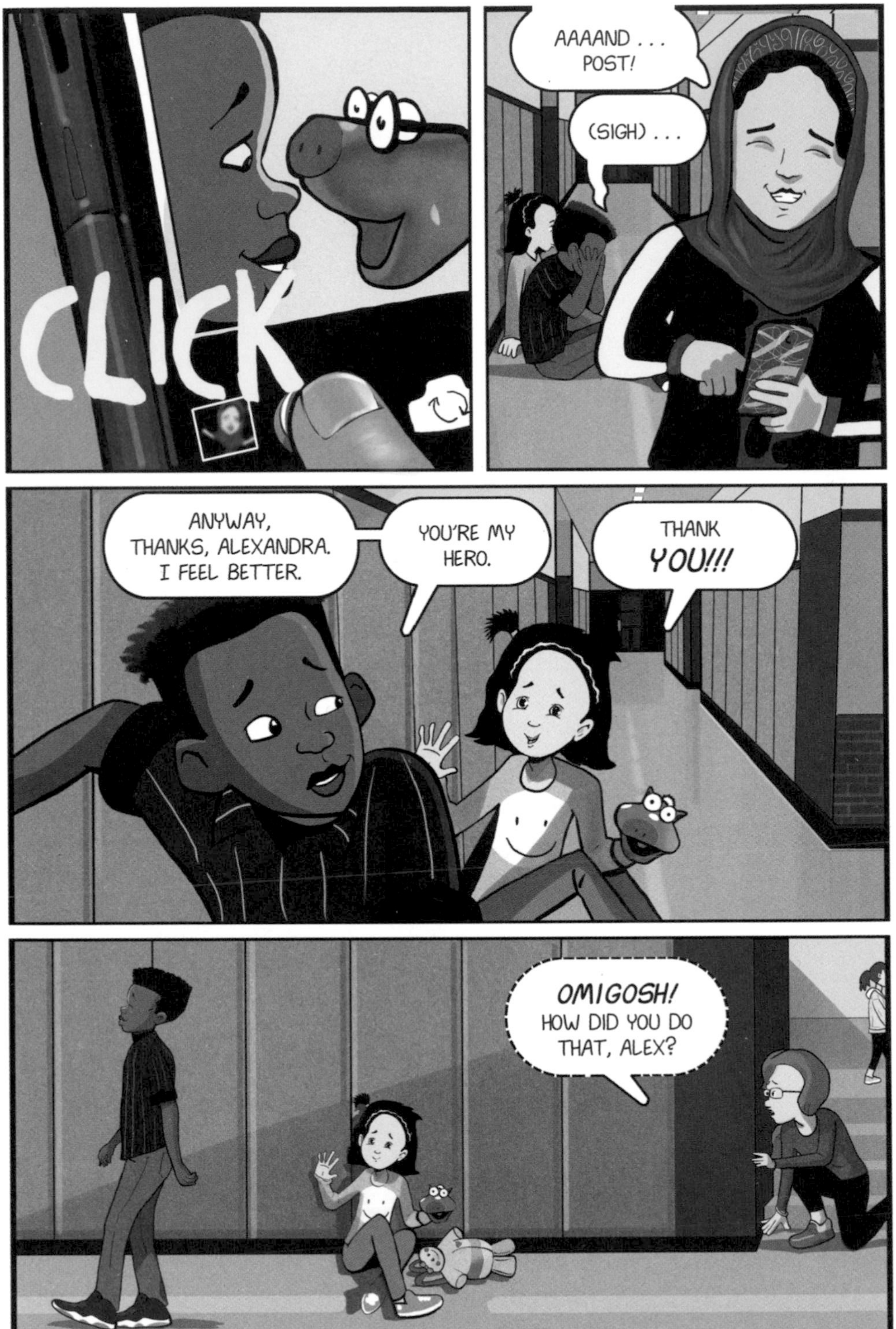
CLICK
AAAAND . . . POST!
(SIGH) . . .
ANYWAY, THANKS, ALEXANDRA. I FEEL BETTER.
YOU'RE MY HERO.
THANK YOU!!!
OMIGOSH! HOW DID YOU DO THAT, ALEX?

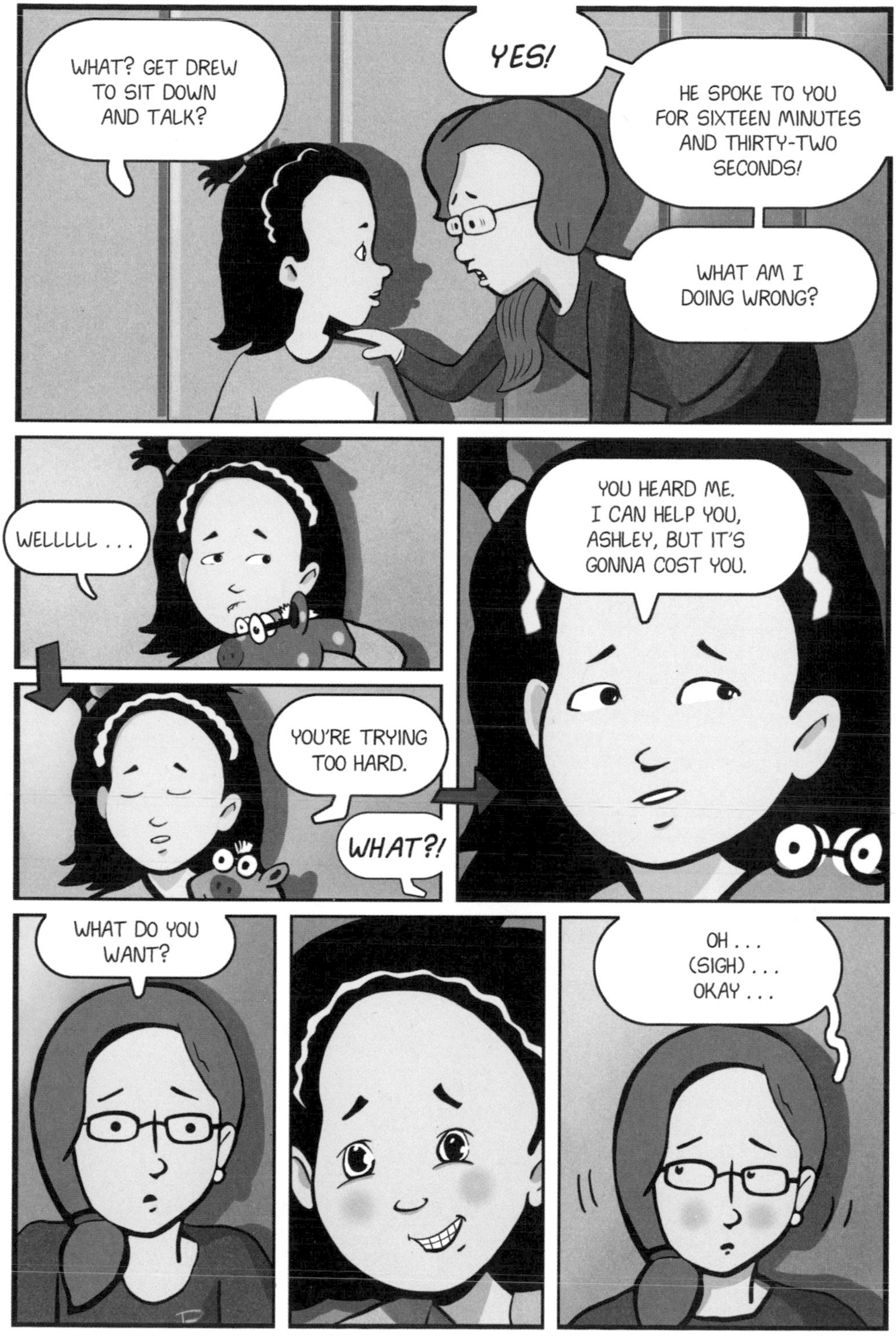
WHAT? GET DREW TO SIT DOWN AND TALK?
YES!
HE SPOKE TO YOU FOR SIXTEEN MINUTES AND THIRTY-TWO SECONDS!
WHAT AM I DOING WRONG?
WELLLLL . . .
YOU'RE TRYING TOO HARD.
WHAT?!
YOU HEARD ME. I CAN HELP YOU, ASHLEY, BUT IT'S GONNA COST YOU.
WHAT DO YOU WANT?
OH . . . (SIGH) . . . OKAY . . .

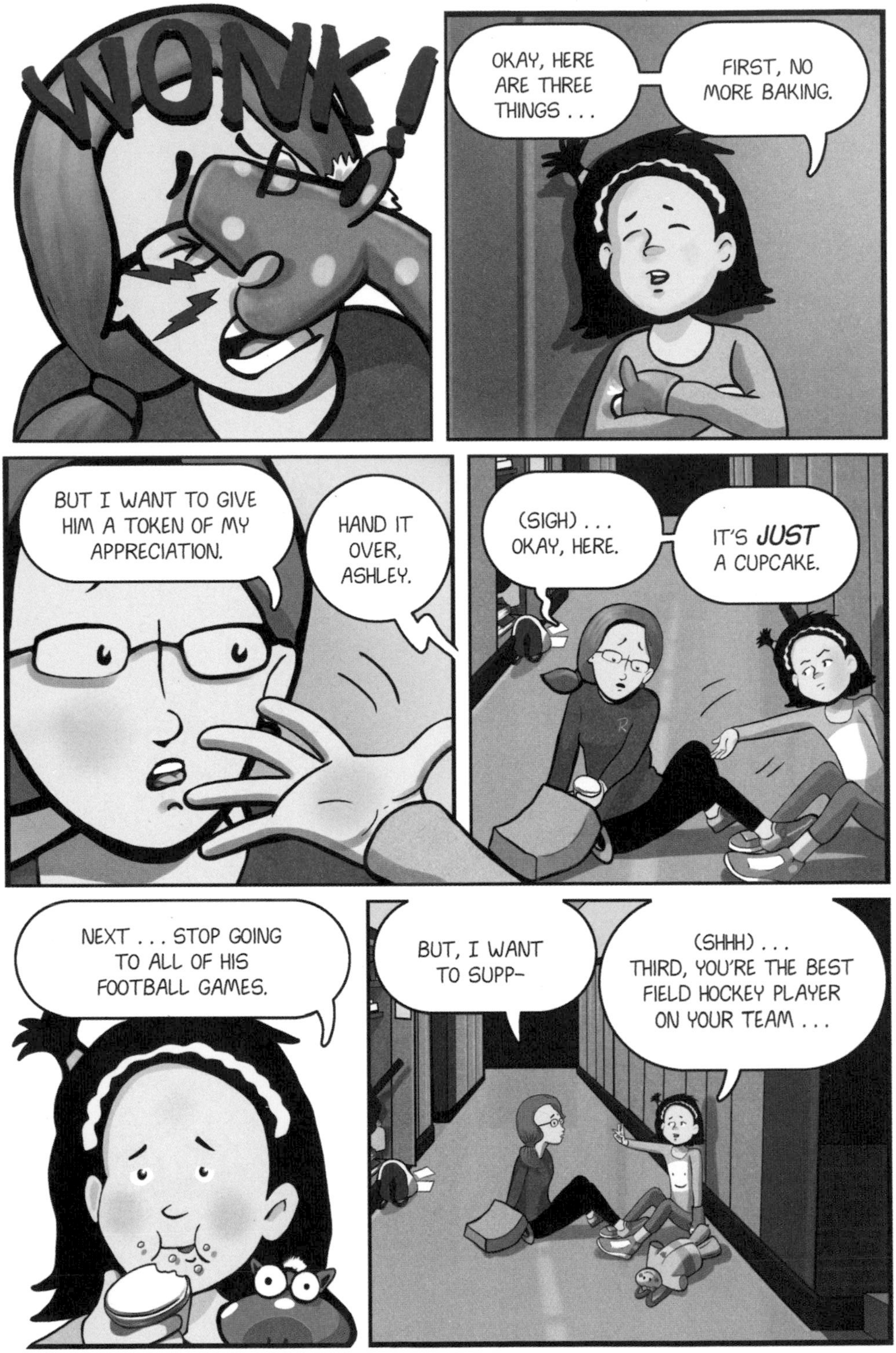
WONK!
OKAY, HERE ARE THREE THINGS . . .
FIRST, NO MORE BAKING.
BUT I WANT TO GIVE HIM A TOKEN OF MY APPRECIATION.
HAND IT OVER, ASHLEY.
(SIGH) . . . OKAY, HERE.
IT'S **JUST** A CUPCAKE.
NEXT . . . STOP GOING TO ALL OF HIS FOOTBALL GAMES.
BUT, I WANT TO SUPP–
(SHHH) . . . THIRD, YOU'RE THE BEST FIELD HOCKEY PLAYER ON YOUR TEAM . . .

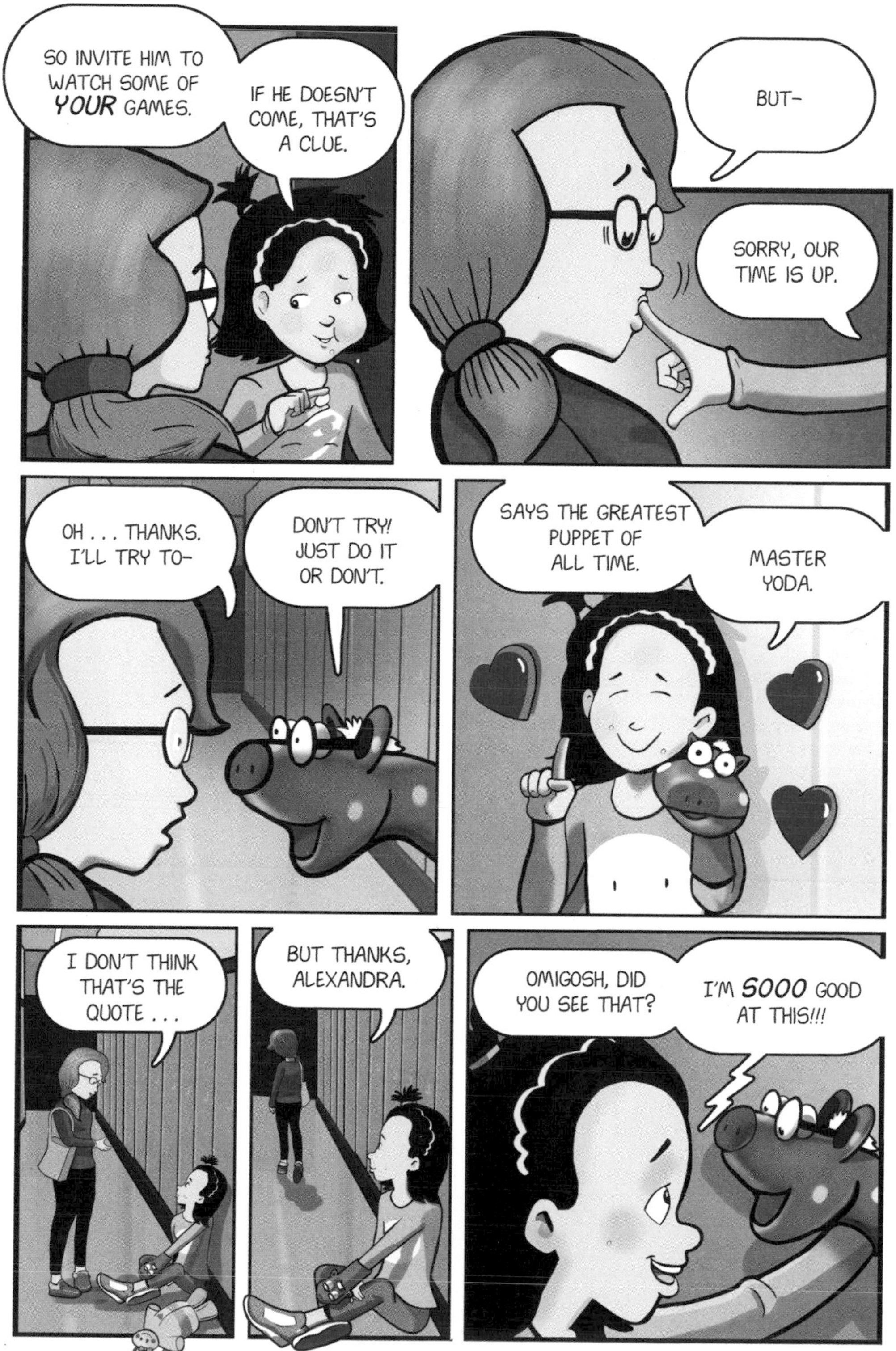
SO INVITE HIM TO WATCH SOME OF *YOUR* GAMES.
IF HE DOESN'T COME, THAT'S A CLUE.
BUT–
SORRY, OUR TIME IS UP.
OH . . . THANKS. I'LL TRY TO–
DON'T TRY! JUST DO IT OR DON'T.
SAYS THE GREATEST PUPPET OF ALL TIME.
MASTER YODA.
I DON'T THINK THAT'S THE QUOTE . . .
BUT THANKS, ALEXANDRA.
OMIGOSH, DID YOU SEE THAT?
I'M *SOOO* GOOD AT THIS!!!

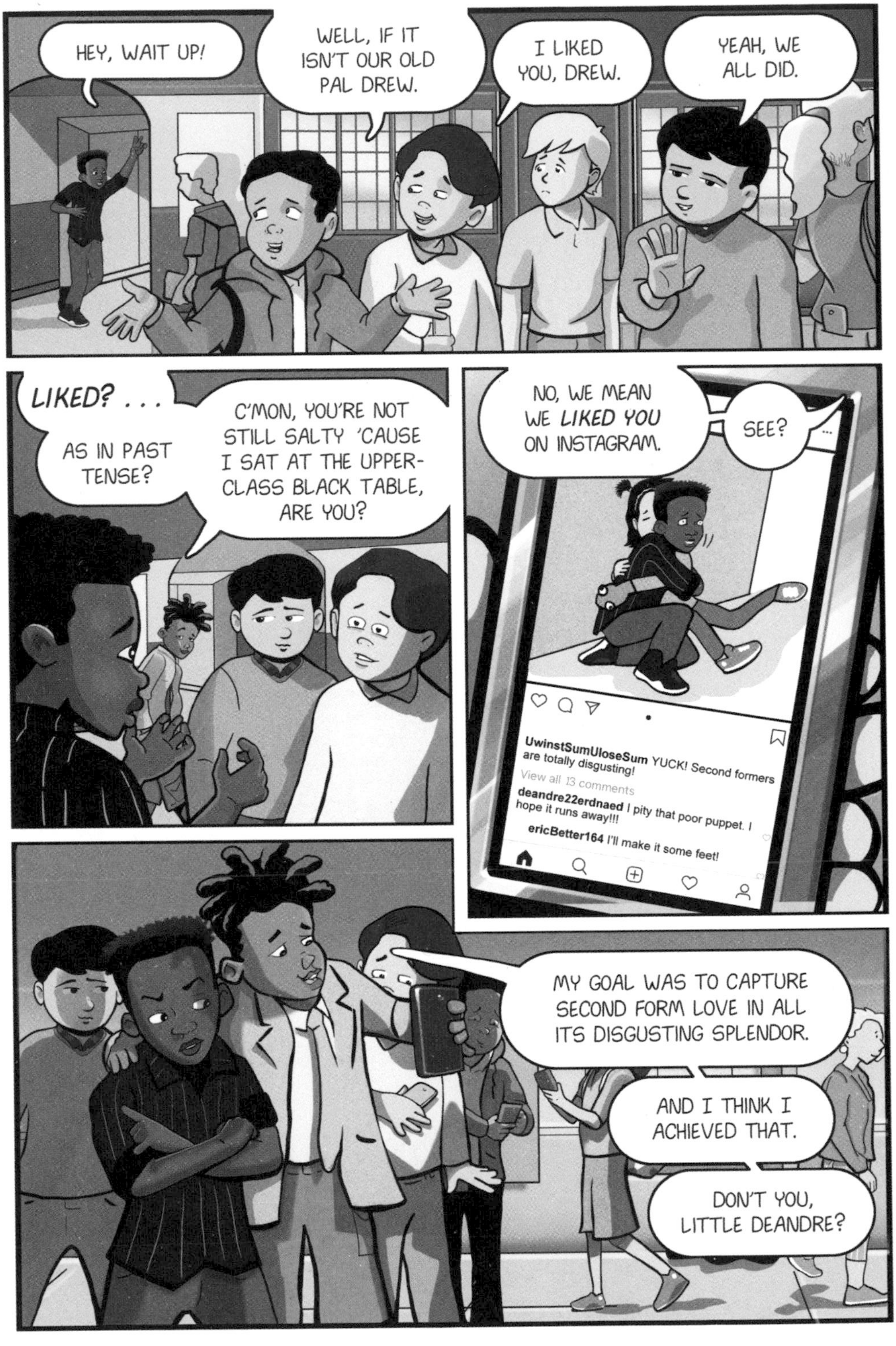
HEY, WAIT UP!
WELL, IF IT ISN'T OUR OLD PAL DREW.
I LIKED YOU, DREW.
YEAH, WE ALL DID.
LIKED? . . .
AS IN PAST TENSE?
C'MON, YOU'RE NOT STILL SALTY 'CAUSE I SAT AT THE UPPER-CLASS BLACK TABLE, ARE YOU?
NO, WE MEAN WE LIKED YOU ON INSTAGRAM.
SEE?
UwinstSumUloseSum YUCK! Second formers are totally disgusting!
View all 13 comments
deandre22erdnaed I pity that poor puppet. I hope it runs away!!!
ericBetter164 I'll make it some feet!
MY GOAL WAS TO CAPTURE SECOND FORM LOVE IN ALL ITS DISGUSTING SPLENDOR.
AND I THINK I ACHIEVED THAT.
DON'T YOU, LITTLE DEANDRE?

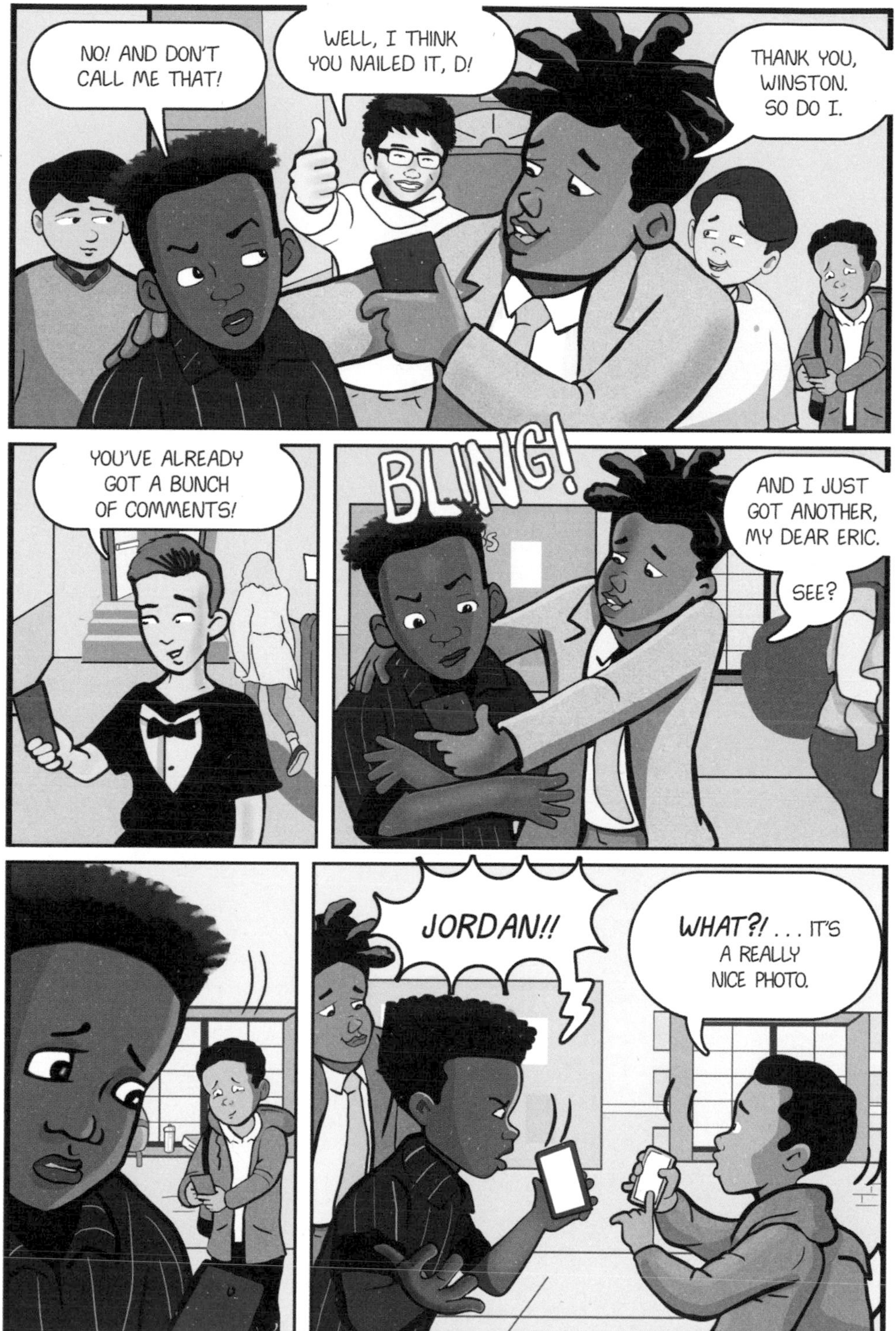
NO! AND DON'T CALL ME THAT!
WELL, I THINK YOU NAILED IT, D!
THANK YOU, WINSTON. SO DO I.
YOU'VE ALREADY GOT A BUNCH OF COMMENTS!
BLING!
AND I JUST GOT ANOTHER, MY DEAR ERIC.
SEE?
JORDAN!!
WHAT?! . . . IT'S A REALLY NICE PHOTO.

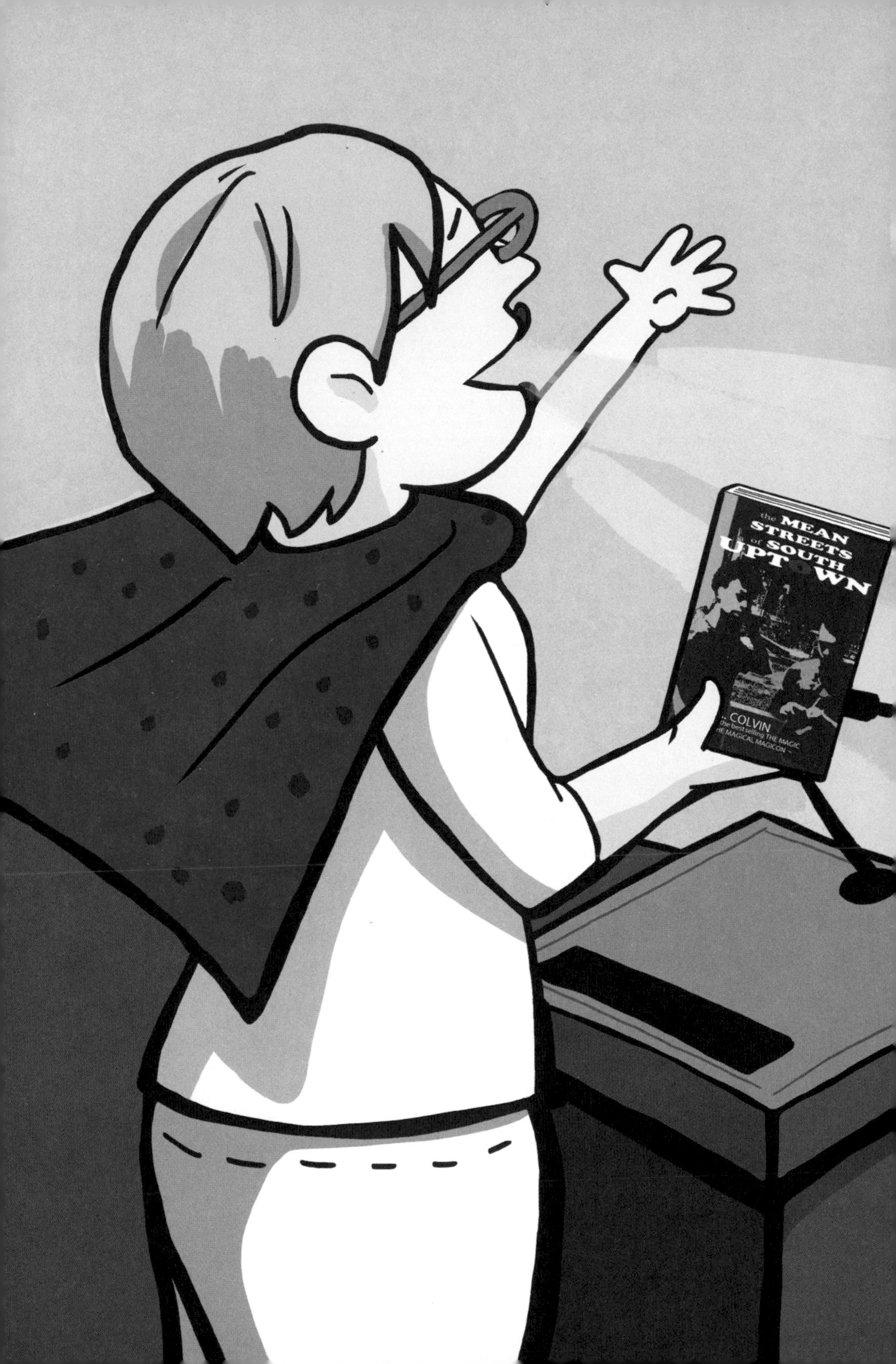

the MEAN STREETS of SOUTH UPTOWN
COLVIN
the best selling THE MAGIC
MAGICAL MAGICON

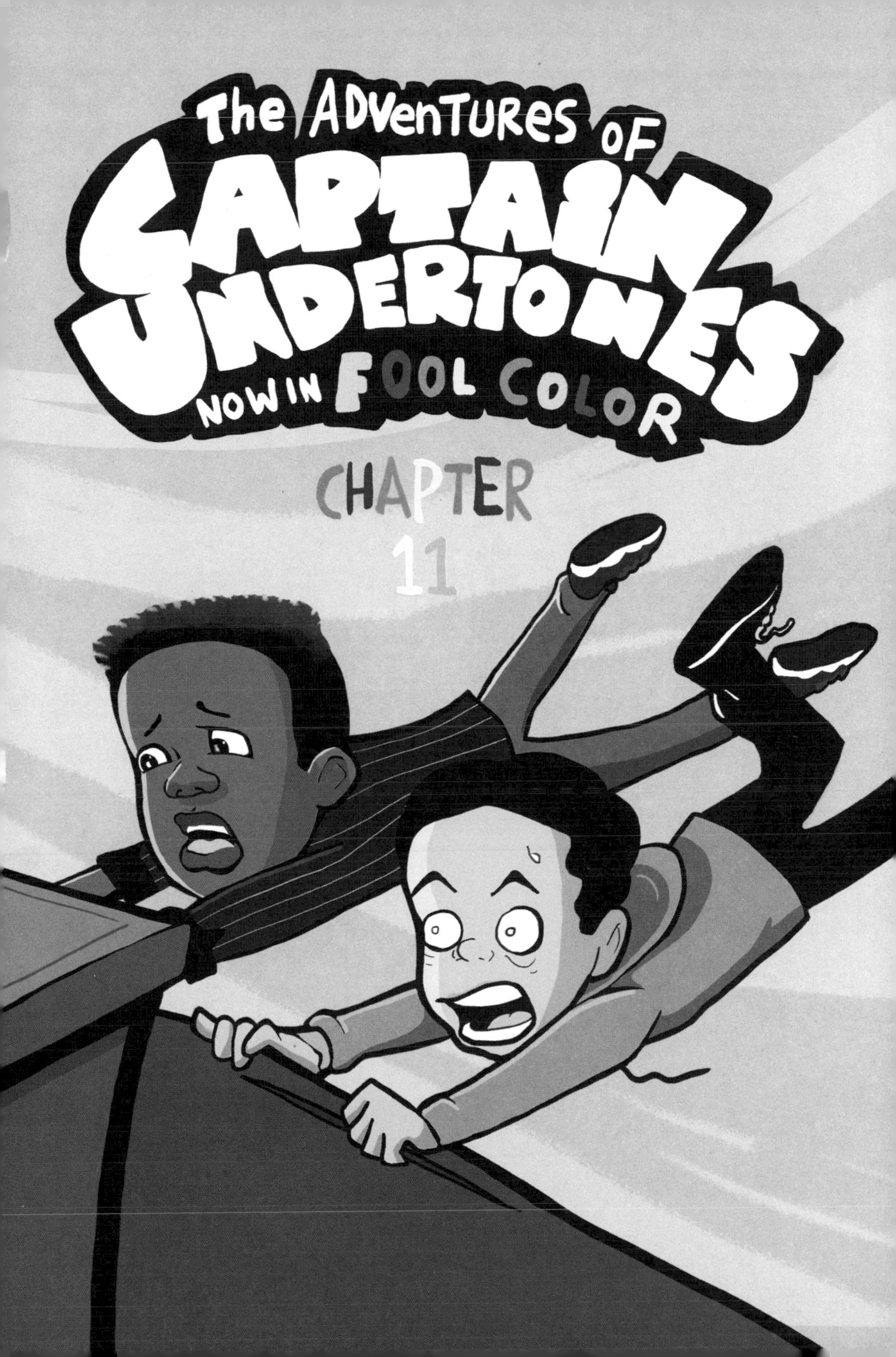
The ADVENTURES OF
CAPTAIN UNDERTONES
NOW IN FOOL COLOR
CHAPTER
11

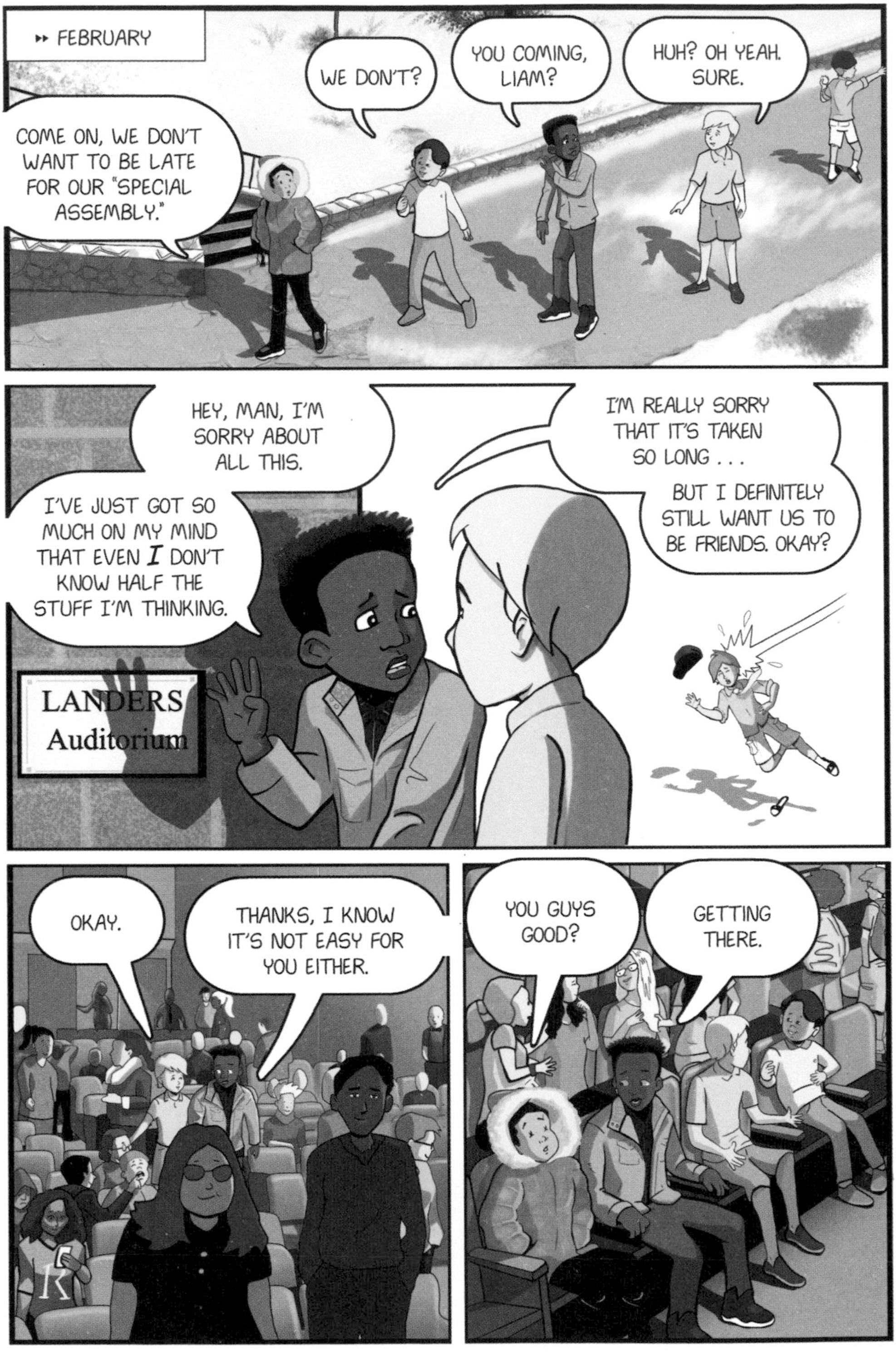
▸▸ FEBRUARY
COME ON, WE DON'T WANT TO BE LATE FOR OUR "SPECIAL ASSEMBLY."
WE DON'T?
YOU COMING, LIAM?
HUH? OH YEAH. SURE.
HEY, MAN, I'M SORRY ABOUT ALL THIS.
I'VE JUST GOT SO MUCH ON MY MIND THAT EVEN *I* DON'T KNOW HALF THE STUFF I'M THINKING.
LANDERS Auditorium
I'M REALLY SORRY THAT IT'S TAKEN SO LONG . . .
BUT I DEFINITELY STILL WANT US TO BE FRIENDS. OKAY?
OKAY.
THANKS, I KNOW IT'S NOT EASY FOR YOU EITHER.
YOU GUYS GOOD?
GETTING THERE.

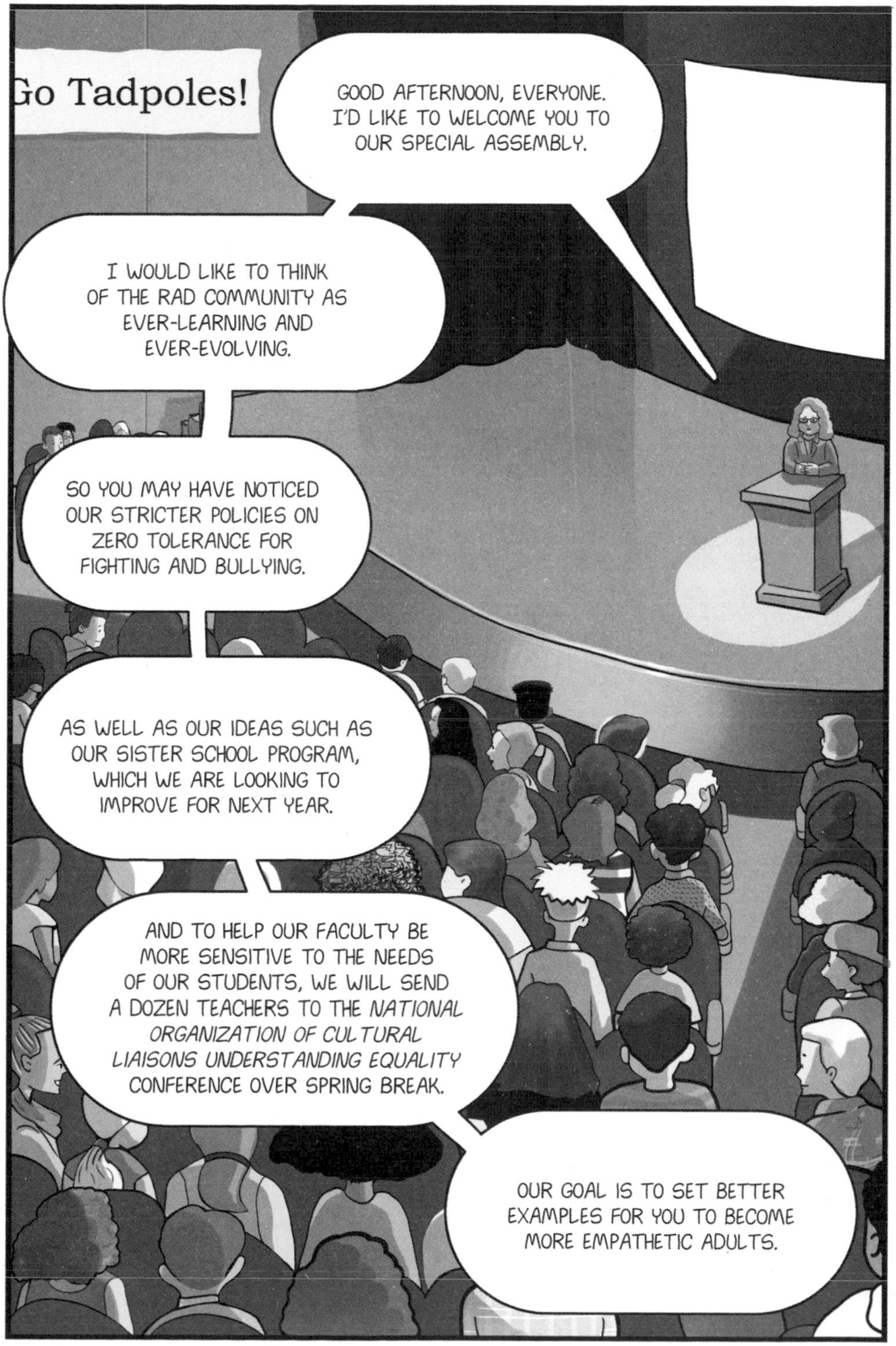
Go Tadpoles!
GOOD AFTERNOON, EVERYONE. I'D LIKE TO WELCOME YOU TO OUR SPECIAL ASSEMBLY.
I WOULD LIKE TO THINK OF THE RAD COMMUNITY AS EVER-LEARNING AND EVER-EVOLVING.
SO YOU MAY HAVE NOTICED OUR STRICTER POLICIES ON ZERO TOLERANCE FOR FIGHTING AND BULLYING.
AS WELL AS OUR IDEAS SUCH AS OUR SISTER SCHOOL PROGRAM, WHICH WE ARE LOOKING TO IMPROVE FOR NEXT YEAR.
AND TO HELP OUR FACULTY BE MORE SENSITIVE TO THE NEEDS OF OUR STUDENTS, WE WILL SEND A DOZEN TEACHERS TO THE *NATIONAL ORGANIZATION OF CULTURAL LIAISONS UNDERSTANDING EQUALITY* CONFERENCE OVER SPRING BREAK.
OUR GOAL IS TO SET BETTER EXAMPLES FOR YOU TO BECOME MORE EMPATHETIC ADULTS.

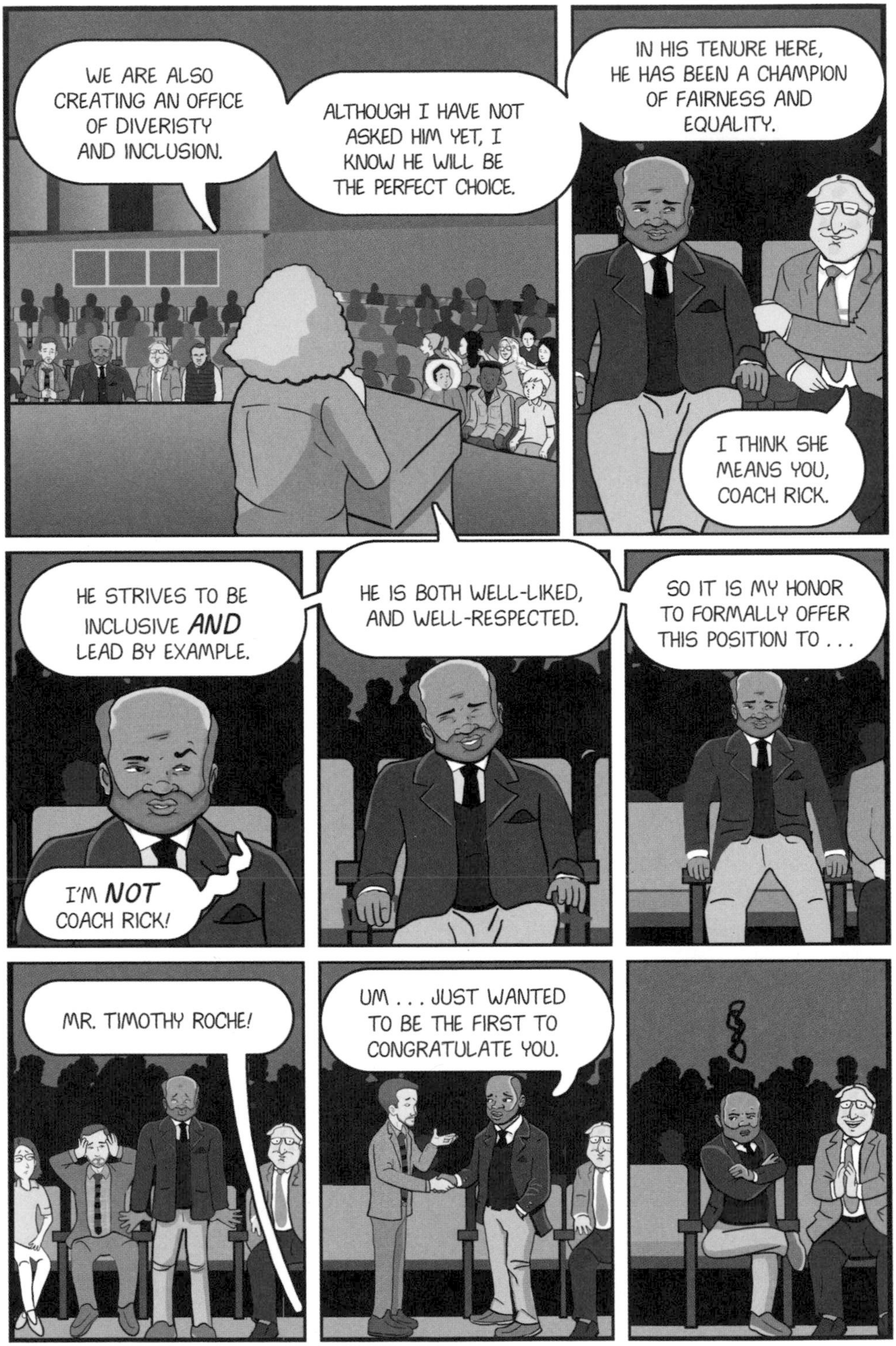
WE ARE ALSO CREATING AN OFFICE OF DIVERISTY AND INCLUSION.
ALTHOUGH I HAVE NOT ASKED HIM YET, I KNOW HE WILL BE THE PERFECT CHOICE.
IN HIS TENURE HERE, HE HAS BEEN A CHAMPION OF FAIRNESS AND EQUALITY.
I THINK SHE MEANS YOU, COACH RICK.
HE STRIVES TO BE INCLUSIVE AND LEAD BY EXAMPLE.
I'M NOT COACH RICK!
HE IS BOTH WELL-LIKED, AND WELL-RESPECTED.
SO IT IS MY HONOR TO FORMALLY OFFER THIS POSITION TO . . .
MR. TIMOTHY ROCHE!
UM . . . JUST WANTED TO BE THE FIRST TO CONGRATULATE YOU.

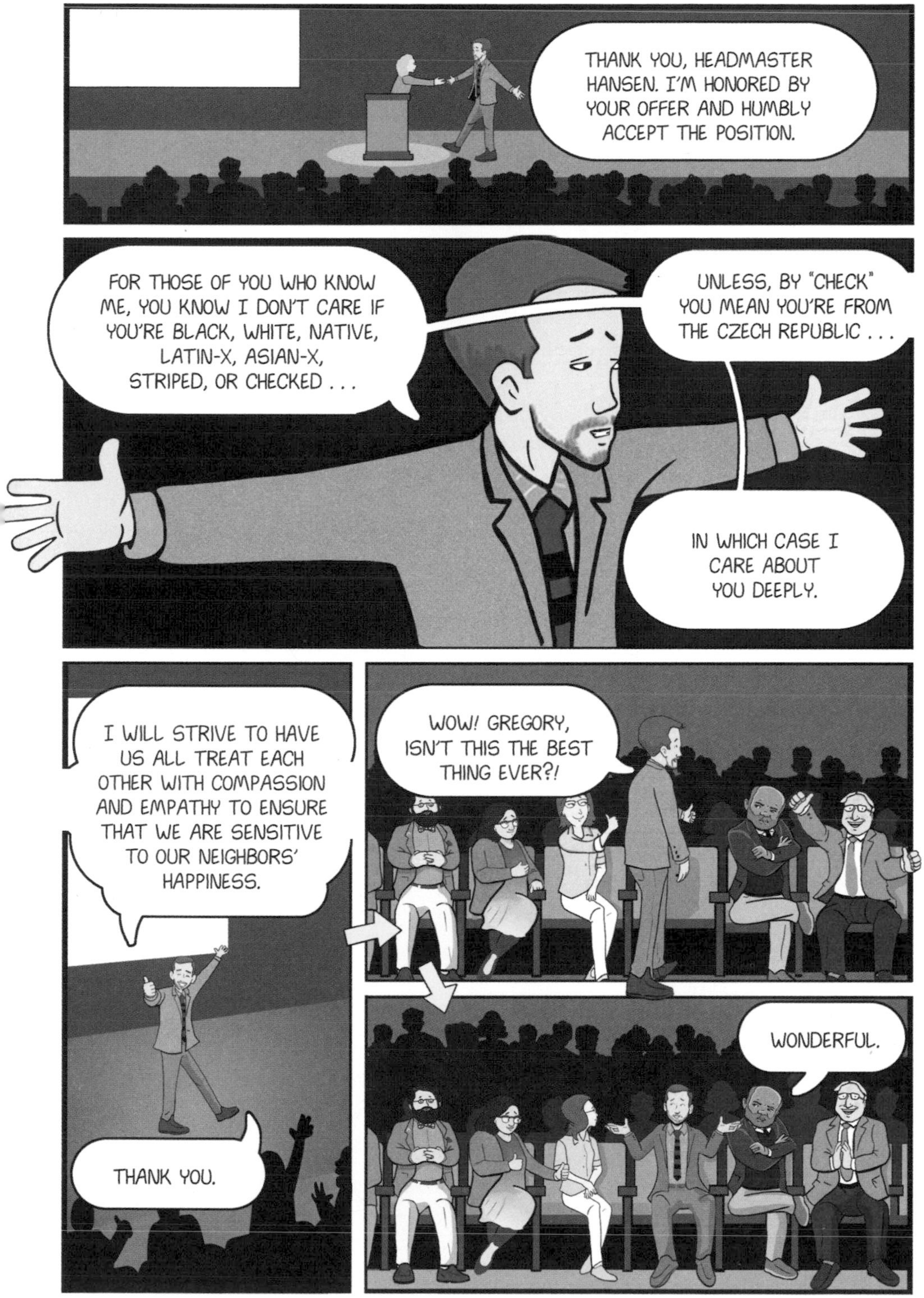
THANK YOU, HEADMASTER HANSEN. I'M HONORED BY YOUR OFFER AND HUMBLY ACCEPT THE POSITION.
FOR THOSE OF YOU WHO KNOW ME, YOU KNOW I DON'T CARE IF YOU'RE BLACK, WHITE, NATIVE, LATIN-X, ASIAN-X, STRIPED, OR CHECKED . . .
UNLESS, BY "CHECK" YOU MEAN YOU'RE FROM THE CZECH REPUBLIC . . .
IN WHICH CASE I CARE ABOUT YOU DEEPLY.
I WILL STRIVE TO HAVE US ALL TREAT EACH OTHER WITH COMPASSION AND EMPATHY TO ENSURE THAT WE ARE SENSITIVE TO OUR NEIGHBORS' HAPPINESS.
THANK YOU.
WOW! GREGORY, ISN'T THIS THE BEST THING EVER?!
WONDERFUL.

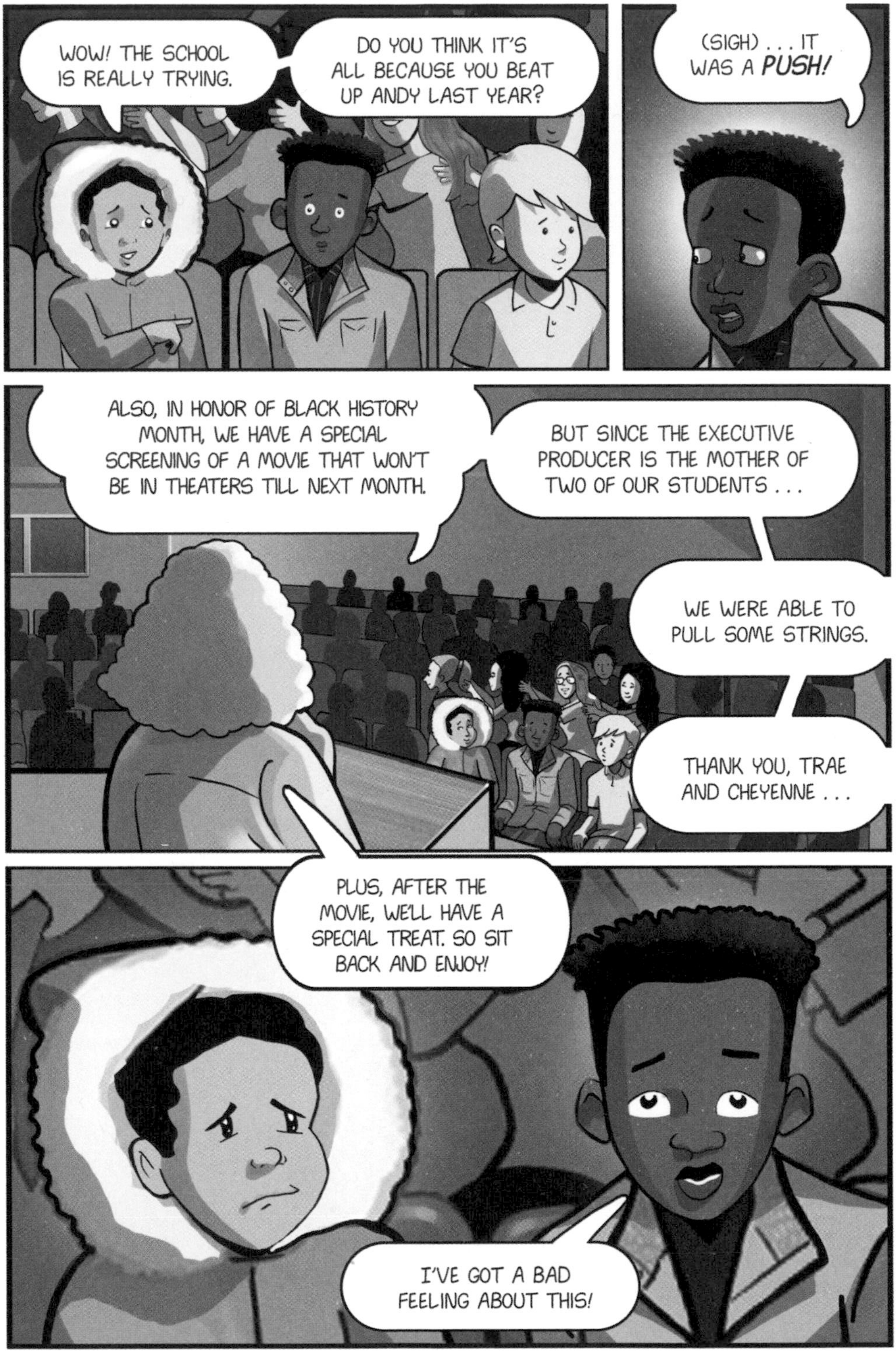
WOW! THE SCHOOL IS REALLY TRYING.
DO YOU THINK IT'S ALL BECAUSE YOU BEAT UP ANDY LAST YEAR?
(SIGH) . . . IT WAS A PUSH!
ALSO, IN HONOR OF BLACK HISTORY MONTH, WE HAVE A SPECIAL SCREENING OF A MOVIE THAT WON'T BE IN THEATERS TILL NEXT MONTH.
BUT SINCE THE EXECUTIVE PRODUCER IS THE MOTHER OF TWO OF OUR STUDENTS . . .
WE WERE ABLE TO PULL SOME STRINGS.
THANK YOU, TRAE AND CHEYENNE . . .
PLUS, AFTER THE MOVIE, WE'LL HAVE A SPECIAL TREAT. SO SIT BACK AND ENJOY!
I'VE GOT A BAD FEELING ABOUT THIS!

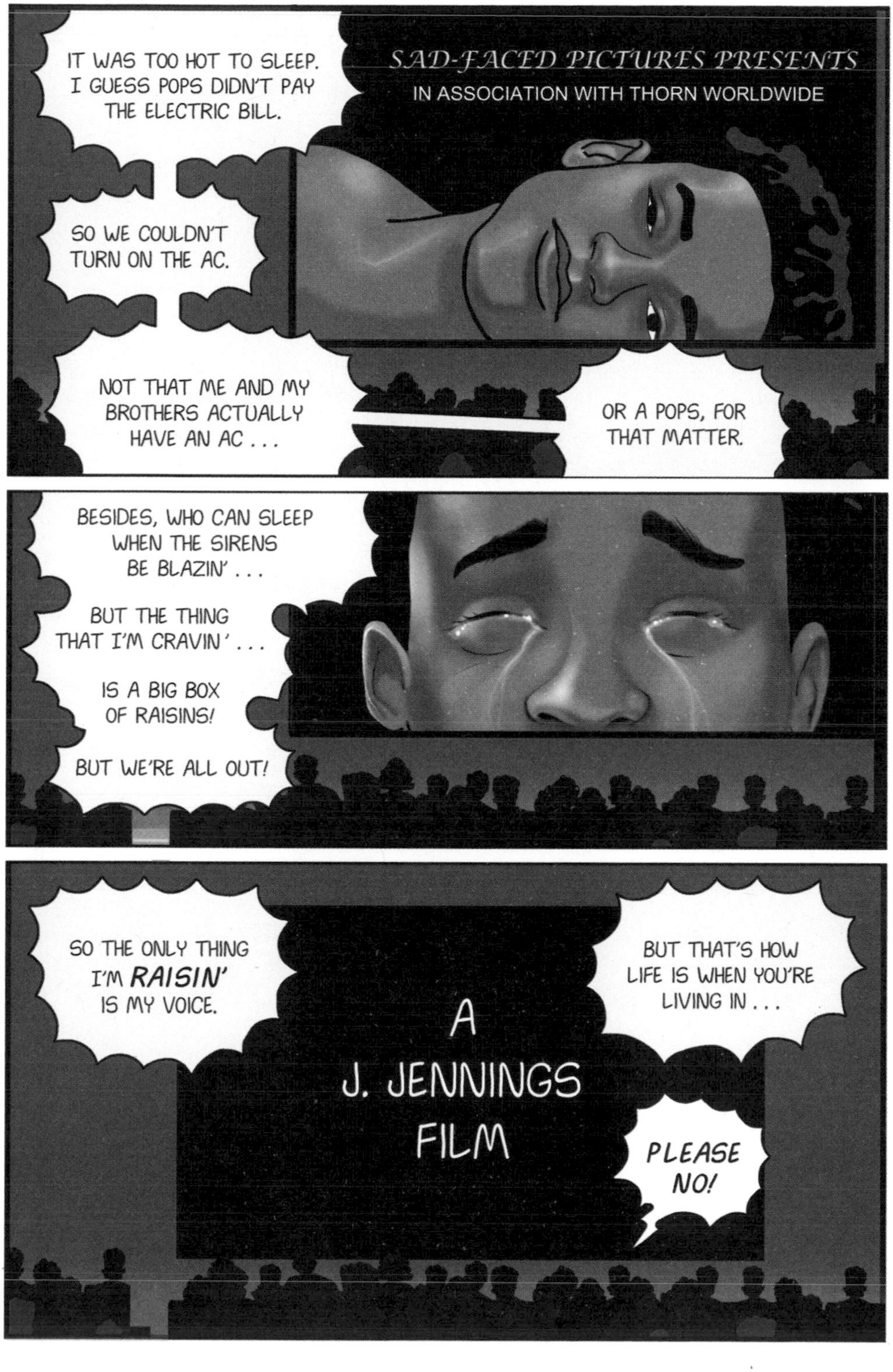

IT WAS TOO HOT TO SLEEP. I GUESS POPS DIDN'T PAY THE ELECTRIC BILL.
SAD-FACED PICTURES PRESENTS
IN ASSOCIATION WITH THORN WORLDWIDE
SO WE COULDN'T TURN ON THE AC.
NOT THAT ME AND MY BROTHERS ACTUALLY HAVE AN AC . . .
OR A POPS, FOR THAT MATTER.
BESIDES, WHO CAN SLEEP WHEN THE SIRENS BE BLAZIN' . . .
BUT THE THING THAT I'M CRAVIN' . . .
IS A BIG BOX OF RAISINS!
BUT WE'RE ALL OUT!
SO THE ONLY THING I'M RAISIN' IS MY VOICE.
BUT THAT'S HOW LIFE IS WHEN YOU'RE LIVING IN . . .
A J. JENNINGS FILM
PLEASE NO!

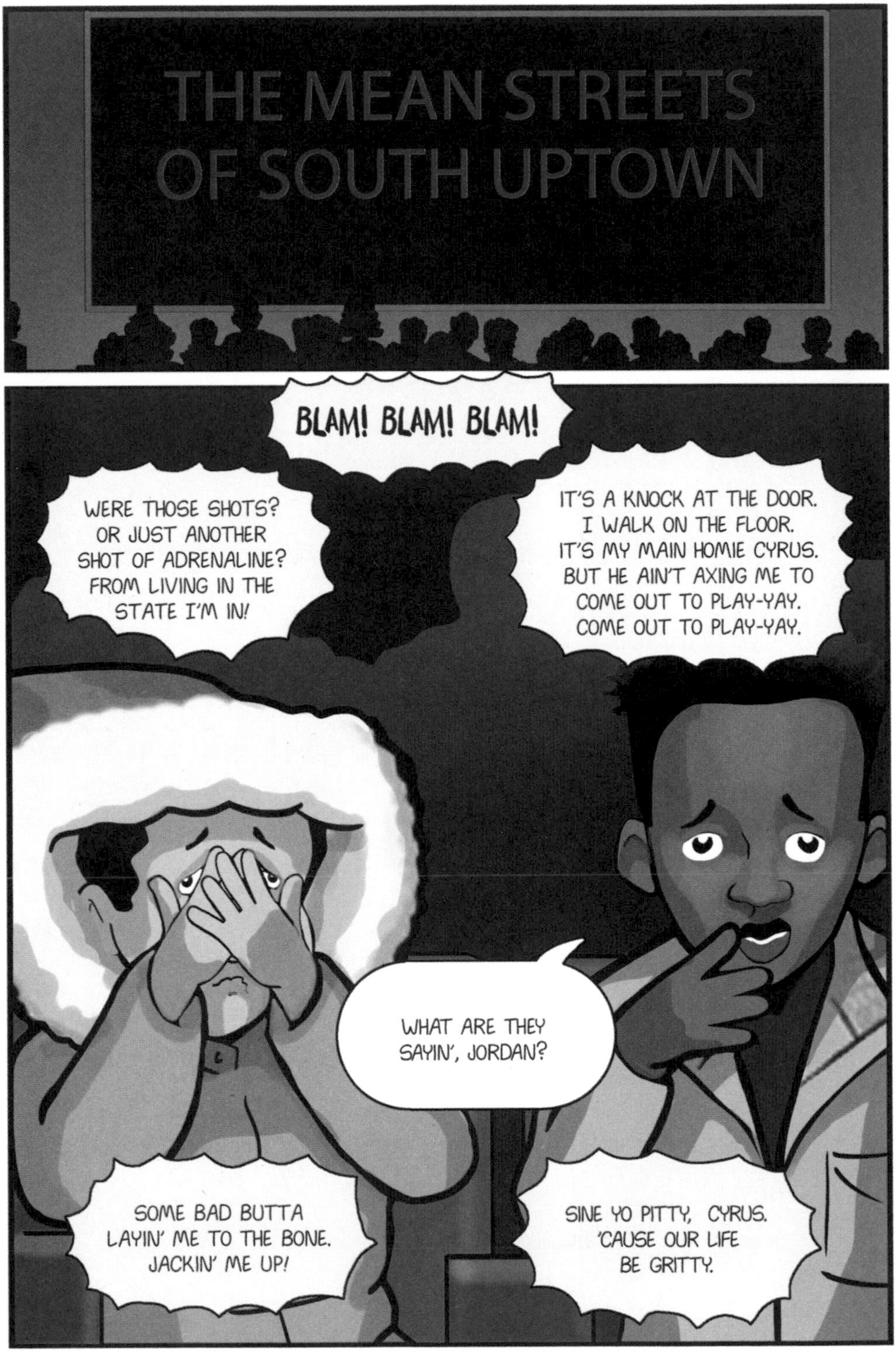
THE MEAN STREETS OF SOUTH UPTOWN
BLAM! BLAM! BLAM!
WERE THOSE SHOTS? OR JUST ANOTHER SHOT OF ADRENALINE? FROM LIVING IN THE STATE I'M IN!
IT'S A KNOCK AT THE DOOR. I WALK ON THE FLOOR. IT'S MY MAIN HOMIE CYRUS. BUT HE AIN'T AXING ME TO COME OUT TO PLAY-YAY. COME OUT TO PLAY-YAY.
WHAT ARE THEY SAYIN', JORDAN?
SOME BAD BUTTA LAYIN' ME TO THE BONE. JACKIN' ME UP!
SINE YO PITTY, CYRUS. 'CAUSE OUR LIFE BE GRITTY.

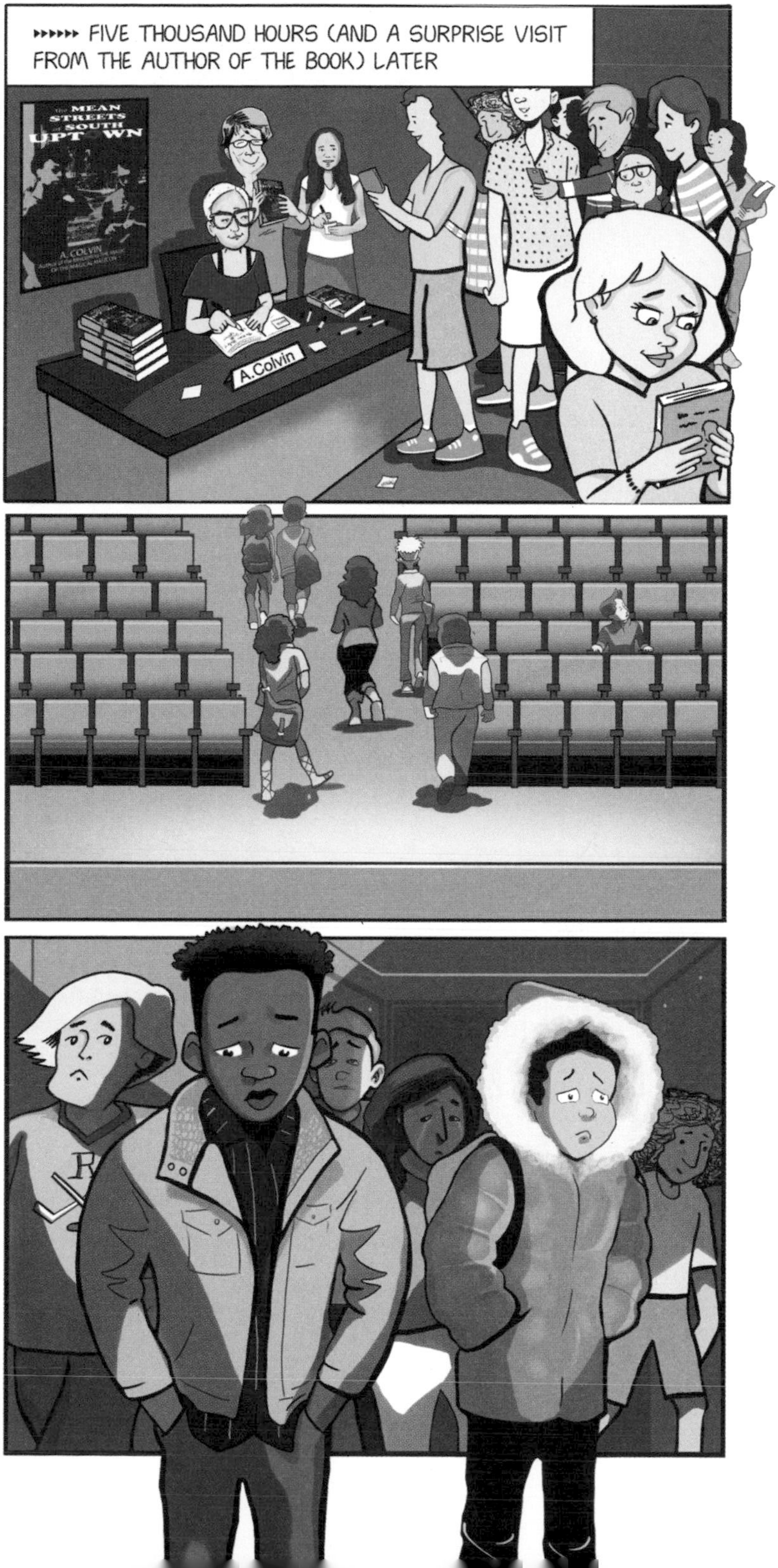
▸▸▸▸▸▸ FIVE THOUSAND HOURS (AND A SURPRISE VISIT FROM THE AUTHOR OF THE BOOK) LATER
The MEAN STREETS of SOUTH UPT WN
A. COLVIN
A.Colvin
A.Colvin

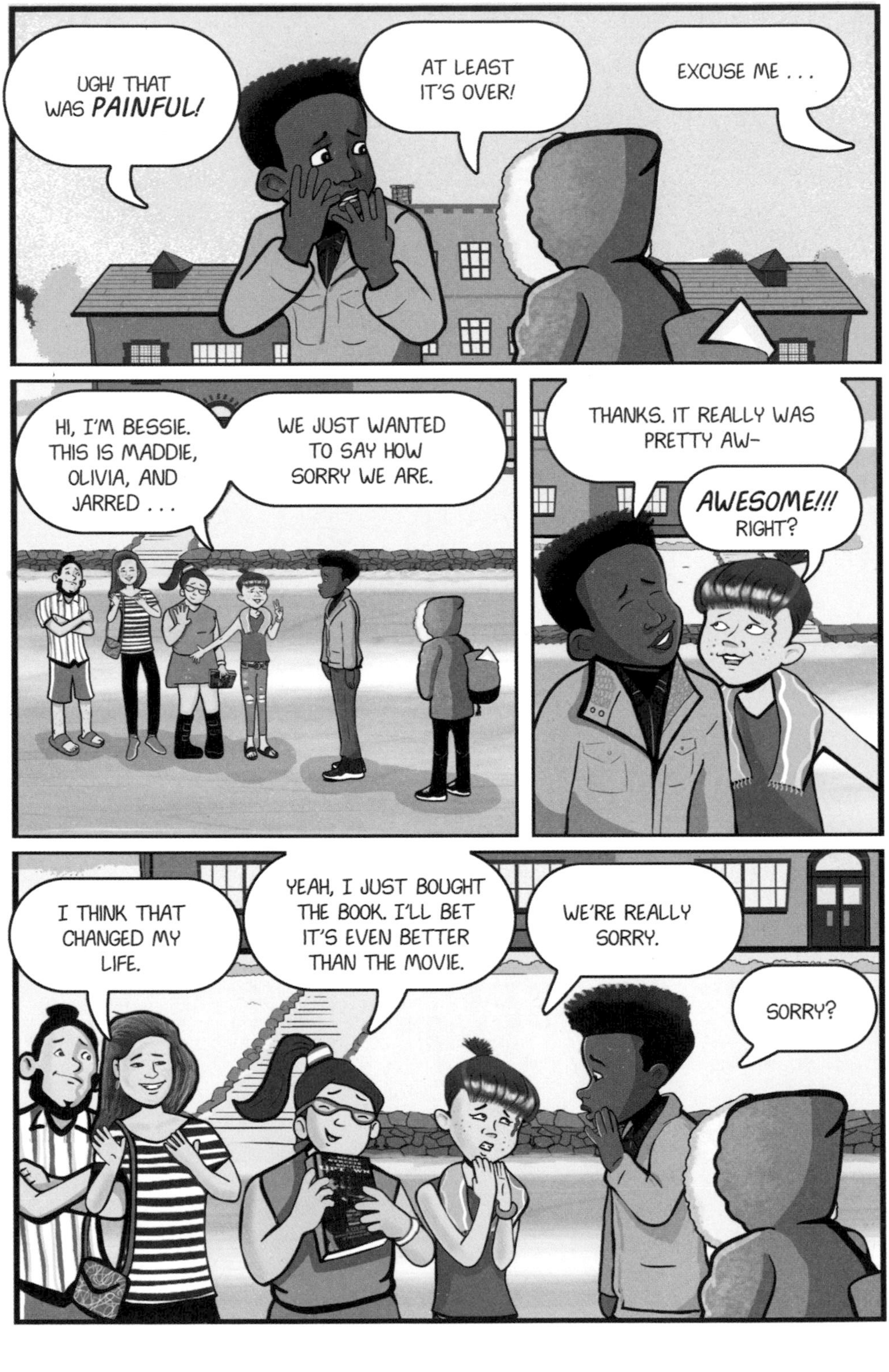
UGH! THAT WAS PAINFUL!
AT LEAST IT'S OVER!
EXCUSE ME . . .
HI, I'M BESSIE. THIS IS MADDIE, OLIVIA, AND JARRED . . .
WE JUST WANTED TO SAY HOW SORRY WE ARE.
THANKS. IT REALLY WAS PRETTY AW-
AWESOME!!! RIGHT?
I THINK THAT CHANGED MY LIFE.
YEAH, I JUST BOUGHT THE BOOK. I'LL BET IT'S EVEN BETTER THAN THE MOVIE.
WE'RE REALLY SORRY.
SORRY?

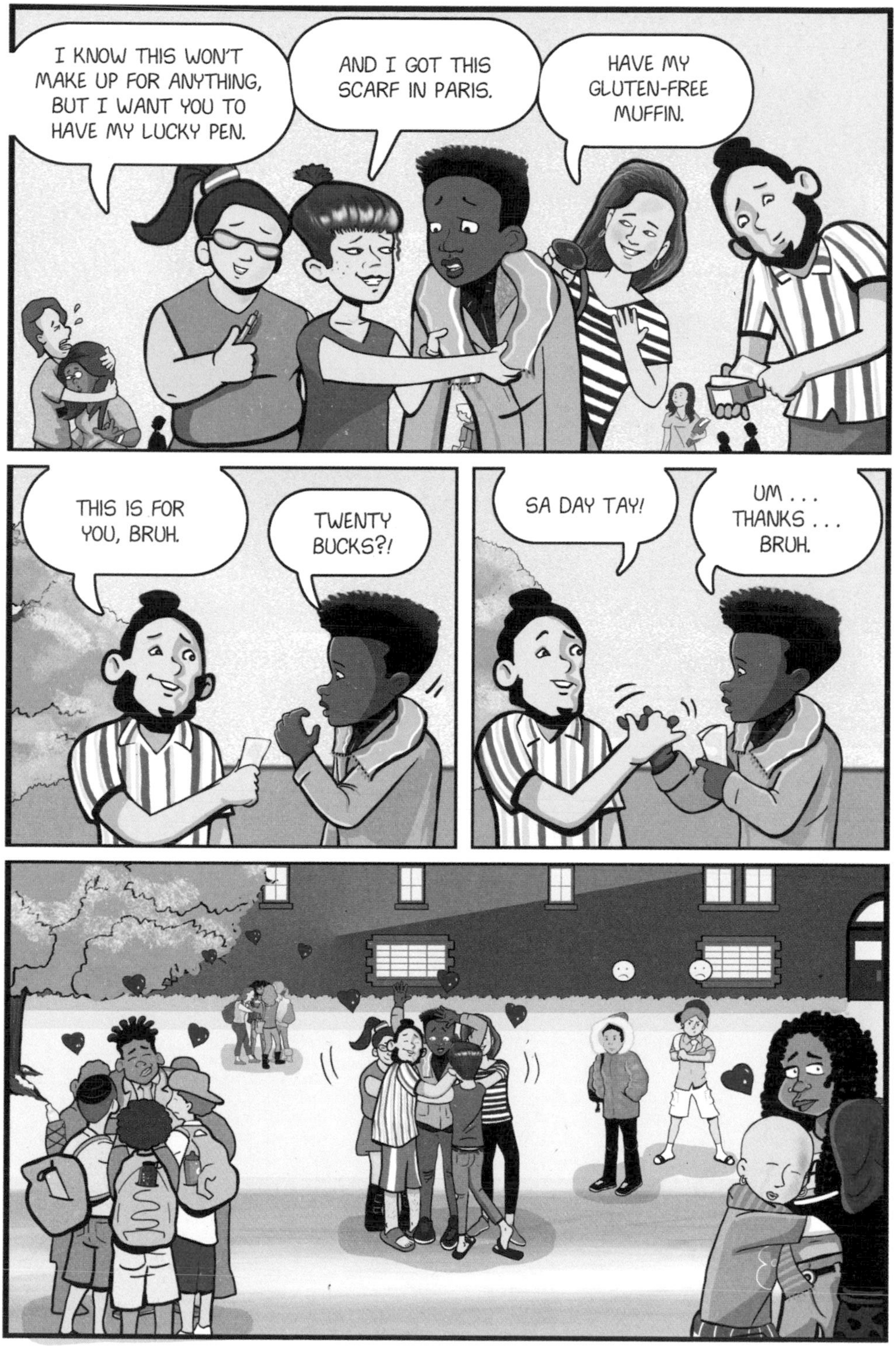
I KNOW THIS WON'T MAKE UP FOR ANYTHING, BUT I WANT YOU TO HAVE MY LUCKY PEN.
AND I GOT THIS SCARF IN PARIS.
HAVE MY GLUTEN-FREE MUFFIN.
THIS IS FOR YOU, BRUH.
TWENTY BUCKS?!
SA DAY TAY!
UM . . . THANKS . . . BRUH.

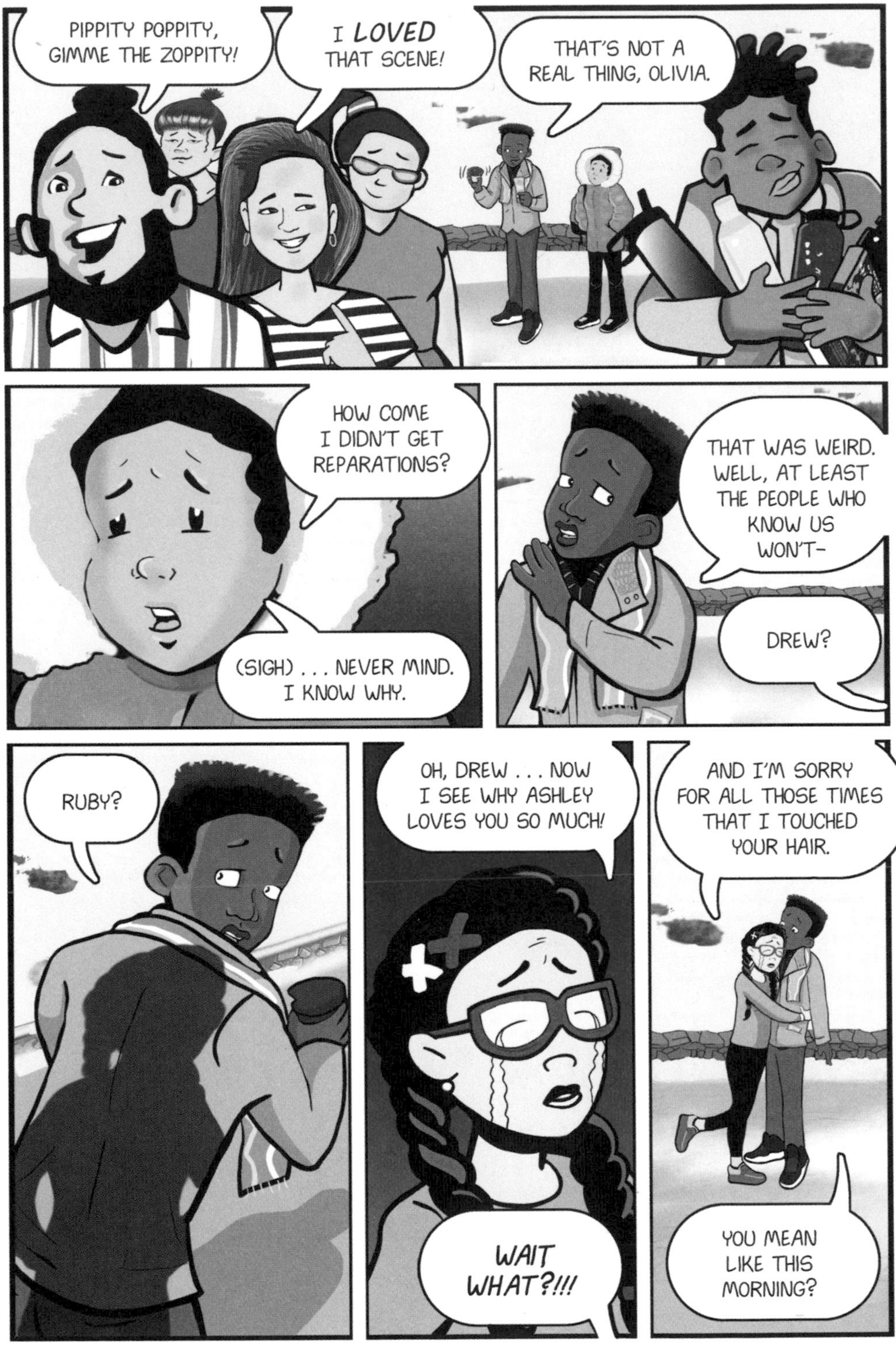
PIPPITY POPPITY, GIMME THE ZOPPITY!
I *LOVED* THAT SCENE!
THAT'S NOT A REAL THING, OLIVIA.
HOW COME I DIDN'T GET REPARATIONS?
(SIGH) . . . NEVER MIND. I KNOW WHY.
THAT WAS WEIRD. WELL, AT LEAST THE PEOPLE WHO KNOW US WON'T-
DREW?
RUBY?
OH, DREW . . . NOW I SEE WHY ASHLEY LOVES YOU SO MUCH!
WAIT WHAT?!!!
AND I'M SORRY FOR ALL THOSE TIMES THAT I TOUCHED YOUR HAIR.
YOU MEAN LIKE THIS MORNING?

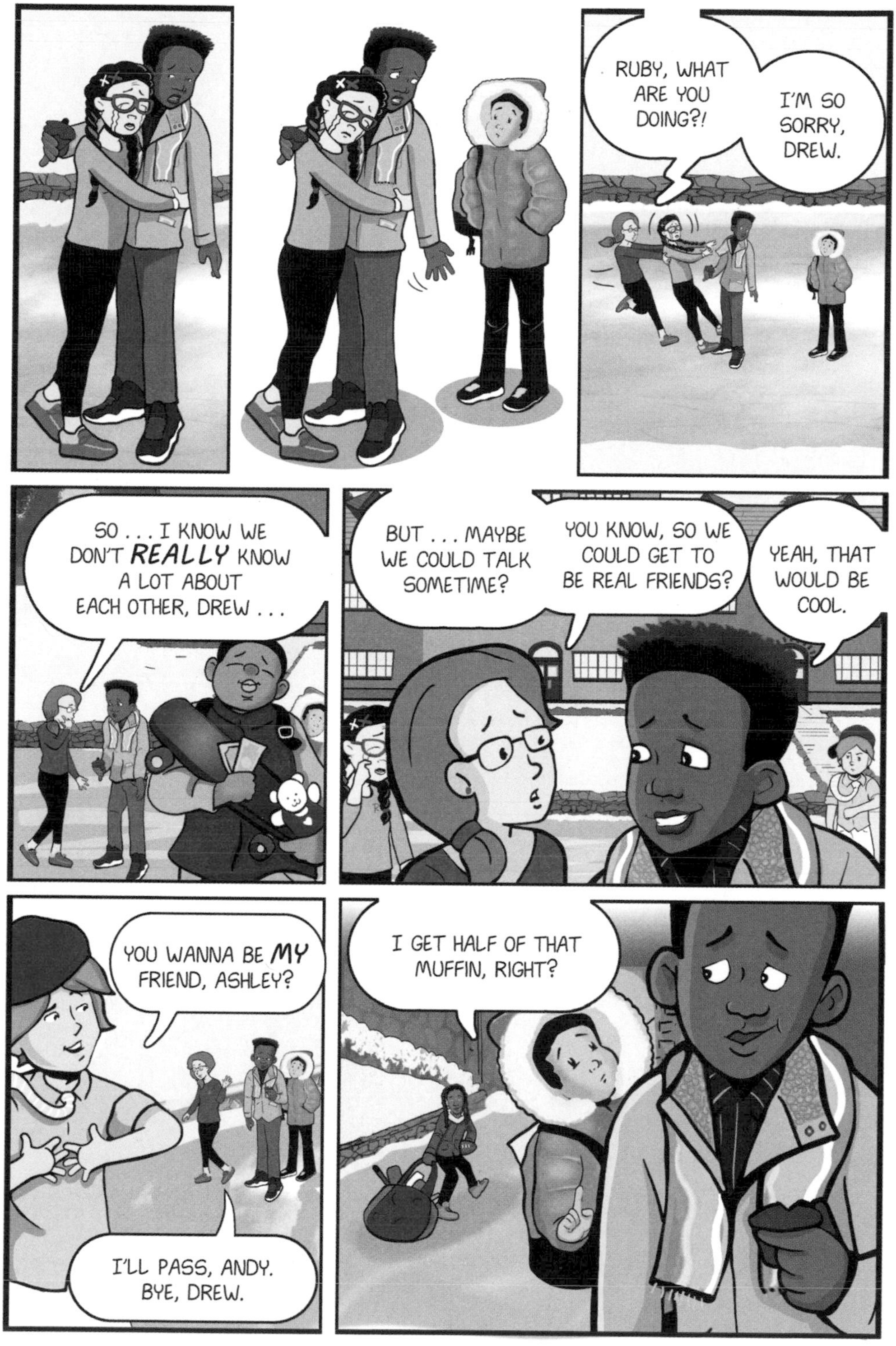
RUBY, WHAT ARE YOU DOING?!
I'M SO SORRY, DREW.
SO . . . I KNOW WE DON'T REALLY KNOW A LOT ABOUT EACH OTHER, DREW . . .
BUT . . . MAYBE WE COULD TALK SOMETIME?
YOU KNOW, SO WE COULD GET TO BE REAL FRIENDS?
YEAH, THAT WOULD BE COOL.
YOU WANNA BE MY FRIEND, ASHLEY?
I'LL PASS, ANDY. BYE, DREW.
I GET HALF OF THAT MUFFIN, RIGHT?

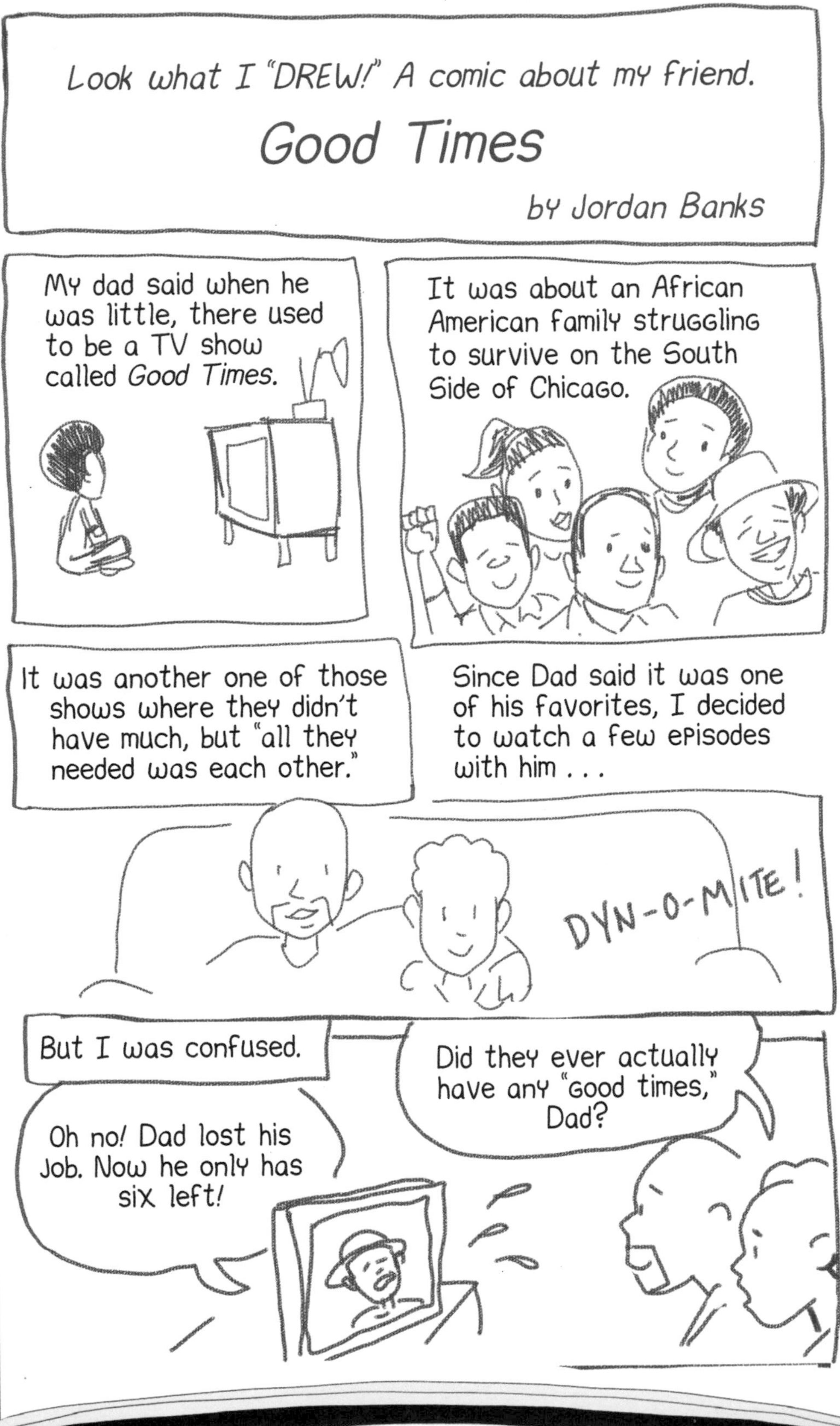
Look what I "DREW!" A comic about my friend.
Good Times
by Jordan Banks
My dad said when he was little, there used to be a TV show called *Good Times*.
It was about an African American family struggling to survive on the South Side of Chicago.
It was another one of those shows where they didn't have much, but "all they needed was each other."
Since Dad said it was one of his favorites, I decided to watch a few episodes with him . . .
DYN-O-MITE!
But I was confused.
Oh no! Dad lost his job. Now he only has six left!
Did they ever actually have any "good times," Dad?

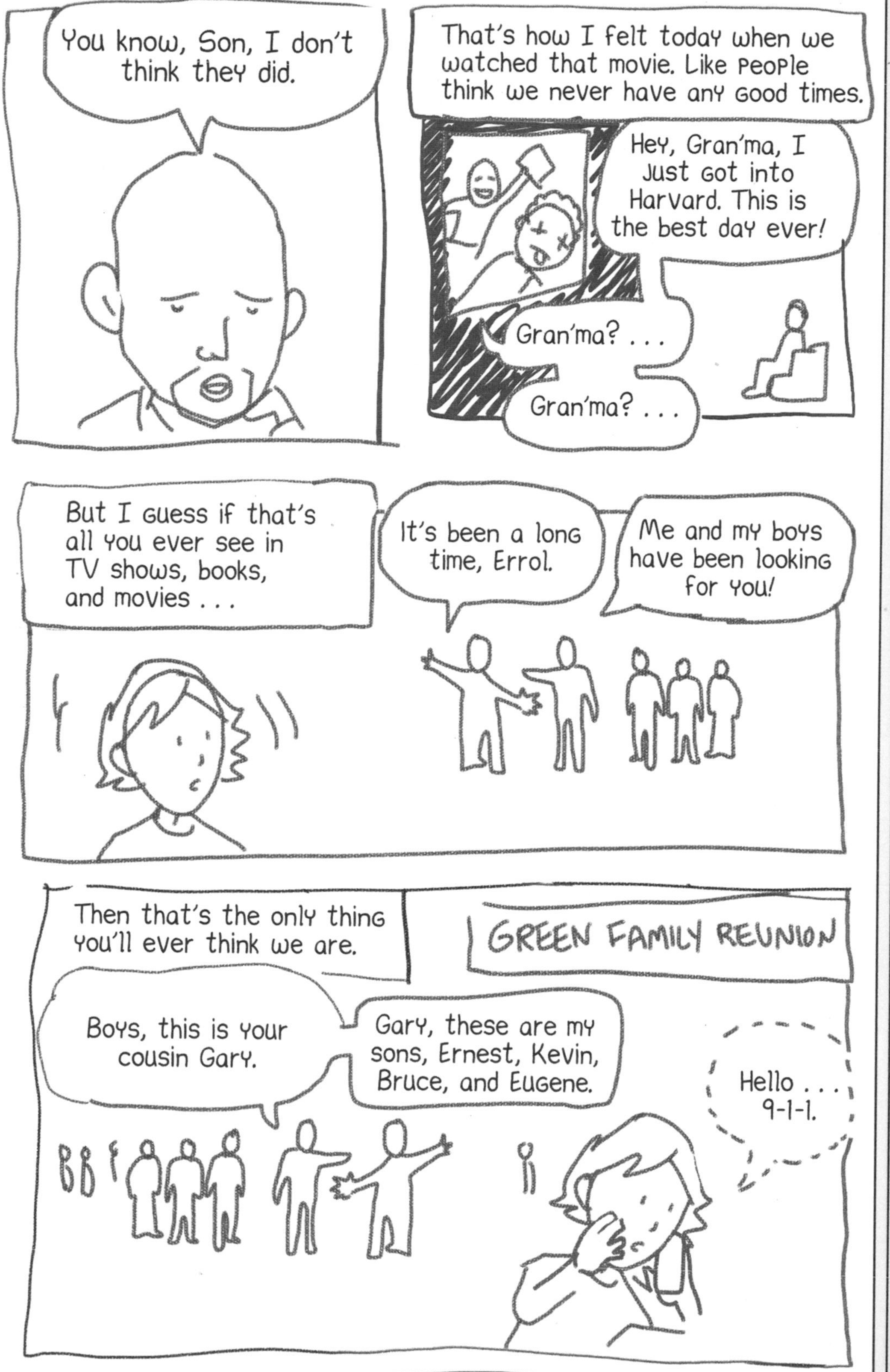

You know, Son, I don't think they did.
That's how I felt today when we watched that movie. Like people think we never have any good times.
Hey, Gran'ma, I just got into Harvard. This is the best day ever!
Gran'ma? . . .
Gran'ma? . . .
But I guess if that's all you ever see in TV shows, books, and movies . . .
It's been a long time, Errol.
Me and my boys have been looking for you!
Then that's the only thing you'll ever think we are.
GREEN FAMILY REUNION
Boys, this is your cousin Gary.
Gary, these are my sons, Ernest, Kevin, Bruce, and Eugene.
Hello . . . 9-1-1.

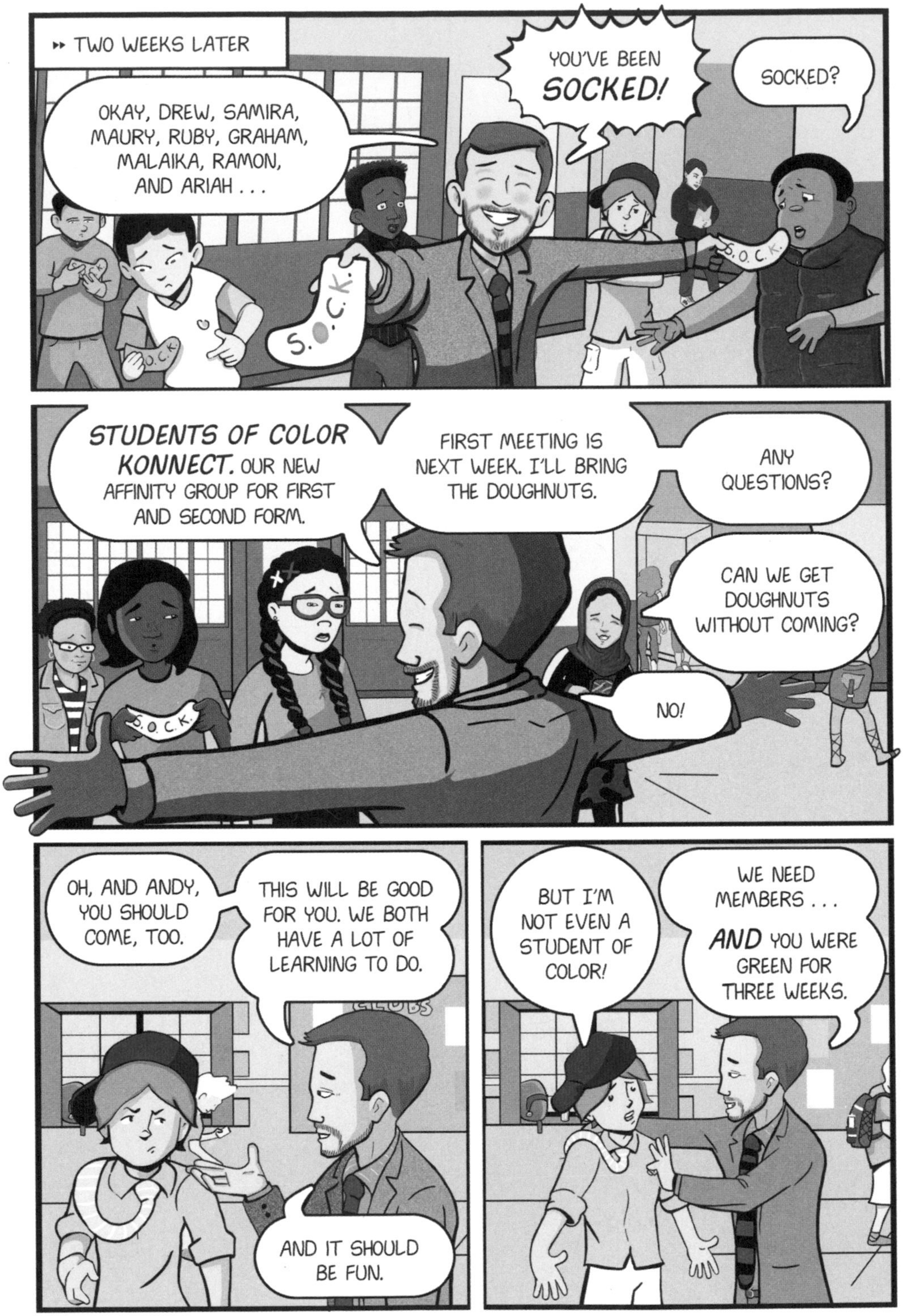
TWO WEEKS LATER
OKAY, DREW, SAMIRA, MAURY, RUBY, GRAHAM, MALAIKA, RAMON, AND ARIAH . . .
YOU'VE BEEN SOCKED!
SOCKED?
S.O.C.K.
STUDENTS OF COLOR KONNECT. OUR NEW AFFINITY GROUP FOR FIRST AND SECOND FORM.
FIRST MEETING IS NEXT WEEK. I'LL BRING THE DOUGHNUTS.
ANY QUESTIONS?
CAN WE GET DOUGHNUTS WITHOUT COMING?
NO!
OH, AND ANDY, YOU SHOULD COME, TOO.
THIS WILL BE GOOD FOR YOU. WE BOTH HAVE A LOT OF LEARNING TO DO.
AND IT SHOULD BE FUN.
BUT I'M NOT EVEN A STUDENT OF COLOR!
WE NEED MEMBERS . . .
AND YOU WERE GREEN FOR THREE WEEKS.

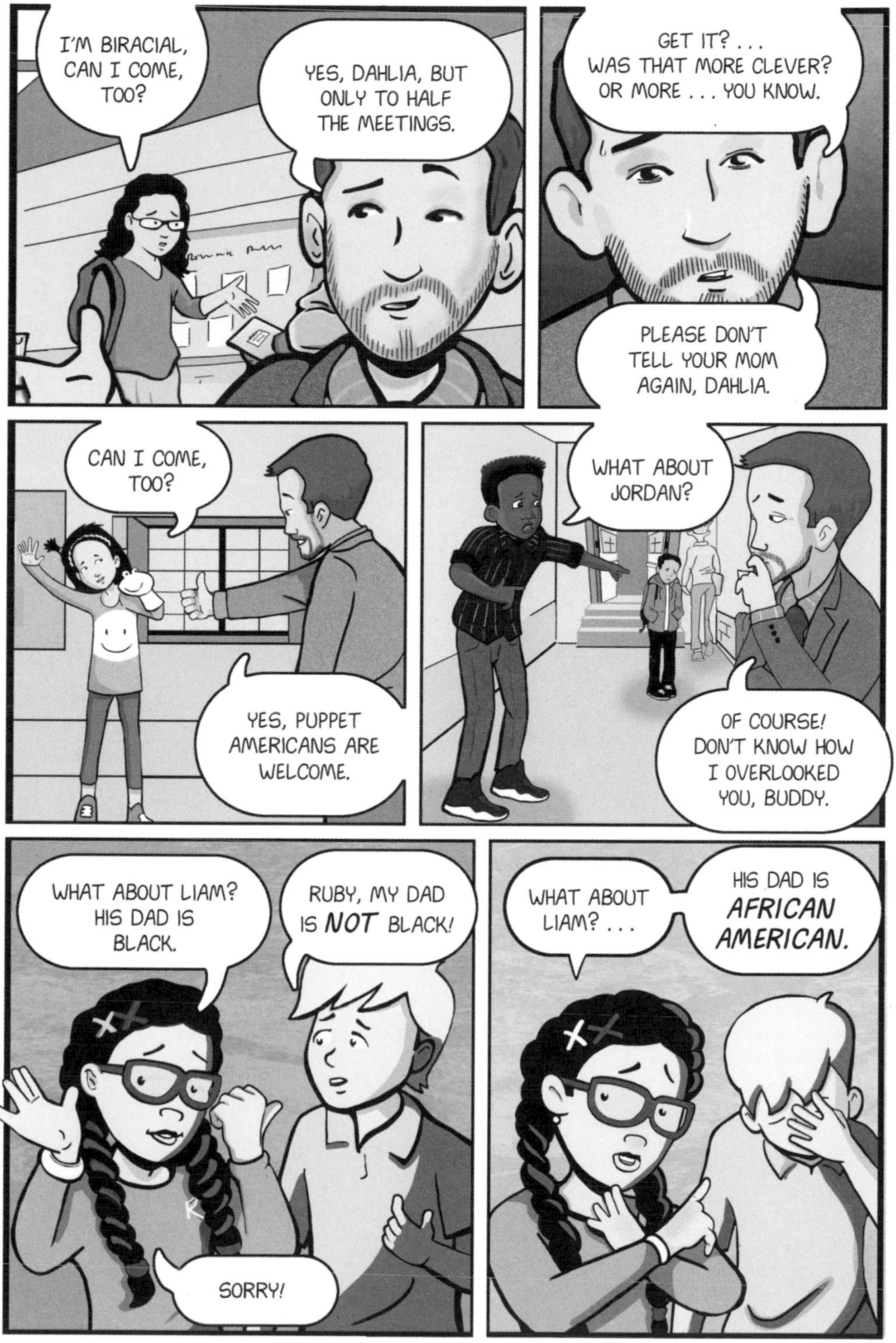
I'M BIRACIAL, CAN I COME, TOO?
YES, DAHLIA, BUT ONLY TO HALF THE MEETINGS.
GET IT? . . . WAS THAT MORE CLEVER? OR MORE . . . YOU KNOW.
PLEASE DON'T TELL YOUR MOM AGAIN, DAHLIA.
CAN I COME, TOO?
YES, PUPPET AMERICANS ARE WELCOME.
WHAT ABOUT JORDAN?
OF COURSE! DON'T KNOW HOW I OVERLOOKED YOU, BUDDY.
WHAT ABOUT LIAM? HIS DAD IS BLACK.
RUBY, MY DAD IS NOT BLACK!
SORRY!
WHAT ABOUT LIAM? . . .
HIS DAD IS AFRICAN AMERICAN.

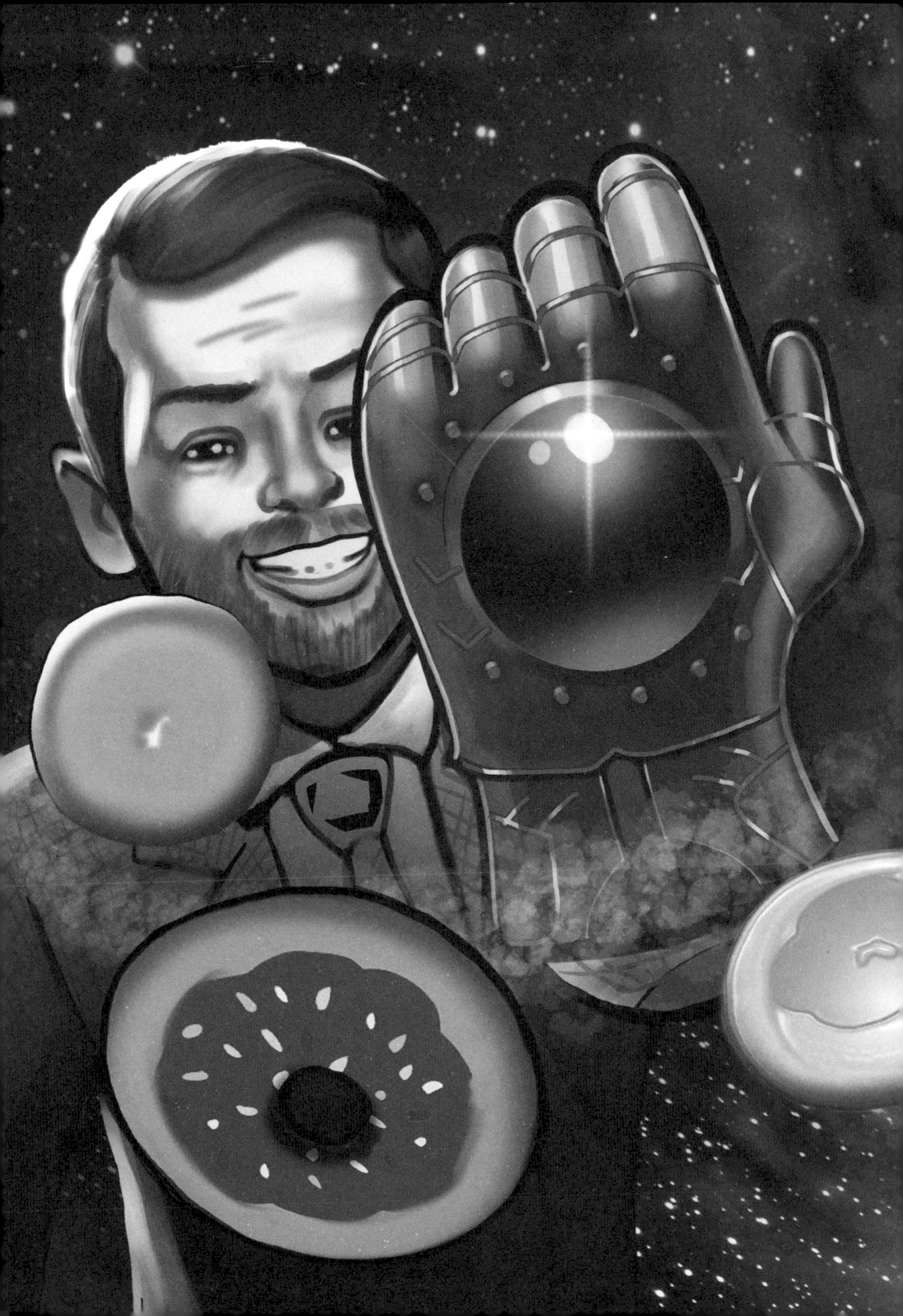

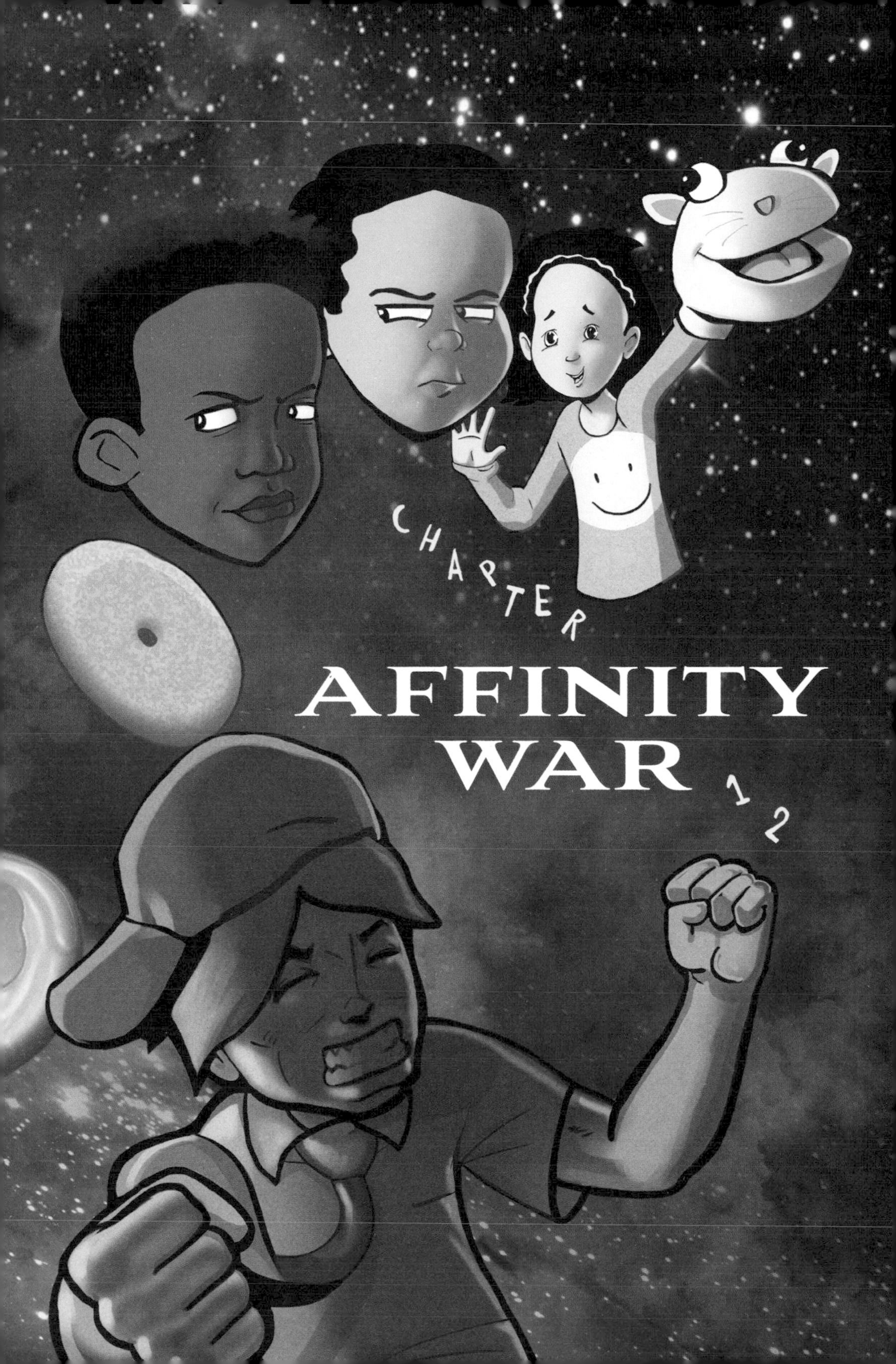
CHAPTER 12
AFFINITY WAR

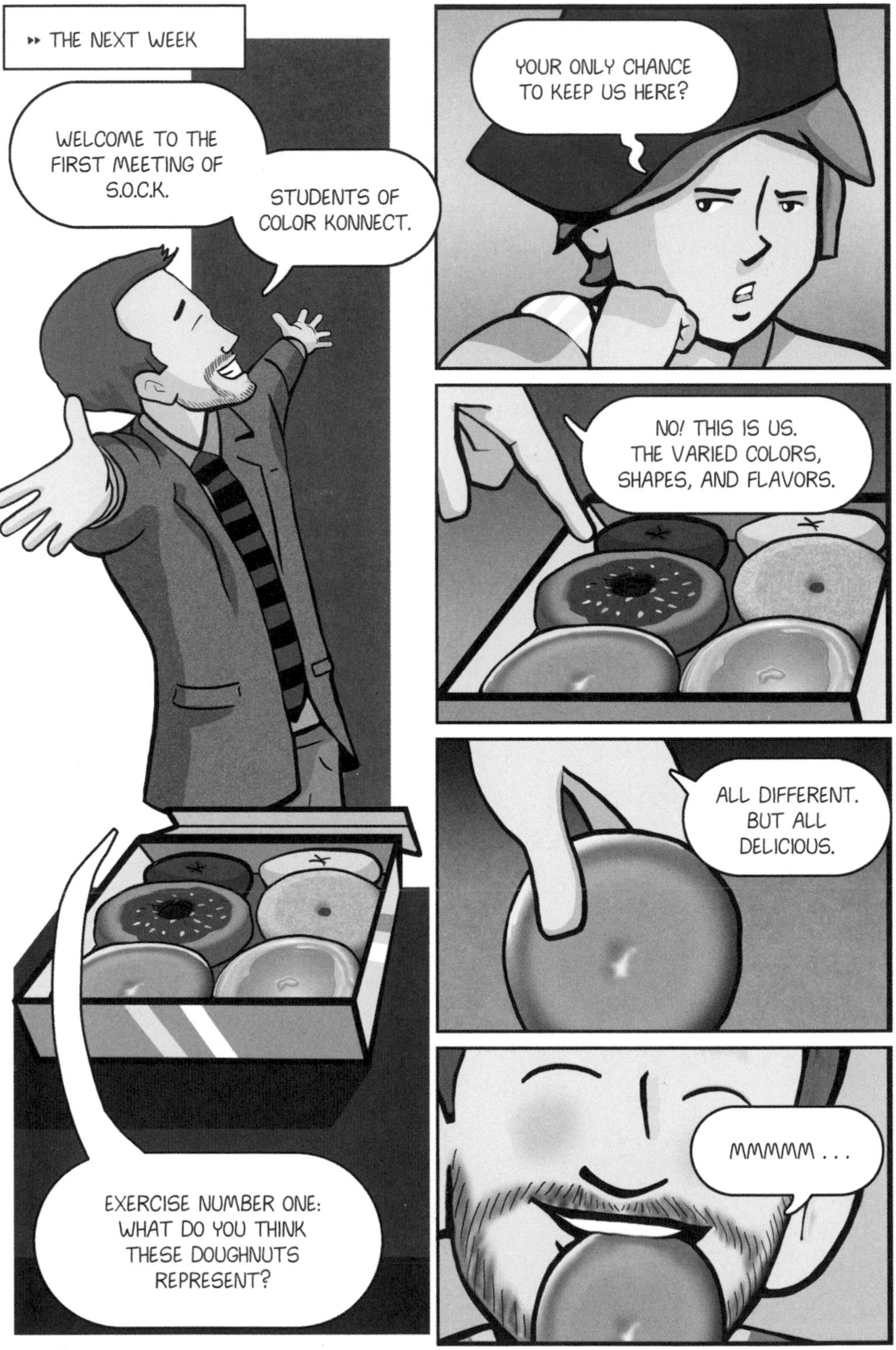
▸▸ THE NEXT WEEK
WELCOME TO THE FIRST MEETING OF S.O.C.K.
STUDENTS OF COLOR KONNECT.
EXERCISE NUMBER ONE: WHAT DO YOU THINK THESE DOUGHNUTS REPRESENT?
YOUR ONLY CHANCE TO KEEP US HERE?
NO! THIS IS US. THE VARIED COLORS, SHAPES, AND FLAVORS.
ALL DIFFERENT. BUT ALL DELICIOUS.
MMMMM . . .

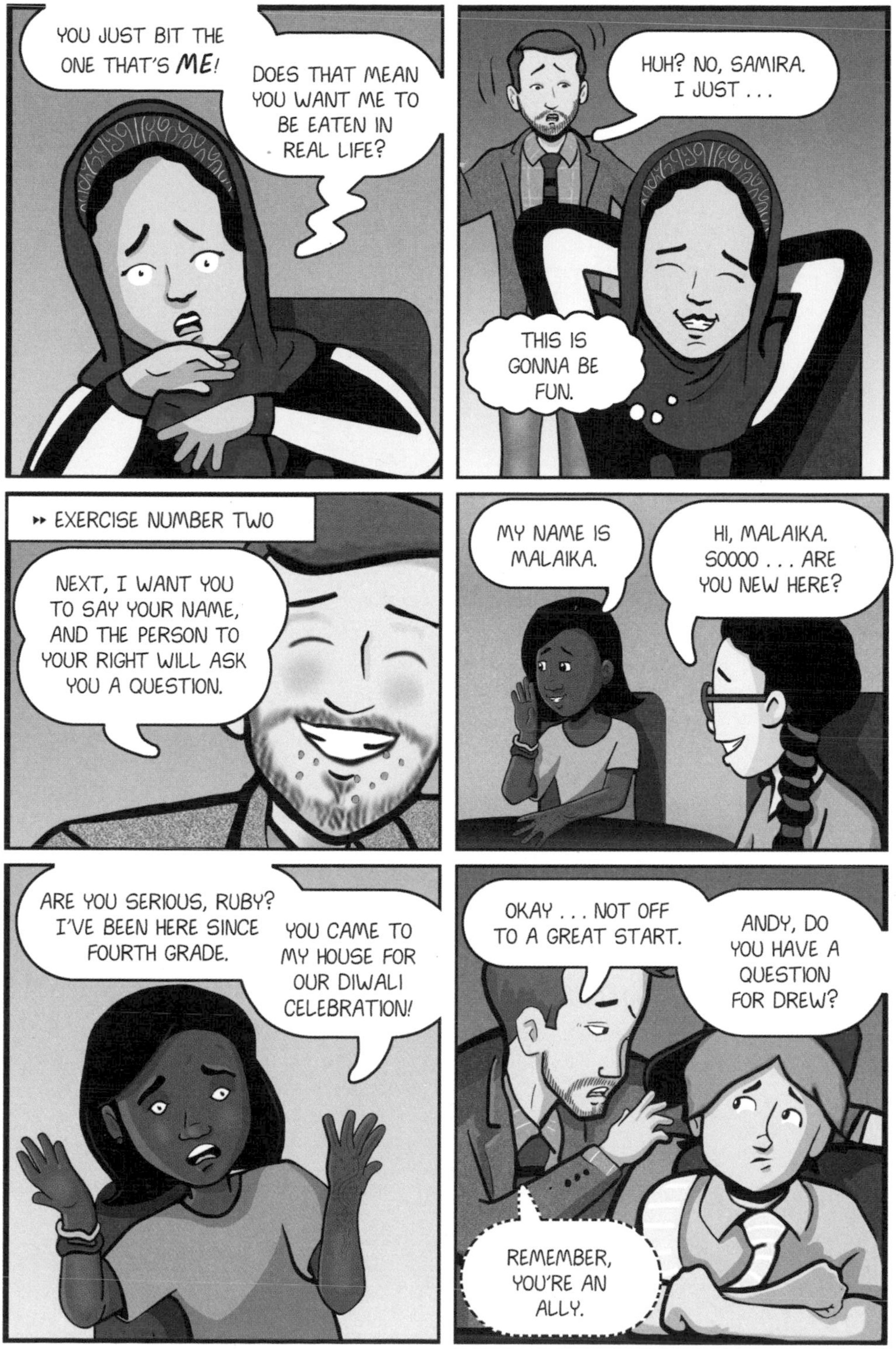
YOU JUST BIT THE ONE THAT'S ME!
DOES THAT MEAN YOU WANT ME TO BE EATEN IN REAL LIFE?
HUH? NO, SAMIRA. I JUST . . .
THIS IS GONNA BE FUN.
EXERCISE NUMBER TWO
NEXT, I WANT YOU TO SAY YOUR NAME, AND THE PERSON TO YOUR RIGHT WILL ASK YOU A QUESTION.
MY NAME IS MALAIKA.
HI, MALAIKA. SOOOO . . . ARE YOU NEW HERE?
ARE YOU SERIOUS, RUBY? I'VE BEEN HERE SINCE FOURTH GRADE.
YOU CAME TO MY HOUSE FOR OUR DIWALI CELEBRATION!
OKAY . . . NOT OFF TO A GREAT START.
ANDY, DO YOU HAVE A QUESTION FOR DREW?
REMEMBER, YOU'RE AN ALLY.

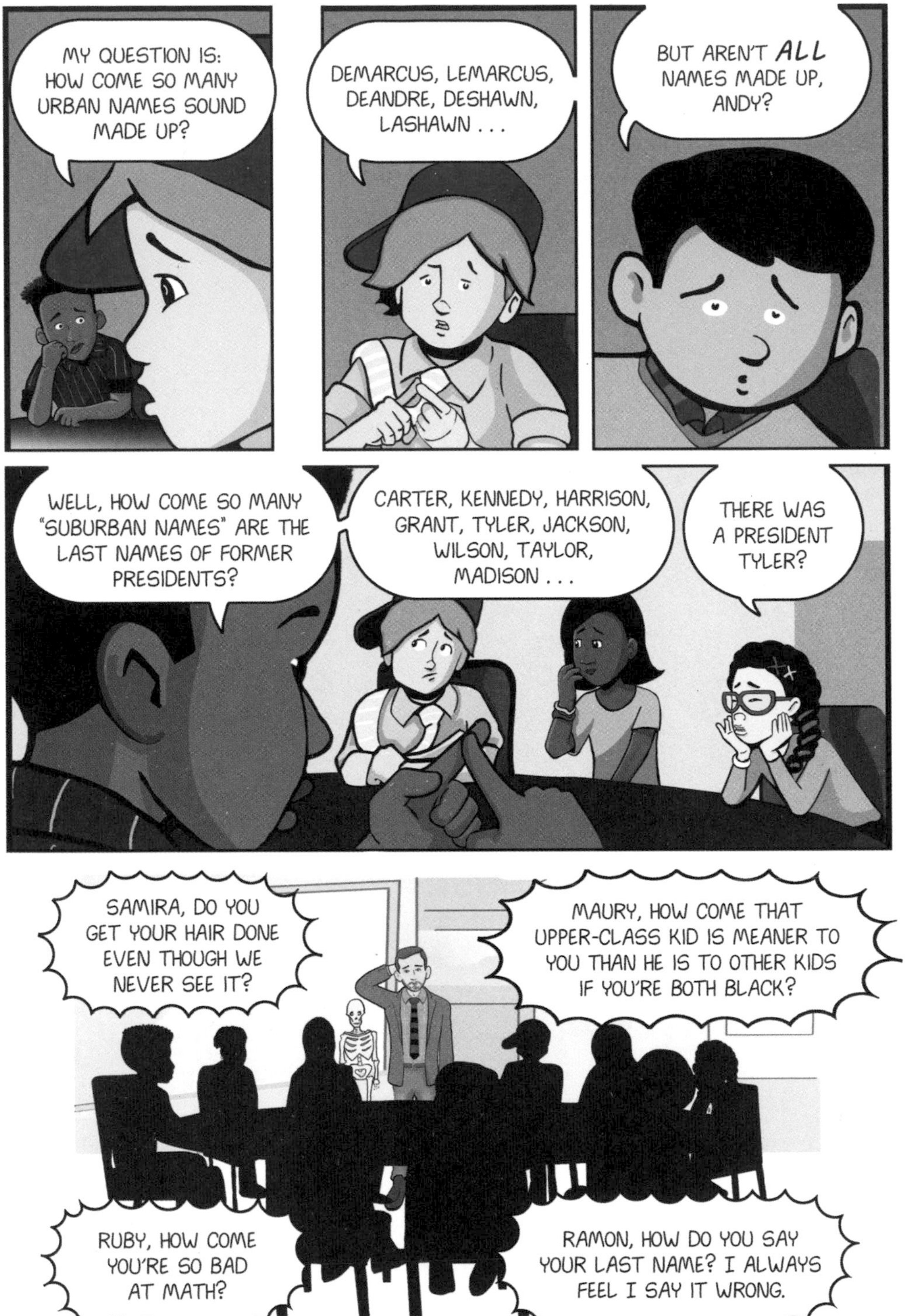
MY QUESTION IS: HOW COME SO MANY URBAN NAMES SOUND MADE UP?
DEMARCUS, LEMARCUS, DEANDRE, DESHAWN, LASHAWN . . .
BUT AREN'T ALL NAMES MADE UP, ANDY?
WELL, HOW COME SO MANY "SUBURBAN NAMES" ARE THE LAST NAMES OF FORMER PRESIDENTS?
CARTER, KENNEDY, HARRISON, GRANT, TYLER, JACKSON, WILSON, TAYLOR, MADISON . . .
THERE WAS A PRESIDENT TYLER?
SAMIRA, DO YOU GET YOUR HAIR DONE EVEN THOUGH WE NEVER SEE IT?
MAURY, HOW COME THAT UPPER-CLASS KID IS MEANER TO YOU THAN HE IS TO OTHER KIDS IF YOU'RE BOTH BLACK?
RUBY, HOW COME YOU'RE SO BAD AT MATH?
RAMON, HOW DO YOU SAY YOUR LAST NAME? I ALWAYS FEEL I SAY IT WRONG.

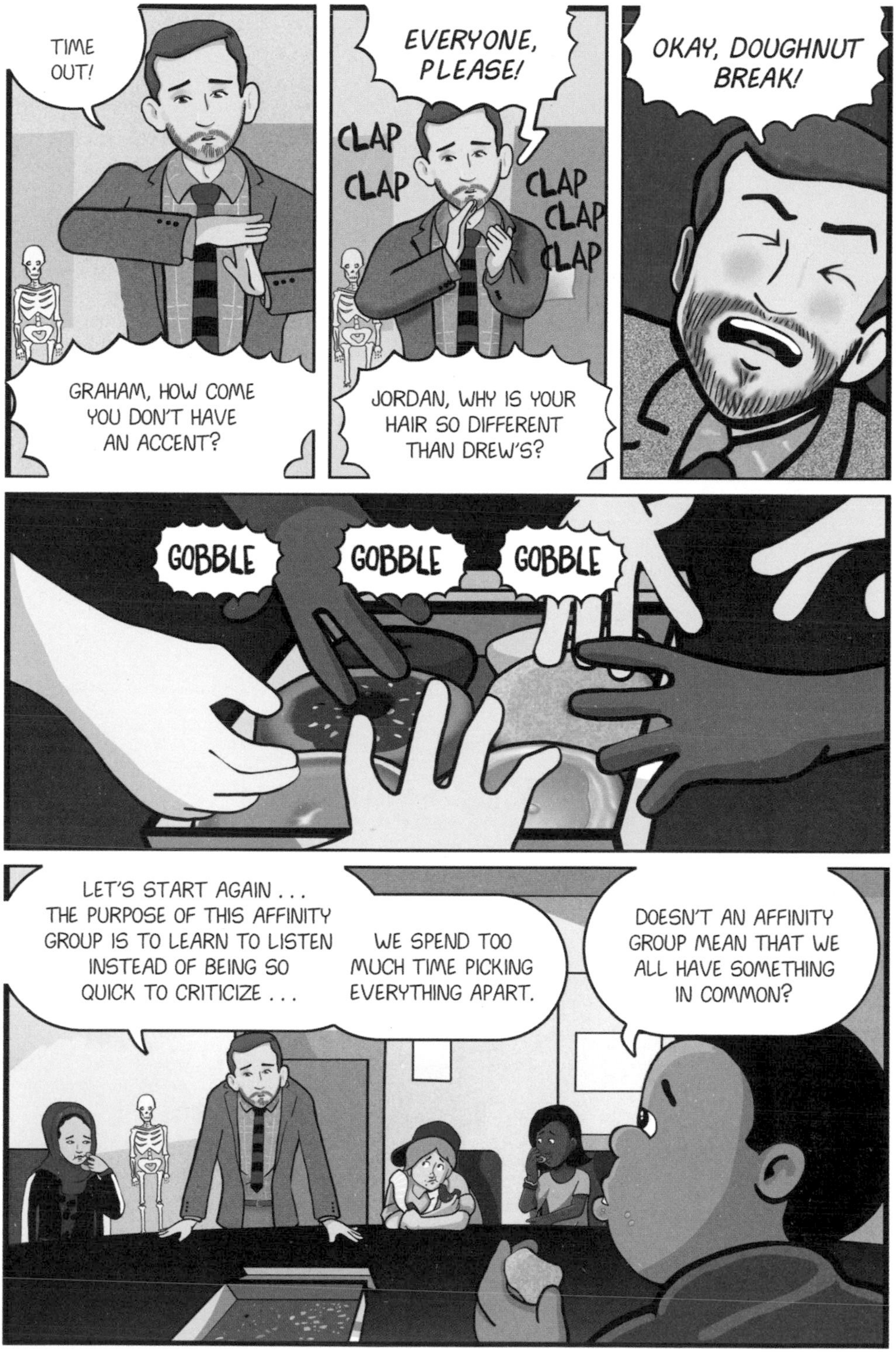
TIME OUT!
GRAHAM, HOW COME YOU DON'T HAVE AN ACCENT?
EVERYONE, PLEASE!
CLAP
CLAP
CLAP
CLAP
CLAP
JORDAN, WHY IS YOUR HAIR SO DIFFERENT THAN DREW'S?
OKAY, DOUGHNUT BREAK!
GOBBLE
GOBBLE
GOBBLE
LET'S START AGAIN . . . THE PURPOSE OF THIS AFFINITY GROUP IS TO LEARN TO LISTEN INSTEAD OF BEING SO QUICK TO CRITICIZE . . .
WE SPEND TOO MUCH TIME PICKING EVERYTHING APART.
DOESN'T AN AFFINITY GROUP MEAN THAT WE ALL HAVE SOMETHING IN COMMON?

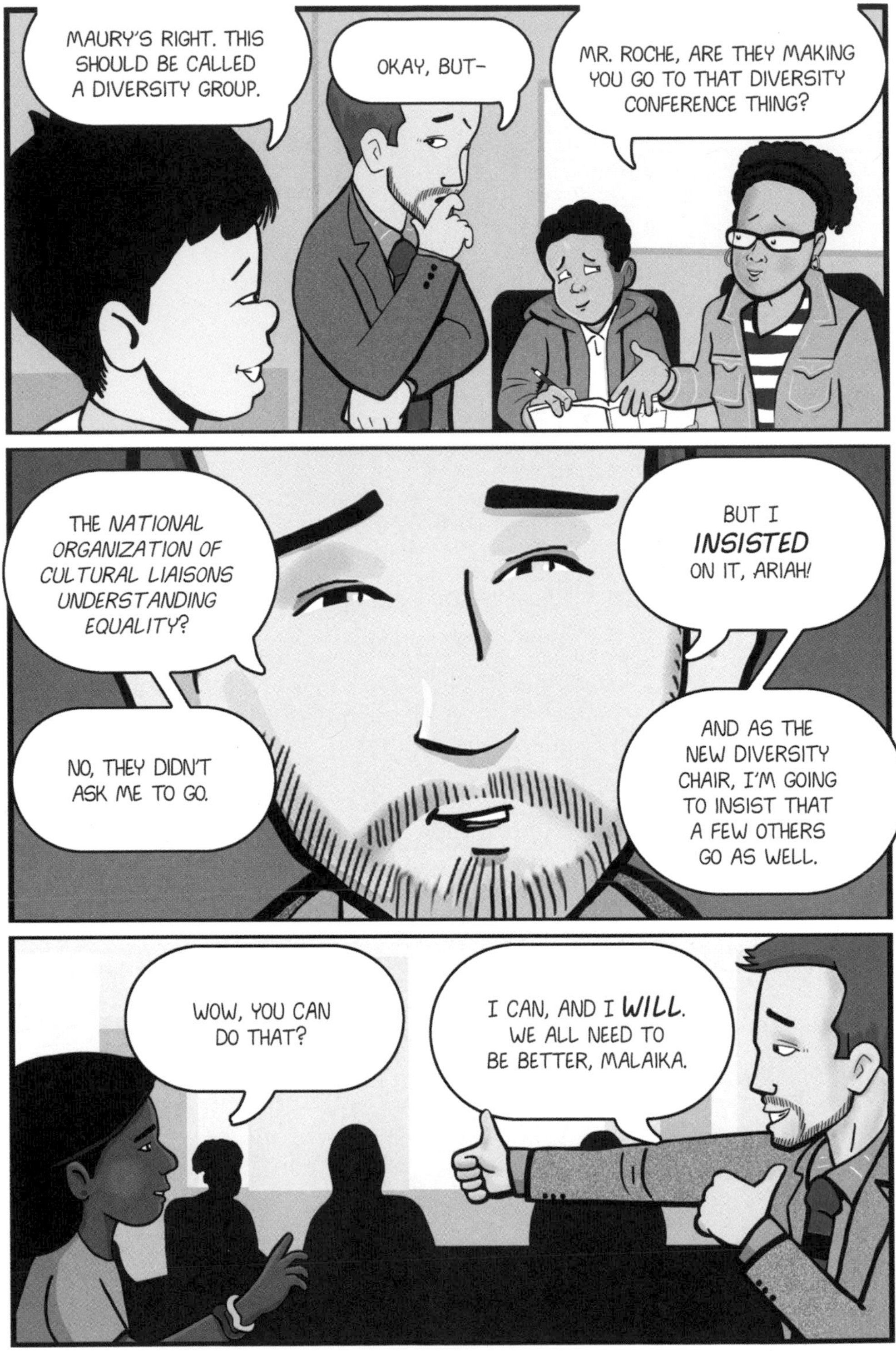
MAURY'S RIGHT. THIS SHOULD BE CALLED A DIVERSITY GROUP.
OKAY, BUT-
MR. ROCHE, ARE THEY MAKING YOU GO TO THAT DIVERSITY CONFERENCE THING?
THE *NATIONAL ORGANIZATION OF CULTURAL LIAISONS UNDERSTANDING EQUALITY*?
NO, THEY DIDN'T ASK ME TO GO.
BUT I ***INSISTED*** ON IT, ARIAH!
AND AS THE NEW DIVERSITY CHAIR, I'M GOING TO INSIST THAT A FEW OTHERS GO AS WELL.
WOW, YOU CAN DO THAT?
I CAN, AND I **WILL**. WE ALL NEED TO BE BETTER, MALAIKA.

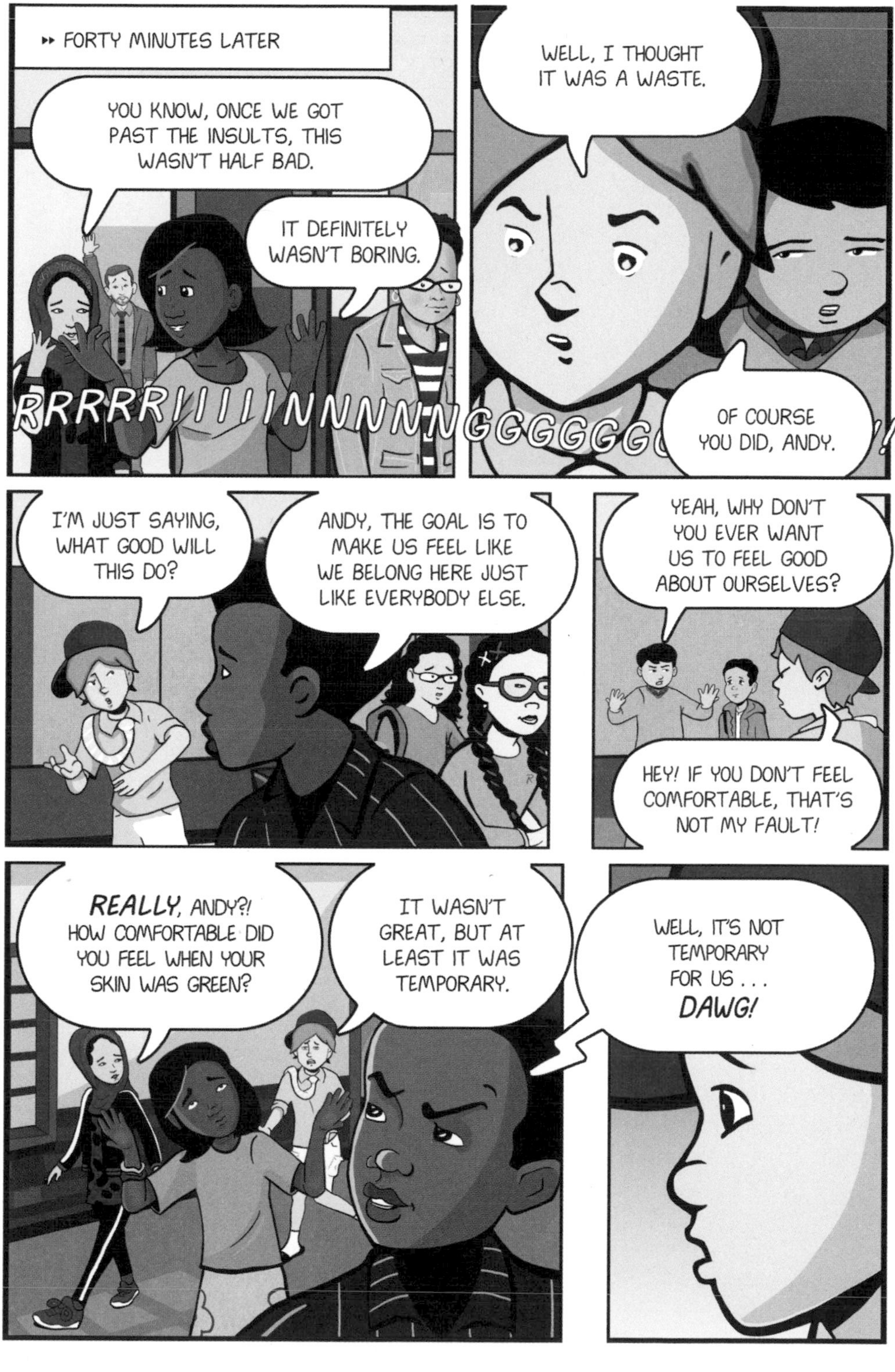
FORTY MINUTES LATER
YOU KNOW, ONCE WE GOT PAST THE INSULTS, THIS WASN'T HALF BAD.
IT DEFINITELY WASN'T BORING.
RRRRRIIIIIINNNNNNGGGGGG!!!
WELL, I THOUGHT IT WAS A WASTE.
OF COURSE YOU DID, ANDY.
I'M JUST SAYING, WHAT GOOD WILL THIS DO?
ANDY, THE GOAL IS TO MAKE US FEEL LIKE WE BELONG HERE JUST LIKE EVERYBODY ELSE.
YEAH, WHY DON'T YOU EVER WANT US TO FEEL GOOD ABOUT OURSELVES?
HEY! IF YOU DON'T FEEL COMFORTABLE, THAT'S NOT MY FAULT!
REALLY, ANDY?! HOW COMFORTABLE DID YOU FEEL WHEN YOUR SKIN WAS GREEN?
IT WASN'T GREAT, BUT AT LEAST IT WAS TEMPORARY.
WELL, IT'S NOT TEMPORARY FOR US . . . DAWG!

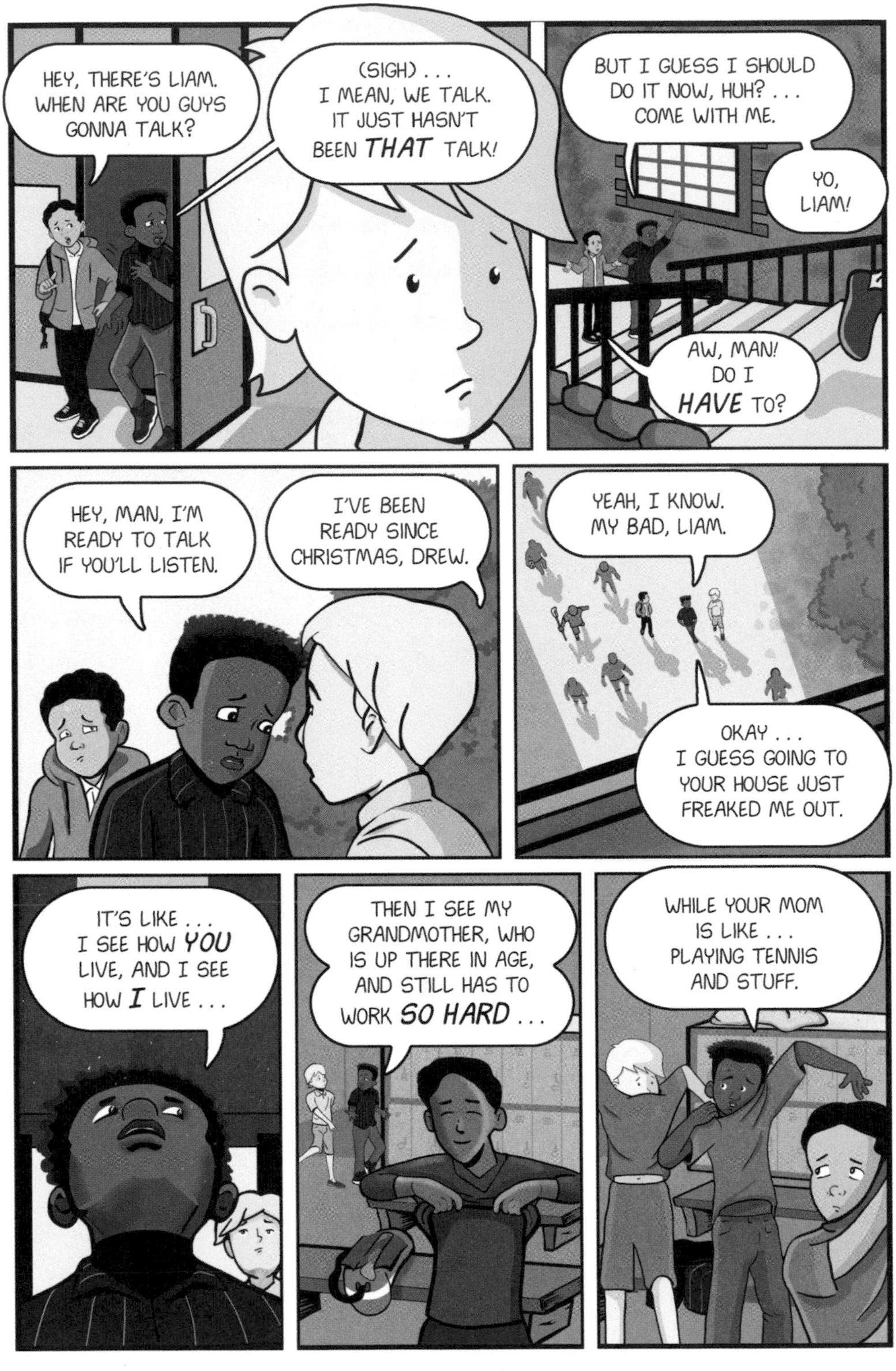
HEY, THERE'S LIAM. WHEN ARE YOU GUYS GONNA TALK?
(SIGH) . . . I MEAN, WE TALK. IT JUST HASN'T BEEN **THAT** TALK!
BUT I GUESS I SHOULD DO IT NOW, HUH? . . . COME WITH ME.
YO, LIAM!
AW, MAN! DO I **HAVE** TO?
HEY, MAN, I'M READY TO TALK IF YOU'LL LISTEN.
I'VE BEEN READY SINCE CHRISTMAS, DREW.
YEAH, I KNOW. MY BAD, LIAM.
OKAY . . . I GUESS GOING TO YOUR HOUSE JUST FREAKED ME OUT.
IT'S LIKE . . . I SEE HOW **YOU** LIVE, AND I SEE HOW **I** LIVE . . .
THEN I SEE MY GRANDMOTHER, WHO IS UP THERE IN AGE, AND STILL HAS TO WORK **SO HARD** . . .
WHILE YOUR MOM IS LIKE . . . PLAYING TENNIS AND STUFF.

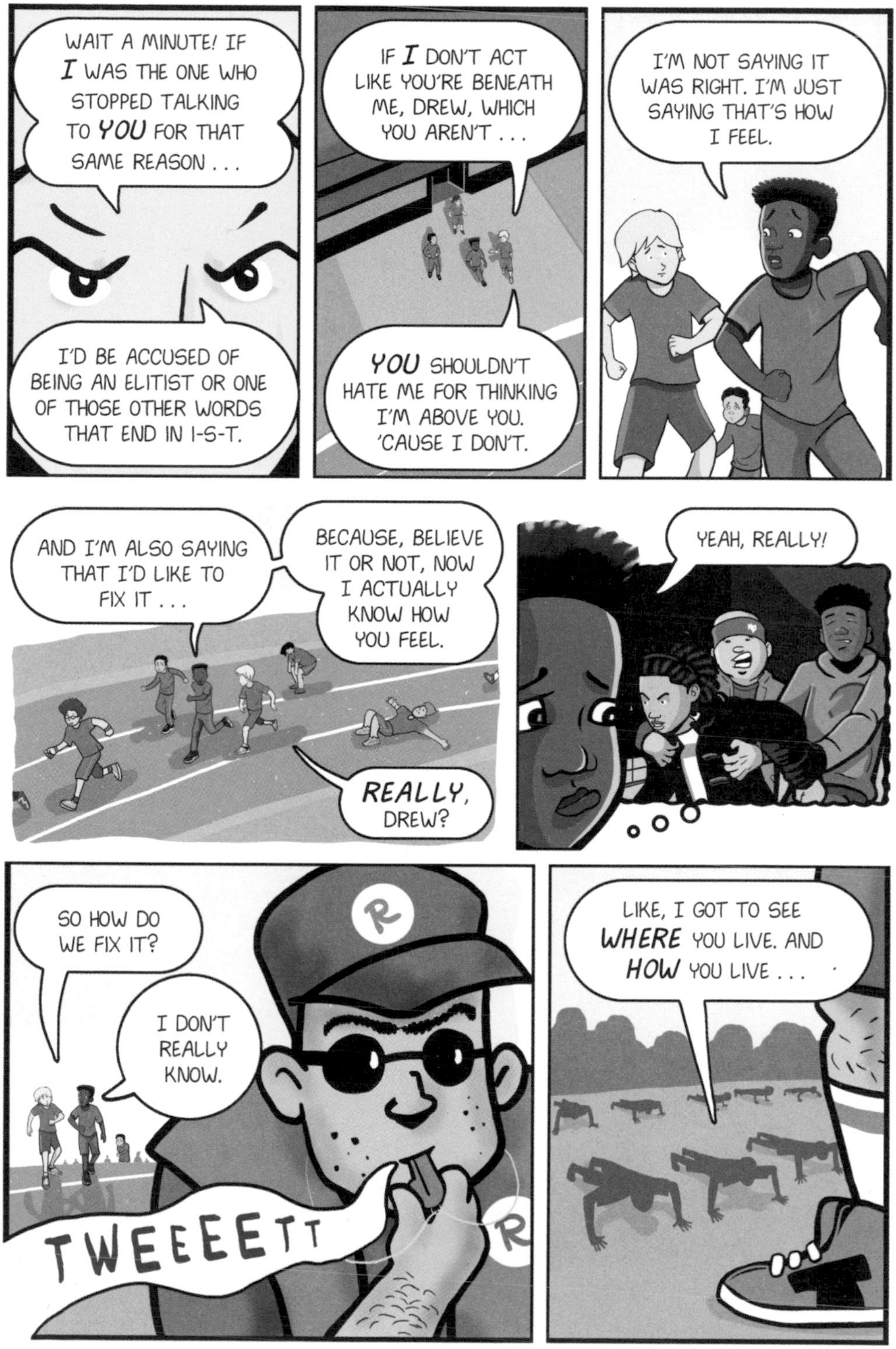
WAIT A MINUTE! IF I WAS THE ONE WHO STOPPED TALKING TO YOU FOR THAT SAME REASON . . .
I'D BE ACCUSED OF BEING AN ELITIST OR ONE OF THOSE OTHER WORDS THAT END IN I-S-T.
IF I DON'T ACT LIKE YOU'RE BENEATH ME, DREW, WHICH YOU AREN'T . . .
YOU SHOULDN'T HATE ME FOR THINKING I'M ABOVE YOU. 'CAUSE I DON'T.
I'M NOT SAYING IT WAS RIGHT. I'M JUST SAYING THAT'S HOW I FEEL.
AND I'M ALSO SAYING THAT I'D LIKE TO FIX IT . . .
BECAUSE, BELIEVE IT OR NOT, NOW I ACTUALLY KNOW HOW YOU FEEL.
REALLY, DREW?
YEAH, REALLY!
SO HOW DO WE FIX IT?
I DON'T REALLY KNOW.
TWEEEETT
LIKE, I GOT TO SEE WHERE YOU LIVE. AND HOW YOU LIVE . . .

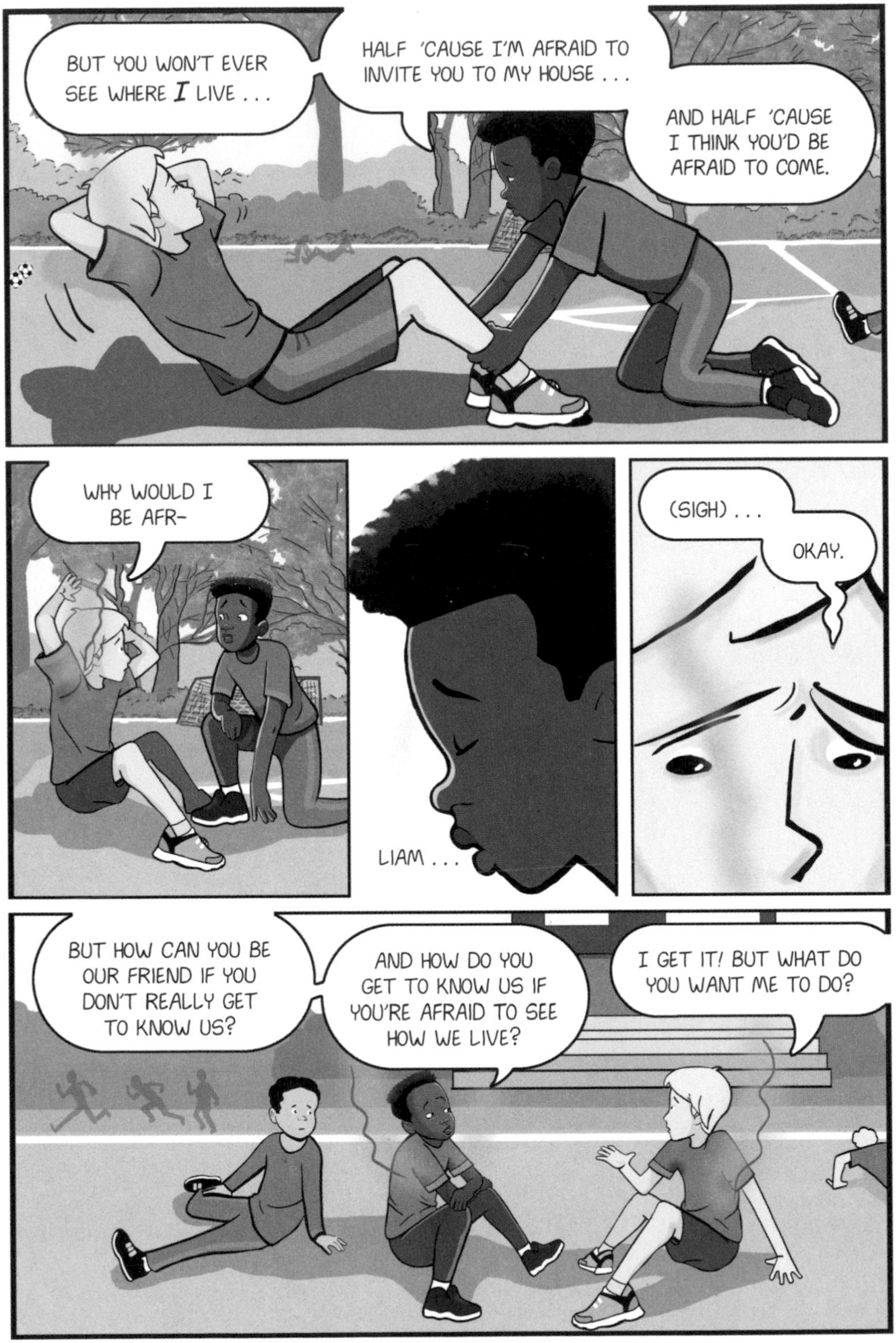
BUT YOU WON'T EVER SEE WHERE I LIVE . . .
HALF 'CAUSE I'M AFRAID TO INVITE YOU TO MY HOUSE . . .
AND HALF 'CAUSE I THINK YOU'D BE AFRAID TO COME.
WHY WOULD I BE AFR-
LIAM . . .
(SIGH) . . .
OKAY.
BUT HOW CAN YOU BE OUR FRIEND IF YOU DON'T REALLY GET TO KNOW US?
AND HOW DO YOU GET TO KNOW US IF YOU'RE AFRAID TO SEE HOW WE LIVE?
I GET IT! BUT WHAT DO YOU WANT ME TO DO?

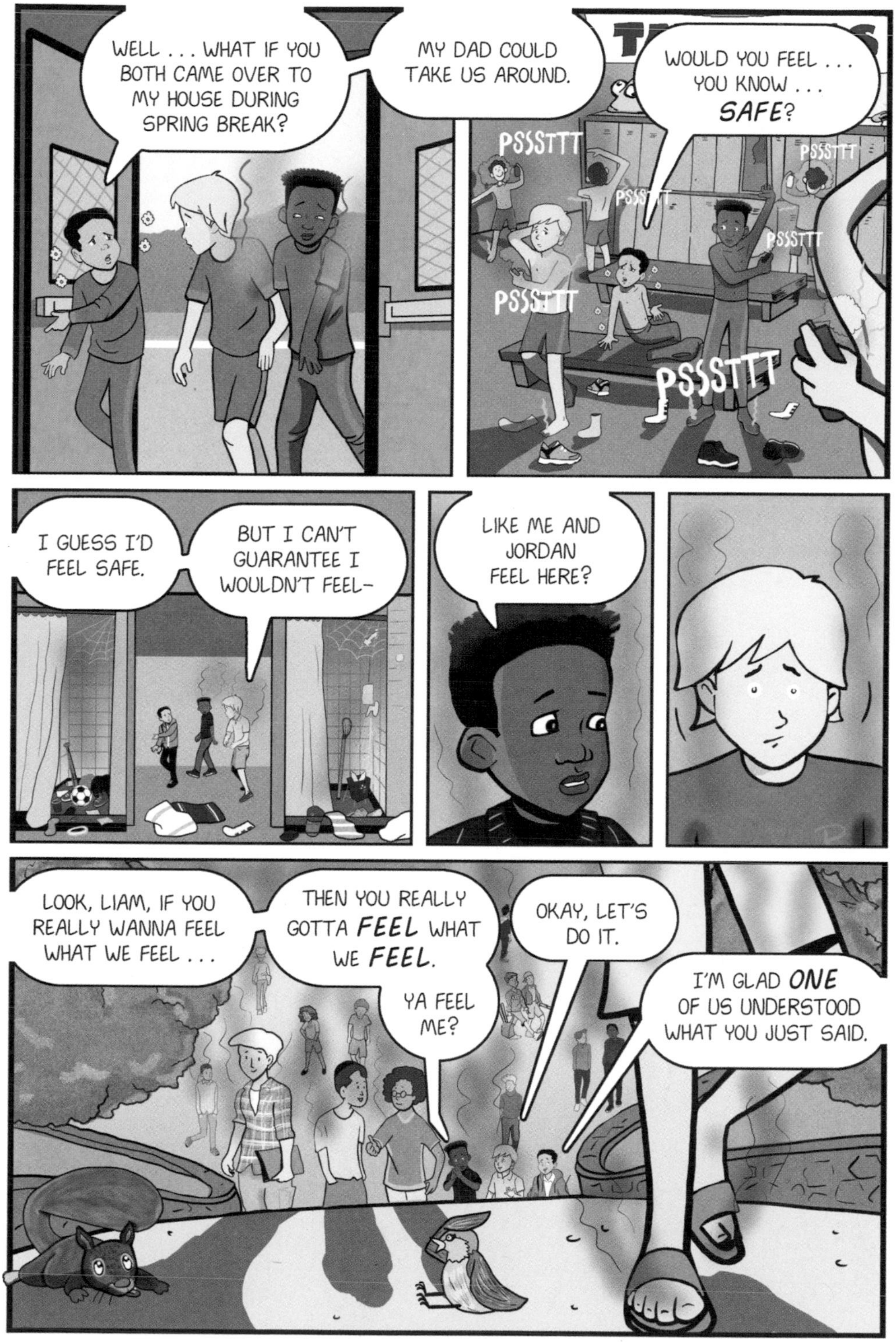
WELL . . . WHAT IF YOU BOTH CAME OVER TO MY HOUSE DURING SPRING BREAK?
MY DAD COULD TAKE US AROUND.
WOULD YOU FEEL . . . YOU KNOW . . . *SAFE*?
PSSSTTT
PSSSTTT
PSSSTTT
PSSSTTT
PSSSTTT
PSSSTTT
I GUESS I'D FEEL SAFE.
BUT I CAN'T GUARANTEE I WOULDN'T FEEL–
LIKE ME AND JORDAN FEEL HERE?
LOOK, LIAM, IF YOU REALLY WANNA FEEL WHAT WE FEEL . . .
THEN YOU REALLY GOTTA **FEEL** WHAT WE **FEEL**.
YA FEEL ME?
OKAY, LET'S DO IT.
I'M GLAD **ONE** OF US UNDERSTOOD WHAT YOU JUST SAID.

NAY, KIDDO

CHAPTER
13

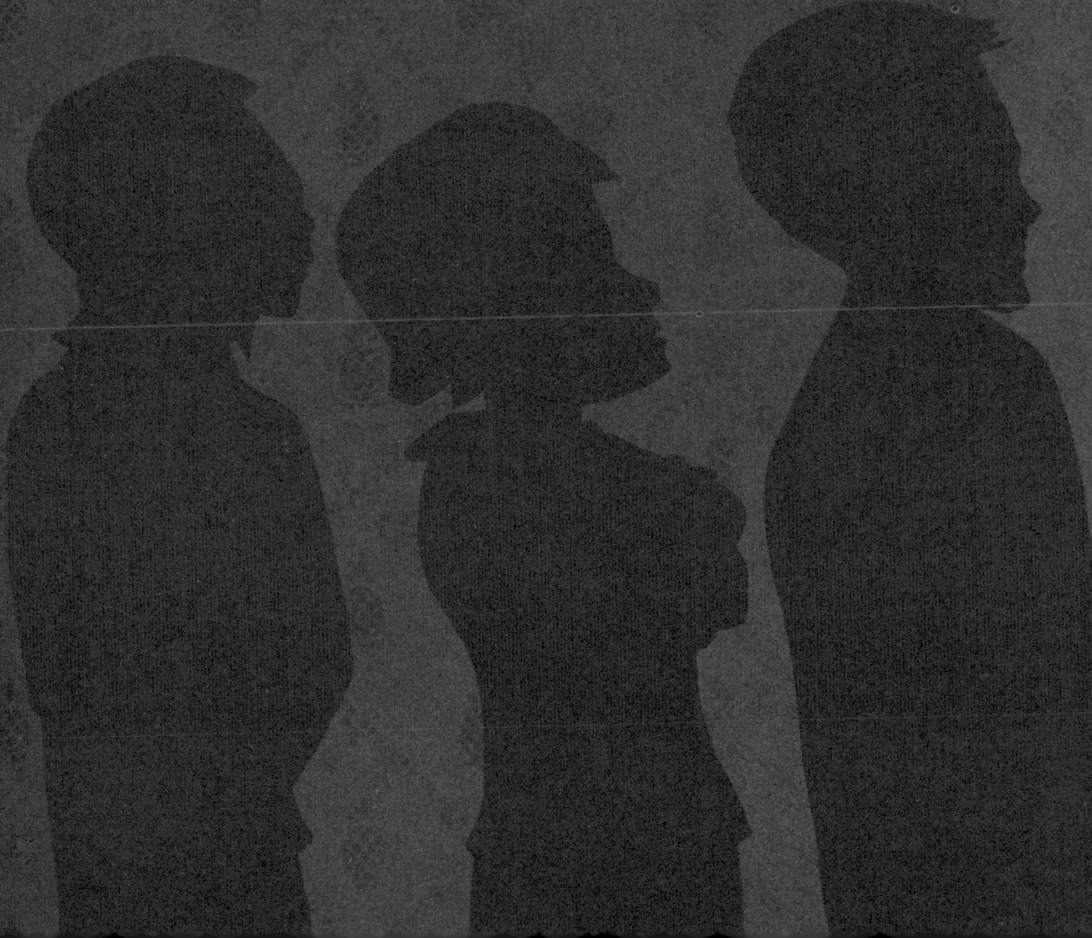

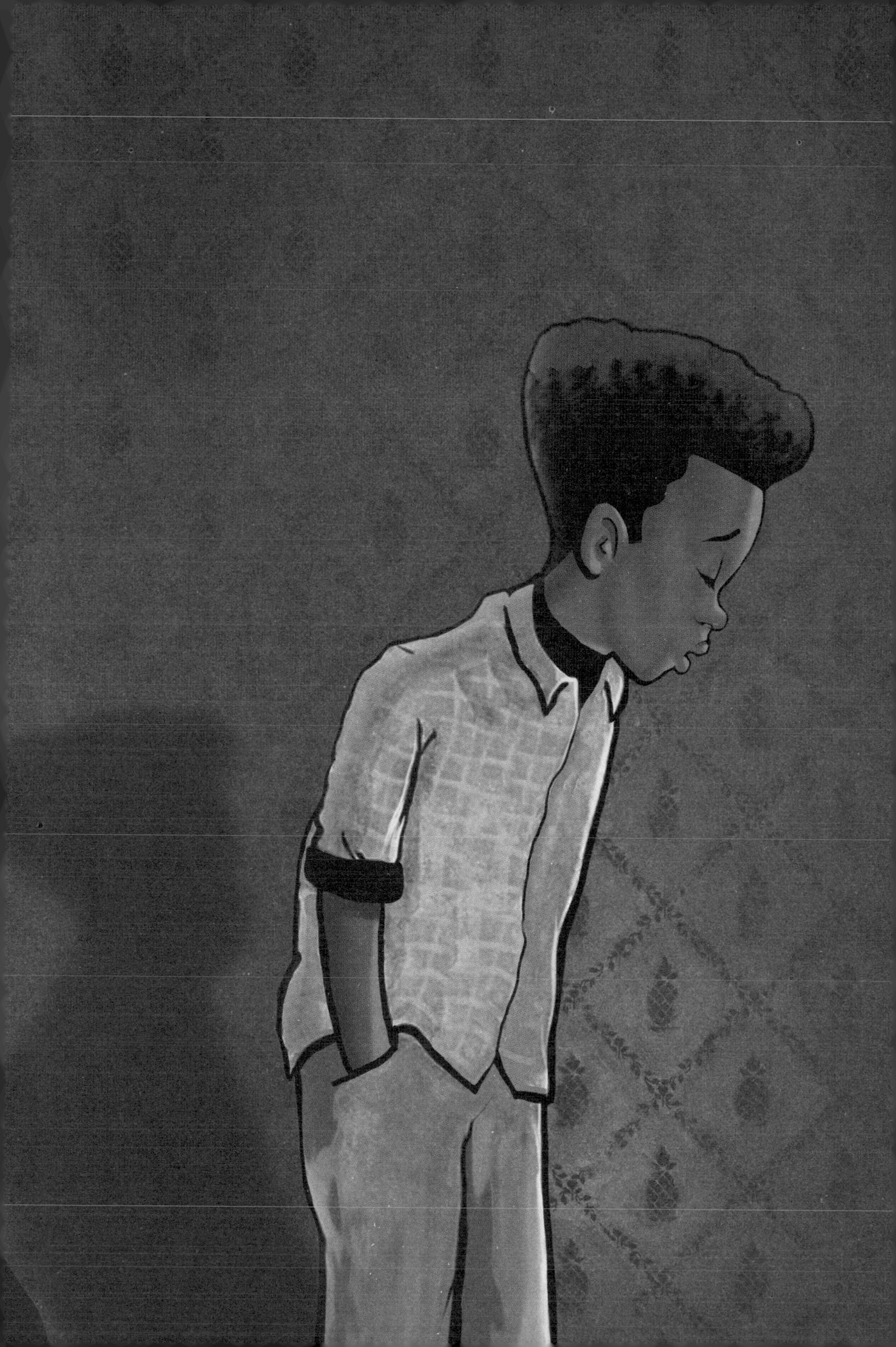

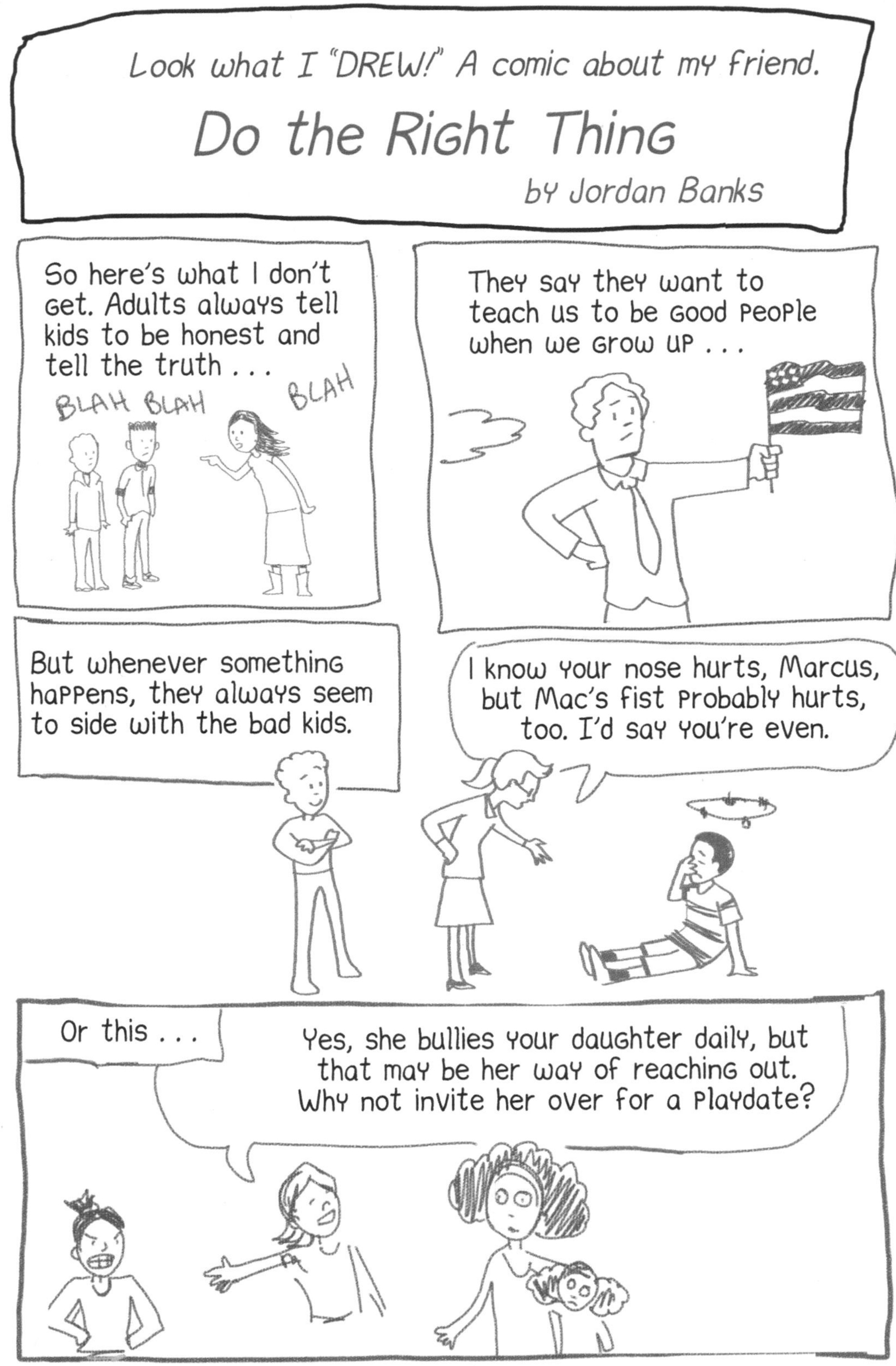
Look what I "DREW!" A comic about my friend.
Do the Right Thing
by Jordan Banks
So here's what I don't get. Adults always tell kids to be honest and tell the truth . . .
BLAH BLAH
BLAH
They say they want to teach us to be good people when we grow up . . .
But whenever something happens, they always seem to side with the bad kids.
I know your nose hurts, Marcus, but Mac's fist probably hurts, too. I'd say you're even.
Or this . . .
Yes, she bullies your daughter daily, but that may be her way of reaching out. Why not invite her over for a playdate?

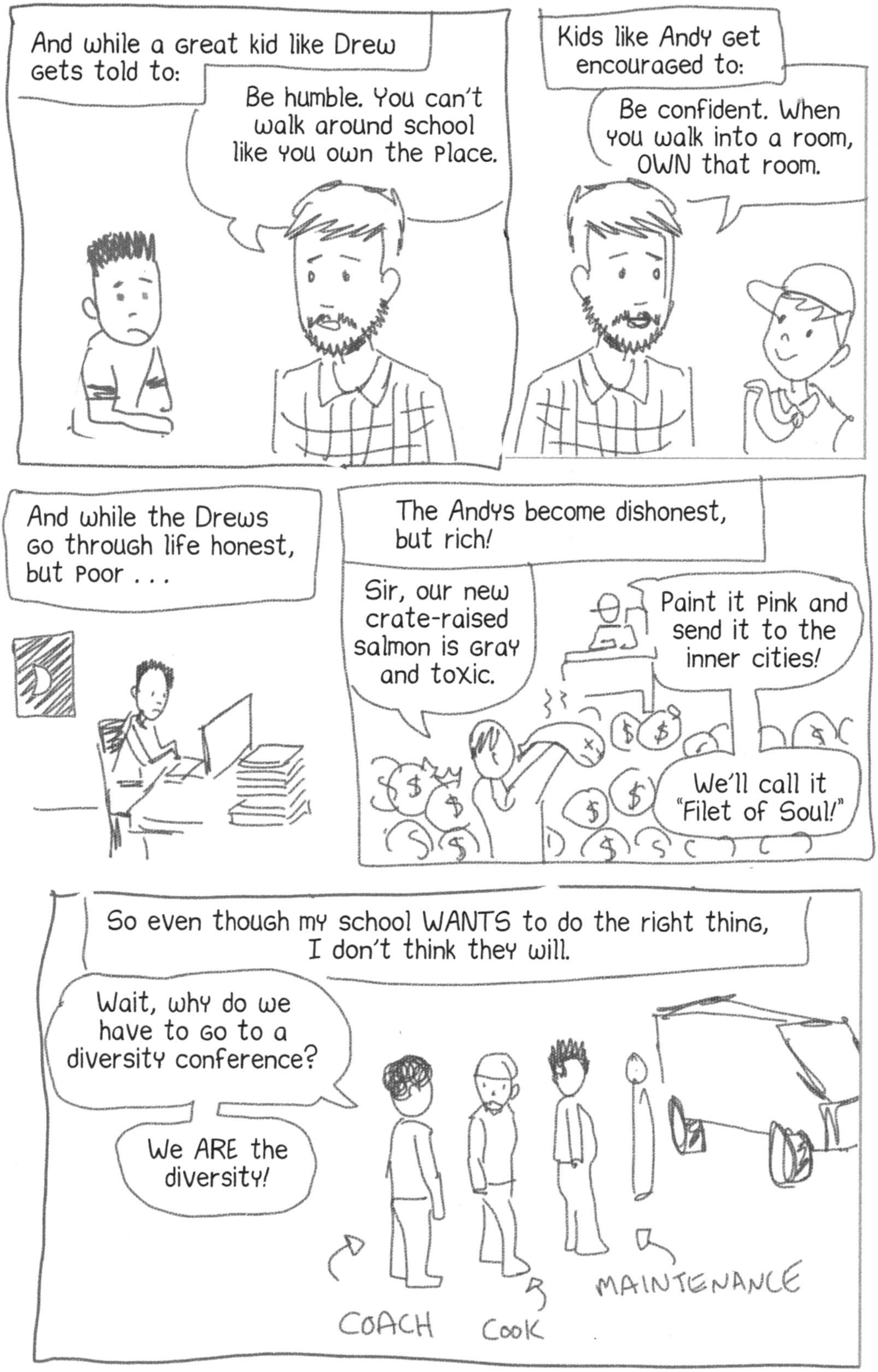
And while a great kid like Drew gets told to:
Be humble. You can't walk around school like you own the place.
Kids like Andy get encouraged to:
Be confident. When you walk into a room, OWN that room.
And while the Drews go through life honest, but poor . . .
The Andys become dishonest, but rich!
Sir, our new crate-raised salmon is gray and toxic.
Paint it pink and send it to the inner cities!
We'll call it "Filet of Soul!"
So even though my school WANTS to do the right thing, I don't think they will.
Wait, why do we have to go to a diversity conference?
We ARE the diversity!
COACH
COOK
MAINTENANCE

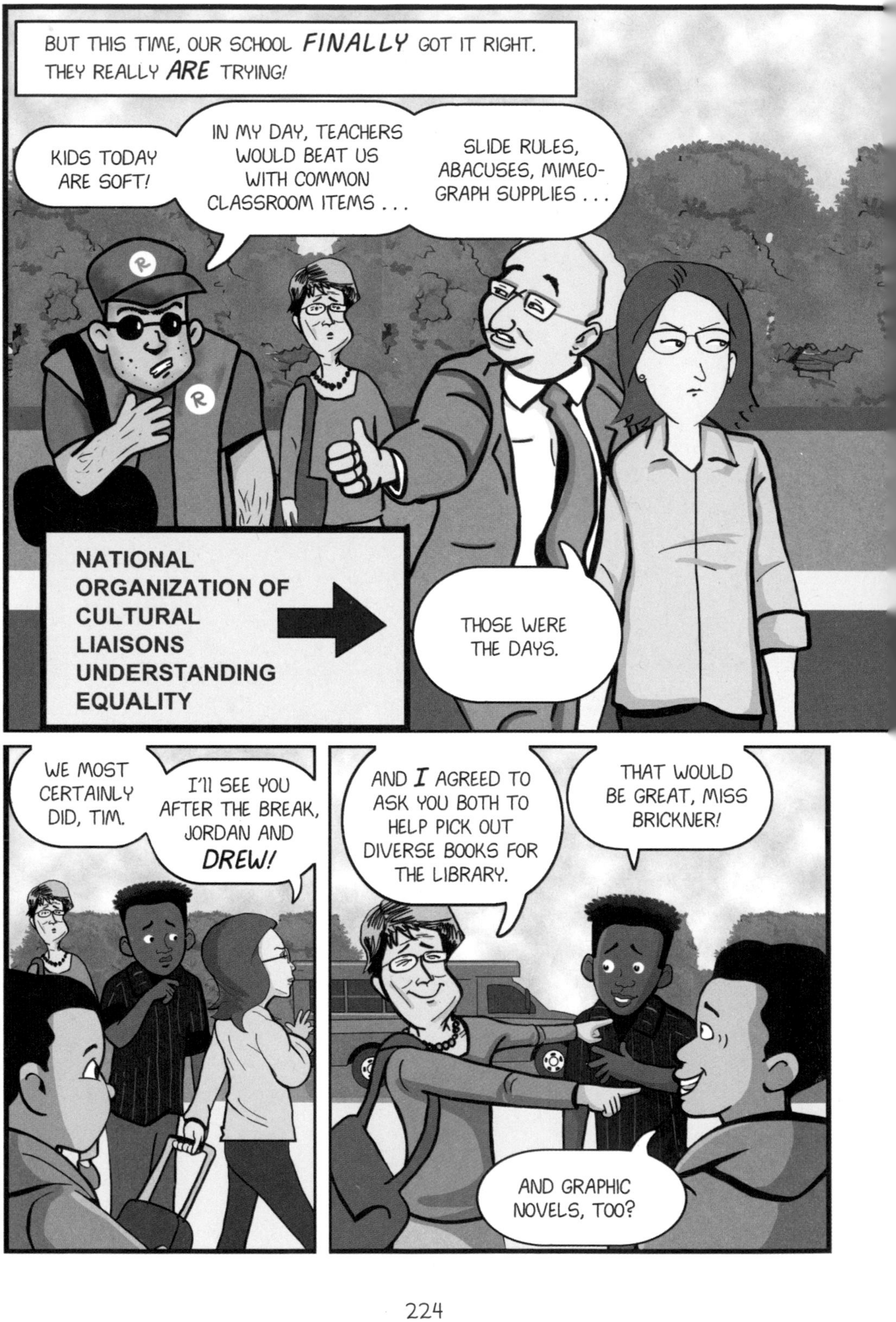
BUT THIS TIME, OUR SCHOOL FINALLY GOT IT RIGHT. THEY REALLY ARE TRYING!
KIDS TODAY ARE SOFT!
IN MY DAY, TEACHERS WOULD BEAT US WITH COMMON CLASSROOM ITEMS . . .
SLIDE RULES, ABACUSES, MIMEOGRAPH SUPPLIES . . .
NATIONAL ORGANIZATION OF CULTURAL LIAISONS UNDERSTANDING EQUALITY
THOSE WERE THE DAYS.
WE MOST CERTAINLY DID, TIM.
I'LL SEE YOU AFTER THE BREAK, JORDAN AND DREW!
AND I AGREED TO ASK YOU BOTH TO HELP PICK OUT DIVERSE BOOKS FOR THE LIBRARY.
THAT WOULD BE GREAT, MISS BRICKNER!
AND GRAPHIC NOVELS, TOO?

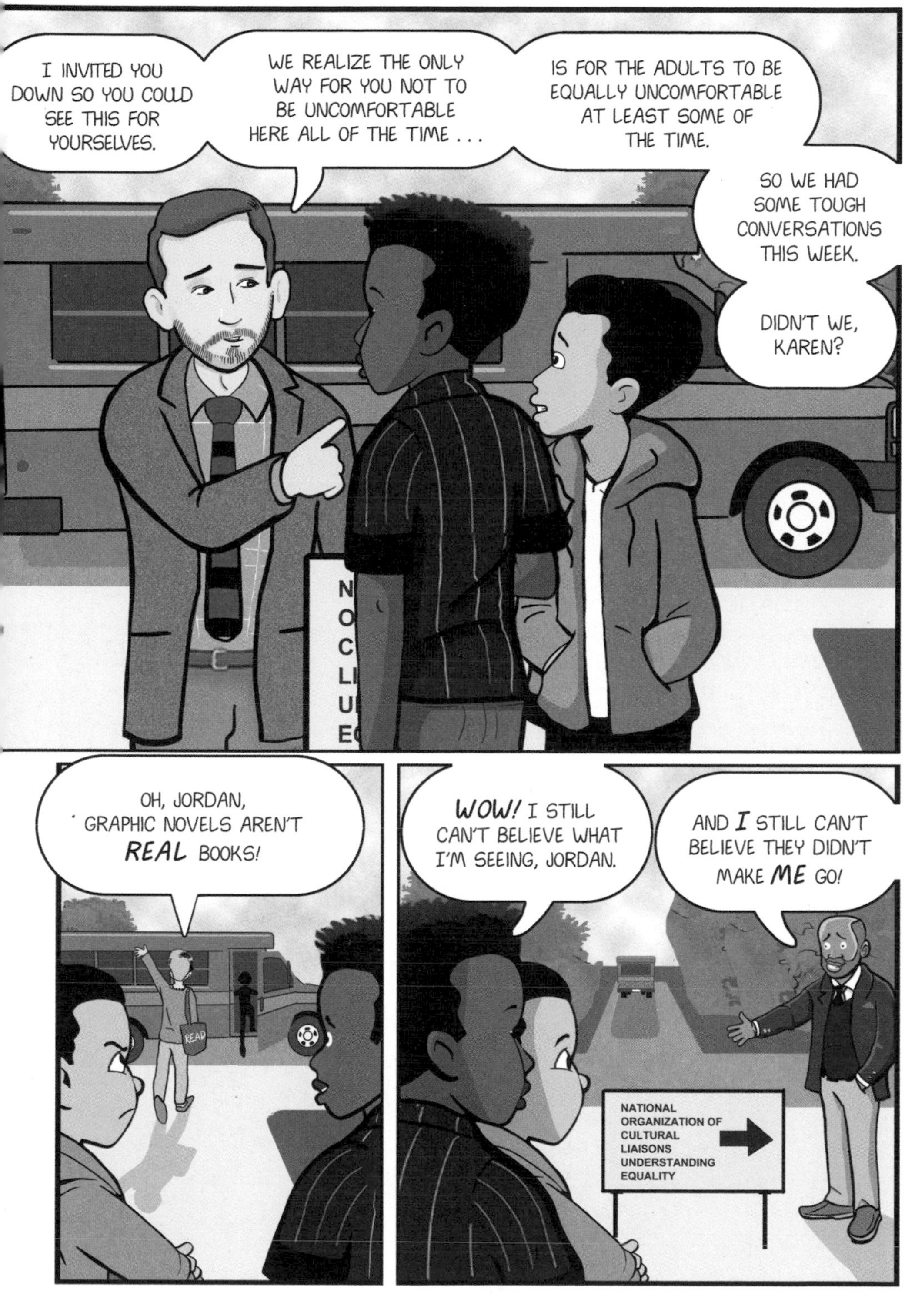
I INVITED YOU DOWN SO YOU COULD SEE THIS FOR YOURSELVES.
WE REALIZE THE ONLY WAY FOR YOU NOT TO BE UNCOMFORTABLE HERE ALL OF THE TIME . . .
IS FOR THE ADULTS TO BE EQUALLY UNCOMFORTABLE AT LEAST SOME OF THE TIME.
SO WE HAD SOME TOUGH CONVERSATIONS THIS WEEK.
DIDN'T WE, KAREN?
OH, JORDAN, GRAPHIC NOVELS AREN'T ***REAL*** BOOKS!
READ
WOW! I STILL CAN'T BELIEVE WHAT I'M SEEING, JORDAN.
AND ***I*** STILL CAN'T BELIEVE THEY DIDN'T MAKE ***ME*** GO!
NATIONAL ORGANIZATION OF CULTURAL LIAISONS UNDERSTANDING EQUALITY

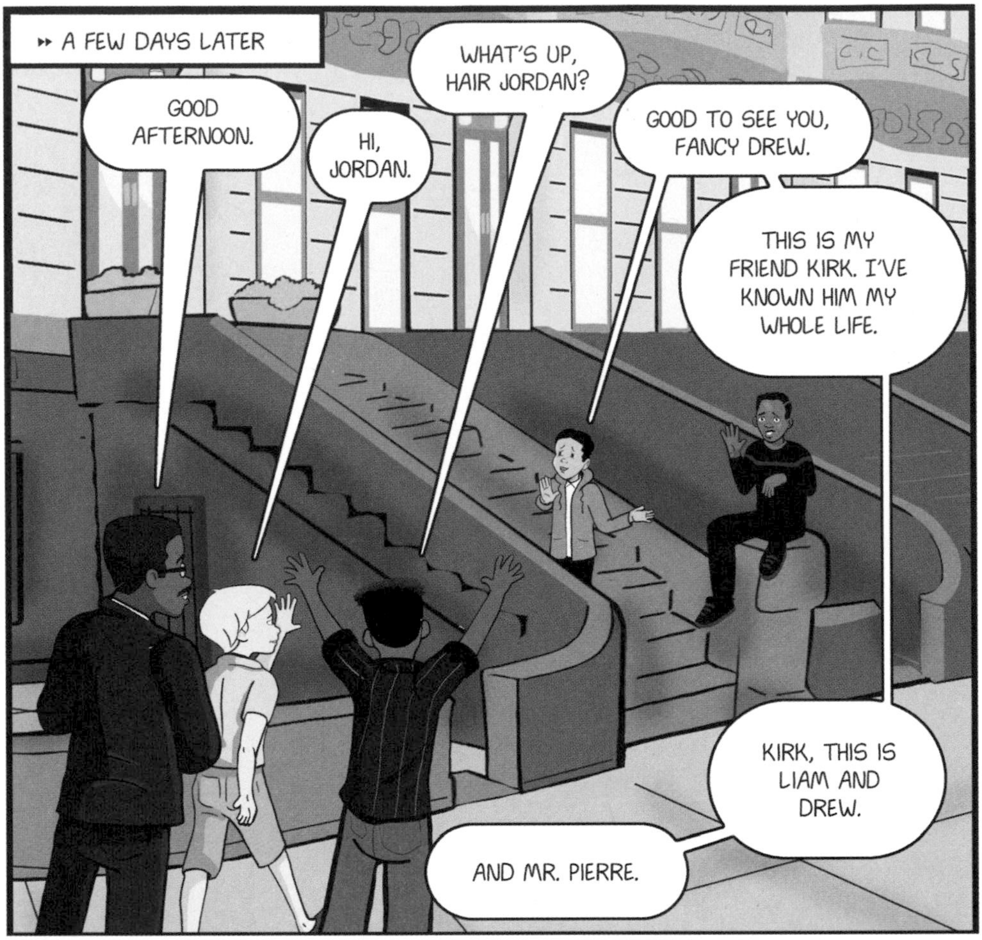
A FEW DAYS LATER
GOOD AFTERNOON.
HI, JORDAN.
WHAT'S UP, HAIR JORDAN?
GOOD TO SEE YOU, FANCY DREW.
THIS IS MY FRIEND KIRK. I'VE KNOWN HIM MY WHOLE LIFE.
KIRK, THIS IS LIAM AND DREW.
AND MR. PIERRE.

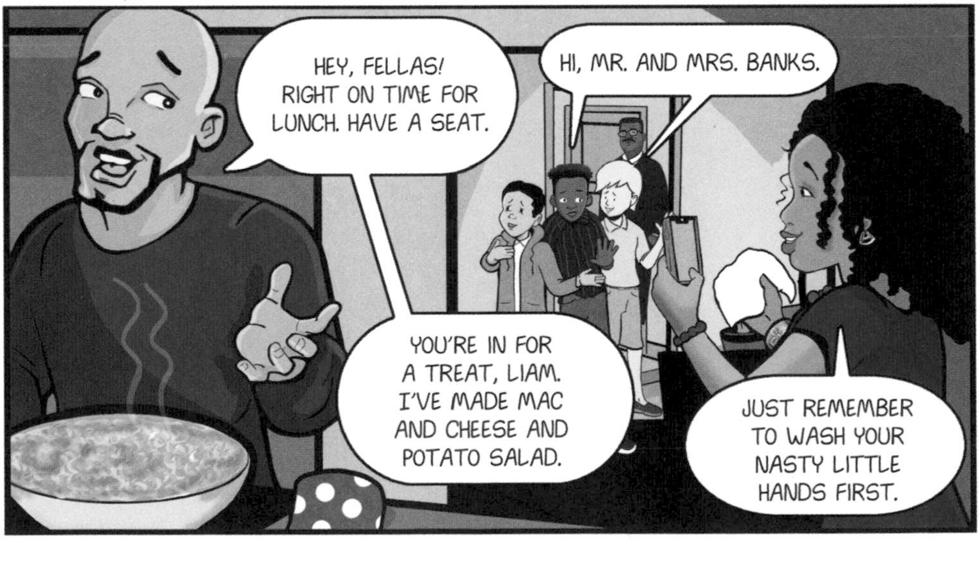
HEY, FELLAS! RIGHT ON TIME FOR LUNCH. HAVE A SEAT.
HI, MR. AND MRS. BANKS.
YOU'RE IN FOR A TREAT, LIAM. I'VE MADE MAC AND CHEESE AND POTATO SALAD.
JUST REMEMBER TO WASH YOUR NASTY LITTLE HANDS FIRST.

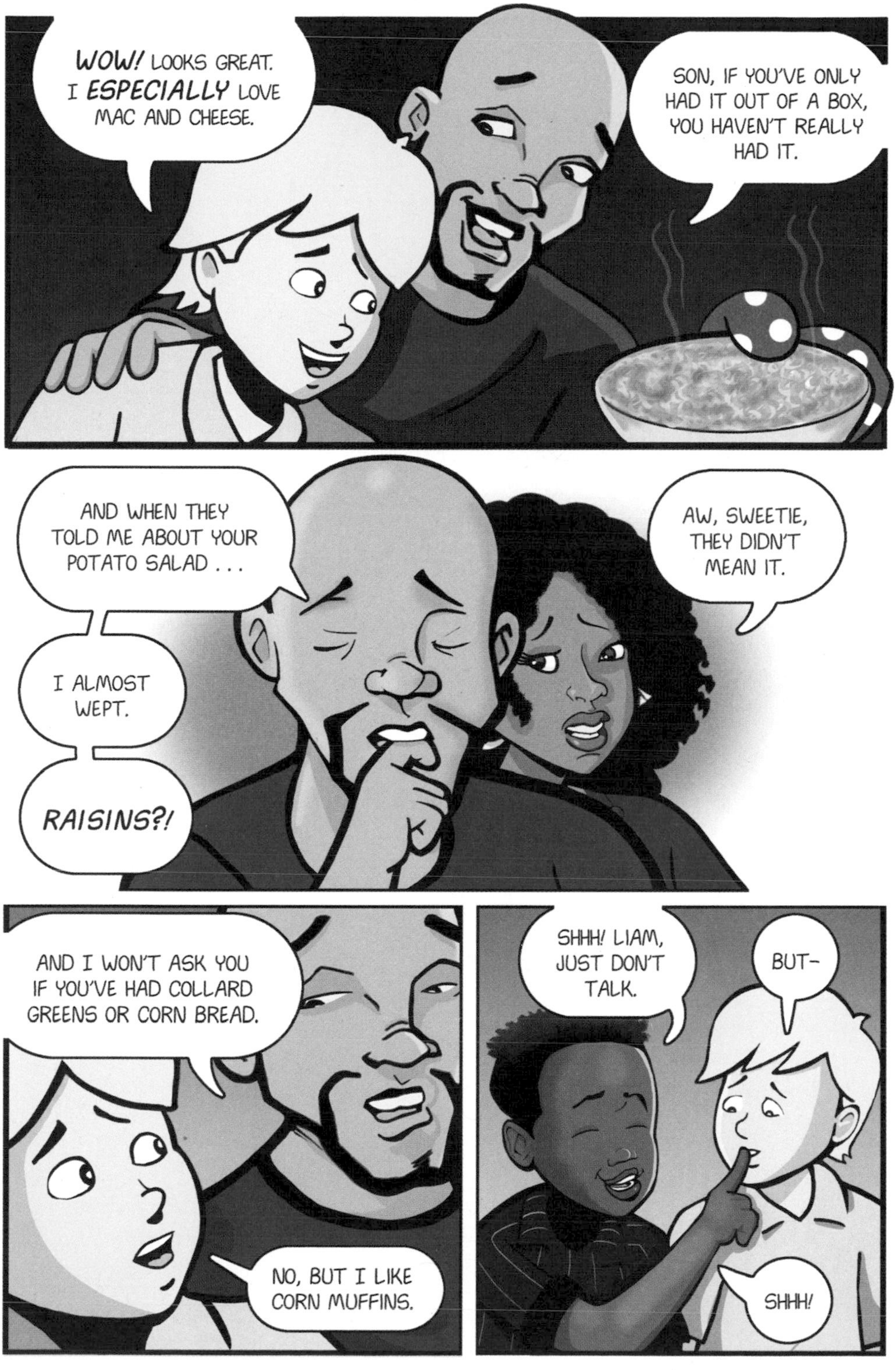
WOW! LOOKS GREAT. I ESPECIALLY LOVE MAC AND CHEESE.
SON, IF YOU'VE ONLY HAD IT OUT OF A BOX, YOU HAVEN'T REALLY HAD IT.
AND WHEN THEY TOLD ME ABOUT YOUR POTATO SALAD . . .
I ALMOST WEPT.
RAISINS?!
AW, SWEETIE, THEY DIDN'T MEAN IT.
AND I WON'T ASK YOU IF YOU'VE HAD COLLARD GREENS OR CORN BREAD.
NO, BUT I LIKE CORN MUFFINS.
SHHH! LIAM, JUST DON'T TALK.
BUT-
SHHH!

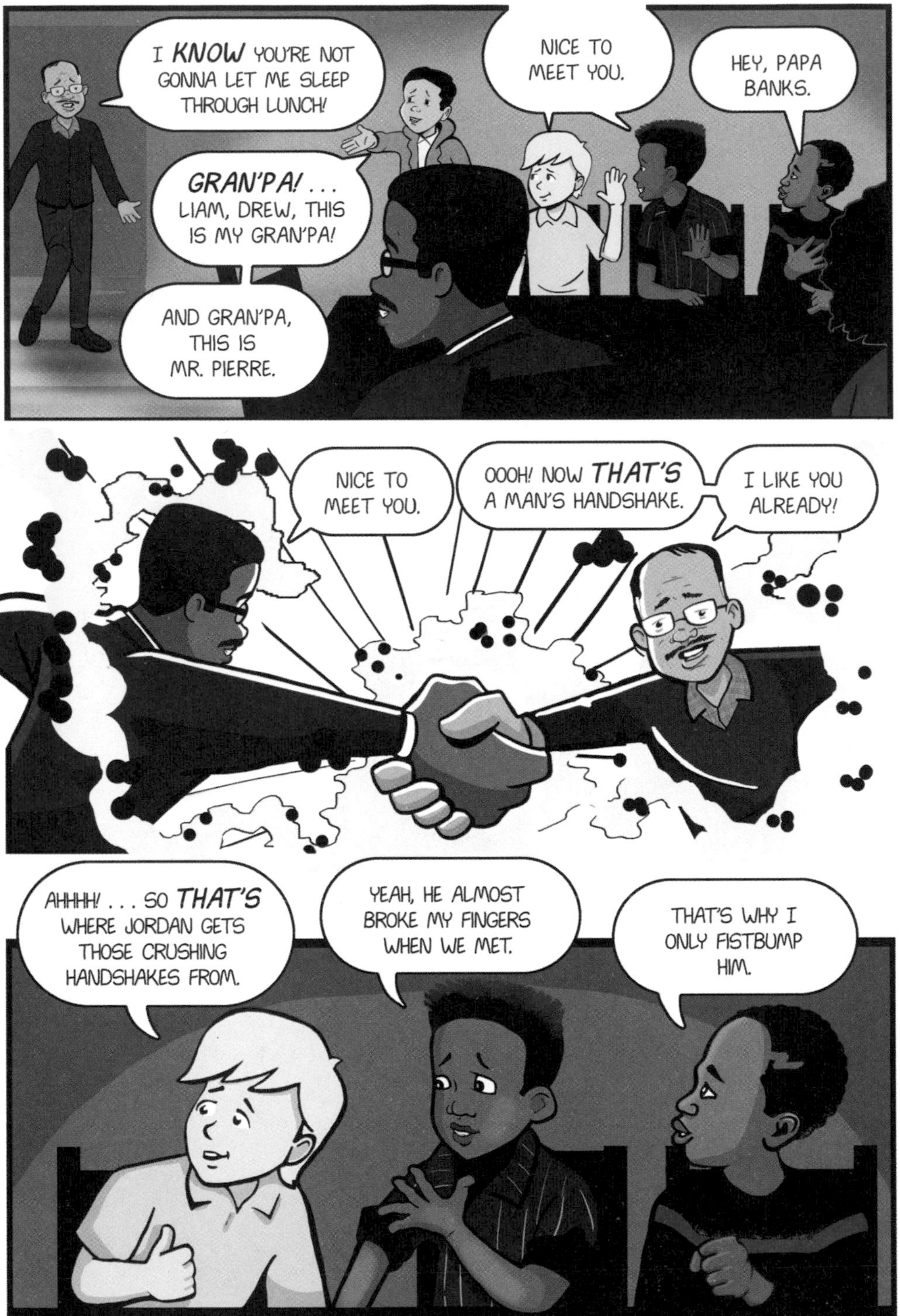
I KNOW YOU'RE NOT GONNA LET ME SLEEP THROUGH LUNCH!
GRAN'PA! . . . LIAM, DREW, THIS IS MY GRAN'PA!
AND GRAN'PA, THIS IS MR. PIERRE.
NICE TO MEET YOU.
HEY, PAPA BANKS.
NICE TO MEET YOU.
OOOH! NOW THAT'S A MAN'S HANDSHAKE.
I LIKE YOU ALREADY!
AHHHH! . . . SO THAT'S WHERE JORDAN GETS THOSE CRUSHING HANDSHAKES FROM.
YEAH, HE ALMOST BROKE MY FINGERS WHEN WE MET.
THAT'S WHY I ONLY FISTBUMP HIM.

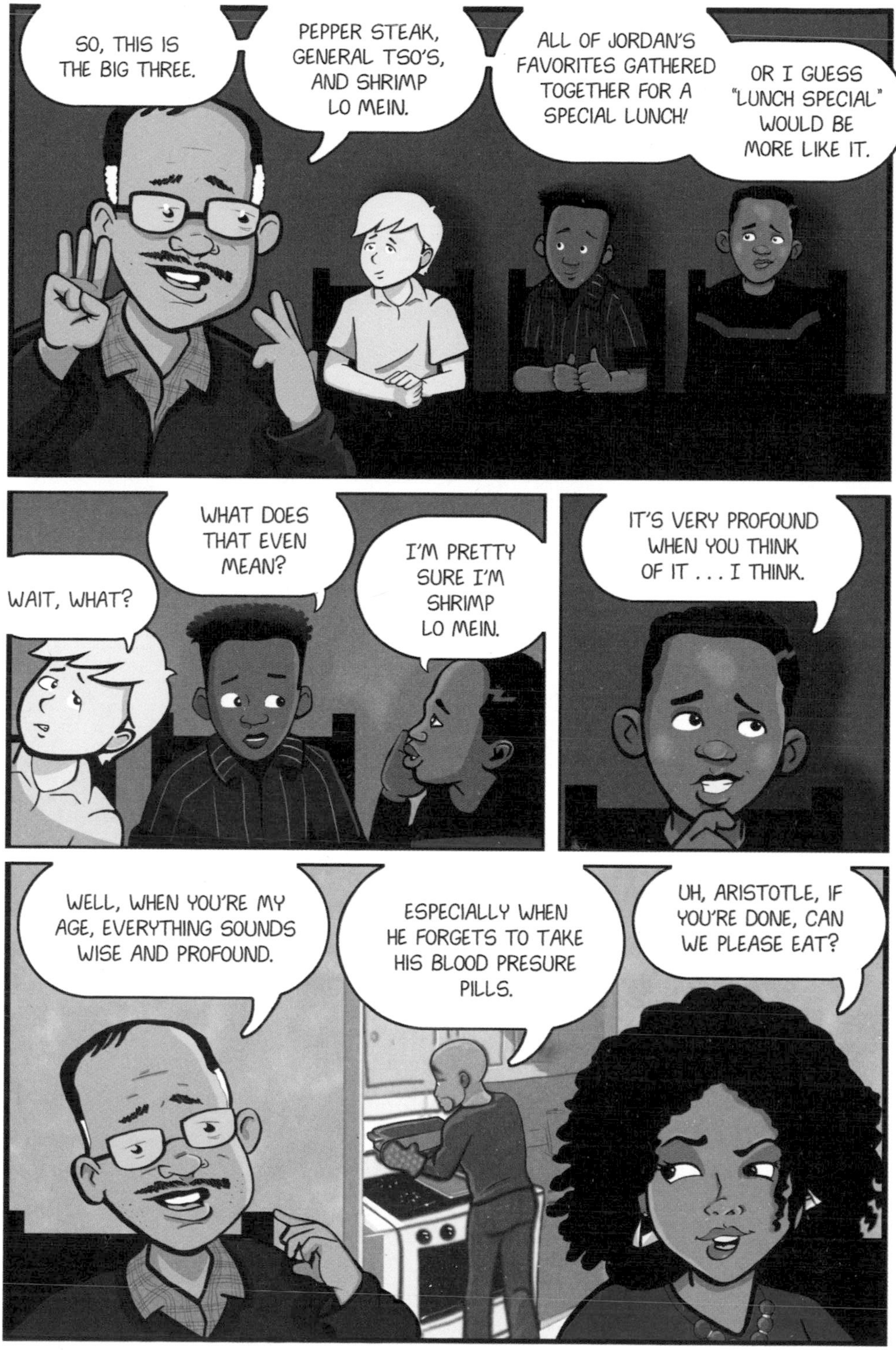
SO, THIS IS THE BIG THREE.
PEPPER STEAK, GENERAL TSO'S, AND SHRIMP LO MEIN.
ALL OF JORDAN'S FAVORITES GATHERED TOGETHER FOR A SPECIAL LUNCH!
OR I GUESS "LUNCH SPECIAL" WOULD BE MORE LIKE IT.
WHAT DOES THAT EVEN MEAN?
WAIT, WHAT?
I'M PRETTY SURE I'M SHRIMP LO MEIN.
IT'S VERY PROFOUND WHEN YOU THINK OF IT . . . I THINK.
WELL, WHEN YOU'RE MY AGE, EVERYTHING SOUNDS WISE AND PROFOUND.
ESPECIALLY WHEN HE FORGETS TO TAKE HIS BLOOD PRESURE PILLS.
UH, ARISTOTLE, IF YOU'RE DONE, CAN WE PLEASE EAT?

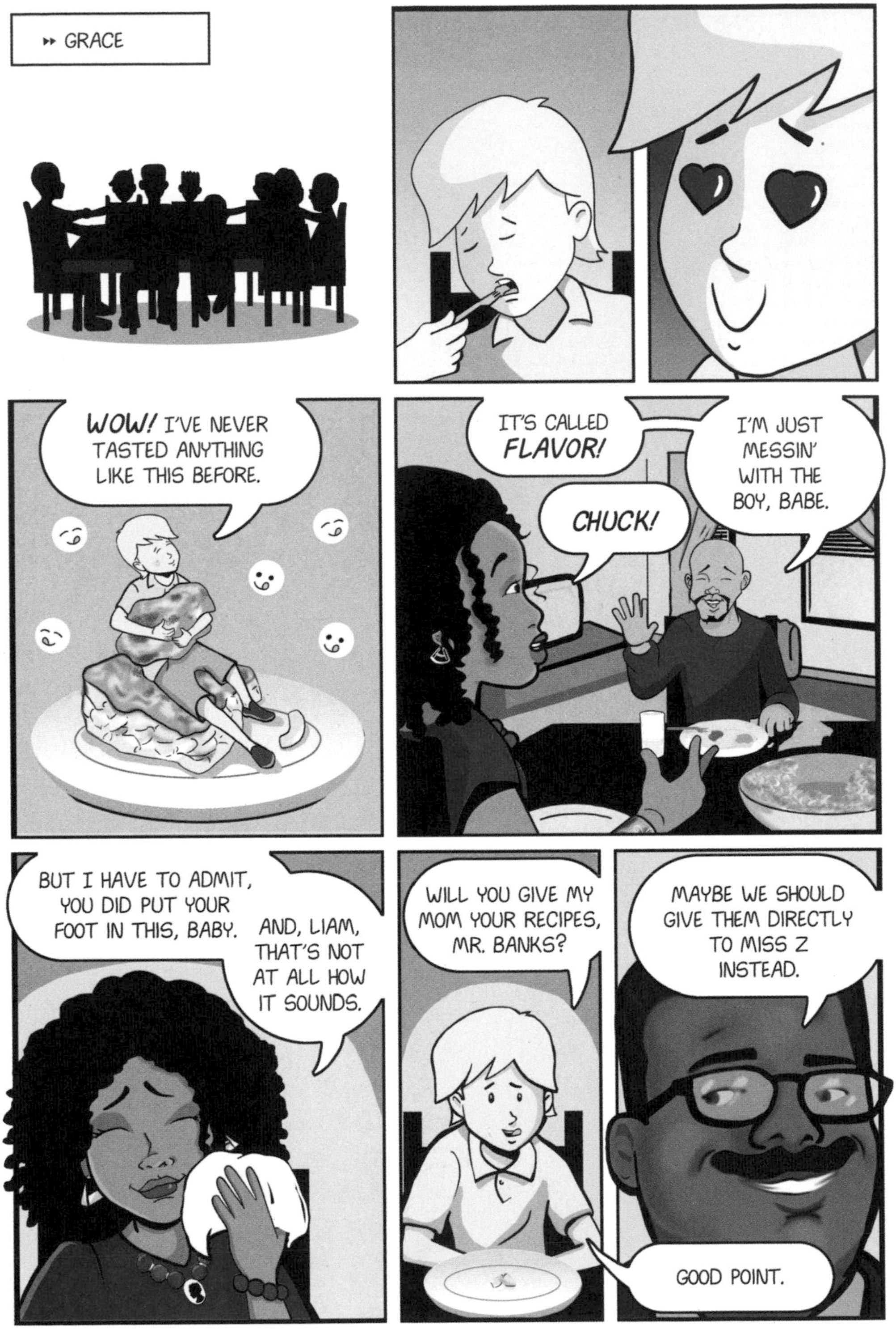
▸▸ GRACE
WOW! I'VE NEVER TASTED ANYTHING LIKE THIS BEFORE.
IT'S CALLED FLAVOR!
CHUCK!
I'M JUST MESSIN' WITH THE BOY, BABE.
BUT I HAVE TO ADMIT, YOU DID PUT YOUR FOOT IN THIS, BABY.
AND, LIAM, THAT'S NOT AT ALL HOW IT SOUNDS.
WILL YOU GIVE MY MOM YOUR RECIPES, MR. BANKS?
MAYBE WE SHOULD GIVE THEM DIRECTLY TO MISS Z INSTEAD.
GOOD POINT.

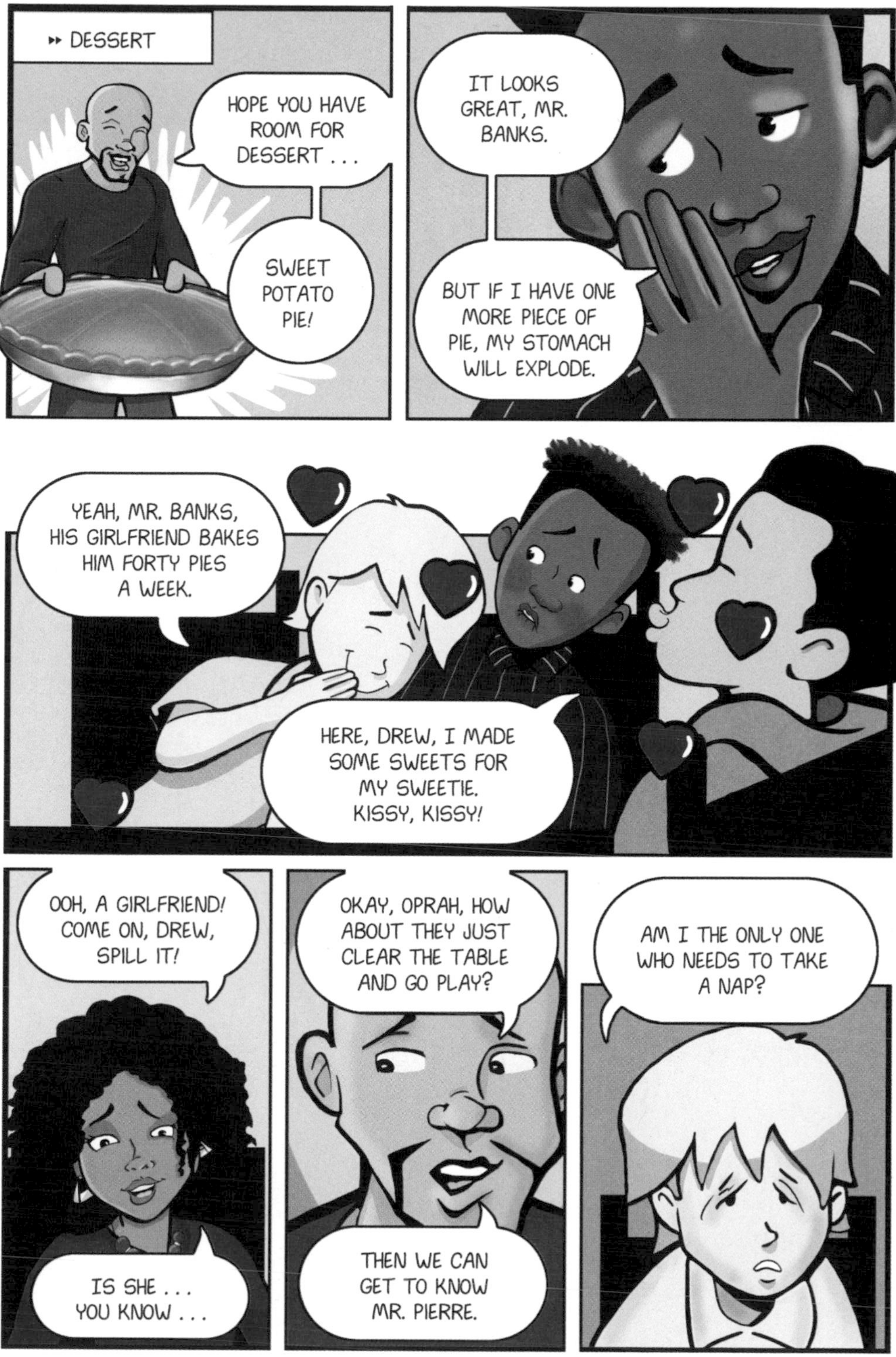
DESSERT
HOPE YOU HAVE ROOM FOR DESSERT . . .
SWEET POTATO PIE!
IT LOOKS GREAT, MR. BANKS.
BUT IF I HAVE ONE MORE PIECE OF PIE, MY STOMACH WILL EXPLODE.
YEAH, MR. BANKS, HIS GIRLFRIEND BAKES HIM FORTY PIES A WEEK.
HERE, DREW, I MADE SOME SWEETS FOR MY SWEETIE. KISSY, KISSY!
OOH, A GIRLFRIEND! COME ON, DREW, SPILL IT!
IS SHE . . . YOU KNOW . . .
OKAY, OPRAH, HOW ABOUT THEY JUST CLEAR THE TABLE AND GO PLAY?
THEN WE CAN GET TO KNOW MR. PIERRE.
AM I THE ONLY ONE WHO NEEDS TO TAKE A NAP?

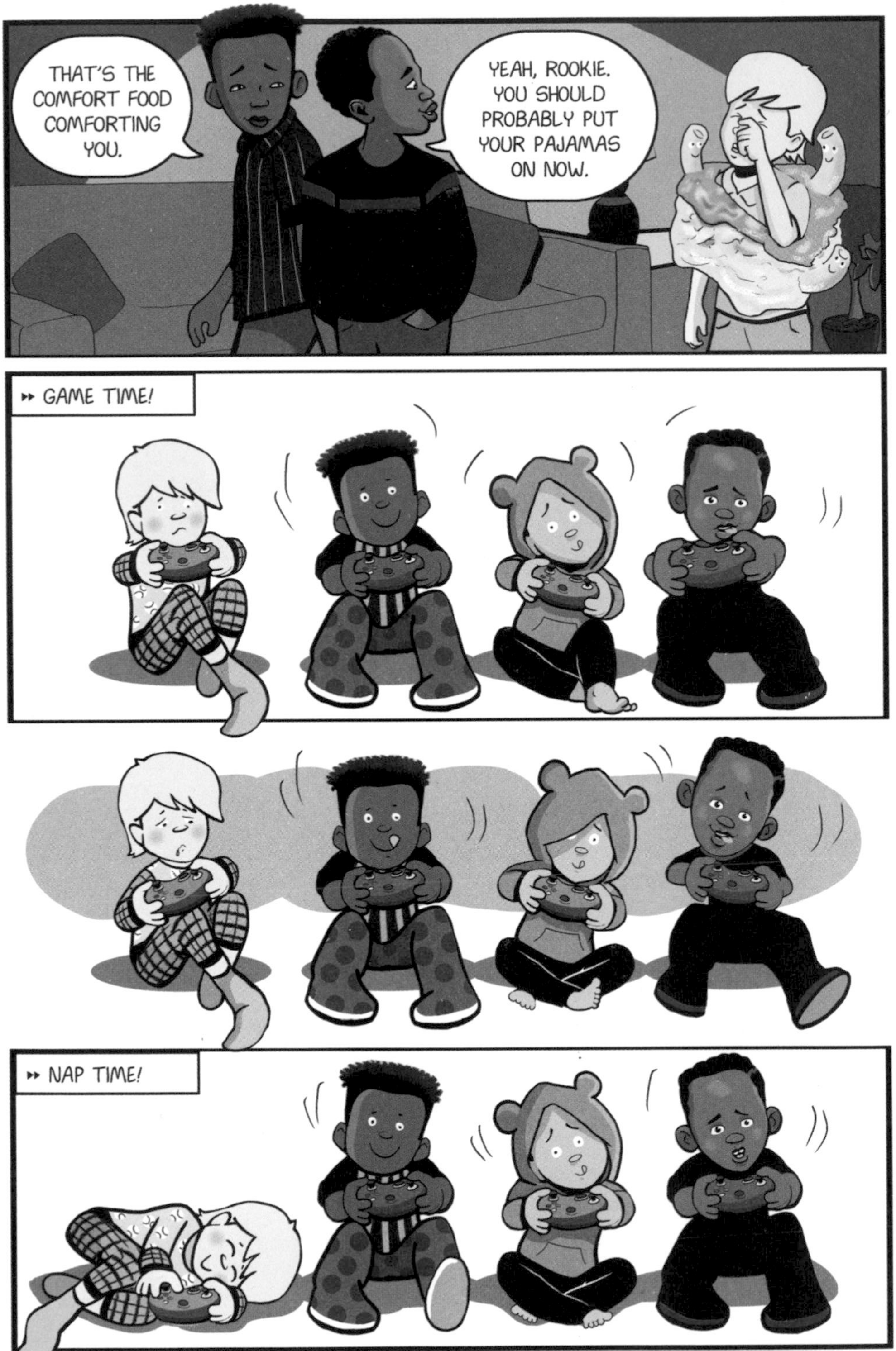
THAT'S THE COMFORT FOOD COMFORTING YOU.
YEAH, ROOKIE. YOU SHOULD PROBABLY PUT YOUR PAJAMAS ON NOW.
GAME TIME!
NAP TIME!

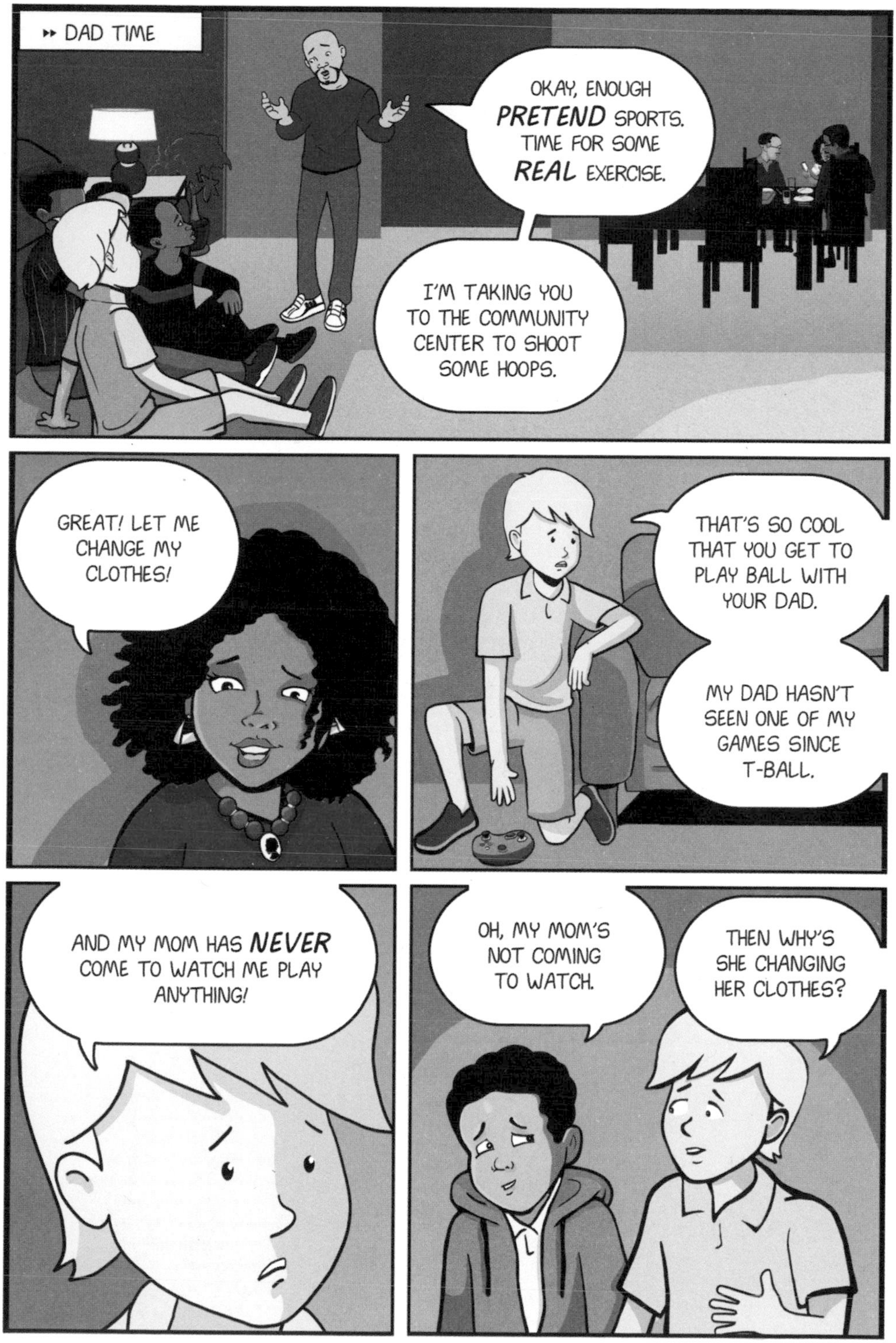
DAD TIME
OKAY, ENOUGH **PRETEND** SPORTS. TIME FOR SOME **REAL** EXERCISE.
I'M TAKING YOU TO THE COMMUNITY CENTER TO SHOOT SOME HOOPS.
GREAT! LET ME CHANGE MY CLOTHES!
THAT'S SO COOL THAT YOU GET TO PLAY BALL WITH YOUR DAD.
MY DAD HASN'T SEEN ONE OF MY GAMES SINCE T-BALL.
AND MY MOM HAS **NEVER** COME TO WATCH ME PLAY ANYTHING!
OH, MY MOM'S NOT COMING TO WATCH.
THEN WHY'S SHE CHANGING HER CLOTHES?

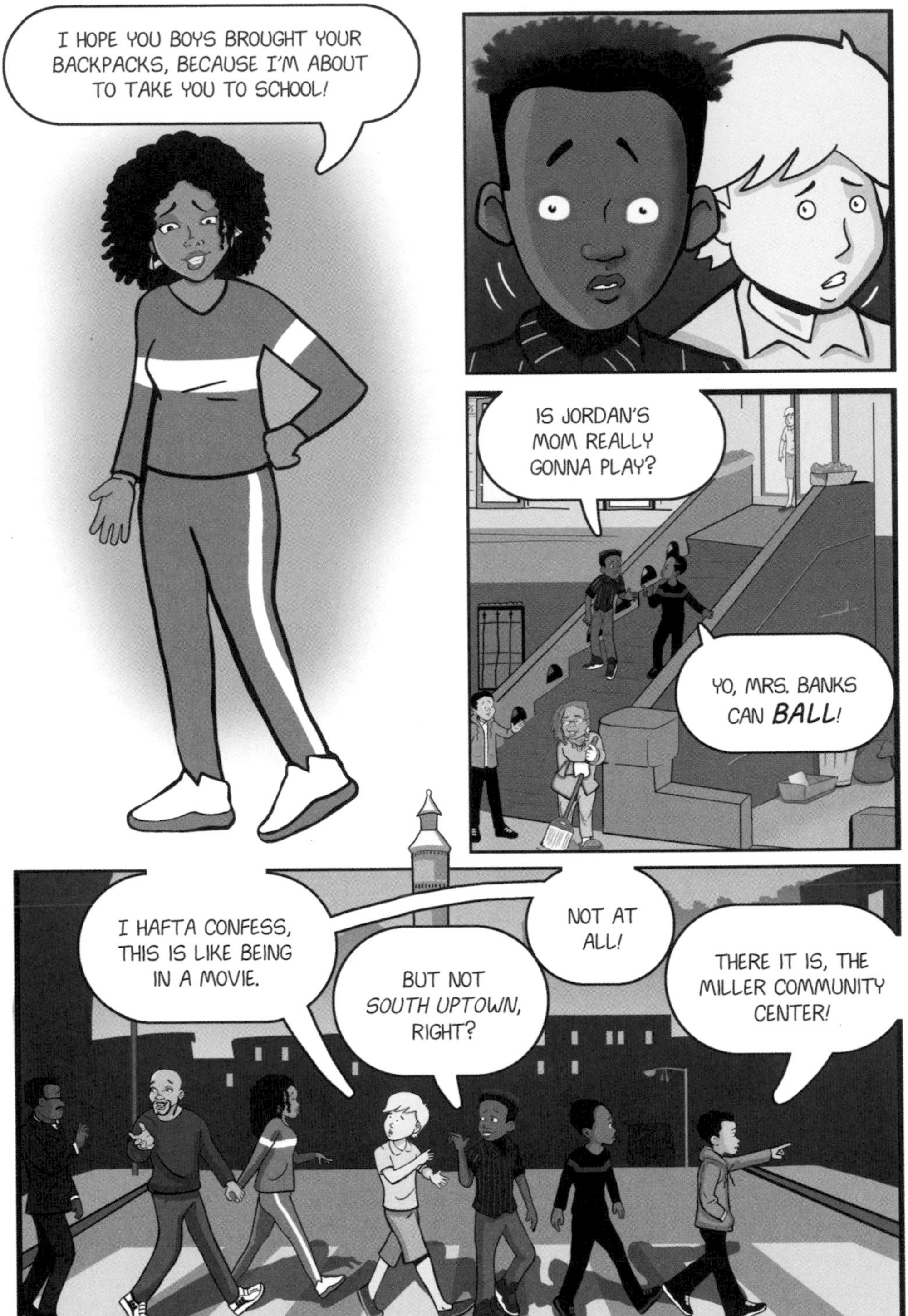
I HOPE YOU BOYS BROUGHT YOUR BACKPACKS, BECAUSE I'M ABOUT TO TAKE YOU TO SCHOOL!
IS JORDAN'S MOM REALLY GONNA PLAY?
YO, MRS. BANKS CAN *BALL*!
I HAFTA CONFESS, THIS IS LIKE BEING IN A MOVIE.
BUT NOT *SOUTH UPTOWN*, RIGHT?
NOT AT ALL!
THERE IT IS, THE MILLER COMMUNITY CENTER!

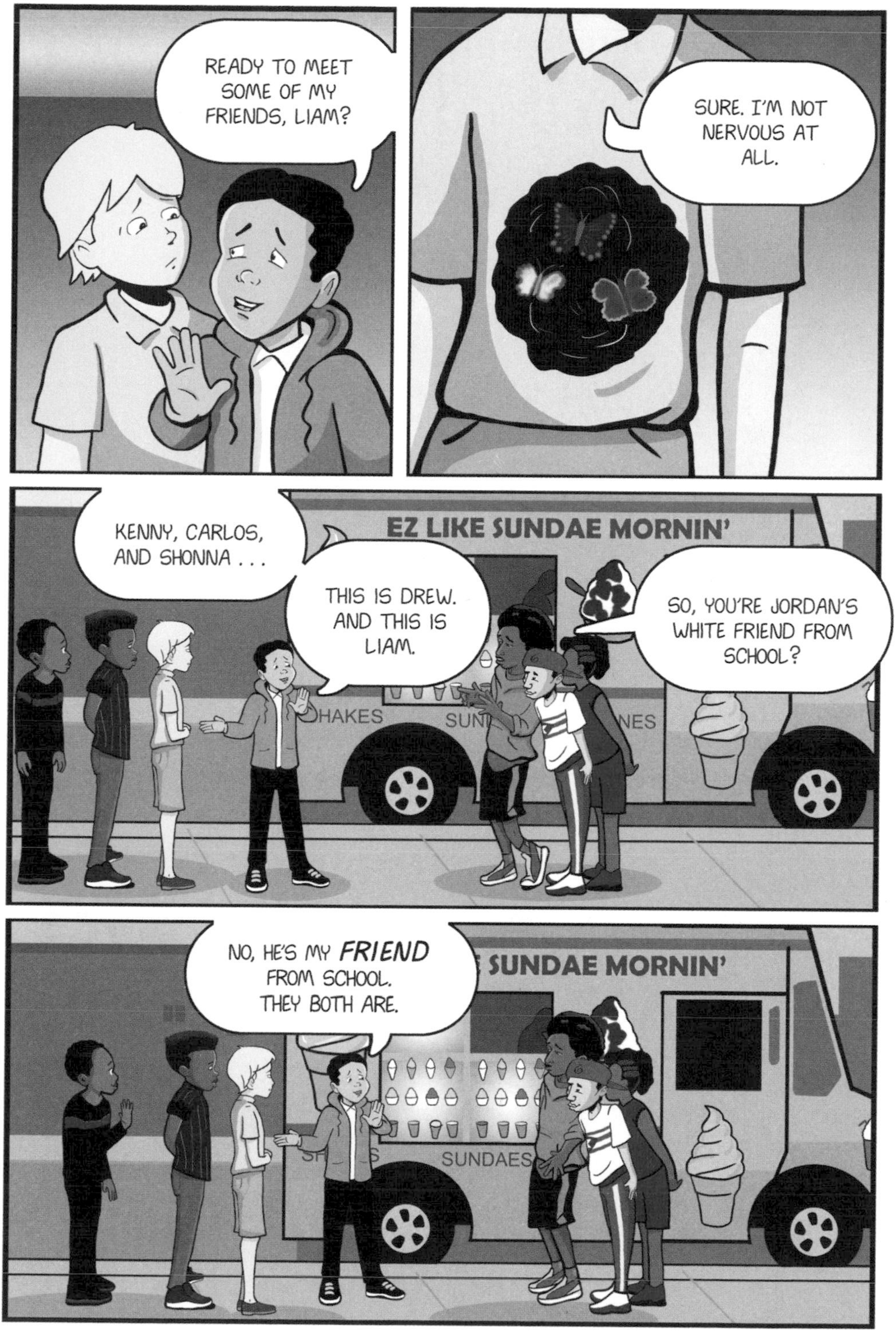
READY TO MEET SOME OF MY FRIENDS, LIAM?
SURE. I'M NOT NERVOUS AT ALL.
EZ LIKE SUNDAE MORNIN'
KENNY, CARLOS, AND SHONNA . . .
THIS IS DREW. AND THIS IS LIAM.
SO, YOU'RE JORDAN'S WHITE FRIEND FROM SCHOOL?
NO, HE'S MY *FRIEND* FROM SCHOOL. THEY BOTH ARE.
SUNDAE MORNIN'
SUNDAES

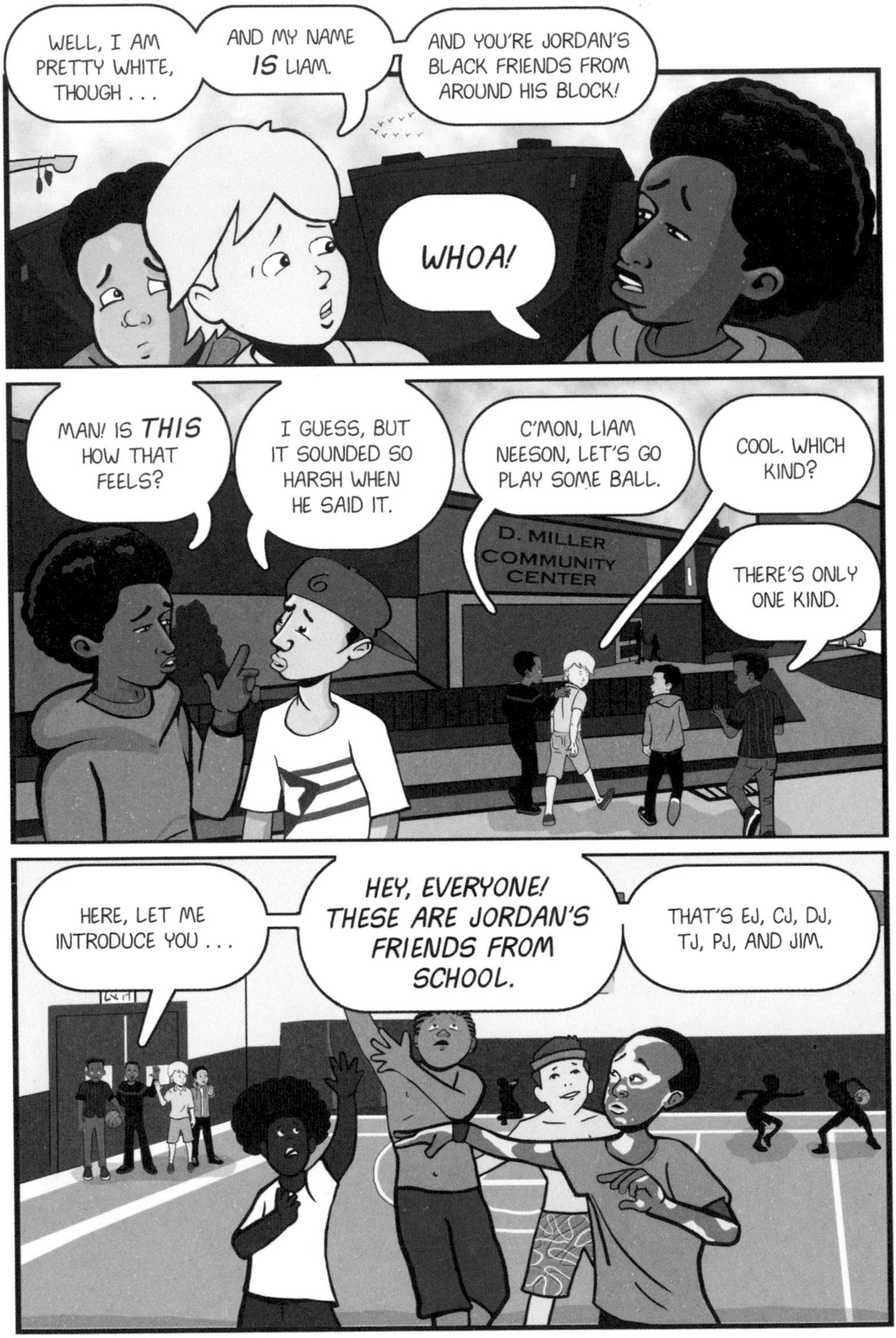
WELL, I AM PRETTY WHITE, THOUGH . . .
AND MY NAME *IS* LIAM.
AND YOU'RE JORDAN'S BLACK FRIENDS FROM AROUND HIS BLOCK!
WHOA!
MAN! IS **THIS** HOW THAT FEELS?
I GUESS, BUT IT SOUNDED SO HARSH WHEN HE SAID IT.
D. MILLER COMMUNITY CENTER
C'MON, LIAM NEESON, LET'S GO PLAY SOME BALL.
COOL. WHICH KIND?
THERE'S ONLY ONE KIND.
HERE, LET ME INTRODUCE YOU . . .
HEY, EVERYONE! THESE ARE JORDAN'S FRIENDS FROM SCHOOL.
THAT'S EJ, CJ, DJ, TJ, PJ, AND JIM.

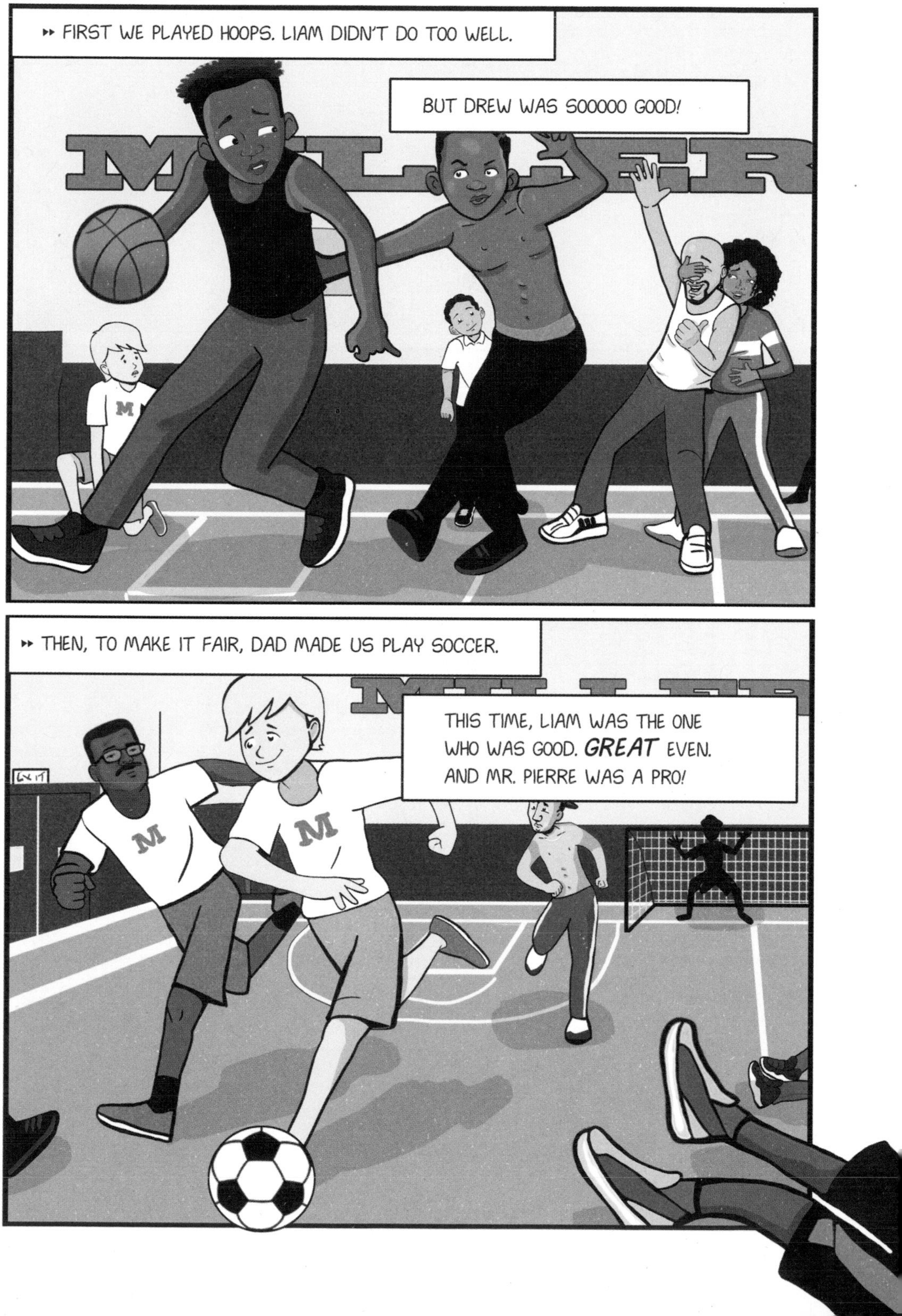
FIRST WE PLAYED HOOPS. LIAM DIDN'T DO TOO WELL.
BUT DREW WAS SOOOOO GOOD!
MILLER
THEN, TO MAKE IT FAIR, DAD MADE US PLAY SOCCER.
THIS TIME, LIAM WAS THE ONE WHO WAS GOOD. ***GREAT*** EVEN. AND MR. PIERRE WAS A PRO!

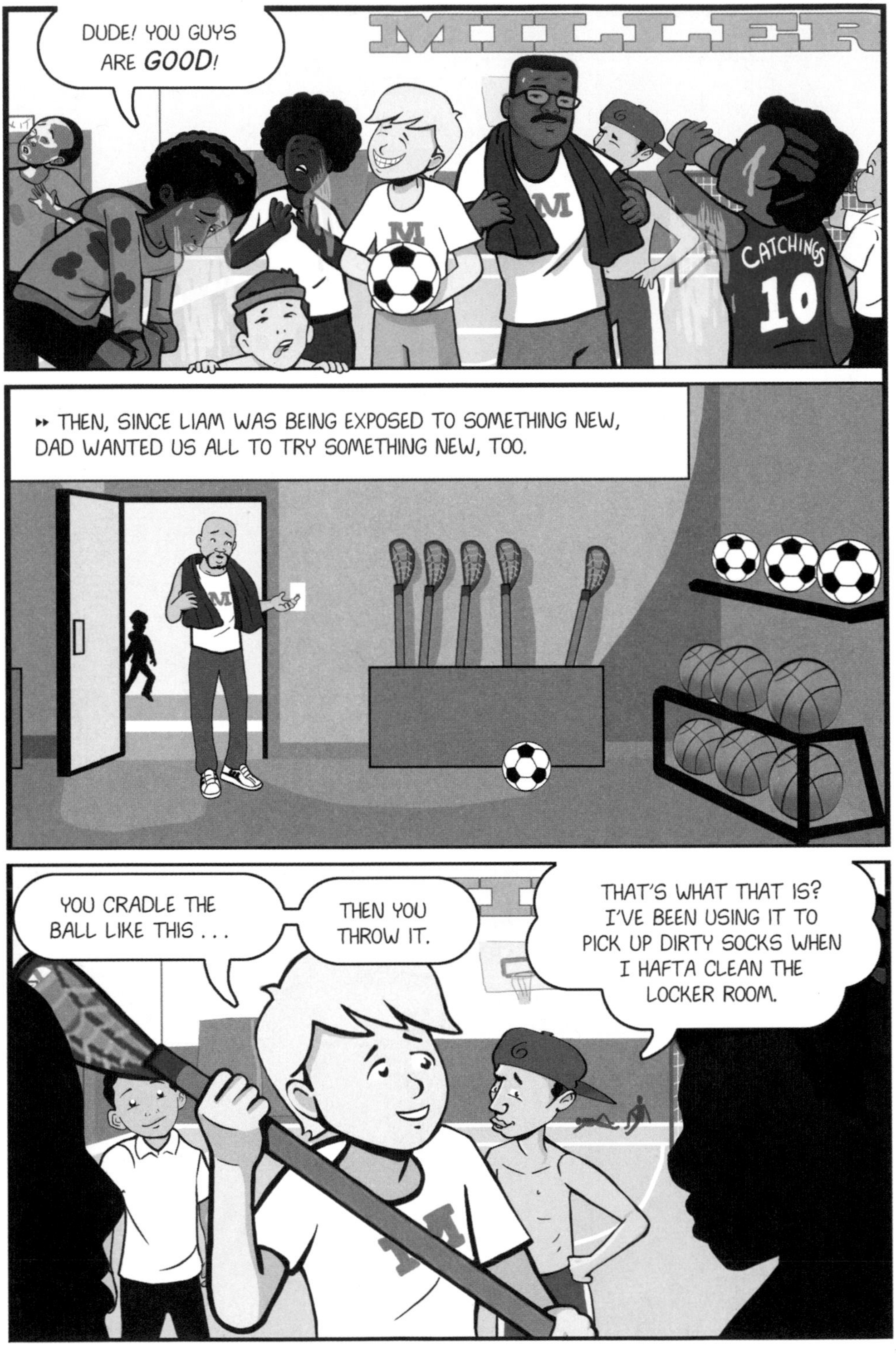
MILLER
DUDE! YOU GUYS ARE GOOD!
CATCHINGS 10
THEN, SINCE LIAM WAS BEING EXPOSED TO SOMETHING NEW, DAD WANTED US ALL TO TRY SOMETHING NEW, TOO.
YOU CRADLE THE BALL LIKE THIS . . .
THEN YOU THROW IT.
THAT'S WHAT THAT IS? I'VE BEEN USING IT TO PICK UP DIRTY SOCKS WHEN I HAFTA CLEAN THE LOCKER ROOM.

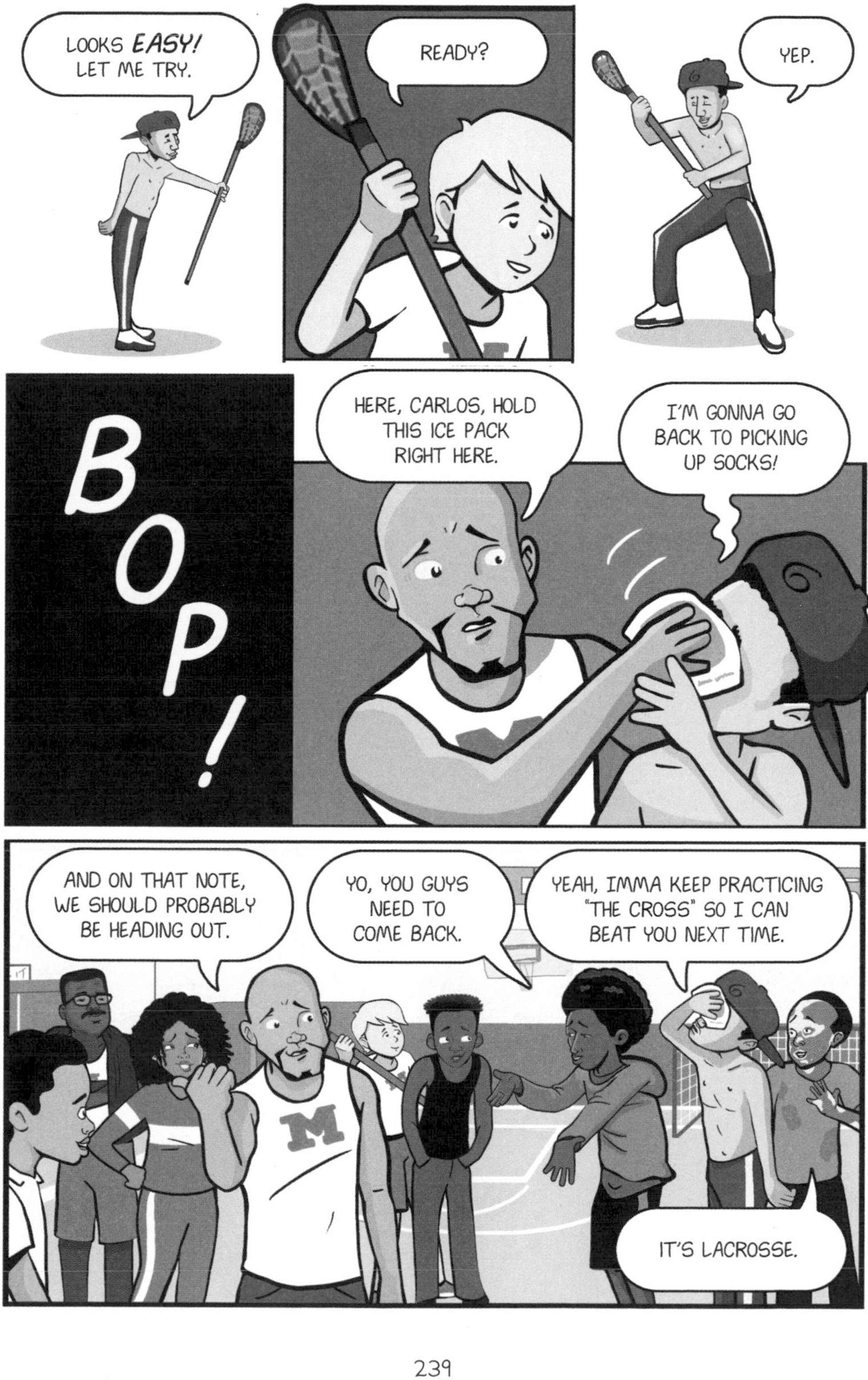
LOOKS EASY! LET ME TRY.
READY?
YEP.
BOP!
HERE, CARLOS, HOLD THIS ICE PACK RIGHT HERE.
I'M GONNA GO BACK TO PICKING UP SOCKS!
AND ON THAT NOTE, WE SHOULD PROBABLY BE HEADING OUT.
YO, YOU GUYS NEED TO COME BACK.
YEAH, IMMA KEEP PRACTICING "THE CROSS" SO I CAN BEAT YOU NEXT TIME.
IT'S LACROSSE.

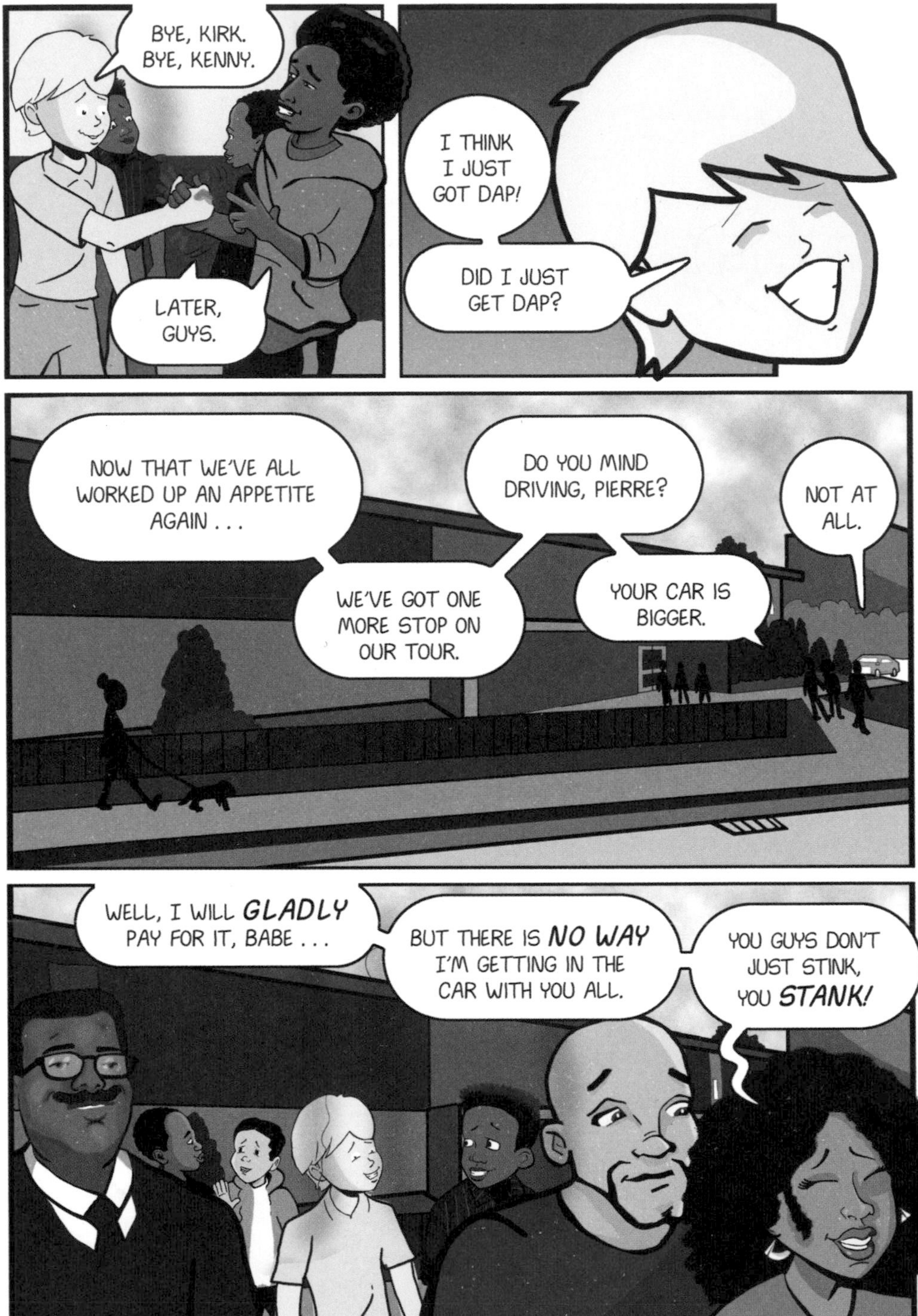
BYE, KIRK. BYE, KENNY.
LATER, GUYS.
I THINK I JUST GOT DAP!
DID I JUST GET DAP?
NOW THAT WE'VE ALL WORKED UP AN APPETITE AGAIN . . .
WE'VE GOT ONE MORE STOP ON OUR TOUR.
DO YOU MIND DRIVING, PIERRE?
YOUR CAR IS BIGGER.
NOT AT ALL.
WELL, I WILL **GLADLY** PAY FOR IT, BABE . . .
BUT THERE IS **NO WAY** I'M GETTING IN THE CAR WITH YOU ALL.
YOU GUYS DON'T JUST STINK, YOU **STANK!**

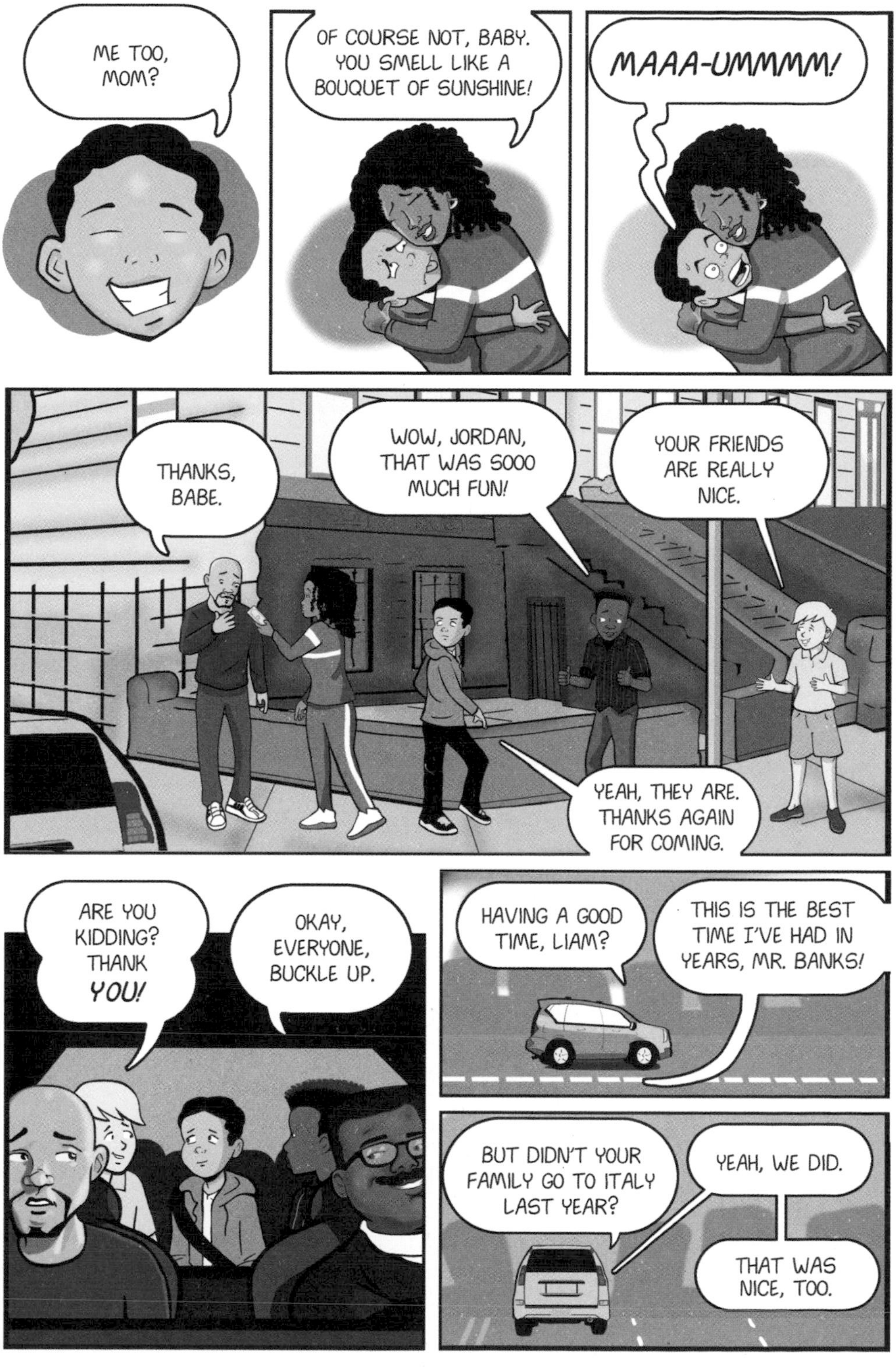
ME TOO, MOM?
OF COURSE NOT, BABY. YOU SMELL LIKE A BOUQUET OF SUNSHINE!
MAAA-UMMMM!
THANKS, BABE.
WOW, JORDAN, THAT WAS SOOO MUCH FUN!
YOUR FRIENDS ARE REALLY NICE.
YEAH, THEY ARE. THANKS AGAIN FOR COMING.
ARE YOU KIDDING? THANK *YOU!*
OKAY, EVERYONE, BUCKLE UP.
HAVING A GOOD TIME, LIAM?
THIS IS THE BEST TIME I'VE HAD IN YEARS, MR. BANKS!
BUT DIDN'T YOUR FAMILY GO TO ITALY LAST YEAR?
YEAH, WE DID.
THAT WAS NICE, TOO.

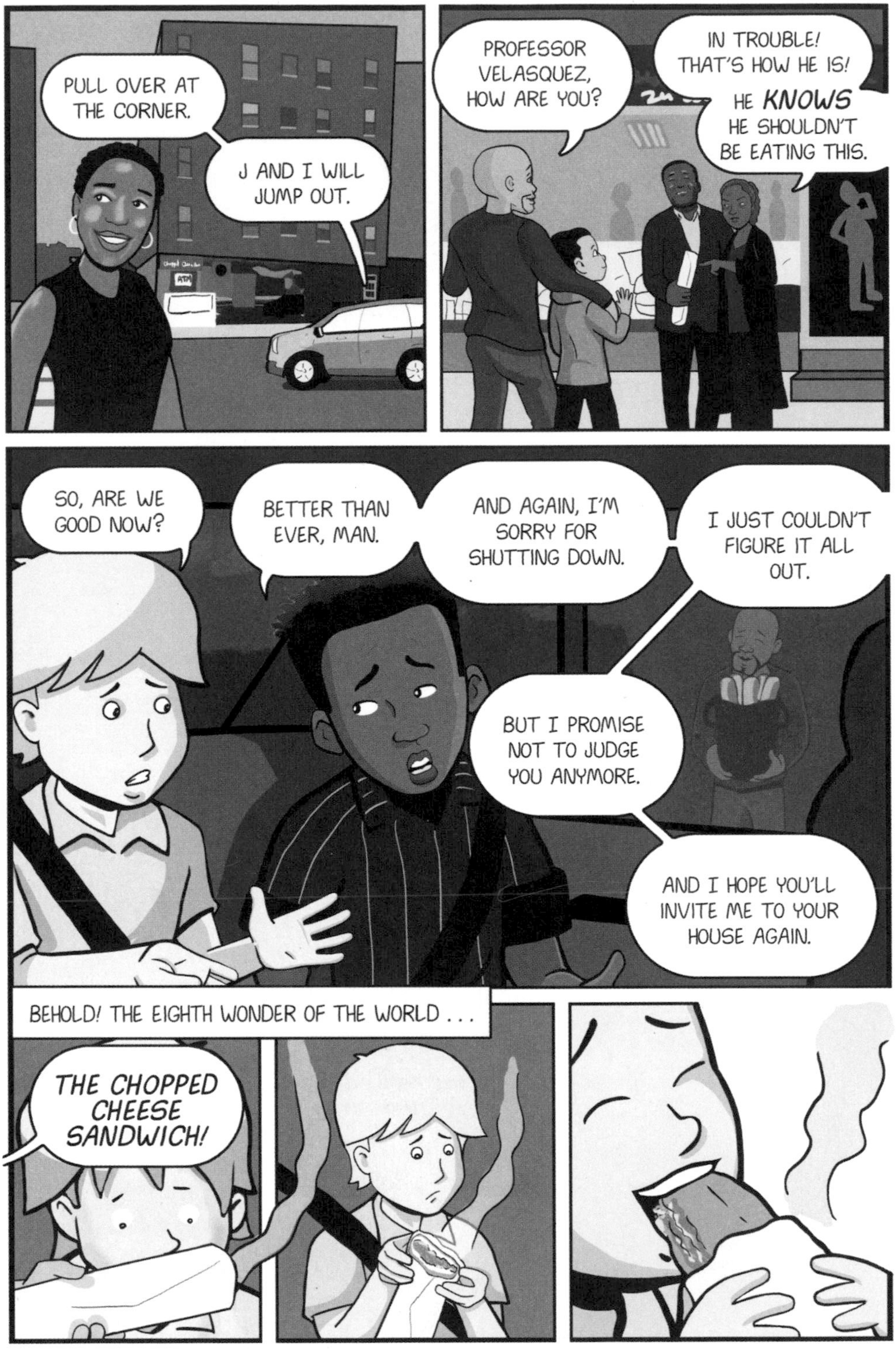
PULL OVER AT THE CORNER.
J AND I WILL JUMP OUT.
PROFESSOR VELASQUEZ, HOW ARE YOU?
IN TROUBLE! THAT'S HOW HE IS!
HE **KNOWS** HE SHOULDN'T BE EATING THIS.
SO, ARE WE GOOD NOW?
BETTER THAN EVER, MAN.
AND AGAIN, I'M SORRY FOR SHUTTING DOWN.
I JUST COULDN'T FIGURE IT ALL OUT.
BUT I PROMISE NOT TO JUDGE YOU ANYMORE.
AND I HOPE YOU'LL INVITE ME TO YOUR HOUSE AGAIN.
BEHOLD! THE EIGHTH WONDER OF THE WORLD . . .
THE CHOPPED CHEESE SANDWICH!

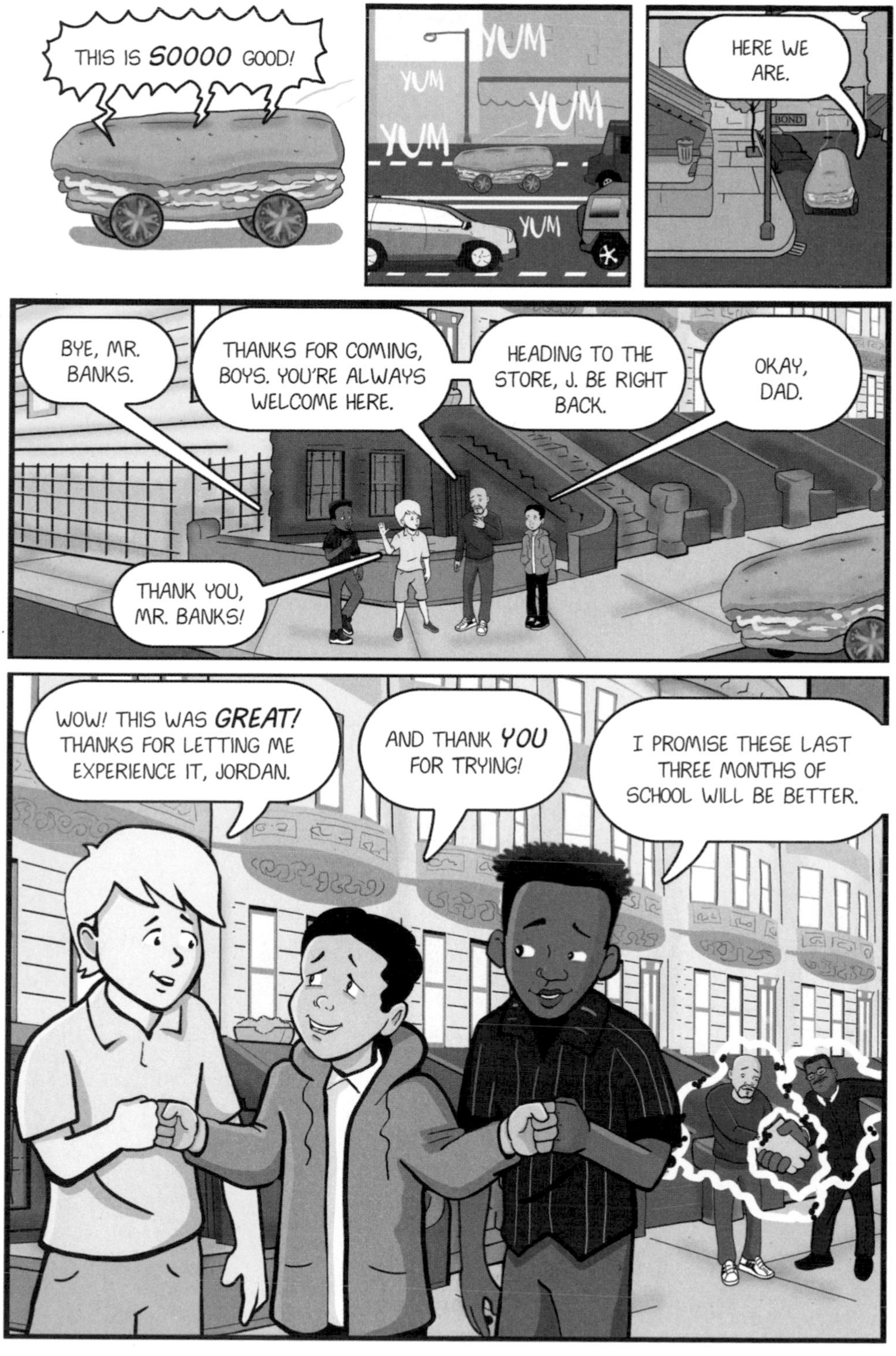
THIS IS SOOOO GOOD!
YUM
YUM
YUM
YUM
YUM
HERE WE ARE.
BOND
BYE, MR. BANKS.
THANKS FOR COMING, BOYS. YOU'RE ALWAYS WELCOME HERE.
HEADING TO THE STORE, J. BE RIGHT BACK.
OKAY, DAD.
THANK YOU, MR. BANKS!
WOW! THIS WAS **GREAT!** THANKS FOR LETTING ME EXPERIENCE IT, JORDAN.
AND THANK ***YOU*** FOR TRYING!
I PROMISE THESE LAST THREE MONTHS OF SCHOOL WILL BE BETTER.

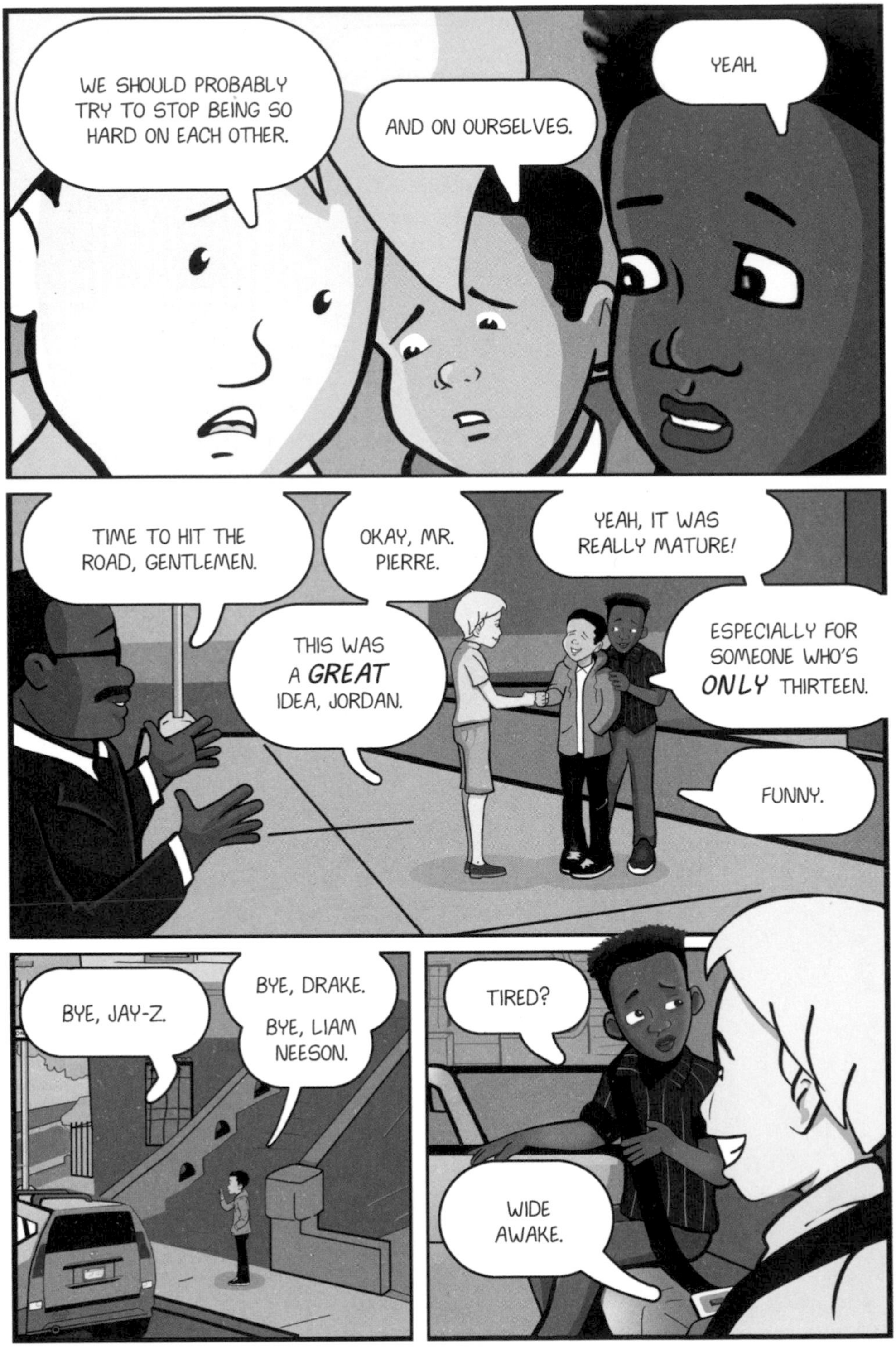
WE SHOULD PROBABLY TRY TO STOP BEING SO HARD ON EACH OTHER.
AND ON OURSELVES.
YEAH.
TIME TO HIT THE ROAD, GENTLEMEN.
OKAY, MR. PIERRE.
THIS WAS A **GREAT** IDEA, JORDAN.
YEAH, IT WAS REALLY MATURE!
ESPECIALLY FOR SOMEONE WHO'S ***ONLY*** THIRTEEN.
FUNNY.
BYE, JAY-Z.
BYE, DRAKE.
BYE, LIAM NEESON.
TIRED?
WIDE AWAKE.

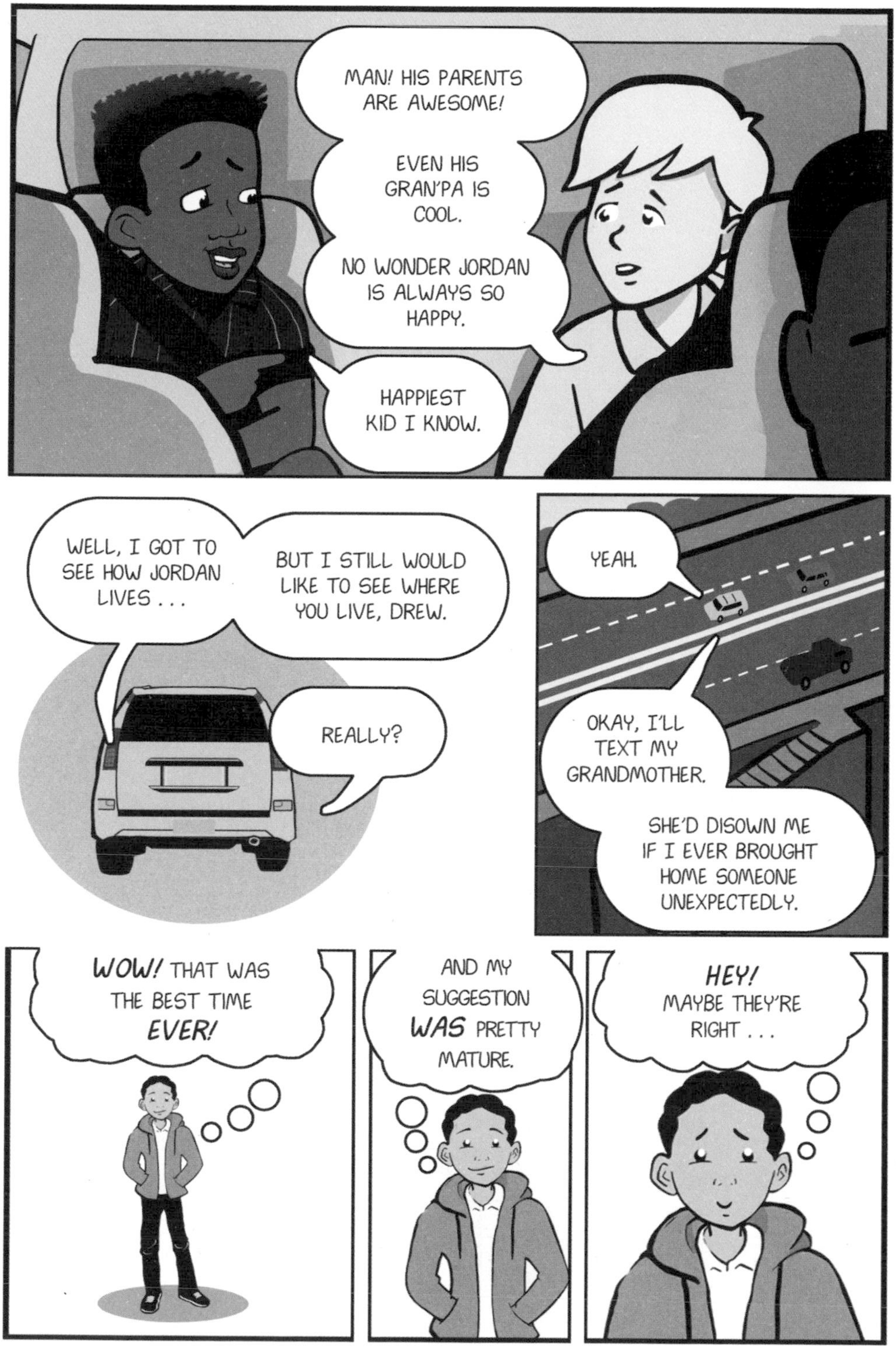
MAN! HIS PARENTS ARE AWESOME!
EVEN HIS GRAN'PA IS COOL.
NO WONDER JORDAN IS ALWAYS SO HAPPY.
HAPPIEST KID I KNOW.
WELL, I GOT TO SEE HOW JORDAN LIVES . . .
BUT I STILL WOULD LIKE TO SEE WHERE YOU LIVE, DREW.
REALLY?
YEAH.
OKAY, I'LL TEXT MY GRANDMOTHER.
SHE'D DISOWN ME IF I EVER BROUGHT HOME SOMEONE UNEXPECTEDLY.
WOW! THAT WAS THE BEST TIME EVER!
AND MY SUGGESTION WAS PRETTY MATURE.
HEY! MAYBE THEY'RE RIGHT . . .

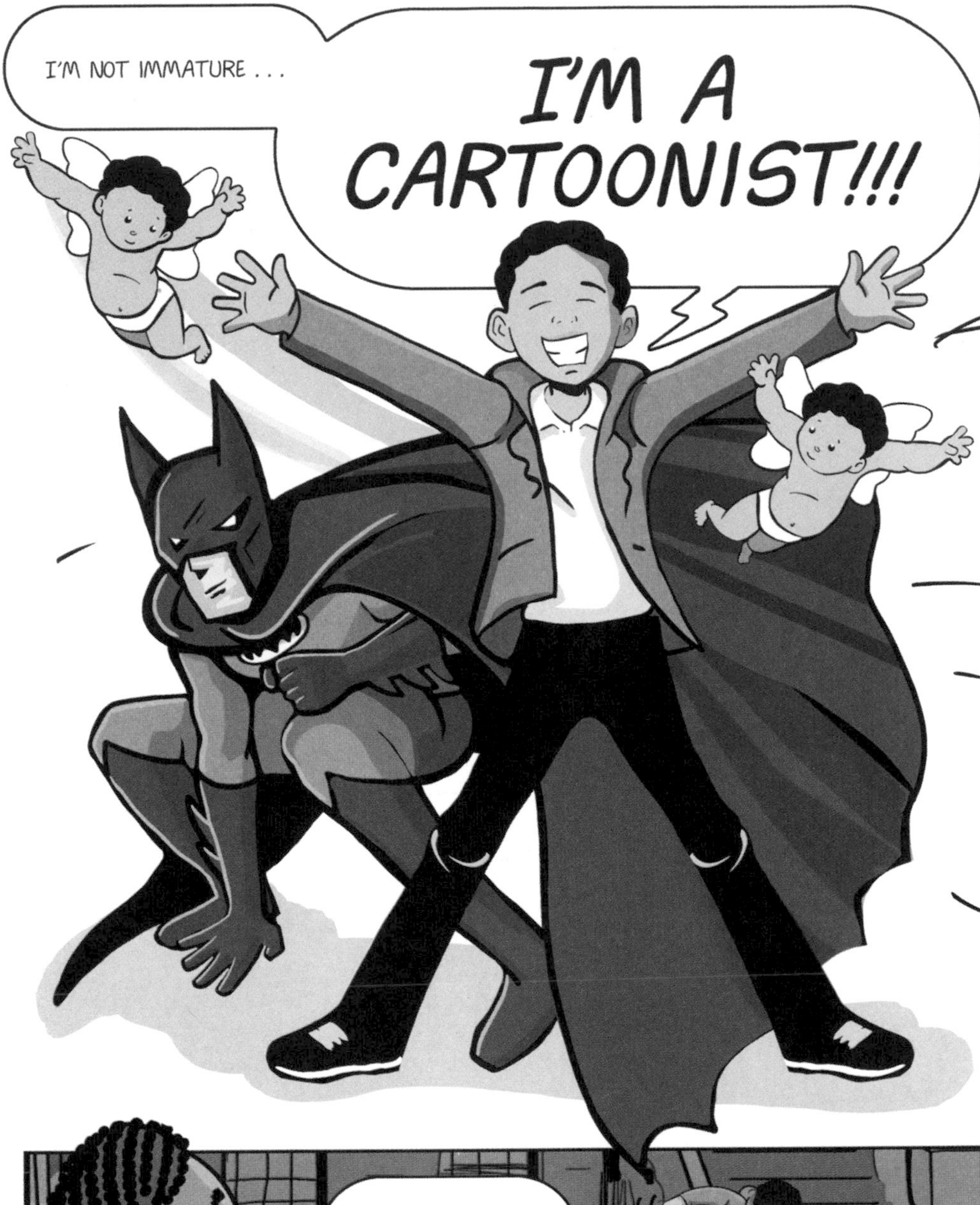
I'M NOT IMMATURE . . .
I'M A CARTOONIST!!!

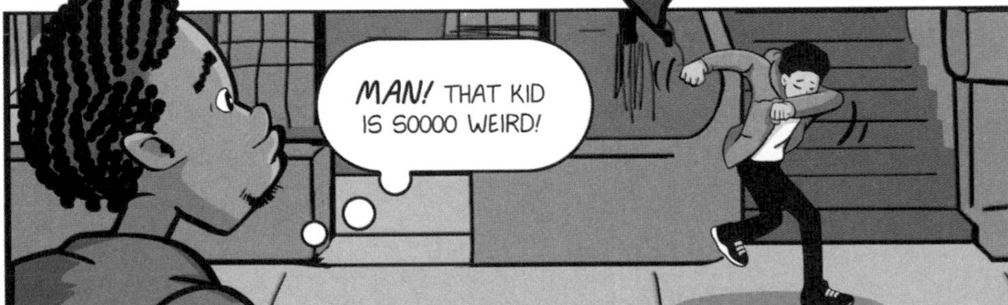
MAN! THAT KID IS SOOOO WEIRD!

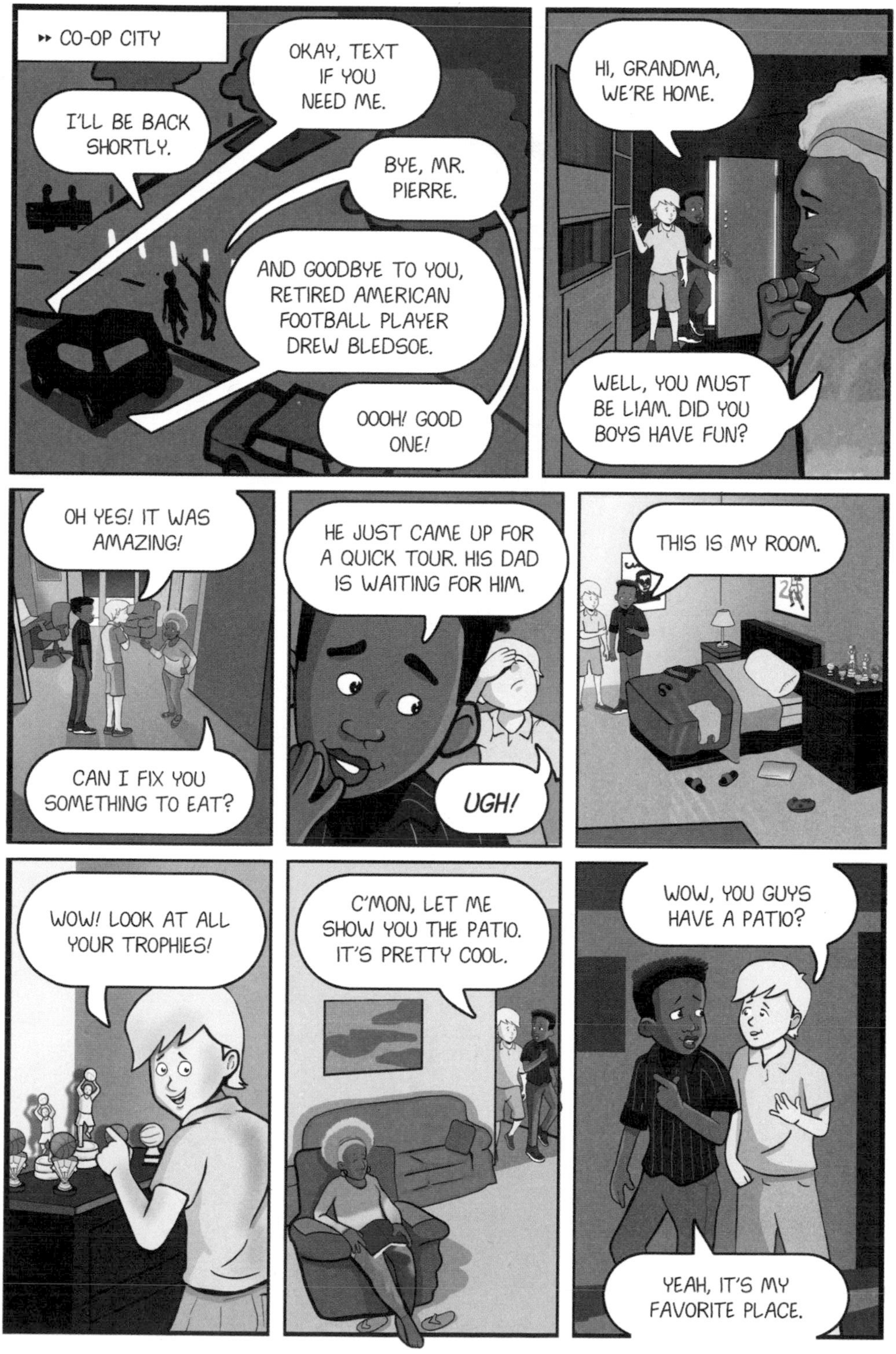
CO-OP CITY
I'LL BE BACK SHORTLY.
OKAY, TEXT IF YOU NEED ME.
BYE, MR. PIERRE.
AND GOODBYE TO YOU, RETIRED AMERICAN FOOTBALL PLAYER DREW BLEDSOE.
OOOH! GOOD ONE!
HI, GRANDMA, WE'RE HOME.
WELL, YOU MUST BE LIAM. DID YOU BOYS HAVE FUN?
OH YES! IT WAS AMAZING!
CAN I FIX YOU SOMETHING TO EAT?
HE JUST CAME UP FOR A QUICK TOUR. HIS DAD IS WAITING FOR HIM.
UGH!
THIS IS MY ROOM.
WOW! LOOK AT ALL YOUR TROPHIES!
C'MON, LET ME SHOW YOU THE PATIO. IT'S PRETTY COOL.
WOW, YOU GUYS HAVE A PATIO?
YEAH, IT'S MY FAVORITE PLACE.

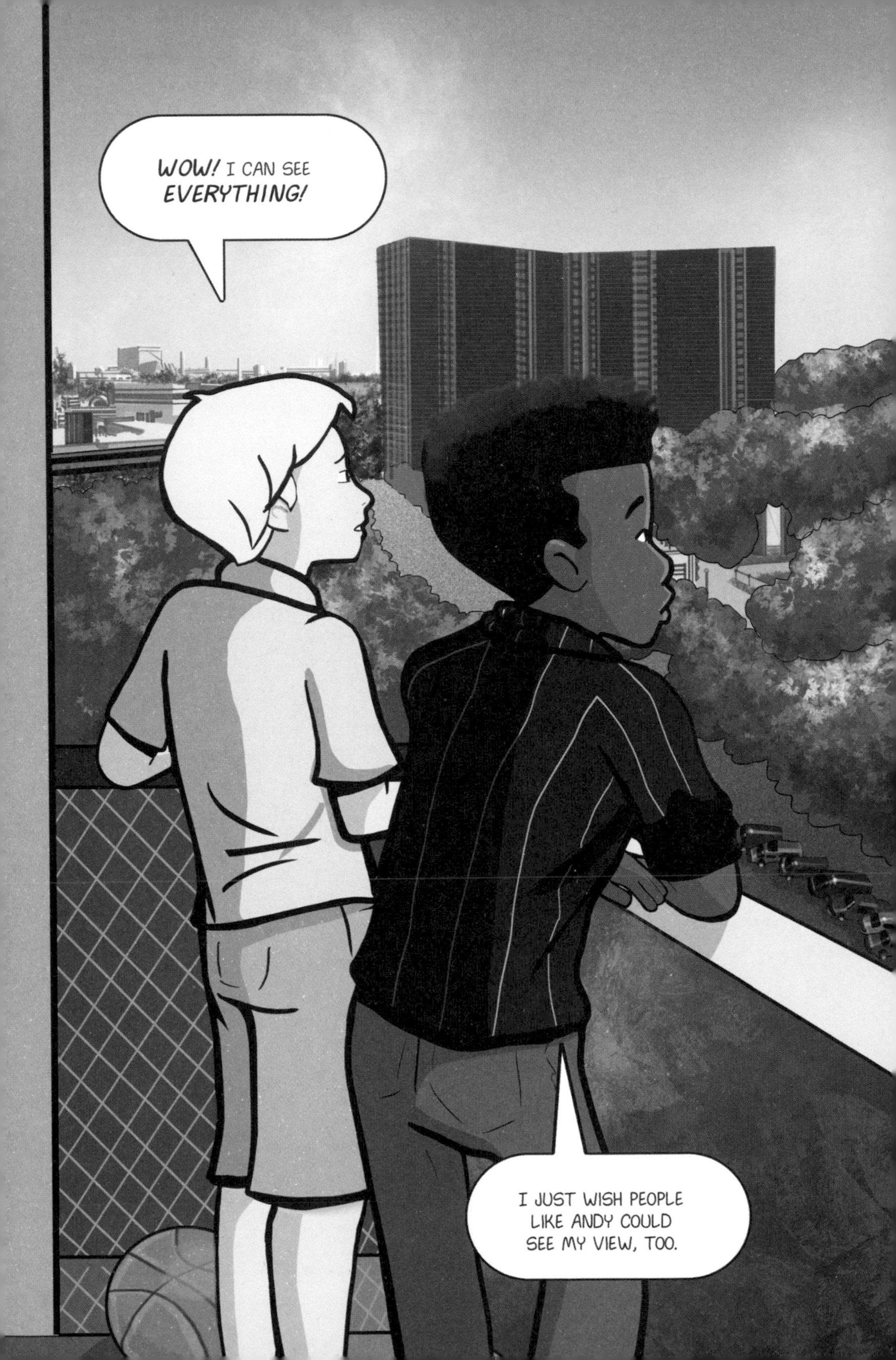
WOW! I CAN SEE EVERYTHING!
I JUST WISH PEOPLE LIKE ANDY COULD SEE MY VIEW, TOO.

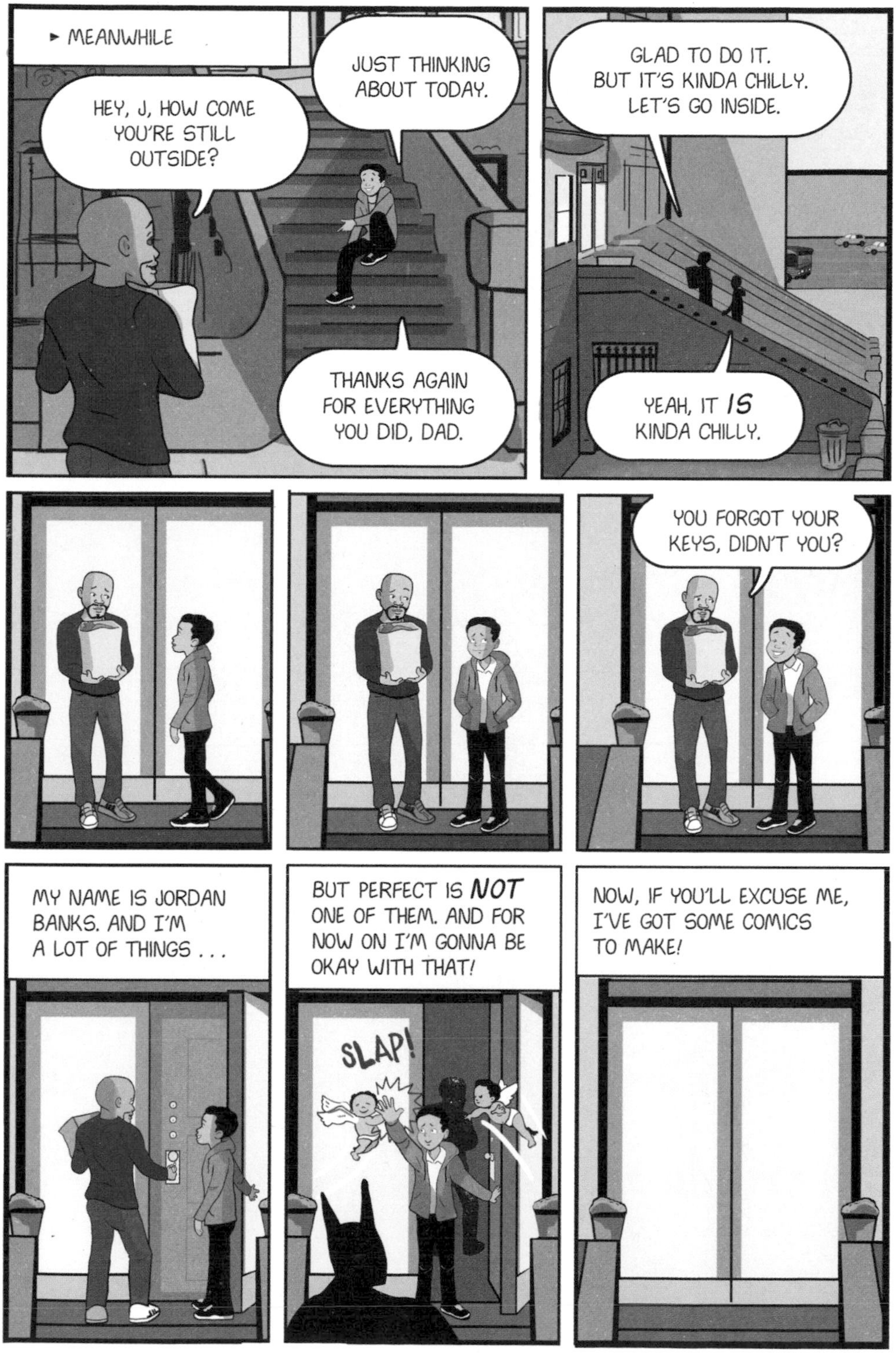
▸ MEANWHILE
HEY, J, HOW COME YOU'RE STILL OUTSIDE?
JUST THINKING ABOUT TODAY.
THANKS AGAIN FOR EVERYTHING YOU DID, DAD.
GLAD TO DO IT. BUT IT'S KINDA CHILLY. LET'S GO INSIDE.
YEAH, IT *IS* KINDA CHILLY.
YOU FORGOT YOUR KEYS, DIDN'T YOU?
MY NAME IS JORDAN BANKS. AND I'M A LOT OF THINGS . . .
BUT PERFECT IS **NOT** ONE OF THEM. AND FOR NOW ON I'M GONNA BE OKAY WITH THAT!
SLAP!
NOW, IF YOU'LL EXCUSE ME, I'VE GOT SOME COMICS TO MAKE!

Thank you to the amazing M'shindo Kuumba
for taking my colors to an entirely different level!

To my family, Aren, Jay, and Autier.
My sons have always been, and continue to be, my inspiration.

Thank you to Suzanne Murphy; Rosemary Brosnan; Patty Rosati;
my editor, Andrew Eliopulos; my publicist, Jacquelynn Burke;
my designer, Cat San Juan; my art director, Erin Fitzsimmons;
and the rest of my amazing team at HarperAlley/Quill Tree Books
for believing in me enough to give me the opportunity
to tell my story my way.

A huge thank you to my agent, Judy Hansen,
who has stood with me from the very beginning
to help bring *New Kid* and *Class Act* to life.

Thank you to all of the authors and artists who gave me
their blessing to use their work in my chapter headings:
Jeff Kinney (*Diary of a Wimpy Kid*); Barry Deutsch (*Hereville:
How Mirka Got Her Sword*); Ryan Andrews (*This Was Our Pact*);
Shannon Hale & LeUyen Pham (*Real Friends*); Kazu Kibuishi (*Amulet*);
Terri Libenson (*Invisible Emmie*); Raina Telgemeier (*Ghosts*);
Dav Pilkey (*Captain Underpants*); and Jarrett J. Krosoczka (*Hey, Kiddo*).

Thank you to my fellow authors who gave me permission to use them
as Easter eggs throughout *Class Act*: Kwame Alexander, Jason Reynolds,
Jacqueline Woodson, Elizabeth Acevedo, Renée Watson, Derrick Barnes,
Nic Stone, Angie Thomas, Tami Charles, and Eric Velasquez.

Thank you to my art assistant, John-Raymond De Bard.

Thank you to Carol Fitzgerald, Andrea Colvin, and most of all
to my fans: The kids. The teachers. The librarians. The parents.
The book groups. The reviewers. The bloggers. The publications.
And the award committees who showed *New Kid* so much love.